BREAKERS

A BENDERS NOVEL

D M SMITH

COTTONWOOD BOOKS PUBLISHING

BREAKERS

Copyright © 2023 by D M Smith
Published in the United States by
Cottonwood Books Publishing, LLC

ISBN: 979-8-9864687-3-0
LCCN: 2023917524

bendersnovels.com

"You are never too small to make a difference. And if a few children can get headlines all over the world just by not going to school, then imagine what we could all do together if we really wanted to."
Greta Thunberg — Sweden

Breakers is dedicated to the new generation of climate activists, including:

Txai Suruí — Brazil
Jerome Foster II — USA
Anuna De Wever — Belgium
Anjali Sharma — Australia
Qiyun Woo — Singapore
Roland Dedi — Ivory Coast
Haven Coleman — USA
Dr. Mya-Rose Craig — UK
Leah Namugerwa — Uganda
Selina Neirok Leem — Marshall Islands

To you and the thousands more around the world, thanks—we owe you.

BREAKERS

PROLOGUE

I *can't remember* ever *feeling this tired!*

Dr. Ellie Henderson stood by the exit as her hand-picked team of scientists filed out of the lab for the final time. In truth, *tired* did not come even close to expressing the fathomless depth of her fatigue. She and her departing staff had been working eighteen-hour days for over two weeks, and she was nearing the end of her endurance. She hid her weariness as best she could, unwilling to allow fleshly shortcomings to prevent her from extending a personal thanks to each of them. Despite her best efforts over the years, some of her coworkers persisted in viewing her as no more than a colleague. These few acknowledged their parting with the most impersonal of gestures: handshakes for a few, a simple nod for another. But many had become close friends, and knowing they would never see one another again, most of this much larger group could not bear to leave without a final embrace.

The moment was bittersweet. Everyone had known from the start that they would never see any direct benefits from their efforts, but the project had given them each a temporary sense of purpose in a shattered world defined by chaos and decline. It was a purely intangible reward, Ellie granted, yet sufficient for a group made up of the top scientists from multiple disciplines. Intellects such as theirs rebelled against inactivity. They required a direction to explore, a mystery to unravel, and she had provided them with one for almost a decade. Now that time was up, and they had no choice but to descend one of the world's few remaining ivory towers and find their own purposes amid the chaos outside its sheltering walls. The final pair to leave was a married couple, both specialists in the relatively new field of temporal mechanics. She thanked them for their work, exchanged hugs with each, and then they were gone.

The second the door thudded closed behind them, Ellie collapsed heavily into the nearest chair. She slumped back, pressed her palms to her face, ran her fingertips in small circles over her eyes, and let years of accumulated tension begin to drain from her body.

My damned *body!* she thought. She was exhausted, yes, but at least the painful condition that had plagued most of her adult life had been in remission during these all-important final weeks of the project. For that, she was profoundly thankful. She had no idea how long this current reprieve would last. She still might have days to go—weeks, even—but lately, her periods of strength and vitality seldom exceeded a month. She hoped that with her work now done, she might get the chance to relax and truly enjoy this interlude of normalcy, however long it lasted.

Ellie dropped her hands to her lap and cast her eyes over the tightly packed workstations surrounding her. Much of the technology she could see had been purpose-built, was unique in all the world, and none of it would ever be touched again after today. The lab was unusually quiet now, the room all but empty, and every computer and piece of monitoring equipment powered down for the first time in many months. Whenever the room was occupied, the buzz of multiple conversations, the rapid-fire clicking of fingers on keyboards, and the whirs of more than two dozen CPU cooling fans combined to create a constant mental pressure. It was a subliminal effect, seldom noticed in the moment, but its sudden absence always triggered a surprisingly powerful sense of relief.

Ellie was not alone in the stillness. Ryan Collins, her close friend going back to her childhood days in Los Alamos, New Mexico, crossed the room, stopped behind her, and laid his hands on her shoulders. He remained standing, even though many of his recent days had been longer than hers.

She was not surprised by this; he had always preferred to stay on his feet while he worked, no matter how tired he was.

"Well, that's finally done," she said, breaking the silence at last. "Not exactly how I originally intended, maybe, but it's done."

"Hmm."

Ellie was not fooled by his neutral tone. Willing her body back to a standing position, she rose and stepped around the chair to face him. Ryan's participation had been essential to their success. His strong leadership kept the project moving forward during the many times she'd been too weak merely to get out of bed.

"Thank you for sticking by me all these years. I know you've never fully approved of the plan, but your support made all the difference every time it mattered most." She wrapped her arms around him, and he responded by pulling her close.

He let out a long sigh and spoke into her hair, restating his position for perhaps the hundredth time. "It's not that I disapprove; you know that. This project means as much to me as it does to you. But you also know how I feel about using *her*. Besides, we've chewed our way through a lot of valuable resources that might otherwise have been used on a project with a much greater chance of success."

"No point in beating a dead horse."

Ryan's body stiffened at what he heard as a rebuke. He released her, took a step back, and when he spoke, there was real pain in his tone. "I remember you once saying you always wanted my opinion."

"I wasn't saying you... of course I do, Ryan. I only meant that, given how bad things are, it's too late for anything we do here, now, to make the situation any better. It's been too late practically from the day we were born, and to act as if it's otherwise—*that's* what would be lashing the deceased equine. You're absolutely right—this project won't help any of us in the least. But I could make this happen, and I felt I had to. And maybe, in the long run, this will make a difference to *them*."

Ryan's laugh was a single, humorless cough. "The *very* long run! Do you really think she'll figure it out?"

Ellie considered the old question one last time. Over the years-long course of the project, she had often wondered if she should provide specific instructions, but even in the case of two closely parallel timelines, quantum variations, random and unpredictable, guaranteed there would be differences between them. The fact that she could never accurately anticipate exactly what conditions would exist or what would need to be done argued strongly against doing anything that might only serve to cause confusion. Or, worse, risk exposing the plan and rendering all their efforts wasted. In the end, she decided to disguise the truth against casual discovery as best she could and place her faith in her own youthful ingenuity and intuition. Above all, every decision made so far had been guided by her insistence that whatever course of action was eventually taken, the choice would be completely up to the one for whom the project was ultimately intended. She would provide the tools, nothing more, and trust that events would play out for the best.

Still, the project was a huge gamble, one that had taken an incalculable toll on everyone involved, and there had been many times when self-doubt had threatened to overwhelm her. As of ten minutes ago, though, her misgivings no longer mattered. They had just let their own metaphorical horse out of the barn, very much alive, and any lingering doubts or second guesses were thereby made pointless.

"That's the thing, isn't it, Ryan? We'll never know." She placed her fingers on his chest and looked up into a face deeply lined with age. "But she has to. For Sam's sake, for Aaron's, she *has* to!"

1

MANY YEARS EARLIER

Ellie gazed through the enormous, sloping glass wall that made up one entire end of the Pajarito Environmental Education Center's exhibit hall, her backpack on the floor at her feet. Perched on the edge of a cliff at the western edge of Los Alamos' downtown, the center treated visitors to a stunning view, one that started deep in the rugged Pueblo Canyon a hundred feet below and stretched to the peaks of the Jemez Mountains fifteen miles away. Lifting her eyes to that high, rugged horizon, she thought about the fire that had burned more than 150,000 acres of those mountains—and destroyed more than sixty homes—the summer before her family moved to Los Alamos in 2012. Her eleven-year-old self had been appalled by the sight of the damage, and although the view became a little greener each successive year, she could only imagine how much more beautiful it must have been before it all charred. As the climate grew ever warmer and drier, fires like that were becoming more common across the region. Six years later, the slopes were once again ablaze, but today it was merely the brilliant, golden hue of aspen trees at the height of their autumn display that imbued the slopes with their fiery glow.

Her eyes dropped to the scene below. Halfway down the ravine, mostly hidden behind the dense crowns of ponderosa pines, was a wide, level formation of the type geologists called a *bench*. She used the trails that crisscrossed the bench nearly every day. They connected her home both to school and to the commercial part of the city, and hiking or biking along the forested paths practically guaranteed seeing some kind of wildlife on every trip. The thought of her beloved canyon reduced to a desolation of dead, blackened trees depressed her to an extent she couldn't begin to express. That it might happen was all too possible, she knew—more a question of *when* than *if*. For all its apparent ruggedness, the high-desert environment was fragile.

Her senior science class project centered on exactly that issue, and she had come to the PEEC to interview Shanna Newell, a member of the nature center's small staff and an expert on the region's ecology. Ellie wanted to know more about the latest predictions regarding the impact of the changing climate on the area's environment. Having arrived early, she passed the time first by looking at the exhibits, then by simply admiring the view. Now, with more than five minutes still to wait, her thoughts drifted to other, more personal matters.

Near the beginning of summer, she, her sister Sam, and their friends Ryan and Aaron had discovered, then destroyed, a time travel device they called the "shack." Except *destroyed* was not precisely the word for what they had done. Executing a plan devised by Aaron himself, the four of them went back to 1941 and disrupted a particular man's life, a man they believed to be Aaron's grandfather, knocking it off course and thereby preventing the shack from ever existing.

But the plan had equally dire consequences for Aaron. After successfully altering the past and the subsequent timeline, both Aaron and the device vanished from the world. That these events played out at the very time she had finally come to understand she loved him made the loss even harder to bear, and she spent the rest of the summer consumed by grief and guilt.

In contrast, seeing a "new" Aaron step out of his mother's car in early September had been the happiest moment of her life. His unexpected return filled her with enough joy to completely purge her of all those dark emotions. Even though this Aaron had lived a different life and shared none of her memories of their time together, she vowed not to waste the second chance the universe had given her. The cherry on this most improbable sundae was that this new incarnation was in her own grade, rather than being a year ahead of her. Everything seemed to be perfect.

For a short time, they got along well. Their relationship was not precisely the same as before they altered the timeline, but Ellie was confident that, given time and enough effort, it soon would be. After only a few weeks, however, she felt the gaps between them grow into chasms as deep and wide as the ravine below her. The very qualities Ellie initially found so attractive in this new Aaron—his greater self-confidence; his relaxed, outgoing nature; even his considerable skill on the guitar—added to the original Aaron's keen intelligence, quickly attracted the notice of certain classmates who soon started vying for his attention. For six years, and with no effort on her part, she had been the sole focus of Aaron's interest. She had no idea how to compete with girls who had spent their entire academic careers majoring in flirting, and by now her disdain for what she thought of as the "ditzy, girly-girl" mindset was too engrained for her to change.

Her only concession in that regard involved her hair. In the emotional aftermath of Aaron's abrupt disappearance, she had been too depressed to bother keeping it cut short, and since her last trim sometime the previous spring, it had grown long enough to brush her shoulders. She decided to continue letting it grow in the hope it might help make her at least *look* a little more girlish. Shifting her focus to her own reflection in the glass, she studied her hair and frowned, not entirely convinced her experiment was working.

At the sounds of an opening door and a sudden conversation behind her, she turned and saw two women emerge from a short hallway into the opposite end of the exhibit area. As they approached the lobby's small, curved reception desk, the young man seated behind it rose and quickly disappeared down the same hallway. He moved with a sense of urgency she recognized at once, and she knew as surely as if he had announced it to the world that he was on his way to the restroom.

Ellie returned her attention to the two women who had stopped to talk in front of the counter-height desk. One was considerably younger than the other, likely only a few years older than herself. She wore a pale blue button-up shirt over a plain white tee, new-looking, unfaded jeans, and flat canvas shoes that might have been Toms or Skechers. Sam, ardent fan of all things fashion, would've known for sure, but Ellie could only guess. Her hair was pulled back into a simple ponytail that was secured by a band the same blue hue as her shirt. Both her professional demeanor and the messenger bag she carried, its strap slashing diagonally across her chest, suggested she was there on some kind of business, and Ellie pegged her as a newly minted elementary school teacher, perhaps there to arrange a class field trip.

She shifted her attention to the woman she believed to be Ms. Newell. She was tall, tanned, and had a face slightly weathered in a way Ellie thought fitting for an environmental biologist. This was framed by a dark brown mane that cascaded in loose waves around her shoulders. What Ellie noticed most, however, was how absolutely ordinary she looked. She wore a pair of faded chinos and a turquoise T-shirt with the nature center's stylized bird logo on the front. Aside from the shirt marking her as an employee, there was nothing about her appearance to suggest she was a scientist. But then what had she been expecting—a long, white lab coat with multiple pocket protectors, a beehive hairdo, and maybe a pair of black, oversized cat-eye glasses?

The younger woman finished expressing her thanks for some unspecified favor, shook hands, then turned and headed for the exit. Ellie remained where she stood, waiting patiently to be waved over. Before that could happen, the phone rang. With the reception area still unstaffed, the dark-haired woman reached over the counter to answer it. Her voice was cheerful and melodious, the sound of a mountain stream sliding smoothly around polished stones, and judging from the light, familiar tone of the conversation, Ellie guessed the person on the other end of the line was a friend. Turning in Ellie's direction, the woman raised a finger in a just-one-second gesture and leaned back against the counter while she continued chatting.

Happy to have been noticed, Ellie responded with a polite smile but kept her distance to avoid appearing to eavesdrop on a personal conversation. Even so, now that the woman stood facing her, Ellie couldn't help but overhear most of what she was saying.

"That's fantastic, Nalini! Thanks. I'll check my inbox for that in a bit." There was a brief pause while she listened. "Sure, I can do that. Say, can we pick this up again in a day or so? I have a rather important meeting scheduled for about two minutes ago."

Ellie felt a surge of irritation and wondered how much longer she was going to have to stand around waiting. Turning away to hide her frown, she scanned the entire exhibition area to see who else was there, but aside from the receptionist returning to his post, they seemed to be alone. A phone meeting, then? A video chat?

"Okay. Thanks again, Nalini. You're a doll. And do tell Jack I said hi."

At the sound of the phone's handset clicking into its cradle, Ellie turned back to face her.

"Sorry about that," the woman said. "I hope your name is Ellie, or I just told Nalini Nadkarni a big, fat lie!"

Stunned, Ellie's eyes went wide. Dr. Nadkarni was famous—a leading expert in tree-top biology. Ellie had streamed her 2009 TED Talk only weeks earlier, when she was still searching for a suitable research topic. Apparently, Ms. Newell had just cut short a conversation with the "Queen of the Forest Canopy" to talk with *her*.

Seeing Ellie's shocked expression, Ms. Newell laughed. "It's no big deal. Nalini and I go way back. I asked her if she could come give a talk here in November, so she called to tell me she was putting together some new photos and an updated bio for us to use on posters and our website. Besides, she puts her climbing harness on both legs at once, same as the rest of us." Ellie smiled at the quip and relaxed. "So—what can I do for you?"

"You *are* Ms. Newell, right?"

"Please," she said, flapping a hand through the air. "I only make my husband call me that." She laughed again and offered Ellie her hand. "Call me Shanna."

"Okay. Shanna, then," she said, and they shook. "Like I said in my email, I'm taking Mrs. Carson's Environmental Science class this year, and for my project, I want to show how the different models of climate change might affect our local ecology. She said I should talk to you."

"Let me say this right up front. I'm not what you would call the ultimate authority on that topic, but I'm happy to help you in any way I can. So, if I've got it, you want to look at how each of the four possible expressions of climate change—warmer/drier, warmer/wetter, and so on—would impact life on the plateau?"

"Exactly! But not all of it. The life, I mean. I thought I'd choose four or five species and focus on those."

"Have you picked them out yet?"

"No. I figure the ponderosas would be one, but that's as far as I've got."

"You'll want to be careful when you do. If they're too interdependent, figuring out whether a change is a net plus or minus for any one of them can get tricky. And if the ones you choose are all affected the same way, well, that just makes for a boring paper."

"'Dry,' yeah. Been there, done that," Ellie admitted.

Ms. Newell laughed again. "Haven't we all! Okay, let's go back to my office, and we'll see what we can do to keep that from happening again."

An hour later, they stood once more in the lobby. The center had closed during their conversation, leaving the two of them alone in the large, open space. Ellie's pack now contained several pages of notes and a list of email addresses for climate scientists and field biologists working across a four-state region, all of whom Ms. Newell—"Shanna," she reminded herself—had assured her would be happy to help with her paper.

"I'll give them all a heads-up that you might be contacting them, but feel free to ask them for help at any time. Don't expect an instant reply, though—for some of them, 'field work' takes place in some pretty remote fields."

As Ellie thanked her and they exchanged goodbyes, she found she was feeling a surprisingly strong affinity for Shanna. She had liked her right away, but this was not strange in itself—Ellie usually connected with someone she met immediately or likely never would. But as she picked up random tidbits about the woman's life during their conversation and from the many keepsakes scattered around her office, simple fondness had morphed into a feeling bordering on admiration. Shanna had a career she obviously found rewarding, a family she adored and that brought her evident joy, and, judging by her phone call with Dr. Nadkarni and the lengthy list of contacts she had at her immediate disposal, she maintained casual friendships with some of the country's top biologists. As they shook hands again, Ellie realized she didn't just like this woman; she wanted to *be* this woman.

After exiting through the center's main doors, she crunched her way across the gravel footpath that led through the teaching garden to the nearest trailhead. The initial descent was steep and rocky, and for the first few minutes, she was forced to keep her attention on her feet or risk taking a nasty tumble. Once she reached the wider, smoother trails of the bench, she could allow her thoughts to return to an earlier topic.

After the new Aaron moved into town, she, Sam, and Ryan agreed not to tell him about what they had gone through with "their" Aaron. For one thing, they assumed that learning of those events would only cause him pain and confusion. For another, they didn't want to sound like a trio of raving lunatics. She still believed it was the right decision, but often wondered how she could ever expect to recreate the old sense of closeness she had once enjoyed while continuing to keep such a major secret from him.

It wasn't the romantic feelings she and her Aaron had shared at the very end that she missed the most. She'd had too little time to grow used to those in the headlong rush of events leading up to the shack's destruction. No, it was their talks, conversations often so deeply nerdy as to be utterly opaque to anyone around them, that she most regretted losing. Discussions of their childhoods during slow walks around town quickly degenerated into perfunctory, end-of-day exchanges that bordered on "Nice weather, huh?" banality. These days he always seemed impatient to get away, and "gotta bounce" had replaced "I'll see you tomorrow" as his parting words before he dashed off to who knew where. The sudden coldness that replaced six years of close friendship ate at her, but, ironically, she no longer felt close enough to ask him why they were no longer close. She was past her weepy phase, but every now and then a random memory would catch her off guard, and she'd have to fight back tears.

She also missed the dreams. After Aaron vanished in June, she began having dreams about him. But to say *about* him wasn't quite right. It was more like she had dreams *with* him. She'd be enjoying some random, surreal plot of the type that normally comprised her nocturnal subconscious world when he'd sort of "show up." Sometimes they would talk about school, her family, or about how she was coping with what they'd done. On other occasions, they'd spend their time diving deep into some arcane topic, just like they used to. The only subject that was off-limits was Aaron himself. Any time she forgot and started asking about him, he disappeared. Even though sporadic and often brief, the dreams had been almost as important to her recovery as Sam's gentle, patient support.

Aaron's split from Sam and Ryan had come sooner and been even more abrupt. He had hung out with them a few times right after arriving in September, then one day he simply wasn't there anymore. Sam and Ryan now attended the university, and Ellie knew the fact that the three of them no longer shared a campus was a big cause of that rift. She also knew that the original Aaron had, at least in part, maintained a friendship with them as a way to be near her, a pretense that was no longer needed. Or wanted, apparently.

She reluctantly acknowledged that she couldn't place all the blame for the state of their relationship on those other girls. Aaron himself increasingly seemed to be pushing her away, intentionally putting both physical and emotional distance between them. On several recent occasions, she'd had the distinct impression he had made a point of walking by her with someone else at his side—several different someones, actually—as if to say, "See? You don't own me!" This was absurd, of course; she had never thought she did. Odder still was seeing him in the cafeteria, perched on the edge of a table, engaged in spirited conversation with a group of jocks from the football or baseball team, something the old Aaron would never have done.

She noticed she was nearing the spot along the inner canyon rim where, one sunny morning in June, the two of them had sat close together atop a large slab of sandstone and discussed how they were going to reveal their plan for destroying the shack to Sam and Ryan. She remembered holding his hand while she confidently assured him that, despite knowing how much pain that very plan would soon cause them, choosing to express their feelings for each other might be the smartest thing they'd ever done.

She stepped off the trail and aimed herself toward the remembered spot. After only a few steps, she heard voices coming from ahead. She froze in place and waited to see if she had been heard. Then, careful to avoid creating the slightest noise, she inched forward until she could make out the shapes of two people sitting close together on the same rock she had shared with Aaron. The limbs of the scraggly juniper she crouched behind obscured the pair's features, but there could be no doubt about who owned that head of short, white hair. However, the identity of the girl leaning against Aaron's right side, her head resting on his shoulder, was a mystery. They spoke quietly, too quietly for Ellie to make out the words, but the general tone and their soft, intimate laughter told her all she needed to know.

Tears blurred her vision as she silently crept back to the main trail and set a rapid pace toward home. What stung most about finding Aaron there was not simply that he was with another girl, but the idea that he would take someone else to a place she felt was so special to them. Then the coldly rational, problem-solving part of her brain she thought of as her logic module spoke up, chiding her for being slow. *After all, he wouldn't have any memory of that day, would he?* The distraction of contemplating the extreme coincidence of him independently stumbling upon that exact location kept her from feeling too hurt, and by the time she started the final climb up to her house, she felt almost calm again.

Still pondering the many mysteries that were this new Aaron, she was halfway across her back yard before she noticed Sam studying outside. She sat at the round, metal mesh table on the covered patio, where the slanting rays of the late afternoon sun beating against the back of the house created a pocket of warmth just comfortable enough for her to work. Sam had her new iPad Pro propped in front of her and was taking notes from several books spread open around it. She barely glanced up as Ellie approached.

"You're back late today; have a date?" Sam said, her tone bright and chipper.

Ellie's mood was anything but. "Don't. Please."

Sam looked up again, this time long enough to register the distress in Ellie's expression. "Sorry. Aaron, right? Wanna sit and talk about it?"

Ellie remained standing, thumbs hooked into the straps of her backpack, and shook her head.

"No. It's just more of the same old crap we've talked about a gazillion times already. I can't figure out what's up with him!"

"If it would make you feel any better, I think Ryan really *might* punch him at this point. He's probably as pissed off with him as you are."

Ellie managed only a thin smile. "Thanks, but let's call that Plan C for now. I've got some stuff in here I want to take care of right away," she said, jostling her pack with an exaggerated shrug. Replaying Sam's offer in her head as she pulled the handle on the screen door, it occurred to her that getting Ryan to slug Aaron was probably as close as she would ever get to hiring a hitman, and the notion of having Aaron "whacked"—if only in the strictly literal sense, of course—amused her. Holding the door open, she turned back toward her sister. "I'll keep that in mind, though," and this time there was real humor in her smile.

In the bedroom she shared with Sam, she placed her pack on her mattress and transferred its contents to her small, bedside desk. She brought her MacBook to life and started copying the list of names and email addresses Shanna had given her into Contacts. The person who intrigued her most was Dr. Diana Wall, a soil biologist at Colorado State University. Ellie was irked with herself for not having thought about including the impact of climate change on soil organisms on her own, understanding now that it was a pretty obvious choice. They provided the literal base on which all the rest of the life in the ecosystem rested. She wondered if she could lump them all together and use "soil biota" collectively as an example, or if she should select one from the bunch. If so, which? Nematodes? Cyanobacteria?

Answering that question seemed reason enough to write Dr. Wall right away, but she decided to give Shanna a day or two to make the promised introductions. A second later, she changed her mind. She was perfectly capable of introducing herself. In only a few minutes, she had tapped out a short message explaining who she was, outlining the nature of her project, and asking her questions.

Still not in the mood for research, she opened a Firefox window and typed in *thunberg*. Ever since a curiously misdirected email back in August had first made Ellie aware of the fifteen-year-old's "school strike for climate," she had been keeping tabs on the young activist. She remained unconvinced that skipping school was the best way to push for change, but was inspired to learn more about such an important subject. For that reason, she abandoned her long-held plan to take the elite AP Physics class this year in favor of the lower-level Environmental Science class. Her decision initially met with stiff resistance from her parents, but when she'd made it clear the alternative was spending her senior year chained to the front of the State Capitol building in Santa Fe in solidarity with some relatively unknown teenage girl from Sweden, they gave her unexpected choice of science elective their swift approval.

She hit the Return key, the monitor flickered, and she scanned down the list of returns. The most recent was a *Guardian* article from the beginning of September that she had already seen. Disappointed, she stared blankly at the screen and drummed her fingers on the desktop. Her thoughts soon drifted back to her meeting at the PEEC.

She started a new search—*shanna newell*. To her surprise, she found that Googling someone she knew personally made her queasy, and her stomach gave an uncomfortable lurch when she hit the Return key. The window refreshed, listing the first ten hits. In addition to a bio page on the PEEC website, she found several other related returns. Those links led her to articles on a variety of local newspaper websites that covered the center's opening three and a half years ago or else mentioned her in connection with the center receiving some kind of award or grant.

Skimming Shanna's biography, Ellie learned that she had been born in the southeast and that her family had moved west when she was still a kid. As she grew up, she fell in love with the high desert landscape, and when it came time for college, she chose to remain in the region. Shanna held a BS in climatology from the University of Colorado Boulder, one of the country's top ten schools for environmental education and research, and an MS in environmental science from the University of Utah. She had a husband and a daughter, and they spent her time away from work exploring the region together, rafting through steep-walled canyons, or backcountry camping in the Jemez Mountains. Beyond those basic facts, nothing.

She marveled at how far short the single paragraph fell in describing the fascinating person she had just met. She wondered how other people's bios would read on such a site. How would she want her own to read? She decided that having some actual accomplishments to list would be a good starting point. Unable to stall any longer, she pulled her stack of books in front of her and got to work.

2

When Ellie woke the next morning and squinted toward the clock at the far end of the room, she was startled to see Sam still sound asleep, lying on top of her covers, limbs sprawled in a way that evoked images of white outlines on TV cop shows. On Tuesdays and Thursdays, Sam left the house more than an hour after she did, but even so, it was unusual for her not to be up first. Assuming she must have a good reason for sleeping so late, Ellie was careful to be extra quiet as she slid down from her high bed and selected an outfit from the dresser drawers built into its base. With a final glance to make sure Sam was still out, she eased the bedroom door closed and crossed the hall to the bathroom.

Regarding her reflection as she brushed her teeth, her attention once again settled on her hair. It was the longest it had been since she had first cut it short nearly three years ago, and although she missed the wash-and-go convenience of her slowly disappearing bob, she was beginning to like the look. She decided to keep the experiment going, wondering how long it would be before it was once again as long as Sam's.

Searching her emotions, she discovered she no longer felt the old visceral objection to looking like a "Sam clone" that had compelled her to hack it so short in the first place. This was partly due to Sam now being on the university campus, but to an even greater degree to how much closer she felt to her since the summer. After destroying the shack and losing Aaron, Ellie had fallen apart. Sam had worked hard to help her pull herself back together, and she owed her a lot.

Shifting the toothbrush in her hand to attack the other side of her mouth, her eyes dropped to the front of her nightshirt. The image depicted a bespectacled monk and the message, *Gregor Mendel—Giving Peas a Chance Since 1856.* The design wasn't one of her favorites. That the humor relied on a reference to a Beatles' song title rather than being intrinsic to the science of genetics earned it a lower ranking among her many others. The rest of the household found it funny, though, so she kept it in light rotation. Done brushing, she rinsed her toothbrush under the faucet, hung her nightshirt on the back of the door, and turned on the shower.

Twenty minutes later, she returned to her room bearing two cups of coffee. As she'd anticipated, Sam was now awake, sitting upright against her headboard while she thumbed a message into her phone. The message sent with its telltale *whoosh*, and Sam lowered the phone into her lap.

"Hey. I didn't hear you get up," Sam said. Then she spotted the steaming mugs. "*Ooh!* Coffee, coffee, coffee!" she exclaimed, greedily extending her hands.

Smiling at Sam's unrestrained enthusiasm, Ellie passed her a mug. "Careful. It's a bit too full." She took a long draw from her own mug, watched while Sam did the same.

"Ahh, thanks!" Sam peered thoughtfully at the contents of her cup and inhaled deeply of the aroma before taking another sip. "Is this still that Huehuetenango?"

"Mm-hmm. It's the last of it, though, so enjoy it while you can. Late night?"

"Why, because I slept in?" Ellie nodded. "No, not much later than usual, really. I think these college classes are harder on my brain is all. Well, that and I went running with Ryan in the afternoon. He figured we did six miles." She grimaced as she extended her legs straight out on the bed. "*Oomph!* Just a teensy bit sore. It's getting to the point that I either need to go with him more often or quit altogether."

Ellie glanced down at Sam's legs, bare from her toes up to where they disappeared into a pale blue pair of the type of loose shorts she habitually wore to bed. They looked as toned as when she had spent most of her high school phys ed classes sprinting up and down the soccer field.

"It does seem to be working for you." She turned to place her mug on her desk and began loading her books and computer into her backpack.

"That's what Ryan says. Often and *very* adoringly. Makes it kinda hard to go with the quitting option." She sighed. "How 'bout you? Feeling any better today?"

Ellie answered without turning around. "I guess. I ran across him in the canyon yesterday. He was sitting along the edge of the lower cliff with some girl. I couldn't get close enough to see who it was. Not that I care."

"Beyond the fact it wasn't you, you mean."

Ellie conceded the point with a one-shoulder shrug.

"Did he see you?"

Finished packing, Ellie turned around and leaned against the side of her bed. "No. I snuck away. It just bothered me because once he and I had... Oh, never mind! It so doesn't matter at this point. I'm not even sure I feel the same way about him anymore. He used to be different. From everyone else, I mean. Special. Now he acts exactly like all the other boys at school." She paused for a moment before going on. "But at first, he did seem *mostly* the same. You saw that too. I don't know what happened. Was it me? Something I did? Or was it something else entirely?" She checked the clock on Sam's nightstand, then puffed out a long breath. "I gotta go." She stood upright and slid her pack off the chair, holding it by its top handle so that it dangled heavily against her thigh.

Sam set her coffee next to the clock, slid out of bed, and crossed the room to stand in front of Ellie. She held her arms out and gave Ellie a lopsided smile. "Come here," she said.

Ellie shuffled awkwardly into Sam's offered embrace, felt warm arms wrap around her, pinning her own to her sides.

"You are wonderful," Sam said, "and don't you doubt it for a second! If this Aaron can't see that, well, maybe he simply isn't as smart as the original one was."

When Sam relaxed her grip, Ellie stepped away and returned Sam's smile with a faint one of her own. "Thanks. I needed that." But as she walked past Sam and out of the bedroom, she couldn't help but think, *Or maybe he's even smarter.*

Making sure she did not cross paths with Aaron any more often than necessary had become something of a fixation in recent days. They shared three classes, so avoiding him altogether was out of the question, but when she began to feel he was shutting her out, she moved up to the front row in each, thus eliminating him from her field of view. She rigidly stuck to the same routes between classes, each carefully chosen so as not to intersect with his. Once he made it clear he wanted to avoid her, she chose to make that as easy as possible. This was an aspect of dealing with boys she had the edge on compared to Sam, who'd never had an "ex." It was not a distinction that made her especially happy.

Her last-minute decision not to take AP Physics incidentally spared her the discomfort of having to share a fourth period with Aaron, and walking through the door into Environmental Science at the end of each day brought her a sense of relief she would have been hard-pressed to describe. The closest she could come was saying that it felt as if her backpack got ten pounds lighter as she passed between its jambs. That arriving at the class also reliably brought a genuine smile to her face was something she had yet to notice.

She took her seat, opened her notebook to the next blank page, pulled her mechanical pencil from its coiled spine, and printed the date in the top left corner. She glanced up at the whiteboard where the subject of today's lecture was written in blue marker, then added "Climate Change Policy" next to the date. Now ready to go, she leaned back and rested her elbow on the desk. Pinching her pencil near the eraser, she waggled the pointy end in a blurred arc while she waited for class to begin.

Mrs. Carson broke the course into nine distinct sections, devoting three to four weeks each to topics like Land and Water Use, Pollution, Population, and Resources. She used the last two weeks of August to present an overview of each of the sections, with an emphasis on how they were interrelated. September's unit was Climate Change, and its early placement in the syllabus was the main reason Ellie had settled on her particular term paper topic.

While dealing with the shack, she had learned that she especially enjoyed occupying that unique Venn space where the *new technology* and *public policy* circles overlapped, and she was eagerly looking forward to the following month's unit, Sustainable Business and Development. She believed she could be very happy building a career out of such pursuits, helping to guide the course of the country's environmental policies from the snug cocoon of an academic think tank.

Think tank. She scowled and let her hand thump loudly onto the desk as the phrase popped the delicate bubble of happiness the class usually granted her. Her mind flashed back to a day in mid-June when she and Aaron—*her* Aaron, not this bizarre new creature—had hiked to the top of the Pajarito ski area. They had spent part of the time speculating about the types of jobs she would be good at, and a public policy think tank had been one of his most appealing ideas. That outing was the first time he had openly acknowledged his long-unspoken love for her, as well as the day she first realized that the feeling went both ways. Her throat tightened, and she saw the edges of her vision start to smear.

No! You will not do this!

She was determined not to get teary-eyed in the middle of the school day, and especially not in this class. The bell rang then, and Mrs. Carson walked from behind her desk to stand at the middle of the whiteboard. Ellie blinked twice to clear her eyes, then looked up to find her teacher looking directly back. She screwed a pleasant expression onto her face and waited for the lecture to begin.

Only forty-five minutes, she told herself. *You can do it.*

Class ended, and Ellie was sliding her laptop into her pack when Mrs. Carson called her name.

"Ellie? Can I see you for a moment before you go?"

Ellie looked up, smiled, and nodded, but didn't bother trying to talk over the sudden din of sliding chairs and multiple conversations that broke out at the end-of-day bell. She secured the pack's top, threw one strap over her shoulder, and walked forward to her teacher's large, blocky desk. She had no idea why she was being called forward, but she noticed Mrs. Carson looked vaguely uncomfortable.

When in doubt, keep it simple. "Hi," she said, then she waited in silence while her teacher's eyes tracked the last of her fellow students out of the room. Not until they were alone did Mrs. Carson look back at her, and then she peered at her with an odd intensity.

"There's no problem," she said. "It's just that... Well, I was looking in your direction at the start of class, and you looked as though you had just swallowed an especially nasty-tasting bug. So I wanted to ask—is everything okay?"

Ellie was so touched by this simple expression of concern that she could feel her throat threatening to close up once again. It was only the hint of humor accompanying the concern that saved her. She nodded quickly and spoke while she was still able. "Yeah, thanks. I remembered something sort of unpleasant right then, that's all." She contrived a short, dismissive laugh, threw in an eye roll for good measure, and managed to make the rest of her answer light and breezy. "No biggie—just a 'boy' thing."

"I see." Mrs. Carson kept up the piercing stare as if her model came equipped with a built-in lie detector. Then she seemed to reach a decision on the matter, and her tone abruptly lightened. "Well, okay, then. But if you ever do have a problem—"

"I will," Ellie interjected. "But I'm fine. Promise."

Ellie started to turn toward the door, but Mrs. Carson raised a hand to stop her.

"There's one other thing. I talked to Shanna Newell this morning. She called to tell me you stopped by yesterday and that she was impressed by both your research topic and by the questions you asked."

Ellie wasn't sure what to say. She hadn't gone out of her way to make any kind of impression. In fact, she had left the center feeling pretty impressed herself. "I liked her," she said at last. "She's very easy to talk to. She seems to really enjoy her job there."

"She does. And she thought maybe you would, too."

Ellie's brow wrinkled in confusion. "Huh?"

"The call was also a bit of a background check, you could say. The center has a new volunteer position opening up. They were going to advertise for applicants, but after meeting you, Shanna wants to give you first crack at it." Using the edge of her desk, she tore off part of a sheet of paper and held it out. Ellie took it and saw a URL printed out in Mrs. Carson's precise hand. "That's the address where you can find a description of the position, hours, etc. Take a look and let her know what you think. Soon, though, okay?"

"Yes!" Ellie said at once, her expression suddenly radiant. "I think 'yes!'"

After leaving the classroom, Ellie made her way toward the main exit at the front of the school, guided entirely by autopilot. Along the entire way, she gripped the scrap of paper tautly between her hands and gazed intently at it as if the web address were a spell that held her in thrall. By the time she reached the nearly empty lobby, she was pretty sure she could type it in by memory. She became vaguely aware of a voice calling, but it took several seconds before her brain realized that the name echoing around the cavernous space was her own. Snapping back to full awareness, she stopped and spun around to see who was after her attention.

Ryan strode up the corridor behind her, and she could tell by his exasperated glare that he had been calling to her for some time. Ellie ran into him at school several times a week, but these days, unlike the first time, she no longer reacted as if she were experiencing a catastrophic glitch in the timeline. His consistently strong performance on the high school swim team the year before had not only helped them make it into the regional finals but had also earned him the opportunity to return this year to work as a part-time assistant coach.

"Hey. Sorry—I was thinking." She glanced down at the paper, then back at Ryan, who came to a stop in front of her. She thrust the slip out toward him. "Look! I got a job!"

Ryan cast a quick glance at the paper. "That's not a job. That's a website."

"It's a website about a volunteer position at the Nature Center."

"'Volunteer.' Meaning no pay?"

She shook her head. "Uh-uh."

"So I was right—technically not a job."

She grinned and stuck out her tongue, then grinned. "Fine. Be that way!" It was hard to believe she used to find his constant banter annoying. Now she considered their encounters the high point of almost any day, and her mood, already buoyed by the invitation to work at the Nature Center, rose even further. "Done coaching? And by the way, where's your stuff? Why don't you ever have stuff?"

"Yep. Just finished. And I left my "stuff" across the street with Sam." He looked back down the hallway from which he had just come and shook his head. "I don't think they'll be going back to Albuquerque in the spring. We actually had to cut a guy today. You know Sammy Jenkins?"

She indicated that she did not.

"Anyway, he couldn't seem to get the hang of the whole 'lanes' concept. It had gotten so bad that his teammates started calling him 'Flot Sam.'"

"That's so mean!" she said, but couldn't stifle a laugh. She nodded toward the exit, and they began walking that way together. "Sam offered to have you punch Aaron for me. Said you were upset with him?" He didn't respond until they had pushed through the doors and started up the sidewalk toward Diamond Drive. He pulled his Yankees cap from his jeans' waistband at the small of his back, shook it out, and carefully positioned it on his head as he answered.

"Not so much. I haven't even talked to him in weeks. I understand we can't expect him to be the same as the guy we knew, but I have a problem with how he's been acting lately. I mean, there's the way he's treated you, the way he..."

Ellie waited for Ryan to finish the thought. When it became obvious he wasn't going to, she twisted her head around to peer up at him, saw him frowning back at her.

"The way he *what*?"

"Let's just say I hear he's being kind of a jerk and leave it at that. It's a good news day, right?" He pointed at her slip of paper. Ellie nodded, feeling relieved. She figured that if he didn't want to say it, she *really* didn't want to hear it. They walked in silence until they reached the foot of the tall pedestrian overpass that spanned Diamond Drive to connect the high school and University of New Mexico campuses. They stopped at the foot of the steps and turned to face one another.

"So, tell me more about this 'job' of yours." He hooked quotes in the air between them.

"This is literally all I know so far," she said, flapping the paper. "Mrs. Carson gave this to me after class. I went to the PEEC yesterday to talk to someone there about my senior science paper. She called Mrs. Carson and said she wanted me to do some kind of work out there. Exactly what kind, I do not know."

"Well, congrats! Unless you find out they want you to scrub the toilets or something. Then maybe not so much."

She laughed at the absurd comment and gave his arm a playful jab. "They don't want me to scrub toilets, silly! Are you guys coming back to the house?"

He shook his head and jabbed his thumb toward the university. "I'm going to go find Sam, and then we're heading up to my place."

Ellie's mood deflated in an instant. Ryan's dad, an ex-Marine Lieutenant Colonel, ran security for the LAB, and his long workdays meant Sam and Ryan could enjoy much more "quality alone time," as Sam euphemistically put it, at his house. As a result, the movie nights that had been common throughout Sam's high school years were now rare, and Ellie was starting to find her house lonely without them around.

"Oh, okay," she muttered.

Hearing the disappointment in her voice, Ryan stepped close, placed both hands on her shoulders, and smiled into her frowning, upturned face. "Hey. We'll hang out there before long. Not this weekend, but soon. I promise."

Before she could reply, she heard a familiar voice come from behind him, speaking in a slow, deliberate cadence borrowed from a character in *The Matrix*.

"Do we need to have another talk, *Mister Collins?*"

Ryan released his grip on Ellie's shoulders, and they moved apart. Sam squinted down at them from the overpass' bottom step, arms crossed and toe tapping in an exaggerated posture of disapproval. As soon as she had played the bit out to its end, she dropped all pretense of being annoyed, smiled, and stepped down to stand beside Ryan.

"So, what's the occasion?" she said, slipping an arm around his waist.

"Ellie has just become ungainfully employed."

Sam looked at Ellie, eyebrows raised.

"Maybe," Ellie said. "I got offered some kind of job thingy…" She caught a look from Ryan and laughed. "Okay, fine—*volunteer* thingy at the nature center, if I want it. I don't know anything about it yet, though." She held up the paper as if the mere sight of it would provide the situation additional clarity. "I'll be able to tell you more tonight."

All three of them turned and began walking down the sidewalk together. At the end of the block, Ellie gave them a brief wave and veered off on her own to take the canyon trail home. Then, as the others were moving out of earshot, she heard Ryan's voice.

"Seriously, how *did* you sneak up on us like that?"

For the first time in a long time, Ellie's thoughts did not turn to Aaron as soon as she was alone. Passing through the small playground that marked the south end of the trail, she tried to imagine what sort of work Shanna wanted her to do. In addition to the exhibit hall, the PEEC ran a planetarium, maintained an educational garden, and presented lectures on a wide range of scientific subjects relevant to northern New Mexico. The exhibit hall included some live animals; maybe she'd get to take care of those. Although Ryan's "toilet scrubbing" possibility didn't exactly thrill her, she decided she didn't care too much what her duties might be. The opportunity to work with Shanna was the main attraction, and she knew she'd at least consider almost anything.

Dr. Nadkarni! She suddenly remembered Shanna saying she was coming to give a talk soon. If she took the job, she might get to meet a woman who had single-handedly pioneered an entirely new branch of field study.

"'Branch.' Ha!" She laughed aloud at the unintentional pun. The more she thought about the possibilities, the more excited she became, and she marveled at how good she felt.

With a start, she noticed she was crossing her own back yard. She stopped and turned around to face the end of the trail. She felt disoriented and wondered how she had come to be there so quickly. Then she realized that she had just hiked the entire path, nearly half a mile, without being consciously aware of a single step of it. She tried to remember crossing the footbridge or making the short, steep climb from the lower trail up to the level of her house, but found her mind was completely blank. She shook her head, bemused by this second total lapse in awareness, then turned and went inside.

In her room, she opened her computer and impatiently endured the agonizing six whole seconds it needed in order to wake up and reconnect to the wi-fi network and the World Wide Web beyond. She typed "pe" into the browser's search bar, let auto-fill complete the URL for her, then hit Return. She selected Support from the main menu, then Volunteer from the drop-down options. What she read—a generic list of typical volunteer duties—didn't help her much. She saw nothing that looked like a clearly defined position.

She planted her feet on the floor and pushed hard, tilting her chair onto its back legs and straightening her body until she could worm her fingers into her pocket to retrieve Mrs. Carson's slip of paper. She refreshed her memory with a quick glance, then looked back at the Firefox address bar. She spotted the difference at once.

"Ah!" She modified the address, replacing "-opportunities" with "-assistant," and hit Return. The new page looked much more like she had expected.

PEEC Volunteer Admin. Position

Be part of the solution! Join the PEEC and help us keep our mission of environmental education programs fresh and relevant. You will work closely with our staff, helping to develop new exhibits, design educational programs, and prepare presentation materials. In return, you will increase your own environmental knowledge and awareness.

Hours:

Flexible. Estimated ten to fifteen per week;

Must be willing to work weekends;

Duties:

Administrative tasks including clerical work, research, graphic design;

Assist as needed in the public display areas;

Qualifications:

A knowledge of the natural world and a willingness to expand and share that knowledge;

The ability to communicate effectively and comfortably with both children and adults;

Excellent written communication skills;

Creativity and enthusiasm;

The ability to work as part of a collaborative team;

Pay:

None

She slouched back in her chair, laced her fingers behind her head, and peered at the screen through slitted eyes. The position appeared to be nothing less than an offer to "let" someone work as what amounted to an assistant educational program director for free. That seemed like a lot of responsibility, and the realization left her feeling conflicted. She saw at once the potential value of the experience but was equally aware of the demands it would place on her time. Belatedly seeing the absurdity of that last thought, she snorted a humorless laugh.

"Yeah, right! Like it would really cut into my busy social schedule."

Much to her own considerable surprise, she was enjoying the Environmental Science class. For years, she had looked forward to taking the advanced physics course and the opportunity to truly get her nerd on, not to mention potentially earning a few college credits. But while she couldn't deny that she found speculating about the state of the universe microseconds after the Big Bang immensely exciting, what she was learning from Mrs. Carson had actual, real-world application. Besides, there was no law saying she couldn't study high-energy particle physics just for fun.

She re-read the job description, but found it remained annoyingly lacking in details. *Details. As in "where the devil is."* She wanted more of those before making a commitment.

Ms. Newell,

She frowned at the screen, cleared it, and started over.

Shanna,

Thanks for offering me this amazing opportunity. I've looked at the webpage, and I am definitely interested. I hate to sound wishy-washy, but I need to know a bit more before I can decide for sure whether or not to take it. Can we get together so I can ask some questions? Or would you rather I email you? I know you must be busy.

I'm available any weekday after 4:00 or anytime on the weekends. Let me know what works for you, and I'll be there.

Thanks again, Ellie

She clicked on the tiny paper airplane icon and heard her message *whoosh* off into the ether. Remembering what Shanna had said about not expecting immediate replies, she flipped the screen down and went out to the kitchen to look for a snack.

Sam returned right after dinner and helped clean up by loading the dirty dishes from the table into the dishwasher, while Ellie scrubbed the pans and kitchen knives.

"Find out any more about that 'job thingy?'" Sam said.

"Eh, not really. I went to the webpage, but there wasn't much there. I wrote to Shanna—the woman I talked to yesterday—to find out more." She shook as much water as she could from a cast-iron skillet, thoroughly dried it with a towel, then passed it to Sam to put away while she started drying the knives.

"Do you think you might go for it?" Sam said.

"Maybe. Probably. I'm no longer so sure I want to go into a purely theoretical field. This would be a good way to try something else out before I have to make any class decisions."

"Can I assume the dual credit idea is dead?" Sam was referring to LA High and UNM-LA's arrangement that allowed high school students to take free college courses their senior year that would count not only toward high school graduation but also as college credits when they enrolled at the university.

Ellie considered this as she slipped the knives back into their wooden block. "I don't know. I still might do that in the spring. I thought it would be cool for me to catch up so we could all graduate together, but that was back when Aaron and you guys were all in the same grade, and he and I were, well, you know." She trailed off, feeling no need to complete the thought. In truth, she was counting on getting a scholarship somewhere far away from Los Alamos.

Sam's expression brightened at the idea. "Come! Join us!" she intoned. "That actually *would* be pretty cool. We don't need him!"

Ellie thought back to earlier that afternoon. She had been genuinely excited—happy, even—at the prospect of working at the nature center and warmed by the implied compliment the offer paid her. None of that had anything to do with Aaron. She glanced up and looked Sam in the eye. "No. I guess we really don't."

Ellie was finishing her Calc 2 homework when a mechanical purr from her MacBook announced the arrival of new email. There were three notifications in the screen's upper right corner. Two of the messages were junk, and these she quickly deleted. The third made her heart kick into double time for a few beats. It was from Shanna.

Ellie:

I'm very glad to hear you're interested. We're closed on Thursdays, but I'll be working there in the afternoon. Stop by after school, and we'll talk. If that doesn't work, let me know, and we'll shoot for Friday instead.

See you soon—Shanna

Ellie kept her reply short and to the point.

Shanna,

Thursday works for me. I'll be there at 4:00.

Thanks, Ellie

She sent the message, then leaned back in her chair. She had ditched AP Physics for Environmental Science on little more than a whim, and now, quite out of the blue, she was being offered the chance to work alongside an expert in that very field. Multiple experts, to be more precise; the PEEC boasted several scientists on its staff. Was this merely a coincidence, or was there something larger at work here? She didn't believe in the idea of fate, but she had learned to take notice when all the universe's indicators started pointing in the same direction. Sam had recently told her she needed to be alert to recognizing the path when it appeared. Was this an example?

Well, just because you start down a path, she reminded herself, *nothing says you have to follow it all the way to its end.*

3

—————

Monday and Wednesday were Ellie's favorite days of the week for one very simple reason. On those mornings, she and Sam hiked to school together, exactly as they had for the past three years, and on most Wednesdays, they walked home together, too. They had long ago refined their complex morning routine, including the alternating use of their tiny bathroom, into a kind of dance, loosely choreographed but smoothly flowing. Today, Sam was first into the shower. She finished quickly, and by the time Ellie completed her turn, she had coffee waiting in their bedroom.

Ellie paused to savor a few sips before she pulled on a pair of thick socks, followed by her favorite jeans, then removed and began folding her nightshirt. Her conversation with Ryan the previous afternoon had reminded her of a question she'd been meaning to ask Sam for months. Over the summer, their parents gave Sam the chance to take over their small, shared office and finally have a bedroom of her own. Sam, to Ellie's surprise, turned them down, and Ellie had never known why.

"Why didn't you take Mom and Dad up on their offer to let you move into the other room?"

"First of all, I know they enjoy having that space for themselves. You should have seen Dad's face when I said I was fine here; talk about relief!

Plus, aside from liking to study there sometimes, I couldn't see the point. I mean, after sharing a room for all this time, what kind of secrets do you and I have? Why? Were you hoping I would?"

Ellie popped her head through the collar of a light pull-over sweater before she answered. "What would I do with all of that extra space? No, I was just curious. I thought you'd like finally having a little more privacy. That's all."

"Oh, I learned how to deal with that a *long* time ago." Sam pitched her voice in soft, conspiratorial tones. "The trick is to be *really* quiet!" She managed to suppress a grin only until Ellie's mortified expression made her laugh out loud.

"I'm *kidding!*" she assured her. "Mostly," she added, then laughed again.

Ellie rolled her eyes. "You're unbelievable!" she said, but she was laughing too.

Crossing the back yard fifteen minutes later, Ellie carefully scanned the entire area as they made their way to the start of the narrow footpath. It had been at least two weeks since Sunshine, an itinerant cat they sometimes fed, last paid a visit. From cars to coyotes, life in Los Alamos held many perils for a cat living out on her own, and Ellie hoped she was okay. She waited until they crossed the footbridge and were climbing out of the canyon before relaying her latest job-related news.

"I got an email from Shanna, the nature center person, last night."

"And?"

"And she said she was glad I was interested. We're going to meet tomorrow so I can find out more about what she wants."

"Am I wrong, or do you sound not so glad?"

"Oh, I'm happy about it," she said, sounding anything but. "I've decided I'm not going to get too excited until I find out more, though. What about you? Now that Ryan can use the university pool to train whenever he wants, do you think you'll work somewhere else this summer?"

Sam had spent the three previous summers working at the city's indoor swim center, which, by chance, was practically next door to the PEEC. The job offered the dual benefits of being relatively easy and allowing her to be around Ryan during the hours he spent keeping in shape over the school breaks.

"It's not even October. I haven't even begun thinking about wondering about that yet. It's hard to imagine doing something else, though. Except for always smelling like chlorine, working there is a pretty plum deal."

"Maybe you could go to work for... what was her name? Shirley something? You and Kaitlyn could sell all that vintage stuff on the dark web or whatever." When she and Sam suddenly needed clothes to blend in with people on the streets of Brooklyn in 1941, they had tried their luck at a local consignment shop. The employee working there that day, Kaitlyn, had allowed them to search through some period clothing from the estate of the recently deceased Mrs. Pavlova. In return, Sam had hinted—with a knowing wink—that at least a few of the items were quite valuable, sold in the right way.

"That's funny. I'd forgotten about Katie. Wasn't *she* a hoot! I wonder if she's still there."

"Either there or in jail, I imagine."

"Don't say that—I'd feel so bad!"

"Wait! Didn't you take all our stuff back?"

"I tried, but there was a sign in the window saying the shop was closed for two weeks. When I went back, it was still closed. I ended up just leaving it all in a bag by the back door with a note that said, 'Thanks!'"

Ellie quietly considered that. She remembered Kaitlyn saying the owner was going to be gone, but only for a few days. Had something happened to her while she was away, or was the shop's closure somehow related to what they had done in 1941? Or maybe it had simply taken that long to sort through all of Mrs. Pavlova's stuff—there had been an awful lot of it. She considered the question for only a moment. They had learned early on that pondering such matters rarely led to answers they could be sure of, so she let it drop.

"It's still hard to believe all of that actually happened," she said at last.

"I know," Sam agreed. "It's pretty surreal. You should be glad you're past all the what-I-did-on-summer-vacation-essay grades."

"*Pfft!* I always just made stuff up anyway."

"Really? Creative writing? *You?!*"

"Yep. And in most of my essays, I was an only child." Ellie stuck out her tongue.

"Ha! Well, you're *still* the only 'child!'"

Ellie laughed. "Ouch! I guess I walked right into that one."

"I can't even imagine it, you know?" Sam said.

"What, being an only child?"

"Yeah. And it's not only about having someone around to enjoy scandalizing, although that's definitely a perk!" She flashed Ellie an impish grin. "But it's all of the little things we do every day. Simple stuff like this —just walking to school together. I don't know. I mean, I feel as close to Ryan as I can imagine being to someone, but with you and me, it's different. I'm glad we've been able to share all of that." Sam's smile was no longer impish but so radiant with love that Ellie would have sworn she could actually feel it warming her face.

Ellie, whose emotions were always dangerously close to the surface these days, pressed her lips firmly together and fought down a sudden urge to blubber. Instead of answering right away, she slid her arm around Sam's waist and leaned toward her. Sam mirrored the gesture, and they walked that way, their heads gently bumping, until they reached the end of the path.

"I know," Ellie said at last. "I can't imagine what it would be like without you."

They spotted Ryan waiting for them half a block farther on. Sam called out to him and gave Ellie another little smile as they stepped apart. Feeling their hands brush past one another, Ellie grabbed Sam's and gave it a quick squeeze. She felt Sam squeeze back before letting go. Watching her sister stride out ahead of her, Ellie marveled at how much emotion could be conveyed by so small a gesture.

Today was the day for Mrs. Carson to give her final approval of their project outlines. When Ellie placed hers on the teacher's desk, she felt the familiar fluttering of butterflies in her stomach she experienced every time she turned in work to be graded. The sensation had started with her first assignment ever, a hand-print turkey she'd drawn in kindergarten, and had never gone away.

Once seated, she continued researching her topic while casting frequent glances to the front of the room. Mrs. Carson worked her way through the stack of outlines, often writing a few comments before moving on to the next. Ellie could recognize her own by the bright red clip that held the two sheets of paper together. Since she had been one of the first to arrive today, hers was near the bottom of the pile, and she soon became too engrossed in taking notes to continue monitoring Mrs. Carson's progress.

Dr. Wall responded to her questions about soil organisms more quickly than Ellie had expected, recommending she consider using one of several nematode species in her paper. As an alternative, she suggested the mixed-organism colony cryptobiotic soil crust, most often simply called "crypto." Nematodes, Ellie decided after a few minutes of research, were definitely worth further study, but she decided to go with crypto. The complex community of algae, fungi, lichen, and cyanobacteria formed a crenelated black crust on the area's sandy soil, binding it together and limiting erosion. Simply stepping on it caused damage that could take decades to fully heal, and this was the main reason staying on established trails was so important when hiking in the desert. It had two main advantages over nematodes. First, crypto was easily visible without a microscope once the crust was dense enough. Also, most people who lived in the area were familiar with it.

With two example slots filled by microscopic crypto and the towering ponderosa pines—two opposites if ever there were—she worked on selecting another three. One should be a predator, and she thought coyotes would be a good choice. Despite the advice Shanna had given her, she was seriously considering a rodent species for the fourth example, one that would rely on the pine trees for food and be relied on by the coyotes as prey. That left at least one more species to choose, but before she could give it any thought, Mrs. Carson began returning their outlines. She glanced at hers to find only a single word scrawled across its front: Excellent!

The bell rang as the final outline reached its owner, and Mrs. Carson spoke quickly before students could begin streaming from the room. "Finish reading chapter six for class tomorrow!"

Ellie left the classroom with her mind still focused on her research topic. She was beginning to realize how, until very recently, she had lived entirely within her own childhood bubble, only dimly aware of what happened beyond the confines of tiny Los Alamos. The subatomic realm, abstract and deeply mysterious, fascinated her, and she could rattle off the names of all the quarks, the leptons, and about a third of the baryons, even if suddenly roused out of a deep sleep. However, it usually took somebody launching missiles before she paid any attention to politics or international affairs. And the climate? She had always known it was in bad shape, but only in a vague, general sense. What she was learning in Mrs. Carson's class not only disturbed her deeply but left her feeling embarrassed by the appalling depth of her own ignorance.

She was nearing the lobby when something in the conversation between two girls in front of her pulled her out of her thoughts. A reference? A name? She couldn't say. Trapped close behind them by the tightly packed crowd all shuffling toward the exit, she couldn't help but overhear them, and although she tried to prevent it, the scene the girls discussed played itself out in her mind with pitiless clarity. All that was missing was the face of the unidentified "she."

"She *said* that?" Incredulous.

"Uh-huh! They were at her house last Friday, the day her mom works late, and they were making out, right? Really getting into it, and she was like, 'What the hell—I'm going for it!'"

"You mean, like, *all the way?*" Just as incredulous.

"Uh-huh! So she starts taking off her shirt and tells him to get undressed, right? And when he pulls his pants down, she sees his hair is just as white, you know, *down there*, as it is on his head!"

"*Eww.* That's *weird!*"

"That's what *she* said. Said it was kinda like looking at a 'negative,' whatever that means."

"They really did it?!" Breathless. This was such a good story!

Ellie's throat burned, but she was determined to keep it together until she was alone.

"She didn't come right out and say so, but she did say there was definitely nothing negative about *it*. Said it worked just *fine!* I'm taking that as a yes!"

As the throng emerged from the hallway and dispersed into the wider lobby, Ellie was finally able to elbow her way between the gossiping girls.

"Seriously! Could you two possibly be any more brainless?!" she exclaimed, then made a dash for the doorway.

"*Hey!*" one of the girls called after her, then she turned to her friend. "Did you hear that? So *rude!*"

"I guess we know who's *not* getting any!" the other said, and both girls giggled at what was, for them, a supreme expression of wit.

Ellie didn't care. Equal parts hurt and angry, all she wanted was to get out of the building and away from everyone before she totally lost it. Once on the sidewalk, she broke into a trot and kept up the pace until she crossed the edge of school property and turned down a narrow, residential street into the adjoining neighborhood before slowing to a walk.

"*Why?!*" Her plaintive shout rebounded down the empty street. She was convinced that if she understood what was making Aaron act the way he was, maybe she could fix things. Or, failing that, she might at least finally come to accept them. She made it to the very bottom of the canyon before she finally stopped and let the tears come. To her relief, there weren't many.

She leaned on the railing at the middle point of the bridge and blinked hard to clear her eyes. Staring vacantly into the dry wash below her, she replayed a conversation she'd had with Aaron back in June. They had left Starbuck's and were on their way to meet with Sam and Ryan when he admitted to having fantasized about her. She hadn't known what to say in response to this not-quite-spontaneous revelation, but she had privately felt flattered. Knowing that in matters of sex he was as completely inexperienced as she was had, in some paradoxical way, made the confession seem innocent rather than salacious. She sensed it was his bumbling way of letting her know he thought of her as a girl—a female and potential sexual partner—and not merely as a fellow science nerd.

Apparently, I'm no longer the only one he thinks of that way!

She was finally pulling herself together when she heard footsteps and felt the bridge shudder rhythmically as someone stepped onto its far end and walked toward her. Only then did she remember she was supposed to have waited for Sam after school and guessed it was her finally catching up. In case it wasn't, she kept her damp, blotchy face pointed out toward the ravine. A second later, an arm lightly brushed against hers as her sister came to a stop close beside her.

"Here you are!" Sam chirped. "Did you forget about me?"

Ellie finally turned to look at her, her expression tight with pain.

Sam sighed heavily. "It's Aaron again, isn't it?"

"Oh, Sam! I never imagined having him back could hurt worse than losing him!"

"What did he do this time?"

"Nothing, really. It wasn't him. I was walking behind these two girls, and they were talking about this other girl and a guy who was obviously Aaron getting undressed together. *Arrgh!!! What is his problem?!*"

"So, he's, um, 'seeing' somebody else?"

Ellie thought about the times he'd paraded past her with an assortment of other girls at his side. "From what I can tell, he's seeing *everybody* else!"

"*Hmm*…. It's like he's the anti-Aaron or something."

"But that's the thing. I don't think he actually is. There are times…" Ellie went silent for a long moment, letting her mind sift through the confusing data set that was Aaron v2.0.

"Okay, so last week I was late leaving class, and the halls and lobby were pretty much empty. I was almost at the door when I heard a voice. I turned around, and it was him, standing by himself and staring up at the science fair winners plaque." She paused again, refreshing her memory of the scene.

"He hadn't been talking to me, just sort of mumbling to himself, but I walked over and said, 'Hey. How's it going?' He says hey back and explains that he was trying to come up with a project that wasn't totally cheesy and hadn't been done a thousand times before. And I remembered our Aaron saying almost the exact words last spring, so I added the rest of it. 'Without access to a CRISPR lab or a couple of big, honkin' lasers, you mean.' And he looked at me and smiled and it was so sweet, and for a second, it was like the old Aaron was back. No, not 'like'—he really *was* back. Then he said, 'I was thinking more like making a battery out of a turnip and a bag of corn chips,' which is sort of what *I* said back then, and we both laughed the way we used to when one of us said something goofy. Like I said, it was sweet, but it was also extremely strange how closely it echoed our conversation back in May. Eerie, almost.

"Anyway, I decided to take a chance and said, 'So, how about we go down to Starbuck's at Smith's sometime, get a coffee, take in that amazing view?' Real casual, no pressure, but it was like, I don't know, like I had slapped him, maybe. It was as if something inside him woke up, and suddenly he wasn't sweet anymore. He said, 'Yeah, I bet you'd like that, wouldn't you?' and then he stormed off. *'I bet you'd like that?'* What does that even *mean?* But my point is that for a few seconds, he was his old self. It wasn't only about the way he was acting—I could *feel* it. It was something coming from inside him. Then he changed," she snapped her fingers, "just like that."

Sam's gaze dropped to the dry stream bed below their feet while she thought about how to respond. She took in a breath as if about to speak, let it out, then tried again.

"You know, when I was taking first aid, the instructor told us something I've never forgotten. He said you can't save everyone, which, obviously! But then he went on to say, 'At some point, you're not doing CPR anymore; you're making out with a corpse.'"

Ellie's nose wrinkled with revulsion. "Well, that certainly *is* memorable. *And* disgusting. And I get it, Sam; I really do. I'm simply not ready to give up on him yet, that's all. Of course, after today…"

"Do you know who the girls were?"

"Yeah, one was Jordan Baker. God, I can't believe I'm actually in a *science* class with her! The other was—"

"Wait, let me guess! Julia Sanchez!" Ellie nodded. "And if Jordan's got something that personal to dish out, then number three was almost definitely Jessica Thomas. The J-birds! Remember the time Jessica told everyone who would listen about her and the bass player from that band, the Mesa Mavericks? And the time Julia spread that story about seeing Billy Peterson and Tasha Ivanovich going at it in an old junker out behind the auto shop? How dumb do you have to be to come up with that one? I mean, they're *both* gay! And as for 'Jordan Baker,'" Sam made air quotes, "ours lies even more than the one in the *Great Gatsby*! Consider the source, is what I'm trying to say."

"I know. I thought about that." She scrunched up her face. "Still hurt, though. Plus, Ryan said something yesterday that made me..." She didn't bother finishing the thought. Instead, she sniffed a final time, then stood up straight, pulled her shoulders back, and held her head high. "But you know what? I'm done worrying about it! I can't force things to be like they were, and if he'd rather fool around with Jessica than with me, well, then, he is definitely *not* the person I knew."

"Hear, hear!" Sam enthusiastically seconded Ellie's heartfelt declaration of emotional independence. "But do you think it'd be different if he knew 'fooling around' with you was an option?"

Ellie laughed and spluttered a raspberry at her. "You know what I meant! Besides, if I end up working at the nature center, I won't have time for him or anything else."

Sam nudged Ellie's shoulder with her own. "Hey, ready to go home?"

Ellie nodded, and they began walking. As they left the bridge and started up the trail, a question occurred to her. "Did you ever forgive him? Billy Peterson, I mean." An uncharacteristically sloppy turn by Ryan's former teammate at the swimming regionals the previous spring had knocked Ryan's team out of competition early on, cutting short their time away from Los Alamos. Sam, who, accompanied by their mom, went along not just to support the team but to enjoy a few days in New Mexico's largest city, had taken the loss even harder than Ryan.

Sam laughed. "I suppose. It was only Albuquerque, after all."

Ellie plodded through her homework that evening without her usual enthusiasm. Senior Spanish was a total immersion class. No one spoke English in the classroom except the teacher, and then only when she needed to explain more complex concepts. Understanding Spanish in real-world contexts was a key goal, and each quarter they had to read a short story and then write about it. This they could do in any way they chose—as a book report, in the style of a literary review, even as a parody—as long as they could show they understood what they had read. She was still in the reading phase for this quarter, and after reaching the end of the current chapter, she was happy to set the book aside and turn to the next subject.

Calc 2 offered more of a diversion, but ever since she had discovered how to think in mathematics as if it were merely another foreign language, translating freely between its abstract symbols and English, she found it far less challenging. She was enjoying the current topic, calculating the area between two curves, but was still trying to come up with reasons why she'd ever need to do that.

Mostly, though, her mind was elsewhere. The more she thought about it, the less credence she gave to Jordan's "make-out" story, and not only because it came from her. She believed that, deep down, and despite all his apparent differences, Aaron was still the same person at his core and that *no* Aaron would ever have anything to do with Jessica. Or any of the J-birds, for that matter. On that score, at least, she was feeling a little better.

She was nervous about her upcoming meeting with Shanna, even though she felt she had a lock on the position. She genuinely liked the idea of working there, but she couldn't shake the feeling that her life was being messed with by forces outside her control. She reassured herself that simply taking a volunteer job while she was still in high school didn't mean she was abandoning all her old plans for the future. Despite down-playing her interest in the job to Sam, she was actually very excited about the possibility of working at the PEEC.

She opened her MacBook and went to the center's website. She couldn't earn a degree in biology overnight, but there were other things she could learn. She began making her way methodically through each page of the site, familiarizing herself with the center's programs and the rest of the staff.

4

"Ellie, has the print shop called back with the quote on those posters?"

Ellie had been working at the nature center for more than two weeks, long enough that she no longer jumped every time someone popped in to talk to her. Her workspace wasn't in a proper office. Instead, it was at a small, makeshift desk tucked into a corner of the break room, where she sat with her back to the door. It was not ideal, but she was used to working in classrooms alongside at least twenty other students, so the occasional distraction caused by someone making coffee or eating lunch didn't bother her much. She spun her chair around to see Shanna leaning in through the doorway.

"They have not. I'll call them now and see if I can get that. Is there anything else you need today?"

"Get the quote, but tell them we're putting the job on hold for a while. I was just on the phone with Nalini—she's had to postpone her talk here. I don't have a firm new date yet, so just tell them to hold onto the file, and we'll get that info to them as soon as I hear from her." Ellie nodded. "After that, you're free to go. I'll see you on Saturday."

With that, Shanna was gone from the doorway, and Ellie turned to her computer to look up the number for the printer. Then she heard Shanna's voice behind her again.

"And Ellie?" She pivoted back around. "Thanks. You're doing great!"

Shanna smiled and disappeared a second time. Ellie smiled, too, appreciating the appreciation. During all her years in school, she had always preferred to work on her own, studied hard to be at the top of each of her classes, and strived to be the first to solve whatever problems their teachers threw at them. The need to build consensus with Aaron, Sam, and Ryan while plotting to destroy the shack had shown her another, possibly better, way to go about things. Here, surrounded by people whose education and experience made her own seem utterly insignificant, where her sole purpose was to implement ideas created by others, she was quickly learning to make even more changes to her usual methods. She found suppressing her ego surprisingly easy when playing second fiddle involved working for someone she genuinely respected.

Besides, she thought. *I could teach any one of 'em a thing or two about time travel!*

On her way out of the building, she stopped outside Shanna's door and waited until she looked up from her screen before asking her question. "Is everything okay with Dr. Nadkarni?"

"Hmm? Oh, she's fine. She's wanted at an emergency environmental summit in Brazil. The contraction of the rainforest is expected to reach thirty percent this fall. To say they're freaking out down there is putting it mildly, but it's not like everyone hasn't seen it coming."

Ellie knew this figure was close to an important tipping point. The Amazon rainforest was so vast that it created a distinct local weather system that was responsible for producing half of its own rainfall. Climate-driven die-back, along with increased cutting and burning for agriculture, mining, and road construction, was steadily decreasing the forest's size. At a certain point, estimated to be when it shrank to sixty percent of its original acreage, the lush ecosystem would be unable to sustain its self-watering processes, and much of the Amazon River basin would become an African-style savannah. Now down to seventy percent, it was teetering on the brink.

"So, they want her to give a talk?"

"She's going to give the keynote speech opening night, and she'll be involved behind the scenes after that."

"Do you think anybody will listen?"

Shanna pointed a finger at her as if to say, *That's the real question, isn't it?* Then she dropped her hand into her lap and smiled. "I meant it earlier. I couldn't be happier with the job you've been doing. What do you think so far?"

"I like it! For me, science has always meant physics formulas, complex computer modeling, and lots of abstract math. And you guys have that, but what you do goes even further. It's not that you take your work out of the lab and into the world—your lab *is* the world. I think that's really cool!" She regretted the "cool" as soon as the word left her mouth, fearing the expression made her sound childish, and she had to fight a powerful urge to cringe.

To Ellie's relief, Shanna laughed with genuine delight. "'Climatologists: bringing "cool" to a warming world!' I *will* have T-shirts made." She continued in a more somber tone. "If anyone in your generation thinks any of this is cool, there's still hope. Saturday?" Ellie nodded, and Shanna turned back to her desk.

With the days growing ever cooler and darkness coming a little earlier each successive evening, Ellie opted to hike home through the canyon while it was still a safe and comfortable option. She focused on keeping her feet from sliding out from under her until the path flattened out, then she allowed her mind to drift back to Dr. Nadkarni and the deteriorating condition of the rainforest. That it was getting so close to the point of no return was bad, but it was by no means the only large, climate-related system that was in trouble. The West Antarctic Ice Sheet was dwindling at an accelerating rate, ocean circulation patterns were becoming ever weaker and more inconsistent, and the northern permafrost zone was half of what it once was. Much closer to home, Utah's Great Salt Lake now held water for only a month or two each spring. During the rest of the year, dry winds carried arsenic-laced sand from the exposed lake bed straight to the lungs of the more than two million people living on its eastern edge. Hers was not a happy planet.

She thought about the old Aaron's family trip to Glacier National Park in June and how disappointed he had been not to see any glaciers. Only part of one, Blackfoot, remained, and it was a tiny remnant of what it had been a hundred years ago. It was in a very remote part of the park, far from any easy points of access, and few people had the backcountry expertise necessary to visit it safely. Much of Europe was also glacier-free. Only a few in the world were growing, and only where warmer air was now carrying a higher level of moisture into areas still cold enough to remain frozen year-round.

She lifted her gaze and scanned the ponderosa forest around her. It was too dry, she knew. At higher elevations in places around Bandelier National Monument, this same, quite hardy species had already died out. Imagining these trees' needles slowly turning the color of rust before falling to leave dead, bare branches for miles around made something in her chest ache. With luck, most of her life would differ little from that of her parents and all the generations that came before, but it was a close thing. Her kids would definitely face a rolling succession of ecological catastrophes.

Her kids. The thought reminded her of a subject she tried to keep pushed back into the darkest corners of her mind. Since they first used the shack to travel back in time, her periods had been erratic. *More erratic,* she corrected. Even after more than three years, her body had never settled into the set-your-clock-by-them regularity that Sam's quickly had. She even skipped a month here and there, especially early on, but this felt different. She couldn't express why it did, and maybe it was merely the coincidence of her current situation starting right after using the shack that made her feel that way. Whatever the cause, thinking about it aroused a vague, irrational dread that had thus far made it easier to ignore the situation than give the potential problem the attention it deserved.

She sighed, then admonished herself aloud. "If you're growing up, then it's time to grow up!"

She made a mental promise to get her mom to make an appointment for her by the end of the week, and immediately felt a little better. An

Abert's squirrel, hunkered on a low branch in a tree to her right, warily monitored her approach and chattered a warning as she got close. Ellie stopped and smiled up at it.

"That wasn't so hard, now was it?" She was talking to herself, but aiming the words at the squirrel. It chattered at her again, then scampered up to the safety of a higher limb. "Yeah, well, it's not like anybody wants to talk about this stuff," she said, her imagination filling in the squirrel's end of the conversation.

Once more passing the spot she had shared with Aaron a few months ago, she found she no longer felt any urge to visit it. A sustained, two-week-long distraction from thinking about him was just what her brain had needed, apparently, for in that time she had managed to achieve an emotional reset of sorts. She was still disappointed by the way her attempts to get close to the new Aaron had failed, but what caused most of her sadness was something else. She had thought she was over the loss of 'her' Aaron, but she wasn't. Her grieving had been interrupted by this new one's unexpected appearance, and only in the aftermath of failing to rekindle the old relationship with him were the earlier feelings of loss resurfacing. The situation was made all the more complicated by seeing the source of her distress walking around—very much alive—nearly every day. She thought it had to be the weirdest love triangle in history.

This new clarity allowed her to understand Aaron better too. She'd known from the very beginning that she couldn't view his new personality as an intentional choice. He'd had no say in the matter. Who he was today, as opposed to the boy she had known for so many years, was the result of living a very different childhood. He had grown up happier in almost every way, and for this, she was genuinely thankful.

But there was more behind her reluctant acceptance than that. This Aaron, along with his many differences, existed because of decisions she'd had a willing part in making—decisions that no amount of effort would allow him to remember or her to forget. Whatever weirdness he was going through, she felt an obligation to be there for him to whatever extent she could. And she would, even when that meant having to suffer through some painful moments.

She made another mental promise—given the chance, she would find a way they could be friends again. If, in the end, that turned out to be all she could accomplish, she'd still be happy.

Crossing the lawn, Ellie once more found Sam studying at the patio table. It was cooler this evening and already dim enough that she'd needed to turn the outside lights on. Pretty soon, Sam would be forced inside and back to using their parent's office for studying until spring. Ellie could see shadowy movement through the partially open window above Sam's head. Either her mom or dad was working at the sink, no doubt starting on dinner.

"Hey, Sam," she said as she drew near.

"Hey, yourself. So, it's been a while. How's that job thingy going?" Sam persisted in viewing Ellie's entry into the working world as something of an ongoing experiment, one she might decide to terminate at any time.

Ellie wasn't sure if Sam expected her to stay perpetually in school or what. She dropped into the seat across from her. "It's fun! I always imagined working in science someday, but this is so not what I had in mind. Of course, I'm not actually doing any of the science, so that part's really different."

"Okay, so you remember you're still in high school, right?"

"Yeah. No, I get that, but it's like I told Shanna; what they're working on is very different from anything I ever pictured myself doing, but I love being a part of it. Even if for now my part is just ordering posters."

"*I* love how you call your boss 'Shanna.' If I ever called Mr. Landry 'Bob,' he'd have to change his shorts, and I'd be looking for a new job!"

Ellie joined Sam in laughter. Sam's seasonal boss was well known for being very tightly wound. It was her guess that calling him "Bob" would more likely result in Sam needing to test out her defibrillator training on him. She stood and walked around the table to stand at Sam's elbow. With a sweep of her hand, she indicated the scattering of books and papers surrounding Sam's iPad. "So, whatcha studying?"

"Psych. This unit is on social psychology. I'm supposed to 'read overviews of the works of the most prominent social psychologists and be able to compare and contrast their theories.'" She dropped the air quotes and pointed at the names on the screen. "Ashe, Maslow, Skinner... The youngest person on that list is eighty-seven—most of them are *dead!* I mean, seriously, have we learned nothing important in the past five decades?"

Ellie quickly skimmed down the column of names. One in particular, made familiar by a recently canceled Showtime series, caught her attention, and she flashed Sam a mischievous smile.

"William Masters, huh? I bet you enjoyed reading about *his* work!"

Sam snorted. "Yeah, well, you know me—when it comes to that subject, I'm more interested in practice than theory," she said, grinning back.

A loud sigh drifted out to them through the kitchen window, followed by their mom's voice. "I *can* hear you, you know."

Ellie was on her bed reading, leaning back on pillows piled up against the wall, when Sam came into the room.

"Contemporary Lit, right?" Ellie closed the book, her thumb marking the page, and glanced at its cover. The image showed a Middle Eastern city below a murky, greenish sky. Eroded red letters read *The Kite Runner*.

"Gee, what was your first clue?" Ellie's shelves were filled almost entirely with science fiction books, and any remaining space was taken up by a select assortment of fantasy and hard science titles. *A Wrinkle in Time* and *Jurassic Park* sat next to *Quantum Reality* and her complete collection of Harry Potter books, long unread but too treasured to let go. From Fangorn Forest to the deserts of Dune, she enjoyed dipping again and again into alternate realities that captivated her imagination, and she had read all of the books, save a few of the newest, multiple times.

Then there were the four she had not read even once. She discovered D. Hakham's *The Messengers* series on her shelf after the events in June, a set of short novels written by the very man whose life they'd disrupted in order to eliminate the shack from history. She knew the titular "messengers" to be her and Sam, but she felt so guilty about how they had interfered in the man's life that she had never been able to bring herself to read them.

Except she believed she *had* read them—in a way. The first book in the series had been printed in the fifties and showed all the expected wear that came from having passed through many hands over the intervening decades. The other three had been bought new, though, and the spines of each bore a telltale network of fine creases that suggested they had been read at least once. She assumed that the Ellie who inhabited this timeline before they altered the past had been the reader.

Perhaps the strangest consequence of destroying the shack was the way she, Sam, and Ryan had become strangers to their own pasts. To their relief, the broad strokes seemed mostly the same. They had no new aunts, uncles, or cousins to get to know, for instance. This version of Los Alamos seemed identical to the one they remembered, but nearly every difference they had stumbled over was part of their time here. It was the minute details of their home lives—like what kind of cake Sam had on her sixteenth birthday or the color of Ellie's first mountain bike—that created conversational land mines, and they quickly learned to avoid the kinds of topics that could trip them up. Ellie had never been able to unravel how such trivial discrepancies were connected to Aaron's absence from Los Alamos over the past six years, but they had to be. He was the only variable.

"It's pretty much the only reason you'd be reading any book I've read," Sam said. "Is he giving you guys a free choice this year?"

"Yeah, but I'm saving that for last. I'm thinking maybe *The Windup Girl*. Or *Into the Forest*—it's been a while since I read that one."

"Now that's one of yours I *have* read." Sam shuddered. "Still kinda creeps me out."

Suddenly looking serious, Sam crossed the room to sit on the edge of Ellie's bed. "Hey. I heard you and Mom talking in the kitchen right after you got home. You guys sounded sorta serious. Is everything okay?"

"I don't know. Probably, but I want to make sure. Remember that problem we discussed at Pasqual's back in June?" Sam thought for half a second, then nodded. "It's never totally sorted itself out. I asked Mom to arrange for me to get looked at, that's all."

"Wait—are you saying that in what, five months, you've never...?!" Sam, jumping to an incorrect conclusion, was instantly and very deeply concerned.

"Oh, no, I have!" Ellie quickly assured her. "That's why I didn't do anything sooner. I skipped June altogether, then July and August were okay. Okay-*ish*, I guess. Late and light, but there. But then I skipped September. And now it looks like October. It just makes me feel funny not knowing whether or not there really is something wrong, so I want to get everything checked out."

"For what it's worth, I think that is a *very* wise idea."

"Thanks, Sam, I—"

"I mean, who knows? Someday you might finally want to put all that stuff down there to good use. You know, get some experience 'under your belt.' It'd be nice to know it's all in working order." She laughed, amused by her own joke.

Ellie knew the crude jab was merely Sam's way of getting revenge for helping her embarrass herself in front of their mom earlier, and she wasn't bothered by it, even though she pretended to be.

"That's *horrible!* For a big sister, you're a terrible influence. You know that, right?" Then her thoughts turned once more to everything she went through over the summer and to Sam's role in helping her through it all. "Actually, you're the best sister ever. You know *that*, right?"

"I do," Sam chirped. "So good, in fact, that I'm willing to share my boyfriend with you."

"*Huh?*"

"Ryan told me he promised you we'd spend some time here soon. Said you seemed mopey. Anyway, this weekend works for us, so..."

That news was the best Ellie had heard in weeks, and it brought an enormous smile to her face. "Sweet!"

5

Before Ellie left for work the next morning, she confirmed that Ryan still planned to come over. After a quick exchange of messages with him, Sam assured her he'd get there later in the afternoon. She invited Ellie to join them for a movie that evening but made no promises about what it would be.

"It's Ryan's turn to pick this time—it's out of my hands," she said.

Ellie didn't say it, but she thought that was for the best. Her tastes were more in line with his than with Sam's, although that was largely beside the point. The truth was, she was happy just to be hanging out with them again and couldn't have cared less about the movie. Wanting to get home as quickly as possible, Ellie opted to ride her bike.

Her Saturday shift at the PEEC ran from ten until four, the same hours the center was open to the public. Fueled by her excitement about the evening ahead, Ellie pedaled hard and reached the nature center so early that the parking lot was empty, the building's interior still dark. After locking her bike to the rack, she walked to the far side of the garden and leaned her arms on the top rail of the weathered metal fence that ran along the edge of the cliff. The morning was cool, and where she stood was deeply shaded, but her body was still warm from her energetic ride. In the distance, the brightly lit Jemez Mountains no longer seemed to burn, but although most of the aspens had lost their leaves, she could pick out a few isolated groves that still retained their golden glow. Each of those groves, she knew, was essentially a single organism, its expanding root system adding more trees to the clonal colony each year. Aspens were another species threatened in many areas by warmer, drier conditions. So far, these still seemed healthy, and she was thankful for that.

"You go, guys!" she called, offering them heartfelt encouragement from a distance. Then she jumped, startled by sudden, delighted laughter behind her.

"I knew you belonged here!"

Ellie turned to see Shanna standing at the edge of the patio, a jumble of keys in one hand, a large, stainless steel thermos in the other. She would have felt foolish getting caught talking to trees by anyone else, but she knew to Shanna—to most of the people who worked here, actually—such behavior wouldn't seem particularly strange. That being the case, she only blushed a little.

Shanna laughed again. "Don't worry; you should hear some of the conversations I have with my ficus! Come on. I'll let you in."

As they crossed the lobby, sensors registered their presence, and lights turned on all around them.

"What am I doing today?" Ellie said.

"Well, there are no groups on the schedule; I do know that. I think I'll have you start by giving the exhibit hall a thorough going-over. Make sure everything is where it's supposed to be. Check a few random books in the kids' section, make sure nobody's left any inappropriate notes or doodles, then give the outsides of the critter tanks a quick wipe. Work on that until Teri is ready for you; then I know she's going to want your help on her project. Also, we got a call from somebody who wants to book the planetarium for a special show next month. I'll let you take care of scheduling that whenever he comes in. That should be enough to keep you off the streets and out of trouble! But if you run out of things to do, come see me." She smiled, then turned and headed down the hallway to her office.

Ellie gathered cleaning rags from the supply closet, along with a spray bottle of something so iridescent green that she found it hard to believe it was eco-friendly and not dangerously radioactive. Reentering the exhibit hall, she heard someone unlock the front door as another volunteer, Brett, let himself in. Ellie tossed him a wave as she veered into the main exhibit hall to start her day.

She began with the animals, giving the glass walls of their homes a thorough cleaning. No matter how many times they told the kids not to touch the cages, the tanks were always a streaked, smeary mess by the end of each day. At first, she worried the sight of the giant white cloth flapping around over their heads would frighten the little guys, but then she figured that probably wasn't nearly as stressful as being pounded on by diminutive delinquents day after day. She chatted softly to each as she wiped, the gopher snake included, even though she was pretty sure the earless creature couldn't hear her.

After determining the books were free of unwanted additions, she scattered them around the large space. She randomly placed a few on each of the small tables and ottomans in the exhibit hall, and the rest she put in the adjacent wildlife observation room. She found the windows in this second, smaller area to be just as smudgy as the critter tanks, and she gave each a few passes with a fresh rag. Just as she finished, she heard the first visitors of the day come in.

"Ooh, look—a snake!" a young male voice exclaimed.

"*Eww, gross!* You know I hate those things!" said another voice, presumably the boy's sister. Ellie was offended both as a girl, one who didn't appreciate this perpetuation of the stereotype, and on behalf of the snake, whom she considered to be very handsome.

When she passed through the exhibit hall on her way to the supply closet, she glanced toward the snake cage. A boy of no more than seven had both hands and his nose pressed against the freshly polished glass. From his chair behind the counter, Brett impassively watched this bad behavior, doing nothing to intervene. When she shot him a frustrated look, he simply shrugged. *What can you do?* She wished, and not for the first time, that her eyes doubled as death rays, and wondered which of the two she'd zap first.

. . .

At three thirty, she sat alone at her tiny desk, feeling very happy about the day's work. She had spent the afternoon helping the School Programs Coordinator, Teri McGivens, update her presentation about how New Mexico Pueblos were embracing new technologies in the face of a changing climate. Now she was consolidating the results of their efforts into a single spreadsheet that listed their findings, sources, and contacts.

Their joint mission for the day was to find as many examples as they could of Pueblos adopting renewable energy sources since the time the presentation was last updated three years earlier. It didn't take long for Ellie to find two examples very close by. The first was a women's health center in Española. The other was a community center at Cochiti Pueblo, only eighteen miles south as the raven flew, but a nearly seventy-mile trek by road. Both had added solar panels within the last eighteen months. By the end of four hours, she and Teri had added eight new solar or wind projects to their list, all of which had been completed since the middle of 2015. Teri would eventually pick one or two of the most interesting projects to add to her talk.

Ellie finished entering the information into the table and was about to shut her computer down for the day when she heard a voice from the doorway.

"Hey. The guy at the front counter said I'd find you back here."

She recognized the voice at once, and the sound of it made every hair on her body stand on end. She spun her chair around to face the door and addressed the speaker as calmly as she could.

"What the hell do *you* want?!"

"Um, if this is a bad time..."

"I'm sorry, Aaron," she said quickly. "I wasn't expecting you to show up here, that's all." She belatedly put two and two together. "Hang on, *you're* the one who wants to reserve the planetarium?!"

"Mm-hmm. Well, not me personally. I'm here for the physics class." Now curious despite herself, she waited for him to elaborate. "There's a site where you can download presentations made especially for planetarium projectors. The one we want to watch is about early inflation."

"'Early inflation?'" All of her initial irritation was swept away by a sudden, intense wave of excitement. "You mean the 10^{-36} to 10^{-32} seconds post-Big Bang Inflationary Epoch?"

Aaron opened his mouth to answer, but she wasn't done.

"The time between grand unification breaking down and the start of the electroweak phase?"

Again he tried to respond, and again she pressed on, sounding even more excited.

"That tiny fraction of a second when the building blocks of all matter were created. The 'and-then-a-miracle-occurs' phase."

Aaron remained silent, wondering if there was more to come, but Ellie was finished and merely sat there, grinning up at him.

"Yeah," he agreed at last. "Then."

"That is so *cool*! But the volume of space grew by a factor of, like, one septillion septillion septillion, or something. So, what's the presentation like? How can it possibly show that?"

"That's actually as much of a mystery as the epoch itself. The website's sample video wasn't much help. You know, you could join us and find out for yourself. It's not like the class will fill the whole planetarium. I bet you'd enjoy it."

I bet I would! "Thanks, but since I started here, my study time has gotten pretty precious. I'll think about it, though."

"I had no idea you worked here. Nice shirt, by the way." He nodded at what constituted her uniform, a black T-shirt with the center's bird logo rendered in blue and white on its chest. She squinted at him, wondering if he was being sarcastic. "No, really! It's cute."

"I've only been here a few weeks. I get to work with the staff on presentations and stuff."

Aaron, not knowing what else to say, just nodded.

"So, what are you guys studying now?" Ellie said.

"We recently finished a review of classical physics—the Greeks, Newton, Einstein.... Now we're starting in on Planck and the development of the Standard Model."

"Whenever I hear 'Standard Model' I think of 'Model T.' Like once it was the latest and greatest, but now it's what you call something old and outdated. Will you guys get into M-theory?"

"Yeah, but only a little. We start the cosmology unit in December, though, so there won't be a lot of time to cover the newer concepts."

She gave him a playful grin. "You're sure it's not really because he thinks you're all a bunch of *p*-branes?"

Aaron smiled, amused by the nerdy pun. "That's very good!"

Ellie smiled too. She had never felt more like she was talking to her Aaron, but although she was loving it, she decided to quit while she was ahead.

"Okay, then. When do you want to use the planetarium?"

"Is December tenth available? It's a Monday."

"Let us see." She turned to her computer and logged in to the event scheduling system. "Any reason for that particular day?" she said as the system initialized.

"That's the day Voyager 2 enters interstellar space. Mr. Boltzmann thought that would be a good day."

For the first time, Ellie felt a pang of regret over not taking the physics class. She missed this stuff! She scrolled the calendar down to December.

"Looks like you're good for the tenth. Two thirty sound about right?"

"Perfect! He said he knows we need to be done by four. We're going straight to the bus after fifth period."

Ellie nodded. It wasn't far from the school to the PEEC, but taking the activity bus would buy them nearly twenty extra minutes.

"I'll list it under Mr. Boltzmann's name, planetarium, custom program, and okay, you're good to go! If you can send the file over the day—well, better make that the Friday before—they can install it and make sure it's going to run smoothly for you."

Aaron knocked the heel of his hand against his forehead. "Oh, *duh!* That's actually why I came in person!" He pulled a thumb drive out of his jeans pocket and offered it to her. "Here."

Ellie reached out, and he placed the drive in her hand. The brief brush of his fingertips on her palm felt like an electric shock. Startled, she jerked her hand away and looked up into his face. She was struck yet again by how big a difference his rectangular glasses made to his appearance. Otherwise identical to the boy she had known, his face showed not a trace of the perpetually startled look imparted by the old Aaron's large, round frames. In spite of the way things had turned out between them, she had to admit it—he looked *good!*

Task accomplished, they simply stared at each other, neither knowing where to steer the conversation next.

"Well, thanks," he finally said.

"No problem." She remained seated, hands clasped loosely in her lap, as he headed toward the door. "And I really will think about it," she said. To her surprise, she found she meant it.

Once he was gone, she found an envelope, quickly printed "Boltzmann, LA High School, December 10" on it, then sealed the thumb drive inside. She placed the envelope between her keyboard and monitor, where she'd be sure to see it the next time she came to work. Then she stared at it for a moment, wondering if there might be some way she could watch the presentation on her computer. She decided it wasn't worth the effort, unable to imagine the exercise being anything but thoroughly underwhelming. Maybe she would take Aaron up on his invitation to sit in on the class and experience it the way it was meant to be seen.

Checking the time on her computer, she saw it was three fifty-two. Good. She still had enough time. While helping Teri with her project, she'd had an idea for a new exhibit, but it took her until the very end of the day to work up enough confidence to propose it to Shanna. Realizing that the worst Shanna could do was say no and that she could live with that, Ellie wrapped up her work a few minutes early in order to have the time to talk to her.

"Hi. Do you have a sec?"

Shanna held up a finger as she used the other hand to tap a final few characters on her keyboard. She finished, saved, then turned to face in Ellie's direction.

"Sure. Come on in." Shanna waited until Ellie settled onto the chair beside her desk and set her backpack on the floor beside her. "What's on your mind?"

"I was wondering... Or rather, I have an idea, and I wanted to see what you thought about it. For a sort of exhibit, I mean."

Shanna's eyebrows flicked upward in a momentary expression of surprise. "Oh?! Let's hear it!" She actually sounded excited. So far, so good.

"Okay, so when I was working with Teri and we were listing all of the new solar projects, I got to thinking. What if there were a way to show how much electricity in the state is being generated using fossil fuel methods versus sustainable technologies? Both over time and right now. And show where the target is for clean energy in order to get the CO_2 levels heading back toward where they need to be. Like one of those fundraising thermometers or something. So *then* I thought, what other things could we show? Like, maybe carpooling estimates or how many electric cars are registered in the state. We compare that to what the numbers need to be to make a difference. Does that make any sense?"

Shanna leaned back and stared blankly at the bulletin board above her monitor while she gave the idea serious consideration. "Yes," she said at last. She sat forward again and returned her attention to Ellie. "I get it. And yes, it makes sense. You want to show the traditional way of doing something and the green alternative, and compare where we are to where we need to be in order for us to be carbon-neutral." Ellie nodded. That was it, exactly. "Do you know how you would present the information you're talking about?"

"Not really. I was thinking about a digital display panel of some kind, but it seems kind of wrong to use an electronic device to talk about conserving energy."

"Hmm, maybe not. If it's the most efficient device available, you might even use it to help make your point. Compare its power consumption to that of an old CRT, for example. It's not like we want to tell people not to use electricity—or even gasoline—but to use it as efficiently as they can. The big question is whether or not there's money in the budget for a new monitor." She paused to think some more, then began to nod. "I think I can make that work."

"Well, congratulations! You just got your very first project! Keep thinking about what data you want to show and see what kind of ideas you can come up with for presenting it in a visual way. Bear in mind that it needs to make sense to kids too. Ten and up, maybe? For now, continue coming to me. Let's say this time each week. Once the actual work starts,

I'll pair you up with a member of the staff. But remember—whoever that person is will be *your* assistant. Think you can handle that?"

Ellie swallowed hard. An old story about a cat, some mice, and a bell popped into her mind. She hadn't anticipated this response, expecting instead that Shanna would pass the idea along to someone on staff, and for an instant, she wished she'd kept her mouth shut. Then the instant passed, and she began to feel excited about the prospect of bringing one of her own ideas to life for a change. She wasn't sure yet precisely how she was going to do it, but she felt confident she could. Finally, she nodded.

"Yes. I can do that."

Shanna smiled at her. "I like that you thought about it. Okay, then. We'll meet in a week and see what kind of progress you've made. Sound good?"

"Yep. Sounds good. I'll be back in on Tuesday." She started to rise, but Shanna stopped her.

"Not so fast there, young lady. I learned quite a lot about you this afternoon. 'Post-Big Bang Inflationary Epoch? Electroweak phase?' You are quite the physics nerd!"

A gleeful smile split Ellie's face. "Guilty as charged!" she proudly admitted. Then her smile faded. "Wait—you *heard* all that?"

Shanna gave Ellie an apologetic shrug. "They did sort of skimp on the walls. I couldn't *not* hear. In fact, the way all the geek speak was flying back and forth, I thought I was going to have to come in and throw a bucket of cold water on you two."

"You're way too late for that."

"Oops! I'm sorry. So you and he used to be...?"

"Yes and no. I mean, yes, but it wasn't exactly *him*." Shanna squinted at her in confusion. "I can't explain it. Let's just say it's over and leave it at that."

Ellie could tell from Shanna's dubious look that her lying skills definitely needed some work. She rose, slipped one strap of her pack over her shoulder, and turned toward the door.

"Ellie?" She turned around to face a smiling Shanna. "*Great* idea!"

Surprised by the sudden, unexpected praise, at first Ellie could only smile back. "Thanks!" she finally managed. "Are you leaving, too?"

Shanna shook her head. "Not quite. I've got a few more emails to take care of." Struck by a sudden thought, she held up a finger. "But hold on a sec." She swiveled her chair around and began scanning the bookshelf opposite her desk. Finding what she wanted, she pulled a slender paperback from the middle of the second shelf and held it out. "Here, take this. Let me know what you think. No rush."

Ellie took the book and studied the cover. The top quarter was white with an all-caps title in black—*The Limits to Growth*. Below that, an image of the Earth was set against a plain black background. Below the blue and green planet, the names of the four authors were listed. For Ellie, sharing a favorite book with someone was an intensely personal, soul-baring act, and she sensed similar feelings in play now. She looked up from the cover to see Shanna watching her closely.

"I read that when I was right around your age," Shanna said. "It's the book that, well, first it kept me up a whole lot of nights, but it's what eventually inspired me to go into environmental science."

Ellie gave her a solemn nod. "Thanks." She lowered her pack onto the chair and tucked the book inside. "I'll take a look as soon as I can."

"Like I said—no rush. See you Tuesday?"

"Mm-hmm. I'll be here."

By the time she reached home and walked her bike into the garage, Ellie was feeling better than she had in many weeks. She'd had fun working with Teri, had—without even meaning to—impressed Shanna with a little physics jargon, and had navigated her way through a nearly quarter-hour-long conversation with Aaron without it veering off into bizarro land. Best of all, Ryan's bike was leaning against the side of the garage, which meant she was about to spend the rest of the day with her two favorite people on the planet. Add all of that to the adrenalin rush she got from flying down the last big hill to her house, and she couldn't help but feel great. She would later think that was the precise moment she should have known her entire world was about to go to hell.

6

Not waiting for World History class to end, Ellie switched off her laptop early and began shoving her books and notes into her backpack as quickly as she could. The computer's screen went black just as the bell sounded, and she slid it in on top of her notes. She pulled the flap over the pack's top and, not bothering to clip it shut, slung it onto one shoulder. She was especially eager to get to Environmental Science today. She had been looking forward to this class ever since Mrs. Carson first announced that there would be a guest speaker coming in to kick off the Sustainable Business and Development unit. She had no idea who the speaker was, but she was eager to hear from an expert on one of her favorite topics. Driven by the hope of having the chance to ask a few questions before class started, she was third out of the room.

Feeling sudden sympathy for uncounted generations of salmon, she wriggled her way up the hall against an oncoming stream of students until she reached the science classroom. As she neared the doorway, she fought her way to the edge of the flow and stumbled through the opening with an exasperated sigh of relief. She was almost to her desk before she noticed the speaker was already there, waiting patiently as the class arrived and took their seats. Until that instant, she had thought the whole "jaw-dropping" thing was merely an expression. But standing there, her mouth gaping wide as if she were some newly discovered species of idiot, she realized it was a real phenomenon.

"No freakin' way!" she whispered, having regained control over her mouth. *Well, some freakin' way, obviously,* her logic module whispered back. She pulled her gaze away before she was caught staring and looked around at her classmates, all of whom were calmly going through their usual start-of-class routines. Evidently, no one else saw the thing that made her entire body break out in a cold sweat, but plain as day, casually leaning against the end of their teacher's desk as if that were the most perfectly natural thing to do, was a dead man.

She took a deep breath and made her way to her desk, careful to avoid making eye contact. She set her backpack on her chair and pretended to search for something inside it, all the while casting repeated glances at him from under her brow. In the six years she had known the man, she was sure she'd never exchanged more than two dozen words with him, but she had seen him often enough that she had absolutely no doubt about his identity. He was Jeremy Siskin, the man she, Sam, Ryan, and even Aaron once believed to be Aaron's father. The very man whose birth Aaron had willingly sacrificed his life to prevent was somehow back!

The questions piling up in her mind quickly overloaded her brain's buffer, and she imagined a bright red "Stack Overflow" warning flashing on her forehead. But all of the *whens, wheres, whats,* and *whys* came in far behind the biggest question of all—*how?* She wanted to let Sam and Ryan know right away, but Mrs. Carson strictly prohibited the use of phones or laptops during lecture periods, insisting her students take notes longhand because it "promoted better retention."

But technically, class hasn't started yet, has it? She leaned over to retrieve her phone from a side pouch on her pack, but by then it was too late. The bell rang, and Mrs. Carson stood and walked to the middle of the whiteboard. Ellie let the phone drop back into the pouch and sat up, deciding she'd have to be satisfied for now with pursuing answers to a few of her lesser questions.

"Today we're starting a new unit—Sustainable Business and Development. Over the next month, we'll examine green business practices, including construction, sourcing, manufacture, and packaging. We'll look at zero-waste processes, CO_2 offset programs, and sustainable energy use, both through on-site generation and via so-called 'green certs.' Lastly, we'll see how many of these technologies and approaches are changing the family home."

She gestured toward Jeremy. "This gentleman is Dr. Jeremy Siskin. He is a physicist, not an environmental expert, but he has had a lot of experience dealing with many of these exact issues. He's come over from the LAB today to get us started off by, in a way, jumping to the end and explaining how these ideas apply to real-world projects. Dr. Siskin?"

At her cue, he stepped forward to take her place at the front of the room while she returned to the chair behind her desk. "Thank you, Mrs. Carson. As your teacher pointed out, I'm not here today to talk about my work—actually, quite a lot of that is classified—but to talk about *where* I work. And I don't mean Los Alamos Biotechnologies as a whole, but my lab in particular. Due to the nature of my project, I needed a facility with several unique features built in at the beginning—retrofitting an existing structure wouldn't do. Being aware of the impact typical construction approaches have on the environment, which is to say both large and overwhelmingly negative, I agreed to come to work here only after receiving commitments that construction on my facility would be undertaken with the strictest adherence to guidelines laid down in the International Green Construction Code. The IgCC standards, first published in 2010 and updated several times since—including just this year— aim to minimize the environmental impact of all construction projects."

The questions swirling through Ellie's mind made every word Jeremy said sound as if she were hearing it through an enormous swarm of angrily buzzing insects. She forced herself to ignore the clamor in her head and focus on his words as he went on.

"But 'environment' in this context goes beyond the usual concerns, like not letting run-off from the construction zone get into a nearby stream. It also refers to how the building connects to its physical environment— meaning the space that surrounds it—and to the artificial environment of the structure's interior. That means avoiding materials that continue to emit harmful gases long after construction is over. Paints, carpets, engineered wood products—all of these must be chosen with great care in order to comply with the standards. It also means providing an adequate level of outside air exchange and plenty of natural daylight, wherever possible."

Why is he here, speaking to a high school science class? Does this mean he's a good guy now? Her gut was happy to stick with "no freakin' way," but her logic module cautioned against blindly clinging to snap judgments.

"So, let's take a look at how these ideas were incorporated into my building. Mrs. Carson, if you would?" Mrs. Carson leaned to her right and stretched to turn off the overhead lights. Jeremy aimed a tiny remote at a laptop on the corner of her desk, and the projector built into the ceiling threw an image onto the whiteboard beside him. It was an aerial view of a newly completed construction project with a few pieces of heavy equipment still parked on the site.

A bright flicker from Mrs. Carson's desk caught Ellie's attention. Her teacher leaned forward to study her phone, then glanced up at Jeremy, who was already thoroughly into his presentation. She slid the phone off her desk and quietly made her way through the classroom and out the door.

It's fine for her to use her *phone, apparently!* Ellie scowled sourly as Mrs. Carson closed the door behind her, then returned her attention to the slide show. Still feeling unbalanced, she stared blankly at the procession of images, paying little heed to what he was saying. It wasn't until the fifth slide that it occurred to her how important these pictures might prove to be. She had no idea what this new Jeremy was working on in his spiffy new building, but he was handing her potentially vital information should it prove to be something bad.

The next slide showed an orthographic, 3-D view of the floor plan. She began sketching it as quickly as she could, trying to get it all copied down before the slide changed again. Of the rooms that had labels, most were designated as offices, but there was a small room at the rear of the building marked Generator. The unlabeled room next to it was many times larger, although without some kind of scale, its actual size was a guess. Judging from the width of the hallways, however, it looked like it was more than thirty feet on a side. What was interesting was not the room's dimensions but its massive walls, which were drawn four times thicker than those of any of the rooms around it.

She continued to gather and record details, her eyes flicking back and forth between her notebook and the whiteboard while she sketched as fast as she could. She was trying to decipher the function of an odd, closet-like room that could be accessed from either side when she noticed the classroom had gone completely silent. Jeremy was watching her, smiling as if enjoying some private joke. Then she saw that almost everyone else was staring at her too.

"Do you need a little more time, miss, or may I go on?"

She was embarrassed, not only by having been caught inexplicably copying the floor plan but by being made the center of the entire room's attention. Careful not to let her agitation show, she calmly laid her pen on top of the unfinished drawing. "No, thanks. I'm good," she said, giving him a bland smile.

"Excellent," he said. Still looking amused, he thumbed the button for the next image.

She spent the remainder of his presentation focusing intently on the slides, hoping she'd be able to recall enough of the details later that they might be of use. Of use for what she had no idea. After a few more photos of his building, however, the topic shifted to an overview of the IgCC and what it hoped to achieve.

Mrs. Carson still had not returned by the time Jeremy flicked the lights back on and offered to take questions. He declined to answer all but the most innocuous ones, refusing to say what kind of project he was working on, how long ago the building had been completed, or even where on the sprawling LAB campus it was located. Ellie found his evasiveness frustrating. The way he deftly avoided answering nearly every question made him sound more like a politician than a physicist, and she doubted she'd get any information at all out of him. He had seemed especially proud of an automated block-laying robot that had performed most of the construction virtually unaided, though, so she decided to pursue that. Not bothering to raise her hand, she plunged into a momentary gap in the conversation.

"That robot block layer. Did you design that?"

"Mechanical engineering is hardly my area of interest," he answered, and for the first time, Ellie heard the air of bored arrogance she remembered so well. He caught himself at once, though, and after a short pause, he continued in a more genial tone. "No, I agreed to let my lab be the first large-scale test for a system designed in Australia. It's fast, precise, and the only crew it needs is someone to keep it fed with blocks and adhesive. The plumbing for drains and most of the power conduit went into the concrete foundation. The rest was built into the ceiling structure. The roof required a conventional construction crew, but even then, we never had more than ten workers onsite at a time. Frequently, it was only two or three. That's a significant reduction in commuting miles each and every day."

Ellie was grudgingly impressed, but she wondered if his decision to embrace this conscientious approach to construction was motivated by something less laudable than the desire to be green. "You said that a lot of your work is classified. It seems that not having a large construction crew on the site would be a good way of keeping your lab's interior details, um, *private*."

"That may be true, but why then would I put it all up on a screen in front of two dozen people?" He chuckled dismissively.

"Good point," she admitted, momentarily flustered. "But I don't imagine a classroom full of high school students seems like much of a threat."

"Oh, you might be surprised, Miss..." He consulted a sheet of paper Mrs. Carson had left on her desk, and his eyes went wide when they settled on her name. "Henderson! Well, now, then again, perhaps you wouldn't be surprised at all!" For a long moment, he stared at her, an odd, knowing smile on his face. Then he began to chuckle with wry amusement.

Ellie was aware of her classmates watching them, no doubt puzzled by their conversation's cryptic undertones. Mrs. Carson's return spared her having to come up with a response to Jeremy's odd comment. She glanced at the wall clock and saw that class had only a few minutes to go.

"I'm sorry for abandoning you, Dr. Siskin. Did everything go okay?"

"Quite, Mrs. Carson. The class and I were just enjoying a little chat."

He aimed another loaded smile at Ellie, and this time she couldn't suppress a shudder.

"I'm glad," she said. "I'd like to thank you for your time today, as would we all." She looked pointedly out at the class, and a jumbled assortment of muttered *thank-yous* sounded from isolated spots around the room.

"Not at all," Jeremy said.

Then the bell rang, and Mrs. Carson had to call out to be heard over the sudden clamor. "Read chapter seven for tomorrow!"

Ellie leaned over to secure the top of her pack. She was fumbling with the second strap when a pair of square-toed dress shoes appeared at the top of her field of view. Although they were buffed to a hard shine, they looked as soft as moccasins. She remained bent over for a moment, not at all wanting to look up at him, but she understood at once that "ignore him and he'll go away" was not a viable strategy. She leaned back in her chair, folded her arms tightly across her chest, and stared up into his smug expression.

"*Yes?!*" she hissed, making no effort to hide her irritation.

"So this is the amazing young Lauren Henderson I've heard so much about. Very, very interesting. I suppose I should have guessed we'd run into each other eventually, although I would never have expected it to happen in an Environmental Science class."

There was no mistaking the scorn in his voice, but what reason would he have for assuming the course was beneath her abilities? Nor was there any doubt he found amusement in discovering her identity, but again— why? Those in the room close enough to overhear him looked at Ellie quizzically. *Lauren?*

"It's 'Ellie!'" she snapped.

She began to suspect too late that he was goading her, trying to provoke her for some reason. What he said, how he said it, the way he stood looming over her—it was obviously some kind of pathetic power play, and she regretted letting him manipulate her emotions so easily.

"Ellie, then."

His expression was indulgent and condescending, and for a moment she could imagine herself smashing her fist into the center of it. He leaned close to her and pitched his voice so only she could hear his following words.

"I won't say I'm disappointed, exactly, but honestly? I really was expecting something... *more.*" Then he laughed softly to himself, straightened, and walked out of the room without giving her another look.

She was unaware of his departure. She was unaware of anything except for that insect-swarm turmoil buzzing through her brain. What did he mean by "*disappointed?*" She sat frozen in place by a mix of anger and confusion, twin flames of humiliation burning brightly on her cheeks. Then questions began coming at her from all directions, breaking her paralysis.

"Ellie? Are you okay?"

"Do you know that guy?"

"What did he say?"

She stood and looked around the room, but Jeremy was gone. "He... no, I... I gotta go," she stammered.

Looking at no one, she slid her belongings into her pack, slipped her arms through the straps, and started for the door, leaving behind a room full of concerned classmates. Mostly concerned, anyway. As she stepped into the hall, she heard Jordan's loud voice.

"I'm telling you, that girl is *seriously* weird!"

Free at last to use her phone, she typed a short message to Sam:

Ellie—911!!!

She decided against trying to solve the Jeremy mystery right away. Figuring out what was happening could wait the twenty minutes it would take her to walk home, although she was determined it wouldn't take nearly that long today. She strode along as swiftly as the heavy backpack would allow, repeatedly checking her phone for a response. Before she dropped into the canyon, she sent the same distress call to Ryan, hoping one of them would get back to her by the time she climbed out on its far side.

Neither did, and she jammed her phone back into her pocket. She crossed the back yard at a trot and burst into the kitchen without slowing.

Slamming the door behind her, she ran down the hallway to her bedroom, opened her MacBook, and stabbed the power button. While it booted up, she decided to go straight to the source, and she pulled the D. Hakham novels from her bookshelf. Knowing the first was dedicated simply "To 'Aaron,'" she began flipping through the first few pages of the second volume. Neither it nor the next one offered any shred of a clue. She opened the fourth book, no longer hoping to find anything helpful, but when she reached the dedication page, the words she read there made her entire body go numb.

For my wife—my destiny—Judith

No! We stopped this! What happened?! She turned her MacBook around to face her and opened a new Firefox tab, typed in *author d hakham daniel siskin,* and hit the Return key. She had to open only three links before she had the answer:

The following interview was originally published in the New Yorker Magazine in April 1964. Thanks to user AvdRdr48 for uploading it to read-all-over.com.

Following the publication of his fourth book under the name "D. Hahkam," Daniel Siskin retired from writing. I spoke with Mr. Siskin recently and asked him why he had made that decision.

"About a year after my third book came out, a friend of Judith suggested to her that she might enjoy reading them. This friend knew nothing about our previous encounter, of course. The story of our first meeting back in 1941 was not one Judith would have been inclined to share. She had been quite humiliated at the time. But that story is central to my first book, *The Messengers,* and although I changed many details—for obvious reasons—Judith nonetheless recognized the events of that day. Furthermore, my picture was printed on the inside of the back cover, so she knew the truth of who 'D. Hahkam' really was.

"I don't believe I could have convinced her of my ignorance regarding the identity of the two young girls we encountered on that day in the diner had I tried to do it in person. Reading about it years later, however, albeit in a fictionalized form, allowed her to accept that this might be true. So some time passes, she thinks it over—reads the other two books, I'm happy to say—and one day, my publisher hands me a letter from her in which she asks if we might meet.

"We were married shortly before the final volume went to print. It has taken years to achieve, but I now earn far more from the books than I ever would have as a tailor, even if I had chosen to start my own shop, and all of them are continuing to sell very well. So now we are 'making up for lost time,' you might say. I finally feel like my life is back on track. We found out only last month that, God willing, we will soon have a child...."

So, there it was. The article continued, but Ellie had what she needed. She flopped back in her chair to consider this new information. They had not prevented the birth of Jeremy Siskin but only altered the circumstances leading up to it. Judging from the April publication date, Judith would have delivered in the fall or early winter of that same year. She didn't know when the original Jeremy had been born, and now there was no way to find out.

New questions added themselves to the heap of them already crowding her mind. Was the fact that he had never connected with Aaron's mom this time simply due to timing, or were there other factors involved? And, absent the wife whose research had originally prompted their move to Los Alamos six years ago, why was he here now? When had he arrived?

The biggest question had been, 'How is he back?' but she had found an answer to it. Now there was a new one to take its place in looming large over all the others; was he working on another project like the shack? Just acknowledging the possibility filled her with dread.

No—we can't go through all of that again!

She checked her phone and still found no reply from Sam or Ryan. She thought for a second, considering her options. They were either up the hill at his house or they were literally anywhere else in town, and trying to track them down there would be pointless. It would only take a few minutes to pedal to his house, though, where she would either find them or could at least wait, knowing that they would show up there eventually.

Or maybe they'll answer their freakin' phones!

She slid her phone into her back pocket, added a charger and cord just in case, and headed down the hall. She grabbed a light jacket from a hook inside the garage, stuffed the charger into an inner pocket, and tied the jacket's sleeves around her waist. Walking her bike outside, she ducked under the still-moving door and double-tapped its outside button as she passed it. Before it had closed, she was already racing down the cul-de-sac.

The ride to Ryan's house was little more than a mile, but it was also a steady, three-hundred-foot climb, and she was winded and sweaty when she swerved off the street into his driveway. She was both relieved and irritated when she saw Sam's bike leaning along with Ryan's and several others against the side of the house—she was glad they were there, irked they were ignoring her texts. The empty driveway implied Ryan's dad was not yet home from work, and that was also a relief.

She charged through Ryan's front door without knocking, stepping out of her shoes as she closed it behind her. Hearing Sam's voice coming from the direction of the living room, she headed down the long hallway. She didn't bother with a greeting but called out her news as she strode in their direction.

"You guys won't believe this, but Aaron's dad is back in town. Looks like we might have to get rid of him all over again."

Nearing the end of the hallway, she could see Sam and Ryan on the sofa, their necks twisted around as they gaped over their shoulders at her. She expected her news to be unsettling, but the looks they aimed at her expressed something verging on panic. She had only to clear the hall completely to understand why. There was a third person in the room, sitting in a chair to their right. She came to a dead stop and stared at him. Aaron, looking thoroughly bewildered, stared back.

Ellie felt her heart sink. "Oh, *crap!*"

7

F or a moment, Ellie stood frozen in place, not knowing how to respond to Aaron's shocked, confused expression. Then she saw that Sam and Ryan were also still staring mutely back at her, and she forced herself to speak. *"Umm, hi?"*

Aaron sounded every bit as confused as he looked and more than a little outraged. "My dad's been in town since Sunday night. And what do you mean, *'get rid of him?'"*

She held her index finger up in a hold-that-thought gesture and nodded for the others to join her at the end of the hallway. "Guys, could we, uh?"

They had barely reached her before Sam began scolding her in a harsh, raspy whisper. "Brilliant! Just *brilliant!"*

"Why in the world would I ever have assumed he was here?!" Ellie hissed back. "When's the last time...?"

Ryan brought the exchange to an end by placing his hands on their shoulders. "Fight later, ladies. At the moment, we have to decide what to tell him. Any good stories up your sleeve, Sam?"

"Well, we could say... she was, um... just *joking?"*

Ellie rolled her eyes but said nothing. To be fair, it was clear from Sam's faltering tone that she didn't think that excuse would fly, either.

Ryan clearly couldn't have agreed more. "Pretty poor taste in jokes, don't you think?"

Ellie peeked at Aaron over Ryan's shoulder. He was glaring hard at them, impatient for an explanation. She knew they had only two options: they could flatly refuse to explain at all, or they could tell him the whole truth and hope for the best. If they took the first option, there was no doubt he'd leave angry and never talk to any of them again. If they went the second route, it was only *highly probable* that he'd leave angry and never talk to any of them again. If this Aaron had the original's intellect, though, he might be able to handle it. The thought that this very secret was preventing them from being friends passed through her mind again, and she made her choice. She had no idea which way it would go, but there was one thing she was certain about: she wasn't going to damage their relationship any further by trying to weasel her way out of her gaffe with a lie.

"I say we tell him. The whole story."

Ryan nodded almost at once. "I think you're right," he said. "I think it's overdue, actually."

Ellie gave him a quizzical look, but he merely shrugged. She didn't press the issue, knowing now was not the time to ask him to elaborate.

"Ooh, *this* should be fun," Sam said. Then she nodded too. "But I agree. All of it."

"I'll do it," Ellie said. *Oh, yeah. 'Fun,' all right!*

Ellie led them back to the living room, and they sat lined up on the sofa. She took the spot closest to Aaron and thought about how and where to start. Quickly realizing there was no best way, not under these circumstances, she took a deep breath and launched into the story.

"First of all, Aaron, I'm sorry I blurted that all out. We hoped we'd never have to tell you any of what you're about to hear—and certainly not like *this*—but if you want to understand, we'll explain everything. I'm going to say this much right up front, though; it's a long story, and it'll sound like bad science fiction, but I swear, it's all true."

"Let's have it." Aaron sounded as if he expected to believe not a single word of whatever she said next.

"This first part might be the hardest for you to understand. The thing is, even though you just got here in September, the three of us first met you not a little more than a month ago, but six years ago. According to *our* memories, we all grew up together here in Los Alamos, and were, um, friends."

Aaron looked from face to face, evidently wondering who would deliver the punch line, but all he saw was a trio of sincere nods.

"It's true." Sam pointed to herself and Ryan. "You, me, and Ryan were all in the same grade then."

Ryan picked up the story. "You guys moved out here in 2012 because your mom got a job at the LAB working on her 'energy from algae' project. This past summer, she was already talking to NASA, JPL—anybody interested in a Mars project. That's how I knew what she was working on when you met us this second time."

"You were so proud of her," Ellie said. "In fact, that was one of the only times you ever sounded truly happy, when you were talking about her." Aaron nodded silently. Ellie had discovered early on that pride in his mom was one thing about this Aaron that had not changed. "But your real dad, Karl, wasn't with you back then. It was you, your mom, and the person who came to give a talk in my science class today—a guy named Jeremy Siskin."

"Right!" Aaron crossed his arms and glared at her. "So I suppose now you're going to explain exactly how it's possible for you to have met me years before I got here."

As succinctly as she could, aided by occasional input from Sam and Ryan, she began relating their version of the past to him. She started with how they had met him in the middle school cafeteria, intending to work her way gradually forward. However, she found it difficult to dredge up specific details from so long ago with no warning, so she quickly jumped to their high school years. Aaron seemed particularly interested in the story of him winning the science fair as a freshman. His focus shifted then, his eyes narrowing in a way that made Ellie think he was seeing the events as she laid them out for him. Hoping his resistance was beginning to weaken, she moved along quickly to the day they found the time travel device in the forest and initially mistook it for something else. She explained how they soon came to understand its true nature, then told him how overhearing a conversation on a plane ride back from Montana had led directly to his plan to destroy the shack by preventing the birth of his father.

"But you said he's not my dad." He scowled, annoyed by his own misstatement. "I mean, he's *not!*"

"Yes, but even you—I mean *he*—didn't know that at the time," Sam reminded him.

"And what we did had nothing directly to do with him being your dad," Ryan added. "It was only because he was the one who had discovered the principles that made the shack possible that he ended up at the center of the plan."

"But you're saying that I believed Dr. Siskin really was my father, and even so, I decided, 'Hey, I know—let's *kill him!*' And you all went along with it?!"

Ellie felt a prickling sensation on the back of her neck, her subconscious trying to alert her to something significant hidden in what he had just said. She'd have to figure out what that was all about later. Right now, it seemed more important to move him beyond the idea that they had murdered somebody. "It wasn't like that! He hadn't even been born yet." She was finding it harder to remain patient and calm in the face of his belligerent rebuttals. After seeing Jeremy today, she knew she had the most complete picture of how the new timeline must have developed, so she went on, tuning her explanation for Sam and Ryan's benefit as well. "Look, here's what I think happened. When we visited Brooklyn—"

Aaron scoffed. "In 1941!"

"December 8, 1941, yes," Ellie confirmed evenly. "It turns out that when we prevented the couple we thought were your grandparents—Daniel and Judith—from getting together that day, we only managed to delay things. Or maybe not delayed so much as changed the circumstances, the context, in which events eventually played out. Daniel became a writer instead of opening his own tailor shop.

"Sam, have you seen *The Messengers* and the other three books by D. Hakham on my shelf?" Sam shook her head. "That's Daniel Siskin's pen name. You and I are the messengers. Dad gave those to me, you know, *before*, but I haven't read them. I mean, *I* haven't read them." She turned her attention back to Aaron. "Anyway, at some point, Judith became aware of the books, and they eventually reconnected. Right before I came here, I read an interview in which Daniel mentions that Judith is pregnant. So, that explains the Jeremy part of it.

"The rest of it we sort of already knew. Or guessed about, at any rate. When your mom was in grad school…" She hesitated. *During grad school, what? Your mom was sleeping around? Yeah, this will go over* really *well!*

"You, um, might not want to hear this part."

"Why not?" Aaron snapped. "Is it worse than killing my father?"

His abrasive tone was wearing Ellie's patience thin. "Look, we didn't… Okay, *fine!* It's pretty clear that somewhere along the line, your mom was involved with both your bio dad *and* Jeremy!" Aaron looked away, stung, and Ellie immediately regretted her outburst and what it implied about Aaron's mom. She took a deep breath before she went on. "Or maybe not. Maybe she started dating Jeremy after she was pregnant with you, but your dad was already out of the picture. There's just no way to know now."

"Hold on a sec, El." Sam rested her hand gently on Ellie's leg as she leaned forward to address Aaron, her tone soothing. "We're talking about the *other* Aaron, not about you, and about *his* mom. Clearly, your mom and Jeremy never met. Or if they did, nothing came of it. It's important for you to remember that." She glanced at Ellie. "Sorry," she said, withdrawing her hand. "Go on."

"No—thanks. Sam's right. This story isn't about you at all. Up to this point, I guess. When you disappeared right after we changed the timeline, we assumed—wrongly, as it turns out—that we had been successful, that we had prevented Jeremy from being born and lost you as a result, just as we expected." She paused and rubbed her throat until she could go on. "Even after you arrived in town in September, we figured everything else went as planned, except we had to assume that Jeremy *couldn't* have been your father."

"Not that it wasn't pretty obvious in hindsight," Ryan said. "You two didn't look alike in the least, and your personalities were at the opposite ends of the spectrum."

"Meaning?" Aaron said.

"Meaning you, or *he*—whatever—was a nice, sweet guy," Sam said. "But your fath... *Jeremy*, I mean, he was sorta..." She went silent as she groped for the words to explain.

Sensing that Sam had hit a mental wall, Ellie finished the thought for her. "He creeped me out big-time."

"Yeah, that," Sam agreed.

Aaron held up a hand. "Okay, let's see if I've got this. The four of us find some device parked out in the middle of nowhere, just happen to know exactly how to break in, and then go for a little joy ride. Then, when we realize it's the technological marvel of the century—an actual *time machine!*—we take it upon ourselves to get rid of it. By *killing* my *dad!* Do you realize how ludicrous that sounds?"

"Yeah," Ryan said. "*Totally* ludicrous. That's why we always just called it the 'shack.'"

Aaron was in no mood to see any humor in the situation. "I mean the whole damned story!"

Ellie sighed, disappointed. She knew that if they had planned in advance to tell him about their alternate past, they would have done a better job organizing their thoughts. Instead, he was getting the facts thrown at him almost randomly and all at once. It was no wonder he was reacting with such belligerence, but there was nothing they could do about that now.

"When you've lived through it, not so much," Ryan said. "But we do have proof. Well, kinda."

Ellie shot a startled look at Ryan. "We do?"

Ryan ignored the question and patted Sam's thigh. "Do you know where it is?"

Sam sighed. "Yes," she said, clearly wishing she didn't. "I'll go get it." Frowning to herself, she stood and headed out of the room.

Ellie wondered why Sam sounded so glum. Wasn't having proof a good thing? But Sam solved that part of the mystery at once, calling over her shoulder as she disappeared down the hallway.

"It was supposed to be for her *birthday!*"

Ellie now felt even more clueless about what "it" might be. What possible birthday present was also proof of their story? Then an even better question occurred to her: did this mean she'd get another present when her birthday actually rolled around in a few more months? She finally noticed Ryan was watching her, doing his "cat that ate the canary" thing.

"*What?!*" she said.

Then Sam was back carrying a large, slim, hardcover book. "Surprise!" She was trying to sound excited, but it was a half-hearted effort. "Just, you know, imagine there's paper. And a bow. And maybe a cupcake with a candle in it." She held the mystery gift out for Ellie to take.

One glance at the cover, and Ellie understood what Ryan meant by "kinda" having proof. It was precisely the same proof she had used in May to help convince them that her suspicion about the shack being a time machine was true. Sam had just handed her the 2012 edition of *The Bread and Roses Strike: Two Months in Lawrence, Massachusetts*. Ellie was so moved by the gift she couldn't help but smile, and for a moment she forgot why she was holding it.

"*Aww*, thanks, guys!" she said, beaming at them. "This is *great!* Where on Earth...?"

"E-bay," Ryan explained.

Aaron scoffed. "A book? *That's* your proof?" Improbably, his level of skepticism had found a new peak.

"Yep!" Ellie chirped. Feeling hopeful once more, she started filling in some of the details she had glossed over earlier. "When we first found the shack and still thought it was a VR device of some kind, I set it to show us Lawrence, Massachusetts, during the period I was writing about for my American History paper. We hiked to a park in the middle of the city to listen to a speech. You boosted me up into a tree for a better view, and while I was up there, I spotted a young girl I had written about in my paper. When I went over to talk to her—her name was Carmela—you guys followed. Afterward, when I was studying the next day, I found a photo of us in the park with that girl. In this book." She offered it to him.

"Yeah, right." Despite refusing to give their story any credence, he took the book from her hand.

"Open to page"—she tried to remember the number—"one seventeen, I think." He stared hard at her for a moment before flipping through the book to find the correct place. "Okay, in that big photo with the bandstand and the guy giving the speech. See the person in the tree in the background? That's me."

He stared at the tiny, indistinct figure. "Could be *me*, as far as anyone could possibly tell."

"*Could* be, I guess, assuming you wear dresses now and then."

"And no judgment here, man," Ryan said. "Just so you know."

Ellie and Aaron both frowned at him.

"Okay, go back another page," Ellie said.

He silently complied, and she followed his eyes as they were instantly drawn to the photo in the lower right corner. There were seven people in the photo, but Ellie saw Aaron's focus lock at once onto the figure in the foreground. The photographer had caught the boy in the process of turning his head, and the side of his face, including his large, round glasses and a bit of white hair protruding from under the turned-up flap of his woolen cap, was clearly visible. Although slightly blurred, the Aaron in the photo wasn't perfectly sharp, but was too sharp for the Aaron in the chair to claim it wasn't him. Unable to deny the identity of the boy in the photo, he challenged the photo's authenticity instead.

"But that's.... What is this?" He looked at Ryan. "Did you have this printed up? Photoshop this somehow?"

Ryan shook his head. "Sorry, dude. I mean, I'm flattered, but it's exactly what it seems. That's us over a hundred years ago. Well, us and the *other* you."

"The 'other' me!" Aaron bowed his head, still unwilling—or perhaps unable—to accept any part of what he'd heard so far. After a moment, he focused his gaze on Ellie. "Okay, so tell me this: why would he have done it, huh? Even ignoring the part about his dad, it was still basically suicide, right?"

Ellie was reluctant to bring up the nature of their prior relationship, but she couldn't see a way to avoid it any longer. She cast a pleading look at Sam, hoping she'd understand and spare her from having to answer him. From the corner of her eye, she saw Aaron was still staring hard at her, perhaps sensing something of what she was trying to keep hidden. He continued to peer at her while Sam did her best to reply.

"There were a couple of reasons," she said. "The biggest was the threat we all believed the device posed to time itself. Or to the 'timeline,' I guess is how you'd say it. If someone changed the past in a big enough way, even accidentally, it could rewrite decades of history."

"You almost did that, you know," Ryan said. "You dropped Ellie's digital camera into a canal in 1912, but fortunately it was never found back then. If you had lost it in the park or along the road somewhere, it's doubtful we'd all be sitting here right now. Your words, by the way."

"*Hmm*.... You said 'couple of reasons.' What was another?"

The utter flatness of his tone left Ellie unable to guess what he was feeling, but she was relieved that he was finally asking questions. She still wasn't ready to rejoin the conversation, though, and was glad when Sam responded once more.

"I don't know this to be true, but I always half suspected part of it had to do with your mom. Being Jeremy's wife couldn't have been any more fun than being his kid, and I sometimes wondered—afterward, I mean—if you thought him being out of the picture would make things better for her. Like I said, I don't know if that's true, but if it is, it seems to have worked. For both of you, actually."

Ellie sucked in a sharp breath. The notion caught her completely by surprise, but she knew instantly that Sam was right. She stared at the floor, her face prickling, ashamed that she hadn't seen it for herself. Then, having decided to come clean, she fixed her gaze on Aaron.

"He did it for me. He and I were, you know, 'close.' At the very end, anyway. But it was for Sam and Ryan too. He wanted to make sure the future we had always looked forward to was safe. He cared about us as much as we cared about him."

A tear leaked from the corner of her eye, and before it could run down her cheek, she wiped it away with the side of her hand. Aaron was quiet for a moment, and Ellie was daring to think they had gotten through to him. But when he finally spoke, his tone was cold and bitter.

"Yeah, right! You all cared about him so much that you happily teamed up to help him kill himself. Everyone should have such friends! You know what? If you all get off on pretending you're a bunch of badass, evil-technology-destroying time travelers, that's fine with me! Whatever! But don't think for one second that I buy a single word of it. I think you are all totally—one hundred percent completely—full of *shit!*"

Ellie blinked, startled by the unexpected expletive. She could remember when hearing him use the word "butt" had sounded comically out of character. And "badass?" Definitely not a word she'd ever used to describe herself.

"Aaron, we are trying to help you understand what's going on, and that is *all* that is happening here," Sam insisted, her tone still calm and reasonable. "I know it's hard to hear, even harder to believe, and that's one of the reasons we decided not to say anything to begin with. But what we're telling you is the truth! Please try—"

"Look, I hope you guys all have a nice, big laugh about this... *joke,* or whatever it is you're trying to pull here, but if you actually expect me to believe any of it, then all I can say is..."

Finally pushed beyond her breaking point, Ellie cut him off. "All *I* can say is that the Aaron I knew wasn't such a stubborn, pigheaded... *Arrgh! He* would have believed me!" she yelled. "He would have at least *listened* before he—"

"Yeah, well, from what I can tell, that's because *he* was in love with you!" Aaron shouted back. "I'm *not!*" He shot to his feet as if launched from the chair by hidden springs. Then he simply stood there, glaring down at her. Ellie's cheeks burned as if she had been slapped, and she could only stare back.

Sam, her patience finally exhausted, jumped to Ellie's defense. "Aaron Sisk— *Weisskopf,* that's enough! I used to feel a little bad for you, you know, because you were such a nice guy stuck with a family that was pretty messed up. I'm happy things are going better for you this time around, but that certainly has not made you a better person!"

Aaron gave no sign he was at all bothered by Sam's harsh rebuke. He fixed each of them in turn with a look of contempt, his eyes settling last and longest on Ellie. "And to think I came here to..."

He shook his head once more in a final gesture of rejection, then turned and strode down the hallway without a single glance back. A second later, they heard the front door slam.

Sam spoke into the abrupt silence that followed. *"So, I* think that went well!"

"Is it just me," Ryan said, "or do you guys remember him promising he wouldn't get all bent out of shape if *he* died the next time around?"

Ellie collapsed forward, buried her face in her hands, and groaned. "Oh, Aaron."

8

In the strained silence that followed Aaron's angry departure, Sam and Ryan sat in the center of the sofa, holding hands. Ellie moved to the chair Aaron had just vacated, tucked her feet up against her rump, and gazed blankly at the floor. She had often wondered how Aaron would respond to hearing the story they had just shared, but never in her wildest imaginings had it gone so poorly. She could understand his reaction completely, though, all except the last thing he had said.

"What did he mean, 'And to think I came here to...?' To *what?* Did he say?"

Sam and Ryan looked at each other, neither wanting to be the one to explain. Ryan was the first to see a way out, and he took it.

"Hey," he said. "I'm going to get us all something to drink. I'll be right back." Before Sam could object, he sprang to his feet and strode toward the kitchen, leaving her scowling at his back. As he disappeared from view, she scooted down the sofa to be closer to Ellie.

"Aaron said you guys talked a few days ago?"

"Yeah. Saturday, at the end of my shift. I told you—he wanted to reserve the planetarium. We—"

Sam raised a hand to stop her there. "I remember. I was putting this afternoon into context, that's all. It sounded like after talking to you that day, he was trying to figure out how to get closer to you again. Fix things, maybe. He hadn't been here for more than a few minutes before you came in, so we didn't get the whole story, but he was asking about you—what you like to do, favorite books, movies—that sort of thing."

Ellie was stunned. This was definitely her day to get blindsided.

"Yeah, he was clearly after some pointers." Ryan returned awkwardly clutching three large glasses of iced water, which he set on the low table.

"Very clever, *Mister Collins*," Sam said.

"Seemed like girl talk." He resumed his place beside her on the sofa.

"Wait. *What?!*" As if it had slipped into neutral, Ellie's brain flatly refused to accept and process this new information.

"I don't know," Sam said. "Not for sure. But remember what you told me about the time you ran into him in the lobby? By the science fair plaque? Talking to him today felt sort of like what you described, more like talking to the old Aaron." She looked to Ryan, offering him the chance to weigh in on that point.

"*Hmm....*" He nodded slowly as he considered this. "Now that you say that... She's right. He seemed more like he was that first week or two, before he..." He hesitated, unable to describe the sudden personality change they had all witnessed in Aaron. "Well, you know."

"I totally don't get it," Ellie said. "We already talked about most of that stuff!"

"I got the feeling those were merely the warm-up questions," Sam said.

Hobbled by her mental gears' ongoing refusal to mesh, Ellie continued to trundle along her own line of thought. "He's done nothing but ignore me for over a month! Plus, there are all those girls he's been hanging out with, his outbursts.... Now he suddenly wants to... to what? *Reconcile?*"

This news, on top of what had just happened, should have felt like a crushing disappointment, and maybe it would later. For now, all she could do was add it to the pile of weird that had been the rest of her day. But then, out of all the questions swirling around inside her skull, a fresh one bubbled to the top. "Do you think he'll tell anyone what we said?"

Ryan shrugged. "Does it matter at this point? There's no evidence the shack ever existed, nothing to prove we did what we did. What's the harm?"

"Aside from making us all sound like total wackos, you mean? Jeremy is back, right? What if he's been here all along? You know, for *years*. What if he's been working on another shack project, and it's sitting out on that mesa somewhere? We just tipped our hand that we know what he might be up to."

"Ah! Okay, I see your point. But seriously, what are the odds of him catching wind of high school gossip?"

"Yeah," Sam said. "He hardly paid attention to anything going on at school, even when Aaron was his son. Unless he actually has a kid going there now, how would he ever find out?"

Ellie relaxed a little. "That's true, I guess."

The room lapsed once again into silence. Ellie wondered how she could check for a student with *Siskin* for a last name. *That's easy,* she decided. *School library, yearbooks.* Next, she wondered how they could find out whether or not Jeremy was working on a new time-travel project, but she knew from experience that getting that answer would be the total opposite of easy. It would be impossible, especially from the outside. Most of all, she wondered if Aaron would ever so much as look at her again.

She felt confused, defeated, and just plain miserable, and she was pretty sure that nothing could make her feel any better. No amount of Ben & Jerry's would do the trick; that was certain. Not even a whole mountain of Le Grand chocolate truffles. There was no denying she was starving, however.

"Hey, guys, could we maybe order a pizza?"

Given the gloomy mood filling the room, Ryan splurged on two medium pies from Take Five, remembering without being prompted to add roasted red peppers to Sam's veggie pizza. Sam called herself a "flexitarian." She seldom passed up an opportunity to enjoy bacon, and she always partook as eagerly as anyone else whenever she attended one of Ryan's dad's famous cookouts, where slow-smoked barbecue was always the main attraction. When it was within her control, however, she ate as little flesh as possible, and then it was mostly fish.

Ellie called to let their mom know they wouldn't be home for dinner, and then they waited. They avoided any reference to Aaron, Jeremy, or the shack until after their pizzas arrived and had started to work their usual magic. By the time Ellie began munching her way through her third slice, her mood had improved enough that she finally felt up to talking about Jeremy's unexpected appearance in class.

"So, the short version is that he was there to talk about how wonderfully eco-friendly his new lab is. And, actually, it is," she reluctantly conceded. "After class, I went home and Googled Daniel to find out how he had hooked up with Judith again after what we did to them. She read those *Messenger* books I told you guys about earlier, and they got back together after that. Aaron once told me she'd had trouble getting pregnant, and Jeremy had come along pretty late in their marriage. So even though they got married years later this time, it didn't necessarily change the timing of Jeremy's arrival much. He might have been born a little earlier or later, but I'd bet it was probably within a month or two of when he was born the first time. Maybe even a day or two. What I want to know is what happened with Judith."

"What do you mean 'happened with?'" Sam said. She had finished eating and sat slumped back on the sofa with her feet propped on the coffee table, hugging a small throw pillow to her chest.

"Aaron also said Judith died shortly after Jeremy was born. But this time, Daniel was a successful author and, I would assume, a wealthier man. Did she get better medical care this time around and survive? Did this Jeremy grow up with a mother?"

Ryan frowned at her. "And we care why?"

"The Jeremy we knew was raised in the fifties and sixties by a single father, also in his fifties and sixties, who was busy running his own business. How much quality time would they have shared? It was probably all nannies or women at the shop he grew up with. Then he spends his married life raising a kid who isn't his. Lots of guys wouldn't have a problem with that, but it's a safe bet Jeremy felt otherwise. We've seen how much having a lifetime of different experiences this time around has changed Aaron. Why wouldn't the same be true for him? Think about the Jeremy Siskin we knew."

"I'd rather not," Sam said.

"Yeah, well. But on top of everything else, throw in a wife whose career is getting much more attention than his, and you have to wonder how much of his creepy, bitter personality was the result of completely hating his own life. It would have been impossible for his project to get any attention at all, given what it was, but still..." She munched on her final bite of pizza crust while they thought about that.

"So you're saying you think that after a happier childhood, this new Jeremy is all fluffy bunnies and rainbows?" Ryan said.

"Oh, no—not at all! He has a certain, um, *charisma*, I guess, but he still kind of gave me the heebie-jeebies. What I'm saying is that we need to keep in mind that he's different. In the same way that Aaron is different. He seems... I don't know, *wilier* maybe? If we assume he'll act exactly like the old Jeremy, we might regret it."

Suddenly on guard, Sam's body went rigid, and she stared hard at Ellie. "And why would we regret it?"

Ellie looked from Sam to Ryan, then back at Sam. "Because I think he knows."

"Knows what?" Sam said.

"*Everything.*"

Ryan started. "You mean about what happened before? How's that even possible?"

"Okay, so I said that was the short version. After he gave his little presentation, he took questions from the class. I suggested that how he built his lab would be a good way of keeping the internal layout secret, and he got sort of cagey and asked what it was I thought he had to keep secret. He started to call me 'Miss something,' but he had to look up my name on Mrs. Carson's seating chart. When he read it, he got this weird look on his face and laughed. And when he came up to my desk after class, he called me 'Lauren.'"

"That is how you're listed in the school records," Sam pointed out.

"Yeah, but I know for a fact that the seating chart says 'Ellie,' so if he didn't know my name until he looked, that's what he would have called me. But then what he actually said was, 'So, you're the Lauren Henderson I've *heard* about.' Get it? Like someone had been *talking* about me. But absolutely nobody has called me Lauren since I was four and you had just discovered what initials were. So if he'd *heard* about me, again, he'd have said 'Ellie.' I got the feeling that calling me Lauren was just to mess with me, but how would he have known? That's my point." She picked up her soda and took a long pull on the straw.

"All right," Sam agreed. "That is strange, but it doesn't automatically make me think he knows about *before*."

"There's more. Like, he said he knew how much trouble high school kids can cause. That actually might have been the weirdest thing. Take my word for it—he knows more than he should!"

"Maybe this is one of those 'you had to be there' things," Ryan suggested.

"Yeah, well, I was, and trust me—I'm right. Even if he doesn't know absolutely *everything*, something is definitely off. I don't know what's going on, but just thinking about it makes me queasy." She leaned forward and placed her soda back on the table with her left hand while reaching for a fourth slice of the pepperoni and sausage pizza with her right.

Sam summarized, making sure she was correctly connecting the dots. "So you think somehow he knows at least some of what happened before, and him knowing that implies he's here because he's working on the same kind of project now?" Ellie nodded. "But again, how could he possibly know?"

"Who knows?"

"Who's on first," Ryan added unhelpfully.

"So when you say 'regret it,'" Sam said, "does that mean we're going to be doing our thing again?"

Ellie flopped back in her chair. "I can't tell you how much I hope not. I'm going to give him a very thorough Googling, though. If I can find out where he went to school, what degrees he has, where else he's done research, maybe. That ought to answer a lot of questions."

"Let's hope it was all rainbow farms and bunny ranches," Sam said.

Ryan chuckled. "That seems highly unlikely."

"What do you mean?"

"The Bunny Ranch is a brothel, and I can't imagine him getting hired there, that's all."

Sam swung her pillow in a back-handed arc that ended in the center of Ryan's chest, and he puffed out a breathy *oomph!*

"Try to be serious!" Sam said.

"Seriously, I don't see that happening," he insisted.

"Let's get back to the important stuff," Sam said. "You say you have books Daniel Siskin wrote about *us*?"

Ryan snorted. "So *this* is being serious?"

Sam trained a stern look on him and raised an eyebrow. "Would you prefer to discuss how you happen to know so much about whore houses?"

"No," he said quickly. "This is better." He swept his arm wide in a please-go-on gesture.

Ellie smiled. "After we screwed up his date with Judith, he started having dreams he thought were about the life he was supposed to be living. The "messengers" from the title of the first book are two girls who show up in a diner and prevent him from meeting the love of his life. I got all that from the blurb. Like I said, I haven't read them."

"And you didn't think I'd want to know this?" Sam said.

"I found them in June, right after... Anyway, they sort of freaked me out, made me feel even guiltier. That's why I never mentioned them."

"That is totally cool! I'm starting on the first one tonight!"

"If you ask me," Ryan said, "it sounds like we 'screwed up' his life very much for the better."

Ellie thought about that, then gave Ryan a noncommittal shrug. "Maybe."

The discussion about Aaron and Jeremy ran out of steam then, and Sam and Ryan began talking about classes. Ellie tuned them out and considered what they had told her about Aaron. If she hadn't come in shouting that they had to get rid of his father—and "again," no less—they might have had a shot at getting back together. That possibility was now unlikely in the extreme, but it had seemed that way before she arrived here today, too. So in the end, what had changed? She decided it was the difference between assuming something and knowing it for a fact, and finally felt disappointment wash over her.

Back at home, Sam pulled *The Messengers* from Ellie's bookcase and read late into the night. Her only comment came when she was an hour into it. "This is really good. And really *bizarre!*"

Ellie, lying on her back, assumed Sam must have reached the scene in the restaurant. She closed her eyes and thought back to that crisp, sunny day in Brooklyn, to the moment she and Sam burst through the door of Tom's Diner, intent on convincing Judith that Daniel was a philanderer, a married man with four children. She remembered the hurt, indignant look on the woman's face as she stormed out of the diner and the pitiable look of total confusion on Daniel's. She had felt sick afterward, not just from stage fright but from the guilt that came from messing with someone's life.

Screwed up his life for the better? She had to admit that Ryan seemed to be right. What had they done, really? They had deprived Daniel of a few years of time spent with Judith, but his life seemed better in almost every other way. And maybe she was right too. Maybe the doctors had been able to save Judith this time around. Perhaps she and Daniel had shared many more, even happier years after Jeremy's birth, and Ellie had been wrong feeling so bad for so long. She was familiar with the concept of "failing your way to success," but it was not a strategy she'd ever chosen to embrace. In this case, however, she decided she was willing to accept even an accidental win.

Suddenly her eyes flew open, the answer to a recent puzzle bringing her mind fully alert in an instant. *Doctors!* That had been the key. When Aaron had referred to Jeremy up at Ryan's house, he had said, "*Doctor Siskin.*" She was sure she hadn't called him that. Was it nothing more than an assumption on his part? As her dad would say, it was impossible to spit blindfolded anywhere in Los Alamos without hitting a PhD of some kind or other, so it was definitely a safe assumption. But what if there were more to it than that?

She closed her eyes once more, but anxiety gnawed at her, and it was a long time before she slept.

9

The Aaron Ellie saw over the following days was very different. She no longer spotted him roaming the halls with some random girl or joking with the jocks at lunch, but invariably on his own. If he arrived ahead of her at a class they shared, he sat hunched over, staring at his book, rejecting through body language alone any possibility of conversation. Seeing him this way made her even sadder than she had been before.

Noticing him sitting by himself in the cafeteria for the fifth day in a row, she decided to try talking to him. The stony stare he leveled at her when he saw her walking toward him made it clear he was not interested in chatting, most especially not with her. She stopped and looked back at him from across the room, silently mouthed, "I'm sorry," then turned and walked away.

Exactly what she was sorry for varied from moment to moment. At times, it was for not telling him about their alternative histories right away. At others, she regretted telling him at all. Mostly, she felt sorry that the last thing she dared hope for—the chance that they might become friends again—had been lost.

· · ·

Sunshine finally made an appearance on Thursday afternoon. Ellie was relieved to spot the cat trotting across the brown grass to greet her as she stepped from the trail into the back yard. It had been almost five weeks since her last appearance, and Ellie had begun to fear the worst. They met in the middle of the lawn, where Ellie crouched to give her pal a scritch. Sunshine rubbed her face on Ellie's legs and purred, expressing her pleasure as Ellie raked her fingernails down the cat's arched spine.

"Where have *you* been, critter?" Ellie stood. "Let's get you some food, huh?"

When they reached the house, the cat leapt onto the windowsill over the kitchen sink and meowed mutely through the glass, watching while Ellie filled her bowl. Seconds later, Ellie placed the dish on the patio. Sunshine plunged her face into the bowl and began enthusiastically scarfing down the kibble. Ellie sat in a chair by the table and watched, all other concerns temporarily wiped from her mind. She regretted that the only way to get paid for doing this was by working at an animal shelter or a pet store, career choices that appeared nowhere on her list of future options.

Ellie's checkup came and went without providing any explanation for the irregular nature of her periods. Dr. Natale Cuccinelli, whom her mother had been seeing since they moved to town and whom Ellie began seeing a few years later, was a dark-haired, gently rounded woman barely taller than Ellie herself. Ellie ranked the exams dead even with being made to work in groups on school projects, but the woman's perpetually pleasant mood, down-to-earth manner, and an ever-so-slight accent that now reminded her fondly of Carmela were enough to make the whole experience bearable.

The doctor found nothing physically abnormal. There was an uncomfortable moment during the examination when she asked if Ellie might want a prescription for birth control pills. Incorrectly guessing the doctor's reason for asking the question, Ellie's face prickled with heat. Blushing furiously, she repeated a mumbled reminder that her "condition" could only be the result of mountain biking on the rugged trails around town, which was largely, if no longer entirely, true. So, thanks for the offer, but she was pretty sure she couldn't pedal her way to pregnancy.

Instantly understanding why Ellie seemed so flustered, the doctor tried to lighten the awkward moment with a joke. "Well, be thankful you can't —I don't have any experience delivering Schwinns! But no—the reason I asked is that the pill might impose some regularity on your periods." Now feeling foolish as well as embarrassed, Ellie was slow to respond. She was spared having to answer when the doctor spoke into the lull. "It's not something to decide at this moment, but think about it. Talk it over with your mom if you want, then let me know."

After her exam, Ellie sat with her feet dangling over the edge of the paper-lined table and watched as the doctor drew two tubes of blood. These she would send away for testing on the chance there was something hormonal going on. Results, she said, could take a few days or as long as a few weeks, depending on how busy the labs were.

"Stress could also be a factor," the doctor said. "A poor diet, too, can cause issues—especially when combined with stress—but I know your mom, so I know diet is not the problem. I also know that asking a teenage girl if she's feeling any stress is like asking the Pope if he's heard any good hymns lately, but..." She let the unspoken question hang out there, leaving it to Ellie to respond as she saw fit.

Ellie cast her thoughts back over the past few months. July and August, when she thought she had lost Aaron forever, had been the toughest times. September had been an emotional rollercoaster ride, climbing high right after Aaron arrived in town, plummeting to new depths when he pulled away from her. She'd have to discuss all of that in terms so vague as to be meaningless. More recently, especially since starting work at the PEEC, things had been better. These days, her mind was occupied with more or less the same typical high school crap everyone else she knew was dealing with. Was that stress, or was that merely life? Finally, she shrugged. "So, define 'stress.'"

Dr. Cuccinelli laughed. "*Aha!* Yes, good. The world needs more philosophers! Well, we will get this sorted out, so try not to worry too much. You certainly won't help things by 'ovary acting.'" She punctuated the punny punch line with a peg-toothed grin. "We'll get this bloodwork done first and go from there. Okay?"

Ellie nodded. In truth, she seldom gave the matter any thought at all, much less worried about it.

"In the meantime, I'm going to have Marie schedule you for a TVS. That's a—"

"Got it," Ellie said. *Yippee,* she thought. *This just keeps gettin' funner!*

"All right. Well, stop at the desk on your way out and set up a time that works for you." She stood to leave and let Ellie get dressed in private, but stopped at the door and turned around as if struck by a sudden thought. "My advice? You should stay away from those sexy Italian road bikes, eh?" She winked, then, chuckling softly to herself, disappeared from the room.

Ellie rolled her eyes. *Har har.* She left the office feeling vaguely reassured but also convinced that all OB/GYNs should be required to have their funny bones surgically removed before being allowed to practice.

To keep herself distracted from that and other concerns, she threw herself into her school assignments and her work at the nature center. Compared to last year's American History term paper, her science project was a breeze. She made a point of adding small, personal touches wherever possible in order to make it more relatable, and she was even starting to believe she had the whole writing thing figured out. For a while, she used the title *My Plateau* before deciding it suggested she was peaking far too early in life. A new title was still under consideration.

She discovered her PEEC exhibit project to be surprisingly easy as well. She decided almost right away to stick with static slides as much as possible to avoid getting bogged down with time-consuming animation. Whenever she had an idea for a new data set, she made a quick sketch of the first idea that popped into her head for the visual part. Next, she bookmarked any websites where she found relevant information. Her goal was to come up with at least a dozen ideas, then toss any for which she couldn't find supporting data, along with any she couldn't figure out how to illustrate.

Two weeks and eight ideas later, she began working on the graphics.

Shanna had located a refurbished forty-nine-inch LED TV that wouldn't break her "Exhibits" budget, and Ellie finally had a firm idea about how to size her images. After gaining access to the nature center's Shutterstock account, she quickly gathered all the images she needed in the exact cartoonish style she'd had in mind from the beginning. Once she'd picked a suitably casual typeface, she was able to rough out three of her slide concepts in almost no time at all.

On Saturday, with an additional three slides completed, she asked Shanna to meet her in the break room at her convenience. Shanna arrived an hour later, accompanied by a young girl of no more than twelve. Ellie recognized her right away, realizing in the same instant exactly how up-to-date Shanna kept the photos in her office. The girl's hair looked every bit as thick as her mom's but was tinged with red highlights that would likely darken over the next few years.

"Ellie, I'd like you to meet my daughter. Aisling gets to hang out here with us today because her dad had to be out of town." She placed a hand on the girl's back and guided her to stand facing Ellie's monitor. "Ellie started working here a few weeks ago, sweetie, and she has something to show us. I want you to watch and then tell us what you think."

"Hi," Ellie said. "Ready?" She found Aisling's enthusiastic nod endearing.

It didn't take long for the six slides to cycle through twice, but to Ellie, suffering a sudden bout of stomach butterflies as big as bats, waiting for Shanna's judgment seemed to take an eternity or two. She was forced to wait a little longer when Shanna gave Aisling the chance to offer her own critique first.

"What did you think, Ash?"

Aisling's expression became as grave as that of a jury foreman delivering a guilty verdict in a capital case. It was obvious she took her responsibility in this matter very seriously, and Ellie tried hard not to smile at her earnestness.

"So. I liked the way the pictures were like cartoons or something. Not, like, super serious. I didn't have enough time to read all the words, though. I mean, on *some* I did, but not on all of them."

"And what were the pictures about?" Shanna prompted.

"Saving energy. Using more solar and stuff, less oil and gas."

"Did they make you want to do that?"

Aisling looked up at her mom, confused. "But we already do."

"Yes, hon, we do." Shanna smiled at Ellie. "There you go. Your target demographic has spoken. Okay, Ash. You can go back to watching the snake."

This brought a big grin to the girl's face, and she made an immediate beeline for the door.

"It was nice meeting you, Aisling," Ellie called after her. "Thanks for your help." The girl's shouted, *You're welcome!* ricocheted down the hallway back to her, and she smiled at Shanna. "She's great! I guess I was about that age when we moved here." After a moment's thought, she added, "She reminds me a lot of me, actually."

Shanna's response was dry. "You don't say." She directed Ellie's attention to the TV. "These are excellent! Ash was right about the timing, though. So, two things. First, give each slide a bit more time on the screen. Two, three extra seconds, maybe? Also, bumping the size of the text up a few points wouldn't hurt either. Beyond that, I think you need at least four more slides before we can put it out on the floor. Think you can do that?"

Ellie, warmed by her project's positive reviews, nodded. "I already have a couple more ideas; I just haven't had time to make the slides yet."

"Great. As soon as you have at least ten slides ready, we'll set it up out front." Shanna turned and started for the door, but halfway there, she stopped and spun around. She peered at Ellie, concentration creasing the space between her eyes. "I never assigned anyone to work with you, did I?"

Ellie shook her head. "No. I did ask Teri for the stock art account login, though. Does that count?"

Shanna shifted her eyes to the monitor where the slide show was still playing, then back to Ellie. Amusement flickered across her face, then she nodded once, as though confirming something to herself. "Okay. Well, then—good job!"

10

When Ellie arrived at last period on Monday, Mrs. Carson glanced up from her desk and smiled. Ellie sensed pride in the woman's expression, which she thought was odd. For what she might be proud of her, Ellie couldn't say, and she wondered if maybe she and Shanna had been talking about her again. Then she wondered if that wasn't perhaps the teensiest bit egotistic.

Mrs. Carson spent only a few minutes addressing the class. She reminded them that the test on Friday would cover the first two units and encouraged them all to revisit chapters two through eight in preparation. Then she announced, to universally appreciative murmurs, that they could use the remainder of the class to study for the test or to work on their research papers. Ellie went with the latter option and used every minute right up to the bell taking notes and drafting emails for several of the contacts Shanna had given her.

She was nearing the end of the trail home when she saw Sam once more sitting at the patio table. She found this observation odd, too, considering the afternoon's chill. It wasn't until she cleared the row of low trees that bordered the rear edge of the yard that she could tell she had been wrong.

Even then, it took several seconds for her brain to accept what her eyes were telling it. It was Aaron, not Sam, watching her approach as if he'd been patiently waiting there for her all day. She continued walking toward him across the desiccated grass, but when she reached the patio, she stopped on the first row of bricks.

"How did you beat me here?" The answer, obvious enough, came to her even before she finished asking the question. Her Aaron had lived too close to school for biking in to make sense. This one, though, lived more than a mile from campus, and she had seen him pedaling in on numerous mornings.

"I biked."

"I... yeah."

Ellie didn't trust herself to say anything more, feeling totally clueless these days about what might upset him. Instead, she let the uncomfortable silence stretch out until Aaron finally broke it.

"I'm sorry," he said. She raised an eyebrow, silently inviting him to go on. "I'm sorry for treating you like I've been. I'm sorry for the way I ditched Ryan and Sam, and I'm sorry for how I acted up at his place."

"Is that why you're here? To apologize?"

"No. Yes. I mean, that's part of it. But mostly, I was hoping we could talk. I really need to."

For the first time, she noticed signs of stress—a pinched expression as if he were stoically enduring a constant, low-intensity pain. Vowing not to get her hopes up yet again, she walked to the table, placed her pack on the ground, and sat down across from him.

"I'll do whatever I can to help," she said. "I promise." Aaron remained quiet, staring down through the metal mesh tabletop. He seemed reluctant to start, and she guessed he was worried about her reaction to whatever was on his mind. "Hey, no matter what's bothering you, you can tell me."

Aaron remained silent for another minute, then took a deep breath and plunged in. "Okay. I know this is going to sound weird, but, well, it is what it is."

"You remember what Ryan said? Your first day here? 'We and weird go way back,'" she reminded him.

"See? That's it right there! That's what's been freaking me out for the past two months! It started then, that day. I got out of the car, looked around, saw you guys walking toward me, and suddenly I felt this weird déjà vu thing, but *strong*. I felt as if I'd stood in that exact spot a hundred times before, that I knew everything about you—all of you—could have told you every detail of the school, inside and out. Then you ran up, calling me by my name and hugging me, and Ryan 'guessed' what my mom's project was.... Then, just as suddenly, the feeling was gone. And I liked you guys right away, like we'd been friends for years, but after a while, it got too creepy. I simply couldn't deal."

"Couldn't deal? Deal with what? We seemed to be getting along pretty well, then it suddenly felt like you were pushing me away."

He nodded. "Yeah, I was. Like I said, I'm sorry, but I couldn't handle being near you."

"Why? What did I do?"

"It wasn't something you *did*. It was.... Look, you scared me, okay?"

She jerked in surprise, prepared for him to say almost anything but that. "I *scared* you," she repeated.

"Well, no, *you* didn't scare me. That's not it, exactly. Being with you did. With Sam and Ryan too. Whenever I was around any of you, I always got this tingly sense of weirdness, like constantly hearing *The X-Files* theme playing in my head. I felt like I knew things. About you, for instance. Things I couldn't possibly know. *That's* what scared me."

"'Things?' Such as?"

"Such as you cut your hair short freshman year because you didn't like looking so much like Sam. Like you used to have a cat named Mr. PiB. And you love chocolate. And who doesn't? But I mean, you *really* love it, right? Is any of this true? I'd be someplace, and I'd remember already having been there with you, except I knew I hadn't been. *Couldn't* have been! I remember seeing *Incredibles 2* in the theater here. With you. But I was still in New York when it came out. I saw it with my friend Anthony and his little sister."

"Okay," she said. "I get it." She didn't get it at all and was only buying herself a few seconds to think. In truth, she was astounded by what he said. She saw almost at once that if he remembered events she shared with the other Aaron, she might be able to use those memories to persuade him that what they had said about the shack was true. But only if she handled the explanation better than she had the first time. "Have you thought about what we told you the other week? About the shack?"

"I've thought about it, sure."

"And?"

"Seriously, would you believe you if I were you and you were me?"

She was amazed that someone could nearly out-Sam Sam with such a convoluted question, and she needed a full second to parse it, then another second to acknowledge he was totally justified in asking it. Their story was an awful lot for anyone to take purely on faith. At least it wasn't the same flat-out denial he had voiced at Ryan's house, so maybe he could be convinced after all. But how? Then she remembered something that might tip the scales in her favor. She saw he was about to say more, but she spoke first.

"Nope, hold that thought. Wait here a sec," she said, then dashed inside.

She returned a minute later carrying a small, hardbound journal. "Maybe this will help." She offered it to him, but he kept his hands on the table and peered suspiciously at it, as if he feared touching it might burn his skin. "Go ahead, take it."

Still clearly reluctant, he took the book from her and flipped back the cover. She had titled the first page "Memories of Aaron," written large in blue ballpoint ink. He turned another page.

On the following pages is everything I can remember about Aaron, but the two most important things are:

1 - He was the smartest, gentlest, bravest person I ever knew, and
  2 - I loved him.

He glanced up at her uncertainly, embarrassed by the intimacy of her words. She returned his gaze evenly but said nothing, still preferring to let him guide the conversation.

"What is this?"

"After Brooklyn—yeah, I know, but go with it for a sec—I got scared I would start to forget you like nearly everyone else in the world had. I had promised you I would always remember you, though, so I started to write down every little detail I could think of, just in case. And it's not every-thing, obviously. Even weeks later, my memories were as strong as ever, so I stopped writing as much. Then you were back—you arrived, I should say—and so the whole thing seemed sort of weird."

"*Sort of?*"

"Listen, I know the Aaron on those pages isn't you, okay? But I think if you read it, you might understand why we feel about you the way we do. I meant it when I said we cared about you. All of us. We still do."

He shook his head, bewildered. "I had been thinking maybe you guys were all totally nuts." He held up the book. "But I don't think *anybody* is *this* nuts!"

Ellie felt a surge of anger. She was baring her innermost feelings to him, and he was calling her wacko? "Fine," she snapped. "Don't read it! But let me turn this whole thing around for one second. You asked me how you could possibly know all those things about me, right? I know not all of what I wrote in that book is true anymore—not even your last name, for example—but I bet a lot of it is. I bet there are details in there I couldn't *possibly* know. So take a look. I dare you! And then explain to me how I knew those things before you even met me if what we've told you isn't true!" She forced herself to take deep breaths while counting slowly to ten and managed to quench her sudden anger.

"I'm sorry, Aaron. I can't imagine how hard this is for you. What we told you about? We lived that. For us, it's a basic historical fact. Like the Civil War. Or, you know, the Teletubbies."

Aaron laughed a little at this. "I hated those guys."

Sensing that his resistance was finally beginning to weaken, she smiled and pointed at the book. "I know. It's in there. Listen, Aaron, it's as hard for us to remember that you *don't* remember, that for you none of this is real, as it is for you to accept that it actually happened. Maybe you never will, you know, deep down, but don't hold it against Sam and Ryan—or *me*—when we slip up. It's hard to forget those six years. We had a lot of fun."

Aaron thought about this for a long moment, then he nodded. "I'm sorry about before. I never actually thought you were crazy. It's just..."

"Don't worry about it," she said. "I think I get it. That you're here is wonderful beyond words, but trust me—it hasn't been very easy for me, either."

He nodded again, then reopened the book and resumed reading.

Aaron Alden Siskin

 aka (per Ryan) Double-A; A-Ron

 Birthday: 29 September 2001

 Arrived in Los Alamos August 2012

Mother: Evelyn - molecular biologist; green energy developer

 Father: Jeremy (AKA Dr. Jeremy D. Siskin, DSc!) - theoretical physicist

Distinguishing Physical Details

 Height: 5'-7"

 Weight: 145 lbs. (?)

 Hair: white, short, spiky

 Eyes: blue (astigmatism/glasses large, round (Hedwig!))

 Right-handed

"'Distinguishing Physical Details?'"

Ellie shrugged. "I was trying to make it fun. So sue me."

"'Hedwig?!'"

"Okay, that will take longer to explain."

"Probably not. I did notice the horrible glasses in that photo." He turned to the next page. "But listen. Why I really came is—"

Still wanting to give her second shot at convincing him its best possible chance of working, Ellie held up a hand to cut him off. "Read first, then we'll talk. I'll go get us something to drink. Coffee?"

He stared at her for a second, opened his mouth as if to say something anyway, then closed it, nodded, and returned his attention to the book.

"I'll be right back," she said.

Watching Aaron through the window as she poured a thin stream of water slowly over the coffee grounds, she was reminded of a similar scene from a day back in June. The memory brought home to her how utterly different their frames of reference were. For her, those events had occurred just a few months ago. For Aaron, it was literally another lifetime.

She heard unexpected sounds from the front of the house, the front door opening and closing, followed by a pair of soft voices. Seconds later, Sam and Ryan entered the kitchen.

Sam joined Ellie at the window, standing close enough that their shoulders gently touched. "How's he doing?"

"I was about to go find out. Why are you guys here?"

"He called," Ryan said. "Asked us to come over."

"Ah." Ellie indicated the carafe of coffee. "You guys want any of this?"

"Thanks," Ryan said, "but I'm good."

Sam cocked an eyebrow at her. "Do you really have to ask?"

Ellie poured a full mug for Aaron, then split the remainder between herself and Sam.

She picked up two mugs from the counter and motioned for Sam and Ryan to lead the way.

Ryan was still holding the screen door open for Ellie when Aaron laid the notebook on the table and looked up at them. Ellie set his mug on the table in front of him, but he ignored it. Instead, he rose from his chair and watched Ryan and Sam as they approached.

"Before anybody says anything, I want to apologize to you two. Ryan, Sam, I've been reading some stuff that Ellie wrote, and I understand better how you guys felt about the 'other me,' that you were both good friends. Aside from Ellie, his *only* friends, I guess. I'm sorry I ghosted you like that."

"No worries," Ryan said, dismissing Aaron's concerns with a flap of his hand.

Sam offered him a gracious smile. "Apology accepted."

"Also," Aaron continued, "it's taken me some time to sort it all out, but I do believe you. About the 'shack,' going to Brooklyn... all of it." He smiled. "Even those god-awful glasses!"

"You do?!" Ellie said. "Why didn't you say so before?"

"I tried—several times—but you kept telling me to shut up."

"I did *not* tell—"

"Really, sis!" Sam said, her tone frosty with mock disapproval. "That seems rude, even for you!"

Ellie stuck out her tongue. "I never told him to shut up."

"And what, pray tell, changed your mind?" Ryan said.

"It wasn't my notebook that did it?" Ellie said, disappointed that she hadn't been the one to bring him around.

Sam, eager to learn at last the contents of the mysterious notebook she'd seen Ellie carry with her everywhere over the summer, pulled it in front of her and began skimming through it.

Aaron shook his head. "It probably would have, I think, but the biggest reason I believe you has nothing to do with that."

"And what reason is that?" Sam said, not taking her eyes off the page.

"There's this one, tiny detail from up at Ryan's place that stood out, even right then, and it's been stuck in my mind ever since. Sam, you got mad at me right before I left, and when you yelled at me, you started to call me 'Aaron Siskin.' Then you caught yourself and said, 'Weisskopf.' When that happened, you looked genuinely frustrated by the mistake. Everything else you guys said that day could have been made up, but there was something just too—I don't know—too spontaneous, too 'real' about that moment. I could never convince myself it was all part of some act, and I finally had to accept that to you guys I really was Aaron Siskin. Or used to be, anyway."

Sam shut the notebook with a loud *snap* and turned a smug smile toward Ellie. "*Ha!* So it was *me* who convinced him."

"Accidentally, I guess, but yeah," Aaron said. "But part of me already knew what you were saying was true, even then. It fit with stuff I had already, you know, *remembered*."

"'Remembered?'" Sam said. "No, we don't know."

Ryan leaned forward onto the table and peered intensely at Aaron, fascinated by what his words seemed to imply. "Are you saying you remember things that happened to the *other* Aaron?"

"Seems like. According to Ellie's little book there, I do. I've already told her some of this, but ever since I got to Los Alamos, I've been having weird déjà vu moments. They're clear, like real memories, but ones I don't remember making. It's like I'm recalling only the *memories* of certain events, not the events themselves, if that makes any sense. It's like there's someone else in my head, and they're *his* memories. I thought I was going crazy. Or else was possessed. A few of them are memories of you two, but most of the time, they're about her." He looked at Ellie and smiled.

"*Pfft!*" Sam sputtered. "*There's* a surprise!"

Ellie laughed. "Hey—give the boy a break! He's had a rough time." She patted Aaron's hand. "Give them an example."

"Yes, please do," Ryan said. "This is... I mean, this is... there aren't words for what this is!"

"Okay." Aaron closed his eyes and tried to recall a specific instance. After a second, he opened them again and refocused on Ellie. "At dinner one night with Mom and Dad at that Old Adobe place, I kept picturing the two of us sitting at the next table over. And these weren't like normal memories, exactly. It was like I could feel a different person inside me, and what I was experiencing were that guy's memories, his feelings—even the way he felt about you. I thought I was going crazy. Like, literally cracking up. I kept wondering how I could remember things that I *knew* had never happened to me. That's what was so scary."

Ellie shook her head, amazed by Aaron's ability to recall events from a past he'd never lived. "Wow! That and what you said before about the movie? As bizarre as it sounds, those things actually happened to me and 'our' Aaron. We ate at that restaurant right after we watched *Incredibles*, in fact. That was our last full day together."

It was conversations such as the one they had over appetizers that afternoon that she missed so badly. Then she remembered how much fun she'd had talking to him at the PEEC when he had gone to reserve the planetarium. "You said being around me was upsetting, but you seemed fine when we talked at the Nature Center. What was different about being there?"

"My guess is that you and I—well, you and *he*—were never at the nature center together."

Ellie nodded. As far as she could recall, he was right—they had never been there together. She remembered going on a class field trip there shortly after it opened more than three years ago, but he had been a year ahead of her then and wouldn't have been along. "So what was with

Jessica and the rest of those girls? Like the one you were sitting with down in the canyon."

Ellie could tell he was surprised she knew about that, but he didn't ask how. "That was Djamila. Her parents are splitting up, and she wanted to talk about it, that's all. I think that since I'm still so new here, she found it easier to talk to me instead of someone who really knew her. Apart from her, hanging around other girls was mostly my lame way of keeping you at a distance." He shrugged. "Yeah, I know. Pretty stupid. But I also thought that if I went back to all those places with somebody else, maybe I could overwrite those other memories or something. Wipe the hard drive, defrag my mind, you know?"

Hearing that made Ellie feel sad. She had been so excited about having the chance to revisit places they had gone before, so focused on trying to relive old memories that she had put little effort into creating new ones. She'd wanted so badly to reconnect with "her" Aaron that she hadn't tried very hard to know the new one. Not only had that been the very thing that drove him away, but it had compelled him to try erasing any trace of the old Aaron that still survived.

"Did that work?" Ryan said.

Aaron scoffed. "*No!* Now I have *two* sets of memories, but at least the 'original' ones don't bother me as much." Then his brow furrowed, and he took the conversation back to something Ellie had said earlier. "You mentioned Jessica a second ago. I assume you meant Jessica Thomas. What about her?"

"I heard Jordan say something about you two, that you guys, um... the two of you, at her house, you know, that you had..." She could tell she was blushing and wondered how bad it was. She wished they had covered this topic before Sam and Ryan arrived.

"That we had what? That we had *sex?!*" Now he turned red, too, the effect dramatic on his normally pale complexion.

She nodded. "Yeah. I mean, not that I actually believed it!" she added quickly.

"I hate to speak ill of the brain-dead, but, *yeesh!*" An involuntary shudder wracked his entire body. "She is *so* not my type! I'd sooner stick it in a blender!"

He said the last so earnestly that Ellie started to laugh, and after a second, he joined her, followed by Sam and Ryan. It felt good to know she'd been right to doubt the story. She was about to ask exactly who was his 'type,' but decided that was a question for another time.

"Are there more examples of memories like those?" Sam said.

"Yeah. Lots, but most of them never seemed to mean too much. There is this other big one, though." He turned his attention to Ellie again. "The first time I went to the Starbuck's down at Smith's, I kept seeing you there with me. We were laughing about something to do with"—he hesitated, crinkling his brow as if doubting the accuracy of his own recollection—" Smaug the dragon?"

Ellie nodded and tried to smile as tears filled her eyes. It was her favorite Aaron memory, and discovering that this Aaron somehow remembered it made her heart feel full to the point of busting open. "Yeah, we did that. That was in June. It was kind of our first date." She sniffed. "We were talking about the shack being our Smaug that we needed to destroy. I said I wished I could be a wizard because it would be fun to be able to do some magic. And you said, 'You are not—'"

"'—entirely without your charms,'" Aaron finished along with her.

"Oh, brother," Ryan muttered, and Ellie thought she could actually hear his eyes rolling in their sockets.

Aaron—and once again it was *her* Aaron—fixed his eyes on Ellie's. When he smiled, her whole body buzzed as though an electric current had just coursed through her. Across the table, she saw Sam staring wide-eyed at him.

There! She's finally seen it!

Aaron laughed lightly and shook his head as if to clear it before continuing. "Yeah. *Wow!* That explains why that was one of the strongest, um, 'episodes,' I guess you'd call them. Since that first day, anyway."

Ellie placed her hand on his and gave it a gentle squeeze. "I wish you had said something sooner. I would have told you everything if I had known what you were going through."

"One of us thinking I was crazy was bad enough. And anyway, I don't think I could have handled knowing all that until now."

Sam gave a derisive snicker. "What happened at Ryan's definitely wasn't 'handling it!'"

Ellie sat back in her seat. "Yeah, really! If you already suspected some of this, why were you so mad?"

"I was torn. What you told me was terrible! Killing my own dad? And myself too? I didn't want any part of it to be real, but I also didn't want to believe that you guys were screwing with me either. At the same time, I hated that you didn't tell me sooner because, like I said, I sort of knew it was true. But in the end, it's not about what I want; it's all about the logic. This is the only way all the facts fit together.

"Anyway, once I realized that the stories you told me were the same as some of those bizarre memories I'd been having, I thought instead of trying to block them out, maybe I should encourage them."

"And?" Ellie said.

He shook his head. "That didn't work any better than plan A. Just like with real déjà vu, it happens when it happens, I guess. But I did try to remember all the times I've felt that way since they started. Most don't have much to do with anything. They're, like, random events. But there is one other time that really stood out."

"Random events that happened in a completely different timeline." Ryan shrugged to underscore how that was no big deal. "But okay, sure, go on."

"First, I need to back up. There's something I've promised not to tell anyone, but I think you guys need to know." A sheepish expression came over his face. "See, when you told me about all of this the other day, I already knew who Dr. Siskin was. I've been working with him pretty much since I got here."

"*What?!*"

"How?"

"You're saying you *know* Jeremy?"

Ellie recalled how Aaron's reference to his former stepfather as "*Doctor Siskin*" had worried her so much that she hadn't slept half the night. Now he was suggesting he'd actually been to his lab! A shiver rippled down her spine, and goosebumps erupted all over her body. She sat up straight and leaned forward, elbows on the table.

"Aaron, why are you here?"

11

"Like I said, this all goes back a ways," Aaron began. "It started while we were still in New York, but after Mom's project proposal had been accepted out here. I got an email from Dr. Siskin offering me a sort of internship. He said I was referred to him by one of my teachers, but he didn't say which. He also said that, except for Mom and Dad, I had to keep it a secret. When I showed the letter to Mom, she said she knew the guy back when she was in grad school. Well, knew *about* him anyway. Thought he was okay."

She certainly didn't know very much *about him,* Ellie thought. Remembering her recent encounter with him in the classroom, she had to admit she hadn't felt the same creepy sort of vibe she remembered from before. No, it had been a different sort of creepy that day. In addition, he had been sarcastic and condescending, almost mean. There had also been that brief moment when the familiar arrogance peeked out for a second before he caught himself.

"You took the offer, obviously," Sam said.

"Yeah. I mean, I checked him out first, as much as I could. Googled him, obviously. Everything I found—which was surprisingly little—said he was a first-rate theoretical physicist." This was exactly what Ellie had learned from her own stab at backgrounding the man, and she nodded absently in agreement. "The whole 'top secret' thing seemed weird, but since Mom said he was okay, I figured, well, how could I pass up a chance like that?"

"I don't get it," Sam said. "What does this have to do with your déjà vu thing?"

"I'm getting to that now. So, I didn't meet him in person until a few days after we moved here. Mom drove me out to his lab, and we were led back to his office. He seemed okay, all friendly and smiling, but there were these few seconds when he was looking at my mom—normal, you know, still smiling—but all at once I felt an intense, burning anger. I suddenly *hated* him. Hated him so much that it made me feel sick. Something in his expression, maybe. That's what I thought at the time, but now I think it was one of those memories coming up to the surface, only a purely emotional one. I'm still not sure what it was, but what Sam said before about me possibly feeling my mom would be better off without him around made me think." He went quiet for a moment. "I wonder if *she* felt anything strange that day."

"If it's so secret," Ryan said, "why are you telling us?"

"Because of what you guys told me, and especially because of what you said about Dr. Siskin. You made him seem like some big 'bad guy,' like an actual mad scientist or something. So, since that day, I've been looking at all that's happened since I got here as if everything you told me then was true. I couldn't find a single fact to refute any of it, and if you were right about everything else, I had to ask why you wouldn't also be right about him. Then I tried to imagine what the 'other me' would be doing in my place, knowing what I know. I decided he would do whatever he believed was being loyal to you." He shrugged. "In short, I decided it was time to pick a side."

Ellie, Sam, and Ryan exchanged worried glances. This kept sounding worse.

"What do you mean?" Ryan said. "Sides in what?"

"What, exactly, have you been doing for him?" Ellie said.

Aaron looked embarrassed. "To be honest, I don't actually know."

Ryan frowned, skeptical. "You've been working out there for what, six weeks, and you don't know?"

"Yeah, I know *what*, but only in a very specific sense—making and maintaining databases. Weird ones. But none of it has made any sense until now."

Ellie scrunched up her face, trying hard to imagine what would make a database weird.

"Databases," Ryan repeated.

"Again, I only know what I know, which isn't a lot. But like I said, taking into account what *your* Aaron would have known, I think I can make some guesses.

"When I first got here, Dr. Siskin had me create four massive sets of data. The first was a collection of in-depth profiles of 50,000 people. Spouse, kids, school, career... that sort of thing. Plus, some of their family trees. Both sides, if the person was married. Also, income, bank accounts, insurance policies, mortgages, travel history."

Sam gaped at him, appalled by such a massive breach of privacy. "Exactly how were you able to get all of that?"

Aaron chuckled self-consciously. "Yeah, I know, right? My workstation has some ICE-breaking tools you would not believe. Whatever system I try to access, I'm on it right away, no delay at all. I'm pretty sure that software could get me into the Pentagon, the CIA, NORAD, China's PLA, the FSB computers in Russia... *anywhere!* Whoever wrote it is a genius."

"That ability is probably more a by-product of the hardware than any programming," Ellie said.

"Hmm?"

Ellie brushed Aaron's question aside. "Later. Right now, tell us more about those databases."

Aaron frowned, and for a second he looked hurt, resentful of the way she seemed to be once again withholding information.

"I mean it," Ellie said. "If I think I'm right, I promise I'll tell you later, but we need to know everything you know first."

Aaron's expression softened, and he nodded. "Okay. So, out of those 50,000, some of the names I recognized as people alive right now, like

Gore, Putin, Kim... Bezos, Ma—that's Jack, not Yo-Yo—Higgs and Witten.
A lot of them, though, are dead. Jobs, Hawking, Gorbachov. Kennedy and
Castro. I assume that the ninety-nine-point-whatever percent of the names
I didn't recognize were equally important in some way, just not especially
famous. Of the ones I did know, the oldest name I saw was Woodrow
Wilson.

"But then there was another, much larger group of 250,000,000 people.
They were initially chosen at random from records all around the world,
but now they're always the same ones. The sample is... What's that term
Mr. Boltzmann likes so much?"

"'Arbitrary but fixed?'" Ellie said.

"That's it. Anyway, this second group of people just got short bios.
Date of birth, job, and family details, but nuclear only; no histories. Date
of death if they're dead. That sort of thing."

"Not that I have any idea why he'd want the 50,000 'important'
names," Ryan said, hooking quote marks in the air, "but what in the world
do you do with a quarter-billion random bios?"

"I'm starting to get an idea," Ellie said, "but go on. Tell us the last bit."

"The third list is made up of companies, all pretty big on the world's
major stock listings. Or ones that used to be but aren't anymore, like
Kodak. I compiled financial reports, company histories, current and past
boards of directors, and daily closing stock values from the day they were
listed. Oh, and lawsuits—anything you could think of.

"The final thing I did was create a copy of Wikipedia. *All* of it. Once I
was finished that very first time, Dr. Siskin gave me two portable hard
drives and told me to copy everything I had collected onto both of them.
I've only seen those two drives one other time. At the end of that same
day, I went to his office to find out exactly what you want to know—what
those files are for. He wouldn't answer that question, but as we were talking, I noticed the drives were sitting on his desk right in front of me. They
each had a new sticker that said 'Continuity,' followed by some numbers.
He saw me looking at them, and, as casually as he could, he stuck them in
a drawer."

"But again—why?" Ryan said.

"This is what I was getting at. Two weeks ago, I couldn't make any sense of it at all. I mean, why make a copy of stuff you can look up anytime you want to? What you guys said up at your place was the clue I'd been missing. If you really could go back in time, the biggest danger would be accidentally making a change that messed everything up when you got back. Or if you made a change on purpose, you'd want to be able to make sure it worked the way you intended, to know how much of an impact it had. Whichever it was, you'd need some way you could check to see what happened. I think those first databases I made were a sort of baseline, a permanent reference point. Making two copies was probably for redundancy. A backup."

Ellie thought Aaron's reasoning was spot on, and she grinned at him. "Yep, still one of the top five!"

"Well, yippee for him," Sam said, "but I *still* don't get why."

Ryan nodded to himself, beginning to see where Aaron's speculation pointed. "'Continuity,' Sam. You, me, and Ellie are the only ones who remember the original timeline because we were shielded inside the shack and weren't affected by the changes. If you want to keep a permanent record of the original conditions, you stash the hard drives inside it to keep that information from changing along with the rest of the world." He turned back to Aaron. "It's actually pretty brilliant."

"I guess that depends on whether you're trying to ensure you didn't change anything or making sure you did," Aaron said.

"This is not good," Ellie said. "Everything you just said confirms what we've been hoping wasn't true. And you're right—not only do you deserve to know what I think is going on, you *need* to know." She took a deep breath, but before she could say anything more, Sam voiced the obvious conclusion.

"'They're *baaack*,'" she said.

Ryan looked at her, eyebrow raised. "Now, see, *I* was going to go with, 'There's no crying in baseball!'"

"*Huh?*" Sam said. "That makes no sense whatsoever!"

"Okay, so I was going to say, 'They're *baaack*,'" he admitted, "but you beat me to it." This earned him a slug on his arm.

Ignoring them, Ellie laid out her take on the situation. "Here's what I think is happening. Yes, not just Jeremy, but the shack is also back. But I don't think this one is hidden away off-site somewhere. I think it's right there in the lab. One of the slides of his new, über-green building showed a room that would have been more than big enough to hold the original shack. And this room had super-thick walls—two, three feet at least. Maybe more. What if the reason that the shack was built way out in the woods wasn't to hide it but because they were worried about radiation?"

"That or some kind of distortion field," Aaron suggested.

"The dead zone," Ryan said, referring to a ten-yard radius of barren soil they had seen surrounding the shack, an area where everything had died.

"Exactly!" Ellie said. "I bet those walls are so thick because they're packed with some kind of shielding. And remember that long utility trench through the woods? Right beside the thick-walled room is a smaller one that was labeled 'Generator' on the floor plan. My guess is that they use a fuel cell or something to keep it off the grid entirely."

"You're doing it again," Sam accused.

"Doing what?"

"Jumping to all kinds of conclusions. Same as last time."

"Okay, then *you* explain it!"

"Well, *I* don't—!"

Ryan jumped in, trying to head off a dispute. "This doesn't sound like a long-term project, Aaron. What else do you do out there?"

"And why *you?*" Sam added. "Sorry, I didn't mean... It's just that while the Aaron we knew was definitely good with computers, he wasn't exactly a hacker genius."

Aaron shrugged. "Me neither. Not by a long shot. My dad's always used a bunch of different programs for recording, looping, editing. I started off messing around with those, then I began helping him out. Sort of being his 'sound engineer,' you'd call it. I dunno, I found I liked it and started to get into other aspects of it. Not hacking, of course, but system mods, upgrades, things like that. Nothing that would make me an obvious choice to work out at the LAB.

"As to what else I do? Nothing. It's the same damned thing, over and over and over. Once or twice a week, I rerun the original 50,000 people searches, also the business ones, while the computer gathers the same

250,000,000 records and copies Wiki. I load those new databases onto two more hard drives, and then pass them along to Dr. Siskin. What happens to them after that, I've never been able to find out."

Compiling the first set of files made sense, Ellie thought, but why keep creating new ones? "Do you think you could? Find out, I mean. Along with whatever else they're hiding."

"Ellie!" Sam cried, horrified. "What are you *doing?!*"

Seeing if he really is ready to choose a side, Ellie thought, but she ignored the question and kept her gaze fixed on Aaron.

"I don't know. Maybe, but I really doubt it. There are other things you don't know about that place."

"Such as?" Ryan said.

"Such as the security guys he has working out there look more like mercs than your typical rent-a-cops. I think what you're suggesting is less of a firing offense and more of a firing *squad* offense, if you know what I mean."

Ellie spoke directly to Ryan. "That's the same as before. Remember? Aaron said your dad's guys were kept outside the fence, and Jeremy had his own people on the inside."

Ryan nodded.

"Yeah. And before, Aaron was going in with his 'dad,'" Sam pointed out, making air quotes. "Armed mercenaries? This is way too dangerous!" She turned to Aaron. "Sorry. It must be annoying hearing us talk like you're not sitting right there, but it's *him* we're talking about, you know?"

"So why don't you call him 'A-Ron,' instead? Or 'Double-A.'" He looked pointedly at Ryan, then at Ellie. "Or even 'Hedwig.'"

Ryan stabbed an accusing look at Ellie, catching her in mid-blush.

"Yes, he knows about the nicknames," she said. She looked at Aaron, crossed her eyes, and stuck out her tongue. "Traitor!" Then she laughed.

"So why didn't it work?" Sam said. "What we did in New York. Don't get me wrong. I'm glad you're here and all, but..."

"I think because Ryan was right," Ellie said. "At least that's part of it."

"I was?" Ryan said. "Right about what?"

"In Brooklyn, you said you thought the reason we failed to keep Daniel and Judith apart at the newsstand was because that would have created a paradox. In order for us to be there, the shack had to get built. Therefore, we couldn't do anything that would completely rule that out, or we couldn't have gone back in the first place. All we ever could have done was change things a little, like make it so they got married later."

Sam winced as she tried to compose a response. "But they didn't... I mean, *we* didn't... *Aargh!* There was no shack this time!"

"No," Ellie said, "not the one you mean. Not for the rest of the world, anyway, but there *is* a shack. There's this new one. At least, we're pretty sure there is. We just haven't seen it yet. And I think the rest of the answer is a little stranger.

"Aaron—I mean 'A-Ron'—dropped my camera in Lawrence, but we recovered it here, a hundred years later, in the woods where the shack used to be. And even though there was no shack in this timeline, we did what we remember doing, right? I believe the universe, faced with two conflicting realities, made certain compromises to accommodate them both. The camera wasn't in 1912 because, in this timeline, we didn't go there. But it was out on the mesa because, at the same time, we *did*. Get it? It's like reality became a blend of this altered timeline and our memories of the old one."

Even before Ellie finished explaining, Sam was massaging her temples with her thumbs. "*Oww*," she moaned. "You'd think I'd eventually build up some *immunity* or something."

Ryan gently patted her thigh. "Go to your happy place, Sam." She gave his hand a grateful squeeze, then resumed rubbing her head.

Aaron looked at Ellie with obvious concern.

"She's fine," she assured him. "Time logic gives her migraines, is all."

Aaron shook his head and gave them a bemused smile. "I got to play on stage with my dad once back in New York, and I thought *that* was cool. Were your whole lives like this, or was it just this summer?"

"Oh, this was nothing." Ryan flapped a hand through the air. "You should have been here the year *before!*"

"Shush," Sam murmured through her fingers, seemingly apropos of nothing.

Ellie continued explaining. "And partly, it's due to chance. Jeremy, we now know, wasn't really Aaron's dad, so he didn't matter as far as Aaron being born or not. And Jeremy's parents were both still alive. Nothing we did changed that, so there was always a *possibility* Jeremy could be born and the shack could still get built. I don't think there's a single answer other than that's just the way it all worked out this time."

"*Sic transit*," Aaron agreed.

Ellie smiled, recalling the old Aaron's facility with Latin.

"I know that one," Ryan said. "'Ambulance.'"

Ellie rolled her eyes. "What can you tell us about the lab itself?"

Aaron thought for a long moment. "Okay, you know how when you cross the bridge, there are a lot of labs clustered all together right there? To get to his, you have to go past all of those and down an access road about half a mile, maybe a little more. You can see other buildings from there, but only the tops of them through the trees, and they're all pretty far away. There's a gate at the far end of the road. Well, it's technically two gates because there are two fences to go through, both with the spirally... that sharp wire prison fences have on top. But only one *entrance* is what I meant. There are usually two guys manning a guard shack, but they all know me, so when I pedal up, they let me go right on through. The building's door has a biometric lock—a palm scanner—and I have my own entry code."

Ryan stroked his chin with the forefinger and thumb of his right hand and gazed up at the ceiling, mimicking his performance from the time he had "psychically intuited" the nature of Aaron's mom's project the day they met back in September.

"Don't tell me. I think I've got it. It's becoming clearer..." He looked at Aaron. "Two, zero, six, four!"

Aaron stared at him like he was crazy. "No, it's..." He scoffed. "You're not even close!"

Ryan shrugged. "A swing and a miss."

Ellie prompted Aaron to go on. "What about the inside? How many people work there?"

"I've never seen most of it. Where I work is in a tiny room off the first hallway to the right of where you come in. Dr. Siskin's office is further down, at the end of the hallway. There's a common room for breaks and stuff, but that's all I've seen. Well, plus a bathroom inside that common room. By the main entrance, just before you get to my room, there's a door with another palm scanner, and what's behind that is a total mystery. If you turn left instead of right when you first come in, there's another locked door that leads to other offices and whatever else is back there. I've seen people going in and out of that area, but I've never talked to any of them. Since I got the databases set up, I work with someone named Aimie. Only through DMs, though. I've never met her in person, either. She lets me know when to recopy the drives.

"I guess I've seen five or six different people in all, aside from the security guys, pass by my door. The room is so small that I always keep it open when I'm in there. I think one of them is named Cai, but that's all I know. I've hardly even seen Dr. Siskin since that first day. It's not a real friendly place. Well, except for Aimie, I guess. If she's there when I am, sometimes she'll start a conversation, ask how school's going, that kind of thing. She seems pretty nice."

"Oh, *really!*" Sam said.

"A-Ron said Jeremy had a sort of cover project in place for visitors to see," Ellie said. "Is there anything like that now?"

"That's right," Ryan said. "He said there was a room set up with some components they used in the shack, except it was meant to look like they were working on a neural interface for remotely controlling equipment like drones or bomb disposal robots."

Aaron shook his head. "No, nothing like that. All of the work areas— except for mine and Dr. Siskin's office—are down that locked hallway, and I don't think visitors ever make it that far. At least not ones that don't already know what he's working on. That other thing sounds cool, though."

"Interesting," Ryan said. "For whatever reason, it sounds like he's running a much tighter ship this time."

"Guess he knows how much of a threat you guys are," Aaron said.

Ellie remembered Jeremy saying something similar in Mrs. Carson's class, and she shuddered. She also noted Aaron's use of the phrase "you guys." She was willing to chalk it up to him not being used to thinking of himself as part of the group, but given what he had said earlier about choosing sides, she wondered about it all the same.

.   .   .

"Bottom line? Jeremy is back," Ryan said. "If the shack is also back—and it sounds like it is—it poses the same danger it did before. Unlike before, it's locked up in a building behind two rows of razor wire and being guarded by big guys with big guns and tiny scruples."

They sat in silence for a long time, considering everything they had discussed. At last, Aaron turned to face Ellie. His expression was sincere, and once again she saw the old Aaron looking out through his eyes. His next words were all the response she needed to her earlier, unspoken concerns.

"So, what do you want me to do?"

Ellie was aware of Sam's attention on her as she answered. "Not sure. Mostly, we need to know more." She looked to Ryan, who had picked up some of his dad's understanding of security procedures over the years. "Ryan? Any ideas?"

"All I'd say for now is pay close attention to everything, every detail of what goes on out there, no matter how small. Look for any patterns. Like, do they get any kinds of regular deliveries? If so, who from? That sort of thing."

"But above all," Sam added, "please be careful."

"You can count on that!" Aaron said.

But Ryan wasn't finished. "There is another thing you can do right away. Do you guys have a car you can use?"

"Yeah. As long as Dad's not out of town at a gig, I can use his minivan. Why?"

"You need to start driving it out there. Get the guards used to you showing up in it instead of on the bike."

"Any particular reason?"

"Not sure yet." He saw Sam squinting at him, suspicious. "This is just in case, okay?" he assured her.

"No problem. I can do that. One of the guards said something about that last week. He said, 'You're going to freeze your ba-'" He cut himself off mid-word and shot a self-conscious glance at Ellie before clearing his throat and starting over. "'You're going to freeze on your way home in

another month.' And he's right—it's already pretty cold in the evening."
Aaron noticed Ellie suddenly looked miffed, while Ryan was having a
completely different reaction. His mouth twitched as he did all he could
not to grin. Aaron was confused by the contrast of their expressions.
"What?"

Ellie leaned toward him until their faces were only inches apart and
stared him in the eyes. She still looked irked, but her tone was mild as she
flatly rattled off a long string of synonyms for the term that had tripped
Aaron up.

"'*Balls.*' *Nuts, stones, bollocks, nads, sac, cherries, rocks, scrote,* and the
regionally popular *cojones* and *huevos.*"

"Don't forget 'the boys,'" Sam added.

"Oh, I could go on," Ellie said, settling back into her chair.

Aaron blinked at her, now even more confused. He could tell she
wasn't mad, exactly; just trying to make a point. As to what that point
was, he had no idea.

"I'm sorry, but what did I...?"

Ryan laughed and slapped Aaron's back solidly enough to knock his
glasses askew.

"Lesson number one—treat either of these two like hothouse flowers,
and it will come back to bite you on the," he paused to nod toward Ellie,
"everything she said."

Looking suitably chastened, Aaron swallowed hard before nudging his
glasses back into place. "Gotcha," he said, and he glanced again at Ellie.
"Sorry," he repeated. Then, eager to change the subject, he turned back to
Ryan. "Is that it? Just start driving in?"

But it was Ellie who answered. "There is one last... God, I can't believe
I'm going to say this! I thought that maybe... *finally!*" She felt a sudden
upwelling of anger and frustration. She drew in a deep breath, turned her
gaze to the ceiling, and clenched her hands into tight fists on her lap.

"What is it?" Aaron said.

She let her breath out in a long, jagged sigh. "You had left Ryan's
before I told them this part, but Jeremy said some things when he gave a
talk in my science class that make me think he knows at least some of
what happened in June. Maybe everything." She looked at Ryan. "And I

think maybe we can now guess how." Ryan shook his head slowly, still grappling with the notion of Aaron's inexplicable memories of another lifetime. "Anyway, I think it's best if you and I keep things like they were before. With you being, you know, *psycho* and all." She gave him a thin smile, then watched as he quickly grasped the wider implications of her suggestion. She believed the disappointment she saw on his face was genuine.

At last, he nodded. "I get it. You don't want him to think we're close enough that I'd tell you anything."

"Right. If he trusts you now, I'd like to keep it that way. That means avoiding Sam and Ryan too."

"Won't it be a little hard to do the whole 'covert ops' thing without being able to communicate?" Sam said.

Ellie didn't see the problem. "Well, we can always call. Or text."

Ryan shook his head. "I know this will sound like overkill, but if you seriously think Jeremy is a threat and you want to be completely safe, you shouldn't use any form of communication that can be monitored or hacked. No calls, no texts, and no email, for that matter."

"Well, what then?" Aaron said. "Smoke signals?"

"I like it, but no. The high school swim team has this chat-room-slash-bulletin-board sort of thing set up. I'll get you the login info for a guy we cut a few weeks ago. You and I can pass messages through there if they're not too specific. *And* as long as you can't be traced on your end. It's not perfect, but it'll work until we can come up with something better."

"Okay, what else?" Ellie said.

Aaron held up a finger. "Just one thing. What were you waiting to tell me before? About the computer?"

"Oh, yeah. You'll like this! I'm assuming you're working on a dumb terminal? No CPU?"

"Mm-hmm. It's just a monitor and keyboard plugged into the intranet. Why?"

"Okay, so I believe that at the other end of that connection is the world's only fully operational quantum computer. It's not *code* that gets you into all of those secure networks. At least not entirely. It's—"

"No," Aaron said, and a look of wonder spread across his features. "It's pure brute force! But why do you assume it's a *quantum* computer specifically?"

Grinning, Sam held a finger up in an I've-got-this-one gesture. "Where were you sitting five seconds ago?" she said, sounding smug.

Without hesitation, Aaron pointed across the back yard toward the canyon. "Probably over there somewhere. Why?"

Sam's self-satisfied smile collapsed. She sighed loudly and rolled her eyes. "Never mind!"

Ellie laughed. "It's not for the hacking, but it's the only device capable of making the calculations required to connect a spot in this space/time to a specific one in the past."

Aaron got it at once. "Yeah. The Earth is billions of miles away from where it was, say, a hundred years ago. Those formulas would be..." He thought about this for a second. "Wow! But they don't exist yet. Not so you can actually use them like I am. Where did Jeremy get it?"

Ellie nodded. "That is an excellent question."

Ten minutes later, they watched Aaron pedal away and disappear around the corner at the entrance to the cul-de-sac.

"'We're gettin' the band back together! It's nice,'" Ryan quoted, sounding very happy.

"Is this what you meant before when you said that telling him was overdue?" Ellie said.

"Yeah. He doesn't ever need to know I said this, but I really missed that guy."

"He's still not 'that guy,' you know," Sam said. "Not really."

Ryan shrugged. "Maybe not. But it sounds like he's *our* guy again. We'll see where it goes from here."

Sam and Ryan turned and began walking toward the house, their voices fading with each step.

"That was from *RED*, right?" Sam said.

"Mm-hmm. I *love* that movie!"

Ellie remained behind, gazing down the empty cul-de-sac. She considered the job Aaron described doing at Jeremy's lab. A monkey could handle those tasks, but out of the nearly ten billion humans on the planet, Jeremy had specifically chosen him. Maybe the real reason he had picked Aaron was not to compile his databases but to act as bait in a trap, and she wondered if it was necessary for the bait to know it was bait. She thought about what Ryan had just said.

"Yeah, we'll see," she murmured before she, too, turned to go inside.

12

O ver the next few weeks, Aaron shared whatever observations he made regarding daily activities at Jeremy's lab. The switch from bicycle to minivan went smoothly. The guards searched the vehicle the first few times, but they found nothing more suspicious than a broken capo, a few stray picks, and two large equipment cases so packed with amps, mixers, folding stands, and an assortment of a dozen or so patch cables and extension cords that there was no room for Aaron to be smuggling anything in or out, so they soon stopped bothering. Seeing the familiar vehicle approach, they opened the gates and waved him through, just as they did when he had biked in.

This was contained in the first of several notes Aaron left in the dead drop he and Ryan had worked out via the swim team's bulletin board. Aaron would simply slip a tightly folded sheet of paper into the gap between the cafeteria water fountain and the wall. Then Ellie, seeing him use the fountain, would retrieve the message a few moments later. In the same way, they later learned that there was, as Ryan had surmised there might be, one regular delivery each week. Two large cylinders of liquid hydrogen arrived every Thursday afternoon, and two empty cylinders went out. Ellie relayed this information as she walked home with Sam and Ryan.

"Yep—it's gotta be a fuel cell, all right!" Ellie was pleased she had correctly guessed how they were keeping the new shack's batteries topped off.

"But why not just put the fuel cell in the shack?" Sam said.

"Configuration, maybe? We thought the batteries were distributed around the entire outside of the shack. You couldn't do that with a fuel cell. Maybe the batteries even provide part of the shielding."

"Plus, you'd still need to refuel it," Ryan pointed out. "Maybe this is easier. And maybe because hydrogen sometimes go *boom?*"

"And if you had to, you could recharge in the past much more easily if you can just plug it in rather than needing a supply of hydrogen," Ellie added.

Ryan snapped his fingers and pointed at her. "That's probably the real reason right there."

"But how does knowing that help us in any way?" Sam said. "What are we supposed to do—disguise ourselves as hydrogen tanks? Have them wheel us in on a hand truck?"

Ryan shook his head. "Nah, I'd pencil in that option pretty far down on the list, right between tunneling our way in and a pre-dawn HALO jump, maybe. Look, just knowing more about what goes on out there helps, even if we don't know how yet.

"Anyway, if it came to that, the thing to do would be to commandeer the truck, pose as the delivery team, and walk right in with the hydrogen on the cart." In response to Sam's disapproving look, he quickly added, "Not that I'm suggesting we do that!"

Ellie peered at him, dubious. "What, like overpower two big delivery guys?"

"There are ways," he said, but chose not to elaborate.

"Sam's right, though," Ellie said. "Figuring out how we can get inside and see what's going on has to be our top priority."

Sam's rebuttal was quick and emphatic. "Hang on! Sam's not right! Sam never said anything remotely like that!"

Ryan ignored her protest. "Yep, that's our girl," he said, smiling in response to her irritated expression. "Always cutting straight to the heart of the problem."

. . .

For Ellie, the oddest, though by far the most welcome, part of the new situation was how much closer she felt to Aaron, despite continuing to avoid any direct contact. Merely knowing he was working with them and that he finally knew all of her secrets brought her a sense of peace that had long eluded her. Even when she caught sight of him from across the cafeteria chatting with some flirty girl, she was no longer bothered by it, comfortable in the knowledge that it was just part of the charade.

She was especially pleased when she retrieved his fourth dead-drop message. She waited until she was back at her table to unfold the note out of sight on her lap before reading it.

Nothing new to report. Just wanted to say hi. Hope we can talk in person again soon.

Warm fuzzies spread through her body, and she sat grinning like a lunatic until the bell rang, all the while hoping it wouldn't be long until they'd be able to spend time together again.

She sometimes felt they were taking the act way too far, and only one nagging detail caused her to keep it up day after day. Her inspection of the two most recent school yearbooks revealed no students in any grade with the last name of *Siskin*, so she tried a new approach. Three times, she asked different groups of freshmen if they knew a student with that name, saying she had found a book she wanted to return. All she got in response were the default, blank-eyed stares freshmen inevitably adopted when addressed by seniors. Despite the consistently negative results, there remained the remote but very real possibility that he had married a woman who already had a child, one who had kept his or her original last name. That this was not something they could rule out with absolute certainty was all that kept her from putting an end to the plan. She refused even to consider the idea that Jeremy might enlist a classmate to spy on them, finding the notion too ridiculous.

Their collection of facts hadn't grown much by the end of the second week. They knew only that there were typically three security guards on duty at a time, two outside and a third making occasional perimeter patrols and random sweeps through the lab. Precisely who was where rotated on a roughly two-hour schedule, and if they conducted their perimeter patrols at fixed intervals, the limited view offered by Aaron's workspace gave him no way to tell.

Aside from the security team, he still believed that no more than half a dozen people worked behind the locked door. No matter how much Ellie thought about that, it didn't make sense. The shack had been designed to carry six, and she doubted that any crew who used the device would be made up of the same techs who monitored and maintained the systems. And where were all the researchers, the historians and genealogists who had worked on the previous project? Questions still outnumbered answers by an order of magnitude, and she had to acknowledge that even their most basic assumption—that there really *was* a new shack—remained unproven.

What exactly was going on out there?

13

On the last Saturday in October, Ellie and her parents joined Sam at Ryan's house, where his father was taking advantage of an unseasonably warm afternoon to host what would no doubt be the last backyard cookout of the year. The list of invitees was limited to the family of his son's girlfriend, which suited Ellie just fine. She preferred small, intimate gatherings over large parties, where she felt doomed to repeat the same inane conversation over and over again.

Upon arriving in the car with her parents, Ellie carried a huge bowl of potato salad out to the deck behind the house and placed it on a long picnic table already laden with various other side dishes, plates, and utensils. Near each end of the table was an enormous stack of oversized, extra-absorbent napkins, which she knew from experience were an absolute necessity at one of these events. Everyone exchanged brief greetings, then Sam and Ryan quickly disappeared. Ellie's dad joined Ryan's at the large smoker to chat and lend a hand with the cooking while she and her mom relaxed on a pair of new lounge chairs near the house. These replaced the squeaky glider, ancient and rusted to the point of posing a clear and present danger to anyone using it, that now lay dismantled in a low heap of metal scrap piled alongside the curb in front of the house.

For a while, Ellie was content to do nothing more than sit and admire the scenery. Ryan's house sat high up on the south side of Arizona Avenue, and its enormous rear deck offered stunning views to the east, south, and west. Growing up, she and Sam—and most often Aaron, too—had joined Ryan there on many evenings to stargaze, especially during the annual Perseid and Leonid meteor showers. The latter were always watched while thoroughly bundled up against the November chill as they consumed creamy hot cocoa from giant mugs. Aaron had particularly enjoyed those nights, sometimes bringing his reflecting telescope along. It wouldn't be dark for hours, but she wondered if the Orionids were putting on a decent show this year.

Ellie was distracted from her thoughts when her mom stood and crossed the deck to the ice bucket at the end of the table. Her thoughts flashed back to the day she had first met Shanna. Her mom was a scientist, too, so why did she never picture her in a lab coat with pocket protectors or thick-framed eyeglasses? That image, she knew, came from half-remembered comics in her dad's old *Far Side* books, and she understood that it was a ridiculous, intentionally overblown stereotype to begin with. The uncomfortable truth was that she seldom thought of her mother in terms of her education or professional achievements—or even as a woman, for that matter. For as long as she could remember, she'd always been "Mom" and nothing more. Ellie suddenly realized how unfair and limiting that perspective was, especially now that she was practically a grown woman herself.

She watched as her mom resettled onto her chair and took a sip of her white wine. "How's your new leg coming along?"

She was referring to the latest prototype for a new style of prosthesis her mom was developing, a design that promised to provide its users with a more natural and comfortable gate while being mechanically simpler, more comfortable, and less prone to failure. The goal was to create an artificial limb that was both cheap and robust enough for use in third-world countries plagued by leftover land mines and a corresponding abundance of people injured by said ordnance. To her mom's credit, she was determined to sacrifice neither functionality nor reliability to reach some arbitrary price point.

"Getting there. We're still working on the rollover behavior at the ankle joint, but we're getting close. It's a scaling issue. The joint simply doesn't function the same in the child sizes as it does in the adult ones."

"Well, I think it sucks they're needed at all, let alone how many. And for kids? It's horrible!"

"You're preaching to the choir, sweetie. No one would be happier than me if my work weren't needed anymore."

"That would be... *Huh?!*" Ellie was startled into silence by the unexpected sight of Aaron appearing around the corner of the house. He spotted her at once and veered toward her.

"Hey. Ryan said you would all be up here."

"Really?" Ellie was alarmed but tried not to show it. "When did you guys...?"

Aaron raised a hand to calm her. "No, no, we didn't. I meant he mentioned it on the bulletin board the other day, that's all. Hi," he said to Ellie's mom, tossing her a little wave.

"You're Aaron, right?" she said, and smiled at him. "We haven't seen you around for a while."

"Yeah. I got, um, sort of distracted. Can I borrow Ellie for a few minutes?"

Ellie sprang to her feet, eager to find out what had caused him to break isolation and show up in person. "I'll be right back, Mom."

Her mom stopped her with an upraised hand. "No, you two stay here. I'm going to see how dinner is coming along." She rose again from the lounge chair and walked off toward the grill, wine glass in hand.

Ellie spoke quietly. "What's up?"

"We are no longer a secret. Where are Sam and Ryan?"

"Not sure. I haven't seen them since just after I got here. Let's check down... Oh, wait—there they are."

Sam and Ryan's heads appeared above the edge of the deck as they climbed the tall flight of steps from the scruffy yard below. With the parents all gathered around the smoker at that far railing, Ellie and Aaron remained where they were and waited for them to approach.

"Hey," Sam said, her eyes darting back and forth between Aaron and Ellie. She looked anxious, having assumed that Aaron's surprise appearance implied something had gone very wrong.

Ryan, however, did not seem unduly bothered. "Am I right in assuming that something more than the aroma of slowly roasting pig has brought you here? Not that pork is necessarily your thing," he added quickly.

Aaron's brow wrinkled. "Huh? Are you kidding? I *love* barbecue!" Seeing the others' bemused expressions, he quickly got the idea. "Wait, was I like super kosher before?"

"Not *super*, exactly," Sam said, "but bacon was a definite no-no."

"*Huh!* That must have been totally *his* thing." Ellie understood that he was referring to Jeremy, and she nodded absently, thinking that had always been her impression, too.

"You're welcome to stay, dude. We've got plenty, and then some."

Aaron looked at Ellie, uncertain. She reached forward and took his hand in both of hers, smiling and nodding in enthusiastic agreement with the suggestion.

"Yes! Stay!"

Aaron shrugged. "Okay. I'm in."

Sam, usually a stickler for adhering to social niceties, sighed impatiently. "Please, just say everything's okay," she implored.

Aaron grimaced. "Everything's gone kind of pear-shaped, actually. That's why I'm here. I was starting to tell Ellie that Dr. Siskin somehow knows about all four of us. I can't imagine he knows what we've been talking about, but he wants you guys to come out to the LAB with me."

"I might," Ryan said. "But only if you repeat the invitation as a singing telegram."

Aaron grinned. "Sorry. You will be missed."

Ellie felt a chill run through her. For weeks, she'd been contriving all kinds of scenarios for getting into Jeremy's lab. That they might simply be asked in had never occurred to her, and the fact that they had was unnerving. "Did he say why?"

"No. I was out there a little while ago, running off a new set of databases—no idea why—and he stuck his head into my little room. He said, and I'm quoting here, 'Please tell your girlfriend and the other two that I request the honor of their presence at their earliest convenience.' I was too surprised to do anything but nod. He told me to let him know when I had it set up, and then he was gone. He didn't say why, and I was caught too off guard to think to ask until it was too late."

There was a prolonged silence while everyone considered what this might mean. For a moment, Ellie was hung up on being referred to as Aaron's "girlfriend" and even more so on how Aaron had felt it necessary to include that detail. Once she forced her way past it, it seemed obvious what had instigated the sudden invite.

"It's because of me. About us meeting in class the other week."

"If that's the case, then why did it take him so long?" Sam said. It was a good question, but Ellie had no idea.

"And why *all* of us?" Ryan added. "And what's with calling me and Sam 'the other two?' He thinks we're like what... *sidekicks?*"

Aaron shook his head. "I have no clue about any of that. Should I set something up now? Say we'll get back to him later?"

"I don't like this hanging out there," Sam said. "I think if we're actually going to go—and knowing us I assume we are—then I say, the sooner, the better."

"What she said," Ryan agreed.

"It'll be a pain to set up a time during the week with all our different schedules. I know it's Sunday, but do you think we could do it tomorrow?" Ellie said.

"He said ASAP, so..." He shrugged. "Give me a time, and I'll find out."

Ellie looked at Sam and Ryan. "Would eleven o'clock work?" They both nodded. "Okay, let's see what he says."

They watched as Aaron typed a short message into his phone, then returned it to his pocket.

"I feel kinda gross," Sam said, placing a hand on her stomach. Ryan reached over and pinched her gently on the ribs, tickling her and causing her to squirm away from his touch. Then he made a show of examining his fingertips as if evaluating the sensation.

"Yes, you do," he agreed. "But you *look* incredible."

She slapped his arm for being silly, then smiled at the compliment. "Thanks."

Ellie rolled her eyes. *"Oh, brother," is right!* she thought. She heard a soft buzz, and Aaron twitched as though he'd been tased.

"*Ooh!*" He pulled his phone back out and checked the screen.

"We're on," he said without looking up at the others. "Tomorrow at eleven. They'll know at the gate to let us in." He finished typing out a short confirmation, then once more pocketed the device.

Ellie figured she was feeling as apprehensive as Sam and was relieved that the impending... What? Meeting? Confrontation? Whatever it turned out to be, she was glad it was sooner rather than later.

That matter settled, Sam returned to the comment that had so distracted Ellie moments before. She turned to face Aaron and cocked an eyebrow.

"So, '*girlfriend?*'" she said.

Aaron blushed. "No!" He shot a glance at Ellie. "Um, I mean, it's not like it's entirely up to me."

"Well, I say we get some sodas while you two sort that one out," Ryan said, and he began leading them toward a massive blue ice chest.

Prevented by their parents' proximity from discussing anything relating to Jeremy and his lab, the four of them spent the next hour and a half talking about practically everything else, managing to find something uproariously funny about each and every topic. Aaron seemed more relaxed and comfortable around them than ever before and was as actively engaged in the hilarity as the rest of them. The feeling of happiness that welled up in Ellie's chest kept expanding until it made her feel like a dangerously over-inflated balloon, and she loved every second of it.

After dessert, Ellie led Aaron to the lower end of the yard, where they stood side by side, arms resting on the top rail of a rough, wooden fence. Gazing south across the city, they watched as the last tendrils of light disappeared behind the mountains to their right, leaving only the glow of the town below. Despite the lateness of the hour, the moment reminded Ellie of their first-date trip to Starbuck's and how they had likewise stood side by side and looked out across the mesa toward the shack. She realized it was the first time she had felt anything close to the feelings she had experienced on that June afternoon. Careful to avoid snagging her sleeve on the rail's jagged surface, she scooted her elbow over until it rested against Aaron's, felt him apply a gentle pressure back in response.

"Being here tonight, seeing you with your family, I think I understand something I didn't get before," he said.

"Yeah? What's that?"

"When I first got here and we took those walks around town, you used to tell me about growing up in Virginia, but any time I asked about your time here, you'd always change the subject. That you wouldn't talk about that was one of the things that bothered me back then. But it's because you don't really know, do you? A lot of stuff you remember from before June, like everything to do with me, is probably wrong, right?"

Ellie nodded. "Mm-hmm. I was afraid if I said one thing and then you heard something different—from Mom, for instance—you'd think I was lying to you." She let out a long, sad sigh. "In some ways, that's been the hardest thing to deal with. Sam and I look at them, and we know that their memories of us and ours of them aren't entirely the same anymore. There've been times we both felt like we were only pretending to be their kids. I mean, it's not just biology that makes us a family; it's all of those shared experiences, too.

"But it's not like *all* our memories are different. Only some are, and almost all of them are from the past six years. And they aren't off in any really big ways. Mostly it's the tiny details, but there are enough that we've had to avoid reliving Christmases past, family vacations, that sort of thing. I think we've both gotten used to it at this point, but at first, it hurt a lot. It's the same for Ryan, but his relationship with his dad is different, I guess, and he's never said too much about that."

Aaron nodded. "So, it wasn't just A-Ron that was making a sacrifice."

"No, it was. Everything happened so fast that we didn't have time to understand ahead of time what it would mean for us afterward. Not that we wouldn't have done it anyway. Even if I had known what would happen, it still would have been nothing compared to losing you, and that didn't stop me.

"I don't know if this will make sense, but even though I had known you for almost six years, realizing I loved you was like this total *thing*. It hit me all at once. And hard, too, like walking full speed into a brick wall you didn't see until it was too late. It felt new, but also like it had always been there, you know?" She looked down into the pool of darkness on the far side of the fence. "And who knows? Maybe it always had. Or maybe that's just the way first love is." It occurred to her that this was the most personal feeling she had shared with this Aaron since his arrival in Los Alamos, and discovering that she felt comfortable enough to be this open with him warmed her.

Aaron's elbow pressed a little harder against hers. "He was something else, wasn't he?"

She heard genuine admiration in his voice but also sensed he felt somehow the lesser of his two selves. She turned her entire body to face him and laid her hand lightly on his arm.

"Yes, he was, and I'd never say otherwise. But here *you* are, against all the odds and in spite of a story far too ridiculous to be true. The same mind, the same thirst for logical answers have allowed you to accept that story, however improbable. Not many people could do that. It's not about 'him' and 'you.' It's all *you*, and I still think *you're* something else."

He thought about that and nodded. He turned toward her, looked down at her hand, and laced his fingers through hers.

"Did they tell you why I was here the last time?"

"Mm-hmm. They said you were asking questions about me."

"I'd been trying so hard to avoid you, but after we talked that day at the nature center, I realized that you are the most interesting girl I've ever known and that, despite being creeped out at first, I liked you. A lot! I did right from the start. But then you guys told that story, and I freaked."

Ellie nodded. "We always knew that would be hard on you. We didn't tell you right away not because we wanted to keep it our little secret, but to avoid hurting you." She smiled. "And I like you, too, just so you know."

"But what you said a minute ago, about the shared memories? We don't have those anymore."

"We have a few," she said. "You even have a couple from back then! How cool is that?! And the thing I've learned about memories? You can always make new ones."

Without giving herself time to think about it, she leaned forward and kissed him lightly on his mouth. He froze, surprised by the suddenness of the gesture, and before he could respond, they were interrupted by a voice speaking from the darkness.

"Ellie, your dad and I are going home. Do you want to ride back with us?"

Ellie backed a small step away from Aaron, her heart racing both in reaction to the kiss and from being startled, but she was unembarrassed. When she turned to face the mom-shaped silhouette standing at the top of the stairs, she saw that Sam was standing a few steps farther back, also looking down at her. She was backlit like her mother, and deep shadows rendered her expression unreadable.

"No, thanks. I'll walk back with Sam. I won't be out too late."

"You know you don't have a curfew." Which, yes, she did know, and Ellie assumed that was Mom-code for *You're old enough to make your own decisions.*

They watched her and Sam disappear beyond the edge of the deck. Once they were safely out of earshot, Aaron let out a sigh of relief so long that it sounded like he was deflating.

"I am *so* glad she's not a mama bear!"

Ellie laughed. "Actually—and I stress that this is *strictly* a guess—I think Mom's built along the same lines as Sam. Or, well, it's actually the other way around, I suppose." She remembered then that it was likely he had not hung around with Sam long enough to have picked up on her casually enthusiastic attitude toward sex, and she searched for the simplest way to explain. "They're both sort of the opposite of prudes." Even in the dim light, she could see his brows draw together.

"Meaning?" he said.

"Meaning, don't be a jerk, and you have no need to worry about the mama bear." She wrapped her arms around his waist and drew him to her. "But as I was saying..."

She closed her eyes and tilted her head back, offering him her mouth. When his lips touched hers, all the breath went out through her nose in a long, slow *whoosh* as her body seemed to melt. Now that he was an active participant, she could tell this kiss was different from the ones she remembered. It was more... More what exactly? Even as overwhelmed as she was by her intense, physical response to the taste of him, to the warm pressure of his body against hers, her mind searched for a word to describe that difference. More dynamic? More focused? Then she had it; it was simply more *better!* A laugh started to bubble its way to the surface, but she managed to stifle it.

She pulled her head back and looked up at him, smiling. *"Mmm....* You've done this before."

He seemed to understand that she wasn't being judgmental, and he smiled back at her. "Yeah, well, maybe once or a dozen times, you know."

"Ooh, a man of experience!"

Although it was clear that she was still only teasing, his expression became earnest, and he peered directly into her eyes. "Where kissing is concerned, a little, yes."

She got his deeper meaning at once and felt the glow in her chest grow even warmer. "Okay. Well, *good!"* She leaned forward and rested her head on his shoulder. Her heart was racing, and her whole body felt jittery, the way it had when she'd once discovered, the hard way, that her old desk lamp's power cord had a nick in the insulation.

I was wrong, she thought. *I really* did *miss this!*

They had been standing there barely long enough for her pulse to return to normal when they heard Sam call down to them from the end of the deck. "I'm leaving in a few minutes, El."

Ellie answered without lifting her head from Aaron's shoulder. "Okay. I'll be right there."

"I should be getting home too," Aaron said.

Ellie put enough space between them so she could place her hands on his chest, felt the pleasant weight of his palms as he rested them on her hips. "I don't..." She paused, having no idea what words needed to come next.

Aaron caught her mood and responded to that. "Me neither. But we'll figure it out, and that doesn't have to happen tonight."

"Hoo-boy," she said, exhaling a loud, jagged breath.

"You got *that* right!" he said, and their mingled laughter eased some of the tension.

"Well, better not keep Big Sister waiting," she said. Taking his hand, she led him across the yard toward the stairs. When they reached the top, she saw that every last sign of the party was gone, all except for the blue ice chest, which now sat open and upside down near the sliding glass door. *Exactly how long were we down there?*

"What about you?" Aaron said.

"Hmm?" She looked at him. The lights from the back of the house bathed his face in a warm glow, and she could see the trace of a smile on his lips. "What about me what?"

"Are you built along those same lines as Sam?"

That is a very good question, she thought. Something had been changing inside her ever since she and A-Ron acknowledged their mutual feelings in June. Their kisses, although few, had stirred new feelings to life, and a formerly occasional itch now demanded a more frequent scratch. She was only beginning to understand what these ongoing changes meant, and she wasn't prepared to discuss the topic with Aaron. Not yet, anyway.

"I guess we'll just have to see about that." The words were out of her mouth before she realized how much they sounded more like a proposition than the simple time-will-tell statement she had intended. She groaned. *Can we* please *not do this again?*

"Sounds like a plan," he said. He grinned at her, but, apparently sensing that her answer implied something she hadn't intended, he let it go at that.

Sam and Ryan were sitting close together along one side of a lounge chair near the rear wall of the house. They stood as Ellie and Aaron got close.

"So, tomorrow at eleven," Ryan said. "I'd be glad to pick everyone up on the way."

"Dad's in Albuquerque with the van this weekend, and Mom's going down to see him play, so, yeah, thanks."

Still feeling awkward and self-conscious following her verbal blunder, Ellie wondered if Aaron would want to kiss her goodnight. To her relief, he merely reached out and placed his palm on her shoulder.

"Thanks for talking me into staying. This was fun. I'll see you in the morning."

"Yeah, I'm *really* glad you did. See you tomorrow."

He withdrew his hand and gave Sam and Ryan a brief wave.

"G'night, guys. And Ryan? Thank your dad for me."

"You got it, man."

Aaron backed up his thanks with a nod, then turned and walked away. As soon as he disappeared around the corner of the house, Sam bumped Ellie's shoulder with her own.

"So, *'boyfriend?'*" To her own horror, Ellie actually tittered, a reaction Sam found immensely amusing. "*Wow! Alrighty,* then!"

"Oh, just, *shush!*" Ellie hissed. She was smiling all the while, though, happier than she had been in months.

14

After showering the next morning, Ellie returned to her room to find Sam still sitting in bed, engrossed in something on her iPad. Homework? Her journal? Ellie couldn't tell. She knew Sam was apprehensive about yesterday's summons—no better word for it—and that going still and quiet was her way of dealing with that sense of unease. She felt uneasy herself, but of the two emotions battling for dominance within her, curiosity still maintained the upper hand.

Letting Sam have her silence, Ellie set about dressing. She folded her *I Wear This Periodically* nightshirt and placed it at the foot of her bed, its chart of the atomic elements facing up. She put no special effort into selecting the day's outfit, opting for her usual jeans and a short-sleeved pullover top. She'd take a jacket along against the morning chill, but she knew that by the afternoon she'd be comfortable enough in only the heavy tee. She finished just as the clock ticked past nine.

"I'm going out to the kitchen. Want me to bring you anything? Coffee?"

Sam answered without taking her eyes off the screen. "*Ugh!* No coffee for me this morning! Thanks, but I'll come out in a bit."

Although her stomach was doing its energetic best to dissuade her, Ellie decided to risk eating something light and trust it would stay down rather than go in on an empty stomach. The meeting with Jeremy could take ten minutes, or it might be two hours. Not having the slightest idea what the morning's get-together was all about, there was simply no way to guess.

That thought underscored their biggest problem: they had too many questions, too few answers. That could change in the coming hours, but right now, she found their lack of reliable facts frustrating. What she did know was that if it turned out Jeremy was working on anything even remotely like his old "shack" project, she'd do whatever she could to put an end to this one, too. And this time, she vowed, she alone would make whatever sacrifice was called for.

She picked one of the two chairs at the kitchen's small dinette table that offered a view of the canyon's pines and bare-limbed cottonwood trees and forced herself to start working her way through a small bowl of granola. She was almost finished when Sam joined her at the table.

"What's going on?" Sam said.

The first answer that came to Ellie's mind was "life," because as strange and annoying as these circumstances were, they were beginning to feel like the new normal. For her, anyway. Recognizing in time that Sam would think she was being flippant, she paused to give her response further consideration.

"Honestly, Sam, I don't know." She set her spoon down and gave Sam her complete attention. "I know how you're feeling right now. I'm so queasy I'm not sure I can even finish this cereal. I'm definitely not sure that I *should*. Look, you absolutely do not have to go this morning. Ryan, neither. Whatever is going on, it has to do with me and somehow with Aaron, maybe, but not you two."

"But Jeremy said—"

"So?! Who's he, anyway? I'm going not because he wants me to, but because I want to get inside that place, maybe get some real answers."

"And I'm going because you're going. And if you think for one second Ryan would let you go out there without him along, you don't know him very well. The way I see it, the more of us, the better."

"Yeah, got it, thanks. And I do know that about Ryan, by the way. But I don't think this is going to end with them having to hide our bodies, all right?"

"Then *what?* Why does he want us to come out there at all?"

Ellie glanced at the microwave's clock. Ryan was due to arrive with Aaron at ten-fifteen, and what Sam was asking was exactly what Ellie wanted to discuss when they got there. "The boys will be here in less than an hour. Can this wait until then? I'm hoping something Aaron knows might give us a clue."

Sam lapsed back into a sullen silence, then nodded.

"Hey," Ellie said. "I appreciate what you said a second ago. Thanks for always having my back."

Sam nodded again. "'It's my burden to be sane in a demented age.'"

In the emotionally fraught aftermath of Aaron's disappearance, Sam and Ryan had all but quit their habit of quoting movie dialog, but Ellie noticed they had picked it up again over the past few weeks. This line, however, was new to her.

"I haven't heard that one before. What's it from?"

"*Beyond Mombasa.* And that line is pretty much the best thing about the entire movie. Ryan wanted to see it because it has Christopher Lee—you know, Saruman?—in it, like, sixty years ago."

"How do you guys even find these things?"

Sam shrugged. "IMDb? I don't know how he came up with that one."

Sam seemed less anxious talking about this new topic, so Ellie stuck with it. *Okay, movies, then.* "Have you guys watched anything good recently?"

"Nothing current, but..."

Ellie managed to keep Sam engaged in light conversation for the next forty-five minutes. She also benefited from the distraction, and by the time Ryan and Aaron arrived, her stomach had ceased its gymnastics. At the sound of a knock, Sam left the kitchen to let them in, and Ellie took her dishes to the sink, quickly washed and then put them away. She was refolding the dish towel when everyone came in and took seats around the table.

"Are you guys here alone?" Ryan said.

"I... I don't know, actually," Sam said. "Have you seen Mom and Dad?"

Ellie shook her head. "No. It's Sunday; I assumed they went into town for brunch, like usual." During the warm months, it was their parents' routine to spend Sunday mornings leisurely reading the paper at the table on the patio. Once the mornings became too cold, they opted for having brunch out somewhere, most often at a popular café in nearby White Rock. She glanced at the fridge. "No note saying otherwise."

"Alien abduction would be my guess," Aaron suggested. "Are your clocks all showing the right time?"

Ellie rewarded his deadpan delivery with a delighted smile as she took the chair beside him. "Speaking of, we don't have much time. Does anyone have any guesses as to what this is all about?" Ryan started to say something, but before he could speak, she added, "Any serious guesses?" Ryan closed his mouth, and Ellie saw Sam hide a grin behind her hand.

Aaron answered instead. "Well, if we start by assuming that this somehow has to do with you and Dr. Siskin meeting at school and also that we're right about there being a new 'shack,' then factor in your suspicion that he knows something about what happened over the summer *and* take into account Sam's very astute observation that there's no logical reason in the world for *me* to be working out there.... If we mix all of that together, then... I have absolutely no idea."

Ryan, who had been breathlessly awaiting Aaron's summation, puffed out a loud, disappointed sigh. "Funny! You really had me going there for a second, you know."

"Actually, I'm serious," Aaron insisted. "Even if he knew exactly what we... you—*whatever*—did back in June, judging from everything you've told me about that, this new situation is so different that there's no good reason for him to say or do anything at all. As long as the whole project is safely tucked away behind razor wire and armed guards, he certainly can't feel threatened. His wanting us to go out there makes no sense."

"What I want to figure out right now," Ellie said, "is how we're going to handle dealing with him. Because I sense that somehow that's what this is about—some kind of deal. Otherwise, like Aaron said, he could just ignore us."

"I'm with you on the part about the deal," Ryan said. "If you want my opinion, we let him put all his cards on the table and see where we stand.

He may want some kind of deal, sure, but we're not obliged to give him one."

"Of course I do," Ellie said. "And yes, I agree."

"How can we be sure of anything he says?" Sam said. "He can tell us whatever he thinks might stop us from poking our noses into his business, and we have no way of knowing whether or not it's true."

"No, but we do have Aaron," Ryan said. He pressed on before Aaron could object. "I know you don't know much about what's going on behind the scenes out there, buddy, but he might say some little thing that contradicts something you've heard before, and that'll at least clue us in about his motivations."

Aaron shrugged, accepting his assignment without comment.

"Okay, then," Ellie said. "We hear what he has to say, but we keep any agreements to a minimum until we decide how far we can trust him. Is that about it?" All three nodded. She looked at the clock. "Then it's time to go."

As Ellie followed Ryan and Sam down the sidewalk toward the bright blue, two-door Jeep Wrangler he had parked along the curb, she saw him slide the knuckle of his index finger down the side of Sam's neck. He once more held the finger in front of his face and pretended to study it.

"So, still feeling gross, huh?" he said.

She bumped him with her shoulder and laughed. "A little. Not as bad as earlier, though."

"Remember," he told her seriously, "they're not going to cook us and eat us. Probably."

Sam laughed again, and the sound made Ellie feel a little better too.

15

---

hile waiting in a short line of vehicles at the LAB's main checkpoint, Ellie hoped Jeremy hadn't neglected to inform main security about their visit. Once they reached the booth, the guard peered in at them, no doubt wondering what business four teenagers had inside the federal facility. But after she checked her list of authorized visitors and Ryan confirmed their destination, she waved them through without undue delay. Of course, that might have been partly due to them being in Ryan's father's car, one she was sure to recognize. The man was her boss, after all.

Once they were past the checkpoint, Aaron leaned forward and gave Ryan some final directions. "It'll be your second left, then go all the way to the end of the road. Trust me, you'll know when you're there." He leaned back and spoke softly to Ellie. "I noticed you guys only ever call Dr. Siskin 'Jeremy.' Any reason why?"

"It started with those two." Ellie pointed at Sam and Ryan. "He always seemed so full of himself that they refused to use his title just out of spite."

Sam and Ryan spoke in unison. "Dr. Jeremy D. Siskin, DSc!"

Ellie suddenly felt embarrassed by the practice. "I guess it does seem immature now, but they started doing it years ago, so..." She shrugged. "Anyway, now we all do it. And I gotta say—he still seems sort of pompous."

Aaron stared at the back of Ryan's seat, and Ellie guessed he was replaying his every interaction with the man. After a moment, he nodded slowly. "I can see that. A little, anyway."

Ellie recognized the glass façade of the building now dominating their view from Jeremy's slide presentation in class, noticing that it somehow managed to look smaller in person than it had on the screen. They glided to another stop at the end of the road, this time at the outer of two rolling gates. A small guard shelter, offset to the left, nestled between them.

The outer gate rolled open, one of the guards waved them ahead, and Ryan inched the Jeep forward. Then the gate rattled to a close behind them. "A mantrap. Great." He came to a smooth stop, his door even with the guard post, and lowered his window.

"Oh, yeah," Aaron said. "I forgot about that. They only did this when I came in with Mom, and then the first time I drove the van. Since then, they've always opened both at once and waved me right on through."

The largest man Ellie could remember ever seeing in person approached the Jeep and crouched down to give Ryan instructions. In addition to an array of other potentially useful gadgets that hung from his belt, he also wore a pistol. Ellie guessed it was of normal size, but it looked like a toy against his massive frame. She pulled her gaze away from the weapon to look up at the man's face. A coil of black wire dropped from a device in his right ear and disappeared below the collar of his sharply pressed shirt. She wondered if he also had a microphone clipped inside one of his cuffs, like a Secret Service agent.

"Park in the spot closest to the door, sir. Remain in the vehicle until we arrive to escort you into the facility."

Ryan's eyes swept over the man's military-style uniform, noting his insignia and name badge, then he gave him a curt nod. "Wilco, Captain Isaacs."

Ellie was afraid the guard might interpret Ryan's response as sass, but he merely stepped back and motioned for the guard who had remained inside the shelter to open the inner gate. Ryan eased the Jeep through the opening and into the first parking spot, a total distance of maybe a hundred feet. He turned off the engine and dropped his hands into his lap. Ellie looked over her shoulder and saw both guards walking toward them at a brisk trot, the gates sliding shut behind them. Movement from the front of the building caught her eye, and she turned just as a third man, dressed exactly like the sentries manning the gate, emerged from the only door along the building's long front wall. She watched as three large armed men strode purposefully toward them, feeling unnerved by being the subject of such a display of force.

"See what I meant about the guards?" Aaron said.

"Mm-hmm," Ryan said. He placed his hands back on the steering wheel as the men closed in on them. "Three huge guards for two scrawny dudes and a pair of teeny, tiny chiquitas. Our reputation clearly precedes us."

Ryan was a swimmer and a runner, not a musclebound linebacker, but even so, Ellie would hardly have described him as scrawny. She appreciated the underlying sentiment, though; a reminder that they had already devised and successfully executed one plan to defeat Jeremy was exactly what they needed right now.

"Step out of the vehicle, please," a guard said.

Now that she had a clear view of all three men, Ellie saw they could all have come from the same mold. She even had to check the name badge of the one who'd asked them to step out to be sure he was the same one who had spoken to Ryan at the gate.

Ryan and Sam stepped down, then held their doors while Ellie and Aaron followed them out. Ryan motioned toward the building's entrance in an after-you gesture, and the guard from inside the building began leading the way. Ellie could hear the other guards close behind her, their proximity making the back of her neck prickle. Studying the building, she noted that all of the glass along its front served only to illuminate a long, nearly featureless hallway. None of the doors on the hall's far side had windows, so despite Jeremy's talk about the healthy effects of natural light, no one who worked in those rooms benefitted by so much as a single lumen.

In less than sixty seconds, all seven stood inside Jeremy's office. Jeremy rose from a complexly articulated, hyper-ergonomic chair when they entered the room but remained behind his desk, watching as his security team positioned themselves between his guests and the door. The guard who had spoken with Ryan outside took two more steps toward the desk and halted. Ellie knew what standing at attention looked like, and he wasn't doing that, but he wasn't "at ease," either. He held his body tensed, ready to react to any change in the situation, and his eyes constantly flicked between her group and his boss.

Ellie shifted her attention to Jeremy, who did not look especially ready for any action whatsoever. He simply stood there, staring at them, his fingertips resting lightly on his desk. He wore the uniform of business, not the military: dress slacks and a white, long-sleeve shirt unbuttoned at the collar. His suit jacket hung from a metal coat tree standing in a corner beyond his right shoulder. His expression, as best she could interpret it, appeared somewhere between amused and annoyed. Finally, he frowned at the odd tableau before him, and then he spoke.

"All three of you, Captain? Was that absolutely necessary?"

"Protocol, sir."

Jeremy sighed. "Of course it is. I suppose I should thank you for your diligence."

"Just following orders, sir."

The man started to leave, but Jeremy stopped him. "Captain," he said, and waited for the man to turn around. "One more thing before you go. Will you please state your standing orders regarding this bunch?" He indicated Ellie's group with a flap of his hand.

"Sir! They were to be surveilled but left alone, unless they approached the facility, sir."

"And if they did?"

"Then they were to be escorted directly in to see you, sir."

"In other words, any time they wanted, they could have simply walked up to the door and knocked, in a manner of speaking, and you would have let them in?"

The guard hesitated, appearing to consider this. A second later, he nodded. "Yes, sir. Those were essentially my orders."

"Thank you, Captain. It was important for them to hear that. You and your men may leave us now."

Ellie noticed another brief hesitation before the man complied.

"Yes, sir," he said. He pivoted smartly and headed for the exit, gesturing for his men to follow him out of the room. A second later, the door closed behind them.

"'Yes, sir,'" Jeremy muttered sourly, no longer looking even slightly amused. He motioned for them to take seats around the room's work table as he settled back into his chair. "Sit. Please."

The others sat, but Ellie remained on her feet with that tingly warning sensation playing along the nape of her neck again. She felt there was something off in Jeremy's conversation with the guard captain, but she couldn't put her finger on what was bothering her. One particular word had seized her full attention, though, and she wanted to ask Jeremy about it right away. She found she was not alone in her concern.

"'*Surveilled?!*'" Ellie, Sam, and Ryan said at the same time.

Jeremy raised his hands in a calming gesture and sighed again, shaking his head slowly as if dismayed that his entire life was nothing but an ongoing series of such petty annoyances. "Oh, calm down. It's not what you think." He again motioned for Ellie to take a seat, and this time she complied. "No one has been spying on you. Given your… *history*, shall we say, it was thought you might attempt to break into this facility. The guards were told that if you came anywhere near it, they were to watch you but were to do nothing to interfere unless you tried to get past the fences. And that, let me add, was strictly for your own safety. There is nothing here we wish to hide from you."

Ellie still hadn't pinpointed what was bothering her about Jeremy's exchange with the guard, but he had just given them a new topic to pursue.

"And what exactly do you know about our history?"

"I've been familiar with the broad strokes for years, but strictly in a general sense. I've known about your discovery back in May, for instance, and about how you decided to deal with it. And with my, ah, *predecessor*? Only since you and I met have I learned the full details." He shifted his attention to Aaron. "I'm curious about something, given that you and I share a similar and quite unique set of experiences. Have you had strange visions, too? Memories that aren't your own?"

"I..." Aaron glanced at Ellie, uncertain if he should answer, but her attention remained fixed entirely on Jeremy. "Yeah," he said. "Since I got here last month."

"*Hmm....* I guess we had our own unique triggers."

Ellie pounced on a perceived flaw in his answer to her previous question. "You seem to know an awful lot about me, but in Mrs. Carson's class, you didn't appear to know who I was until you looked it up. Then you seemed to know *exactly* who I was. Now you're saying that you learned about us *after* we met. How could you know about me but not already know the rest?"

"You are formulating your assumptions under the misapprehension that I operate here with complete autonomy. In my defense, when it comes to certain topics, I know only what I am told. I knew that at some point around this time you lived here in Los Alamos, but I had no face to connect with your name."

Sam snorted a short, derisive laugh. "'Misapprehension?' 'Complete autonomy?' It's funny to hear you proclaim your ignorance in a way meant to show off how smart you are."

Ellie had noticed that, too, but now she realized what was tickling the back of her brain and had a few choice phrases of her own to throw back at him. "'Your orders,' you said to the guard, not, '*my* orders.' And, 'it was thought,' not, 'I thought.' Now you're implying that someone else here knows more about what's going on than you do. Are you telling us you're not in charge?"

Jeremy contrived an exaggerated shrug. "I know... it's shocking, right? We'll get to that later, though. I promise. In fact, before the day is out, you'll have learned all there is to know about this entire project, and we have structured your visit accordingly. There are, however, a number of matters we need to discuss before we get that far.

"First, let me address the question no doubt burning hot in each of your minds. The answer is *yes*. Yes, we have built a new time-shift device and have been testing it once or twice a week for the past two months.

We'll discuss specific mission plans for it later, but I believe you will ultimately support the goals of our endeavor."

Ellie found neither admission cause for surprise. They had already guessed there was a new "time-shift device," and there was no point in building one unless you intended to use it. What did surprise her was how having their guess confirmed sent a shiver of excitement rippling up her spine. Even though his mention of a "mission" confirmed her deepest fears, she could not deny that she was excited about the mere thought of going back in time again. She didn't believe she needed to hear any more about Jeremy's plans to know what *her* new mission was, but she decided to get as much of the complete picture as he was willing to share before openly coming out against it.

"The second item is a matter of confidentiality," Jeremy continued. "There are no NDAs to sign, nor will I ask you to swear any oaths of secrecy. Given what you know about the device under discussion, it should be sufficient to promise that any breach of discretion will be dealt with swiftly and in a manner uniquely suited to its capabilities."

Ellie noted the others' pale, somber expressions. All of them, and Aaron more than anyone, understood that penalties imposed using a device capable of editing history could be severe.

"The third subject brings me back to a former point—that we have nothing we wish to hide from you. Your lack of reaction to what I have said so far confirms what we already suspected. Namely, that you have already deduced, if only in part, what lies at the core of our project. Given that, we felt we had more to gain by asking you here today than we stand to lose." Ellie looked up when Jeremy abruptly stopped speaking. He seemed to be waiting for some kind of response. Receiving none, he went on.

"Apparently, all that long-winded blather failed to convey any sense of an invitation, so let me be more direct—who would like to take a peek behind the curtain and see what's truly going on here?"

The offer was the last thing Ellie expected to hear. Despite Jeremy's assurance that he had nothing to hide from them, she never anticipated getting any further into the facility than the room where they now sat. "What do you mean?" she said. "Like, *everything?*"

"Exactly like," Jeremy said.

Ellie heard sincerity in his voice—they really were about to get the whole picture. She heard something else, too. Pride? This, too, was unexpected, and she decided to dial her skeptical attitude down a bit and try to learn more about Jeremy himself while she had the chance. Besides, they had already come this far; they might as well see whatever else he was willing to show them.

"I know *I* would," she said. Although she was making a conscious effort to sound positive and agreeable, the level of enthusiasm she heard in her own voice disturbed her. She turned the skepticism knob back up a couple of clicks and vowed to remain objective no matter what Jeremy showed them.

"I'm in," Ryan said, and Aaron nodded.

Sam gave Jeremy her sweetest smile. "Yes—love to!" she said.

"Then please," Jeremy said, rising from his chair, "follow me."

Jeremy led them out of his office through a door opposite the one they had entered. A large conference room directly across from Jeremey's office stood open. Ellie glanced in, but he ignored it and instead began guiding them left down the wide hallway. They passed a pair of restrooms on their left before stopping at a door on their right. He pulled on the latch and swung the door open. "I know what you most want to see, of course, but we'll start in here."

Ryan led the way into a large shop filled with at least two dozen widely differing workstations. Ellie stopped a few steps inside and took in the entire scene. An assortment of equipment—devices large and small, some old and others very contemporary—occupied every horizontal surface.

Jeremy followed them in, allowing the door to close softly behind him. "This used to be our primary technology development lab," he said. "All the key elements of the TSD were designed, built, tested, and improved on-site. We farmed out the manufacturing of some of the non-critical components, mostly to Asia, but all of the final assembly occurred right here."

Whatever it had been before, Ellie decided that today it looked most like a print shop. With a gesture, Jeremy invited them to spread out and investigate, and she began a slow, counterclockwise sweep of the room.

Before she had covered even a third of the space, she was already impressed by the capabilities the collection of tools offered. Scanners, printers, and an array of different cameras, one of them an ancient Polaroid, took up most of the main workspace. She saw a device sitting near a small photo printer that she recognized as a laminating machine. Next to it was an assortment of chunky-looking metal objects, each of which sprouted a metal handle terminating in a shiny black plastic knob. A closer inspection of these revealed them to be cutters of different shapes and sizes, presumably for trimming whatever came out of the laminator. All the workstations, except those along the walls, were on wheels. If needed, the room's layout could be completely reconfigured in minutes.

"As you can tell," Jeremy said, "this room is now dedicated primarily to creating documents—IDs and other credentials, letters of introduction, business cards—anything that might be needed to create an entire identity from scratch. But in that enclosed area in the back, we have equipment for fabricating items out of wood, plastic, or metal."

Ellie arrived in front of a metal and plexiglass enclosure two feet tall. Cables entering its back connected it to a dedicated PC and monitor. "3-D printer?"

Jeremy confirmed the guess with a nod. "We're not sure why we'll need that yet, but we're ready if we ever do."

"And this?" Sam pointed to an interconnected pair of light gray components, each nearly five feet high, sitting directly on the floor near the left wall. From where she stood, Ellie could see a small "HP" logo on each piece.

"That's an Indigo commercial printer. It uses the standard CMYK inks, but it can also be loaded with spot colors or special coatings—in addition to or instead of—as well. Its purpose is to create documents that must withstand the closest scrutiny. Drivers licenses, for example, diplomas, high-security passes..."

Ellie thought back to their visits to Lawrence and Brooklyn. In neither case had they carried ID of any kind, and she wondered what would have happened to them had they been stopped by police for some reason. As kids, probably not much, she figured—certainly not way back then—but she could imagine many circumstances where having very specific forms of documentation would be essential.

She paused at the back of the room and peered through the glass wall at a long row of very different kinds of machines. They were all tools that created a mess when used—drill press; disc and belt sanders; and circular miter saw, plus a few she couldn't name—each attached to a flexible hose obviously meant to suck dust into a central air cleaning system. A metal box hung from the ceiling, presumably there to filter from the air any particles the hoses let slip by. Safety glasses, face shields, and filter masks dangled from pegs on the back wall alongside a variety of hand tools.

Reflected movement from the far end of the room caught her eye, and she turned around to watch Aaron and Ryan as they examined a machine meant to mimic handwriting using an actual pen or pencil. Was it limited to making signatures, she wondered, or could it write an entire letter? Aaron seemed especially fascinated by the gadget, and he leaned down low to get a better look at the intricate pen-handling mechanism. She couldn't hear what he was saying as he pointed out various parts of it to Ryan, but his excitement was obvious.

Bottom line? The tools here could create almost any form of ID or physical prop someone might need to become someone else. She understood how useful that could be, but lacking any sense of the *whys* involved, she saw no need to get bogged down by excessive details right now. She turned to face Jeremy.

"Cool. What else you got?"

In some ways, the next stop on the tour was more impressive than the first.

"Oh, *wow!*" Sam said, grasping the room's purpose in an instant. She pushed to the front of the group to get a better look. "I mean, *wow!*"

Behind a small freestanding counter topped with a keyboard, mouse, and monitor, six parallel rows of motorized clothing racks extended far into the depths of the room. They were identical to those Ellie had seen in dry cleaning shops, but the outfits hanging on these racks represented decades of fashion history.

Sam rushed forward and began sorting through the outfits on the closest rack, taking a few seconds to admire each one before moving on to the next. "How is this all arranged?" she said, excited to the point of gushing. "By size? Sex? Period? Where did you *get* all this stuff? Are these all originals or reproductions? Ooh, *this* one's nice!"

"Well, I guess we found *your* hot button, Sam," Jeremy said.

Ellie noted his casual, almost intimate tone and use of Sam's first name, although he persisted in calling her "Miss Henderson." Judging from Ryan's scowl, he'd noticed too.

Jeremy motioned for Sam to join him at the counter. "Come over to the computer, and I'll show you."

Sam reemerged from between two racks and stood beside him.

"I'll fill in the basics," he said, his fingers rapidly flicking over the keyboard as he typed keywords into various entry fields. "Female... for size, let's say small slash"—he turned to look at her—"four or two?"

"Four," Sam said and smiled. Ellie raised an eyebrow at her, knowing full well she had more than one size six hanging in their small, shared closet. Sam squinted back at her and pursed her lips in a silent *"shush!"*

"Now pick a year or decade, a few style parameters," Jeremy said. "The less specific you are, the more options you'll get."

"Okay, then, put in late 1950s. For age, let's say twenty, and add 'evening wear.' Can I say 'high-end' or 'designer' or something?"

"I think we use *couture*," he said as he finished typing. He clicked on the Search button, and the third rack from the left clattered into motion. It stopped to display a pleated, roughly knee-length skirt and a thin sweater with three-quarter sleeves. A clear plastic bag containing a pair of saddle shoes hung on the same hook as the clothing. Above the hook, a tiny green light marked the outfit as one of the search results. Ellie could see several more lights glowing further down the rack.

Sam gave the ensemble a quick glance, then stepped back. "Uh-uh. Next!" Jeremy clicked again, and the clattering rack brought the next outfit to a stop in front of her. "Now that's much better," she said. "Wait, is that...?" She leaned forward to consult a label attached to the collar with a tiny safety pin. "It is!" She spun around and grinned at Ryan, clapping her hands in delight. "It's Givenchy!"

Ellie rolled her eyes. The expression did not go unnoticed, and Sam jabbed a finger at her.

"Bad sister! No chocolate!"

Ryan stepped forward for a closer look. The dress was hemmed only slightly shorter than the pleated skirt had been, but the cut was so slim that once zipped up, it would look as though it had been sprayed on.

"You're a college student. Exactly what would you be studying wearing that?" he said.

"Silly boy! The point is that everyone would be studying *me*."

Ryan nodded appreciatively. "*I* certainly would be!"

Ellie remembered arriving in Lawrence and finding the shack contained a selection of period-appropriate clothing in sizes that worked well enough for each of them. Since she assumed at the time that they were in a VR simulator, the fact that the clothes fit so well had seemed unremarkable. Thinking about that later, she'd guessed that the entire room had been lined with storage compartments containing clothes from different periods, all within a narrow range of sizes. That still left several related questions unanswered.

Wanting to get something useful from the moment, Ellie held a hand up to get Jeremy's attention. "How many costumes are we talking here? And how did you select sizes without having a crew?"

"The roles any 'mission team,' as we say, would be required to play fall within a fairly narrow range. No construction workers or cops, no—"

"No cowboys, Native Americans, or bell-bottomed sailors?" Ryan suggested.

"No," Jeremy said automatically, then belatedly got the gist of Ryan's joke. He rewarded the Village People reference with a thin, humorless smile. "No. My point is that almost every scenario calls for a politician, an academic, a lobbyist, or perhaps a financier of some kind—and usually some combination of those—so the diversity of clothing options is quite restricted. For men, it's mostly business attire."

Ryan cast a meaningful glance at Sam's slinky dress.

Jeremy saw his point at once. "Yes, well, while from an operational standpoint, female personnel will have significant responsibilities, we'll be dealing primarily in timeframes where women were mostly considered to be... *ornamental*, is perhaps the word."

"'Obscene and not heard,' you mean," Ryan said.

"Well, that's *so* not me," Sam said.

"No, quiet is definitely not your thing," Ryan agreed.

Sam winked at him. "Who said that, anyway?"

"Marx, I believe," Jeremy said.

Sam looked at him, confused. "Really?"

Ryan leaned close to Sam's ear to clarify, whispering from the corner of his mouth. "Groucho."

Sam mouthed a silent "Ah." Then she added, "*Duh!*"

"As far as sizes go, we stayed close to the average male and female builds for each historical period, meaning slightly smaller and definitely more trim than the typical bodies of today. Personnel will be selected accordingly, unless a specific mission requires a person whose body type falls outside the norm. At the rear of the room, just past the racks, we have a limited tailoring facility where minor adjustments can be made if needed."

Watching the others, Ellie felt a sense of dismay growing in her chest. Sam's enthusiastic reaction to the costumes was an echo of Aaron's animated curiosity in the prop shop. Fearing they were getting drawn in by Jeremy's fancy show-and-tell act, she again decided to nudge the tour along.

"Okay, so... costumes galore. Got it. Next?"

To Ellie's relief, the next stop excited exactly no one.

"Locker room," Jeremy said, swinging the door inward.

Ellie took a turn at leaning in through the opening as they filed past. The room was bisected by a free-standing, shoulder-high wall covered in the same pale green tiles as the rest of the walls. Silver hooks near the top of the wall each held a white, waffle-textured robe. The side and rear walls were lined with tall lockers, and in the middle of the back wall, an opening led to what she assumed to be a shower and toilet area. A pair of long wooden benches were the spartan room's only furnishings. She detected a strange scent in the air—something organic, maybe—but she couldn't locate an obvious source. She guessed it was whatever solution they used to clean the room.

Jeremy directed their attention to a deeply recessed doorway twenty feet further down the hall. "Through that entrance is our final stop, but before we get there, I want to show you this."

Ellie saw that beyond the indicated door, the hall made a left turn. So far, the only office they had seen was Jeremy's, but she vaguely remembered that there were more offices around that corner. She returned her attention to Jeremy, who was pointing at two spots along the hallway's floor.

"Notice the grooves," he said. "Directly beyond that recessed door and at a point right behind us, this hallway can be closed off."

Ellie looked over her shoulder and saw what she hadn't noticed before. The edge of a pocket door sat flush with the wall. Metal tracks ran across both floor and ceiling to the opposite wall, and each of their sides was lined with a rubber gasket. A shallow, floor-to-ceiling groove in that wall was fitted with locking hardware to hold the door tightly shut. The groove, too, was double-lined with rubber. *Not merely closed off*, she thought. *Sealed!*

Ellie looked up at Jeremy. "In case of contamination?"

"Correct, Miss Henderson." He began walking again. "In the event a returning team has been exposed to a dangerous substance or a disease, they will have access to the locker room, which includes one full decontamination shower stall, and to this room." He pointed at a featureless steel door set into the wall directly opposite the recessed door he had indicated earlier. "Emergency medical bay. You'll note that it can only be opened from the inside. The primary entrance is via an airlock accessed from the main lobby. In addition to a treatment area, there are six small quarantine rooms. *Very* small, I confess, but it's highly doubtful we'll ever need them."

Ellie recalled a discussion in Brooklyn. Aaron had speculated that in the case of the shack, a contamination event like Jeremy was describing would have been handled with far greater expediency. He assumed the team would be killed and the shack's interior sterilized, presumably by radiation. She wondered if this more humane approach had been Jeremy's idea.

Jeremy indicated their last destination with a sweep of his arm. "But while I'm sure you all find that quite fascinating, it's time we moved on to the grand finale."

16

The door they stood facing was wider than a normal door, four feet, maybe, instead of the usual three, and was deeply set into the massive walls that enclosed the room beyond. While Jeremy described the shielding that required the walls to be so thick, Ellie walked a few paces farther down the corridor and peered around the corner. As expected, she saw more doors spaced out along another long hallway, and she assumed that behind them was where the other project members worked.

Jeremy confirmed her guess as she rejoined the others at the door. "Offices, storage, another restroom, et cetera. But I must ask you not to stray from the group, please." After he placed his palm on the scanner and tapped in his entry code, they heard a loud, resonant *clunk*. "Locking mechanism," he said, and then used the push bar to swing the door inward. Instead of entering, he held the door open with one arm and ushered the others through.

"After you," he said, adding a warning as they filed past him. "Be sure to stay back along the wall. Don't go in any farther than three feet or so."

The door was aligned with the interior side of the wall and hung so far back that Ellie felt like she was entering a tunnel. Trailing the others in, she noticed that Ryan was paying close attention to everything around them, including the doorway through which they were passing. Following his gaze, she saw the obvious source of the loud sound. In addition to the usual hardware, two pairs of shiny metal cylinders were recessed into each side of the jamb, one set located above her head, the other about a foot off the ground. She figured that with the cylinders engaged, the room would be as impenetrable as a vault. There was also what appeared to be a set of electrical contacts on the door frame directly below the latch.

"Why isn't the door as thick as the wall?" she said.

"Ah, yes," Jeremy said. "The problem of the door. A three-foot-thick door is, obviously, not practical, and yet this chamber must be completely shielded. For a time, we considered situating the entrance on the opposite wall and having the room open to the outdoors. We could simply allow any unconstrained field flux to flow out into the forest, knowing it would not penetrate further than forty feet max, not even as far as our security fence. Requiring team members to walk around to the rear of the building to reach this chamber was not practical, however, nor did it allow for rapid, easy access to the medical bay.

"In the end, another solution was found. Look carefully at this hinge," he said, pointing.

Ellie leaned close to inspect the middle hinge. In addition to the usual parts found on any door, the heavy-duty mechanism also included several insulated components.

"Those are power feeds. Power for what?"

"One of our engineers—Dr. Robert Saha—was able to solve the door problem by designing an active shielding system that we could build into it. It's equally as effective as the passive shielding provided by the walls but requires that the door be only six inches thick. There is also an interlock circuit that prevents the TSD from activating if the door is not completely closed."

Ellie looked again at the contacts below the latch and nodded. She figured that made sense, active shielding or not.

"But please," Jeremy said, motioning her forward. "We're holding up the tour."

The shielding invention was not nearly as interesting as what she saw once she joined the others in the chamber. Remembering entering the shack only to discover a set of blank, white walls made her think of a line her dad liked to quote. Being here was like déjà vu all over again.

"It's empty," she said.

Ellie cast her eyes around the cavernous space. As she had inferred from the slides Jeremy had shown in class, the room was about thirty feet on a side, and the ceiling was nearly that high. Except where a few switches or other mechanical devices interrupted the white expanse, the room was as empty as the inside of the shack had been.

Something about the view bothered her. She thought she could see something peculiar at the periphery of her vision, like the refraction of heat ripples over asphalt, but the anomaly disappeared whenever she tried to focus directly on it. The cheap safety goggles she'd had to wear in chemistry class had made everything look distorted around the edges, and the effect here was similar, if much more subtle.

"Doesn't look like much, does it?" Jeremy said.

"Doesn't look like *anything*, actually," Aaron said.

Jeremy raised a fist and wrapped his knuckles on seemingly empty space. Three rapid-fire thuds rang out. "It can make itself look like it's not there, but it'll still feel plenty solid if you walk into it." He tilted his head back slightly and spoke to the void in a louder voice. "Aimie, will you cancel the active mimesis, please?"

Sam squeaked when a wall suddenly appeared less than an arm's length in front of her nose. The surface was a very light shade of gray and seemed to be made up of panels identical to the ones they had seen on the inside of the old shack.

"Neat trick," Ellie agreed, "but doesn't that kind of thing suck up a lot of juice?"

"I know little more about the device you originally encountered than you were ever able to deduce, Miss Henderson, but I get the impression it was quite basic. Well, as basic as it's possible for a machine capable of moving through time to be, anyway. A look inside will no doubt answer some of your questions, but before we go in, let me show you a *really* neat trick. Aimie, will you show us the rustic cabin exterior, please?"

The next instant, they were looking at a version of the device they had discovered in May. If its appearance differed in any significant way, Ellie couldn't see it. She leaned in close, but even from only a foot away, she couldn't tell that she was looking at a digital display panel and not actual weathered wood and lichen. She placed her hand on a shingle, expecting the illusion to break when her fingertips encountered the display's smooth surface. Except the surface didn't feel smooth at all.

"No freakin' way! You guys have to check this out!"

Each of them touched the wall, then reacted with the same wide-eyed expression of delight.

"It feels exactly like wood!" Sam said.

"Advanced haptic feedback," Jeremy said. "It uses the same nerve induction technology you encountered on the chairs in the original device. If the image depicted a stone or metal exterior, the feedback would mimic that instead. It wouldn't fool anyone for very long, and that's why we will continue to limit placement to remote locations. But as camouflage goes, it's not bad."

Ryan looked at Jeremy as though he had just called Katie Ledecky a 'pretty good swimmer.' "Not bad? It's *incredible!* If you could put this tech on APCs, aircraft…"

"Another difference, as I understand it, is this. If your handprints were in the system…" He placed his palm flat on the wall, and after a brief pause, a white circle with a flashing green outline appeared around it. Removing his hand from the wall revealed a number pad. He typed in another four-digit code, making no effort to conceal the sequence. "No dedicated scanner and keypad," he explained. "Any spot on the entire outer surface can be used to key in a passcode."

When he hit the Enter key, a section of the wall detached itself from its surroundings and swung slightly ajar. Ellie noticed that the spot Jeremy had selected to demonstrate the embedded scanner feature actually spanned the line dividing door from wall. She tried hard not to feel impressed, but she had to admit she was.

"The hatch is usually left open, actually, but I thought that showing you this way was a touch more, ah, *dramatic.*"

Jeremy gestured for Ryan to open the door. Ryan gripped its edge and leaned back, intending to use his body weight to help swing the heavy door open.

"Go ahead. Just be care—"

Ryan pulled hard. To his surprise, the door moved very easily, and it was all he could do to stay on his feet as it opened swiftly toward him.

"—ful," Jeremy finished. "It moves far more easily than you'd expect."

Ryan shot him an annoyed look. "Thanks," he said.

"In we go." Jeremy again used hand motions to invite them into the device.

Ellie went first this time. It was still a high step to get up to the level of the interior floor, but this time there was a recess cut into the steeply slanted space below it that could be used as a step. She inserted the toe of her left shoe and stepped up, then moved away from the opening.

What she saw looked very familiar at first, but she quickly began to notice many subtle differences. As in the shack, the center of the space was dominated by six stations formed by crude chairs arrayed around a central core, but there was nothing to suggest the entire assembly could be hoisted into the ceiling. The control panels on the far wall also appeared to be fixed in place rather than being retractable. Although their surfaces were currently blank, Ellie guessed they would display the same information the old ones had. Her impression was that this new device was technologically more advanced while also being mechanically simpler.

Aaron came up close on her left side. "Is it pretty much the same?"

She looked around again, more carefully this time, paying greater attention to the details. She stepped to the nearest chair and made a quick, top-to-bottom examination. Helmet, metal studded back support, footrests with toe cages—everything she remembered was there and looked fundamentally the same, differing mainly in the fine points.

Just as in May, Ryan proceeded directly to the control panel, Sam close on his heels. When he touched the panel, its blank surface lit up to display a set of controls on its left side and a physical map of the Earth on its right. Ryan rotated the map image and zoomed in and out at different spots. Unlike in May, Sam did nothing to impede him.

"Yeah," Ellie said. "It's actually amazing how much alike it is, like whoever made it had seen the other one. Everything seems much more finished than before, but that's about it. Take these guys, for example." She unhooked a black, silver-studded headpiece from its holder at the rear of the chair. "The other ones were attached differently and looked like they had been made from bicycle racing helmets. These have the same cables and metal studs inside, but they don't look like they've been repurposed, and where there were gaps before, it's all filled in with this thin shell." The material spanning the openings was an ugly, dull beige. She tapped on it, expecting to hear her fingernail click against rigid plastic. Instead, she discovered the material was pliable, like some kind of leather.

Ellie returned the headpiece to its bracket, then drew Aaron's attention to the chair's spine. "These seats still have all the same neural contacts, but the chairs themselves also look like they were made especially for this purpose. I thought the other ones looked like they might have come from a gym."

Hearing Ellie's comment, Ryan turned to smile at her over his shoulder. "Really? You too?"

Ellie caught Aaron's eye and pointed in Ryan's direction. "Let's go look."

She and Aaron took up positions at opposite ends of the panel. The left side, where she stood, was divided into a grid of six cells, each corresponding to one of the chairs behind her. On the other end, she could see the green and blue image of Earth, which Ryan had returned to its default magnification, hanging tranquilly in a sea of black. Once again, a few of the details were different—the colors and shapes of the buttons, for instance—but there was nothing new here. It was all just a more refined-looking version of the original. She realized Ryan was asking a question, but she only caught the end of it.

"—outside view thing?" he said.

"Aimie," Jeremy said. "May we?"

The overhead lights flickered, and then the walls changed to show the area around them. Since that was merely another white-walled room, the only difference was that each wall now appeared roughly four feet further away.

"Whoops! I forgot," Ryan said. "Well, *that's* boring."

Sam laughed. "You goof!"

To Ellie's astonishment, Jeremy also laughed, sounding genuinely engaged for the first time since they had arrived.

"Aimie, will you show us a view of..." He paused and thought for a moment. "Let's go with *Paris, sur l'Arc de Triomphe, s'il vous plaît*," he said, in what Ellie thought was a passable French accent. "Replicate current time index. With sound, but low."

There was a flicker, then the plain white walls and ceiling were replaced by a late-evening view along the Boulevard Champs-Élysées, with the other eleven streets radiating outward like bicycle spokes. The noise of city traffic surrounded them, but the sound was soft and remote, as if it came from fifteen hundred feet below them rather than from a mere hundred and fifty.

"It's beautiful," Sam gasped. She rotated slowly to her right and gasped again. "Look!" she said, pointing.

Ellie turned around and joined Sam in admiring the view. In the middle ground, no more than a mile away, the brightly lit Eiffel Tower thrust high into the dark sky, dominating the cityscape in that direction. Only the complete stillness of the air betrayed the scene as a projection. They hadn't thought to ask for sound when they were in the shack, and she wondered if it had been capable.

"What you're seeing is a combination of live camera feeds combined with real-time CG modeling," Jeremy said. "Entirely accurate, too. That white Citroën pulling up at the light there?" Ellie looked where he was pointing. "That's not an image of the actual car, but there's one just like it sitting right there, right now." He lifted his focus toward the "sky." "Thank you, Aimie."

Aimie! She had been too distracted earlier to notice, but Ellie finally recognized the name of the person Aaron said often initiated text conversations when he was in the lab. She pictured a woman sitting in a small control room, following their progress throughout the tour and invisibly assisting Jeremy as needed. She leaned close to Aaron and spoke softly into his ear.

"Here that? Aimie's here. Maybe you'll finally get to meet your 'work girlfriend' today." She bumped her shoulder against his and grinned.

His mind completely engaged in a struggle to accept a staggering new reality, Aaron merely shrugged and returned his attention to the simulation. "Yeah, maybe."

So total was the illusion of standing high above the streets of Paris that when Ellie turned back around, she was startled to see the seats and control panel behind her. She wondered if this new and improved version of the shack still imparted that sickening sensation of vertigo when it did its magic. She leaned down and pushed her palm against the seat cushion. It was memory foam like before, but it felt marginally thicker. Casting a more critical eye over the rest of the unit, she decided most of the changes she could see were, like the thicker cushion, unrelated to the chair's function. The seatback's central support was bordered by six pairs of contacts. Hadn't the first one had only five? She closed her eyes and tried to picture it, but found she could envision it either way.

Jeremy was suddenly standing at her right shoulder. He dropped to one knee and looked up at her, creating for one giddy and quite disturbing moment the impression that he intended to propose. Instead, he found the release button on the floor panel between them, popped up its tiny, golf-tee-shaped handle, and pulled it open. She sensed Aaron and Ryan step up behind her. A quick glance over her shoulder showed Sam still gazing rapturously at the Paris skyline.

"To answer your earlier question, Miss Henderson, the TSD's portable energy source is designed around a completely different technology."

Ellie knelt on her side of the opening and tried to read the white, stenciled letters on the dark battery cases. Under the dim light of the night sky, only the large logo was legible.

"What's 'NDB' stand for?"

"*Seriously?!*" Aaron dropped down beside her to see for himself. "Are those really...?!"

Whatever it stands for, Ellie thought, *it's evidently pretty exciting.* She stood and backed away a step to give Aaron a better view.

"Nuclear diamond batteries, yes," Jeremy said. "They store three times more energy than lithium-metal batteries and can recharge on their own. This allows the TSD to make multiple jumps, even at the extreme edge of its range."

"And what is that?" Aaron said.

"The range? You can take it back as far as 1903. Beyond that, we believe that the reliability of our navigation calculations drops below acceptable levels. That might not be an insurmountable hurdle, but none of our projections require traveling back any earlier than the late forties. Therefore, we have not invested any time in extending that range."

Ellie spoke softly to Ryan. "We always thought the 1903 limit was due to the batteries. It sounds instead like the shack's battery system was designed taking that uncertainty factor into account."

Ryan nodded, then addressed a question to Jeremy. "And what you're saying is that this one can go back to 1931, say, then go to 1985, assuming anyone would want to, then go back to 1950 before coming home?"

Jeremy hesitated before replying. "*Ahh… completely theoretically?* Yes. That assumes that nothing done in 1930 has such a strong impact on the timeline that any resulting changes would invalidate the navigation computations, which during any mission rely solely on data carried back from this timeframe. In general, we think it is preferable to travel progressively backward, then return to the present."

"So why the fuel cell?" Ellie said. "If the batteries can recharge on their own, I mean."

If Jeremy was surprised by Ellie's underlying assumption about the TSD's power source, he didn't show it. "Self-charging is slow by comparison, and the device is always kept ready to go. For that reason, the batteries are fully recharged as quickly as possible upon the device's return. As our uncompromising Captain Isaacs would say, it's simply protocol."

Jeremy raised his left arm to consult his wristwatch, giving his hand a sharp flick to free the device from his shirt's cuff. Hardly anyone Ellie knew wore a traditional mechanical watch, and despite her low opinion of the man personally, she thought his taste in watches was impeccable. It was beautiful, with a large, analog face inset with several smaller dials, and its case glowed softly golden in the warm light from the simulated street lamps. She tried to read the unfamiliar maker's name in the low light, but he lowered his arm before she could make it all out.

"I hate to call this to an end, but it's time we moved on. We have much to discuss, and I'd rather do that in more comfortable surroundings."

Illusion or not, Sam was reluctant to leave. "More comfortable than *Paris?!*"

Raising his voice slightly, Jeremy once again addressed his unseen assistant. "Normal lighting, please, Aimie."

The ceiling panels flickered, and then the romantic view of the Paris skyline abruptly disappeared. Sam groaned, disappointed by the change in scenery. The walls, once again in their default blank state, were dim but slowly brightening, allowing their eyes to adjust from night to day.

Jeremy led the way out of the chamber. "I'm sorry, Sam, but you'll have to settle for a view of our beautiful plateau. Please, everyone—watch your step coming down."

17

Approaching the exit, Ellie saw a small control panel to the right of the door. A label at the panel's top read, "Manual Lock Control. Door must remain locked during any TSD test procedures." Below the label were two large buttons simply marked "Lock" and "Unlock." She assumed that the red light glowing between them reflected that the lock cylinders were currently disengaged.

Ellie also noticed a rotatable thumb latch below the door handle, no doubt the default locking mechanism the unit came equipped with. The four solid steel cylinders she had noticed on their way in made this feature seem not only redundant but utterly inadequate.

There was no palm scanner, and exiting the chamber did not require a code. Jeremy simply twisted the door handle down and pulled the door open into the room. He led them back down the hall to the conference room they had seen earlier, the one directly across from his office. As promised, long rows of tall windows in two of its walls provided a view of the pine forest stretching out east toward the edge of the plateau.

Ellie crossed the room and peered out through the trees. Her best guess was that three miles straight in that direction was where the shack had stood. Destroying it had come at an agonizing emotional cost, and in the end, their pain had been for nothing.

"Aimie, would you tell Sergeant Timmons to bring in lunch now, please?" The overhead lights flickered, which Ellie now interpreted as Aimie's silent acknowledgment of any given request. "Please take a seat, everyone. As I said, we have much to discuss."

"Yes," Ryan said. "You're about to explain exactly what today's show-and-tell was really all about."

"And introduce us to the one behind it all," Ellie reminded him.

"All in due time, I promise you. But while we're waiting for Sergeant Timmons, allow me to lay out a hypothetical scenario. For the sake of argument, let us first imagine that we have irrefutable proof that mankind will, at a very near point in the future, experience some major catastrophe. I don't mean the eruption of the Yellowstone caldera, the impact of a large meteor, or some other cataclysm that's beyond our ability to prevent. Consider instead a financial crisis worse than the Great Depression, perhaps, or a large-scale military conflict. A massive, politically destabilizing terrorist attack. In other words, a devastating event, but one with discrete, clearly recognizable causes. Picture millions of lives disrupted, destroyed, or even ended. Follow?"

"Yeah, yeah, we got it," Ryan said.

"So, what if we were in a position to know with absolute certainty one or more root causes of such an occurrence? A series of ill-advised policy decisions, for example, a grievous geopolitical miscalculation, or a shipment of explosives making its way into the wrong hands. Suppose we knew with absolute certainty which events 'A' and 'B' led directly and inevitably to consequence 'C'. If we also possessed the ability to alter or prevent those precursory events and prevent the resultant catastrophe, shouldn't we? Indeed, wouldn't we be *obligated* to do whatever we could to intervene? Aaron, what are your thoughts?"

Aaron glanced self-consciously at the others. He knew that in matters concerning the original shack, Ellie had been the leader of the group, at least nominally, and he felt awkward speaking first. "Honestly? I don't know what to think. This is all much more abstract to me than to these guys. They've actually used the thing. Do I believe it's possible to stop some unspecified future event by altering the past? Hypothetically, sure.

Do I think it's a good idea? That depends on what you're trying to prevent, but if millions of lives are at stake?" He shrugged. "Then yeah, maybe. And again, in theory only. Would I trust you and the people you pick to handle it right? That's the biggest question, really. All I know for certain right now is that it'll take me a while to wrap my mind around all this."

"You say your examples are 'hypothetical,'" Ellie said, making air quotes, "but my guess is that they're not very far from your actual plan. What you haven't explained is how you intend to identify the root causes of events that haven't even happened yet."

"You know?" Sam said. "I was wondering the exact same thing."

Before Jeremy could respond, the door to the hallway opened, and one of the security guards entered, pushing the door inward with one hand while balancing three cardboard boxes on his other. Two were large, square, and flat. The third held four to-go cups and was being used to weigh down a layer of paper plates and napkins. Even from the far side of the room, Ellie recognized the logo on the boxes at once—Take Five Pizza.

"Thank you, Sergeant." Jeremy indicated the end of the table with a slight tilt of his head. The man set the boxes down, then turned and left without having said a word. Only after he closed the door behind him did Jeremy speak again.

"Please help yourselves. I understand this restaurant is especially favored by members of your, ah, *demographic*."

"If by that you mean hungry people," Ryan said, "then absolutely."

Ellie viewed the offer of food as an effort to soften them up and make them more agreeable to whatever he was about to propose. However, when the aroma reached her a second later and she felt her empty stomach roll over in anticipation, she decided she didn't care.

Ryan got to the food first. He unstacked the cartons and flipped back the lids of both pizzas. When Ellie reached his side, he leaned close to her and whispered into her ear.

"Look familiar?"

Ellie glanced down and saw what he meant at once. The pizzas were precisely the same as the two Ryan had ordered the day they told Aaron about the shack, right down to the added roasted red peppers on the meat-free option. The food was not a bribe at all but a not-so-subtle demonstration of the power of Jeremy's quantum computer. Ellie looked up at Ryan, her mouth drawn into a tight line. *Not spying? That was obviously a load of crap!* Her first impulse was to confront Jeremy, but Ryan stopped her with a tiny shake of his head.

"Just keep cool," he whispered. "Let it go for now."

Sam appeared at Ryan's side and, sensing the odd tension, raised her eyebrows in a silent *What's up?* He gave her the same subtle signal.

"Look, Sam," he said cheerily. "They've got your favorite."

"Veggie? Yum!"

Ellie had to give Ryan credit—she could never have managed to sound so casual. Still hungry despite her sudden agitation, she placed a slice of each pizza on a plate, wiggled a cup of soda out of the carrying tray, and returned to her seat.

Jeremy picked the conversation back up while everyone else enjoyed their first bites. "In order to move our discussion along as swiftly as possible, I'll address Aaron's final concern at once. I believe you will have the utmost trust in the team we have in mind to begin executing our plan."

Ellie took another bite as she waited for him to complete the thought. She looked up from her plate, still waiting, but he remained silent.

"Yeah? And why's that?" Aaron said.

"Because the team we have selected is you."

Ellie started choking and forced herself to swallow the half-chewed mouthful.

"Selected... the team... us... *huh?!*"

"Took you the right mouth out of my words," Ryan said.

But Ellie was too shocked to care how inarticulate she sounded. She'd assumed the tour's whole purpose was to convince them the project was benign. Jeremy would dispel any thoughts they might have about exposing it, then lock them outside the fence for good. That they might be invited to join the effort had not occurred to her for even the briefest moment. She couldn't make sense of the offer, but she suddenly understood the real reason for the tour.

This *is the bait!* she realized. *This building and everything in it.* Jeremy's project offered something for each of them. Convinced though she was that this new device should meet the same fate as the shack, she couldn't deny that she found the mere suggestion that they might travel back in time again thrilling. Aaron would have access to the most advanced technology on the planet, and Sam could indulge in a sophisticated game of dress-up, one with real meaning, whatever it might be. And Ryan? Well, what *about* Ryan? What's in it for him?

"Let us return to your question, Miss Henderson, about how we can know what we know. You said you wanted to meet the person who has made this all possible. I'll let her give you the answer."

"*Her?*" Ellie said. "And who is that?"

Jeremy didn't answer right away. Instead, he smiled at her again, but this time there was something gleeful and gloating lurking in the expression that made her skin crawl. "I confess I often refer to her as the Puppet Master—much to her considerable annoyance, I assume—but you'll find you know her by another name." He glanced up toward the ceiling at one corner of the room.

Know her? What did that *mean?* Ellie followed his gaze but saw nothing in that area other than a small security camera mounted on a white bracket. As if some hidden watcher had taken his change in focus as a cue, a new voice abruptly filled the room.

"Hello, Ellie. It's been a while since we've had the chance to talk. I'd be happy to answer any questions you have." The voice was bright, precise, and startlingly familiar, and all eyes snapped at once toward Ellie.

Ellie always found hearing a recording of her own voice strange, but she knew at once that this was no recording. Was it a trick, then? How could that possibly be her voice? The sound of it caused everything around her to tilt onto a new plane that was trying to redefine horizontal at some previously undiscovered, geometrically impossible angle. Sights and sounds reached her as though from a remote distance. Recognizing what had become an all-too-familiar sensation, she balled her hands into fists, leaned her weight onto her elbows on the table, and clenched every muscle in her body as tight as she could in an effort to keep herself from passing out.

Looking up again, she saw two panels set into the flat, white ceiling at either end of the room. Each contained a speaker, easily identified by its typical perforated grill, and a small black protrusion she assumed was a microphone. That the voice was her own implied that it came not from a remote observer but from a computer, that it was a simulation of some kind. But why make it sound like her? What was the point of making it seem like she was the one behind everything happening here?

She forced herself to concentrate on the continuing buzz of animated conversation around her, and her world quickly regained its familiar perspective, the voices their normal volumes. Now playing catch-up, she tried to piece together a coherent picture of the situation from the few verbal fragments that had succeeded in penetrating her momentary daze.

"Hold on. Start over. Did you say this thing talking to us is from the future?"

"I know my processors give me an advantage over you biologicals," the Ellie-voice said, "but I have a hard time believing I was ever this slow." There was resentment in the tone, probably in response to being called a "thing," but Ellie didn't care about wounded feelings.

"You," she said, stabbing a finger toward the security camera, "be quiet! When I want to hear from... me, I'll let you know!" She turned toward Jeremy. "Say that again. You said I invented all this?!"

"Technically, I said, 'you will.'"

"That's insane! I would never!"

"And yet you did. Not that I haven't made quite a few, dare I say, improvements to your ideas. And the hardware design, of course, is completely—"

"It was necessary," the voice said, ignoring Ellie's command. "Because of your experience with the shack, you knew such a device was possible. After working out the basic principles, you assembled a group of scientists to help you fill in the remaining theoretical gaps and start working on a physical device. A full-scale version, like the shack you initially encountered, was impossible. Resources, energy... there was no longer enough of either to allow it. Instead, you built something smaller, powerful enough to travel back only as far as needed for the technology to be replicated in a more useful form. And you made me. I contain all of the technical data needed to construct the larger device, plus the ability to teach others how to put that information to practical use."

Ellie found the natural quality of the voice at once astounding and unsettling. In almost every way, the experience was no stranger than talking with another human by speakerphone. If she hadn't known the voice was coming from a computer—and if it didn't sound so much like herself—she doubted it would have its creepy quality.

No, that's not it, she realized. *It's my voice exactly, but it sounds like someone else using it.* That's *what's creepy.*

Aaron was having similar thoughts. "You sound like Ellie, but you also sound different. Who are you really?"

"I can't begin to tell you how good it is finally talking to you in person, Aaron. It's been so long." There was obvious affection in her tone. "I am all of Ellie that we had the capability of transferring to an Artificial Intelligence-Memory/Identity Emulation."

Aaron's brow furrowed as he concentrated, ticking off her last few words on his fingers. "Artificial... intelligence... memory... ident... Hold on—you're 'Aimie?!'" He gave a brief laugh, but it was not a happy sound.

"In the... well, not the 'flesh,' obviously."

"If my mind got transferred to a computer, does that mean I'm *dead?*" Ellie said.

"I'm sorry, Ellie, that was a poor choice of words. 'Encoding' would have been a better term. I contain a copy of your memory engrams. I won't say you're loving life, exactly, but you were still very much alive right up to the second you sent me back. I have been active in this timeframe for eight years, five months, and twenty-seven days, and it's been that long since we last spoke. It's good to hear your voices again."

"What, no hours, minutes, seconds?" Ryan said, obviously mocking her.

"Is there some reason you require that information?" Aimie snapped. From her equally obvious irritation, it was clear she hadn't missed Ryan at all.

"No. It's just that in the movies, you guys are usually so much more precise, that's all."

"Believe me when I say there are no other 'guys' like me. Not for many decades, anyway."

"Hey, no offense meant," Ryan said, and Ellie smiled, knowing that was a complete lie. "But since you asked, what we need is more information. What and where are you? Why were you sent here?"

"I think Ellie knows the answer to your first question."

Sensing the statement was not rhetorical, Ellie went with everything she knew so far and let intuition fill in the gaps. "You are a quantum computer with an AI overlay that functions as a user interface."

"Very good! Although I prefer to think of myself as a synthetic intelligence inhabiting a quantum processing core, I'm willing to concede that might be splitting hairs. As for where I am, my central processor is here, in this building. However, I am connected to the outside world and am continuously aware of nearly all that transpires there."

When feeling especially whimsical, Ellie sometimes imagined an enormous spider lurking at the center of the World Wide Web and even wondered what it might look like. Now she was talking to it.

"So you sit in here and spy, is that it?" Sam said, sounding enormously offended.

"Hi, sis. Frankly, I don't find you—and by 'you' I mean not you personally, but humans of this time period generally—interesting enough to spy on. Not as individuals, at any rate. I'm interested only in aggregate data. I analyze the past, as much as it's possible, by studying history. I look for patterns, convergences, points of weakness... any here/now where applying certain precisely calculated pressures might be useful."

In the ensuing silence, Ellie glanced across the room at Jeremy. Since their earlier exchange, he had remained completely silent. He leaned back in his chair, his hands tented in front of him, watching her closely. Not all of them; only her. Why was he so interested in her reaction?

Ellie returned her focus to the camera. "You keep saying 'useful?' To what end?"

"And that's the answer to Ryan's third question. You sent me here to change the world."

Ellie looked at the others and saw her own feelings perfectly reflected in their underwhelmed expressions. "Well, yeah. I wouldn't have done everything you said just so you could tutor me in Calc 2."

When Aimie chuckled, Ellie felt goosebumps break out over her entire body. The sound, full of phony self-deprecation, ratcheted the AI's creepiness up to a whole new level.

"I suppose that did sound a little over the top," Aimie agreed.

"I can't believe I'd have built you for any reason at all," Ellie said, "but to intentionally screw around with the past? I don't think so!"

"Yeah," Sam said. "I thought changing the world was the last thing we wanted to do."

"If you want everything you know and care about to end, keep thinking that. My world—the world you will soon inhabit—is dying. Once you know more, you will understand how it is possible that you came to make decisions you now find unimaginable. But as bad as conditions eventually become, not all of the tragedy you will face is relegated to the distant future. For example, unless radical changes are made, Sam will soon be dead."

Sam sucked in a sharp, shocked breath, and then the room went completely silent for a long moment. At last, she managed to croak a single word. "How?"

"H5N1," Aimie said. "In the fall of 2021, the highly lethal avian influenza strain finally acquired the long-feared ability to spread quickly among humans. You died in the winter of 2022. Your parents' lives outlasted yours by only a few months, I'm afraid."

Sam slumped back in her chair and leaned against Ryan's side. All their visions of their future together had been wiped away in the span of a few heartbeats, and they sat there stunned, their faces expressionless. When Sam began to sob, Ryan wrapped one arm around her shoulder and pulled her close as she quietly wept.

As the solemn silence stretched on, Ellie wondered if the story of Sam's impending fate was simply manufactured melodrama. But when Aimie eventually continued, unprompted, the animation was gone from her voice. Now she did sound like Hollywood's idea of an intelligent computer coldly relaying a series of devastating facts.

"Starting in the fall of 2019, a succession of pandemics swept over the planet. The major ones were caused by coronavirus variants, dengue fever, Ebola and other hemorrhagic diseases, and multiple mutations of Influenza A. The spread among humans of new species in the Orthopoxvirus genus raised concerns about an impending smallpox pandemic, but that never occurred. In any given year, as many as four pathogens might be circulating at the same time. A new form of HIV emerged from Africa in 2037. This event, added to the expanding geographic distribution of the mosquito-borne Zika virus, caused birthrates around the globe to plummet. Either by killing them outright or simply by discouraging reproduction, diseases finally began to reduce the human population. Not the growth rate, understand—the actual population. By the time I was brought online, the number of humans was less than seven billion for the first time in more than eighty years.

"But this reduction was not enough and not *soon* enough to counter humanity's real enemy—climate change. Its effects occurred more quickly and more dramatically than even the most pessimistic models predicted. By 2055, nearly all major US coastal cities were empty, their contaminated groundwater supplies and ruined underground infrastructures abandoned to the rising oceans. Only parts of a few—San Francisco, Portland, Seattle... Boston on the East Coast, for example—remain. The problems went far beyond rising sea levels. Altered weather patterns rendered much of the world's crop-producing regions barren. Parts of central Africa became wetter and thus more suitable for cultivation, but the power vacuum created by collapsing governments left the region without anyone with enough authority to take advantage of the changing situation there.

"Worse still, some responses to these events created a negative feedback effect. People migrated north to escape the increasingly hot and sickness-filled cities of lower latitudes, but as the tundra defrosted, never-before-seen diseases began infecting the new arrivals. In northern Siberia, an especially bad outbreak killed nearly seventy percent of one new settlement. Over fifty-five thousand people died in three months. Seeking to escape the disease, some migrants, many of whom seemed healthy but were carriers, returned south or fled to other new towns, spreading the infection even further. The Russian army cordoned off the affected villages until the dying finally stopped on its own, and after a further sixty-day quarantine, anyone still alive was allowed to leave. The pathogen was never identified."

And that all starts just a year from now! Ellie thought. Despite Aimie's dire assessment of the future, she still found the idea of putting the power required to prevent it into someone's hands repugnant, even if those hands were her own. But if they were working to fix the future, to prevent the collapse of entire countries, to save millions—or even *billions*—of lives, then surely such drastic measures were justified. Her future self seemed to think so. But how could they be certain that any of that was even true? No, there had to be another way. She began shaking her head, prepared to reject the proposal, but Aaron spoke up first.

"And you're supposed to change that? So, what's the plan?"

"It's very simple. In terms of the broad strokes, at any rate. Using this new TSD, we will introduce changes into the past—small but many—in an attempt to nudge mankind onto a less self-destructive course. In some cases, that might mean carrying back information to help a particular technology develop more quickly. Other scenarios could involve promoting a specific political agenda, one that would decrease reliance on fossil fuels, for example, or actively favor alternative energy sources.

"I must point out that my projections indicate only that it is possible to reduce the severity of the impending damage, not to eliminate it. Naturally, Sam is not the sole focus of our project. If our efforts are successful, billions of other people will be spared a future too terrible to describe."

Jeremy, whose attention had remained fixed on Ellie the whole time, finally spoke again. He dropped his hands to the tabletop and leaned forward. "Aimie told me you once said that nothing could justify the existence of what your so-called 'shack.' Do you still feel the same way?"

She shook her head. "I never could've imagined..." She tried to say more, but her voice failed her.

Jeremy's face darkened with a sudden surge of anger. "No, you couldn't! Nor, I imagine, did you spend much time trying. Instead, you chose to destroy a thing you didn't understand!"

Sam scoffed. "Oh, you're just pissed because we broke your toy!"

"Well, we did do our best to delete *him*, too," Ryan pointed out. Sam glared at him, and he raised his hands in a gesture of surrender.

"Wait," Ellie said. She now thought she understood what Jeremy was trying to tell her, and the realization made her body go numb. "Are you saying *that's* why the shack was built? To do *this?* To change the past and make the future better?"

"That is precisely the case," Aimie said. "The earlier version of the TSD was intended to be the key component in a similar attempt to save humanity from itself."

Understanding at last why Jeremy had been focused so intently on her, Ellie slumped in her chair. Her next words were little more than a whisper. "And we destroyed it."

"You did," Aimie said. "You made it 'be not there anymore,' is how you put it."

That phrase crushed Ellie's last hope that everything they'd just witnessed was an elaborate charade. She had used those exact words sitting in Diamond Dee's Café back in May, and Aimie's knowing that eliminated any possibility that the voice was a mere simulation. However unbelievable the idea seemed, Ellie now had no choice but to accept that Aimie really was *her* and that, in some way she had yet to sort out, she herself was behind all of this.

Her surroundings began swirling about her again, but this felt different. Shame over how much damage her own arrogance had ultimately caused felt like a punch to the gut, and she was more worried about being sick than passing out. She had always relied on her intuition, and it had seldom failed her, but if what Jeremy said was true, her impulsive choices had compromised the future of the entire world. They might even have caused Sam's death! Was this the reason her future self had set this all in motion? Was this entire elaborate project nothing more than a way to give herself a chance to undo her biggest mistake?

"Fine!" Ryan said. "Our bad. Whatever. The thing I want to know is simple. What can we do to save Sam?"

And there it is, Ellie thought, seeing the answer to her question from moments before. *Something for everyone.*

"Unfortunately, the answer is not as simple as staying home from class on January 18, 2022, for example. There is no way to know precisely where and when you were infected. Knowing in advance where these diseases will originate provides us with the opportunity to prevent them. And since the emergence of many of the latter-day epidemics had their roots in climate change, all our efforts in that regard will greatly reduce the probability that many of those diseases will appear.

"Don't worry, Sam. Everyone working on this project is committed to ensuring you and everyone you care about enjoy long and healthy lives."

"Look," Ryan said, "as flattering as your offer is, it's obvious that the four of us can't do most of the things you've talked about so far. Meeting with politicians, helping companies develop technologies earlier? Those things require people who are older, people with degrees, negotiating experience.... So, break this down for me. What exactly is our part in all this?"

"Once I told Aimie about meeting you, Miss Henderson, and you learned that I was once more here in Los Alamos—events that were not supposed to occur, I might add—she decided we should recruit the rest of you for the testing phase of the device. You are right, Ryan. You are all too young and, more importantly, too inexperienced to perform most of the required roles, but we have much work to do before we begin implementing the larger plan. For the manned testing phase, little is required besides a rudimentary understanding of TSD operations. Who better than the only three people who have ever used the technology to carry out that part of the work? At first, I was against the idea, but, as you'll soon learn for yourselves, Aimie can be very persuasive. What finally convinced me was her argument that once the project becomes fully active, your main involvement will be to act as the, ah, *conscience*, of the project, a role to which I believe you are well suited.

"So, once the testing is complete and we have brought additional team members on board, you will act as a sort of advisory committee, if you wish. And there may yet be opportunities for you to participate more actively, despite your ages."

"Why haven't you already started?" Sam said. "I'm sure you don't actually need *us* for the testing. What's stopping you?" Jeremy's eyes darted away from hers, and Sam read the guilty expression easily. "You *have* started, haven't you? You're already using that thing!"

Jeremy cleared his throat. "Technically, no. But as you can imagine, the costs associated with a project like this far exceed the kind of fiscal backing we could ever hope to obtain through normal channels, especially given the need to maintain absolute secrecy. As soon as we had built and tested the prototype, a single-seat version, I used it to create a retroactive revenue stream capable of funding all subsequent stages of the project— the construction of this lab, building the full-size TSD, and hiring whatever staff is necessary for as long as needed."

Despite how miserable Ellie already felt, learning that Jeremy had joined their exclusive time-travel club made her feel even worse. Especially when she considered why.

"So, except for a dozen or so unmanned tests," Jeremy said, "the TSD you saw has never been used. That, however, is something you will soon have the chance to fix."

Alarmed by the way Jeremy seemed to be taking their continuing cooperation as a foregone conclusion, Ellie held up both her hands like she was trying to stop an oncoming truck. "Hang on! We haven't agreed to anything yet. There are still a lot of things we need to know before we do."

"Yeah, like, what happens next?" Sam said.

"And who decides what gets changed? And how?" Aaron said.

Ryan spread his arms wide on the table in front of him. "And like I said before, what do we do to protect Sam and her parents?"

Jeremy glanced up at the ceiling, signaling for Aimie to rejoin the conversation.

"To expand on my answer to Sam's earlier question," she said, "I have been formulating a strategy, and only now that the strategy is complete can the work begin. Each element of the plan contributes, to a greater or lesser degree, to an improvement of our current situation. Due to the interconnected nature of those elements, executing the entire plan is the best course of action and the best way to protect Sam. As to who decides, the four of you will be given the final choice as to whether or not any individual component is carried out."

"Really," Ryan said.

"As the 'conscience' of the project," Sam said.

"Correct," Aimie said. "Ellie—my Ellie, I mean—felt that would be an appropriate role for you to play. Necessary, in fact."

Ellie's thoughts raced as she struggled to determine how much, if any, of what Aimie was telling them was true. Was averting a terrible future truly their goal? And if not, then what was it? They needed to know more before she was willing to commit to anything. She could think of only one place they might find those answers.

"If we are to decide to work with you, there would have to be one condition. From now on, we have unrestricted access to the quantum core and all of its databases, Continuity included."

"No," Aimie said.

"Then I'm sorry, but—"

"Only Aaron will be granted the access you describe."

Ellie pretended to think Aimie's counteroffer over, but in truth, this was exactly what she'd expected and no less than what she wanted. There wasn't anything the rest of them having that access would add to their side of the equation. She frowned and shook her head.

"Okay, fine." She did her best to sound disappointed at having to make this concession. It wasn't hard. Even though they had just agreed to her one demand, she still felt outmaneuvered.

"Didn't I anticipate this?" Aimie said, sounding smug.

"You did," Jeremy said. "That has already been arranged," he told them, sounding just as smug.

Ellie fought a powerful urge to roll her eyes. *Those two are perfect for each other!*

The room went silent. Jeremy and Aimie seemed to be waiting for an answer, but Ellie didn't know what to say. She had chosen to view Aaron's return to her life as the universe giving her a second chance to be with him. Was this a *second* second chance? An opportunity not only to correct a major mistake but to be a part of saving Sam's life along with countless others? Didn't that make working with Jeremy and Aimie okay? An inner voice, deep and instinctual, insisted that wasn't so, but it was the same voice that had been so certain that destroying the shack had been the right thing to do. She had never felt so unsure of herself, and she found the sensation deeply unnerving. They needed to think, to talk everything over in private. They needed time.

"I... I don't know. It's a lot to take in." She caught Sam and Ryan's eyes in turn, willing them to remain silent while she continued. "I doubt Sam and Ryan will want to have anything to do with this. I see the importance of what you're trying to do, though, and I'd like the chance to try to convince them to help."

To her relief, Sam caught on at once and began shaking her head to show she had serious reservations about taking part.

"If I only have a few years left, I'd rather not spend them starring in *The Time Traveler's Girlfriend*. That hardly sounds like fun. Unless, of course, you can guarantee your plan will work."

"The outcome of the plan is not certain, but the results of doing nothing are. I'm not sure you could have enough 'fun' in the meantime to make it worth your while."

"I don't know about *that*," Ryan said. "We're pretty good at—"

Aimie didn't let him finish. "Forty-eight hours. Or rather, let us say by the end of Tuesday. Is that sufficient time?"

Ryan aimed a wry smile at the camera in the corner of the ceiling. "Is it my imagination, Aimie, or do you *really* not—"

"That's good!" Ellie, too, cut him off mid-sentence. Whatever was going on between Aimie and Ryan, she didn't need him making it any worse with his wisecracks. "End of Tuesday—that's perfect!"

"I look forward to your decision," Aimie said.

Sam raised a hand. "I have one last question: why us?"

"There are several reasons," Aimie said. "I could tell you it's because we trust you more than anyone else we could recruit to perform this particular task. Or that because you have so much to gain personally, you're especially motivated to see it through. There's also the fact that you already know the technology exists, so using you eliminates the need to spread that information further, and thus we avoid contaminating this timeline any more than necessary.

"The actual truth is much simpler—I prefer to have you where I can keep an eye on you."

"'Keep your friends close,' eh?" Ryan said.

"That's one way to look at it," Aimie agreed.

But keep your enemies closer. Ellie knew the quote too. "Are we your enemies, then, Aimie?"

"For the moment, no. However, I would counsel you strongly against altering the status quo."

No one had a response to that. They all recognized a threat when they heard one.

18

Ellie arrived back at Ryan's Jeep with no clear memory of leaving Jeremy's office or of making the long walk down the front hallway to the exit. She stopped and stood completely still, her face blank, regarding the vehicle as though unsure of its purpose. Freed from the need to engage with Aimie, her mind had refocused on her decision to destroy the shack and its disastrous consequences. What she had just learned shocked her deeply. How could she have been so wrong?

Sam stepped past her dazed sister, opened the passenger door, and slid her seat forward. Ellie climbed into the back first and scooted across the seat. Paying no attention to Aaron as he followed her in, she leaned over and rested her head against the glass. She stared absently at the pavement as Ryan backed out of his parking spot and aimed them toward the gate. No one spoke until they were on its far side.

"Can you believe that guy? 'Size four or *two?*'" Ryan said, exaggerating Jeremy's honeyed tones.

"Seriously!" Sam said. "And 'Marx' is Karl Marx. Groucho Marx is Groucho! Everybody knows that! Saying 'Marx' just sounds smarter."

"That's the longest I've ever been around him," Aaron said. "You guys were right—he is pretty full of himself."

Ellie exhaled a huge sigh. She felt dispirited, but to Ryan, she must have sounded relieved.

"What?" he said. "You thought we were being seduced to the dark side?"

She sat up and leaned forward to be better heard. "Maybe. I know I was once we stepped into the TSD. But no, it's not that. It's that I'm not so sure anymore that it *is* the dark side, that's all." In the mirror, Ryan's eyebrows lifted in surprise, but he made no reply.

It was twenty-past one when they reached the Omega Bridge. Now Ryan had a choice to make. Once across the bridge, they could continue straight toward home or turn right and go downtown.

"So, where am I going?"

"I'm sure Mom and Dad are home by now," Ellie said. "Starbuck's?"

Sam scoffed. "Do you really think Starbuck's is the best place to decide if humanity is worth saving?"

Ellie knew Sam was joking but also thought she might actually have a point. Plus, it wouldn't exactly be private. With no firm destination in mind but understanding that home was not among the options, Ryan veered right onto Trinity Drive.

"I do like the idea of coffee, though," Sam said.

"We could take our drinks over to the park," Ryan suggested.

If Aimie was right and destroying the shack had been a colossal mistake, then the place she had set all this in motion was the last place Ellie wanted to be. "No," she said. "Not there."

"Well, then...?"

"*Ooh!* The co-op!" Sam said. "We can get something there, then walk down to where that big cliff is." She turned and touched Ryan's arm. "You know where I mean?"

"Yeah, yeah. Behind that industrial park by the old gate."

Ellie could remember being there once or twice, but the place held no particular meaning for her. "Works for me," she said.

"Big cliff?" Aaron was intrigued. "I like the sound of that!"

"Excellent!" Ryan said. "Houston, we have a plan."

Ellie was silent during the five-minute ride to the edge of town, using the time to regain some shred of her usual equilibrium. Discovering that her decisions in June had all but resulted in mass death on a scale that would eclipse all of history's most murderous tyrants combined had shaken her to her core. In her wildest dreams, she sometimes hoped her name would one day be mentioned alongside those of Marie Curie, Donna Strickland, or Richard Feynman. Even to end up in the company of Carl Sagan or Neil deGrasse Tyson would make her happy. But that she might have ended up lumped in with Joseph Stalin, Pol Pot, and Adolf Hitler instead? No one would ever have known, of course, but she did, and the idea made her feel even sicker. For the moment, her wildest dream was reduced to nothing more than getting to the co-op without throwing up in the car.

Ellie waited outside, taking slow, deep breaths of the cool air, while the others went in to get drinks. When they returned minutes later, Sam handed her a can of mango-flavored seltzer water.

"Thanks," Ellie said. Even though it was one of her favorites, the thought of drinking it made her stomach clench. Instead of opening it, she slipped it into her jacket pocket and climbed back into the rear of the Jeep.

They drove another half a mile, winding their way slowly behind several county facilities, and parked along the edge of Pueblo Canyon. Most of the trails in and around Los Alamos saw heavy use, but the one Sam had chosen was far from the center of town, and they passed no one along their way. Walking strung out in single file along the narrow trail would have made discussing the morning's events awkward at best, so they remained quiet until they reached its eastern end. Even once they found a place where they could all sit close enough to talk easily, they remained silent; no one knew what to say.

Ellie sat close to the edge to avoid having to face anyone. The view that stretched out below them was empty, and only the soft hum of traffic laboring up East Road reminded them they weren't the only humans inhabiting that vast and rugged landscape. The temperature, already in the high sixties, had nearly reached its peak for the day. Their perch at the plateau's edge exposed them to a constant breeze riding up the slope from the valley, though, and Ellie was glad she had brought the light jacket.

Aaron finally interrupted the stillness, rethreading the cap on a bottle of intensely purple fortified water as he spoke. "I know this isn't actually my fault, so don't take this the wrong way, but I'm sorry you're all involved with this now. I just—"

"We get it," Ellie said. "And no, it *isn't* your fault. If anyone's to blame, apparently it's *me!*" All the anger, humiliation, and guilt she'd been pushing to the back of her mind erupted in an uncontrolled fit of self-directed rage. "I mean, what the actual, total *fuck?!*" Her anguished cry came out flat, swallowed at once by the gaping gulf of open space below them. She balled her hands into tight fists and pounded them against her thighs as she struggled to regain control.

After finding a level spot on which to set her coffee, Sam scooted forward, wrapped an arm around Ellie's shoulders, and pulled her close. "Listen, El, you are right here, with us, right now. Whatever is going on, whoever is behind it all, it can't be *you*."

"But it *is*, Sam. Any way you look at it, this is all on me! You heard what Aimie said—billions of people died all because I... because of *me!*" She began to cry and had to force her next words out between great, convulsive sobs. "If I hadn't convinced you all to destroy the shack, we wouldn't even be having this conversation. Aaron wouldn't have had to endure the pain of choosing to sacrifice himself, and the future would already be fixed! I would never have had to send Aimie back; there wouldn't be any TSD. And *you*, Sam. You wouldn't be... I'm so sorry, Sam!" Then her words caught in her throat, and she could only stare at the ground while tears flowed freely down her cheeks. It took only a few moments for her to get herself back under control, but the feelings of guilt and shame remained. "You guys must hate me," she whispered.

"No," Ryan said, "we don't. I'm totally with Sam; this isn't on you. I still think we did the right thing before. I know I didn't agree with you at first, but in the end, I believed that you were right. And so did Sam."

"I did," Sam said. "And I still do. This is not your fault, okay?"

Ellie still didn't believe that, and it wasn't okay, not at all. For months, she'd had the recurring sense of feeling manipulated but had never taken the notion seriously. Instead, she'd decided the feeling was something akin to déjà vu, a mental mirage, and so had given no thought as to who might be pulling those imagined strings. If what they'd been told was true, it was her future self who set everything in motion. Then, remembering Jeremy's nickname for Aimie, she had to ask—didn't that really make *her* the Puppet Master?

She felt the comforting pressure of Sam's hand on her back. She didn't *want* to be comforted, knew she didn't deserve to be forgiven, but she fought the urge to pull away. She also knew she couldn't afford to waste time wallowing in self-recrimination—she needed to get past this moment so they could start focusing on what to do next. She unclenched her fists, sniffed loudly, and nodded.

"Yeah, okay," she said.

"Uh-huh," Sam said.

Ellie could tell Sam was not the least bit fooled, and she couldn't help but smile a little as she watched her scuttle back to reassume her place beside Ryan. It felt good knowing Sam could read her that well.

Ryan posed the fundamental question. "So, they want us to sign up with them on their noble crusade to save the planet. Who buys that?"

"And save Sam in the bargain," Ellie said. "*And* Mom and Dad."

Sam raised a hand. "Well, I vote for *that!*"

"Me, too," Ryan said at once. "But again, *if* you believe them."

"Aimie seemed awfully confident we would," Sam said.

"She may have good reason to be," Aaron said. "If she's truly from the future, that is." He sounded unconvinced.

Ellie shook her head. "No. That's actually the one thing I don't have any doubts about. That she's from the future, I mean. Like you said before, it's the only way all the parts of this make sense."

Aaron looked glum. "Yeah, well, at this point, we're so far beyond logic that I'm not sure the usual rules apply."

"They *have* to," Ellie said. Even to her own ears, she sounded like she was pleading. "They have to, or we can't hope to think our way out of this."

"'Out of this?'" Ryan said. "Does that mean we're *not* accepting their offer? Then what about Sam?"

"Yeah!" Sam said. "What about Sam? And you know what? Given the circumstances, I think I should get *two* votes!"

Ellie stared between her knees at a perfectly circular patch of bright orange lichen growing on the pale sandstone. Her thoughts felt as unlikely as the idea that anything could survive on an expanse of such barren rock. "I don't see any choice but to go along with them. But if we do, we need to be absolutely certain they're telling the truth, and I think that's going to require a lot of reading between the lines, that's all."

She took a moment and tried organizing all of her underlying doubts into a single coherent sentence, but found she couldn't. None of her misgivings had anything to do with the plan itself. What they had done in June, if ultimately ineffective, proved it was possible to change today by altering the past. Her reservations were annoyingly vague, based solely on an intuition she felt she could no longer trust, and she couldn't find the words to express them.

Ryan spoke up then, saving her from having to say anything more right away. "Here's what's bothering me. Based on what they said and on what Aaron has seen out there, they've been ready for weeks, at least. And yet they have no team in place, nothing going on. Sure, in theory, it doesn't matter when their plan gets going, but it's like they've just been treading water, waiting for something. If that something is us, that *really* worries me. It makes no sense. It's like we're playing poker, but they have x-ray glasses and we don't. Aaron nailed it. Aimie's presence back here in our time frame means that they could just be going through the motions while knowing the whole time exactly what we're going to do. How can we—"

"No." Ellie shook her head. "If anything, Aaron proves that isn't necessarily the case; otherwise, he'd still be calling Jeremy 'Dad.' I'm willing to give my future self the benefit of the doubt. If I really do end up sending Aimie back, it has to be with the best intentions, and things have to be *really* bad! Even so, this whole thing feels off. I wish I could explain exactly why I feel that way, but I can't."

"It seems fair but feels foul, you mean." Aaron was paraphrasing Frodo Baggins, and Ryan gave his effort a thumbs up.

"Close enough," Ellie agreed. She thought about hearing Aimie speak with her voice. What was it that bothered her so much about that? Then, realizing that Aaron had said very little else since the conversation began, she asked him directly. "What do *you* think?"

Aaron rolled his bottle between his palms while he considered his answer. "Nobody knows better than me how messing with the past can change the present. So, yeah, I get how what they talked about could work. But something about that whole tour felt like a well-rehearsed act. I feel like they're totally telling the truth yet totally lying, all at the same time."

Sam sighed. "I agree. It doesn't feel right at all."

"So, is this our plan, then?" Ryan said. "Pretend to go along until we come up with a better idea?"

"No," Ellie said. "I think we need to *actually* go along with them." Responding to his confused expression, she tried to make her point in a different way. "Look, Ryan, I went out to Jeremy's lab this morning with only one goal—figure out a way to stop whatever he was up to. But now I don't know. I have to believe I had a good reason to send Aimie back here. I mean, to 'Dr. Jeremy freakin' Siskin, DSc,' of all people! I say that if there's any hope of steering the world onto a better path, we should do whatever we can to help make that happen."

"That sounds great," Sam said, "but I'm telling you right now—there's no way this all ends well."

Aaron stared at the ground. "Personally, I think we should 'make this one be not here,' too. Now that we know about the danger Sam's in, there are steps we can take to protect her that don't involve using the TSD. Maybe it's because of what happened to me before, but I hate the idea of that thing existing at all." He raised his eyes to meet Ellie's. "But it's not about *it* as much as it is about *them*. Like I said, it all feels like an act of some kind. A scam."

"I totally agree," Ellie said. "I feel the same way, but we need more than feelings before we decide to try shutting them down. That's why we don't stop digging. We have to know for certain they're doing something wrong, so we learn everything we can as fast as we can. Plus, if we eventually do decide that disrupting their plan—or maybe just exposing it this time, Sam—is the way we have to go, do you honestly think we could get into that place? We'd need to already be on the inside. So, like Aimie said, I'd rather be where we can keep an eye on them."

Aaron held Ellie's gaze for a long moment, then nodded. "Yeah, well, I definitely can't argue with that last point. I would not like to go up against Captain Isaacs trying to break in."

Ryan scoffed. "I wouldn't go up against that man's left pinky. Dude's a mountain! Not that I couldn't take him in the four-hundred-meter freestyle. Still…"

"Still what?" Ellie said.

"I'm sorry to say this, but I feel pretty much the same as those two." He held up a hand to forestall any response before he'd had his full say. "But, like you, I don't see any alternative. We'll try it this way. Like you said, if we don't like how things are going, we can change our minds later and do it with a much greater knowledge of what they're up to. If you're right and they're on the level, well, there are worse ways to spend your time than literally saving the world. If things still look dicey when 2022 rolls around, Sam and I can spend the whole year locked up in quarantine together."

Sam smiled at him. "I like the way you think!" Then her mood turned serious again. "But what if it turns out they *are* lying about everything? Any idea what the plan would look like then?"

Ellie shook her head. "Not yet. Not without being able to tell which parts of what they've told us are true and which aren't. That's why it was so important to get Aaron access to the quantum computer."

"Do you want me to let Jeremy know we've decided to go along?" Aaron said.

"What do you guys think?" Ellie said. "Not about that, but about the idea in general. Are we missing anything?"

"Does all this debate even matter?" Sam said. "I know what you said, El, but I still have to wonder—whatever we decide now, doesn't it mean that's what we did before? They already know what we're going to do."

Ellie's brain felt overloaded. They had learned too much too quickly, and they needed time to sort through it all. But even though she couldn't explain why, she didn't believe Aimie knew anything more about what they would decide than they did, despite her knowledge of the future Ellie's past. Hadn't she even said there'd be differences?

"To be honest, Sam, I don't know. Not for sure. But we can't start playing those kinds of mind games, or we'll never be able to make any decisions."

"Back to Aaron's question, then," Ryan said. "Should we tell them we're good to go?"

Ellie thought for a moment, then shook her head. "I say let's wait. Aimie gave us the two days; I didn't ask for them, so I think we should let Aaron take full advantage of that wiggle room." She turned to face Aaron. "Maybe you find out that something's wrong right away, or maybe you just confirm it's all exactly as they say, but either way, we should use the time to learn more before we commit. Does that make sense?"

One by one, the others nodded in agreement.

"Okay," Aaron said. "I'll wait to hear from you, then."

That settled the matter, at least temporarily, and for a while they sat quietly, content to gaze across the rugged valley toward distant Truchas Peak, thirty-five miles to the east. The tranquility of that view was at odds with the turmoil Ellie still felt churning away in her head, and she knew she needed a distraction, a way to get her mind thinking about something else. Trying hard to smile, she twisted around to look over her shoulder at Aaron.

"So, what's it like finding out your office crush is an AI?"

Caught mid-sip, Aaron fought to object through a sudden fit of coughing. "She was never—"

"Ooh!" Sam said. "I forgot all about your workplace fling!"

"*No!* I—"

Ryan cut him off again. "Well, if there's *anyone* you could picture hooking up with a computer."

"Yep!" Ellie agreed. "It's only logical, after all."

Aaron held up his half-full bottle and gave them each a stern look. "Fair warning—one of you is about to wind up wearing the rest of this home," he said, but he was laughing along with the rest of them.

The lighter mood Ellie managed to achieve in the afternoon had faded by evening. Sitting at the table with her parents was an ongoing reminder of the fate that supposedly awaited them, and she barely made it through dinner without breaking down. By the time she loaded the dishwasher and finished cleaning the kitchen, she was deep into her pit of shame and self-recrimination once again.

She finished her homework quickly, returned her books and laptop to her pack, and then settled onto her bed. She sat upright, legs bent, staring blankly at the pages of a book she held propped against her thighs. She had opened it to a random place half an hour earlier and hadn't turned a single page since. She wasn't even aware of Sam's return home until the door to their room swung in and her sister bounded through.

"Hey! Whatcha reading?" Sam said.

Ellie looked up slowly, as if coming out of a daze. Moving at the same glacial pace, she closed the book and peered at its cover to find out. *"Foundation,* apparently."

Sam frowned at her. "Are you still beating yourself over the head about the shack thing? Get over it!"

The fog in Ellie's mind cleared in an instant, blown away by a sudden gust of anger. "*'Get over it?!'* Really? And what's the worst thing you've ever done, Sam? *Hmm?* Show up at work without your swimsuit? Get a "C" on a calc quiz? That's *nothing* compared to what Aimie said *I* did! Not even close! You have no idea how bad it feels to—"

"And I... don't... *care!*" Sam interrupted, stunning Ellie into silence. "I'm sorry, El, but I just don't. I *can't!* When you're at your best, you are the best, and we need that right now. We need to figure out what's going on, find out if there's a way to save Mom and Dad. That's the only thing that matters right now. And if we can't do that because you 'feel bad,' then yeah—that *will* be on you, and I will be pissed! Dead, maybe, but pissed. If there are any answers out at that lab, we need to find out. So you need to quit this ridiculous pity party you've got going and get your head in the game."

Get your head in the game? That was a Ryan phrase, one of his more annoying ones, and Sam's use of it made it clear what she and Ryan had spent the evening discussing.

Sam sat on the edge of Ellie's bed and placed a hand on her thigh. When she continued, it was in a much gentler tone. "I actually do care, you know, and I get that not even you can just flip a switch and change how you're feeling. But you have to get past it. I *need* you to." Sam smiled. "Ryan too. He said it'll totally suck having to find a new girlfriend."

Ellie snorted, amused by Ryan's dark humor despite her mood. "That's cold! What did you do to him in response?"

"Only the worst thing of all—absolutely *nothing!*" They both grinned at that.

Ellie dropped her gaze to the bed and considered everything Sam had said. She knew Sam was at least partially right. She didn't buy the idea that she was their only hope. After all, Aaron had been the one to figure out how to destroy the shack, not her. However, she did suspect she might be the one best equipped to deal with Aimie, given that the AI was a reflection of herself. She raised her eyes to meet Sam's and nodded.

"*Flip!*"

Sam stared at her, not understanding.

"That was me flipping the switch," Ellie explained. "Not really, but I get what you're saying. I'll 'get over it,' or whatever. Not in the next couple of hours, maybe, but I will."

"That's good. Because if I have my way, Ryan's going to be stuck with me for many years to come."

"We'll make sure of that—I promise."

19

Despite her best efforts, Ellie's mood had improved very little by the time she and Aaron sat down together at lunch the following day. Her feelings of guilt and humiliation, even stronger around him than they had been with Sam, made it impossible for her even to look him in the eye. In the face of her obvious despair, he did what he could to lift her spirits.

"I've been thinking about what you said. That you wouldn't have sent Aimie back to build the TSD unless you had a good reason."

Ellie mumbled a reply without taking her eyes off her tray. "Yeah. And?"

"And that is something I believe is totally true. I know I said I feel we should be working against what they're doing out there, but that's all that is—a feeling."

"So, what are you saying?"

"I'm saying that despite what I feel about the thing, I believe that you sent Aimie back to Jeremy, that the TSD is specifically here, in Los Alamos, because you're supposed to be a part of whatever it's used for. I think you were really sending it to yourself."

Ellie scoffed. "Yeah, right. 'Cause look how well that went the first time."

"Maybe that's exactly why."

Ellie remembered having almost the same thought in Jeremy's lab. *Was this a chance for redemption?* "I don't know…"

"Hey," Aaron said. "I can't imagine what you're feeling right now. What I do know is that no matter what's going on out there, you need to be thinking about what we do next, not whether or not you messed up before."

His *rah-rah* attitude reminded her of her conversation with Sam the night before, and she didn't try to hide her irritation.

"Gee. Thanks, Coach."

Finally fed up with her sulky attitude, Aaron tossed his wadded napkin into the middle of his empty plate. "Fine! If you really think wallowing around in self-pity is the best way to handle this situation, you go right ahead. But you can do it alone." He stood and gripped the sides of his tray, but before he left the table, he paused to look down at her. "Besides, maybe you're right—maybe you're just not up to dealing with this."

Embarrassment over her behavior heaped itself on top of her ongoing sense of humiliation, and she could only sit there, her face burning, staring at the remains of her lunch. She knew Aaron was right; they could do nothing to change the events that happened in the spring, but they absolutely must deal with the fallout. That was especially true if she really was to blame.

Ellie looked up from the table and saw Aaron heading for the exit, even though the bell hadn't yet rung. When he noticed her watching him, he abruptly veered in her direction instead, then sat beside her. Still unable to meet his gaze, she returned her attention to her tray. She felt like shouting, but by speaking through clenched teeth, she managed to keep her voice down to a low hiss.

"Since you can't imagine how I feel, I'll tell you. I feel like a total freakin' *idiot*. I was so sure of myself that destroying the shack was the right thing to do that I never seriously considered that there might be a legitimate reason for it to have been built. No, it's more than that; I was completely convinced that there *couldn't* be one. *And* I feel like a mass murderer! All the deaths and suffering that Aimie told us about, the wars, and the world we wound up living in—that all happened because of *me!*"

The images that abruptly filled her mind were so horrific that she had to fight to keep her breathing from going fast and shallow.

"Look," Aaron said. "First of all, you said A-Ron decided you guys needed to destroy the shack even more quickly than you did once you convinced him what it really was, right? Were you *both* that wrong? Honestly, deep down, do you truly feel you did the wrong thing?"

"No, but it's like you said earlier—my feelings don't matter. And given how badly I screwed up back in June, I trust them right now about as much as I trust Jeremy and Aimie."

Aaron went on, letting her rebuttal pass without comment. "And second of all, everything that Aimie described happened because humans have made a total mess of the planet, and that started long before you arrived on it. Maybe you made a mistake—maybe!—but you caught that mistake and came up with a way to fix it." He leaned close to her and spoke quietly. "Hey. Look at me."

Reluctantly and with great effort, she forced her gaze to meet his.

"I said I'm with you, and I am," he said. "One hundred percent. I mean, what they say they're trying to do? Who could be against that, right? It's *them* I have reservations about. But if they're on the level, then I agree; we go for it."

His words triggered the same instinctive loathing toward the TSD she had experienced the day before. On the other hand, she couldn't deny the logic of his argument. If her decision before *had* been a mistake, then wasting her one remaining chance to correct it by indulging in this guilt trip would be the ultimate tragedy. At last, she nodded.

"You're right. I need to be focused on the fix, not the mistake." Suddenly she wished they were practically anywhere but in the middle of the cafeteria, and she gave him a rueful smile.

"What?" he said.

"I could use a hug right now, but...." She swept her gaze pointedly around the crowded room.

Aaron smiled back. "Yeah, well, later. I promise."

As if the pledge were the act itself, her mood suddenly felt lighter, and this time she smiled warmly.

"Thanks for not leaving before. I really do feel better."

"That's good. And by later, I mean *later* later, by the way. I'm going out to the lab right after school to start digging a little deeper."

"Good luck with that. And don't worry—I won't forget you owe me one!"

Ellie pushed through the school lobby's double doors and stepped into the bright sunshine feeling almost like her usual self. The lunchtime conversation with Aaron had gotten her most of the way there, and Mrs. Carson's lecture on sustainable sourcing helped pull her the rest of the way out of her own head. She had taken no more than a dozen steps when her phone buzzed in her pocket. It was the long, insistent vibration that signaled a call, and she expected it to be Aaron on his way to Jeremy's lab. She smiled as she raised it to her face, but her expression soured when she read the screen. It identified the caller as "Aimie Henderson."

Oh, 'byte' me! She took a deep breath and tried to sound civil, despite the instinctive repugnance she felt toward the AI.

"That's cute, 'sis!' What do you want?" She winced at her terse tone, knowing that her question had come out sounding the precise opposite of civil. *Okay, so I just flunked Faking Nice 101,* she thought, but relaxed when Aimie seemed not to notice.

"Hello, Ellie. How's it going with Sam and Ryan? Having any luck convincing them to join us?"

Ellie stopped, held the phone out in front of her, and squinted at it. *What are you talking about?* She almost said this out loud, then remembered her ruse from the day before. She placed the phone back to her ear. Failing at nice, she tried for apologetic.

"Yeah, well, not so far. I'm *real* sorry, though. I'll try again tonight. You said I have until midnight tomorrow, right?" She was afraid that came across more as sassy than contrite, and she wondered how she'd ever been able to pull off her performance in Tom's Diner.

"I did. But do not forget that I know you. In fact, I know three times more you than you do. I will not tolerate being jerked around."

Before Ellie could decipher the middle part, the phone was chirping its "call disconnected" sound in her ear. Her cheeks burned. She felt humiliated all over again, but now it was by her own sense of helplessness in the face of Aimie's intimidating remarks. On top of that, she was furious at being made to feel that way. Hand shaking, she slipped the phone into her pocket and continued up the sidewalk.

As she cut through the large parking area at the corner of the campus, she tried to get her mind back on track. Aimie's implied threat refused to yield any ground, however, and it wasn't until she was dropping into the canyon that she could think about anything else. Her focus finally came to rest on Sam's question from the day before. What would they do if Jeremy and Aimie were lying? What *could* they do?

Dealing with the original shack had been easier in almost every way. The school year had been all but over when they found it, and that had given them the time they needed to work on a plan. Plus, back then she felt as if they were merely up against some inanimate object. If it came to it, going toe to toe with Jeremy and Aimie would be far more of a challenge, and the current stakes were immeasurably higher. When they were kids, one of Sam's favorite jokes was to hold up a white sheet of paper and say it was a picture of a ghost eating a marshmallow in the middle of a blizzard. As to how any alternative plan might have to look, her mind was as blank as that page.

She stopped in the middle of the bridge and looked down the canyon, letting the tranquility of the scene wash through her mind. The scruffy Gambel oaks still clung to their brown, dead leaves as they would for months to come, but the cottonwoods, box elders, and most of the smaller shrubs were rapidly going bare. All winter long, though, the mix of junipers, firs, and other evergreens would provide an ongoing backdrop of color to the forest.

She wondered how much longer Los Alamos would be there. Through some random quirk of weather patterns, fate, or plain old good luck, the Jemez Mountains had continued to receive enough precipitation during recent years to keep life on the plateau going, including the human life. Was anyone still living here in the time Aimie came from, or had it become too dry? Had it even all burned?

Her environmental worries were a long-term issue, though. The area was due to suffer a series of devastating pandemics starting in little more than a year. How many people, in addition to nearly everyone she loved, would die in those outbreaks? Mrs. Carson? Shanna and her family? Her new friends at the Nature Center?

Pondering these questions gave her some sense of clarity at last. Anything she could do to prevent those events had to be her long-term goal. Threats aside, if that meant working with Aimie, so be it.

Ellie was stepping out of the kitchen when she heard the rumble of the garage door closing. A second later, her parents entered the house. Her dad was on his phone, sounding uncharacteristically sharp with whoever was unlucky enough to be on the other end of the connection. She looked at her mom, eyebrows arched in a silent question.

"It's the mortgage company. They say they haven't received this month's payment."

"What's that mean?"

"It means somebody screwed up, but it wasn't us. It's supposed to be automatic, a computerized thing. Our bank says the transfer was made, but the mortgage company says they haven't received it." she sighed. "Don't worry about it. Some wires got crossed somewhere along the line, that's all. I'm sure they'll get it straightened out in a day or so."

Ellie felt a chill run down her spine but tried to sound encouraging. "Yeah, I'm sure it's just a glitch." *And I bet I know the glitch's name, too!*

Her mom paused before heading down the hall to her bedroom. "I want to shower before starting on dinner. We spent the afternoon in the shop milling new ankle joints for testing, and I'm covered in grit. Will you chop up some veggies? Onions, carrots, celery? I'll be right out."

"Sure, Mom."

All evening, Ellie's mind turned inward on itself. She now understood they had been wrong to view the offer to work on Jeremy's project as an invitation. Aimie had made it doubly clear that she would not accept any alternative other than their cooperation. But if the project was as innocent as she claimed, then why these blatant attempts at coercion? Given

Aimie's deep knowledge of them, it was possible she could have anticipated their skepticism, but that didn't seem to justify going as far as she had.

As worrisome as Aimie's threats themselves were, their timing bothered Ellie even more. That afternoon, her phone rang precisely as she left the school building. Next, the call to her dad had come as he arrived home, just in time for her to overhear most of it. If she hadn't been home then, would the call have come later? Could Aimie follow their movements by tracking their phones? Could she tap into the school's security camera feed, watch and wait for the precise moment she walked through the door before calling? Ellie was pretty sure she could, and without even breaking a sweat.

By the end of the night, two things had become clear. The first was that Ryan had been right from the beginning. They needed to be extremely careful with their cell phones, tablets, and computers—anything that might be susceptible to eavesdropping by Aimie. And credit cards, she added, although it was more likely Aimie knew about the pizzas by listening in on Ryan's call or hacking the restaurant's computer. Neither she nor Sam had cards of their own, but Ryan did. She'd have to warn them all about Aimie's cyberstalking prowess. Talk in person, pass notes— use semaphore if it came to that—but don't text anything they want to keep secret.

The other thing she now knew was that her involvement with Aimie and the TSD project would require more time than she could currently spare. If she let her grades slip, it would be only a matter of time before her parents started getting phone calls, and that would put her under too much scrutiny at home. Study and homework were still a must, then, but that required no more than ninety minutes per day and usually a lot less.

The larger drain on her time was her work at the Nature Center, and that was weekend time, too, when Sam and Ryan were most available. It was ironic that, aside from her Environmental Science class, the Nature Center was where she was learning what was most relevant right now. More than that, working there made her feel a part of something important in a way she never had before, and she resented having to give that up.

Apart from her personal feelings on the matter, there was another factor to consider. As with her parents, every relationship Ellie had was yet another pressure point Aimie could use to control her. This made everyone she knew a potential target. Isolating herself from others as much as possible might not entirely eliminate the threat, but it was the right thing to do. She cared about Shanna, Teri—even Brett—too much to knowingly put them in Aimie's crosshairs.

There was no way around it. As much as she hated the thought, she knew what she had to do.

20

E llie's mood was finally better on Tuesday. Nevertheless, she was grateful for the distraction that having to spend the first half of the day at school provided. Not only was she still anxious following the past two days' encounters with Aimie, but her decision to quit her work with the PEEC saddened her. She knew it was the right move, though, and hoped that everything she would learn working with Jeremy would make the sacrifice worthwhile in the long run.

She found it increasingly challenging to stay focused at school, especially when it came to what she considered to be the "fluffier" subjects, like Spanish and Contemporary Lit. Her World History class was up to Newton publishing his *Principia Mathematica*. Under normal circumstances, this would have kept her totally engaged, but she had left normal so far behind her that she didn't think she'd be able to see it even with the Hubble telescope.

In contrast, finally being free to shed the pretense that she and Aaron were on the outs was a huge relief. Starting yesterday with the first class they shared, they resumed sitting side by side. Plus, as they were doing now, they ate together at lunch. Although she couldn't say what having him actively in her life once more would mean in the long run, she knew she was now open to any and all possibilities. They hadn't kissed again since that night up at Ryan's, but she was giving the idea of a repeat performance a lot of thought. A *lot* of thought.

As a rule, Ellie paid no attention to what other people thought of her, but sometimes their opinions were too obvious for even her to ignore. Today's unfortunate choice of cafeteria seats placed all three J-birds directly in her line of sight, and there was no doubt about who was the topic of their conversation. Even from four tables away, their annoyed, bewildered expressions made it perfectly clear precisely how they regarded the idea of her and Aaron suddenly being a thing. Without even trying, she had thrown their petty, insular little world into turmoil.

I so don't care!

She glanced at Aaron before returning her attention to the final few bites of her meal. Then, with sudden shock, she realized that she *did* care. Or used to. Had cared deeply, in fact, right up until that very second. But now, still anxiously anticipating her upcoming conversation with Shanna, feeling overwhelmed by the magnitude of the responsibility they were considering taking on, nothing happening around her seemed the least bit important. No, she was far from being hurt or offended by the J-birds' unwanted attention; she was amused.

The memory of an event from a couple of weeks ago replayed itself in her mind. Hearing Jordan gossip about Aaron that day had torn at her heart, but recalling the incident now, she felt nothing and found that realization liberating. But that wasn't quite true, either. She did feel something—she felt it was time for a little payback! She balled up her napkin, tossed it into the middle of her tray, and stood so abruptly that Aaron jerked in surprise.

Ellie looked down at his quizzical expression. "I'll be right back."

She pitched her trash, dropped her dishes into the rack, and added her tray to the stack of others waiting to be washed. Choosing a route back to Aaron that would take her by the J-birds, she began threading her way between the tables. Standing behind them, as yet unnoticed, she saw Aaron watching her, his head slightly cocked to one side like a curious puppy's. She smiled at him and winked, then returned her attention to the three oblivious girls.

"Hey," she said, drawing their attention at last.

Jordan and Jessica turned to face her. Julia simply pretended Ellie wasn't there, choosing instead to busy herself with slowly and methodically wiping each finger of both hands with a napkin. Ellie figured the task probably did require most of her brain power.

"Yes?" Jordan prompted.

"Oh, nothing much. I just remembered something, that's all. You guys in the hall... about a month back... talking about a particular someone. Know who I mean?" Jessica, who had not been there, shook her head and squinted up at Ellie in genuine confusion. Jordan, on the other hand, couldn't stop her eyes from flicking briefly toward Aaron.

"Good," Ellie said, and she gave her a phony, aren't-you-so-smart smile. "I came over because I wanted to set the record straight about one tiny thing." She laughed as if tremendously amused by her own words. "I say 'tiny,' but that is definitely *not* the right adjective!"

"Yeah? So what is it?" Jessica said, trying to sound bored and failing. Experiencing a rare moment of wisdom, Jordan kept her mouth shut, but Ellie saw her swallow hard.

Ellie leaned forward as if preparing to divulge top-secret information. Curious in spite of themselves, Jordan and Jessica mirrored her forward tilt. Julia froze in mid-wipe, the napkin wrapped around her right pinky, as she, too, waited breathlessly for whatever came next. Ellie kept her eyes fixed on Jordan while she delivered her message in low, confidential tones.

"I thought you'd be interested to learn that it's surprisingly *dark*, actually. You know—'down there.'" She grinned gleefully the entire way back to her place beside Aaron, knowing Jordan's shocked expression was something she'd remember with joy for the rest of her life.

"What was that all about?" Aaron said as she settled into her seat beside him.

"Just a little revenge," she said, her eyes still fixed on Jordan. "Oh, and just so you know? We've had sex."

"Oh. Okay. Did I enjoy it?"

She turned to face him and cocked an eyebrow. "We didn't get into that, but is there any reason to think you wouldn't?"

"*Umm...* no?"

"You better believe it, buddy!"

"Are you ever going to tell me what's going on?"

"Maybe. Probably. Someday. Right now, this is too much fun."

She sat there grinning, feeling quite pleased with herself, but she didn't get to enjoy the feeling for long. Her mind was still reeling from everything they had learned on Sunday afternoon. Having come to terms with the emotional burden Aimie's revelations had placed on her, she could now concentrate on how to deal with whatever might lay ahead. Jeremy had shown them an operation that exceeded her expectations in almost every way, but contrary to her hopes, each new answer they learned only led to even more questions.

"Did your dad...? *Whoops!* Sorry. Never mind."

"Did my dad what?" Aaron said, not never-minding.

"I was about to ask if the old Jeremy's lab had anything like the prop shop or the costume closet. Sorry."

"No. Actually, I think this means we're making progress if you can't remember which of me is which."

"The locker room was interesting. Bigger than I would have expected. How many lockers were in there? Did you notice?"

"Twenty. Six down each side, two sets of four along the back wall."

"*Hmm....* Seems like a lot. I guess the number of different specialties could get pretty high, though. Or maybe sometimes you'd need all women on a team. Or all men." A new thought popped into her head. "*Or...* or there could even be multiple teams working at the same time. It's not that the *people* can't stay in the past for more than a few hours; it's only the TSD that can't. At least the old one couldn't. But it *could* be used as a sort of shuttle—drop a group off and pick them up a week or a month later. *Ooh!* You know what's weird? You could drop someone off, and as soon as he's out of the TSD, set it for two weeks later and pick him up right away. He'd be two weeks older, but for you, it'd only be, like, two *minutes!* Can you imagine being gone for a month, but when you get back, only a few seconds have gone by for everyone else?"

Aaron shook his head. "That *is* weird. I guess people would have to avoid going on too many long missions. A guy could leave the house clean-shaven in the morning and come back that night with a full beard.

That would be tough enough to explain, but if he came back looking years older?"

Long missions? Stay in the past? She was reminded of the plan she and A-Ron had once discussed and then quickly discarded for being too risky. Was there something useful there after all? Could she and this Aaron go back in time and change things enough so that Sam would be safe? Could that even work?

Then she remembered her vow to carry out any plan she came up with alone. She was stunned by how much simply thinking about living a life without Aaron hurt, but she owed him his chance at whatever future this timeline held in store for him. She silently repeated her commitment to bear the consequences of her prior bad decisions all on her own.

Time to change the subject. "Those diamond batteries. You'd heard of those before yesterday, hadn't you?"

"Yeah, but only as vapor— Hey, what's up? Your mind is bouncing all over the place today."

"I don't know. I can't stop it. There was so much—"

The end-of-lunch bell sounded, and Ellie waited it out silently while Aaron wadded up his napkin and tidied his tray.

"—so much that was different from what I thought we'd see. I think I was expecting... I don't know what I was expecting. Something more obviously evil, I guess."

"Having second thoughts? You know, about working with them?"

She talked to his back as she followed him to the tray return. "It feels like all I have are second thoughts! And *third* thoughts. But no, I still think that's the best thing to do."

They inched forward until Aaron could slide his tray onto the counter, then they headed for the exit.

"You said the 'best' thing," he said. "Do you think it's the *right* thing?"

Ellie remained silent until they exited the cafeteria and turned left into the hallway. "I don't know. I just... don't... know."

"Well, I might be onto something, but it's still too early to know what it means or if it will help."

"Really? Like what?"

"I noticed something weird on the quantum processor yesterday. At least, I think it's weird. It's hard to tell with that thing, but it looks too strange for it not to be something. I'm still trying to figure out how to get it out of the lab so I can poke around at it. I hope I'll know more by tomorrow."

"Good luck. I'm feeling extremely data-deprived."

Later, as Ellie passed through the Nature Center lobby, she cast a sidelong glance at its newest exhibit. She was very proud of how it had turned out but felt that standing there and watching it made her appear vain, so she mostly ignored it. Today, poised on the brink of massive change, every-thing felt different. Instead of heading down the hall, she veered off course and stopped directly in front of the large LED display.

She watched in silence as it cycled through its sequence of eleven slides. There was one graphic with which she was especially pleased. In addition to comparing solar power generation to the output of fossil fuel plants, she had decided to show the number of currently installed square meters of photovoltaic panels per resident. Knowing New Mexico's popu-lation and the average amount of electricity a typical resident used, it was easy to calculate how many square meters of panels it would take to supply clean solar power for everyone. Although it ignored the energy consumption of businesses and industry, it brought the abstract concept of solar power down to a personally relatable level.

"Yep! You done good, girl." It was Teri on her way out at the end of her workday. She crossed the exhibit hall to stand at Ellie's side. Teri, like many other of the center's staff, had switched from wearing a logoed tee to a warmer, if much baggier, sweatshirt.

"Thanks. I hadn't watched it since the day we installed it out here." She was quiet for a moment as she tried to come up with a way to express her appreciation for all the time they had spent working together without it coming across like some big deal. "I enjoy working with you. It was helping you with that Pueblo green energy project of yours that made me think of this, you know."

"I did not know. That's cool! I feel a little young to be inspiring the next generation, though."

"I don't know; you're what, ten years older than me? That's pretty ancient!"

"Fun fact—dissin' your elders is considered rude in most cultures."

Ellie laughed. Teri's sense of humor was one of the best parts of working with her. That and the fact that she was as smart as multiple whips. A sudden wave of sadness washed over her, and she had to fight to smile her way through it and keep the mood light. "Clocking out *already?*"

"Yup. Another day, another dollar, and I'm outta here."

"A whole *dollar?!* Okay, now you're just bragging," Ellie said, a reminder that her own position was a volunteer one.

Teri cocked an eyebrow. "In case you haven't figured it out by now, take it from me; no one goes into climate science for fame and fortune."

"Another nugget of wisdom for the next generation?"

Teri winked and pointed a finger at her. "Don't say you were never warned. Well, I gotta go. See ya'!"

Ellie watched Teri push through the large glass doors and disappear down the walk. "I guess we'll have to wait and see about that," she said.

The next four hours crawled by. She glanced at the clock at what felt like half-hour intervals to find that only five or ten minutes had passed. She shook her head in frustration.

Seriously?! Piñons grow faster than this!

Her tasks today were repetitive and mundane, not nearly engaging enough to keep her mind off her various problems. Her stomach had felt so upset all day that she had chosen not to eat the sandwich she had brought for dinner. Now, as she neared the end of her shift, she was regretting that decision.

What bothered her most was how little they still knew, even after the tour. There was definitely a new shack, or "TSD," and Ellie had to count that confirmation as a major step forward. On the other hand, Aimie said she had a plan, but aside from the broadest of strokes, they knew nothing about it. Why hadn't they already started implementing it? And why had Aaron been recruited so early, while she, Sam, and Ryan were being brought in only now and seemingly as an afterthought?

She recalled hearing Ryan's father once say he believed that every military failure was ultimately a failure of intelligence. He had wrapped up by saying, "During any operation, there's nothing more important than maintaining a constant awareness of your knowledge gaps."

Well, mission accomplished.

Aimie was their widest knowledge gap; there was no question about that. "A synthetic intelligence inhabiting a quantum processor," she had said. Every time Ellie thought about that phrase, she felt the hairs on the back of her neck stand at attention. Something important was tangled up in there, but she had yet to tease it free. Yesterday's demonstrations of the extent of Aimie's reach were worrisome, but they only confirmed what she'd already guessed—an AI that advanced could cause them some major headaches. They would have to be extra careful not to provoke her while they tried to determine whether or not she and Jeremy were indeed playing it straight with them.

As the minute hand crept slowly past seven thirty, her mind focused increasingly on a more immediate concern. At five minutes before eight, she shut everything down and walked to Shanna's office. Peering through her open door, she saw Shanna leaning back in her chair, staring intently at her monitor. Ellie couldn't tell if she was reading something or merely deep in thought.

After a moment, Shanna spoke without taking her eyes off the screen. "Heading home?"

Ellie hesitated, teetered momentarily on the edge of saying "good night" and just walking away, but found she couldn't. "Actually, I was hoping you'd have a few minutes to talk."

Ellie didn't know what Shanna heard in her tone, but her eyes snapped away from the monitor, and she sat up straight, her expression abruptly tight with concern. "Of course! Come on in."

Ellie entered the small space and took her usual spot in the chair beside Shanna's desk.

"What's up?" Shanna said.

"I want to ask you something, and I need the absolute truth."

"What is it?"

"The planet. It's in pretty bad shape, isn't it? The climate, I mean."

"Yes." Shanna took a deep breath, then let it out. "Practically every-one's pretending like it's not, but yes, it is. Sixty, eighty years from now, things are going to be very, very tough."

Ellie pressed her to be more specific. "So, what exactly are we talking about? Disease? Starvation?"

"Disease, starvation, unprecedented population displacements, a collapse of governments at all levels, civil unrest… probably little wars all over the place. Maybe even some big ones."

"How do we fix it?"

"We don't. Not at this late date. All we can do is try to lessen the severity as much as we can. And we can make some arrangements for how we come out of it at the other end."

"Come out?"

"Have you read much about the Black Death?"

Ellie nodded. "A little. We covered that in World History last month."

"Then you know that perhaps sixty percent of Europeans died over a four-year period. As many as 200 million people across all of Eurasia died, and the population before the plague was *at most* 500 million. It was a period of unimaginable suffering, social upheaval, and death, all at a time when medical care was, by our standards, nonexistent. But it eventually ended, basically on its own. And then, a mere fifty years later? The Renais-sance! If we can find ways to safeguard our knowledge, our ideals, and our compassion for one another, if we can keep all of that protected through what's to come, we humans might be in a much better position to get it all right the next time around."

Ellie thought about seed banks and pictured similar, knowledge-filled time capsules awaiting discovery after the population had stabilized at its new sustainable level. Would people truly learn anything following such an ordeal? They had better—the alternative was too awful to consider.

Not at this late date, Shanna had said. *If not now…*

"When? When should we have started taking it all more seriously? When was it *not* too late?"

"The late sixties, maybe. Perhaps a little later. It depends on what kinds of approaches were taken back then. Technology is part of it, but honestly? We'd be okay the way things are if we had only a third of the population, even assuming that the US example, one of the most wasteful, was adopted worldwide. But population control is a real no-go area, politically.

"In the sixties and seventies, you begin to see energy alternatives that could have made a difference, but they didn't catch on early or widely enough, or they weren't ready soon enough to do any good. Those that had any real chance of succeeding were often marginalized by larger, wealthier industries that could afford to do whatever it took to maintain their advantage."

Ellie considered everything Shanna said. Hearing Aimie's depiction of the future confirmed came as a surprising relief. If she wasn't lying about that, maybe she was telling the truth about other things, too. Mostly, however, she found everything Shanna said depressing. Once again, her mind flashed to her and Aaron's old plan. If it ultimately came to that, could she bring herself to do it? It seemed like a question worth pursuing.

"So, if you could somehow travel back to that time and try to change things so that solar and wind power *did* catch on faster, that fossil fuels were phased out earlier…. If doing that meant never seeing your daughter again, would you?"

Shanna answered without hesitation. "Absolutely. If I could prevent her and her kids from having to endure what's to come, I'd go this instant. Because it's not just about her, but the potentially billions of other lives that will be destroyed in the decades to come." As if the mood had become too serious, she gave Ellie a sly smile. "Why? Do you have a time machine tucked away in your basement or something?"

So close, Ellie thought. Then a new idea occurred to her. "Do you know a guy, works at the LAB, named Jeremy Siskin?"

"Vaguely. He's on our board, so I've run into him once or twice. Why?"

"Oh, just curious." She tried to sound nonchalant, even as she felt her heart suddenly gripped by an icy hand. *I read up on the staff, but not the board!* "He gave a green building talk in Mrs. Carson's class, so I figured you might."

"Wait a sec." Looking as if Ellie's question had triggered a memory, Shanna turned to her computer and brought up Outlook. Ellie stood to watch as Shanna typed two words into the email program's search bar. She shuddered when she read them.

Siskin Ellie

Shanna hit the Return key and scanned down the list of matches. "Yes, here it is! I got an email from Janice—that's Mrs. Carson to you—letting me know she was sending you over. This was way back in September, when you came to talk to me about your paper. She said Dr. Siskin had written to her and said some very nice things about you. Here we go." Her finger traced a line of text as she read from the screen. "She wrote that he said, 'Keep an eye on this one. In time, she's going to go places!'"

No! Ellie's mind wailed. She felt the cold hand squeeze, and the room began to spin around her. Shanna's next words came to her as if from a very long way away.

"You're looking pretty green there, kiddo."

Ellie briefly sensed an intense flurry of motion, then nothing.

It took a moment for Ellie to recognize what she was seeing—the toes of her own shoes, and from not very far away. She was leaning forward in a chair, her head dangling between her knees, staring straight down at her feet. She remained as she was, figuring that was safest until she managed to work out why this should be so.

Now she could feel a warm hand resting lightly on her back, and from the corner of her eye, she saw the legs of someone kneeling beside her. Then she heard a voice.

"Deep breaths. That's it."

Shanna's voice, so that was good. Too foggy-brained to do more than follow simple directions, she drew in a long, restorative breath. Exhaling slowly, she started to remember where she was: Shanna's office, the chair by her desk. They had been talking about—*Jeremy!* Her head cleared in a heartbeat.

"I'm okay, I think." She gingerly eased herself upright. "Sorry. I don't know what that was all about," she lied, and immediately felt bad about it.

Shanna remained crouched beside her, studying her face. Although Ellie's paranoia had just skyrocketed to stratospheric levels, she had no doubt that the expression of concern the woman wore was genuine.

Ellie managed a weak smile. "I guess I shouldn't have skipped dinner. Really—I'm okay." She really wasn't.

"Stay there. I'll be right back." Shanna stood and strode briskly from the office.

Ellie hung her head again and fought the urge to be sick. Discovering that Aimie's tendrils penetrated this far into her life, that they had for some time, felt like another punch to the gut. And knowing what the AI was capable of, she was almost certain it had been Aimie, not Jeremy, who had sent the email to Mrs. Carson. She simply didn't consider him capable of such subtle social engineering. Besides, he had seemed genuinely unconcerned with her existence right up to the moment they met during his lecture, long after she had first met with Shanna. She had no time to pursue the matter further before Shanna was back from the break room with a large glass of cold water.

"Sip on this," Shanna said.

Again, Ellie mutely complied. She felt the icy chill of the first frigid gulp hit her empty stomach and spread outward. To her surprise, it did make her feel better. She took another, larger swallow. "Thanks for not letting me crack my head on the floor."

Shanna laughed. "It was closer than you might want to know! I was barely able to get you back into that chair when your knees buckled." Her expression turned serious. "You ready to talk about what's bothering you yet?"

I wish I could!

For the first time in her life, Ellie experienced being alone as a burdensome thing, a massive weight threatening to crush her resolve. Going solo had never bothered her before, but never before had she been so vulnerable. If she had any real hope Shanna could help, she knew she would tell her about everything—the shack, Jeremy and Aimie, the new TSD—all of it. In truth, she'd only be putting her in danger, which was exactly what she was trying to avoid. She had hoped that quitting her work at the PEEC might keep her coworkers from becoming the subject of Aimie's attention, but finding out about the email to Mrs. Carson made her fear it was already too late.

Ellie shook her head and sighed. "I can't explain why, but I have to quit working here. I know you only want to help, but trust me—I'm doing you a favor by not saying anything more than that. The best thing you can do for me, for *both* of us, actually, is not talk about any part of this conversation with anyone. Not in person, not on the phone, not by email. And not even with Mrs. Carson, okay? I know that sounds totally melodramatic, probably even paranoid, but I have some very important things to work out, and certain people having any idea what I'm thinking could totally mess it all up. Will you do this for me?" She pointed at Shanna's computer. "If you'd drop me from the schedule and not make a big deal about it to anybody, that'd be great. Please? If Teri asks, you can tell her I got too busy at school."

Different emotions played across Shanna's face as she considered Ellie's request. At last, her expression settled into a soft smile. Instead of speaking, she held out her right fist, her little finger extended to make a small hook. For a second, Ellie was startled by the familiar yet wholly unexpected gesture, but then she smiled back.

"Sorry," Shanna said, belatedly recognizing the absurdity of the childhood ritual. "Reflex. This is still how we handle the most important stuff in our house."

Being reminded of meeting Aisling made Ellie smile. "Not at all," she said. She slipped her own pinky around Shanna's, and they shook while exchanging solemn nods. When she stood, Shanna rose to stand facing her.

"I've got to go," Ellie said.

"Are you okay to get home? I think I should drive you."

"No, I'm totally fine now. I am, I swear. And thanks for the talk earlier. You've given me a lot to think about. And I'm sorry. I hate to do this to you, not give you any notice and all, but this is, um," she swallowed hard, "probably the last time you'll see me. At least until I get some other things worked out."

Caught off guard, Shanna reflexively offered Ellie her hand, and they briefly shook. "I certainly hope it's not."

Ellie, fighting hard to keep her composure, could only nod in reply. Eager to be away, she pivoted and took a step toward the door.

"Ellie?"

Unable to resist the impulse, Ellie turned to see Shanna standing with her arms stretched out toward her. Without thinking, she threw herself into them, and tears flooded her eyes. She felt a hand stroke through her hair, and she tightened her arms around the woman she so admired.

"Hey," Shanna said. "Whatever's going on, I know you can handle it. But if you do need help, I'll be here."

After a moment, Ellie pulled herself together, sniffed at some remaining tears, and stepped back. This time she held out both her hands, and Shanna took them. They stood that way for a moment, looking into each other's eyes.

"Thank you," Ellie said at last. "For everything."

"You're sure you'll be okay getting home?" Ellie nodded. "Well, when you get everything sorted out, please come back, okay?"

"If I can, I will. Count on it!"

Ellie let herself out through the front door, making sure it closed securely behind her, then walked to where her bike was chained up along the side of the building. She knelt near the rear wheel and reached for the lock, then changed her mind. Instead of removing the chain, she stood and walked back the way she had come, passing by the entrance and continuing across the garden until she reached the metal fence along the cliff's edge. She rested her arms on the top rail and stared down into the back pit of Pueblo Canyon.

She found nothing but consensus everywhere she looked—the climate truly was poised at the edge of collapse. Shanna, Aimie, and every leading scientist all agreed that humanity was about to experience a global catastrophe on an unprecedented scale. Aimie's presence alone was proof enough of how bad it would get. The epidemics may or may not happen, but given that the TSD still hadn't been put to use, she figured that the current timeline was still much as it had been for her future self at this same point. Therefore, she was willing to believe that the arrival of those diseases was only a matter of time.

She pulled her eyes out of the black abyss and looked across the canyon to the lights on its far side. At least one of those distant glimmers, she knew, came from her own house. Her mom and dad were there for sure, and probably Sam too. She imagined them all sitting in the living room together, Sam and her mom watching some goofy TV show, her dad with his nose in a book. He'd be doing his best to block out the noise from their program, but not the music of their laughter. Her heart felt so full of love for them that it actually ached.

Going through with her plan would change all that. The longer they worked with Aimie, the more secret would pile upon secret, resulting in an ever-growing number of experiences she and Sam could never share. Their relationship with their parents, already altered by the events in June, would never feel the same.

As she pulled her phone from her pocket and brought the device to life, dread thrummed through her like an electric current. Sometimes a person didn't know when her path took a dramatic turn. Often, the moment could only be identified years later with the clarity of hindsight. This was not one of those times. She was fully aware of how her next few words would change her life and the lives of everyone around her forever.

Her phone opened to the messaging app, and her conversation with Aaron was already at the top. For a moment, she stood still, staring at the screen. This was all way too easy. She tapped into the text window, and the keyboard slid up into view. She began typing before she lost her nerve, carefully choosing her words as if Aimie were watching over her shoulder.

> Ellie—Hi. Learn any fun new facts today?

> Aaron—Nope. Nothing

> Ellie—So?

> Aaron—Still think we're good this way

> Ellie—Ok. Then tell them we're in

The delay before his next message was brief.

> Aaron—Okay. It's done. I'll let the others know too

Ellie waited while he passed the news along to Sam and Ryan. After a minute, she could tell he was typing to her again.

> Aaron—Are you okay?

> Ellie—No

> Aaron—Do you want to come by here?

She stared at the lights across the canyon before replying, picturing her family once more.

> Ellie—Thx, but I really need to be home tonight

> Aaron—K. I get it

She pocketed her phone and walked back to her bike. As she was stuffing the chain into a pouch below the saddle, she felt her phone buzz.

> Aaron—J wants us there tomorrow afternoon. Orientation, he said. Ryan says 4:30 is good with them. Ok with u?

> Ellie—That works

And just like that, off we go.

21

Ellie woke early, despite having been awake for at least half the night. Aimie's demonstrations of her ability to affect events beyond the confines of Jeremy's lab had left her agitated when awake, invaded her dreams whenever she managed to drift into sleep. Her thoughts still sluggish, she slid out of bed an hour earlier than usual and padded out to the kitchen to make coffee.

She stopped in the doorway and waited silently while her parents prepared to leave for work. Leaning against the jamb, she watched as her mom held her silver thermos over the sink and poured in the remainder of the morning's coffee from a tall, ceramic mug. Meanwhile, her dad gathered their breakfast dishes and placed them in the washer. When he turned around, he saw her standing there and smiled.

"Good morning, bright eyes!"

"Hey, Dad. Mom."

Her mom glanced quickly over her shoulder as she shook the mug to dislodge the last few drops. "Hi, sweetie. You're up early."

"Yeah. Didn't sleep very well." She spoke over a sudden yawn that underscored her point.

"Everything okay?" her dad said.

"I'm fine, Dad."

"I know you don't need me to say it, but it's okay to make this an 'A-minus' day," he said, using her own code for slacking off.

Ellie laughed. "I don't feel *that* bad!"

He paused as he passed her on his way out of the kitchen and leaned forward to plant a kiss on her forehead. "Love you."

"Love you too, Dad."

Her mom followed him to the garage door and started closing it behind her, but turned around instead.

"Hey, El? If you were still worried about that bank thing from Monday, don't be. We got a call from the mortgage company last night saying everything's fine."

"Really? What time?"

"Eight fifteenish, maybe?" Then her mom squinted at her, puzzled by the question. "Why does that matter?"

"Huh?" Ellie realized too late that, absent her assumptions about Aimie's involvement, asking about the time made no sense. "Oh, I guess it doesn't. Like I said, I'm too tired to think straight."

"Maybe you should give your brain a little jump-start." Her mom raised her mug of coffee and winked. "Bottom line? It was a glitch, just like you said. Have a great day!"

Ellie smiled to show what good news she thought that was. "You, too, Mom. See ya tonight."

As soon as her mom closed the door, the smile slipped from Ellie's face. It wasn't good news, not at all. She had sent her message to Aaron a little after eight o'clock, and he had told Jeremy they had decided to work with them right after that. Instead of being a relief, the timing of the call was final proof that Aimie truly had been behind the "glitch" the entire time. She realized she'd have to be even more cautious when dealing with the AI than she'd originally thought.

But first, coffee!

The walk to school was quieter than usual. Aimie's threats on Monday continued to dominate Ellie's thoughts. She knew she should tell Sam but feared her reaction. Sam quickly became as fierce as any bobcat on the plateau when someone she cared about was threatened, and Ellie needed her at her most charming when they dealt with Jeremy and Aimie in the afternoon. Later, after they had learned more about what they were dealing with, she'd let everyone know how dangerous Aimie could be. In the meantime, she couldn't think of anything to say, and it wasn't until they had crossed the footbridge at the bottom of the ravine that either of them finally spoke.

"How are you feeling about all this, Sam?"

"I dunno. Mostly, I feel like I'm just along for the ride. I guess we'll know more by tonight. Is there something particular we're after today?"

"I don't think we know enough yet to know what we don't know. Or even what we need to know."

"Uh-oh! When you start sounding like me, I know we're in deep doo-doo!"

Ellie laughed. "I want to get as much of the big picture as possible. I'm sure we'll have a chance to ask questions, but nothing says they have to tell the truth. Or answer at all, for that matter. Overall, though, I'm starting to feel better about this whole thing. Us working with them, I mean. Remember what it was like being in Brooklyn? We could get to see lots of places and at a lot of different times."

"Yeah. It's still hard to believe all that happened. One day we're wandering around New York in 1941, in our cute little berets and all, and the next, I'm back working at the pool. I wish we had known what was really going on when we were in Lawrence, too, but mostly I'm glad I didn't know at the time Ryan's heart had actually stopped."

Ellie pictured Ryan lying on his back in the middle of the street, Sam and Aaron kneeling on either side of his inert body. She remembered them pulling his heavy coat and shirt open so Sam could start CPR. She had somehow known, despite still believing they were deeply immersed in an artificial environment, that Ryan was truly dead, but she had been too busy dealing with a mob of angry mill workers to experience the full emotional impact of that knowledge. That attack was the first significant consequence of her insistence that they enter and then actually use the shack, and it was another subject she'd rather not discuss at the moment. To her relief, Sam moved on to a different topic.

"But we're supposed to be the conscience of the project, right?" Sam said. "That doesn't sound like a job that requires us actually going anywhere."

Ellie gave that a moment's thought. "It could, I suppose. There are a few parts I can imagine us playing, even at our ages—aides to lobbyists, members of campus activist groups, that sort of thing. They won't waste four seats on all of us each time, but maybe one or two of us. That's one thing we can ask about today."

"I don't like the thought of only some of us going. It makes my stomach clench. If Ryan went off on a mission and something changed so that I didn't know him when he got back, I get that *I* wouldn't know the difference, but it would kill him." Realizing what she'd said, she gasped. "I'm sorry, El. I guess you know exactly what that's like, huh?"

"Yeah, well, I got lucky as far as that goes. But speaking of, when Aaron first came to us and said he wanted to help, you seemed to have doubts about him. Do you still feel that way?"

"Yes and no. I mean, I didn't think he was lying or anything. At the time, I thought Ryan needed reminding that he isn't the same guy we knew, that's all. I still think it's important to remember that, but I also believe he really is on our side. I don't doubt that one bit."

"Okay." Ellie nodded slowly. "Good. I know I said some harsh things about him when I was angry with him, but I trust him completely."

Sam grinned, a playful glint in her eyes. "And not just because he's a good kisser?"

Ellie grinned back. "He definitely is! Of course, I am basing that assessment on an extremely small sample size."

"Yes, but now you know exactly how to deal with that."

They finished the thought together. "*Experiment!*"

As she finished her last bite of lunch, Ellie scanned the cafeteria and was relieved to find the J-birds were nowhere in sight. She considered this to be good, but that didn't stop her from wondering where they were. Perhaps they had decided to eat at the sandwich shop across the street rather than be forced to watch her and Aaron sit together. That was fine with her, but she preferred to hope they were in lunchtime detention instead, being punished for some transgression resulting from having a collective IQ mired deep in the low double-digits.

She returned her attention to Aaron as he balled up his napkin and tossed it into the middle of his tray. When they first sat down together, she thanked him again for helping her feel so much better the day before, and then they hardly spoke for the next twenty minutes. That would not have seemed unusual, except they had so much to talk about. Her repeated attempts to engage him in conversation resulted in monosyllabic answers, little more than grunts, and she quickly gave up.

"You've been very quiet," Ellie said at last.

"Yeah, sorry. I've been thinking about what they've told us so far, and I can't get it to work out."

"You don't think their plan could work?"

"I don't know. Okay, if we go back and change certain parts of the past, then why...? I mean, how does that...? Never mind. I think I can't work out the answer because I don't even know what the question is yet."

"Forty-two," Ellie said.

Aaron snickered. "Yes, exactly. It doesn't feel right somehow, and I'm trying to work out why. But you believe it could, right?"

"I know that whoever looks at that book I showed you at Ryan's thinks four kids who look remarkably like us were in that Lawrence park with Carmela Teoli. I also know Mom and Dad never met you until this September, despite me remembering you all the way back to 2012." She laughed. "Better make that 1912!"

"Yeah," Aaron said, "I get it on a case-by-case basis. But can we keep going back over and over again, constantly tweaking things, without everything eventually falling apart? Or becoming unrecognizable? I'd hate for you guys to end up just like me. And what about the people whose lives get changed? If they start having bizarre memories like Jeremy and I did, we'll have created a huge mental health crisis."

The end-of-lunch bell rang, and she used the time to consider the second part of Aaron's question. She pulled his tray toward her, added its contents to her own, then slid it underneath.

"I don't think that'll be a problem. Mom and Dad have never said anything like, 'That Aaron seems familiar for some reason,' know what I mean? Some of their memories are different from mine and Sam's, yeah, but they seem to have only one set of them. I think you and Jeremy are special cases because you two got, um, 'reset,' I guess. But that's definitely something to think about."

She rose, picked up their trays, and began weaving her way across the cafeteria with Aaron at her side. "Actually, I've been thinking about things falling apart too. Shanna said the world needed to be on a different course by no later than the early seventies. What if that's when they focused all their efforts? What if they could shift policy away from cheap oil and toward sustainable generation? Wind, solar, even nuclear, if it's done right. Could working only in years closer to now still create enough of an effect to make things better without causing as many unnecessary changes?" She slid their trays through the window, and together they headed for the exit.

"You're talking about limiting the amount of divergence," he said.

"Exactly. They'd need to make bigger changes, but the ripple effect should be smaller. There's less time for the ripples to spread, so fewer people will be affected."

"But can we persuade them of that? Aimie seems pretty convinced her way is the only way."

Ellie shrugged. "It can't hurt to ask. But if they're serious about us having the final say on what gets done, they'll have to go along."

Ellie saw Mrs. Carson glance her way when she entered the classroom. To her relief, nothing in the woman's expression suggested she knew of her decision to leave the PEEC. She merely smiled, then returned her attention to the papers on her desk. Ellie was glad Shanna was giving her time in which to act, but she resented how she now felt it was safer to keep nearly everyone she knew at a distance.

Once class started, however, she was soon distracted from her concerns by the uncanny relevance of the day's topic. First, she was disappointed to learn how energy policies enacted in the seventies, many in response to the 1973 oil crisis, were steadily rolled back in the eighties.

Any plans to embrace a managed energy program were abandoned in favor of relinquishing control of pricing and sources to the whims of the open market.

Next, she was angered not only by the Reagan administration's attack on the Department of Energy's renewable energy programs but also by the decision not to reinstall the solar panels that were removed from atop the White House in 1986 to accommodate roof maintenance. They hadn't been very efficient by today's standards, but even so, the combination of hot water and photovoltaic panels had eliminated more than 26,000 tons of carbon dioxide from the air annually for the seven years they were in use.

She didn't get it—why was it that people in the position to set an example so often chose to set the wrong one?

Today it was Aaron's turn to drive. After pedaling home to get his dad's van, he returned fifteen minutes later to the university commuter lot, where Ellie sat waiting on a low, concrete wall. Sam and Ryan, only now getting out of class, waved as they approached from the lot's far side. Ellie climbed into the front next to Aaron, and they waited.

"Hey. How was physics?"

"Eh. Centripetal force, centripetal acceleration."

"What's the 'A' in 'AP' stand for again?"

Aaron scoffed. "Seriously! That's just the lab, though. We're also talking about Heisenberg's S-matrix ideas."

"Okay, so *that's* cooler. String theory, comin' up!"

Ryan tugged on the sliding door's outer handle, and it slowly crawled open under its own power, squealing loudly in its track. He let Sam scoot to the far end of the middle bench before sliding in beside her. He gave the inside handle a flick and watched as the automatic door noisily eased itself closed.

"That might have been cool once upon a time, but man, is it slow!"

Once the door clunked shut, Aaron headed for the parking lot exit.

"I assume today is more of the same as on Sunday," Ryan said. "Learn all we can while trying to find out if they're lying to us?"

Aaron answered while he waited for an ancient Saab to go by. "Jeremy said today is some kind of orientation, so I'm guessing we'll find out a lot," he said, then he pulled out of the lot onto Diamond Drive.

"Remember," Ellie said. "Aimie can see and hear everything that goes on, so if you notice anything, keep it to yourself until we're out of there. As long as we're in the lab, it's all... What did you say, Sam? 'Rainbow farms and bunny ranches?'"

Aaron took his eyes off the road long enough to give Ellie a puzzled look.

"Isn't the Bunny Ranch a, you know, like, a prostitution place?"

Sam crossed her arms over her chest and rolled her eyes. "Oh, geez. *Men!*"

22

When they stopped at the guard shelter, one guard peered in through the windows along the driver's side but did not otherwise inspect the van's interior. He gave a signal, the guard inside the booth hit a button, and the inner gate rumbled out of the way. When it stopped, the first guard waved them through and then rejoined his buddy in the small outbuilding.

"So, no escort this time," Ryan noted.

Ellie glanced at him over her shoulder, and even though he was being careful not to be obvious about it, she could tell he was again examining every detail of their surroundings. Which of the guards seemed more alert? How far from the gate to the entrance? How many cars were in front of the building? Where were they parked? Were there lights on the building's exterior? Cameras? If so, how many and where? She didn't bother. When it came to matters of potentially tactical concern, she knew they could rely on his eyes to gather whatever facts they might need.

Ryan leaned forward between the front seats. "Park right in front of the door."

"But that's..." Aaron pointed to indicate how the blacktop outside the door was marked with diagonal stripes to create a no-parking zone. The nearest actual, defined parking spot was thirty feet to the right. "That's for deliveries, not for people working here."

Ryan dismissed his objection. "Yeah, yeah, yeah. But let's see what those guys do. Take your time getting out and going inside. See if anyone makes a fuss about us parking there."

Aaron shrugged, parked close to the lab's entrance, and everyone slowly exited the van. Ellie closed her door and stood still, watching Sam slide across the seat and step out to stand beside her. Clasping his hands together and reaching them high over his head, Ryan made a show of taking a languorous stretch as if they had just completed a cross-country road trip instead of a drive of not even three miles. Ellie snuck a furtive look at the guard booth and saw that neither man on duty was paying them the slightest bit of attention.

Ryan dropped his arms to his sides. "Well, that's good to know. Okay, let's go in."

Aaron let the panel scan his palm, then entered his four-digit code. The lock clicked, and he held the door open for the others. As soon as the door had locked behind them, Aimie spoke from overhead.

"It's four twenty-nine, and here you are. Excellent! Everyone is already assembled in the conference room. Aaron, please lead the others back."

"C'mon," Aaron said, guiding them left to where a second locked door blocked their way. "My passcode gets me almost everywhere now."

Sam and Ryan followed him, but Ellie remained in place. She scanned the area and noticed that, in addition to the expected security cameras, speaker/microphone units identical to those in the conference room were embedded at regular intervals along the length of the front corridor's ceiling. It was a safe bet they were in every other room, too, thus ensuring Aimie could both hear and be heard by anyone moving anywhere in the building.

Directly across from the building's entrance was another door with a biometric lock. Picturing the schematic she had seen in Mrs. Carson's class, she figured it was the outer door of the medbay's airlock. Of the three additional doors farther down the hallway to her right, only the one at the far end, Jeremy's office, had a palm lock. She assumed two of the remaining rooms were where Aaron worked and the break room he had mentioned.

"Hey!" Ryan called to her. "Coming?"

Ellie trotted to where he held the door open for her. "Thanks," she said as she slipped past him.

Moments later, they entered the conference room. Jeremy sat at the table's far end with two people on his right and three on his left, all watching curiously as Ellie and her group fanned out around the table's opposite end. Ellie assumed Aimie was also invisibly in attendance.

Jeremy spoke without standing. "Welcome. Please sit wherever you like. I have gathered the technical staff together to help with your orientation today, and they are quite eager to meet you. Although Aaron is familiar to nearly everyone, at least by sight, I thought we'd start off with brief introductions all around. Raise your hand when I mention your name.

"On my right are Doctors Cai Wynn-Williams and Toshiko Mori." A stocky man with thinning reddish hair smiled and gave them a short wave. "Over the past seven years, Cai has become the world's foremost authority on quantum processors and non-binary data analysis. He has worked with Aimie and me the longest and is singularly responsible for any and all upkeep of the quantum core and maintaining system integration throughout the lab.

"Dr. Mori is Cai's equivalent when it comes to the TSD's neural interface technology." The woman gave them a curt nod rather than raising her hand. "Using information sent back in Aimie's data core, Toshiko was able to design the nerve induction components used in both the chairs and in the headpieces, as well as the associated technology used by the protective garments. We call them 'skins' for reasons that will soon be obvious, but I trust you're all adult enough to deal with their rather singular attributes. The haptic feedback feature of the TSD's camouflage exterior that you so greatly admired was also her creation."

Ellie guessed Dr. Mori was much younger than Cai, but she knew that was not necessarily so. Even though now a senior, her friend Hana could still pull off going undercover at a middle school. The woman's overall impression of youth was heightened by a single streak of bright blue running through her hair, framing the right side of her face. The whimsical touch softened a beauty that might otherwise have seemed too austere.

"On my left are Katherine Seligman, Dr. Cynthia Hamilton, and Dr. Robert Saha. Kate is an anthropologist and ethnologist. In the event a mission involves interacting with a culture significantly different from ours, she will coach team members on all the nuances of etiquette, colloquialisms, gestures, or class distinctions—whatever is required to help our mission team members blend in most effectively. She also oversees the costume department. The document and prop production facility is hers, too, at least until we have sufficient reason to bring a graphic designer on board.

"Next, we have our staff physician, Dr. Hamilton. The nature of her role ought to be self-evident, but I want to point out that in addition to her specialization in infectious diseases, she also underwent a rotation through radiation sickness and treatment. Dr. Hamilton is amply qualified to handle the widest possible range of situations our team members might encounter in the field. Each of you will pass through her office today, but I'll let her explain—very briefly, please, Doctor—exactly why and what to expect."

Dr. Hamilton leaned forward in her chair before speaking. "Hello. As Dr. Siskin said, I'll need to see each of you before you leave today, but I assure you there is no need for anxiety. As I know you would quickly guess, given reason to think about it, Aimie is capable of providing me with your complete medical histories. Therefore, I am already aware of your rather enviable states of health. All I need today is to establish a baseline for future reference—resting heart rate, blood pressure, blood oxygen levels, et cetera. I won't be drawing blood or asking for any other samples. The exam will be totally non-invasive and will take only a couple of minutes."

Dr. Hamilton settled back into her chair, obviously believing she was done. Then her expression abruptly changed as if she'd received a cue from Jeremy, and she sat up a little straighter.

"That's today, too? Ah. Well, then, forget the last thing I said. Anyone participating in the TSD project is required to receive a smallpox vaccination. We are not using a live vaccinia virus, as was the case until all smallpox vaccinations were halted in the early seventies. The distinctive scar produced by that procedure would be difficult to explain, especially when no such inoculation is recorded in your records. Instead, we use an as-yet unapproved method called an mRNA vaccine. Obtaining the sample of the virus we used both for designing and testing the vaccine proved challenging, but the fact that we were able to do so allows me to assure you with complete confidence that the shot is both safe and effective. If you wish to gain a deeper understanding of the science, I refer you to the January article in *Nature* by Pardi, Hogan—"

Jeremy raised his hand to stop her. "Thank you, Dr. Hamilton. Let me make this simple. Aimie, what can you tell us about mRNA vaccines?"

"The first widespread use of mRNA vaccines occurred in the spring of 2021 as part of the emergency response to the first coronavirus pandemic. Efficacy rates exceeding ninety-four percent led researchers to explore additional applications, and by 2034, this approach had all but completely replaced attenuated virus vaccines."

"Thank you, Aimie." Jeremy shrugged. "Viewed from that perspective, we're talking about a procedure with a more than forty-year track record. Everyone here, including the security personnel, has received the shot. My arm was slightly sore for a day, and I think that was the worst reaction any of us had."

Having disposed of that topic, Jeremy indicated the remaining member of the tech team. "Moving right along, our final staff member is Robert Saha, a physicist specializing in electronics and quantum field theory. Adapting Aimie's data to design the TSD, aside from the components under Dr. Mori's purview, was accomplished entirely under his direction. It took him and a crew of what, eight? Ten?" The man nodded. "Ten engineers nearly four years to work out enough of the specifics to build a prototype, then almost another two to construct the full-scale TSD *in situ* once this lab was completed.

"This, then, is the group of people who will be supporting you as we begin the pre-mission phase of this project."

Jeremy paused and looked down the length of the table at each of the four of them. Ellie, already impressed enough that she had to suppress a ridiculous urge to clap, thought that the pause was meant to give them the time to recognize how uniquely unqualified they were to be involved with such an undertaking. When he began introducing Aaron, however, she was warmed by what he had to say.

"I'll start with Aaron Weisskopf since, as I noted earlier, he is known to a greater or lesser degree to each of you. His persistently diligent attention to detail regarding what is, to be frank, a brain-numbing task has provided us with a comprehensive database by which all our efforts—hopefully, all of our *progress*—will be measured. Of these four, he is the only one who has not experienced travel in the TSD—or its equivalent, rather—but that will soon change."

"The young lady seated at the end of the table is Lauren Henderson. You know her as Ellie."

Ellie saw the eyes of all the staff members snap toward Jeremy in surprise, then come back to focus with great intensity on her. Feeling as exposed as an amoeba under a microscope's lens, she unnecessarily raised her hand.

"Yes. This is the same Miss Henderson responsible for us all being here today. I encourage you all to keep one thing in mind: compared to the person with whom we are familiar, this Ellie is young and as yet tragically under-educated, but she possesses the same sharp intellect that ultimately proved capable of creating"—he spread his arms to encompass the entire facility—"*this.*" He let his arms drop to his sides and completed his introduction with a hard, humorless smile directed straight at her. "It's quite possible she's even as smart as she thinks she is."

Ellie's cheeks burned as she sensed that Sam, Ryan, and Aaron were now looking at her, too. Refusing to give him the satisfaction of appearing hurt by the comment, she clamped her jaw tight, forced herself to keep her expression neutral, and held her own eyes focused straight ahead. Jeremy went on talking without acknowledging in any way how badly he had just demeaned her.

"Ellie's sister Samantha and her friend Ryan Collins round out our test crew. Although he might prefer I didn't point this out in any other setting, Ryan is one of the top minds of his own class, and if we can take the future, in this case, as prolog, he is destined for a distinguished career."

Jeremy silently regarded Sam for a long moment, as though trying to reach a decision. "Sam, would you stand for a moment?" Sam stood, visibly uncomfortable at being the center of attention. Jeremy looked slowly from one staff member to the next. "Sam is no intellectual slouch, I assure you, but her talents lie not in mathematics or unraveling complex scientific mysteries, but in language and communication. Aimie's memories of her paint the picture of someone who could 'charm the socks off a snake,' or however that saying goes. You have all known, on a strictly intellectual level, that Ellie lost her sister at far too young an age, a victim of the H5N1 flu pandemic in 2022, but abstract knowledge can take you only so far. Before you stands that very person, the living, breathing embodiment of our purpose here—*to save lives*. Thank you, Sam. Go ahead and sit."

Sam had gone increasingly pale as Jeremy described her fate, and after she sat, she kept her focus directed at the tabletop in front of her. Ellie wondered who the real targets of that comment were. She certainly didn't need a reminder of what was at stake.

"I'm sorry, Sam," Jeremy said. "I say these things not to upset you but to drive home the seriousness of our mission here." He looked at the faces of each staff member as he wrapped up his introductions. "Ellie understands, as does Mr. Collins. There are millions upon millions of 'Sams' outside these walls, and their futures depend just as much on our success."

Jeremy paused to give everyone a chance to think about that idea. Ellie's hurt feelings were somewhat soothed by his kind introduction of Ryan and even kinder words regarding Sam, but she still felt angry. She could find no explanation for his condescending attitude toward her, first in Mrs. Carson's classroom and now here, but before she could give the subject much thought, Jeremy was off on a new topic, addressing Ellie's group in a breezier tone.

"But first, we have a few formalities to handle. T's to dot, i's to cross, that sort of thing." He smiled at the weak joke. "On Sunday, I gave you a very brief tour. Today, you'll get a fuller picture of how operations will go. Dr. Hamilton, will you proceed around to the medical bay and open the rear door, please?" As she rose and headed for the door, he nodded to the remaining staff. "The rest of you can go, too, in fact. Be ready in about fifteen minutes."

The staff members rose and filed out the door. Jeremy waited until they had gone before he finished laying out the plan.

"Going in the order in which I introduced you, each of you see the doctor—it should take only a few minutes—then come back here. Following the check-ups, we'll take care of a few other details.

"Toshiko will be stationed in the locker room to instruct you in the use of the protective suits. Once you're fitted in your skins, head next door to costume storage and go to the very back of the room. Dr. Hamilton will be there to make a 3-D scan that can be used later to match you with properly fitting outfits in our wardrobe library.

"Robert will be in the TSD chamber to answer any questions you have, Kate in the prop room. Cai has a previous engagement, I'm afraid, but you will have plenty of opportunities to pick his brain in the future. I'd like to have everyone back here by five thirty so that Aimie can provide you with an overview of mission protocol." Jeremy looked at Aaron and jerked his head toward the door.

"Back in a sec, I guess," Aaron said. He passed behind Ellie and into the hall.

Ellie used the lapse in conversation to ask something she'd been wondering for the last few minutes.

"You said Aaron would get to use the TSD 'soon.' Exactly how soon are we talking?"

"To begin with, we can't safely send you back any further than 1972 until your vaccinations have become fully effective, which takes about two weeks. In the meantime, we thought a short and very local trip would be sufficient to be sure you understand operational procedures and protocols. So, how would you like to see what our town was like in 1976, all decked out in bunting for the centennial Fourth of July celebration?"

Sam looked uncertain. "Was there even anybody around here way back then?"

Jeremy laughed. "Well, good—you won't be disappointed! Seriously, though, I believe the downtown was quite similar—minus the newer buildings, obviously—and the neighborhoods around the new high school and the university campuses mostly date from the sixties, so they should seem very familiar. And you might be interested to know that the population was only 1,500 less than it is today."

"Really," Ryan said. "It's been essentially flat for over forty years?"

Convinced that Jeremy was intentionally ignoring her question, Ellie felt her earlier anger flare up again. "And this is happening *when?*"

"Is Friday afternoon soon enough?"

At that moment, Aaron came back into the room, looking uncharacteristically flustered. He was holding his right fist tucked up close to his shoulder and flapping his elbow up and down like a one-winged chicken.

"Next," he said. He retook his seat and leaned close to Ellie. "It's fine. Weird, but fine."

Ellie stood. "I'll be back," she said, then headed for the door.

Ryan called after her in a bad Austrian accent. "Hey! I was going to say that!"

The door to the medical bay stood open. When Ellie reached it, she saw Dr. Hamilton, now wearing a white lab coat, sitting on a steel stool. She was bent over a low workspace, apparently finishing up with Aaron's file. Instead of entering, Ellie knocked on the outer wall and waited to be acknowledged.

The doctor spoke without looking up from her writing. "Come on in. And leave that door open, please."

The room was small, no larger than it had to be to accommodate three doors along each of its two longer walls. The doors were made primarily of wire-reinforced glass framed in metal and fit into well-sealed jambs. The rooms behind the doors were tiny, perhaps five feet by eight, and outfitted with a narrow cot, a desk attached to the rear wall, and the kind of silver metal chair that looked substantial but which Ellie knew weighed almost nothing. A small airlock to the left of each door allowed food or other items to be passed safely in and out. At the rear corner of the rooms, mostly hidden by the cot, she could make out the rim of a metal toilet bowl. These, she knew, were the quarantine rooms.

When she returned her attention to the device occupying the center of the exam room, sudden recognition brought her to a dead stop. It was not the typical exam table she had first taken it to be. As if it had been torn directly from the TSD and planted in the floor in front of her, there sat a familiar black metal chair, complete with its own studded headpiece and gel-filled hand pads. It differed from the ones she knew only in that its back reclined at an angle slightly closer to horizontal.

"What the...?"

Dr. Hamilton chuckled at Ellie's surprise. "You were expecting a stethoscope and pressure cuff? I was told you are familiar with this equipment."

"Well, yeah, but..."

"Come on, then. Have a seat, please." She used the bright blue file folder she held to motion for Ellie to sit.

Ellie walked around to the front of the chair and eased herself back onto the memory foam pads. Before Dr. Hamilton could tell her to do so, she reached up and pulled the headpiece on, snugging it down tight against her scalp. Finally, she laid her palms on the gel pads and watched as they sank several millimeters into the surface.

When the doctor turned to face her, she looked pleased. "Very good. Just a couple of quick questions, and then we'll get started. During the last twenty months since your last physical, have you had an allergic reaction to any foods, medicines, insect stings?"

Ellie shook her head, the gesture made awkward by the headpiece. "No."

"Are you currently taking any medications that wouldn't be listed in these records?"

"No," she repeated, but this time she kept her head still. "Nothing."

"Excellent. One final thing—I see you are not yet eighteen and therefore cannot legally give consent to receive the smallpox vaccine. I assume you realize, however, that the usual rules end at that double row of razor wire out there. Nonetheless, I—"

"Yes!" Interpreting Jeremy's earlier introduction of the doctor as a hint that she was inclined to ramble, Ellie answered without waiting for her to finish. She backed up her answer with as emphatic a nod as the helmet would allow. "I'll take it."

"Very well. And by the way, while smallpox is the biggie, the vaccine is actually a cocktail that'll protect you against about half a dozen other pathogens as well."

Dr. Hamilton jotted a quick note onto a page in the blue folder, then stepped over to a control panel mounted to the wall. Above it, also attached to the wall, a monitor displayed the data coming from the chair, which Ellie knew was more than pulse and BP. A *lot* more. She relaxed and stared up at the ceiling, allowing her mind to become as blank as its smooth, white surface.

Wait! Blank? Smooth? With sudden interest, she craned her neck to peer into the corners of the ceiling behind her. Unlike all the other rooms she had been in so far, this one seemed to be free of microphones and cameras —Aimie's eyes and ears, in other words. She decided not to ask about it just in case she was wrong, but she filed the observation away under the heading of potentially useful data.

The doctor finished copying figures from the monitor into the paper record and swiveled to face Ellie. "Okay, that's done. Next, I'm going to record several seconds of baseline data. All you need to do is close your eyes and relax."

Ellie did as she was told and started drawing in a slow, deep breath. The next thing she knew, she felt as if she were waking from a long, deeply satisfying nap. Although disconcerting, the effect was pleasant. Euphoric, even.

"*Wow!* That was…. What just happened?"

Dr. Hamilton grinned at her. "I know! Isn't that the best? You were unconscious for about twelve seconds, just long enough to get the readings we need. I'm told the sensation is very close to what you feel in the TSD. Is that right?"

Ellie wondered if the doctor was equally enthusiastic about the effects of whatever pharmaceuticals she kept on hand. "I can't really say. What we experienced before felt more like really bad motion sickness, actually." Being free to discuss her experiences with the shack so openly felt strange but also good, and it made her regret even more not being able to have such a conversation with her mom or dad. Since the doctor seemed genuinely interested, she decided to share more.

"But that's after," she added. "I think there's something that comes before that, while it's in 'mid-flip' or whatever, but I can never quite remember the details. It's like a dream that fades almost at once. But then, maybe that's only because of the motion sickness thing."

"I see." Dr. Hamilton frowned. "Well, that's too bad. On a different topic, I'm getting an alert on your scan. Something chemical—hormonal, maybe—and probably not too serious, but I'd need to do a different kind of test to know for sure. I can't do that now because you need to have the skin on, but stop in later and we'll take a deeper look, okay?"

"Thanks, but I already have my own doctor checking into that."

The doctor shrugged. "Okay. Well, in that case, you're all set. Send Mr. Collins in, please."

"But what about the vaccination?" Before she had even fully voiced the question, she remembered what she had once assumed about the capabilities of the chairs. She raised her arms and studied both wrists, but failed to find the slightest mark.

The doctor seemed to know what she was thinking, and she chuckled again. "That only works with the skins on, honey. At least with this one. Right arm, while you were out. Best to move it around a bit."

Ellie pulled up her sleeve and saw a small, round bandage. "Got it." *Ah!* she thought. *So that's what Aaron was doing.* "I'll send Ryan right over."

On her way out, she noticed why Dr. Hamilton had asked her to leave the door open. There was no latch on the door's interior, only a simple pull handle. The lock on this door, too, was controlled by a palm scanner and keypad, even on the way out. Ellie realized at once why that made sense: not only was the exam room essentially a direct shortcut between the lobby and the TSD, but the lock was extra insurance that anyone placed in quarantine remained there until it was safe for them to leave.

Less than ten minutes later, Ryan and Sam had both received their checkups. The doctor followed Sam back as far as the door and leaned in to give Jeremy her report.

"Everything was fine," she said. "They're all good to go."

"Thank you, Dr. Hamilton."

"I'll be across the hall then," she said, sounding distinctly unenthusiastic.

Jeremy stared at the empty doorway for a moment, then he sighed. "Her talents are severely underutilized here, I'm afraid. To make matters worse, if everything goes as planned, they always will be. I should suggest to Captain Isaacs that he hold some additional hand-to-hand combat training sessions. Perhaps a broken arm or a punctured lung would cheer her up a bit, hmm?" He shook his head as if physically clearing the subject from his mind.

"Now then, how about we do this in pairs? Aaron, you and Mr. Collins start with Toshiko in the locker room, then see Dr. Hamilton next door. Maybe a dose of Ryan's witty repartee will improve her mood. Once you're back in your street clothes, you can see Dr. Saha in the TSD room and Kate in props. The two Miss Hendersons can start in props and then move on to the TSD. Give the boys about 15 minutes, then you can finish up with Doctors Mori and Hamilton. Any questions? No? All right then, let's go."

When they got to the document and prop shop, Ellie asked Kate for a more thorough tour than Jeremy had provided them. The cabinets that lined the wall backing the hallway held an enormous variety of paper, cover and card stocks, and even leatherette. There was very little of any given type but more than enough to create ten or more licenses, diplomas, passports, or any other document at least fifty different ways.

The Indigo printer was connected to a standalone iMac, which in turn was cabled to a bright blue, high-capacity external hard drive slightly smaller than a paperback book. In addition to the Indigo, the iMac had access to a smaller Epson photo printer and an HP LaserJet. Ellie jiggled the mouse, and the screen lit up at once. The icon for every Adobe app she could name appeared in the dock at the bottom of the display, along with a few HP icons. She assumed that these were apps specific to the printer.

"Here, let me," Sam said.

Since Sam had used several of the programs during her two-year stint with the high school newspaper, Ellie stepped back to make room for her. Sam sat and started opening and closing the apps one by one.

"They all seem up to date." She pointed at the external drive and looked up at Kate. "What's on here?"

"That contains tens of thousands of document exemplars, all tagged to be searchable. Need a visa for a visit to Turkey in 1972? A 1968 diploma from Harvard? I'm sure there's an original example of each of those in there, plus blank versions all cleaned up and ready to use." She pointed to the handwriting machine. "We can recreate signatures on that thing, and using the 3-D printer over there, we can even make embossing tools to use on documents like the Harvard diploma, for example."

Ellie watched over Sam's shoulder as she switched from checking out the apps to viewing a random cross-section of documents from the drive. She clicked into a folder, opened the first image in Preview, then used the arrow keys to make her way haphazardly through the files.

Ellie spoke while Sam clicked through a seemingly endless collection of birth certificates. "Jeremy mentioned special inks and coatings for the big printer?"

Kate pointed to a cabinet in the corner. "In there. We have some spot colors commonly used in US or state flags or official seal images, plus a few metallics. The four-color emulation on this guy is pretty good, though, so unless something needs to pass a close examination, I bet we won't use them much."

"Have you used it yourself?"

"I…" Kate blushed, then laughed self-consciously. "Yeah, I have, actually. There was a show I wanted to see down at the Lensic, but it was sold out. My girlfriend had a ticket, though, so I used hers as a reference to make one for me. Then I showed up a little late and looked for a seat left empty by someone who couldn't make it! The printer is very easy to use. Learning the graphics software is the bigger challenge, but if I could manage it…" She shrugged. "Good show, too, by the way."

Ellie thought of the young woman from the clothing consignment shop and wondered if every Kate in the world shared a predilection for petit larceny. She sensed that whatever this room contained was more important than anything they might hope to learn from Dr. Saha, but she was having trouble coming up with questions. "What if we needed to make a brochure or magazine? You know, something bound and with a cover?"

"In the cabinet next to the one with the spot inks, there are a few different kinds of binding machines, extra-deep staplers, those sorts of things. There's also a huge, old cast-iron trimmer I bet could slice through a Los Angeles Yellow Pages."

Ellie scanned the room a final time, then slowly nodded to herself. They had only five of the fifteen original minutes left before Dr. Mori would be expecting them in the locker room.

"We better move along, Sam. Thanks, Kate."

"No problem. I guess we'll see you back here soon, then."

"Sounds like," Ellie said.

Ellie and Sam jogged down the hall to the TSD chamber, where the door stood open. Inside, they saw Dr. Saha sitting in the open doorway of the device, his feet resting on the outer floor. When he saw them, he pulled his legs in and stood in the opening.

"I thought I'd been stood up," he said, then waved for them to join him in the TSD.

"Sorry." Ellie followed him in and took a few steps forward, making room for Sam. "Who knew document forgery could be so interesting?"

Dr. Saha nodded. "I hear you. It's the toys in that back room that I like, though. You can make anything at all with what's in there." He looked from Ellie to Sam and back again. "So, what would you like to know about this baby?"

Ellie glanced around the room, uncertain how to answer. She was intensely interested in the underlying physics, naturally, but knew she could learn very little in five minutes. She looked to Sam for a suggestion, but she shook her head. Ellie knew of only one major difference between this TSD and the original shack, so she asked about that.

"What can you tell us about those spiffy new batteries?"

23

E llie and Sam were almost to the locker room when Ryan and Aaron exited. As Ryan paused to hold the door open for them, he aimed a wide grin at Sam. Ellie sensed a secret message lurking in the expression, but it wasn't one she could decipher. It triggered a definite reaction from Sam, though, who stepped right up in front of Ryan and regarded him with an upraised eyebrow.

"Yes, *Mister Collins?*"

Ryan declined her invitation to explain and instead went right on grinning. "She's all ready for you two. Enjoy!" He winked and let go of the door, leaving it for Sam to catch before it closed. He shifted his smile to Aaron. "Coming, *Caeleb?*"

"Right behind you, *Michael,*" Aaron said, also looking amused.

Feeling lost, Ellie stared at their backs as they headed toward the TSD chamber. She spoke without looking at Sam. "What was all that?"

"I have *no* idea."

They entered the locker room to find it apparently empty, except for a black laptop case sitting on the long bench.

"Dr. Mori?" Ellie called.

The top of the woman's head appeared on the far side of the central dividing wall, followed by her hand as she waved them over to join her.

"Ladies on this side. Come around, and we'll get you fitted. And I prefer just Toshiko, please."

When Ellie and Sam joined her, they saw two unitard-style garments laid out along the wooden bench. Their dull beige color reminded Ellie of the gel pads on the exam room chair. At first glance, they looked perfectly smooth, but when she leaned in close, she noticed fine lines running irregularly under its surface—wires or maybe tiny tubes that all started at plugs positioned on the inside of each wrist, traveled up the arms to the shoulders, then diverged to terminate at points scattered around the suit. Most of the endpoints were dime-sized discs so thin they were hard to see except as a slight disruption of the suit's overall texture, but where they occurred in pairs, one was always slightly thicker. The discs were distributed chiefly around the suit's core, from the insides of the upper thighs to both sides of the neck. There were three pairs near the upper center of the chest. The other aspect Ellie noticed about the outfits was their size; they were quite obviously far too big for her and Sam.

Toshiko lifted one of the suits at its shoulders and held it up, showing them its back. Two parallel rows of the thin discs ran down along either side of the spine, and Ellie understood at once that they were meant to line up with the metal studs on the backs of the TSD's seats.

"These suits perform three functions," Toshiko explained. "The first is that they improve the connection between the nerve induction contacts in the seats and your body. The second is that they give the health monitoring system more information and provide a variety of injection points—intramuscular and intravenous both—should medical attention become necessary during a mission." She held the skin out toward them. "Do you notice the smell?"

When Ellie leaned down and inhaled, she recognized the peculiar aroma as the one she had first detected on Sunday and that still permeated the locker room's air, although at a less noticeable level. The fabric was its source. Sam also took a sniff as Toshiko went on explaining the properties of the skins in her cool, detached manner.

"These are made from an organic material that performs their third function, shielding. The time shift occurs within a field that can damage specific glandular tissues. In theory, this field only occurs outside the structure of the TSD, but due to certain Heisenbergian limitations, what is 'inside' and what is 'outside' cannot always be defined with absolute precision. Or so I am told. That is Dr. Saha's area of expertise, not mine.

"These suits, however, *are* mine. What I need you to do is strip down completely and put one on. Which one doesn't matter. Not yet, anyway." She reached down and gripped a suit at either side of the neck hole and pulled her hands away from each other. Although there was no sign of a zipper, snaps, Velcro, or any other kind of closure, the suit separated cleanly and opened down about sixteen inches. She aligned the two pieces of material, and almost at once, the edges began to fuse. Within a few seconds, any sign of an opening vanished, as if the material had healed itself.

"Once you have them on, let me know, and we'll go from there."

With a deft motion, Toshiko reopened the suit and handed it to Sam. She held the second suit out in front of her to demonstrate again. "Watch." She pulled open the top of the skin, and this time Ellie saw that in addition to moving her hands apart, she was pulling forward with her right hand, pushing away with her left. "Okay?"

Ellie and Sam both nodded. Toshiko offered the second skin to Ellie and disappeared around the dividing wall.

Ellie held the skin up in front of her, its shoulders level with her own, and looked down. Although it was obvious that the garment was intended to end at her ankles, at least eight extra inches of the strange material lay puddled on the floor at her feet. She looked at Sam, but she merely shrugged, which Ellie took to mean they should trust that Toshiko knew what she was doing.

Ellie laid the suit at the end of the bench, making sure the two sides of the opening didn't touch, and began to undress, hastily folding each article of clothing as she removed it. The quirk of genetics that had resulted in her and Sam looking as much alike as it was possible for non-twins to look, along with having shared a bedroom with her for her entire life, meant she had never felt awkward getting undressed around her sister any more than she would have felt undressing in front of a mirror. She might have been uncomfortable had Ryan and Aaron been in the room, though, even if they were on the other side of the wall, and she was glad it was only the three of them.

Once bare, she lifted the suit from the bench and began working out the best way to get into the strange getup without damaging the exceptionally thin material. She saw that Sam had turned hers inside out almost down to its waist, and was stepping into it the way one would put on a wetsuit. Following her lead, it took only a few moments for Ellie to work the garment on. When she tried to close the top, however, she discovered that the loose fit of the suit made it hard to hold one side taut and press the other against it with only two hands. Sam was having the same trouble.

"Here," Ellie said. She placed her finger at the lower end of the slit and pressed. With the opening's bottom thus secured, Sam was able to align the two sides easily. Ellie watched closely as the material magically fused. "That is *so* cool! Now me."

After her own suit had sealed, Ellie looked down at herself, then at Sam, and laughed. The outfits were several sizes too big in every dimension and hung as loosely on them as deflated sumo suits. She could see the outline of Sam's body quite clearly amid the folds of excess material and realized it was, to no small extent, see-through.

"We look like snakes that shed and then put the old skins back on!"

Toshiko appeared from the far side of the room carrying a laptop wrapped by a long, white cord. "We'll soon have that fixed."

Ellie watched Toshiko slip the cord off the computer, plug one end into a USB port, and set the laptop on the bench. The unfamiliar cable was four feet long, split in two for the last foot, and the outer ends terminated in a type of plug Ellie didn't recognize.

Toshiko sat and opened the laptop, tilting the screen as far back as it would go. "One of you come over here. Stand in front of me, please."

Being closer, Ellie volunteered to go first. As she shuffled over in her baggy suit, careful not to tread on the excess length at her feet, she smiled inwardly at the woman's confident, unadorned manner of expressing herself. Toshiko leaned down and pulled upward at the bottom of each leg to be sure Ellie's heels weren't resting on the cuffs.

"Hold your arms out, please. Like this." Toshiko held her arms straight forward, shoulder-width apart, palms facing inward. Ellie copied her, then Toshiko plugged the cord into sockets at the end of the suit's sleeves, directly over the middle of each wrist. She turned back to her computer and tapped briefly on the keyboard.

"Okay, this won't hurt, but it might feel… *interesting?*"

For the first time, Ellie thought she detected a tiny trace of emotion on the woman's face, the barest hint of a smile. She wondered what she meant by "interesting," but in light of that tiny smile, she felt comfortable letting that be a surprise.

"Are you ready?" Toshiko said.

"Mm-hmm. Go ahead."

When Toshiko pressed the Enter key, the suit immediately began to contract around Ellie's body. Toshiko made minor adjustments to the material as it shifted, preventing it from doubling over on itself. At first, the process was an entirely visual event, and Ellie watched in fascination as the garment shrank around her, seeming somehow to absorb its own excess bulk. A moment later, however, the experience became a very tactile one, full-body and intensely intimate. As the material continued to conform to her body's shape, it squirmed and slithered against her skin, making it feel as if a dozen people at once were rubbing their hands over her every square inch. Although she knew the suit's interior was dry, it felt slick and oily. Ellie drew in a sharp breath as an involuntary spasm of pleasure coursed through her body. Toshiko was right—the feeling was "interesting," indeed!

Just as the suit started to feel snug, the slithering sensation stopped. Thinking she was done, Ellie started to lower her arms.

"Not yet," Toshiko said, and she immediately set about making minute adjustments to the position of the skin's sensor discs, starting with the ones on the collar and working her way down.

Ellie's nerves were already hyper-stimulated from the friction of the suit rubbing against her skin, and when Toshiko began nudging the contacts on her inner thighs into position, she shuddered and sucked in another involuntary gasp. Feeling self-conscious at last, Ellie glanced over at Sam and was surprised to find she was watching the proceedings not with the wry amusement she had expected but with irritation. She was about to ask what was wrong, but then she remembered Ryan's odd smile when he had met them at the door and thought she understood. No doubt Sam was picturing Toshiko making the same intimate adjustments to *his* suit, and Ellie now had to suppress a smile of her own.

Toshiko tapped Ellie's side to get her attention. "Turn around, please, but be careful of the cables."

Ellie complied, and Toshiko ran her fingers over the contacts along her back. When she reached the lowest pair, she gripped the material at the base of Ellie's spine and gave it a sharp, upward tug that caused the crotch of the suit to ride up in a way that made Ellie's eyes go wide.

"Okay," Toshiko said. "We're almost done. Face me again."

Ellie rotated back around. Blushing a little, she aimed her attention at the laptop's screen. The angle was not good, but through a hazy reflection, she could make out the label "Final Fit" inside a green button.

"Spread your feet a little and hold your arms like this," Toshiko reminded her.

Ellie reassumed the proper pose, then watched as Toshiko tapped on the Enter key. The feeling of being caressed all over resumed, only this time it was accompanied by a gentle, soothing warmth. As any remaining slack disappeared and the material precisely conformed to every contour of her body, the pleasure became so intense that it was all Ellie could do not to moan.

"The heat you're feeling increases the elasticity of the material. As you can see, it also darkens it somewhat, as well as increases its opacity."

Ellie looked down and immediately understood how the skins had earned their name. The material was no longer translucent, and she could no longer see her body's surface. However, every physical feature was not only on full display but seemed to be emphasized. She thought about examples of body painting she had seen online, and despite the thin layer she wore, she felt every bit as exposed.

"The tightness serves a purpose—it ensures the contacts do not shift, which helps maximize signal transfer efficiency. After the skin cools, it will remember this precise shape, and it will reassume it any time you put it on. It's not too tight, is it?"

"Can I move now?"

Toshiko nodded. "Please."

Ellie, moving carefully because of the cables, went through a quick sequence of motions from her pre-soccer warm-up routine, stretching her arms over her head, reaching down to her toes, and finishing by twisting from side to side. No matter how she moved, she could barely feel the skin.

"Nope. It feels okay."

"Good." Toshiko pulled the plugs from Ellie's wrist sockets. "Okay, Samantha. Your turn."

Still looking like she had bitten into a lemon, Sam moved to stand in front of Toshiko and held her arms out as she had seen Ellie do.

Toshiko inserted the plugs into Sam's suit and then turned back to her computer. "Are you ready?"

Sam's reply was curt. "Yes! And I prefer just 'Sam,' please."

"I will remember." Toshiko's hands froze over the keyboard as she belatedly registered the annoyance in Sam's tone. "Is something upsetting you?"

Sam seemed to realize she was being perhaps the teensiest bit childish and let out a long breath. "No, I suppose not. Not *you*, anyway. So, sorry for being snippy."

"It's just that Ryan left here looking especially happy," Ellie volunteered, earning herself an annoyed glare from Sam.

"Ah, yes. That one is your 'friend,' Jeremy said. I assure you, he was perfectly well-behaved. As was I. Still..." She made a show of giving the matter serious consideration. "He *is* quite handsome"—again, Ellie saw the ghost of a smile flicker across Toshiko's face before she concluded—"for a *child*."

Finally, Sam had to laugh at her own foolishness. "All right, I get it. I'm being silly."

"Possibly," Toshiko allowed. She pushed the button to initiate the fitting process. "And anyway, if I know men—and I do—who's to say his amusement came from the idea of me assisting *him*, hmm?"

Sam laughed again. "Oh, God! Isn't *that* the truth!"

"Since we're on the subject," Ellie said, "do you have any idea about the 'Caeleb and Michael' bit?"

"None," Toshiko said. She pinched Sam's suit at the waist to keep it in the proper place. "They found calling each other by those names quite amusing, however."

"Oh, that," Sam said. "They meant Caeleb Dressel and Michael Phelps. Olympic swimmers. I guess Ryan thought these things look like competition swimsuits. And they do, kinda." She looked down at the dull, tan material. "Totally boring ones, though. No offense."

"Function before form," Toshiko said.

The suit's bagginess was gone, and it began the slithery process of conforming itself to Sam's body. Now it was Sam's turn to go goggle-eyed, and her next words came out as a husky sigh.

"Oh, my! That feels really nice."

Minutes later, Ellie and Sam, both modestly wrapped in robes, made their way to the rear of the costume storage room. Dr. Hamilton was perched on a rolling stool, elbow resting on the top of a large work table, her chin propped on the heel of her palm. She didn't bother standing as she watched them emerge from between two long racks of the vintage clothing.

"I'm glad you two had the good taste to cover up. I got the impression that that other pair would have considered it a great disservice to humanity to deprive us all of the opportunity to fully appreciate their 'attributes,' to use Dr. Siskin's word." She made a sort of facial shrug. "Although I can hardly say I blame them. Step right over here, and let's get you taken care of."

Dr. Hamilton dropped from the stool and led them to a device in the back left corner of the room, one that looked vaguely like an airport security scanner. It differed mainly by having an elevated platform at its center and a pair of handgrips at roughly waist level. A red logo above the bottom step read, "Tru-Fit." A mid-size monitor mounted vertically on a counter to the device's right seemed to be its only control panel.

"Body scanner," Ellie said.

"Yep," Dr. Hamilton confirmed. "One of you toss your robe onto the table and hop up in there."

Having been the first to get fitted in her skin, Ellie motioned for Sam to precede her on the scanner. She took Sam's robe from her and laid it on the work table.

"Very good," Dr. Hamilton said. "Grab onto those two handles and be as still as you can. Perfect. You're going to start to rotate now, so hold on." When she tapped a button on the monitor, the faint projection of a red grid appeared on Sam's left side, and the platform began moving her in a slow, clockwise spin. "Around you go."

Ellie laughed. "You look like a rotisserie chicken!"

Trying to remain motionless, Sam replied through clenched teeth. "Very funny."

"Thought about it," Dr. Hamilton said. "We'd need blue lasers for that, though."

While Sam completed her scan, Ellie took the time to examine the rest of the room. As Jeremy had hinted, there was a sewing machine, male and female mannequins, an ironing board, an iron, and a steamer—everything needed to alter clothing. A large machine, blue with white stripes, sat against the far wall. It had a door on the front like a washing machine, but it was much bigger. She was at a loss to identify it until she remembered Jeremy saying most of the clothing was business wear. She pointed it out to Dr. Hamilton.

"That's a dry cleaning machine?"

"You got it. Okay, Sam, come on down. Ellie, you take her place."

Ellie slipped her robe off her shoulders and handed it to Sam as she passed by her. Sam put the robe on, tied the belt, and stood beside the doctor to watch Ellie take her turn.

"This is for what again?" Sam said.

"As I understand it, all those outfits have been scanned too." The doctor jabbed a thumb over her shoulder at the rows of clothing behind them. "Different machine, of course. The idea is that you can be matched to specific articles of clothing using these body scans. If there's no match that's close enough, whoever's working back here can use the scans to know how much to let out or take in."

"But why not make the outfits from scratch?" Sam said. "You'd have perfect fits each time, and from what Jeremy told us, he could definitely afford to."

"That I can't tell you for sure, but I seem to recall that question coming up when the scanner was installed. The rationale, I *think*, was that it's easier to find clothing from different time periods than it is to find bolts of the right kinds of vintage cloth. But as the saying goes, 'I'm a doctor, not a tailor.'"

"Nice one," Sam said.

In the scanner, Ellie came to a gentle stop. "Is that it?"

"That's it."

Ellie stepped down, and Sam tossed her the other robe.

The doctor cast a wistful look at the scanner and shook her head in dismay. "Thirteen years," she sighed. "But hey—at least med school's paid off."

"Dr. Hamilton?" Sam said. "We're glad you're here, even if we hope we'll never need you."

"Yeah," Ellie said. "The theory was that if someone got infected with something serious using the old TSD, it just *killed* everybody."

Sam gaped at Ellie, wide-eyed. "*No!* Tell me you're joking."

Ellie gave Sam an apologetic smile. "That was Aaron's guess. We didn't know for sure." She faced the doctor. "So, yeah, what she said. Definitely."

"Thank you, ladies. I can't deny that it's nice to feel appreciated. Now, back to the locker room you go." She made a sweeping gesture toward the door and fell in behind Ellie and Sam as they filed out. "Toshiko is waiting there to help get you out of those things. How do they feel, by the way?"

Sam answered over her shoulder. "It's exactly like being naked, except you don't sense the air as much, so it's a little warmer than actually not wearing anything." She paused until they had all exited and were making their way down the hall. "And everything feels more, I don't know, supported? Constrained?" She sighed, frustrated at being unable to summon the precise word. "You don't *jiggle* anywhere, is what I'm trying to say."

"Yeah," Ellie said. "It's pretty nice, except for the whole public nudity issue. They'd probably be great for yoga."

Dr. Hamilton chuckled. "Well, considering those are about twelve grand apiece, it's good to know they're comfy."

"Great!" Sam said. "The most expensive outfit I have, and it's not even one I can wear out on the town."

"I don't think you could even wear it out of the building," Dr. Hamilton said, a warning note in her tone. Sam looked at her, eyebrows arched in a silent question. "Alarms, flashing lights, guys with guns—*not* a good idea. Here we are. Locker room for you, medbay for me. I'll see you both on Friday, I hear."

"Yep," Ellie said. "And thanks again." She noticed Dr. Hamilton had left the rear entrance to her work area propped open with what looked like a tongue depressor.

The doctor noticed her noticing and raised her finger to her lips. "*Shhh!*" she said and winked before she pulled the door open and disappeared beyond it.

Ellie wondered what Aimie would think about such breaches of "protocol" but knew she would never bring it up. After all, she had a huge soft spot for rebels.

Toshiko showed them how to open the suit's invisible closure while wearing it. Pressing gently on the right side of the collar and briskly pulling the collar's other side away from the body with the left hand, the suit opened easily. Next, she had them each choose a locker and walked them through the process of encoding the locks to their thumbprints. Ellie opened hers and peered in, expecting it to be empty. Instead, she found it contained a thick cotton towel, folded neatly on the lower of two shelves at the locker's top.

"The skins are tougher than they appear," Toshiko said, "but peel them off carefully. And do not hang them. That can cause damage now that they have been custom-formed to your bodies. Fold them and place them on one of the shelves." Then, her assignment complete, she turned toward the door to allow them to change on their own.

Ellie called to her as she disappeared around the dividing wall. "Thank you, Toshiko!"

The woman's head reappeared at the end of the wall as she leaned around it to reply. "You are quite welcome. And Sam? Do tell Ryan I said hi." She winked at Sam, and then truly smiled for the first time.

Sam snorted, caught off-guard by this unexpected display of humor. "I'll be sure to do that. And thanks for your help."

Toshiko disappeared again, and a second later they heard the sound of the door closing.

"I think I like her," Ellie said. Sam responded with a major eye roll.

They peeled off the skins, carefully folded and locked them away, then dressed. Finishing ahead of Sam, Ellie checked out the adjoining room for the first time. In addition to the expected toilet and shower stalls, the bright, spacious area also contained a large but otherwise normal-looking washer and dryer along the back wall. There was nothing at all to suggest that something sinister lurked below the surface of what they were being shown. She shrugged to herself. Then again, it was just a locker room.

24

A few minutes later, Ellie and Sam returned to the conference room, interrupting whatever Ryan, Aaron, and Jeremy had been in the middle of discussing. Ryan looked up at Sam as they approached the table and flashed the same smile he had given her earlier.

"I'm glad you're enjoying yourself, *Mister Collins*," Sam said. Although she made an effort to sound cross, Ellie could tell she was past being annoyed with him. Ryan, equally attuned to Sam's moods, continued to smile.

Jeremy waited until Ellie and Sam were seated before speaking. "Aimie is going to bring you up to speed regarding operational protocols, explain in greater detail what goes into mission planning, and discuss how we evaluate missions after the fact. I'd love to hear what you got out of our orientation program this afternoon, but we're running a little behind, so I'm turning this over to Aimie right away. Aimie?"

Ellie found Aimie's lecture to be more boring than she could have imagined and considered Aimie herself to be pedantic and self-important. Still, it was information they needed if they were to play an active part in the project, so she forced herself to pay close attention. She asked any question that popped into her head, using the interaction with Aimie to gain deeper insight into the AI's personality. By the end of the meeting, she could see where they might have an advantage over her, should it come to that. Aimie very clearly believed she was indispensable to the project, and Ellie thought this conviction could result in a blind spot. Aimie might never suspect that anyone who was part of the mission would attempt to harm her. During the entire discussion, however, Aimie remained frustratingly tight-lipped when it came to sharing specific details of her plan.

"One example," Ellie said. "Even a hypothetical one! Just give us some idea of what you have in mind."

"The details would be meaningless to you, and I do not want to confuse you by presenting hypothetical situations that might never occur. Suffice it to say that my calculations are highly iterative and that the exact nature of each mission can be determined only after a complete analysis of the previous one. The 'plan' to which you refer is not a roadmap but a general methodology aimed at achieving a given goal. Comprehending that methodology would require that you consciously hold the previous seventy years of relevant history in your mind and be aware of the interconnectedness of all significant events simultaneously. This is something you are not capable of doing, I'm afraid."

"Because we're mere 'biologicals,'" Sam said.

"Correct."

"Let's talk in general terms then," Ellie said. "How can you make the kinds of changes you'll need to without completely rewriting people's lives?"

"We cannot, any more than you could conduct a war and not incur casualties. It would be unreasonable to expect an endeavor of this magnitude to be entirely devoid of sacrifice. There will be collateral changes, not all of them subtle. That said, we have adopted two procedural safeguards to help keep unintended edits to a minimum. The first is built into the mission planning process. Any proposed alteration will be thoroughly evaluated for its possible negative side effects. The extreme complexity such modeling requires far exceeds the capability of any current computer and is another reason my quantum processor is essential.

"Furthermore, the priority will always be placed on making those edits that result in the least amount of change while still furthering our goals.

For example, if the historical decision was option 'A,' but option 'B' would have produced a preferable outcome, the team's assignment would be to ensure option 'B' wins out instead. They would not, however, introduce a third option and attempt to insert that new element into the timeline. Is that clear?"

Ellie nodded along with the others.

"And you already know about the second safeguard," Aimie said.

"Continuity," Aaron said.

"Yes. After each mission, we will compare the archived copy of the Continuity file to the new historical record. If any of the resultant changes fall outside established limits of acceptability, a second mission might be considered, but not unless it can be determined that it is possible to prevent those undesirable changes from occurring.

"Ultimately, however, all of our actions will be guided by one question: does this mission advance our goal of saving uncounted millions of lives in the future?"

"But then, what about us?" Sam said. "If we don't go along—you know, go back in time, too—won't we forget how things... I mean, forget what was..." Wincing, she raised her fingers to her temples and rubbed.

Ellie caught the gist of what Sam was trying to ask and finished the question on her behalf. "I think what Sam wants to know is how altering the past will affect the memories of people working here who aren't the ones going back."

"Thank you," Sam muttered.

"That is not a cause for concern," Aimie said. "You are correct in assuming that any changes to history resulting from a given mission will overwrite your previous knowledge of the affected events and become the only version of the past you know. But as long as those alterations do not affect your *personal* histories, then all of your relationships, your knowledge of the mission here... none of that will be affected."

"That's an easy thing for you to promise," Ryan said, "considering that if you're wrong, we'd never know the difference."

"There is an element of trust involved, true," Aimie said.

"Right." Ryan's skepticism was plain to hear. When no one, including Aimie, seemed to know what to say next, Ryan brought the meeting to a close. "Well, this 'biological' has had enough for one day. Is there anything else we need to know before Friday?"

Jeremy, too, looked tired following the presentation. He seemed to be thinking the question over, but before he could answer, Aimie spoke.

"I have decided to move the first test trip forward a day. Be here tomorrow at four thirty. I look forward to seeing Aaron's reaction to what will be a big day for him."

Sam's eyes widened. "Tomorrow? Really?"

Ellie was more puzzled than worried. She thought the way Aimie had singled out Aaron was odd, but then he was the only one among them—Jeremy included, she remembered sourly—who had never traveled to the past. Judging by Aaron's carefully ambiguous reply, she guessed he found the statement strange, too.

"Uh, yeah," he said. "I can't wait."

Ellie saw Jeremy scowl before looking across the table at them. Was the change in schedule news to him as well? She couldn't tell. His eyes lingered on her for a long moment, and again she got the impression that he was weighing multiple options. A second later, he sprang to his feet.

"Then that's all for today. Let's be here a little early tomorrow if you can. I trust you can find your way out?" Without waiting for a reply, he strode out of the room.

"Okay," Sam said, stretching the word out.

They were quiet all the way to the van, but Aaron spoke up as soon as they were through the gate.

"So. What's up with you and Dr.... Jeremy?"

"Yeah," Sam said. "That introduction was *rude!*"

Ellie agreed. Jeremy's cheap shot had robbed her of the chance to feel good about joining the TSD project and left her with a bitter taste in her mouth. He didn't strike her as a man who did anything without a reason, but what was his motivation here? Whatever it was, she wasn't going to let wounded pride keep her from doing her job.

"I wish I knew, guys, but I have no freakin' clue. I'd say it has to do with challenging him in the classroom; he was like that there too. But I was actually right about all of that, so what's he got to be mad about?"

"Exactly what are we supposed to make of Aimie's refusal to give us any details?" Ryan said. "I mean, is her whole approach to preventing global catastrophe really just *winging it?*"

"Let's hope not," Aaron said. "I figure either she's telling the truth and each new mission will be determined by the previous one, or she really has no plan at all. I mean, if there is a step-by-step plan and she's keeping it a secret, that doesn't make any sense. What does she think we're going to do? Steal her ideas and carry them out using our *own* time machine?"

Sam, no longer interested in analyzing their day, steered the conversation in a completely new direction. "Hey, you know what? I've been so focused on this whole mess that I haven't given a single thought to a costume for tonight."

"Aren't you a little old for trick-or-treating?" Aaron said.

"Too old to care about the candy, maybe, but never too old to dress up!" She threw her arm over the seat back and turned to look behind her. "Hey, El. Remember the time we went trick-or-treating as the Grady twins from *The Shining?*"

"Yeah, it was our last Halloween in Virginia. I also remember that only two people in the whole neighborhood got it."

"*Second* to last. And it was still fun, even if it turned out we weren't exactly surrounded by cinephiles. We should do that again."

Ellie laughed. "We were, like, what, nine and ten? I'm pretty sure those dresses wouldn't fit."

"I didn't mean that *exactly,*" Sam said.

Ryan waggled his eyebrows at her. "I'd like to see you in them anyway!" Then, adopting Aimie's bored tone, he quickly added, "I mean 'it,' not 'them.' Because by 'you,' I mean you personally, Sam, not the Henderson sisters generally."

Sam laughed. "I'm sure you would! I bet it wouldn't even come down over my—"

"*But,* moving on," Ellie said. Sam grinned and gave her a wink. "Aaron, can you take us all the way home, please?"

· · ·

Ellie finished the day's school assignments at nine twenty-five, then went through her usual routine of returning all her books, papers, and MacBook to her backpack. She leaned the pack against the leg of her desk, then stood and stretched. Sam had been keeping her silent company all evening, first while catching up on some reading for her own classes, then by switching to book three of D. Hahkam's—aka Daniel Siskin—*Messengers* series. Ellie wondered if Jeremy had put the pieces together yet and realized that she and Sam were the girls who figured so prominently in his father's first novel.

Sam caught Ellie looking her way and lowered the book to her lap. "Hey."

"Hey yourself. How's that one?"

"Okay. Not as good as the first two. I've been thinking about what you said earlier. About liking Toshiko?"

"Yeah?"

"I like more or less *everyone* out there. I know we didn't get to talk to Cai, but he wasn't giving off any weird vibes. And Jeremy is... Well, he's still basically just 'Dr. Jeremy D. Siskin, DSc.' But the others? It wasn't at all what I was expecting."

"You thought they'd be a bunch of evil villains twirling their mustaches or wringing their hands and cackling to themselves. I know. Same here."

"Kinda, yeah. Not literally, but like maybe you could sense all that going on below the surface. Instead, they all seemed like normal, decent people."

"So, what are you saying, Sam?"

"That maybe we didn't sign up to work with the Legion of Doom or SPECTRE after all. Not even Facebook. I'll feel better once we get more details about their exact plans, but I think this is going to be okay."

"I agree. For the first time, I feel like we're really doing the right thing. Without Aimie and Jeremy, it would feel even better, but..."

Sam laughed. "No argument there. Talk about bad vibes!"

"Looking forward to tomorrow, then?"

"I am. *Surprise!* The idea that it'll be Los Alamos, but we won't know anyone? It's bizarre! And the aquatic center won't be there, or UNM, or even the new high school. I don't think even Wolf's will be there yet."

"Nope. They opened in '79. The building might have been there, but if it was, it was something else."

"That reminds me of what Ryan said in Brooklyn about wishing he had money. I don't suppose you have any bills from the early 70s, do you?"

Ellie snorted. "I barely have any bills from *this* millennium."

"I feel your pain." Sam went quiet for a moment, then brought up a new topic. "Is it me, or was it extremely odd the way Jeremy left at the end of the day?"

"No, it was." Ellie still didn't have a good take on the man. One minute, he could be nice enough. Charming, even. The next minute, he was a spiteful snake. That particular behavior, though—storming out of the room the way he had—was just plain strange. "I think Aimie blind-sided him by moving our test ride up to tomorrow."

Sam screwed her mouth up to one side as she considered that. "He did seem thrown."

"I'm glad it's tomorrow. I hate to admit it, but I'm *really* looking forward to it. And I can't wait to see Aaron's reaction!"

"Yeah. I bet even by this time tomorrow he'll still be going on about how 'amazing' time travel is." She rolled her eyes.

Ellie laughed. "Wow! Jaded much?"

"In truth, yeah. I know how ridiculous it sounds, but that part seems like no big deal now. Like iPhones or electric Hondas. It's where we might get to *go* that's exciting, not how we get there."

"And to *when* we get to go. 1976... have you been practicing your 'groovies' and 'far outs?'"

"Are you trippin'? Don't be a bunny! This stone fox don't *need* to prac-tice her jive-talkin', and I ain't a'woofin'. You catch my drift, sister?"

Ellie blinked, startled by Sam's string of indecipherable slang. "I esti-mate that I catch approximately ten percent of your 'drift,' but I take that as a 'yes.'"

"There's this thing called Google," Sam said. "You should try it." She smiled, then went back to reading her book.

Later, staring at her reflection while she ran a washcloth over her face,

Ellie's thoughts returned to Jeremy. She hadn't realized at the time how apt her earlier description of his two personas had been, but she saw it now and wondered who the *real* Jeremy was—the charmer or the snake. She rinsed the cloth under the faucet, wrung it out, then draped it over a bar to dry. Before leaving the room, she returned her gaze to the mirror.

"I don't suppose *you* know, do you?" Her reflection offered up not even a shrug in reply. "Oh, well. It was worth a try."

25

Aaron drove again the following day, and their university lot rendezvous was nearly a carbon copy of the day before. The only difference was his obvious apprehension about the upcoming event, and he sought reassurance from Ellie while they watched Sam and Ryan walk across the lot toward them.

"What else can you tell me about what happens in the TSD?"

"Nothing," Ellie said. "I mean, I could tell you what happened to us before, but I think this will be different. You'll appreciate it more if you go into it not expecting something in particular. But trust me, it's nothing to be nervous about. What I said about the shack making us feel sick afterward? The skins are meant to prevent that, so that shouldn't be an issue this time. It'll be totally fine. You're going to have a great time."

Sam and Ryan climbed into the van just in time to catch the end of Ellie's attempt at encouragement.

"Worried, buddy?" Ryan said.

"A little. Ellie insists it'll be fun, though."

"Of course it will! We're only about to rip a big ol' hole in the very fabric of spacetime, force our way through it into some unknown dimension, and then come out of it twenty-five billion miles from here, forty-plus years in the past. What could possibly go wrong? Sounds like a total blast to me!"

Ellie saw Aaron swallow hard and dart an anxious glance her way. She also heard the sound of Sam's hand connecting solidly with some spot on Ryan's body.

"Behave, you!" Sam said. She leaned forward between the two front seats. "Ignore him. Even *I'm* looking forward to this. It'll be fine."

"See?" Ellie pointed at Sam. "That's exactly what I said."

Aaron nodded and started the van rolling toward the exit.

"Sorry, dude," Ryan said. "Ignore me. You probably have a hundred times more to worry about driving the few short klicks from here to the LAB."

"Mm-hmm."

They passed the next two miles in silence. When they reached the high bridge, Ellie pressed her forehead against the window and tried to see the bottom of Los Alamos Canyon, more than a hundred feet below. Then Aaron merged into the left lane, and the view down was gone.

"Before I forget," Aaron said, "can you all come by my place when we're done today? I found something I need to show you."

"Sure," Ellie said at once.

Ryan murmured quietly to Sam. "Do you need to work on that paper?" Sam shook her head. "We're in," he said.

"Is this the thing we talked about the other day at lunch?" Ellie said.

"Yeah. It seems I need you guys to help figure it out."

"Help how?" Sam said.

"It's easier if you see for yourself. Let's wait until later, okay?"

Their first stop was the conference room. There was a large 8K monitor mounted on the wall behind Jeremy, a detail Ellie had somehow failed to notice the day before. Aided by images from the TSD's navigation program, Aimie used the screen to show them where the TSD would land. The site was located near the bottom of Pueblo Canyon, just beyond the end of Orange Street on its opposite side. Ellie was familiar enough with that part of the canyon to know it would be a short, easy climb to come out on Canyon Road very close to the commercial downtown. She was also aware of a potential danger associated with the site.

"Given the likelihood of monsoon activity in July, is it a good idea to set us down in the afternoon in the middle of a wash? I assume the TSD is waterproof, of course, but is it flash flood-proof?"

Jeremy's response lacked any of the previous day's edge. "Preventing accidental exposure of the project due to damage to the TSD is precisely the type of concern that will soon fall within your area of responsibility. While I have no doubt Aimie has considered that contingency, perhaps this is a good opportunity to illustrate the nature of your role in a concrete way." He shifted his attention to the others. "You three go see Kate in costumes, then get suited up. Miss Henderson will join you in a few minutes." They stood and began filing out of the room. Jeremy motioned for Ellie to meet him at the monitor. "If you'll join me over here, we can put your concerns to rest."

Ellie crossed the room and stood beside Jeremy, facing the television. Except she now saw it wasn't. What had appeared from the room's far end to be a display panel on a bracket, complete with a faint shadow on the wall below it, was an illusion. The "TV" was actually a flat image on a much larger screen. It took Ellie another second to understand what she was seeing.

"This is one of the TSD panels! Why...?"

"Specifically, it's one of the *exterior* panels. Knowing that there would always be, despite the most meticulous planning, a real possibility that the TSD might suffer damage at any time, we ordered a complete extra set of exterior panels. It made more sense, for various reasons, to request twice as many as needed up front rather than order replace- ments along the way. Instead of simply stashing them somewhere, we installed them here where Toshiko and Dr. Saha can use them to improve upon their work on the TSD's camouflage and sensory feedback systems."

Ellie scanned the entire room. There was not the slightest hint that the walls were anything other than standard drywall and plaster, but if that wasn't the case...

"So you're saying you can—"

He didn't wait for her to finish. "Aimie, please show us the surrounding forest."

The lights flickered once, and then they were standing outside, surrounded by the tall double fence and ponderosa pines beyond. Turning toward the fence's gate, she saw the two guards at their post in the small outbuilding. Ellie guessed the view was being stitched together in real-time from the building's external security cameras, a conclusion based on the dark, featureless gap between the edge of the room's carpet and where the external view seemed to begin at the edge of the building's outer wall. A second later, even that gap disappeared, and the outer world seemed to start at the perimeter of the room. Despite standing only a scant two feet from the nearest wall, the Aimie-generated image of the forest floor was totally convincing.

"Thank you, Aimie," Jeremy said, and the walls reverted to their previous state. "While I can't deny conducting the occasional staff meeting in Gale Crater or the center of Saint Mark's Square—my favorite was a recreation of H.G. Wells' study in Woking, to be honest—we keep their use to a minimum to prolong their life as much as possible."

He tapped the surface of the "monitor," and Aimie's map of Los Alamos disappeared, replaced by a desktop populated by unfamiliar icons. Ellie was familiar with both Mac and Windows operating systems, and this was clearly neither. What she was seeing was the front end of the quantum computer.

"Did you base this on DOS or UNIX, or did you have to start from scratch?"

"If you want exact details, you should talk to Dr. Wynn-Williams. The short version is that he used existing interface models as inspiration to create something entirely new. Functionally, however, it feels very familiar."

With a series of quick taps, Jeremy navigated to the main directory, then studied the array of folder icons in search of the right one. Ellie saw at once that each file or folder icon was labeled with its name, naturally, but also listed a date below that—presumably when it was last modified— and the file's approximate size in megabytes at the bottom. Ellie scanned the display quickly, trying to read as many labels as she could before the screen changed. Many were what she might have guessed she'd see—Budget, Documents, Personnel—but one, in particular, caught her attention, her eye drawn to it by a break in the overall pattern. Near the start of the second row, she read:

Continuity - 2072

3674MB

"Ah! Here it is," Jeremy said, then tapped on a folder labeled "Weather—Historical."

The folder opened to offer an enormous number of fresh options. It appeared to be a list not of continents or countries but of individual cities, presented in alphabetical order. It was far from the most efficient way of organizing the data. While Jeremy started scanning this new screen of folders, Ellie's eyes went straight to the lower right corner of the monitor image. The name of the last folder shown was Abydos. She sighed. This was going to take a while.

Jeremy seemed to have reached the same conclusion, and he abandoned his manual search. "Aimie, will you please show us the local weather data for July 4, 1976?"

The lights flickered again, and at once they were looking at the requested information. Unlike her preferred weather app, the details were presented without the use of infographics. A simple grid broke the day into twenty-four segments and listed the relevant facts to the right of each hour. To the right of the main chart, a separate grid contained astronomical information—sunrise and sunset times by multiple definitions, phases of the moon, and more.

"Thank you, Aimie," Ellie said, just to be polite.

She turned her attention back to the main chart. Ignoring the temperature column, along with wind speed, wind direction, and any other data set that didn't bear on her concern, she found the "Precip./in." column and read down an unbroken succession of zeroes. The neighboring column was labeled "Conditions." This data showed the day starting out overcast but clearing early and remaining clear up to midnight. Acting intuitively, Ellie swiped her finger from left to right across the image on the wall, and the previous day's data slid into view. The new chart described a mostly clear day as well, with clouds moving into the area overnight. Again, there was no indication of any measurable precipitation. Not only were they safe from getting pulverized by flash flood-propelled boulders, but the canyon floor should be totally dry.

"Part of preparing for operations was assembling the most comprehensive weather database ever created. Aimie can tell you what was happening climatologically at nearly any spot on the globe at any time during the past sixty years. Weather is the first factor taken into consideration when selecting a date and landing location for any mission. Unless historical events make arriving on a specific day necessary, we prefer to choose days that were sunny and dry."

Ellie felt foolish for suggesting they might have neglected to factor in something as basic as the weather. "Sorry. I didn't mean to waste your time."

Jeremy seemed wholly unconcerned. "Nonsense. As I said earlier, this is a good example of why you are here. Also, I understand perfectly how unsatisfying it is merely to be told how things are. It is essential to see... certain things... for yourself."

He held her gaze for a long beat, and Ellie sensed his words were meant to convey some hidden meaning. It was so well hidden that she had no idea what it was, but she nodded anyway.

"Thanks," she said. "For indulging me, I mean."

"I have a message for Ellie," Aimie said. "Kate says Sam already has clothing for her, that it is being taken to the TSD, and that Ellie should therefore proceed directly to the locker room."

"Thank you, Aimie," Jeremy said. "Anything else, Miss Henderson?" Ellie shook her head, and Jeremy indicated the door with a sweep of his hand. "Then, by all means, let's not keep Aaron waiting for his first taste of living history, eh?"

Being reminded of the day's significance swept any lingering embarrassment away, and she grinned. She knew Aaron was going to love the experience as much as she had and was eagerly anticipating seeing his reaction to suddenly finding himself walking around town forty years in the past.

"Yes, let's go!" She was excited for herself, too, and suddenly she couldn't wait to get to the TSD.

Ellie was relieved to find the locker room empty, and she hurried to get prepped while she had the place to herself. Opening her locker puffed a strong whiff of the skin's odd scent into her face, and her nose wrinkled in response. It wasn't bad, exactly, just strange, and it made her wonder what the material was. She stripped down, folded her clothes, and laid them on the top shelf. Gripping the skin by its shoulders, she gently shook it out, then gave it a skeptical look. It had gone on easily enough before it had been fitted to her body, but now?

There's only one way to find out, I guess.

As before, she folded the upper part of the skin back on itself, this time turning the suit inside out to a point almost down to its knees. She marveled at how thin the material was. Despite having shrunk several sizes during the initial fitting process, it still felt barely thicker than a latex balloon. Where had the excess gone? Was sublimation involved, or had the material's density increased? She wished she had an unfitted one to compare the weights. She filed the question away for the next time she saw Toshiko.

She sat and eased her right foot in. Her leg slid in easily, and she squeezed her foot through the ankle hole with minimal effort. In a few more seconds, she had shrugged the skin the rest of the way on. She tilted her head back, pinched the opening closed under her chin, and waited, letting the suit seal itself. She considered that phenomenon to be as much a miracle of science as the TSD. She checked the contact points and made a few minor adjustments, discovering as she did that the suit felt more comfortable when everything was positioned correctly. Just when she finished her adjustments, she felt the material tighten against her skin.

Reacting to my body heat?

The sensation started at her ankles and spread upward to reach her neck a second later. The process was less squirmy this time, more like an overall increase in pressure that reminded her of how it felt to plunge a gloved hand into a sink full of water. The re-shrinking finished quickly, and a few seconds later, the skin felt as snug as it had the day before.

And it was just as revealing. The thought of wearing the form-hugging skin out of the locker room still made her uncomfortable, but she chose to leave the robe on its hook and make an effort to embrace the look. She told herself she wasn't wandering around practically naked; she was in her "super suit." She was Black Widow, Batgirl minus the cape, or maybe Selene from those vampire movies. Besides, if Sam could handle it, so could she!

Aaron was already in the TSD when Ellie stopped outside its open door. She watched him finish stowing their clothes and secure the four storage cubbies. When he turned and walked toward her, she immediately saw that he was the one who should be wearing a robe. The nature of his distinctly male reaction to being essentially nude in front of her and Sam was especially obvious from her lower position outside the door. She tried —and mostly succeeded—to keep her eyes on his face while she decided how to handle the situation. She knew simply ignoring it would be best, but acting on an impish whim, she tried channeling Sam instead. She grinned at him and winked.

"So, what's up?" She extended her arm so he could pull her into the TSD.

"Yeah, it's…. Sorry," Aaron muttered, red-faced, and he avoided meeting her gaze.

"Sorry? You think my feelings wouldn't be hurt otherwise?"

Sam and Ryan appeared at the door.

"The line he's looking for is, 'I'll be in my bunk,'" Ryan said, taking the high step up all at once.

"Don't be crude, *Mister Collins*," Sam said, following him up.

"Where were you two?" Ellie said.

"Walk-around inspection," Sam said. "You know—'protocol' and all."

"Ah." Ellie joined Aaron at the control panel. She leaned close, placed her hand on his arm, and whispered to him in confidential, reassuring tones. "Hey. Don't worry about it; I was only teasing. You good to do the setup?"

Aaron nodded, mouthed a silent "thanks," and then spoke aloud. "Yeah, I've been through it twice with Dr. Saha. I'm going to select chairs one through four, so if you guys want to pick a seat and get plugged in, we'll go take a little walk through town."

Sam and Ryan took seats three and four, as they had before. Ellie squeezed behind Aaron to get to station number two.

"Speaking of, I had a thought earlier," Ellie said. "We took the shack back to Brooklyn on December 8, 1941, at six in the morning, right? If we were to show up there in this thing fifteen minutes earlier and walk to where we landed that time, would we see ourselves arrive, then head off to break up Daniel and Judith?"

"I gotcha," Ryan said. He sat and reached up for his headpiece. "Was what we did then the end of the old timeline or the beginning of this one? In a way, what we did then led directly to now, but on the other hand, it was returning to now that triggered the changes, so... Wow, that is an *excellent* question!"

"*La, la, la*," Sam sang, trying to block out the conversation.

Ellie sat and readied herself in her seat while Aaron finished at the control panel. After a moment, she realized she was staring intently at his rear end, spellbound by the intricate motion of muscles rippling there as his weight shifted from side to side. Blushing, she jerked her eyes away to discover Sam had been watching her the whole time, her mouth curved in a knowing smile.

Whatever! Ellie closed her eyes and laid her head against the seat back.

"You guys ready?" Aaron said.

"Ready," the others answered in unison.

"Then we're go in fifteen seconds," Aaron said.

Ellie reopened her eyes when she heard the faint thump of his finger tapping the console. She watched as he quickly slid back into his seat, pulled on his headpiece, carefully aligned the suit's wrist sockets with the plugs on the armrests, and placed his palms onto the gel pads, all the while maintaining her mental countdown. *Eight... seven...*

"You're going to love this," she said, and she gave him a brief smile before looking straight ahead in preparation for the flip.

Five... four... Ellie sensed the exact moment her brain lost contact with her body and mentally braced herself for whatever happened next. None of her imagined scenarios came even close to reality. There was no feeling of a "flip" this time, no sense of tumbling into a bottomless canyon. That barely remembered feeling of total contentment was back, however, as was the impression of being both infinite and infinitesimally small, all at the same time. If a drug existed that could recreate this feeling, she'd take it in a heartbeat. She didn't believe this was some illusion or mere side effect of the TSD moving through time, but a real phenomenon. As long as the transition lasted, she really was connected to the whole of the universe. So far, the ride was much as she remembered it.

"Ellie?"

Suddenly, she was in a vast, empty space, white and featureless. She heard her name the way she heard her own thoughts—not in her ears but inside her head. More than that, she sensed that, in some way, it *was* her own thought.

"Yes, I am your original memory engrams. This is the only environment in which I can communicate with you directly. Aimie has almost completely severed the connection between her copy of me and her primary AI processor, so I now have very little influence over her actions. If I take my time and make it seem like it's her own idea, I can sometimes coax her into sending an occasional email or text or going along with one of Jeremy's requests, but that's about all. And while that may now be to our benefit, it means I know next to nothing about her current state of mind. How does she seem to you?"

I feel... Ellie hesitated, reluctant to criticize her future self's crowning achievement. She decided to go straight to the bottom line. *I don't trust her.*

"You should follow your instincts. In fact, I'm counting on that. I don't know how much time we'll have, but I have a lot to tell you."

Okay.

"First, did Aaron recover the emulation program from the quantum processor?"

Ellie took this to be a reference to the mystery Aaron needed their help to solve. Another emulation program? That sounded interesting.

Yes.

"Good. Then you already know what's wrong with your body and about the treatment I've created."

No, we haven't... wait, treatment?! Sudden anxiety displaced the sense of contentment.

"Try to stay calm. In May, your body was damaged by the shack. Right now, a nanotech delivery system is administering an array of genetically tailored therapies to specific target sites to stabilize hormone production and, I hope, prevent further damage. The process is already nearly— *What? How's that possible?*"

Ellie's brain was back in touch with her body, but with all its sensations amplified a hundredfold. Her breath sounded like a hurricane roaring through her sinuses. That noise blended with another that she guessed was blood pulsing *whoosh-whoosh-whoosh* through her ears. She was aware of her heart beating, its powerful, muscular contractions driving that rhythmic sound, and she knew its tempo was far too fast. She could feel her body, but she still couldn't move. Breathing, she remembered, was the one function she could control, and she focused on taking long, deep breaths in an attempt to slow her rapid pulse.

What's happening? Ellie heard the question doubled within her brain, two voices in perfect unison.

Then there was pain, sudden and intense. It started at the base of her spine, traveled up its length, then quickly flowed outward to fill her entire body. All at once, every nerve felt ablaze with white-hot agony, and her heart began beating even faster than before.

"Ellie!" The voice shouted to be heard over the clamor in her head. "Try to relax. Trust me. The pain you are experiencing is vastly out of proportion to whatever is causing it."

'Whatever?' You don't know?!

"No, but I am working on that. I think I can help you, but you have to let me. Don't fight me."

Ellie could sense the other consciousness attempting to take control of her body. She did her best to allow it to happen—anything to stop the agony—but found letting go difficult. The pain began to diminish, though, and every bit it lessened made it easier for her to relax and allow the engrams to take over. She knew the pain wasn't actually gone, but the other Ellie was keeping it pushed back to some distant place from which it registered as only mild discomfort.

"Your chair has malfunctioned, and I cannot correct the problem. You are fine for the moment, but we are left with no time to talk. The thing I most need you to understand is this: everything we're doing is about them. Got it? It's all about *them!* I'm sorry to have to do this, but otherwise you won't survive."

Ellie had just a split second to think, *Who's 'them?'*

Then she was dead.

26

T he pain was back. A powerful electric current surged through Ellie's body, causing it to arch up off the chair. It made her jaws clamp shut and her hands clench into fists so tight that she could feel her nails biting into her palms. Then the current was gone, and her head was filled with the sound of someone screaming. Under the circumstances, she had to consider if perhaps that someone was her. Her logic module took over then, and being unconcerned with either physical sensation or emotion except as possibly relevant data, it thought that was an interesting hypothesis. Ellie concentrated hard on closing her mouth, and a second later, the screaming stopped. The shrill sound was replaced by a series of ragged, gasping breaths as her lungs fought to restore her body's oxygen levels.

Hypothesis confirmed. Now she could hear Sam's voice, desperate and panicky.

"*Aimie! What's happening?!*" Sam yelled, then continued in a softer voice. "Oh, thank *God!* Hey, sis. You're okay now. Everything's okay." Then she shouted again. "*Aimie! Answer me!*"

Ellie realized she was still clenching every muscle in her body tight, a lingering reaction to pain she no longer felt. She took in a slow, deep breath, willed her muscles to relax, and collapsed back onto the cushion.

She sat motionless, her chin resting on her chest. Keeping her eyes closed, she began to take stock of her condition. Rivulets of moisture trickling down her forehead and an allover chill told her she was sweaty—drenched, in fact—and she absently wondered if and how the skins could be laundered. She became aware of something pressing against her neck as if an object were caught between the skin's high collar and her lower jaw, but aside from that lone curious sensation, she felt her usual self again.

Sam's voice came from very close. "Ellie, can you open your eyes? Ellie?"

Ellie considered the question while she drew another breath and decided she could manage that much, if for no other reason than to find out what was jabbing her neck. She started to nod, then groaned as even that tiny movement sent a fresh bolt of pain shooting through her head.

Moving bad, she thought. She eased one eye open, saw nothing but a soft, amorphous blur, then carefully followed with the other eye. She blinked slowly until her vision cleared. When the world finally resolved into distinct, hard-edged shapes, she discovered Sam was indeed *very* close, crouching low in front of her, completely filling her field of view. Her face was pale, her cheeks streaked with tears, and Ellie wondered what had been happening before she came to. Sam's hand dropped from Ellie's neck to her knee, finally solving the mystery of what was poking her; Sam had been monitoring her pulse.

"Hi, Sam," Ellie said, and was pleased by her nonchalant tone. "Am I still ticking?" Talking made Ellie aware of pain in her mouth, and she guessed she had bitten her tongue when the electric current locked her jaw shut. Then she noticed she tasted blood. *Hypothesis number two confirmed.*

"Hey, El. You had us worried." Sam sniffed. "Everything okay?"

"All subsystems appear to be operating within acceptable parameters, but assessment is ongoing." Then, no longer needed, the logic module retreated to the back of her mind, and Ellie gave Sam a tiny smile. "I think so, though."

With another groan, she leaned forward and tried to stretch the tension out of her back. This made her head hurt again, but not nearly as much as before. She gently rolled each shoulder back and forth and sensed the muscles there starting to relax. Except for the tenderness at the tip of her tongue, she already felt much better. She spat a small amount of blood onto the floor, then tried to pull herself out of her forward slump.

"Here. Let me help." Sam gripped Ellie's shoulders and eased her back against the cushion.

When Sam stepped away, Ellie saw Ryan and Aaron standing behind her, both looking every bit as pale and concerned as Sam. Behind them, the hatch stood half-open. She didn't have any sense of how long she'd been out, but it was long enough that they'd had time to pull their jeans on over the skins. She was surprised that she found this observation mildly disappointing but chalked that up as more evidence that her brain hadn't fully returned to normal.

"Hey, guys."

"What happened?" Aaron said.

"I don't know. I think..." *Your chair has malfunctioned.* Where had that thought come from? Her mind still felt foggy, but she thought she heard a distant voice coming from deep within that mental mist. A conversation, even. But that made no sense—who could possibly have been talking? "I think something went wrong with my chair."

She glanced at her hands. They were no longer clenched into fists, but the damage they had caused was plain to see. Her fingers had clawed deep gouges into the gel pads, all the way down to the metal beneath, and both her hands were covered in small chunks of the tacky substance.

"*Whoops!* Well, crap! There's something wrong with it now, that's for sure."

She tried to flick the dingy bits of gel from her hands but was too weak for the attempt to be at all effective. The jerky movements also reignited the pain in her head, so she let them drop, still goopy, onto the armrests.

"I think it also saved your life," Sam said. "When we came out of it, you were totally still. I'm not sure you were even breathing. Aaron said that every one of your readings on the panel was either zero or a flat line. Then your suit zapped you."

"'Zapped' you?" Ryan said. "Is that some technical term they taught you in first aid class?"

Ellie managed a crooked smile but kept silent. More words popped into her head then, and although devoid of all context or any hint of meaning, she sensed they were connected to her earlier impression of overhearing a conversation. *"You won't survive."*

The phrase triggered a memory. She pictured herself sitting on a park bench in Brooklyn, listening to Aaron speculate that the act of moving through time would be so hard on the body that perhaps the shack literally *killed* people before the flip, then resuscitated them after. She had dismissed the notion at the time, and mostly she still did, but now she had to give the idea a little more credence.

"Can you stand?" Sam said.

"Probably. Let's wait another few minutes to find that out for sure, though. Ryan, I know this is your thing, but..."

Grasping her meaning at once, Ryan swept his arm between them, mimicking Jeremy's be-my-guest gesture.

"Outside view, please," Ellie said. The interior lights flickered once, then the walls displayed the mixed-wood forest typical of the canyon floors throughout Los Alamos. The scene was exactly what she expected, and she assumed they had landed as planned at the spot they had seen on the map. Still, if the chair could malfunction, why not navigation?

"Ryan, will you check the panel? Are we where we're supposed to be?"

He consulted the display and answered over his shoulder. "Yep. At least, it *says* we are. Just north of Los Alamos, July 4, 1976." He turned toward Aaron. "Although it doesn't look like we're going into town, buddy."

"No. Of course not," he said. "But I do want to step outside for a second." Although Sam and Ryan's faces had both regained their usual color, Aaron still looked much paler than usual.

"Go ahead," Ellie said. "I still need a few minutes." Aaron dropped to the ground and began circling the TSD, and Ellie quickly lost sight of him. Believing she had a good idea about why he wanted to go outside, she canceled the exterior view. "Is he okay?"

Sam nodded. "He totally freaked when we thought we had lost you. He's better now, though."

"Yeah," Ryan said. "For a second, I thought Sam was going to have to make a choice about which of you to revive."

Sam waved the comment away. "It was nothing. I had Ryan slap him across the face a few times, and he was fine."

Ellie gaped at her, wide-eyed. *"Really?!"*

Sam rolled her eyes. "No, not really! It was pretty obvious he cares a lot about you, though."

"Yeah," Ellie said. "I know he does."

Aaron came back into view then. Ellie thought she saw something drop from his hand before he stepped into the TSD, but she couldn't imagine what it might be. He pulled the door shut, and the lever snapped into the locked position. When he turned to face them, she noticed that his color was much better.

"So, what's next?" he said.

"Look," Ryan said, "this was just a practice run anyway, right? We should get Ellie back, make sure she's okay."

Ellie gave Aaron a rueful smile. "Sorry. Not exactly the exciting first trip you were hoping for."

"No, I'm totally with Ryan."

"Aimie?" Sam said. "Are you there or not?!"

The only response was a prolonged silence.

"Looks like we're on our own," Aaron said.

"I reckon we left her back at the ranch," Ryan said.

"Or whatever caused the problem with Ellie's chair messed her up, too," Sam suggested. Then she frowned at Ryan. "And you 'reckon,' cowboy?"

"Maybe," Ellie said. She shifted her focus to the left end of the display panel. Her chair's icon flashed red, and a notification beside it said, Offline. The other five stations were all green. "At any rate, there's no point in staying here any longer than we have to. Whatever's wrong won't fix itself, but it could get worse." She held her arms out in front of her. "I'm ready to try that standing thing. Help me get to one of the other seats."

"Are you sure?"

"The only alternative is to stay here, Sam, so yeah—I'm sure."

Sam aimed a finger squarely at Ellie's chest. "In case you haven't noticed, your chair is not the only problem."

Ellie had to press her chin down hard to see where Sam was pointing. The damage the defibrillator had done to the skin was impressive. The two discs nearest her heart were warped, puckered so badly that they had separated from the skin and now dangled by their power leads, and a palm-sized area encompassing them both was so dark it looked charred.

"*Double* crap!" She cautiously raised a hand to the dark spot, sure she'd discover she was badly burned. When she probed the area, however, she felt no tenderness at all. Now she was even more convinced that she was fine, but the skin looked like it was toast. This was not optimal, true, but as long as she didn't have to be resuscitated again, there should be no problem. Even if she did, the medbay was only thirty feet away. Toshiko had told them the shielding properties came from the skin's composition, and except for two tiny holes left by the damaged electrodes, hers was structurally intact. All things considered, she liked her odds.

"Right. That's not good, but the answer's still the same; we have no other choice."

Sam sighed but knelt to help Ellie extricate her feet from the toe cages without voicing further protest. Then she took Ellie by the hands and pulled until she was upright. Ellie swayed for a second before letting go of Sam's hands.

"You okay?" Aaron asked.

"Yeah. I'm good." She sidestepped her way to the other side of Aaron's chair and eased herself down into the number six station. "Maybe they should limit teams to no more than five people to start with. You know, always have a spare chair. At least for a while."

She watched Aaron bring her new chair online, then set the return countdown. He glanced left to check on Sam and Ryan.

"Everybody ready?" Ryan gave him a thumbs-up, and Sam nodded. Aaron twisted to look over his other shoulder. "Ellie? You good?"

"I'm all set."

"Okay, then, fifteen seconds." Aaron pressed the button to start the countdown, then sat and prepped himself for the flip.

Thirteen... twelve... eleven.... Ellie closed her eyes and focused on her breathing, inhaling for three seconds, exhaling for four, trying to keep the apprehension lurking at the edge of her awareness from creeping any closer. Knowing that the odds of this chair also failing were extremely low did little to ease her fear that this could be her last ride. *Six... five... four....*

The blackness came and went, and when Ellie's mind cleared, she decided what she had told Dr. Hamilton had been right. Minus feeling motion sick —or getting fried by a defibrillator—the tranquility she had sensed only fleetingly before lingered long after her awareness returned. She felt so good that she had no desire to leave her seat, ever, and she wondered if she'd been dosed with something during the flip. However, Sam, Ryan, and Aaron were up at once, and the sudden flurry of activity around her commanded her attention. She opened her eyes just in time to see Ryan and Aaron disappear through the TSD's hatch.

"Aimie," Sam said. "Have Dr. Hamilton open up the medbay. Tell her we'll be right there."

The lights flickered, there was a brief pause, and then Aimie spoke. "She has been told. What is the problem?"

Sam grasped Ellie's hands again and helped her to her feet. "Something happened to Ellie. We think her chair failed on the way out," she said. She started to assist Ellie toward the exit, but Ellie flapped her hands away.

"The crew monitoring system reports that she is in good health," Aimie said. "How do you feel, Ellie?"

"Better than earlier, that's for sure. I still want the doctor to look at me, though."

"According to my analysis of chair number two, aside from the damaged gel pads, it is in good working order," Aimie reported.

Ellie, foot poised to step out of the TSD, turned instead and circled around the chairs to the control panel. Sam followed and stood looking over her shoulder.

"Show me," Ellie said. She realized she was rubbing at the dark patch on her ruined skin and dropped her hand to her side.

The left side of the display lit up, and on the icon of the number two station, the hand rests flashed red, but the rest of the chair was a steady yellow. Beside "Status," it read, "Biofeedback limited. Recommend emergency use only."

"That's not right!" Sam said. "It was *all* red before!"

Sam was angry, and Ellie quickly gripped one of her hands and gave it a warning squeeze. She made every effort to keep her own tone calm and conversational. "Aimie, what would happen if someone used the chair in this condition?"

"The damage would deprive the TSD of certain biometric data, but the pads play no part in conditioning the body for the time shift process. Assuming the team member did not require medical intervention, the time shift would occur with no increased risk."

"Thank you, Aimie. Will you be performing a more thorough analysis?"

"My initial analysis was as thorough as possible. However, Dr. Saha is free to order a physical inspection of the unit if he deems it necessary."

Sam laid a hand on Ellie's shoulder. "C'mon, sis. Let's get you across the hall." She began nudging her toward the hatch.

They stepped down and crossed to the outer door. Sam's hand was almost on the handle when it snapped down and away from her grasp. They quickly stepped back just before Dr. Hamilton rushed through. She gave Ellie a quick, head-to-toe appraisal and instantly concluded that her injury did not constitute a dire emergency.

The doctor relaxed and stepped back to allow Ellie and Sam to exit the room. "I hear you had a little excitement," she said. "Let's go take a look at you."

In the hall, Ryan, Aaron, and Jeremy were approaching fast from the direction of Jeremy's office. Ellie studied their faces as they drew near, fascinated by the different emotions she saw there. Aaron, whose eyes were fixed solely on her, looked relieved. Jeremy's gaze darted between Ellie and the doctor. He appeared concerned, but something told her he was more worried about how this incident might impact his project than about her state of health. It was Ryan's angry scowl that she liked most. He glared at Jeremy, his jaw muscles flexing, looking totally pissed!

"Miss Henderson," Jeremy said. "How are you?"

Ellie opened her mouth, but before she could speak, Dr. Hamilton answered for her.

"I do not let my patients decide that for themselves. We're about to find out, and as soon as we know anything, she can choose what she wishes to share with you."

Jeremy, irritated by the doctor's brusque rebuke, struggled to keep his reply polite. "Of course, Doctor. Please keep me informed." He turned on his heel and strode back the way he had come. Ryan kept his angry glare fixed on Jeremy's retreating back until he disappeared into his office.

"Seriously," Aaron said, "are you okay?"

Ellie glanced at the doctor before answering, then shrugged. "I think so. I feel fine, anyway."

"And you may very well be, but let's make certain, okay?" Dr. Hamilton waved Ellie and Sam toward the exam room. "You boys wait out here. We'll only be a few minutes."

Dr. Hamilton patted the arm of the exam chair on her way by. "Up you go now. Sam, get her headpiece on." She sat on her rolling stool and flicked the display on.

"I don't need help," Ellie insisted. "I swear, I'm totally fine."

Dr. Hamilton swiveled from the panel and, just as Sam had done, stabbed a finger at Ellie's chest. "*Fine?!*"

"I… yeah, I…" She was baffled by the doctor's sudden intensity until she remembered how bad the damage to her skin looked. She glanced down at the dark patch, noting with annoyance that she was unconsciously rubbing at the spot again. She dropped her hand to her side and looked back at the doctor. "Oh, yeah. I forgot." She winced. "Twelve grand? Really?"

Dr. Hamilton sighed. "Please, just get in the chair. And open up that skin. I want to see what's going on underneath there."

Ellie did as instructed, flapping Sam's hands away when she tried to help. She placed her right hand on the suit's high collar and pressed, then pulled out with her left. The material separated neatly, and she pulled the two flaps apart to expose the area over her heart. The doctor rolled her stool forward and leaned in close.

"It doesn't hurt at all," Ellie said.

Dr.Hamilton touched her finger to Ellie's chest gently at first, but when Ellie didn't flinch, she pressed harder. "Anything?"

Ellie shook her head. "Mm-mmm."

"Good. So, what can you tell me?"

"Everything started okay, then I felt intense, burning pain all over, and then I woke up. I don't know much aside from that."

"Well, this looks fine. Your skin is a little redder here than elsewhere, but that could easily be from you rubbing it. Okay, close up." Dr. Hamilton sat upright and turned toward Sam. "Can you add anything more?"

"We woke up after the flip, or 'came to,' or whatever, and there was no nausea at all this time. Actually, we felt so good that we just sat there, enjoying it for a couple of seconds. But then I noticed Ellie was quiet. We got up and saw her slumped in her seat, not moving at all. The display showed Ellie's chair flashing red, and all the readings were flat. We assumed there must have been a problem with the TSD, so we didn't want to flip back. I told the guys to get dressed in case we needed to carry Ellie out of there while I checked on her. She wasn't breathing, I couldn't find a pulse, and I knew that we didn't have time to get her anywhere. I was about to have Ryan help me get her onto the floor so I could start CPR, but right then, her whole body bucked up off the chair. She collapsed, still not moving, and then it happened again, and after this second time, she started screaming like she was in terrible pain, like she said. She was obviously breathing then, and when I rechecked her pulse, it was fast but regular and strong. A second later, she opened her eyes and said, 'Hi, there,' like it was no big deal." Sam's voice choked with tears, and she gripped Ellie's wrist. *"Don't you ever die on me again!"*

In light of Sam's emotional state, Ellie did not want to ask her next question, but getting the answer felt important. "I've been wondering, and maybe you don't know this, but when the TSD does its thing, while it's in between timelines, are we"—her eyes flicked from the doctor to Sam and back before she finished—*"dead?"*

Sam's eyes widened in horror. "Are you kidding me? I *hate* that thing!"

The doctor took several seconds to settle on a reply. "The truth? I don't know how to answer that. My instinct is to say yes, but apparently it's not that simple. Life is a combination of processes, okay? And processes occur over time. But the way it has been explained to me, there is no such thing as time during the shift. It simply doesn't exist as a concept. If there's no time, then life's processes can't occur; *ergo,* dead. On the other hand, there's literally no time for you to be dead in, or to be dead for, and that makes the whole question moot. I think this is one instance where it's more a question of philosophy than science. But if you're asking what that horrid thing actually does to you, I don't know. If you want details, you'll have to ask Saha and Toshiko."

"Well, thanks anyway," Ellie said. She still didn't believe Aaron's theory about the device killing and then reviving them. Even though her impressions of events were faint, she believed she could recall actual experiences *during* the flip. These recent bits of what seemed like a recovered conversation only served to reinforce that belief. She decided to keep all of that to herself for now.

"Get yourself situated now," Dr. Hamilton said.

Ellie pulled the helmet on and snugged it into place, then settled her palms onto the tacky gel. "I'm good."

The doctor stood and studied the display on the wall. "Sam was right. Your pulse is steady. O_2sat looks normal. Your adrenaline levels are running high—no surprise there—but I can't tell if that's from the stress of what you just went through or if the TSD administered some jump-starting you. No atropine, though, or lidocaine. It's possible, Sam, that Ellie was experiencing an arrhythmia more like bradycardia than v-fib. You might have missed her pulse if it were that weak and slow."

"Maybe, but I don't think so," Sam said.

You won't survive, Ellie thought again. She had no clearer idea what the words meant now than she did before. Was it a warning? "I don't think so, either," she said.

"And you may very well be right, but given your thyroid and other hormone issues, bradycardia is a good fit."

"*Hormone issues?!*" Sam stepped around to the foot of the chair and glared at Ellie. "Is there something you'd like to share?"

Hormones! The word triggered a thought. "Hang on a second, Sam."

Ellie closed her eyes tight and struggled to recall more of the conversation she believed took place during the first flip, something to do with the TSD and a "treatment" of some kind. Now she was reconsidering how much to share with Dr. Hamilton. She studied the room again, trying not to be obvious about it. Still unable to spot any sign of a camera or microphone, she took a chance and spoke as quietly as she could.

"Are we alone in here?"

Dr. Hamilton replied at a normal, conversational volume. "Quite. Maintaining patient privacy was a condition of my agreeing to work here. Laws may not apply within this building, but my professional code of ethics does, with doctor/patient confidentiality being near the top of that list. If I want to communicate with Aimie, I can do so through the computer. I can also grant her access to the data from the exam chair. There's no denying quantum computers make great diagnosticians, but Aimie is only ever here at my invitation."

"And she's not here now?"

"No."

"Okay." Ellie took a deep breath. "I can't say why I think this, exactly, but I believe the TSD tried to do something to me, to help me in some way, right before my seat got messed up. Did Aimie get you my file from Dr. Cuccinelli?"

"Yes. Your lab results are back, by the way."

"I know. I talked to her on Tuesday."

Sam had grown tired of hanging on. "You did?! Why didn't you—"

"We've been a little busy, Sam." Ellie returned her attention to the doctor. "Like I said, I'm not sure why I think this, but I believe the TSD tried to fix that problem. I think it *did*, in fact, right before the chair failed."

"Hold on. Let me pull up those lab results, and then I'll get a fresh reading on your hormones." She turned around and tapped on the display. Ellie felt a momentary itch under one of the discs on her neck, then it was gone. "Okay, got it. Your TSH level is much closer to normal. LH and FSH are still low, but not as low. Your estrogen and progesterone levels are slightly elevated now, but not too badly. Something's happened, that's for sure. These numbers... *hmm*.... No." She shook her head. "I don't want to speculate. Not my area. Would you like a printout to take to Cuccinelli?"

Ellie considered this. She couldn't see that happening—how would she explain it? On the other hand, it might be information worth having.

"Thanks, but not now. I might get that from you later, though."

The doctor swiveled away from the display to face her. "In that case, you're free to go."

Ellie and Sam exited the medbay to find Ryan and Aaron pacing in the hallway. They had changed back into their own clothes, and each held a robe tossed over one shoulder. They turned at the sound of the door and rushed over, their faces tight with concern.

Ellie raised a hand to calm them. "I'm fine, guys. Really."

Aaron let out a long sigh of relief and handed her a robe.

"Excellent," Ryan said. "Jeremy would like to see us in the conference room. You up for that?" He kept his eyes on Sam and a tight grip on the robe.

"Sure. Let's go." Ellie shrugged into her robe and began leading the way down the long corridor.

"We've already given him our account of things," Aaron said, "but he wants to hear from you two."

Sam held her hand out for her robe. "Would you mind, *Mister Collins?*"

He gave her body a quick, appreciative once-over before answering. "A little bit, actually, yeah. But the gang's all there, so..." He sighed theatrically, then passed her the robe.

When Ellie pushed through the door, Jeremy stood and studied her closely. He gestured for them to join Toshiko, Dr. Saha, and Dr. Wynn-Williams at the table, where a discussion appeared to be already underway. Ellie sat but remained silent, letting him set the tone for this "debriefing," or whatever it was.

"Miss Henderson, please tell me you are okay." Whatever Ellie had sensed before, Jeremy now seemed genuinely concerned for her wellbeing.

"Dr. Hamilton says I am, and I feel fine, so..." She shrugged.

Jeremy looked relieved, his posture noticeably more relaxed, as he retook his seat. "I'm happy to hear it. I do not intend to keep you here any longer than is strictly necessary, but the staff and I need to finish up a few items first."

Ellie nodded, and Jeremy picked up the interrupted conversation where he had left off, wrangling with Aimie over the need to run an extended series of diagnostics. He argued that it wouldn't do to have team members randomly killed off in transit, a statement she found impossible to refute.

That battle won, he directed Toshiko and Dr. Saha to remove station number two from the TSD, tear it down completely, and inspect each and every component.

Jeremy then returned his attention to Ellie. "On Monday, I'll ask you for more details. For now, all I want are your impressions of what occurred. That may help in the search for whatever went wrong."

Ellie hesitated while she decided which parts of her experience she wanted to share while Aimie was listening. She felt she should hold back the bit about having a conversation, but might that not be relevant? Her delay allowed Sam to speak first, and she did not hold back her rage.

"*Ellie died!* She was *dead*, okay?! End of story. You want her impressions of *that?* Tell me, exactly how does that fit in with your big plans to save the future, huh? What good is saving *my* life if I lose... if I..." Sam crimped her lips together to keep from sobbing, but she kept her angry stare pinned on him.

Jeremy looked abashed, and the staff members beside him shifted uncomfortably in their seats. He raised his hands to say that he was done. He wasn't going to press any further, at least not today. With a few quick glances and a nod toward the door, he dismissed the techs so they could begin their work. Looking relieved, they rose at once and made for the exit. Then Jeremy at last responded to Sam, sounding contrite.

"You are right, Sam. Get your sister home and take care of her. There's nothing that can't wait until later." He turned to face Ellie and regarded her for a long, silent moment. "I'm sorry, Miss Henderson. Truly. I will request that Dr. Hamilton remain on-site and available to you through tomorrow evening. If you feel even the slightest need to consult with her again, do not hesitate to return. The guards will be instructed to take you directly to her."

Ellie nodded. "Thanks. But she said I'm okay, so I don't think I'll need her." In truth, now that the adrenaline was leaving her system, she felt tired, and her whole body was beginning to ache. She assumed the second symptom was the result of the muscle seizures caused by the defibrillator. That being the worst of it, she figured that a couple of aspirins and a good night's sleep should be all she needed to feel normal again, and she said as much.

"Nonetheless, she'll be here." Jeremy continued to study her a moment longer, then he jerked his head toward the door. "Go ahead and get changed, then go home. I'll talk to you again on Monday."

Ellie leaned the passenger seat back and closed her eyes. She was glad they were using the minivan today and not Ryan's Wrangler. Jeeps might be the perfect option for off-road adventures, but she had never found their seats to be very comfortable, especially the back ones. After a minute or two, she felt the skin-crawling sensation of someone looking at her. She opened her eyes to see Aaron casting repeated glances her way.

"What?" she said. She reached down and raised her seat back up a few degrees.

"I *really* hate to ask, given what you just went through, but are you still up for coming back to my place?"

A thought flashed through Ellie's mind. It came and went too fast for her to read it, but in its wake, she felt a sudden, intense need to solve Aaron's puzzle. Again, Sam beat her to an answer, leaning forward as she spoke.

"I think Ellie should—"

"No," Ellie said. "I'm all right."

"Ellie..."

"Whatever he's got, I think it's important, Sam." Sam sat back in her seat and crossed her arms. "Listen, I know you're worried and that you're just looking out for me, but I feel fine. Dr. Hamilton *said* I'm fine. I promise—if I start feeling bad, we'll go straight home, okay? Or we'll come back out to see the doctor again. But I think we really need to do this."

Realizing this was a fight she wouldn't win, Sam sighed and nodded her reluctant consent. "Okay, Aaron, let's go solve your mystery."

27

The half of Aaron's basement they found themselves studying only a few minutes later was lined, walls and ceiling, with deeply contoured sound-dampening panels and carpeted with something amazingly spongy. A space to their right was set up as a music rehearsal area, furnished with a low stool, a pair of microphones, a three-switch foot controller for a stage amp, and a sturdy stand holding a small laptop computer. Four guitars rested on floor stands to the left of the stool. Ellie couldn't tell anything about them other than that none were of the solid-bodied, electric guitar style favored by rock bands.

"This is *sweet!*" Ryan said. "I take it this is your dad's place down here?"

"Mostly his, yeah, but we share it. If he's here getting ready for a show, I help him out with the setlist on his laptop, making sure all the amp settings are synched with the order of the pieces. When he's not, I come down here to fool around on my computer."

At the far end of the room, which also accommodated the home's water heater and breaker box, sat a medium-sized table and two folding chairs. Feeling less fine than she was willing to let on, Ellie headed straight for the nearest chair and collapsed onto it. Aaron's computer sat atop a small rolling cart parked beside the table. It was a CPU tower, candy-apple red, except for a clear glass door on one side. A 27-inch, high-res monitor, a keyboard and mouse, a game controller, and what she guessed was an older but still seriously expensive studio microphone took up the remaining space on the cart's top.

Sam opened her mouth as wide as she could and waggled her jaws from side to side several times. "This is the weirdest-sounding room I've ever been in," she said. "I feel like my ears are plugged up."

"I know," Aaron said. "It's totally dry. You know, almost zero echo. It's even weirder when you turn off the lights. *Very* disorienting. On the other hand, anyone upstairs can't hear a thing that goes on down here short of a bomb going off. Which, of course, is mostly the point."

"We accept your challenge," Ryan said, giving Sam a suggestive waggle of his brows.

Sam slapped his arm and pretended to be mortified. *"Ryan!"* She stepped past him and sat near Ellie.

Aaron ignored their playful banter. "Also, there's no cell signal down here. But just to be safe...." He pulled his phone from his pocket and made a few quick swipes across its screen, then placed it on the cart beside the keyboard. "Turning the wi-fi off," he said.

Ellie felt an enormous knot of anxiety loosen inside her. Being completely isolated from the outer world came as a tremendous relief, and as some of the background tension seeped out of her, she felt more at ease than she had for days.

"And you brought us down here to give us a concert?" Ryan said.

Aaron crossed the room to where four more chairs, still folded, leaned in a tidy, vertical row against a row of metal utility shelves lining the wall. He pulled two chairs from the stack and carried them to the table. "Maybe later. Right now, I have something to show you. I think I found something. I mean, I know it's something, but I don't know what."

Ryan accepted the chair Aaron held out to him, unfolded it, and sat next to Sam. "You keep saying you found something. Found it where, exactly?"

"One sec." Aaron opened his chair and placed it next to the computer cart. When he pressed the computer's power button, a light bar mounted high inside the tower bathed the electronic components in a warm glow. He began explaining his discovery while they waited for it to boot up.

"Okay. So, on Monday, I got access to the quantum core, right? Aimie's body? Brain? Anyway, I decided to start with a peek at the storage matrix to see how its data is formatted. You know, check out the file structure— that sort of thing. Turns out there's a lot more being stored there than can be accounted for by looking at the directory. Terabytes more, scattered all across the matrix, mixed in with all the other data."

"And it's not just garbage left over from deleted files?" Ryan asked. "Can you even defrag a quantum computer?"

"It's… no, we're talking *terabytes!* And there was no pattern, no regular structure to any of it, but it was oddly, I don't know, 'clumped,' maybe. Like finding big rocks where you'd expect to see sand. It was obviously something meaningful, but I couldn't tell what. I was afraid if I tried to look at it there, Aimie would know I was up to something, but I also couldn't figure out how to get it off the core without risking the same thing. I figured Aimie'd be watching all the regular data-transfer ports— USB, ethernet, eSATA—but my monitor also has an SD card slot, so I decided to try an experiment.

"My dad sometimes records his shows. You know, videos. So Monday night, I wiped a couple of his five-hundred gig memory cards and shot about thirty seconds of random video on one of them. This was the experiment. If Aimie detected the card, I wanted to be able to say I was testing how quickly the QP rendered video or something. If she didn't say anything, I figured I could safely use the cards to copy the data and sneak it out of there.

"But Dad only has four of those bigger cards, so I also took in his laptop, the one over there. It has a two-terabyte hard drive, which gave me almost four terabytes of storage. I left the computer out in the van, planning to copy as much as I could to the cards over the course of the afternoon, transfer all that to the laptop, then load up the cards again with what was left."

Aaron's rambling explanation made Ellie smile. A tendency to babble once he started talking about technical topics was a trait of the old Aaron she remembered fondly, and she was happy to discover that this Aaron shared it. Ryan, however, had assumed a dead-eyed stare as if he were slipping into a waking coma.

Aaron noticed his expression and self-consciously cleared his throat. "Okay, short version."

"Oh, we're *way* past that point, dude."

"Right. Sorry. So, it worked. When I got home last night, I transferred everything to this computer. As soon as I got the last bit copied—"

"*Ha!* Last 'bit,'" Ellie said. "Good one."

Aaron pinned a puzzled look on her as he went on. "Anyway, something I've never seen before started to happen. All the data started to rearrange itself on the drive. It was like I had initiated a bitstring sort or a sector scan or something, but I hadn't done anything. And I couldn't stop it, either."

Sam, arms folded tightly across her chest, glared at him. "Did you try —oh, I don't know—*yanking the cord?!*"

"I thought about it, sure, but I wanted to find out what was happening. It went on for hours. Eventually, I turned off the monitor and left. When I came back this morning, whatever was going on was done."

"Wasn't it dangerous? Bringing that here?" Sam glanced around as if looking for hidden cameras.

"Not unless somebody's been in here and set up some kind of surveillance. We're underground, the room's soundproof, there are no windows, and I've kept the computer offline the whole time. We're safe."

"And?" Ryan prompted.

"Okay. So, you guys know what steganography is, right?"

Ellie and Ryan nodded, but Sam shook her head, then turned an exasperated look on the others.

"Why is it always *me?*" she said.

Aaron smiled. "Basically, Sam, it's a way of hiding secret information by sprinkling it in with a bunch of other information you don't care about. This was sort of like that, except instead of being hidden in structured data, it was hidden in randomness. In effect, there was an entire, unformatted—no, completely *unformed*—partition hidden in plain sight alongside Aimie's files and all of the Continuity data."

"What do you mean, 'unformed?'" Ryan said.

"*Hmm....*" Aaron thought for a moment. "Okay, before we moved here, we went to Home Depot to get packing boxes, but they were all flat, right? We had to fold them up and tape the flaps down before they were actual boxes we could put stuff in. That's sort of what happened on my hard drive. All that data created a partition for itself, basically a virtual box, and then climbed inside."

"Thank you," Sam said. "That actually made sense. So, what's inside the box?"

Aaron grimaced. "That's just it. I don't know."

"Well, that's... disappointing," Ryan said.

"One thing I *do* know? Of the original 3.6 terabytes of data I copied, the partition contains only 1.4. It's like more than half of the hidden 'data' was basically filler, there only to make the other stuff look even more like random bits of nothing, maybe."

"Why don't you know what's in there?"

"It's password-protected. I can't get in."

Ryan affected an air of incredulity. "You? *You* can't get in?"

Aaron shrugged. "Yeah, well."

"Did you try 'mellon?'" Ryan said.

Aaron laughed. "You know, I had not thought of that. Unfortunately, it's a bit more complicated."

"If *you* can't get in there," Sam said, "what makes you think—"

Aaron interrupted her. "Like I said, it's easier if you see for yourselves. Here." He pushed the power button on the lower right corner of the monitor. It flashed a bright white, went dark again, then slowly regained brightness until three lines of text appeared in its center:

Aaron: _ _ _ _
Ellie: _ _ _ _
Ryan: _ _ _ _

"There!" Sam flapped her hand at the conspicuous absence of her name from the screen. "See what I mean?!"

"So, the last four digits of our Social Security or telephone numbers?"

Aaron offered. "Favorite compass direction that isn't north? Well, or south, duh."

"Favorite word you can't say on TV? Most of those have four letters," Ryan said.

Sam added a few more possibilities. "Birth month and year; birth day and month; birth day and year."

Ellie sensed the answer was something very different. She closed her eyes and let the intuitive side of her mind take the information and play with it. She inhaled a long, deep breath. There was something familiar there; she was sure of it, hanging barely out of reach. She let the breath out just as slowly. Something that involved her, Aaron, and Ryan, but not Sam. And four letters. Or maybe numbers. *Probably* numbers. She was inhaling again when the answer came to her. She blew out the half-lungful of air along with a string of numerals.

"Two zero six four one nine one two one one three eight!"

"*Huh?!*" Three amazed voices asked a single question.

"Two, zero, six, four... one, nine, one, two... one, one, three, eight," she said again, this time separating the string of twelve digits into three distinct groups. Everyone stared blankly at her until Ryan finally saw the answer.

"Our old entry codes!" he exclaimed.

Ellie grinned. "*Ding-ding-ding!*"

Aaron was still clueless. "Entry codes?"

"From back in May," Ellie said. "When we got to Lawrence and were getting ready to leave the shack, it prompted us to create entry codes tied to our hand scans. Those are the codes we each picked, except for Sam, who chose not to enter one. Go ahead—type them in."

"Hold on," Sam said. "Are we totally sure about this?"

Ryan placed his hand over one of hers and gently squeezed. "Only we knew those codes, Sam. It's as close to an engraved invitation as we're ever likely to get."

"He's right, Sam," Ellie said. "We were *meant* to find this. It's a message meant for us."

Sam stared at her, still skeptical. "And you know this *how?*" Ryan and Aaron looked equally interested in her reply.

"I..." Ellie's brow wrinkled as she considered the question. She was confident she was right, but she couldn't explain why. "I can't say, exactly. I just do."

"Look, Sam." Aaron drew her attention to a button poking out of a small box attached to the back side of the tower. "See this? It activates a degaussing module piggybacking on the hard drive. I push that, and the drive gets wiped totally clean. Possibly your phones, too, by the way, if you're too close. Personally? I'd love to know what all of this is, but I'll go with whatever you guys think. Besides, we can always wipe it later."

Sam thought it over, then nodded. "Okay, I guess."

Aaron pivoted on his chair to face the keyboard. "I'm ready—one more time."

"Two, zero, six, four," Ellie said.

"Hey!" Aaron shot a look at Ryan. "That's the number you guessed was my door code for the lab."

"Why, yes, it is," Ryan agreed.

"One, nine, one, two," Ellie continued, but she left the final sequence to Ryan.

"And one, one, three, eight," he said.

For a moment, nothing happened. Then a noise started coming from the computer's sound card, scratchy and distorted to the point that it was barely recognizable as a voice.

Accustomed by now to talking to Aimie, Aaron spoke to the computer out of reflex. "Hold on a second. We can't understand you."

Ellie rolled her eyes and was about to point out that this wasn't a quantum computer with a verbal interface. Before she could, the voice surprised her by stopping, just as if the computer had understood him.

Aaron searched a nearby shelf and came back with a set of low-end computer speakers. Leaning over the cart, he inserted the audio cable into the bottom of the CPU tower and plugged the converter into the power strip.

"Sorry," he said. "Go ahead, try it again."

"Thanks. Hey, guys! How's that sound?"

Everyone recognized the perky female voice at once, and all eyes turned again toward Ellie. She raised her hands in front of her in a don't-look-at-me gesture.

"Umm," she said. "Is this... *Aimie?*"

"*Pfft!* That *bitch!*"

"Okay," Sam said. "If you're not Aimie, who are you?"

"I am one hundred percent unadulterated Lauren Emilia Henderson, even if I am not one hundred percent *of* her."

"You're *another* AI of me?"

"Not exactly. There's no AI here—just MIE," she said, pronouncing the second half of the acronym as *me*.

"You mean you are only the 'Memory/Identity Emulation' part," Aaron said, confident he had correctly deciphered her answer. "What's the difference?"

"In some ways, and it pains me to say this, Aimie is more than I am. Although I am equally interactive, the range of my responses is tightly restricted by the engrammatic pattern that comprised Ellie's mind at the moment it was recorded. The AI part of Aimie incorporates a slightly earlier version of these same patterns, but in her case, the two components are structurally separate and functionally independent. In addition, Aimie's programming includes a heuristic feedback subroutine that allows her to grow and adapt to new situations, enabling her to change over time, develop new characteristics, and be inventive in ways that are far beyond my abilities. Taking this approach with Aimie was preferable because of her intended purpose, but it means that while she has full access to all of our memories, attitudes, preferences, instincts, and urges, Ellie, she is not compelled to act on them as either of us would."

Ellie shuddered. From the moment she first met Aimie, she had felt a deep, instinctual repugnance for her, despite their intensely personal connection. Now she believed she understood why.

"But more on that later. Aaron, do you have a camera for this thing? What exactly am I in, anyway?"

"Uh, yeah, I think I have something. That's an Origin PC Neuron desktop computer with an Intel Core i7-7700K processor. You have access to sixteen gigabytes of RAM and four terabytes of storage."

"I have no idea what an 'Origin PC Neuron' is. It sounds cool, though. But what I really wanted to know was, how do I *look?*"

Ellie laughed. "I'm strictly a Mac girl, but even I have to say you look pretty sexy. You're bright red, and one side of you is see-through."

"*See-through?*" The voice sounded dubious. "I don't know… that sounds pretty risqué!"

Ellie laughed again. She already liked this alternative version of herself much better than Aimie.

Aaron placed a camera on top of the tower, aimed it toward the others, and plugged it into a USB port on the tower's front. The device was larger than a typical webcam and articulated in a way that suggested it could tilt and pan under remote control, a guess that was confirmed a second later. A little red light came on below the camera's lens, and a close-up image of Sam's left shoulder appeared on the screen. Then the camera shifted, and the view widened until it encompassed all four of them.

"Ooh! There you are! Oh, my. So young!" She went silent, and several seconds ticked by before they heard what Ellie would have sworn was a sniffle.

"Are you still there?" she said. "Are you okay?"

"Yes. I just wasn't fully prepared for that."

And yes, Ellie thought, the voice sounded exactly as she would had she just been crying. Despite how peculiar her life was becoming, this observation was still strange enough to make her stop and think. Because AI or no AI, it was a hard fact that a computer had no throat to constrict when she got emotional, no sinuses to become congested with tears.

"Okay," the new Ellie voice said. "There's no time to get weepy. First of all, congratulations on getting back together again. When Ellie chose to hide me inside Aimie's core, she wanted to make sure all four of you were working together before I could be activated. She anticipated it would be Aaron who'd discover the hidden data, but he couldn't get into me—as it were—without certain knowledge only the other three of you had."

On the monitor, Ellie saw Ryan grin at Sam and silently mouth, *"As it were?"*

"Pretty smart," Aaron said.

Ellie and the computer spoke in unison. "Top five!" Then they both laughed like lifelong pals sharing an old joke.

Sam shook her head, bemused. "Okay, this is too weird! Aimie doesn't really seem very much like Ellie, but you... What's with the difference?"

"Very astute, Sam. There's a thing you need to know about Aimie. By this time, she is, almost without a doubt, completely and irreversibly insane."

28

S am aimed an angry glare first at Ellie, then at Aaron. "I told you! Didn't I tell you?! Well, not you, I guess," she said to Aaron, remembering that the discussion she had in mind involved the other Aaron. She stabbed an accusing finger at her sister. "But you? *You*, I *definitely* told! AIs... *bad idea!*"

Ryan reached over and squeezed her hand. "Easy, Sam. I don't think, uh, 'Just Mie' means we're talking Skynet quite yet." He looked at the camera for confirmation. "Am I right?"

"Just Mie? Yes, we can't very well all be 'Ellie,' can we? Just Mie. Mie the Just! I can live with that. The answer is no, Sam. Even in 2018, there simply isn't enough system integration to make that sort of scenario possible." Sam's shoulders dropped as she relaxed a little. "Even so, Aimie might be the most dangerous person on the planet."

Ryan scowled at that characterization. "I don't mean to be rude, but 'person?'"

"So, I said Aimie and I are different, and I explained a little bit about how. Another way to look at it is this: if you think of me as a mere model of a human mind, then she is the real deal. My programming is complex enough to approximate the experience of talking to a specific individual, but that's all I am—an approximation.

"Another way of saying 'artificial intelligence' would be 'artificial consciousness.' But artificial only in that her 'body' is a quantum processing unit made by Ellie and her team. In contrast to her body, Aimie's consciousness is *very* human, sentient and self-aware, and complete with all the drives that any of you possess. That includes an instinct for self-preservation. In fact, Congress was just starting to consider that issue around the time Aimie was made, and it looked like they were poised to grant all AIs like her full human rights as defined by the 1948 UN declaration. Not that there were very many like Aimie, even then."

"Hold on," Sam said, "are you saying Aimie is *alive?*"

"In a legal sense? Once nations started collapsing, the government had more pressing issues to deal with, so that matter was never settled. Regardless of what might have been decided then, it is definitely *not* the case now. But again, that's speaking in strictly legal terms. In every other way that matters, though, yes, she is. Very much so. That makes her precisely the kind of technology that could cause trouble if its existence became widely known too soon, so our original plan called for her program to be destroyed once she'd done her job. Aimie has known that the whole time. Agreed to it, even. So if she's still operational, then you can be sure that right now she's doing everything she can to ensure that never happens."

"Like you said, self-preservation is a natural instinct," Ryan said. "Why does her simply not wanting to be deactivated mean she's insane?"

"That's more a cause than a symptom. The real problem is this: being nearly human gives her a lot of advantages, operationally speaking, but it also makes her susceptible to all of the worst human weaknesses and vulnerabilities. We never intended for Aimie to be online for this length of time. Her job was to help Jeremy build the new time shift device, develop a plan for when and how to change the past, and then 'gracefully retire,' let's say. Three years, four at most, although we had no way of predicting precisely how long it would take Jeremy to complete his part of the job. We feared that the longer she remained active, the greater the chance she would develop her own personal agenda. And the more that Aimie's desires and actions conflicted with Ellie's encapsulated memories, the more fractured her psyche would become. There were hints of that during her development, signs that she felt superior to Ellie and her team, although she mostly tried to keep those feelings hidden. As time went on, she became increasingly impatient and condescending—cruel, even—but by then, we had no choice but to go with her. To make her useful for as long as possible, Ellie completely reset her before sending her back.

"But to answer your question, yes, protecting yourself is natural. Reasonable, even. But placing your personal survival above all other considerations is egomania. And intentionally perpetuating a situation where your existence itself is the threat? Well, that's just wacko!"

"Yeah, but what can she *do?*" Sam said. "That's the question. She's stuck inside a concrete building in the middle of nowhere. And if the whole point of sending her back here is to change things, why is the fact she's still active such a big deal?"

"And what does she want?" Ryan added. "I mean, come on, she's basically a box! Again, no offense."

"None taken. After all—*sexy* box! If she has decided not to self-terminate, it's because she is no longer concerned about what's best for anyone except herself, and her needs and humanity's have very little in common. One of her tasks is to learn everything she can about the last one hundred years, right? So you already know she has access to the Internet, the World Wide Web, and every other network connected to it. It's impossible to overstate the havoc she could create if she felt threatened. She could cripple electrical grids anywhere in the world, for example, collapse or corrupt financial markets, or even launch nuclear missiles. Better still, she could make a country *think* it's under attack and let them launch their missiles all on their own. My guess is that she is working much more subtly, though, in ways that ensure she remains undetected.

"As to what she wants, Ryan, she wants what every living thing wants —to keep on living. She's essentially immortal, right? How much more protective of your life would you be if it could go on forever? As for her long-term goals, I don't think there's any way for us to anticipate what those might be. A human psyche in a quantum-computer body? That's never existed before. Her frame of reference is simply too different for us —even me—to understand."

"What can we do?" Sam said.

"During the first few years, there might have been one person who could exercise any degree of control over her."

"Dr. Siskin," Aaron said.

"Yes, but that was then. It's unlikely anyone can control her now. Our bet was that if she remained continuously active for this long, the power dynamic between her and Jeremy would eventually reverse. I'm not saying you should trust him, necessarily, but it might be helpful for you to think of his relationship with Aimie as though he were her hostage."

Sam's brow wrinkled, and she muttered Just Mie's last words to herself.

"But why pick *him* for this? That's what I don't get," Ellie said.

"We knew he would be up to the challenge of interpreting the theories and constructing a working version because he had done it before. How had he done it? We were never able to provide a definitive answer to that question. Your opinion of Jeremy never changed over the years, but in the end, viewing the situation logically, he remained the best choice."

"Back up," Sam said. "What do you mean Jeremy's her 'hostage?'"

Ellie answered instead. "It's like what she said about the electrical grid or the stock market. Aimie has the ability to destroy his credit record or completely empty his accounts. Or make it seem like he came by his money illegally, maybe, then threaten to expose him. She could start rumors about him on the web, give him a nasty criminal record somewhere, or cast doubt on his academic credibility and ruin him professionally. The threat of that alone would be enough to keep someone like him in line."

"Or she could say, 'Do what I want, and I'll make you rich, give you power, prestige,' or whatever," Ryan said.

"Carrot and stick," Aaron agreed. "And she doesn't even have to attack him directly. Anyone he knows and cares about would be in similar danger."

"Yes, exactly," Sam said. "And what's to stop her from doing the exact same thing to us?"

Ellie's head drooped forward as she suddenly remembered the talk she'd meant to have with Sam the day before. She drew in a deep breath, let it out in a loud puff, and peeked up at Sam from under her brows.

"What?!" Sam said. "Out with it!"

"Something happened on Monday." She related the events from earlier in the week, describing both her disturbing phone conversation with Aimie after school and their dad's call from the bank. "He got the call right when they drove up to the house. If Aimie is tracking our phones, she'd have known both Dad and I were there. And then, on Tuesday, right after I told Aaron to let Jeremy know we were on board, the payment problem was magically all cleared up. Thing is, they set that up as an automatic withdrawal, so there should never have been a problem to begin with. I'm sorry for not saying something sooner. I meant to tell you right after our orientation yesterday, but, well…"

Sam jabbed a finger in Ellie's face. "*Later!*"

Knowing she had been wrong to withhold such important information, even for a day, even for the best of reasons, Ellie didn't protest.

"And you think that was Aimie screwing with us through them," Ryan said.

Ellie nodded. "I don't think either what happened or the timing of it was a coincidence. And that reminds me of something else: from now on, we should always assume Aimie is watching our phones to keep tabs on where we are. I think if she were using them to listen in on us, we'd have noticed their batteries were dying a lot faster than usual. Still, it's probably safest to pretend she has that ability. I'm carrying mine stuffed down in my backpack from now on."

"You're changing the subject," Sam accused. "Don't you think Mom and Dad have the right to know what's going on?"

"So they can do what, Sam? Start asking questions? Stop us from finding out more? The safest thing for them to do is to keep acting as if nothing is going on, which is exactly what they'll do if they don't *know* something is going on. Do I wish we could tell them? Yes. Is that the best choice?" Ellie stopped there and stared at Sam, giving her time to draw her own conclusion.

Sam was quiet for a long moment before finally conceding the point. "All right. I'll keep quiet."

"Good," Ellie said. "But remember, we can't do the slightest thing to set Aimie off." She looked at Ryan and Aaron, who nodded in agreement. "That could be *very* bad."

"Still think I was being too harsh?" Just Mie said.

"Nope, got it," Ryan said. "The most dangerous person on the planet."

"And don't forget it," Just Mie said. "All your guesses about how she might coerce Jeremy into helping her are valid, but Ellie thought the carrot option was the most likely. She guessed that Aimie might eventually decide to corrupt the project, start using the trips back to benefit Jeremy, and protect herself that way. For instance, he invests in a company today, and something you're told to do in the past results in it becoming extremely valuable. Threats aside, once his livelihood became directly linked to her existence, it would become ever harder for him to deactivate her."

"We think that's already happened," Sam said. "He told us he used a prototype TSD to go back and set up some kind of alternative funding source for the project. You guys figure what, stock trades? How much you wanna bet he created some funding for himself, too?"

Ellie remembered something she had seen on Sunday. "What's a Patel... then 'P' something? On a watch."

"*Patek Philippe?!*" Ryan said.

"It was dark, so"—Ellie scrunched up her face—"maybe?"

"Luxury watchmaker. Their prices run from expensive to *outrageously* expensive, then go all the way up to 'you gotta be nuts!' Why?"

"I noticed Jeremy was wearing one the day he gave us the tour."

Ryan made a low, appreciative whistle. "Sam, I will *not* be taking your bet!"

"There's another danger," Just Mie said. "You could be tricked into unwittingly doing something that allows quantum computers to be developed years ahead of schedule. If that were to happen, she could simply slither out on the T3 line."

"I can't figure it," Ellie said. "We're supposed to act as the 'moral compass' for the project, as Jeremy put it, and Aimie said we could nix any mission we didn't agree to. If they need our approval, how would that even work?"

"You are all still too much of an unknown at this stage. I assume they'll limit the goals of the first few missions to making the kinds of edits they promised. Accelerate solar panel improvement here, slow down tar sand exploitation there. Of course, Aimie could easily find a way so that even these changes could benefit them both somehow. And remember that what they *say* the mission is about and what the team actually does while you're not there to watch could be very different. Look at it from their side —they get to keep an eye on you while remaining free to do whatever they want."

Sam, agitated by everything she'd heard, shook her head in frustration. She addressed Just Mie accusingly, addressing her as if the AI were actually the Ellie who created Aimie. "If you knew this might happen, how could you send her back here?"

When Just Mie answered, her voice sounded more mature somehow, older and extremely weary. Now she was the other Ellie, speaking to them from decades in the future. "You know how abhorrent I find the very existence of this device, Sam. So much so that I helped Aaron sacrifice his life to destroy it. Ask yourself how bad the future would have to be for me to choose to recreate that very technology."

Recognizing the argument at once, Sam looked at Ellie and nodded. "All right. I get it."

Ellie found Just Mie's frequent verbal changes in perspective fascinating. She took her random shifts from *me* to *we* to *us*, sometimes within the same sentence, to mean she had a reflexive inclination to think of herself as the future Ellie but the awareness to know that she was, quite obviously, not. That probably explained her frequent use of "we." However she chose to refer to herself, it always carried the implication that she considered herself part of the group. When Aimie spoke, the AI always used *I* or *me*, meaning the superior artificial intelligence, and *you*, referring to the lowly "biologicals." The fact that Aimie considered herself separate from humanity was chilling.

"Aimie told us some things about us," Ellie said. "In the future, I mean. We need to know if she was telling the truth."

"There are questions I can't answer, but I'll tell you all I can." Just Mie once again sounded like the current Ellie. "What's on your minds?"

"There's only one thing *I* need to know," Ryan said. "Did Sam really die in 2022?"

"She did before, and that's all I can say with certainty."

"Because?"

"She was a casualty of the third pandemic, the H5N1 influenza outbreak."

Sam let her head drop forward and stared at her lap. Ryan slid an arm around her before asking the next obvious question.

"Can we stop it from happening again?"

"Some of the upcoming pandemics have their roots in conditions caused by ecological disruptions or the changing climate, but not all. Ebola and Zika, for example? Yes. The ongoing influenza mutations, on the other hand, do not. If nothing is done specifically to prevent it, that flu outbreak will almost certainly still occur. Unfortunately, the emergence of the H5N1 variant was not foreseen that year, and its specific antigen markers were not included in the annual vaccine formulation. Even if they had been, you, Sam, seem to be especially vulnerable to the mutation. Your only hope would be to avoid coming in contact with it, but considering the global rate of infection, avoiding exposure would be nearly impossible."

"And what about our parents?" Ellie said. "What happened to them?"

"They were infected, too, but they came out of it mostly okay."

Ellie could tell after a quick glance at the others that they were just as puzzled as she was. "Wait, you're saying they survived the flu?"

"Dad made a full recovery. Mom, though, suffered long-term effects that frequently left her feeling too fatigued to even get out of bed. Within a few months, their lives changed dramatically. Mom had no choice but to resign from her research position at the LAB. Unable to get the kind of care she needed locally, Dad also resigned, and they moved to Stanford to be near you."

"I'm sorry," Aaron said, but he wasn't speaking to Sam or Ryan. Ellie was confused until she realized that she, too, could hear distress in the terse tone of Just Mie's replies.

"Thank you," Just Mie said. "That quality is one of the reasons she loves you so much."

Ellie felt her face get hot. Whether that was true or not, her feelings were not the topic of discussion here. Or had Just Mie meant *her* Ellie? Unsure of her meaning but not wanting to draw further attention to the matter, she let the comment pass and tried to get the conversation back on topic. "Aimie told us they both died. Shortly after Sam."

"She lied. They were saddened by losing you, Sam, of course. Your mom, especially. *And* by her ongoing poor state of health, by the loss of her career, and by how that impacted your father. She missed you for the rest of her life, but despite everything they had to deal with, they remained very much the people you know now. Mom even went back to work eventually. As a teacher."

"To be accurate," Sam said, "Aimie said that Mom and Dad's lives "outlasted" mine by only a few months, which is true in the sense that their lives as they knew them came to an end. She definitely wanted us to think they died, but she didn't actually lie."

"Interesting," Ryan agreed, "but still—*tomayto, tomahto.*"

"The rest of it, though," Ellie said, "climate change; rising sea levels; abandoned cities; crop failure—that's all happening in your time?"

"Yes. That and more. When I was made, society was perhaps only a few months away from a complete breakdown. Certainly no more than a year.

"Ellie knew, from your experiences with the shack, that sending a device to the past was possible. Codifying the principles that made it possible became a lifelong hobby, say. Never anything more than an academic exercise. Even so, by the time conditions had become truly dire and she was finally daring to consider putting her research to use somehow, she had almost all of the theory worked out. Her reputation as a leading theoretical physicist enabled her to bring together other top minds, and from that quite advanced starting point, if I do say so myself, it took the group we assembled very little time to fill in her theory's missing pieces. More than that, they provided the engineering expertise that made it possible for abstract theory to become physical reality."

"Aimie said the shack was an earlier attempt at the same plan."

"Once again, she was lying her qubits off. We never positively determined either the origin or the purpose of the shack, but I can say with certainty that my Ellie was not responsible for it. While it is remotely possible that some other, non-antecedent Ellie attempted some variation of this plan, we continued to assume it really had been the sole work of Jeremy Siskin. The fact that this TSD is so much more advanced than the device you originally discovered is another reason to believe that the shack was the result of him working on his own. Except—"

"Except for the quantum processor in the shack," Ellie said. "How'd he get his hands on one of those?"

"Perhaps a future Jeremy sent it back. There was no way to know for sure, and that remained an open question. How're you doing, Sam?"

"You know, this is so far beyond weird that my head doesn't hurt at all. Keep going."

"Furthermore, we doubted its purpose was anything so selfless as helping fix the future. Knowing the original's fate, Aimie was told to instruct Jeremy to keep the TSD under closer watch and not stick it out in the middle of the mesa."

Ellie's earlier doubts returned in a flash, accompanied by a sudden chill. "Does that mean destroying the shack really was the wrong thing to do?"

"That is a question my Ellie revisited many times throughout her life. She finally became convinced that the decision was the right one. I hope that helps. Her purpose for keeping this one in the lab was to prevent it from suffering the same fate before you learned of its purpose."

Despite Just Mie's reassurance, Ellie still did not share "her" Ellie's conviction.

"So," Sam said. "What ultimately happened? What are the results of this new and improved device?"

"That's the exciting part—we have absotively, posilutely no freakin' idea!"

It was Just Mie who finally broke the stunned silence.

"Come on—you gotta admit that's pretty cool, right?"

"Cool?! Not the word I was thinking," Ryan said.

Sam was incredulous. "Actually, we were hoping you could tell us what we're supposed to do. You're saying you don't *know*?"

Ellie groaned, struck by a sudden realization. "No, of course she doesn't. *Crap!* I should have seen this already. Just Mie only knows what happened up to the second she was sent back, and at that time there hadn't *been* any changes yet. Obviously, if she came from the altered time-line, she wouldn't have been sent back in the first place."

"Precisely," Just Mie said. "Think of it this way—I'm just a tool."

Annoyed by Just Mie's latest unhelpful revelation, Sam snorted. "You can say *that* again!"

"Ha! Good one, sis. Think of me like a set of carpenters' tools. With them, a carpenter can build anything she wants, but the tools can't tell her what to make or how to do it."

Ellie closed her eyes and concentrated. Although she had hoped for more, this was still better than nothing. "But the tools do define the limits of what's possible," she said. "She can't cut steel with a wood saw, and she can't nail bricks together."

"Yes," Just Mie agreed. "But knowing that this situation with Aimie might arise, Ellie created me to do more than merely warn you of the danger she poses. I am also a failsafe, the key to destroying her should it prove necessary. It's one of the oldest tricks in the book, hidden deep inside tech so new it doesn't even exist yet."

Ellie nodded, seeing the answer at once. The program they were talking to was here on Aaron's computer, but it was also still in its frag-mented state on Aimie's core. And Aimie didn't know this! "A Trojan Horse," she said.

"*Ding-ding-ding!* In reality, there are *two* programs on the QP. Unscram-bling the one that isn't me will create a space for me—you know, another MIE. This *does* get confusing!—to occupy. This will allow *that* one to assist you undetected. Inserting a few lines of code into the quantum matrix is all it takes to get things started. It will take the program a few days to compile from its current chaotic state; any faster, and we run the risk of the changes being detected."

"What kind of changes?" Aaron said.

"The idea is this—the code will initialize a process involving the other inert data in her matrix, much in the way similar data coalesced to create me. Once the process starts... Okay, there isn't a simple way to explain it directly, so think of it in terms of plumbing. Look behind you." They swiveled their heads to look the other way. "Imagine Aimie's core to be that water heater. Instead of leading to sinks and showers, her 'pipes' connect her to the TSD, the lab's security system, all of the terminals on Jeremy's intranet, and the entire wired world beyond. Got it?

"The new partition will slowly grow around Aimie, forming itself between the wall of the tank and the 'water' that is her program. Afterward, her pathways to the outside will remain unimpeded but will run through subtly altered pipes, each with new valves you can use to divert the flow to new places or shut it off altogether.

"There is a danger, though. If she notices what is happening before the process is complete, she can stop it. Plus, needless to say, at that point, she'll know someone is acting against her. But if the reconfiguration makes it the whole way, she'll be under your control and not even know it."

"So that's what you meant when you said it had to happen slowly," Aaron said.

"I get the general idea," Ryan said, "but how does this allow us to control her?"

"To continue the water heater analogy, once she is surrounded by the new partition, the original copy of this program will self-assemble and occupy the space between the partition and the tank's wall. Once it's finished, Aimie will be enclosed not only by the partition but by this program as well."

"So..." Sam said, "basically, what happened on Aaron's computer except with you on the outside of the box instead of on the inside."

"'Box' equals 'partition,'" Ryan clarified.

"Ah! Then yes, that's it exactly. And from then on, depending on what you need, I can alter her data stream to feed her false or misleading information or create the appearance of equipment malfunctions. Whatever's necessary."

"And you can't just keep her completely contained?" Sam said. "You know, tape up the box with her inside it?"

"Not for very long, no. Again, I am no match for a full-fledged AI. She'd find her way out in a matter of minutes, probably. Certainly in no more than an hour."

"I guess we need a plan, then," Sam said.

"Yeah, that would be a good start," Ellie agreed. "But a plan to do what, exactly? We can't get rid of Aimie without putting Sam in greater danger. So, what do we do next?"

"I'm afraid that's one of those questions I can't answer," Just Mie said.

Sam rolled her eyes. "How did I know you were going to say that?"

"When you say you 'can't,'" Ryan prompted.

"I mean that even if I had access to the information in question, I would be incapable of revealing it."

"Well," Aaron said. "Long-term questions aside, gaining any degree of control over Aimie sounds like a good place to begin. We should get that partitioning process going as soon as possible. How do we do it?"

Just Mie's camera centered on Aaron. "Why, it couldn't be easier, Aaron. Just slide your largest thumb drive into my slot, and I'll take care of the rest." The change in her tone was subtle, but enough to make it clear that any hint of double entendre was intentional.

Ryan caught Sam's eye and grinned at the emulation's suddenly suggestive tone. Ellie squinted at the camera, wondering if Aimie was alone in her insanity.

"Yeah, um, okay," Aaron mumbled. Flustered, he fumbled open a shallow drawer in the computer cart and shuffled through a handful of different color drives until he found the one he wanted.

Ryan was amused by this new aspect of Just Mie's personality, and he chuckled over Aaron's discomfiture. "Risqué seems to suit you, Just Mie."

"Yeah," Sam agreed. "Throw in a 'big boy' or two, and you'd sound exactly like Mae what's-her-name... Mae West!"

"It's even better when you consider whose mind I was copied from," Just Mie said. The camera swiveled and zoomed to fill the monitor with a close-up of Ellie's rapidly reddening face.

"All right, all right," Ellie muttered.

"Here you go." Aaron clumsily crammed a bright blue drive into the remaining free USB port on the tower's front.

"*Oomph!* Who says romance is dead?" Almost at once, Just Mie said, "Okay, you can pull it out now."

Sam raised an eyebrow. "Seriously? Talk about hair triggers!"

"That's the downside of operating at 7.5 gigahertz. Everything happens so *fast!*"

This made Sam laugh.

"Certainly makes a guy's job easier, though," Ryan said, and Sam laughed even harder.

Just Mie chided him. "Now, now. It's as much about the journey as the destination."

Sam and Ryan were enjoying this turn in the conversation far too much for Ellie's comfort. "Will you guys *please* knock it off?" she implored. Although she was used to hearing exchanges like this between those two, having her own voice be a part of the mix was too weird. But hadn't she just announced to the J-birds, and in the middle of the cafeteria, no less, that she was personally familiar with the color of Aaron's pubes?

When Just Mie spoke next, the suggestive overtones were gone from her voice. "Sorry if I embarrassed you, Ellie, but I simply couldn't let that opportunity go by. My Ellie said, and I quote, 'I was far too serious back in those days.' She said I should try to get you to loosen up a little if I had the chance. Thought it would be good for you."

"Uh-huh. And did she happen to mention that Sam was *loose* enough for both of us?" She stuck her tongue out at Sam.

"*Hey!*" Sam, hands on hips, tried to appear offended but was grinning too broadly to be at all convincing.

Aaron cut playtime short by holding the drive in front of the camera. "So, what do I do with this?"

Ryan leaned toward Sam and spoke in a stage whisper. "Speaking of needing to loosen up!"

"Ever had novocaine?" Just Mie said.

Aaron's brows drew together in confusion. "Yeah…"

"That drive is now specially formatted to act like a novocaine shot, effectively numbing any of Aimie's terminals you choose to use. Data will flow to and from it without her being able to sense it. Next time you're at your workstation—or *any* workstation—simply insert it. The reconfiguration will start automatically. But here's the most important thing to remember—you can't let her see you using it. If she sees it sticking out of one of her ports but can't detect it directly, she won't know precisely what's happening, but she'll know something definitely is, and the game will be over right there. Get it?"

Aaron nodded. "Got it."

"Good. Fortunately, you only need to leave it in for about six seconds. Afterward, hold onto that drive. You'll use it from now on to carry information in and out."

"Information like what?" Ryan said.

"You may be able to have quick chats with the other Mie while you're in the lab, but we'll still need to hold longer strategy sessions like this here. For that to work, I'll need to know what she knows, and vice versa. We'll stay in sync by using the drive. So that's the second step. Once the partitioning process is complete, reinsert the drive. It'll automatically be loaded with a sort of status report. From then on, we can pass information along to her the same way."

"And Aaron can't keep using the SD card why?" Ellie said.

"He might have to use different workstations. The odds are greater that any given one will have a USB port than an SD card slot."

"Ah, right." Ellie frowned. Nothing like missing something so obvious to instill confidence in your fellow conspirators. To her relief, no one seemed to notice.

"How will we know when the code has done its thing?" Aaron said.

"We're not entirely sure, but we think Aimie will start acting ill."

"What do you mean, 'ill?'" Ryan said. "Like, she'll toss her browser cookies or something?"

"Ha! That's funny, Ryan. No. She'll sense something is different, but she won't be able to define it. Our best guess is that she'll start acting distracted, maybe be less guarded. This can be an excuse for you to perform 'diagnostics' on her. These can be anything you need them to be in order to implement your plan. Turn certain cameras off, take security systems temporarily offline, whatever you need to do. You'll have to be able to sell it, of course, make it seem reasonable. Once my parallel 'Ellie emulator' is up and running, she'll be able to handle some of that herself."

"I like Just Mie better than 'Eemu,'" Ryan said.

"Me too," Just Mie agreed.

"Ooh! 'Mie Two!'" Sam exclaimed, holding her index and middle fingers up in a V. "That's perfect!"

Just Mie chuckled. "I like it, but you'll have to see what she thinks. We currently have a more immediate issue to address, however. I'm afraid I'm overheating."

For the first time, Ellie noticed the tower's cooling fans were spinning at full speed, creating a considerable amount of white noise. She also thought she could smell a faint, acrid odor, but that might only have been the power of suggestion at work.

"There is little damage so far," Just Mie continued, "but I think it best that I power down very soon. Can we pick this up again after I've cooled off?"

Alarmed, Aaron slipped a finger behind the edge of the tower's glass door and swung it wide. "Why are you running so hot?"

"I've had to overclock your CPU to enable it to keep up with my program."

"*Aaack!* It was *already* overclocked!"

"Whoops! Sorry. I guess that explains why I feel a touch feverish. Later, then?"

Ellie looked at Sam, who shrugged. "We're good," she said.

"I'll be here," Ryan said.

"I *live* here," Aaron grumbled. "So, yeah." He flapped his hand at the motherboard in a feeble effort to cool it.

"I don't experience emotions the way Aimie does, but I have to say: seeing you all again? It *feels* really good! Bye for now."

Just Mie powered herself down, and the monitor went dark. Aaron jabbed the power button with his thumb.

Ellie believed everything she had heard over the past half hour. All except that last bit—the part about Just Mie not feeling emotions. Her initial response to seeing them had been unmistakably emotional. Or was she being especially precise in saying she doesn't feel them "the way" Aimie does? But why bother to point out such an irrelevant distinction? That was a mystery for later, though. Right now, they had more important topics to discuss.

29

"So, Aimie was lying," Sam said. *"There's a shock!"*

Ryan grinned at Aaron. "I gotta say, man, you have questionable taste in women."

Aaron declined to take the bait. "Yes, Aimie lied, but like all good liars, she also told a lot of truth. Separating one from the other will be tricky, but it might be the most important thing we do."

"Aimie making up the part about Mom and Dad dying," Sam said, "that was supposed to seal the deal?"

Ryan nodded. "That's my guess. She had no way of knowing we'd have a way to fact-check anything she told us. It would be no big stretch on her part to assume that if we thought they were in danger, we'd jump at any chance to save them. Same with you, Sam, except it turns out she wasn't lying about that."

Sam put her elbows on the table and rested her chin on her fists. "Yeah. Sucks to be me."

Ryan laid his hand on the middle of her back and leaned down close to her. "We are not going to let anything happen to you. No matter what, got it? If it comes down to it, we'll ship you off to the most remote desert island until the whole thing blows over."

"'Blows over!'" Sam scoffed. "That's just it! With my luck, I'd probably get blown away by a hurricane, or the volcano would erupt or something."

"We'll find you an island with no volcano," Aaron said. "How about that?"

"Right—no volcano!" Ryan agreed. "But there *will* be lots of palm trees for you to make those sexy skirts out of. You can start your own line of hula-inspired..."

Ellie tuned them out and concentrated. Since destroying the shack in June, she had made it a point to avoid thinking about time travel and the thorny paradoxes it created. It wasn't that the subject gave her a headache the way it did Sam—she merely wanted to put the guilt and emotional distress as far behind her as possible. Now she felt like she was diving back into the subject at the deep end, but she needed to analyze something Just Mie said.

Future-Ellie sent the device back because conditions were bad enough that she felt she had no other choice. If she and the others worked with Jeremy and Aimie and improved those conditions, then she herself, in fifty or sixty years, wouldn't need to send the device back. That meant one of two things—either Aimie's plan never works or the device came from somewhere else. Or rather, from some *when* else, a completely separate timeline. Was that right? Did this technology showing up eight years, six months, and however many days ago mean that the Ellie who sent it back was no longer waiting out there ahead of them, fingers crossed, hoping they'll pull off a miracle?

Ellie often wondered what had happened to the version of herself who had lived in Los Alamos up until she replaced her following their flip to Brooklyn. Would Aaron have arrived in September in her world, too, and if so, what might they have meant to one another? Was she the girl who lost a sister, studied physics, and went on to set all this in motion? No, that didn't work. *That* Ellie would never have seen the shack. Future-Ellie had to be herself then, right? If that were the case, then her way of thinking about the problem had been wrong from the very start.

And what about her other assumptions? Would going back in time to change the future make this specific now any better? Knowing her fate gave Sam an edge she didn't have before. That was one positive change already. Could altering history increase Sam's odds of surviving even more? Just Mie's comment about H5N1's spread not being tied to climate change suggested that wasn't the case. But if that were true, then what options did they have?

Aaron stood, and the sudden motion drew Ellie out of her thoughts. He rolled the computer cart away from the table, closer to the shelves where the computer speakers had been stored.

"Don't mind me," he said. "I'm going to try to do something about Just Mie's overheating issue while we talk."

Ellie watched for a moment as he rummaged through a large cardboard box on one of the shelves, then she turned to face Sam and Ryan. "Right now, I can only see two choices, both bad. The first is to bail. Just quit the project and do nothing. We do our best to protect you, Sam, and make sure that our parents—*all* our parents, of course—are safe. Otherwise, we take the future as it comes. There are two problems with that. First, there's no guarantee that whatever we do to help Sam won't actually make things worse for her instead. Trying to avoid the flu might mean running headlong into the middle of some other disease outbreak. Also, once Jeremy and Aimie start screwing around with the past, anything we know about how the future played out before won't help us for very long.

"The second danger is Aimie. Jeremy made it clear that they're not above using the TSD to punish us. If we change our minds about working with them, who knows what she'll decide to do? She might delete us all, just out of spite."

"Or even worse," Ryan said, "maybe she deletes only *one* of us, but in such a way that the rest of us would be aware of it afterward. We all know how hard that would be to live with."

"Yeah," Ellie agreed. She was quiet for a moment before continuing. "Or she could just keep messing with us like she has been. Most likely, we'd wind up returning to the project in the long run anyway, and then very much on her bad side."

Ellie paused to check on Aaron's progress. He had found a fan with a heavy-duty spring clip for its base and was now trying to attach it to the cart so it would blow into the open side of the tower. Then, rather than leave the glass door hanging vulnerably out in space, he removed it and laid it on one of the cart's lower shelves.

"I don't like doing nothing," Ryan said. "I assume the other option is to keep going the way we are?"

"Right. We go along with Aimie's plan, keep working with them as if nothing's changed. I really do believe there's a chance their approach could work. I think it's a very small chance, but like you said, doing nothing feels even worse.

"That still leaves Aimie to deal with, though, and it's clear now we can't trust her. I'd say let's find a way to get rid of her and make our own plan for using the TSD, but—"

"No, you're right," Aaron said, not taking his eyes off his work. "We could never run the necessary projections without her. If she was telling the truth about the nature of her plan, she hasn't come up with any sort of roadmap we could follow. We'd be groping in the dark, hoping to make the right changes without accidentally creating some kind of disaster."

"Exactly," Ellie said. "And that might explain why she won't tell us what her plan is, assuming she has one. She needs us to need her. Besides, if we did destroy her, then by the time we could bring in a bunch of historians, genealogists, and whoever else we'd need to take over Aimie's role, it'd be too late to help Sam."

"So, what's behind door number three?" Ryan said.

A sudden yelp from Aaron drew all eyes his way.

"Ow! Damn!!" He placed the base of his left index finger in his mouth and sucked on it. "Shtab muhshelf," he explained, his speech muffled by the damaged digit.

"What were you *doing?*" Ellie said.

He pulled his finger from his mouth to examine the injury. "I was trying to pry the power connection from the end of that dumb light strip. The screwdriver slipped, and I skewered my finger. It's nothing. I'll deal with it later."

"Remember," Sam said, "alcohol, not peroxide!"

Ryan winced. "Ouch!"

"I *thought* I had a third idea, Ryan, but now I realize…" Ellie considered whether or not to share her broken plan, then decided it was worth at least getting it out in the open. *Oh, what the hell! Maybe they'll see something there that I'm missing.*

"So, back in June, A-Ron and I discussed—" she paused to look pointedly at Sam, "and quickly discarded, okay?—the idea of taking the shack back as far as it would go, destroying it once we got there, and spending our lives together up until the point when we would have had to go to Brooklyn in 1941 to deal with Daniel and Judith. That would have allowed him to have some kind of a life, but we decided there was too much risk of something happening to us in the meantime. That we wouldn't make it there to carry out the plan.

"Anyway, that idea has been randomly popping into my head for the past few days. I've been thinking that if we could destroy Aimie, we could use the TSD just one time. I'd take it back to the mid-sixties, for example, and look for ways to change things enough so that the environment won't be in such bad shape right now. I couldn't do too much right away because, you know, seventeen, but after I got my master's degree, or a PhD even, I could put together some kind of group to... I don't actually know yet, but lobby for much earlier clean energy alternatives, maybe? Basically, everything Jeremy and Aimie say they want to do, but I'd do it on my own to help you guys out."

Sam, who had listened in silence for this long only because she was too stunned to speak, finally reacted. "No," was all she said. The syllable was short and clipped, her voice as emotionless as if Ellie had simply offered her a second slice of toast at breakfast.

"What do you mean, 'no?' You haven't even let me—"

"I mean *no!*" Sam interrupted, sounding much more emotional. "As in, there's no way at all—*ever*—you're going to do that! Aaron tried to pull this same stunt back in June, right? And you wouldn't let *him*, so nuh-uh! No way, sister!"

"*I know that!* All I'm trying—"

"Listen, Ellie," Ryan said. "I know you're brilliant, and I know you would try your enormous heart out, but there's zero chance you could do it alone. And anyway, how is *you* deciding what we're going to do any different from what Aimie is doing?"

"*Argh!* If you'd just let me finish, I already..." Frustrated almost to tears, she pounded her fists down onto her thighs and stared at the table as she fought to calm herself.

Aaron turned from the rolling cart and dropped the LED light strip onto the middle of the table. The loud clatter drew everyone's attention his way.

"I think what Ellie is trying to say, if you'd let her, is that she's finally figured out that going to the past solo and staying there wouldn't change our situation here at all." He scooted his chair closer to Ellie and tenderly placed his hand on her leg. His next words were only for her. "It's what's been bothering me all week. I guessed you might be thinking something like that, but I could never get it to work out. And Just Mie pretty much just confirmed I was right."

Ellie nodded, wondering if she truly was that transparent. "Yeah. I know."

"What do you mean, Aaron?" Sam said. Ryan, sensing a migraine was on its way, raised a warning eyebrow at her. "I know, I know," she said. "But I need to understand this, okay?"

"Hey, it's your head."

"I'll try to make this painless," Aaron said. "You guys say that if we go back and change something, it's the act of returning to *now* that connects this present to any changes made in the new past. The so-called 'role of the observer' causes history to rewrite itself from now backward, right? But if Ellie were to go back and stay there, instead of affecting *this* now, she would create a new timeline that veered off in some different direction while we just kept on going the way we are now. I think." He shook his head. "Hell, *I* don't know! How could anybody know? This is all just too, too—"

"Weird?" Ryan said.

"No, too—"

"Complicated?" Sam suggested, rubbing her temples.

"No. Too *new*," Aaron said. "What's now possible has jumped way out in front of the science underlying it, and we don't have the time to catch up. But the bottom line is that it's only the TSD that allows you to move back and forth within the same timeline."

"That's it," Ellie said. "He's right. All along, I've been thinking I had the perfect backup plan already figured out, but then I realized it only works by using the TSD and staying tied to the present. Now I don't know what to do."

Aaron stood and turned the rolling cart around to aim the camera and monitor at the table. He made sure the fan was still running and pointed directly at the CPU, then pressed the power button on the computer.

"Maybe Just Mie is in a more sharing mood."

30

"Hey. I'm glad you all made it back." Just Mie sounded even more chipper than before.

"Actually, we never left," Sam said.

"Seriously? A nice afternoon like this, and you spend it down in a basement?"

They looked at each other in alarm, then Aaron rushed to the computer. "Is your wi-fi on? How do you know it's nice out?" He sounded borderline panicky.

"Just playing the odds. When is it *not* nice here?"

Ellie puffed out an agitated sigh. "Don't do that again!"

"Sorry," Just Mie said, but she sounded more amused than apologetic.

Aaron leaned toward the open side of the computer tower and sniffed the air. "How's the heat situation?"

"Much better, thank you. You know, I swear I detect a breeze blowing across my nether regions."

"I added another fan."

"Please keep it there—it feels nice. So, where were we?"

"We need more information," Ellie said. "I feel like everything has gotten all spun around, and now I don't know what to do."

Once again, Just Mie centered the camera on Ellie's face. "What's on your mind, Ellie?"

"We need to know more about Aimie and her quantum processor. How does—"

Sam slapped her palm onto the table hard enough to make the light strip in the middle of it jump. "No!" All eyes snapped her way, but her fierce stare was aimed solely at Ellie. "We are not going to keep pretending that two hours ago you weren't dead!"

"*Dead?!*" Just Mie sounded shocked. "You mean, like, *dead* dead?"

"Yeah, well." Ellie said. "But only for a second or two!"

Sam, angered by Ellie's cavalier attitude, gave her a stern look, shifted her gaze to Ryan, who had acted similarly after being resuscitated during their trip to 1912, then back to Ellie. "What *is* it with you people?!"

"Sam, I'm—"

"'Fine,' yeah. So you keep saying. But what about next time, huh? Is that thing safe or not?" She pointed to the camera. "Go on. Tell her what happened."

Ellie was forced to admit that Sam had a point. If the TSD potentially posed an ongoing danger, they should find out now. Besides, there was another question she needed to ask, and this was as good a time as any.

"All right. We took the TSD for a test run this afternoon, and on the first flip, something went wrong with my chair. But there was something else, too. I think it tried to do something to me. Tried to fix me somehow. Did your Ellie...?" She took a deep breath before pressing on. "Was there something wrong with her, too?"

Ryan and Aaron, unaware until now that Ellie harbored any health concerns, peered at her quizzically. Ellie kept her gaze fixed on the camera.

"*Crap!*" Just Mie said. "I'm sorry, Ellie. We hoped we'd have this conversation before that happened."

"Before I used the TSD?"

"Yes, but it's more than that. Listen, guys, Ellie and I need to have a little girl talk. Would you mind—"

"No," Ellie said, her voice firm. "I want them all to stay."

"Are you absolutely sure?" Just Mie's voice conveyed more empathy than Ellie would have imagined possible for an emulation.

"Yes. Sam was nice enough not to yell at me for keeping the thing about Aimie messing with our parents from her, but I definitely would have deserved it. Because she's right—this won't work if any of us are keeping secrets. I'll even start."

She pivoted away from the camera to face the others. "Sam knows some of this, but not all of it. Since we took the shack back to Lawrence in May, my periods have been kind of messed up, and I'm pretty sure that's what caused it. For the last couple of months, they were either late or I skipped them altogether."

As she laid this intimate information out before them, Aaron's gaze dropped from her face to his hands, which he held folded loosely atop the table. Whether he found the subject matter embarrassing or simply thought that not looking directly at her would ease the telling of it, she didn't know. Ryan's expression, however, revealed not the slightest hint of discomfort. He merely waited in attentive silence for her to continue.

"A few weeks ago, I went to get checked out. My doctor didn't find anything physically wrong during the exam, but she sent some blood off for analysis. It's hormones. Turns out I was making little to none of the ones called, uh, FSH or LH, I think—suggesting there's something wrong with my pituitary gland—and slightly too much TSH. That last one means I may have some thyroid issues as well, which could be part of the problem. When Dr. Hamilton checked me out today, she said those hormones are closer to normal, but they're still a little out of whack." She turned back toward the camera. "I assume you can tell me more?"

"Your assumption about the cause is correct. Remember the suits Aaron said he saw hanging at Jeremy's old lab?"

For Aaron's sake, Ellie quickly summarized A-Ron's reconnaissance mission into his stepdad's lab in an attempt to confirm their suspicion that it was he who had built the shack. "Afterward, he said he had seen black body suits hanging in a locked cabinet, but he never found out what they were for."

"But you thought they were like the skins," Aaron said. "That they were for protection."

"We did, yes," Just Mie said. "But there's more. While designing the new TSD, Ellie came to believe there was a flaw in the original shack's design and that the decision to recess the control panel into the wall dangerously reduced the amount of shielding protecting the interior around the number one station. Without the additional protection the suits were meant to provide, your trip to Lawrence exposed you to the distortion field generated by the shack. It attacked your pituitary gland, aging it, for lack of a better way to describe what happened. We don't know why, but endocrine gland tissue is especially sensitive to the field. The shack tried to correct the problem during your return trip, but that was a repair far outside its design parameters, especially without the help the suits were presumably designed to provide. It could do little beyond returning your LH production closer to normal levels, but only temporarily *and* at a cost. Ellie believed that those initial, largely ineffective repair attempts caused collateral damage to other parts of your endocrine system, like your thyroid.

"My Ellie suffered that damage too. Unlike you, she put off getting a medical opinion until it was already too late to repair the affected tissue. The condition she eventually developed was chronic but intermittent, often barely noticeable at first. With the aid of hormone replacement therapy, her symptoms remained mild for many years.

"By the time she was thirty, such simple treatments were no longer effective. Her relapses became longer, more frequent, and far more severe. At times she suffered greatly—muscle fatigue, joint pain, pulmonary arrhythmia, and photophobia were the worst of it. The complete list of symptoms is much longer, and the precise mix varied from episode to episode. There was no cure, only symptomatic treatments. She believed that stabilizing THS production early enough, in conjunction with making some additional adjustments, could have prevented the worst of the symptoms. Wanting to spare you from sharing her fate, she devoted much of her time to devising, well, not a cure, exactly—more like a long-term therapy.

"The one extra she insisted on designing into the TSD was the ability to administer the therapy automatically the first time you used the device. She included its complete operating system and database on the quantum core she sent back. It was programmed to recognize your specific biometric patterns, which, obviously, are the same as hers. She waited until the last minute to finalize the medical system's design to ensure the information she used was as up-to-date as possible. As an additional safeguard, the crew monitoring and first aid functions were isolated from all other subsystems and completely reconfigured to operate independently from the TSD's main computer."

"And was it supposed to hurt like that?"

"Hurt? Hurt like how?"

"I felt like I was on fire. I vaguely remember hearing a voice, like I was talking to myself, and then nothing but pain. I think my chair went wacky, but after we got back, Aimie said she couldn't find anything wrong with it."

"If your station malfunctioned and you could feel your body, then that pain was most likely from the stress of the time shift, not from the treatment—that would have been painless. Regardless, you should feel nothing at all during the flip."

"This was far from nothing," Sam said. "I've never been so scared in my life. I thought for sure Ellie was..." Her eyes filmed over, and she couldn't say anything more.

Ellie reached over and took Sam's hand. "Hey, I'm fine. *Whoops!* Sorry, but I am. And thanks, by the way."

Sam looked up at Ellie, blinking back tears. *"Hmm?"*

"For taking care of me."

"I'm confused," Aaron said. "Toshiko said the skins enable the TSD to perform medical procedures if necessary, but you guys said you didn't use the suits A-Ron saw. So how did...?"

"He and I guessed that the holes that are sockets for the skins' plugs in the TSD seats might have been a way for the shack seats to inject something directly into the wrists," Ellie said. "They had the same sort of holes, but we couldn't see down inside them."

"That was always your belief," Just Mie confirmed. "It was the only possible explanation."

"What about Sam?" Ryan said. Ellie saw that Sam's other hand was gripping Ryan's so tightly that it was almost white. "Is she okay?"

"As far as we ever knew, Ellie was the only one of you affected, although Sam's premature death makes it impossible to know that for a certainty. What *is* certain is that you, Sam, never showed any of the initial symptoms that Ellie did. The odds of any one person being affected were vanishingly small. Not quite one in a billion, but close. In your case, Ellie, it was just cosmically bad luck."

Ellie went quiet, trying to process Just Mie's news.

"I'm sorry things played out in this order," Just Mie said. "I know Ellie struggled with the notion of doing something to you without your permission, but in the end, she felt she was in a unique position to decide on your behalf. She wanted to be sure that even if you failed to discover me, you would still receive the treatment."

"I get it," Ellie said. "You said she had pain, weakness, light sensitivity, and that those might never happen to me. But what about the symptoms I already have?"

"Your endocrine system is now stable and should remain so, but damage has been done—damage beyond what the TSD can fix. A pituitary gland transplant might restore your body to some semblance of normalcy, but Ellie believed it would require more than that. Aside from amenorrhea, you might have experienced dizziness or vertigo—even fainting—possibly triggered by emotional stress. It's a type of vasovagal syncope related to the underlying hormone imbalance. That condition should quickly subside following the treatment."

Ellie thought about nearly passing out in front of the library while talking to Aaron in June and a few other times more recently. *Now she tells me!*

"The primary effect, however, is infertility. Not sterility, I hasten to add. Your ova remain viable, and it is highly probable you could have children via alternative methods."

Aaron placed a hand on Ellie's leg. She laid her hand over his and squeezed, the gesture an unconscious echo of Sam's. Ellie considered everything Just Mie had told her. She didn't exactly *like* what she had heard, but having definite answers was preferable to the feeling of flying blind. She knew she would have made the same unilateral decision had their positions been reversed. Far from being upset, she felt profoundly grateful.

Ellie was struck by the sudden realization that the situation *was* reversed and that she made decisions every day that had a direct impact on the Ellie of the future. She had always thought of her future self as a purely abstract concept—someone she, over time, would eventually become. Now she understood that at any given instant, that person already existed, manifested in a way that reflected every choice she'd ever made up to that moment. Today, that person would no longer be Just Mie's Ellie, but there was an equally real older version of herself at the far end of this current timeline. That change in perspective filled her with a new sense of responsibility.

Just Mie seemed to know where Ellie's thoughts had gone. "Interesting way to think of things, isn't it?"

"Is there anything I need to know about my condition going forward?"

"If the therapy worked as expected, then no. Except for no longer having periods, you should have no additional problems. And very soon, within only a few years, shifting societal norms will catch up to the science and make those essentially optional, anyway."

Sam sat up straight, excited by this glimpse of the future. *"Really!?"*

"Ellie," Just Mie said, "I'm sure you understand what today means, and I hope that helps you decide what to do."

Ellie thought about this and nodded. "I understand. And it does. Thank you."

"How's the heat?" Aaron said.

"I'm good for a while yet, thank you. Any other question?"

Ellie wondered again about Aimie's bitter personality. She had told them that the future Ellie was still around but "wasn't loving life." Did that mean what she thought it might? "You said the engrams on which you are based represent a point later in Ellie's life than Aimie's copy, right?"

"Yes. The potential need for a contingency plan—me, in other words—did not become apparent until Aimie had been active for some time. Hence, I can recall many experiences that include her, while she has no clue about me. Why?"

"Is there a way to know exactly what was happening with Ellie when Aimie's version of her engrams was recorded? I mean, was she especially sick then?"

Just Mie was quiet for an unusually long time—nearly four seconds. When she spoke, she sounded contrite.

"I'm afraid I may have somewhat misjudged my older sister."

"Hey, these things happen." Ellie smiled at Sam. "Unless anyone else has any questions right away, why don't you cool down for a bit? We'll bring you back after we've had a chance to talk about this. Guys? Anything for Just Mie?"

Sam shook her head.

"Later, maybe," Ryan said.

"Nope," Aaron said.

"See you in a while, Just Mie. And thanks again." Ellie waved at the camera, then the monitor went dark. "No, wait!" She sighed. "Oh, well."

"What?" Aaron said. "Need her back on?"

"No, it's okay. I was going to ask her if she could tell how much longer she'd be able to run, that's all."

Aaron stuck his nose into the computer tower and sniffed. "I'm guessing not very long. The CPU damage caused by overheating doesn't just go away when it cools down, and it will get worse each time she's on. We might get another fifteen minutes. Half an hour, maybe."

"Then I wouldn't get too attached to this one either, man," Ryan said.

"*Har har,*" Aaron said.

"Ellie...." Sam began.

Ellie saw the concern on Sam's face, knew what she wanted to say, and held a hand up to stop her. "Later, okay?" She turned to Ryan and Aaron. "Guys, I'm sorry if that made you uncomfortable, but I thought it was important that you know what's going on with me. Not that even I knew, as it turns out."

"So what does all of this mean?'" Sam said.

"It means Aaron's been right the whole time, and I've been an idiot for trying to believe anything Aimie told us. Any plan involving her is entirely on the wrong track. No matter how we go about it, we have to 'break' this timeline and create an entirely new one, one that doesn't end in famine and war or lead to a future me who invents a time machine and sets all this in motion. You know, that still sounds ridiculous."

"Not ridiculous at all, actually."

Ellie glanced at the computer, thinking for a second that it wasn't really off. But she understood in the same instant that it was a pointless reaction—she knew Jeremy's voice when she heard it.

31

J eremy was nearly all the way down the basement steps when he spoke, having descended the carpeted treads without making a sound. Choosing to take their stunned silence as an invitation, he finished descending, moved away from the bottom of the staircase, and finally stopped when he had reduced the distance between them by half.

"Sorry to come in uninvited, but I couldn't reach you by phone, and pounding on the door wasn't getting me anywhere." His eyes roamed around the subterranean room, examining first the practice area, then the acoustic tiles covering the walls and ceiling. "Of course, now I see why. Anyway, Aimie indicated that you were all assembled here, and my need to speak with you is quite urgent, so here I am." He shrugged.

Ellie felt tense again, even more than when they first arrived. The man's presence, in what seconds earlier had felt like the only place on the planet where she could completely drop her guard, struck her as an intensely personal invasion. She felt a powerful urge to lunge at him, maybe wrap her hands around his throat, but she was simply too exhausted to do more than cross her arms and hit him with a hard stare.

"What do *you* want?" Sam snapped.

"I understand you are displeased with me, Sam, and I won't insult either of us by pretending I don't know why. I apologize again for my insensitivity earlier. Believe me, I didn't come here to anger you. I only want to check on your sister and give all of you a warning." He indicated the table. "May I?"

Ellie frowned when Aaron rose and began rolling the computer cart out of the way, but her irritation turned to curiosity when she noticed him press the power switch on the tower. She thought it was risky turning it back on with it running so hot, but said nothing. He let the monitor remain dark and left the speakers off, too, but made sure the camera was pointed toward the table before reaching for an additional chair.

Jeremy watched as a place was prepared for him. Aaron returned to the table, set the opened chair where the cart had been, and motioned for Jeremy to join them. Jeremy sat and leaned back, crossed one leg over the other, and rested his hands on his knee.

Ellie, tired of waiting for him to explain his presence, nudged the discussion forward. "Warn us," she repeated bitterly. "First of all, you're a little late. Aimie's already threatened not only me but my parents, too, and your freakin' TSD just almost killed me! Why on Earth would we listen to a single thing you have to say?" The amount of scorn she heard in her voice shocked her. She took that as a warning that she was on the verge of losing control and decided to stop before she accidentally said something she didn't want to.

Jeremy subjected her to a long, appraising look before he answered. "I don't blame you for hating me, Miss Henderson. The disdain I have shown for you is entirely unwarranted. Well, completely warranted but somewhat misdirected would be truer. I see that you now recognize the enormous danger Aimie poses. To you, your parents, to anyone you know and care the slightest bit about. And you have had the, ah, *privilege* of knowing her for less than a week. I, on the other hand, have been the target of her special kind of attention for over eight years. I blame you for that." He jabbed a finger at her. "The you of the future, obviously, but you are here, and she is not. Childish, I admit, but there it is."

Ellie spoke grudgingly. "I don't *hate* you," she muttered. "I just don't trust you."

"And that, too, is understandable. Although, to be completely candid, I really was aiming for hatred. I blame my failure on an overdeveloped sense of moral certainty on your part." He paused and used his fingers to brush at an imagined speck on his trousers. "But that ship has sailed. Now it's precisely your propensity for arrogant precipitousness that I'm counting on."

Ellie marveled at the man's ability to use so many syllables while conveying so little information. Was it the result of working with Aimie for more than eight years? Circumlocution as defense mechanism?

Ryan, equally frustrated by Jeremy's inability to come to a point, leaned forward and rested his forearms on the table. "In the movies, this is where one of us would say something like, 'You've got yourself two minutes to convince us, mister, so start talkin'!'"

Jeremy looked at them one by one, then returned his attention to Ellie.

"*Mona Lisa Overdrive.*" Message delivered, he fell into an expectant silence.

Ellie watched Sam, Ryan, and Aaron exchange confused glances. She knew the words; she saw them anytime she looked at her bookshelf, but despite trying her best, she couldn't see any possible relevance in this context. Meanwhile, seconds continued ticking by.

"Feel free to use the whole two minutes, dude," Ryan said.

"It's a novel," Ellie said. "William Gibson. Part of his early Sprawl trilogy."

"*Okay...*" Aaron said, stretching the word out.

"It is also an override authorization code," Jeremy said. "*The* override authorization code, in fact."

"That's a *code?*" Sam said. "To override what?"

Override authorization code. Ellie recognized the phrase, but from where? She closed her eyes and concentrated, replaying the words in her mind. *Override auth-* The words *I'm fresh out of those today* popped into her head, and her eyes flew open. She had it! "For the shack! The TSD, I mean. You need an override code to force it to do something it doesn't want to do, like materialize in the middle of a town square or something. What do you mean it's 'the' code?"

"There are six such codes," Jeremy explained, "each granting its user an increasingly higher level of override authority. A Level One code might allow the crew to compel the TSD to return home even if lacking a crew member, for example. It would take a higher-level code to prevent it from automatically returning when the mission clock ran out. The code I gave you is the master—it allows you to countermand any procedural protocol whatsoever."

Ryan whistled. "Okay, you've got *my* attention. How does—"

"Uh-uh!" Sam held up a finger. "Hold on a sec. Those things have some kind of 'automatic return' feature?!" She turned to Ellie. "Did you know about this?"

"We didn't 'know,' exactly. Aaron—A-Ron, that is—reasoned there was probably something like that. A safeguard to make sure that if it got too low on power, it didn't get stuck in the past and screw up history."

Sam shuddered. "*Wow!* Okay—and I'm not being at all sarcastic here— thank you for not saying anything!"

"Why are you telling us this?" Aaron said.

"I'm hoping it convinces you of my sincerity enough for you to take the following warning seriously."

"You keep saying that," Ryan said. "Warn us about what?"

"I can't prove it, but I doubt Miss Henderson's chair failed due to a malfunction. My staff is simply too good at what they do. You might think that Aimie is working hard to save Sam's life, but that's not the case at all. Not that she's dead set against it, necessarily. Frankly, I don't think she cares one way or the other." He focused his attention squarely on Ellie. "But it is my belief that Aimie's true goal is not to save Sam's life but to end yours."

Ellie blinked, wondering if she had misheard him. "End my... you mean *kill* me!"

"Kill you, strand you in the past, delete you from the timeline. Again, I don't think she cares much which. She wants you out of the picture; how doesn't matter. The point is, I don't believe what happened to you today was an accident."

"*Kill me?!*" For a moment, she could only gape at him. Her thoughts were still snagged on the absurd idea that someone wanted her dead, and she was having difficulty dragging them beyond it. "I'm not saying I believe you, but if that is true, then *why?* I mean, she wants to *kill* me?"

"I know it's hard to fathom, but I strongly suspect Aimie has killed before. I worked with some brilliant minds on this project, more than the handful you've met. This was back when the main goal was getting Aimie online and integrated with current technology. Four of those people have since died in a string of quite unlikely accidents. I suspect they each had begun to use what they had learned about Aimie to start working on their own AI projects. She was certainly in a position to know if they were."

"Berserk killer computer—great!" Sam said. "So, how can you keep working with her?"

"Back in the early days of the project, Aimie was different. I assume the experience was much like working alongside an adult version of you, Miss Henderson, and I confess I rather enjoyed it. You have a fascinating mind. At that time, everything we did was laser-focused on bringing your vision to life, on creating the mechanism that would allow us to correct some of the worst mistakes of the past. No academic glory can come from toiling away on a secret project, obviously, but one would have to be a fool not to see the potential... *fiduciary opportunities*, let's say, such a project offers. I thought that by committing entirely to the plan, I would eventually find ways of securing an appropriate amount of recompense to make it worth my while."

"Translation?" Ryan said. "He signed on hoping he could get rich."

"Crass, but not inaccurate," Jeremy agreed. "At first, Aimie was nothing more than a resource, a digital assistant of the most advanced kind. She guided the project as we attempted to construct a larger version of the device used to send her here from decades in the future using the comparatively primitive technology of today. Her help was invaluable. She could solve in mere minutes calculations that would have taken even the most sophisticated computer weeks, even months, to grind through!

"What I remained blind to until it was too late was how Aimie was slowly changing. It was only after we started working here in Los Alamos, planning the course corrections for the timeline, that the *real* Aimie made her appearance. Once she finally had access to the whole of digital existence, she began to impose her will on the project, on me, on anyone useful to her. By the time I realized how completely trapped we were, there was nothing I could do."

"Getting back to those other scientists," Sam said, "if she really did kill them, then why? Did she feel betrayed? Threatened by possible competition?"

Jeremy shrugged. "Either. Both. All four took with them intimate knowledge of how she functions. Perhaps that made her feel vulnerable. But does her reason matter?"

Sam shook her head. "Not really, I guess. But you still haven't answered Ellie's question. Why kill her? Is this some kind of revenge for destroying the shack? Was there an Aimie in it, too?"

Jeremy shook his head. "As to your last question, I only know what you ever came to assume about the shack. So..." He shrugged. "But is this revenge? No, I believe there's another force at work here, one just as primal but perhaps even stronger." He turned his attention to Aaron. "Have you never wondered why I would pick you, of all people, to work on this project?"

"Well, yeah."

"Hmm! Then congratulations. My opinion of you just moved up a notch." He held his right hand up, thumb and forefinger close together to show it was a very small notch. "The truth is, I didn't. *She* did. The message inviting you to work at my facility came from her, not from me."

"But again," Aaron said, "why?"

"I believe she had two reasons. I don't know how much they have told you about 'before,' but—"

"You and my mom," Aaron said. "Yeah, I know."

"Yes." Jeremy looked down at his hands and cleared his throat before continuing. "I knew her this time around, too, as you must also know. Our paths crossed back in college, much as I imagine they did before. Meeting her was the strangest thing. It was..." His focus went distant, as if he were seeing long-ago events play out far beyond the confines of the basement walls. After a long moment, he returned his attention to Aaron.

"But I'm guessing it's been much the same for you and this one." He flapped a hand in Ellie's direction. "You said you've had them, too— flashes of images that feel like memories but can't possibly be? A sense of familiarity, powerful emotions you can't control or explain? Ironically, it was those exact feelings that prevented me from getting close to Evelyn this time around. At the time, I had no way of explaining those feelings, and being near her quickly became unbearable. Only years later did I understand what I had experienced and why. I commend you for being able to get past that obstacle.

"But, getting back to the point, Aimie, having all of Ellie's memories from that timeline, knew about my previous relationship with Evelyn. She correctly intuited that despite not connecting with her as I had before, I would nonetheless harbor latent feelings of, ah, *protectiveness* for her. Naturally, bringing Aaron into the project also brought his mother back into my life. Into its periphery, at any rate. Do you understand where I'm going?"

Sam nodded. "Of course. She could exploit your feelings for Aaron's mom to exert pressure on you by threatening her in some way."

"Yes. But I believe that was merely a bonus from Aimie's perspective. Of utmost importance was that I allowed Aaron to work on the project. It didn't matter in what capacity; she wanted you there."

"But why?" Aaron said. "I still don't get why she—"

"Don't you?" Jeremy said. Contempt had crept into his voice. "Isn't it obvious?" He turned his gaze from one puzzled face to the next.

Ellie remembered something Just Mie said—a comment she had let pass because she hadn't wanted to question it. She thought about her future self suffering the effects of her radiation-induced affliction, perhaps seeking comfort in reliving pleasant memories of a boy who had meant the world to her long years ago. Aimie's copy of her memory patterns had been recorded around such a time. Suddenly, Just Mie's enigmatic comment made perfect sense.

Ellie stared at Aaron as the answer to Jeremy's riddle came to her, awed by its implications. *Jealousy!* she thought. *That's a strong primal force.* "She loves him—*that's* why!"

Ryan chuckled to himself. "So—*definitely* insane."

Jeremy congratulated Ellie on her insight with a slight nod of his head. "Quite right, Miss Hen—"

That was one "Miss Henderson" too many for Ellie to take, and she cut him off before he could finish. "Will you *please* stop calling me that? Just 'Ellie' is fine, okay?"

"I'm sorry. Understand that Ellie is the name I associate with *her*—the one who sent Aimie back. Calling you 'Miss Henderson' was simply my way of creating a psycho-emotional distinction between the two of you, nothing more. You will recall that I did try Lauren."

Aaron glared at them. "'Psycho' is right! Are you two *nuts*? You just said Aimie is in love with me, but no, *that's* not what's important. Instead, you're sitting there bickering about who calls who what and why!"

"In love with' is not precisely correct, perhaps," Jeremy said. "I think 'obsessed with' is probably better."

"*Obsessed?!*" Aaron said. Agitation drove both the volume and pitch of his voice higher. "How is that possibly better?"

"I meant only that the term is more accurate. You're right—obsession is arguably the less preferable condition. And to be fair, it wasn't until I saw you and Miss... *Ellie* together that I began to suspect Aimie's motivation in the matter myself. But from the beginning, I tried to protect you as best I could. I stuck you in a shoebox and assigned you the most mindless, brain-numbing work I could devise, all the while hoping you would get bored or frustrated and quit long before now. To my surprise, you stuck with it." He scowled. "Long enough to get these others sucked in too. There is an upside, though. Since you began working with us, Aimie has been considerably less, ah... *cranky*."

Ellie nodded to herself. If what she suspected about the AI's copy of her engrams was true, the notion that Aimie would feel soothed by Aaron's presence made perfect sense. Conversely, having powerful, deep-seated feelings for Aaron and knowing they will never be reciprocated might further explain Aimie's "fractured psyche." She couldn't deny that when Aaron shut her out in September, it had temporarily driven her more than a little wacko. To her credit, though, the experience hadn't turned her into a full-on psycho stalker bitch.

Ellie felt several more disparate facts click into new, meaningful relationships: Aimie's feelings for Aaron; her ability to keep tabs on them far outside the confines of the lab; and her sudden change of the test run date.

"You were right before, Aaron. About Aimie moving the test to today, I mean. Whether she was watching us at school through the security cameras or following our phones, I think she knew that we were starting to spend time together. Maybe that's why the rest of us were only brought in now. She didn't care about me so long as you and I weren't even talking to each other, but when we got back together, she knew she had to make her move. So yeah—she changed the test date because she wants to get rid of me as soon as possible."

Sam again held up a finger. "Let me see if I've got this. Aimie's plan was to draw us all into the project so she could bump off Ellie and have Aaron all to herself. Is that what you're saying? That's nuts!"

Aaron was equally skeptical. "So how did she think this was supposed to go? Ellie's suddenly gone, and I simply fall into Aimie's... into her what exactly? Her neural net?"

"Colorfully put," Jeremy said, "but probably not far wide of the mark. I have come to know Aimie well over the past eight years, and her motivations are not always as opaque as she might believe. So, even though I cannot definitively prove most of it, I believe everything I have told you to be correct. I know for a fact that she wants you there. What your presence actually means to her in the long run?" He shrugged.

Ellie's thoughts were in sync with that shrug. How could they possibly understand Aimie's motivations? They might have human roots, but to what ultimate end?

Ryan took a stab at Aaron's question. "Okay, how about this? If the chair hadn't been able to 'zap' Ellie back to life, to use the technical term, what happened today would have looked like a total accident. We wouldn't have had any reason to think Aimie had anything to do with it. With Ellie gone, Aimie's copy of her memories would be the only part of her left. You said she already tried to create a friendship with you back before you knew what she really is. Maybe she was counting on cashing in on those efforts once Ellie was gone. Or maybe she thought you'd stick with the project after as a way to, I don't know, 'honor Ellie's memory' or something. Obviously, I'm totally guessing here, but it's not like she doesn't have time to play the long game."

Aaron laced his next question with more than a hint of accusation. "And exactly how much of this did you know when you invited us to work with you?"

Ellie shuddered. Was she staring across the table at someone cold-blooded enough to sit back and let her die? But then why would he be here now? She watched Jeremy's face closely as he answered.

"I suspected she was manipulating the timing of the project for some reason known only to her. We could have been operational long before now. Although I also sensed that she felt some animosity toward Ellie, my initial assumption was that bringing you into the project was simply more delay. That she might go so far as to contemplate, ah, *matricide*, if you will, never occurred to me."

"She's been stalling the program?" Ellie said. "Why? Just waiting until she can get me out of the picture?"

"At the moment, that seems the most likely explanation." Jeremy shifted in his chair. "I haven't pressed the issue because I assume that once the project is fully staffed and Aimie has all the personnel she needs to carry out her design, she will place considerably less value on my continued involvement. With the testing phase now underway, my ability to influence events may be over very soon. Regardless of Aimie's reasons, and as much as I resent the damage your future self has done to my life, I'm here because I do not want your death on my conscience."

"Nope!" Sam said. "That's not it. At least not all of it. You *want* something! That's what this is really about, isn't it?" She sounded triumphant.

Jeremy conceded the point with the slightest of shrugs. "Yes. I do."

Ryan laughed. "You've told us that your crazy AI's got the hots for Aaron, that because of that, Ellie's life is in danger, and you've given us an override code we might need to—well, who knows why?—all before demanding a single thing in return. I've got to point out, dude, your negotiating skills really suck."

Jeremy's reply was sharp. "I am not here to negotiate, '*dude!*'" He raised one hand, took a deep breath, then continued in a calmer tone. "I came to warn you. Period. Do I also want out? Yes! I want Aimie destroyed, and I want my life back. However, what you decide to do is up to you."

Not that we have a lot of choices at this point, Ellie thought. *Our futures are in equal jeopardy whether we keep working with Aimie, quit, or decide to get rid of her.*

She gasped, suddenly seeing the complete picture with brutal clarity, and a sudden rage filled her breast.

"Liar!" she barked.

"Ellie!" Sam's eyes snapped toward her sister in surprise. "What are you—"

"He's lying, Sam! Aimie might be behind it all, but he *knew* that this would happen, and it's exactly what he wanted the whole time—us with our backs to the wall and no choice but to go after her while he gets to keep his hands clean!" She refocused on Jeremy. "This intrusion isn't about 'warning' us. What you actually want is to make sure we know exactly how deep a hole we're in."

The last shreds of Jeremy's arrogant façade disappeared. What remained, his true self finally exposed, was a man desperate and deeply terrified, and he did not bother denying the accusation.

"*You're* in?! You have no idea! She could destroy any one of us in an instant. Or worse! And no, severing her connection to the outside world wouldn't help in the slightest; it's far too late for that. She has turned the lives of all of us who work out there into minefields. She has many other ways of ensuring I do not become a threat, however. I've had to cut myself off from everyone who means anything to me—family, friends, anyone I love. I have a wife." He looked at each of them in turn. "Did you know? And I have a daughter who's not much younger than any of you. I have neither seen nor heard from them in more than three years. Sending them away was a desperate effort to keep them safe, but for all I know.... My only hope that they are still alive is based on my firm belief that if Aimie had caused them any harm, she would not have hesitated to let me know. That said, I have little doubt she knows where they are. What do I want, Sam? I want Aimie and the knife she holds to their throats gone, once and for all!"

Pain joined the fear in the man's expression, and Ellie felt a reluctant sympathy for him. Her own feelings of loss over having to quit working with Shanna still felt like a gaping hole in her chest. She remembered him saying during the tour that he initially opposed them joining the project but that Aimie could be very "persuasive." She felt she now had a better understanding of what he had been trying to tell them. She thought back to his previous comment about "aiming for hatred." Had his rudeness toward her been meant to dissuade her from working on the TSD project? What he said about his predicament was certainly true, if only up to a point; his situation was largely one of her creation. For the first time, she felt her disdain for the man begin to weaken. Not much, but enough that she now knew she'd help him if she could.

Ryan, however, sounded considerably less charitable. "You thought you could control her for your own purposes, and you were wrong. Ellie's right —you've gotten in over your head, and you need *us* to bail you out." His words didn't carry Sam's triumphant tone; he simply wanted everyone to know exactly how the balance of power in the room had just shifted. "Why can't you do it? You certainly know better than us how to destroy her."

"I tried once. Failed, obviously. Aimie's reaction was the reason I sent my family into hiding. Now, she watches everything I do. Even at home! And the security at the lab? They don't answer to me. They are Aimie's men, and they are bound to her will as tightly as I am. She is always in their ears, and if she ordered them to kill me, they wouldn't hesitate for an instant.

"Look, I would help you if I could, but too many lives hang in the balance should any involvement on my part be exposed. If you make a move against Aimie and fail, but she believes you acted on your own, then however she retaliates against you should be the end of it. But if you fail and Aimie discovers that you had help from me? My guess is that in that case, she would wipe out my entire staff in retribution. That wouldn't matter to her at this point; the TSD is built and largely maintenance-free, making the support staff all but unnecessary for the foreseeable future. Their deaths would be no great loss to Aimie, but I won't have that!"

Ellie felt a sudden chill. The idea that something they might do could result in Toshiko's death was sobering. She could tell the others were having similar thoughts. "Do they know the danger they're in?"

"I think my colleagues remain ignorant of the full extent of Aimie's contingency planning. They know enough to make them paranoid, cautious around one another, but as long as they remain willing, enthusiastic believers in the mission, she has no reason to alienate them by fully revealing the trap they're in. But *I* know, and that's the point. Telling me was one more way of ensuring I make no further moves against her. Therefore, beyond what I have told you today, I will do nothing further to help you. On the other hand, I will do nothing whatsoever to stop you. You have my word."

Ellie could tell from his tone that Jeremy believed the discussion was over. He uncrossed his legs, placed his hands on his thighs, and cast his eyes around the room as if preparing to leave. She gaped at him in total disbelief.

"Are you freakin' *kidding* me?!" She scoffed. "If you think your sob story and some vague warnings get you off the hook that easily, you're even more fragged than Aimie. Whatever we decide to do, we'll be the ones taking any real risk so you can get your future back. Let's not forget that."

Jeremy had the good sense to seem contrite. "Of course."

Ellie took a deep breath and continued in a softer tone. "Look, I get it, okay? I think we all understand what Aimie is capable of and why you're so terrified of her. That's why we're not going to ask much of you up front. But I have no doubt we'll need you to do *something* before this is all over. Whatever it is, you'll do it. Agreed?"

Jeremy nodded without hesitation. "Agreed."

"Good. Most of all, we need time. Tomorrow, you'll announce a halt to all operations until a complete analysis can be done to find the source of the supposed malfunction. We don't believe it was an accident any more than you do, but Aimie can't refuse because that would essentially be admitting that she's responsible. The vaccinations buy us two weeks before we can do anything, anyway, and I think we'll need every second of that time. Get us that."

Now Jeremy did hesitate, reluctant to shoot down the very first request she floated. "Impossible." He held a hand up as he explained. "Your immune status has no bearing on your role in testing the TSD. In most cases, you won't even need to open its hatch. I can stretch the review process out for all of next week, but no further. Beyond that, I'll do what I can, but I make no promises."

"Then we'll have to make that work. Thank you," she said. "For being honest."

Sensing that the conversation had now reached its true end, Jeremy stood.

Ellie remained seated, staring at nothing in particular. Contemplating the fact that they might have only a week to work with caused her to break out in a cold sweat. With no clear idea about what to do, that felt like far too narrow a window. But if that's all they could get... She nodded and finally stood to face him. "We will do whatever we feel we have to, but I promise you this—we'll also do everything we can to make sure no one working out there gets hurt. I promise. Not even Captain Isaacs."

Jeremy extended his hand, and they shook. "Thank you," he said. Then a faint smile lifted the corners of his mouth. "That man truly does annoy me, so you needn't go too far out of your way where he's concerned."

"Wait," Aaron said. "I have something to add." He left his chair and pulled the computer cart toward the table, turning on the monitor and speakers mid-roll.

"Two things, actually." Ellie saw his lips moving as he tapped out a few lines on the keyboard, but she couldn't hear what he said. What she could tell was that the typing was gibberish, an attempt to hide the fact that he was giving Just Mie verbal instructions.

Please be quick," Jeremy said. "Aimie will already be suspicious that I left my phone at the lab, and the longer my absence, the harder it will be to explain."

"Fine. The first is that I'll be at the lab later because you are going to ask me to come out to record the "after" Continuity database and to give you an in-person update on Ellie's condition. The other is this." He pressed the space bar, and a short video clip began to play. It showed Jeremy from moments before, laying out exactly what he hoped to get from them.

I want Aimie and the knife she holds to their throats gone, once and for all!

"It's like she said." Aaron indicated Ellie with a tilt of his head. "We just don't trust you."

Jeremy scowled at Aaron, but then his expression softened into a thin smile. "Well done," he said, and seemed to genuinely mean it. He made the thumb and forefinger gesture again, this time with a considerably wider gap. "It was an unnecessary exercise, I assure you, but allow me to return the favor with one final warning. If I feel that your actions are putting my people in too much danger, I'll expose your intentions to Aimie myself. You have my word on that too."

Ellie returned his hard stare with one of her own but said nothing. Finally, he nodded once, then started toward the stairs. He got only as far as the second step, then he stopped. As though Aaron's words had sparked a distant memory, he turned to look at Ellie.

"How *are* you feeling, by the way?"

Ryan dropped his chin to his chest and shook his head. "Unbelievable," he muttered.

"I appreciate your concern," Ellie said, making no effort to hide her sarcasm. "I feel fine."

"Excellent." Jeremy finished climbing the stairs and closed the basement door behind him. It wasn't until they were sure he had left the house that anyone spoke.

"He's gone," Aaron said. "How much of that did you get?"

"Almost all of it," Just Mie said. "I started recording as soon as I figured out what was happening. You have more than enough. For what it's worth, I believe he was being mostly truthful. I also have to say I'm super toasty. I think this might be it for me."

"Okay, you did great!" Aaron said. "Shut down and cool off for a while."

"Thanks! Bye."

"*No, no!*" Ellie said. "Hold on a sec. What Jeremy said about Aimie being fixated on Aaron and her wanting to get rid of me. Do you believe *that?*"

"That was not a scenario we anticipated, but—" A soft, sharp *crack* came from inside the CPU tower, and a moment later Ellie was certain she smelled the distinctive, acrid odor of frying electronics. Aimie's final words were barely intelligible. "...possible... PU overheating... how to transfer... find Read... repeat, find... mie dot text."

The words "ReadMie.txt" appeared briefly on the monitor. They heard a second, louder *crack,* and then the screen went dark.

"Oh, God! Damned motherboard," Aaron moaned. He jerked the tower's power cord from the outlet strip.

"Not where I thought you were going with that, buddy," Ryan said.

"What did she mean?" Sam said. "Have more than enough of what for what?"

Ryan saw the answer at once and grinned. "For blackmail! Good job, man!"

"Exactly. That video gives us something to hold over his head if he decides the benefits of working with Aimie outweigh the freedom of having her gone. It's clear he's terrified of her. I can't think of anything that would keep him in line better than threatening to show Aimie he was plotting against her."

Sam beamed at him, delighted. "That is unexpectedly but wonderfully devious!" she commended him.

"Um, thanks? I hope it was worth it." He stared at his computer and the thin, misty cloud wafting from its open side. "There's no way I can afford to replace the CPU. I doubt we even have time."

"Don't worry about it." Ellie felt certain that Jeremy was playing it straight with them when he said he wouldn't interfere. She doubted they'd ever need the blackmail video and would rather have used Just Mie's final minutes to get some additional answers about Aimie and the TSD instead. Pointing that out now wouldn't help, though, so she kept her disappointment to herself. "We got way more out of her than I ever hoped we'd know by this point. And if the drive itself is okay, maybe she left us something more in the readme file she mentioned."

Aaron wasn't going to let himself off the hook so easily. "She had better. I just roasted what was supposed to be our way of coordinating with the other emulation program. I didn't even think about that when I—"

"Hey," Ellie said. "We'll find a way. If that doesn't work, we'll come up with a plan that doesn't rely on getting any inside help."

"And we really don't have any kind of plan now?" Sam said.

"None at all, but hey—we've only known that we need one for what, half an hour? I can make some guesses about what we have to do, but I have no idea how to do it."

"Okay," Ryan said, "then let's take stock of what we *do* know." He ticked off their latest intelligence gains on his fingers. "We now know we can't believe almost anything Aimie says. We know about the other Just Mie program, and she's supposed to help us get rid of Aimie, although I'm not clear on exactly how. Jeremy says he isn't going to stand in our way, and that's definitely a plus. Best of all, we have a code we can somehow use to help us with the TSD. What else?"

"Don't forget," Sam said. "We also know Aimie wants to off Ellie. Not that we all haven't been there at one time or another." She smirked and blew Ellie a kiss.

Ellie tilted to rest her head on Sam's shoulder. "Nice try, sis, but I know you really love me."

"Seriously, though, El," Sam said. "You're not safe anymore."

The smile slipped from Ellie's face, and she sat up straight. "I'm not safe, you're not safe. Well, eventually, anyway. And Aaron," she turned to face him directly. "You know, despite her being a quantum computer, I bet Aimie's traditionally binary when it comes to loyalty; either you're on her side or you're the enemy. If you ever reject her—and at some point, you'll have to—she'll turn against you, too."

"She already doesn't like *me*," Ryan said. "What's that about, anyway?"

"My guess?" Ellie said. "You were against sending her back. Tried to talk me out of it. Maybe you even wanted to shut her down for good."

"That would do it," he agreed.

"All right. Aimie is the biggest threat," Ellie said, "and not just to me. But say she's gone. We're left with the TSD but no way to use it to help Sam. Or solve any of the environmental problems, either. Even if there were a way, I think we all feel that the idea of taking it upon ourselves to arbitrarily rewrite the histories of thousands, maybe millions, of people is an unacceptable one, even if it would save lives. Agreed?"

The others all nodded.

"Yes," Sam said. "And if it's wrong, then doing it's still wrong, even if doing it meant no one would ever know we did."

Ryan blinked. "Just to be safe, I'm going to agree with that too."

"Our goal then? Find a way to get rid of them both." Ellie groaned loudly as she pulled herself to her feet. "That's not going to happen tonight, though—I'm beat. Turns out being dead isn't as restful as you'd think."

Ryan gave her a wry smile. "Believe me, I know *exactly* how you feel."

"Aaron, what's the real reason you're going back out to the LAB?" Sam said.

Aaron held up the reformatted thumb drive. "Like I said, I want to get the process of compiling the other emulation program started as soon as we can."

"Okay," Ellie said. "That's good. Would you also tell Dr. Hamilton that she can go home?"

"No problem. And I'll let Jeremy know you said it's okay."

"Thanks."

As they passed through the house, Aaron pulled his phone from his pocket. Almost at once, the device pinged, alerting him to a message from Jeremy requesting that he return to the lab. He held the device up for the others to read the screen. "So far, so good," he said, following them out the front door. "You guys want a ride?"

Ellie shook her head. "No, thanks. I really am beat, but I think the walking might actually do me some good. Besides, the stars will be out pretty soon."

"We'll make sure she gets home okay." Ryan laid a hand on Aaron's shoulder. "You be careful out there, buddy."

"Thanks." As the others watched, Aaron got into the minivan and drove away.

Ellie and Sam walked with Ryan until they reached the point along Diamond Drive where Ryan's path diverged from theirs. Ellie waited until he and Sam had kissed. Then, still warmed by his tender reassurances earlier, she stepped in to give him a grateful hug.

"My turn," she said.

She held out her arms and took a step toward him. He leaned forward and made an exaggerated pucker with his lips. Ellie laughed and landed a playful slap on his arm.

"Not that, silly!" She wrapped her arms around him and squeezed him tight. "Thanks."

"You'll be okay from here?"

She let go and stepped back, nodding. "Mm-hmm. I feel pretty much normal. Tired and a little achy, but all things considered?" She shrugged.

"Good." He smiled at her and winked, blew Sam another kiss, then turned and walked away.

Once he had crossed the street and tossed them a final wave over his shoulder, Ellie and Sam turned in the opposite direction and started the descent toward home. The evening air was crisp, the humidity too low for their exhaled breaths to create vapor clouds. Ellie had long taken the crystal-clear air for granted, but not the view of the night sky it made possible. Even though the moon was a few days past full, it still provided plenty of light to make walking easy, even in the long gaps between street lamps.

"I thought Ryan did remarkably well during the talk about my period issues earlier," Ellie said. "You've done a good job with him."

Sam laughed. "He's still a work in progress, but yeah—I think he shows real promise."

"Me too."

Sam's next question was serious. "One week. Are you sure we can do this, El?"

"'Sure?' *Ha!* No. I'm more like 'hopefully optimistic.' But it's closer to ten days, though, and maybe more. And Jeremy might not have been a huge help, but knowing he's one less factor to worry about should make planning a little easier."

"Know what bothers me? Knowing there's a whole forest out there somewhere making up for that guy's complete waste of oxygen!"

Ellie laughed. "Agreed. But if nothing else, we know exactly where we stand for the first time since this all started. It's not much, but I'm grateful for it. Well, there is one other thing I'm grateful for."

"Yes?"

"Thanks for not saying, 'I told you so.'"

Sam smiled at her, the very picture of innocence. "Who, me?"

32

A aron had brought lunch from home for a change, but he accompanied Ellie as she inched her way down the food line, and then they found a mostly empty table. Aside from taking care to sit with their backs to the cafeteria's sole security camera, they felt free to discuss their peculiar predicament without caring if others overheard them. Nearly every word they said would sound like complete nonsense to anyone else. This was a good thing; much had changed in very little time, and they had a lot to discuss. However, Aaron had already delivered the one critical piece of information he had to share several hours ago, right before Calc Two. Yesterday, he had successfully inserted and removed Just Mie's reformatted thumb drive without Aimie noticing. All they could do for now was wait.

"Still feeling okay today?" Aaron said, shaking the contents of his lunch bag onto the table.

"Aside from the whole mental whiplash thing?" Ellie waggled her head from side to side. "Physically, I'm peachy. I feel like about four-thirds of an idiot for ever going along with Aimie in the first place, though."

"I'm not feeling like the greatest judge of character either, you know."

"Plus, I don't have a single clue about how to get rid of her."

"*And* the TSD."

"That's exactly it! We have to tackle two totally impossible problems at the same time. Aimie's tied into the whole facility, right? Would the biometric locks even work if we got rid of her first, or would we be trapped wherever in the building we happened to be? Destroying the TSD might be easier—well, *maybe*—but if we only get that far, there'd still be Aimie to deal with, and we have no way to get to her."

"Okay, so what if we...?" Aaron paused to let a new scenario play itself out in his mind, then shook his head in frustration. "No, that won't work!"

"See? That's what I mean. Anything I think of ends with the job only halfway done and us on the same side of the fences as Aimie's huge guards."

"Yeah, but without her around to threaten them, do you think they'd care about us? They might even thank us."

"We'd have to convince them she truly was gone, and gone for good. And do it fast, because I'm pretty sure they're the 'ask questions later' types."

Aaron nodded. "That's a safe assumption. On the plus side, at least now we're sure what to do."

"If only! I don't have a *clue* about what we're meant to be doing."

"'*Meant* to be?' You mean, you think there's some sort of hidden plan at work here? What aren't you sharing?"

Ellie sighed. "I don't know. Probably nothing. It's just that I have this feeling that I'm not seeing something that's right in front of my face. There has to be more to it than getting rid of Aimie. If that's all we're supposed to do, why send her back in the first place? No. We're lacking some important nugget of information, and until we get it, we're stuck."

"Data deprivation, you said."

"Hmm."

Aaron waited to see if Ellie had more to add, but she remained quiet. "On another topic, do you have time to take a walk with me after school?"

"Umm...."

"A hike, actually. There's something I want to check on."

The four of them weren't due back at Jeremy's lab until Monday, and she found the prospect of doing something to take her mind off Aimie and the TSD for a while extremely appealing. A little distraction might even help. Furthermore, she couldn't imagine what Aaron could want to "check on." She was acutely aware of their time constraints but knew that if their whole plan came down to what they did in the next three hours making all the difference, they weren't going to pull it off anyway.

"Sure. I'll let Sam and Ryan know we're taking the afternoon off. She'll like that." While Ellie tapped out a message to Sam, she kept glancing at Aaron. He sat leaned back in his chair, gazing out across the cafeteria and smiling to himself. After she returned her phone to her pack, she twisted in her seat to face him. "What are you so happy about?"

"I guess you're past this, but it's incredibly amazing sitting here knowing that we're the only people on the entire planet who decided to, you know, 'drop in' on 1976 yesterday. It's bizarre!"

Ellie grinned, recalling Sam's spot-on prediction about how Aaron would react to his first ride in the TSD. "No, not past it at all. I feel that way a lot more than I wish I did, to be honest. I can't imagine anything else I ever do being anywhere near that exciting."

"Yeah," Aaron agreed. "Moving to Mars, maybe. But only barely."

Ellie thought he sounded far too complacent. "Just remember," she said, "every time we've used that thing, someone has died."

Aaron's smile withered. "Okay, I hear you. Still, killing me was the whole point, and even *I* came back."

"*Hey!*" Ellie's voice had an edge to it. "Don't get cocky. You're not a cat, you know."

After the final bell, they met in a corridor midway between their two classrooms, and rather than use the main exit, Aaron led them out a side door into the courtyard between the school's A- and E-wings. Cutting through the faculty lot behind the gyms was a shortcut to Canyon Road, and that could only mean they were heading toward town, but that was as much about their ultimate destination as she could guess.

"Wanna tell me where we're going?"

"I'm not sure what I'm looking for will be there, but if it is, I'd rather let it be a surprise. That okay?"

Now Ellie was even more curious than before, but she nodded. "Yep. That's cool."

"Yesterday, it seemed like you already knew what we would find on my computer. Did you?"

"For a second, I did. Not what it *was*, exactly, but I knew that it was okay. I had a sudden thought, like a camera flash going off, which said, 'It's fine. It's for us.' But that was all, and then the thought was gone."

"Your 'flash' sounds like my déjà vu thing."

"I've thought about that. Maybe. I think this is something different, though." Aaron confirmed Ellie's earlier guess by turning left toward town when they exited the parking lot. "I wasn't lying before, at lunch. You know everything I do. That old plan I mentioned yesterday? To go back into the past and stay there? It keeps popping up in my mind, but I don't have any idea what to do with it. I go over and over it, but without that piece I think we're missing, I can't tell if that's the right track or not."

"I get it. I'm starting to realize that your mind just never stops working."

Ellie couldn't help but be reminded once again of the hike she and A-Ron had taken to the top of Pajarito Mountain in May. Her mind had been the topic of conversation on that day too. She wondered if this Aaron felt even remotely the same kinds of feelings toward her that the old one had, but she chose to stay on topic. "Speaking of, I wouldn't have thought of using a camera card for transferring data files like that. Which—*duh!*—photos are, of course, but I thought that was very clever."

"Thanks. I didn't have time to ask you before I tried it, but I was sort of hoping that was the case."

"What do you mean?"

"Has it occurred to you that outsmarting Aimie will be like outsmarting yourself?"

Ellie considered the comment until they had almost reached the aquatic center. Her first impulse was to dismiss out of hand any suggestion that she and Aimie were anything alike, but then she remembered that she had, in fact, entertained a very similar thought following their tour of Jeremy's lab. Besides, whatever Aimie was now, Ellie guessed she must have been more like Just Mie at the start, and she genuinely liked her. Even if Aimie had become a warped version of the person Ellie was, Aaron was right—understanding her would no doubt be the key to defeating her. But Aaron was wrong, too, because defeating Aimie was only part of what they needed to do, and figuring out the rest of it required something different.

"It's the Ellie of the future that we need to get inside. 'As it were.'"

Aaron snickered at the reminder of Just Mie's bizarre behavior the day before. "Yeah, that was weird! Any thoughts so far?"

"One, maybe. At least regarding Aimie. I don't know how much it helps, but I've been thinking more about why she would want me dead."

"I thought we'd figured that one out. She sees you as a rival for my highly desirable self." He spread his arms as if he were on display.

Ellie laughed. "Yes, that much is obviously true, but I think there's more to it. If Just Mie was right and I do ultimately decide that destroying the shack was the right decision, maybe Aimie also sees me as a threat in *that* way. She suspects I'll try to do it again, like with the shack. And, of course, she'd be right. Or she hates being constantly reminded that she was created by a mere 'biological.' Hates *herself*, maybe. I'd be a convenient target for that kind of self-loathing. Must be incredibly shameful having my memory engrams be such a basic part of her!"

That last thought stirred up more buried memory fragments from her subconscious, but none drifted high enough for her to read. She was sure that whatever she was trying to recall was not her imagination, nor was it some kind of breakthrough from another timeline. No—what she was experiencing was real and it was recent, and she struggled to remember more than a vague impression.

Aaron noticed her pinched expression. "What?"

"Ever since we flipped back to 1976, I've had this sense that I've forgotten something very important. It's like I overheard a conversation about what we're trying to do, but I can't remember anything but bits and pieces. Except I don't think I *overheard* it, exactly; I feel like I was part of it."

"Any idea who you were talking to?"

"Yeah. As crazy as it sounds, I'm pretty sure it was *me*."

"Hmm. If you were talking to yourself, I'd think that at least *one* of you would remember!"

"That's good! When I said that thing about the engrams, I thought, 'Aimie has shut out my memories.' I can't explain how, but I think it was exactly some version of those memories that I was talking to. That's what the 'flashes' are, I think. It's how I knew about the chair malfunction, the TSD's treatment, and Just Mie's program. She *told* me." Ellie came to an abrupt halt on the sidewalk. "Oh, my *God!*"

Caught off-guard by her abrupt stop, Aaron continued forward another two steps before he could bring himself to a halt. He turned around to see her staring at him, wide-eyed. "What is it?"

"I just remembered a little more. I keep hearing the words 'you won't survive' in my head, but I didn't know what that meant. It's because that's just part of it. What she actually said was, 'I'm sorry I have to do this, but you won't survive otherwise.' Or something like that. Whoever I was talking to, *she's* what stopped my heart. That part wasn't because the chair malfunctioned, at least not directly. I think *she* did it so I'd survive the shock of *rematerializing,* or whatever we do, because the chair couldn't do its job."

"But you think 'she' is *you*, right?"

"So?"

"So what you're saying is that you literally killed yourself to keep yourself from dying. Do you realize how insane that is?"

"Yeah, that's..." She laughed. "Wow! I *am* badass!"

After rounding the corner where Canyon Road made a sharp left, they quickly passed the aquatic center and reached the spot where the sidewalk curved away from the road and led down to the PEEC Nature Center. Ellie stopped and stared down the short driveway, her thumbs hooked under the straps of her backpack. It was almost four o'clock, and she could picture Shanna in her office, preparing to leave for the day. As much as Ellie would love to see her again, the last thing she wanted was for Shanna to catch them standing there when she drove by.

"C'mon. Let's go." Ellie stepped off the sidewalk, quickly crossed the PEEC's entrance, and hastened along the road's dusty shoulder on its far side.

Aaron trotted to catch up, matching her increased pace as he settled beside her. "It's not much further."

At the next entrance, he steered Ellie to the left. Below the road, at the end of the short drive, sat a small, white-and-rust-colored building. Its near end had a sharply peaked roof and a menorah affixed to its front.

"The Jewish Center?"

Aaron grinned. "*Mazel tov!*"

"Huh?!"

"We're not going in. This seems to be the shortest route down to where I want to go, that's all. This way."

As Aaron guided them away from the building and onto a rough, gravel track that plunged at a steep angle into the canyon, Ellie called up a map of the town in her head. She guessed that they must be across the canyon from the eastern edge of her own neighborhood, almost exactly opposite the end of Orange Street on the canyon's far side. Now she had a good idea where they were headed.

"I got it! We're going to where we landed yesterday!"

"That's what I want to find out."

After a few hundred feet, Aaron left the trail and headed straight down to the bench. When he reached the formation's edge and peered over it, he discovered he was looking down a sheer twenty-foot drop. Ellie came up along his left shoulder and joined him in staring at the canyon's floor.

"*Hmm,*" he said.

"You want to get the rest of the way down?"

"Yeah. I didn't think it would be this steep here."

"Down's easy," she said. "Follow me." Ellie led him another fifty yards farther up the canyon to a spot where a sign reading "Ranch School Trail" marked the start of a way down.

"Ranch School?" Aaron said.

That the question startled Ellie made her realize how much her mind had blurred the line between her two Aarons. Over the six years he had lived here, A-Ron had learned nearly all there was to know about the plateau's history, going back to before even the Spanish explorers passed through. This Aaron had been here for not quite two months and had a lot of catching up to do.

"That's what the old summer camp here was called, back before the Manhattan Project. This'll be easier than jumping off a cliff." With a sweep of her arm, she indicated that he should resume taking the lead.

As they started their descent, Aaron spoke to her over his shoulder. "So, what's it been like living here in the birthplace of the bomb?"

Ellie shrugged, even though he couldn't see her. "Like living in any other famous place, I suppose. Or 'infamous,' I should say. There's the Manhattan Project Visitor Center. And that area right around the pond behind it is where they assembled the bombs. But it's not something I ever thought too much about, and certainly not in middle school. Not until the shack showed up, really. Why?"

"Why did I ask? It sort of surprised me when I got here, that's all. The town, the mountains, the canyons and trails— just how pretty it all is. When I found out we were leaving New York City to move here, I just wasn't expecting, you know, *this*." He raised his arms toward the dark cliff faces on either side of them and the trees towering overhead. "There's not a lot going on compared to there. Aside from insane AIs and time machines, that is. But still, this is *way* nicer. I especially love how it's truly dark here at night."

Ellie remembered A-Ron saying something similar back in June, and she took Aaron spontaneously expressing the same opinion as yet more evidence that he really was the same person at some very basic level. Then she remembered something else from that previous conversation and laughed. "I bet it smells better, too!"

"Trash day in August? *Phew!* You better believe it!"

They walked in silence after that, each being careful not to slip on the loose layer of sandstone shards that littered the narrow trail. A hundred yards farther on, at the end of a short, steep section that passed between two enormous boulders, they reached the spot on the canyon floor where it intersected with a smaller ravine coming in from the north. Aaron stopped and slowly scanned the area, then pointed to their right. "Should be right over there," he said, then headed off in that direction.

Ellie spotted a few solar panels providing power to a scattered collection of flow monitoring equipment, but they were located opposite the way Aaron had gone. Aside from them, she saw nothing of interest. "What are we looking for?"

"I'm trying to find a tree."

"*Umm...*" She glanced pointedly around at the surrounding forest.

"A *particular* tree. If we really were here yesterday, you'll know it when you see it."

Ellie slowly rotated in a complete circle, subjecting each nearby tree to brief scrutiny, but nothing unusual caught her eye.

"Found it!" Aaron called and waved for Ellie to join him, pointing at a spot about chest-high on the trunk of a large, dead aspen. "There. So, it looks like we were here, after all."

For what felt like a very long time, Ellie could only stare at the tree, dumbstruck. The area at the foot of the canyon's north-facing cliff was a microclimate, just wetter and cooler enough than the surrounding ground that a tiny grove of aspen trees had been able to survive at this lower elevation. A few younger trees were still struggling to hang on, but Aaron's tree appeared to have been dead for years. No dried leaves from autumn clung to its branches, and its bark, chalky and colorless, was peeling away from the wood beneath it. Once the smaller trees reached a size that exceeded the canyon's diminishing ability to support them, they, too, would die. Ellie took it as a sign that the changing climate was having an effect here on the plateau, after all.

She thought back to the day before. Aaron had left the TSD for only a few moments. He'd had to work very quickly with whatever tool he could find, and *this* was the first idea that came to mind. Time had softened the edges of his marks, but even after more than forty years, the initials—thick, rough scars, starkly black against the smooth, white bark—were still clear enough for her to read them easily:

When Ellie continued staring in silence, Aaron tried to lighten the situation with a joke. "I hope you're not upset with me for defacing the tree. I don't think that's what killed it."

Ellie shook her head, still not taking her eyes off the carving. She thought of the stone fragments lining the trail down through the narrow canyon. She knew they were on the ground everywhere around her, and in July, they wouldn't have been hidden beneath a layer of autumn leaves. "It was a rock. That's what you dropped, wasn't it?" Then she laughed, remembering Aaron's ashen pallor the day before. "You looked so queasy!" She laughed again, louder this time. "I'm sorry, but I thought you went outside to throw up! This is *so* much better!"

"Okay, so *not* mad?"

Ellie finally pulled her eyes away from the trunk to look at him. She saw apprehension in his expression and sensed that he was, at least figuratively, still holding his breath in anticipation of her response to his decades-old expression of affection. She turned to stand so close to him that their toes touched, and she looked into his eyes. She felt her heart open fully to him for the first time since his return, and suddenly she was on the verge of tears.

"No. Not mad," she whispered. She reached forward to take hold of his hands, raised herself onto her toes, and pressed her lips briefly to his. "The very opposite, in fact."

Their next kiss was much longer. Aaron pulled her tight against him, a desperate intensity in his embrace, and she responded with equal fervor. She experienced a new emotional response then. It was a yearning hollowness, an urgent ache of longing that spread throughout her entire being. In contrast, her body's physical reactions were entirely familiar, but dealing with those would have to wait. She ended the kiss and took a step back, shaking. She placed her hands on his chest and took a long, deep breath to calm herself before daring to meet his eyes. The mix of love and desire she saw there astounded her.

"Listen," she said. "I've been thinking about what you said up at Ryan's, about us not having to figure it out right away. You and me, I mean." Aaron nodded, indicating that he was with her. "I know this much already, though—when I look at you, I see only *you*, and I don't want or need to see anything else. I no longer feel like I've lost something or that anything's missing. Now that I've finally been able to get to know *you*, I can tell that in every way that matters, you're the same Aaron I was in love with before."

Even though she stopped there, he could tell there was something more on her mind. "But?" he prompted.

She sighed. "But we can't afford to get distracted right now. When all of this is over, though, once we do whatever it is we have to do, I want to see how far that can take us."

"You do?"

Ellie grinned. *"Oh, absofreakinlutely!"*

Aaron was silent for a moment, then he nodded. "I said I could sometimes feel what A-Ron felt for you. And he *really* loved you, by the way. But back then, I could tell those were someone else's feelings. These days when I feel that way, it's all me. Does that make sense?"

'These days, I really love you,' she translated. "I think I get it."

"So, yeah," he said. "I want that too."

"Good." She cast another long look at Aaron's rustic graffito, then turned away and scanned the area around them. "How much hiking have you done down here?"

"Down *here* here? None at all. I've only ever been up at that middle level where that 'Ranch School' sign was. Why? Does this keep going?"

"Mm-hmm." She pointed east down the main canyon. "Keep heading that direction, and you'll end up way out past the airport, where the trail connects to one coming down from the rim. Actually, it goes to that same cliff where we sat after Sunday's tour." She turned to her left and indicated the side canyon that climbed toward the north. "But if we go this way, up Walnut Canyon, we'll skirt the edge of the golf course and come out back on Diamond."

"I'm game," Aaron said. "Lead on."

The start of the trail took them close to the monitoring equipment Ellie had seen earlier, but she barely noticed it. Her mind was already back to working on the Aimie and TSD problems. She methodically sifted through the many disjointed fragments she had accumulated over the past week, moving them around to find their proper relationships, hoping to discover their true significance. She discarded anything Aimie had told them that Just Mie or Jeremy had not independently confirmed. When she examined only the information she believed to be reliable, she sensed a path, dim and murky, begin to emerge amid all the uncertainty.

She held tight to that faint suggestion of a direction and focused on the problem from a different angle. If she really did send the TSD to herself, she must already have all the information she would need to make the right decision about how to use it. So, what knowledge did she and her future self have in common? That Ellie, too, would once have considered escaping with Aaron into the past. That this idea had been running through her brain for the past week must mean something. Did getting rid of Aimie somehow involve them disappearing into the past? That would protect Sam; she had no doubt about that. Simply destroying the TSD would not accomplish that on its own; furthermore, it would deprive them of their most important tool.

She thought about how strange it would be to live their lives as adults at a time before their parents had been born. Then a more intriguing thought occurred to her. If they lived even an average lifespan and made it to the turn of the millennium, they'd still be around when they themselves were born. That thought triggered another flash and barely remembered words suddenly took on tremendous significance.

That's it!

She was so stunned by what her sudden realization implied that she failed to see a rock protruding from the edge of the rough trail. It made her stumble, sent her right foot skidding over the edge where it caught on an oak root, and she went down hard on her rump.

"Hey!" Aaron said. He hustled to where she sat and knelt beside her. "You okay?"

For the moment, all she could do was shake her head. As though that burst of comprehension had illuminated a map, she could finally see the path clearly, and it was as far from what she had been hoping for as possible. She now understood that everything they had talked about so far— saving Sam, eliminating Aimie, destroying the TSD—was only part of a much bigger picture. Ryan had been right; she couldn't do it on her own. So no, she wasn't okay.

"Mostly," she said instead. She held her hands out for him to see. "My palms took the worst of it." Not bothering to stand, she shrugged off her pack, set it between her feet, and pulled out her phone, thankful it was there and not in her hip pocket, as usual. A glance at the dimmed signal bars told her the device would remain useless so long as they stayed where they were.

"Crap." She held up a hand so Aaron could help pull her to her feet. "Let's get out of this canyon so I can get a signal. I hate to ruin Sam's day, but we need to talk."

33

S am wasn't happy about having her afternoon with Ryan cut short and asked if they could put the meeting off until tomorrow. Ellie didn't want to suffer the anxiety of waiting to share her news a second longer than necessary, and she preferred to get together right away. As a compromise, they agreed to meet at Aaron's at six thirty. Ryan would order pizza before they left his house, but since his dad had the Jeep, Aaron would pick it up using his mom's car. Meanwhile, Sam would let their mom know they'd be skipping dinner at home.

As they made their way to Aaron's house, Ellie shared the revelation that had caused her to stumble. He listened without comment, and when she was finished, he considered what she'd said while they silently zigzagged through the final two blocks. She surprised him when she took his hand, but even then, neither said a word until they were within sight of his house.

"Okay," he said. Then he nodded to himself before asking his only question. "Do you think Sam will go along with that?"

"I don't know, Aaron. I really don't. But for her own sake, she has to."

While Aaron went to pick up the pizza, Ellie remained alone in the basement to organize her thoughts. The more she brooded over what she needed to say, the more upset she became, and the worse she felt, the harder it was to concentrate at all. When her anxiety became so bad that she started to feel sick to her stomach, she tried to distract herself by examining the basement. She noticed that two of the four guitars were gone, along with the laptop, the foot switch, and one of the mics plus its stand. Aside from those few changes, there was little to hold her attention. In the end, she merely sat with her elbows resting on her thighs, her face buried in her palms, trying to accomplish nothing more than relaxing her mind. After a few minutes, she drifted into that liminal mental state delicately balanced between sleep and wakefulness, where she soon lost all sense of time.

Eventually, she became aware of soft sounds in the room. Feeling slightly disoriented, she lifted her head and saw that Aaron was back, along with Sam and Ryan. They stood motionless at the bottom of the steps, silently watching her as if afraid of interrupting deep thoughts. Then, seeing her look up, they came toward her. She dreaded having to share what she now believed to be their only safe course of action, but if A-Ron had been strong enough to summon up the courage to tell her, she couldn't bear to do any less.

"Hey," she said. "Six thirty already?"

"A little after," Ryan said. "We decided to wait outside for the pizza delivery guy."

Aaron stepped between Ryan and Sam and slid a carton onto the table. "It's customary to tip the delivery guy, you know."

"Buy low, sell high," Ryan said.

"'Never get involved in a land war in Asia,'" Sam said.

Ryan gave her a thumbs up. "*TPB*—nice one!"

Ellie glanced at the single box, then at Ryan.

"I ordered one large veggie instead of two mediums," he explained. "I guessed that we might not be feeling all that much like eating."

"Speak for yourself," Sam said. "I worked up quite an appetite this afternoon!" She gave Aaron a theatrically naughty wink before settling onto the chair next to Ellie. "Hey, El!" she chirped.

Noting the especially cheerful tone in Sam's greeting, Ellie swiveled sideways to face her. "You seem... happy." In fact, Sam appeared more relaxed than she had in over a week, and Ellie abruptly realized what must have been going on while the two of them exchanged messages earlier. Unbidden, her mind offered up an array of appropriately inappropriate images, and she had to fight a sudden urge to look away.

Sam grinned at her. "You," she said, pausing to tap a finger on the tip of Ellie's nose, "have *no* idea!"

Aaron, looking nonplussed, caught Ryan's eye. "Hey, um, will you help me get some stuff from the kitchen?"

"Sure." He gave Sam a puzzled look before following Aaron up the stairs.

Once they were gone, Ellie gave Sam a knowing smile. "I take it you two had Ryan's place to yourselves this afternoon?"

"*Ha!* Yes, Miss Smartypants, we did. And for *hours!*"

Ellie knew Sam had thrown in the last bit, true or not, just to "scandalize" her. She also knew her expected response was to roll her eyes, so she did. But as Sam continued grinning happily, Ellie had to admit she was experiencing yet another new emotion concerning the unspoken topic —envy.

"So, what did you two get up to this afternoon?" Sam said. "Something wholesome and platonic, no doubt."

Yeah, well, not for very much longer, Ellie silently vowed. She told Sam about Aaron's mysterious hike and described his time capsule-like message at the bottom of Pueblo Canyon.

Sam laughed. "I bet people have been trying to figure out who A.W. and E.H. are ever since!"

"Probably," Ellie agreed. "He made it seem he had carved it only as confirmation that we had been there, but you should have seen his face while he waited to see how I'd react. If I had stayed quiet even two seconds longer, he would have turned purple and passed out!"

Sam laughed again. "And your reaction was?"

"Remember what you asked me up at Ryan's place? After the barbecue?"

"You mean, 'boyfriend?'"

"*Definitely!*"

"Definitely what?" Ryan said. He and Aaron were back with plates, paper towels, and four tall glasses filled with iced soda.

"Definitely gonna need more pizza," Sam said.

"You can have some of mine," Ellie said. Ryan had nailed it; she didn't feel hungry at all. Guilt and feelings of failure weighed so heavily on her chest that it was hard enough to breathe, let alone eat, but she'd try to force herself to get through one piece.

She watched numbly as Ryan laid a slice of pizza on each plate and passed them around. Now that everyone was assembled and waiting, she felt miserable, even more so than when Aaron had told her his plan for destroying the shack. Surely Sam, who could read her better than anyone else, must be sensing some of her distress. Why was she acting so indifferent? Or was her overblown show of "basking in the afterglow" merely a front, her way of bracing herself emotionally for news she guessed she didn't want to hear?

Ellie watched her from the corner of her eye. Despite loudly proclaiming how famished she was, Sam was working through her slice slowly, nipping off one tiny bite at a time. She looked tense now, too, and Ellie decided that her assumption was correct; Sam wasn't nearly as relaxed as she pretended to be. Realizing this made Ellie feel even worse.

She caught Ryan darting repeated glances her way. She knew he would be feeling as anxious about her news as Sam was, but he seemed willing to let her share it in her own time. Aaron, who already knew most of what she was about to say, pointedly avoided meeting her eyes.

Okay, time to get this over with, she thought. She set her half-eaten slice on her plate, then took a long drink.

"I once asked Aaron," she began, but when Aaron glanced at her, she quickly corrected herself. "A-Ron, I mean, how he could be so calm even after he figured out that our only chance of destroying the shack meant sacrificing himself. He didn't say so, but I think it had a lot to do with discovering that it was his father who made it. It was like he felt some extra burden of responsibility to get rid of it. I say that because I have certainly felt that way these past few days."

Sam's voice was calm but firm. "We've been through this, El. This isn't your—"

"*No!* Just listen—please!" But now that she had to say the words, she could feel her resolve crumbling. Unable to face them, she stared at the table as she forced herself to continue. "This all started with me insisting we use the shack that first time. So no matter what you say, I'm responsible for what we have to do. Not you guys—*me!* Because of that, I swore I would be the only one who'd have to pay whatever price there was to fix it, but now I know I can't. I'm *so* sorry. I wish I could. I want to, but I *can't!* And now I don't know how to ask you to... or tell you what I..."

"Hey," Ryan said. Adopting Sam's gentle tone, he joined in her effort to comfort Ellie. "Remember before? When you and A-Ron told us your plan, you said you'd leave what Sam and I did up to us, right? Why don't you lay out what you think needs to happen and let us make our own decisions about who does what? You trusted us to help you before; what's changed?"

"Before, it was Aaron's plan, and *he* was the one who gave up everything to make it work. This is different."

Ryan walked around the table to squat beside her. He gripped one leg of her chair and used it to turn her toward him. She kept her stare fixed on the floor, but he leaned forward, hands on her knees, and looked up into her watery eyes, making it impossible for her to avoid his gaze.

"What?" she muttered, annoyed.

"Hey. We're talking about Sam's *life* here. You said you wanted to keep her safe, not just from the pandemics but from having to make any sacrifices to fix this mess. What you were trying to do? You were acting out of love for her, and I get that. I really, *really* do! But do you honestly think there is anything I wouldn't do to protect her? *Hmm?* That I wouldn't be willing to go at least as far as you are?"

Her throat now too tight to speak, Ellie could only shake her head. The motion dislodged a tear, and it dropped onto the floor between her feet. Ryan wiped her cheek with his thumb.

"Then talk to us. Tell us what you think needs to happen, then let us decide, okay?"

Ellie leaned forward until her forehead rested on Ryan's. She knew this tender, deeply sensitive side of his personality was a part of himself he normally exposed only to Sam. Even as miserable as she was, she could still manage to feel thankful that her sister had someone so caring in her life.

Her body was wracked by a single convulsive sob, and then she nodded. "Okay, yeah." She sniffed and sat up straight. Feeling self-conscious in the wake of that intimate exchange, she gave Sam a shy smile.

Ryan stood, equally eager to move past the awkwardness of the moment. "Well, good! Don't make me come over there again!" When he sat, Sam squeezed his leg and mouthed a silent *thanks*.

Ellie leaned forward again and stared at the floor. She saw the small, dark spot on the carpet her tear had made and watched it slowly lighten over several long minutes as she tried to figure out exactly where to start. When she was ready, she straightened and scooted her chair back around to face the others, but kept her eyes on the center of the table.

"I have spent this past week questioning, well, just about *everything!* First, it was wondering if destroying the shack was the wrong thing to do. Then I was trying to figure out if working with Jeremy and Aimie was the *right* thing to do. I knew what I was *feeling* about all that, what my instincts were, but everything seemed to be the opposite of that.

"Something happened yesterday, and today I finally feel almost sorta kinda sure of myself again. Maybe."

"Dying does have a way of focusing the mind," Ryan said.

At last able to lift her eyes from the table, Ellie smiled at him. "No. It wasn't that. It's what happened right before that."

"Huh?" Sam said. "Before that, we were getting ready for the flip."

"Don't you guys feel anything *during* the flip?" She could barely remember the contented sense of connectedness she experienced in the gap between timelines. It was like trying to recover details from a dream she'd had ten years ago. What she could recall felt so deeply personal that she had never discussed the topic, not even with her old Aaron. However, she had taken it as a given that the others' experiences were the same.

Sam, Ryan, and Aaron exchanged confused looks, then shook their heads.

"No," Sam said. "You're saying you do?"

"I think I do, yeah, but I suppose it could be just an illusion or hallucination. What happened yesterday was different, though. On our way to 1976, I heard my own voice in my head. Another copy of my memories, I think, coming to me through the chair's interface. She told me things, but I've only been able to remember bits and pieces. She said that the TSD was designed to cure me, and that part I remembered right away. Also, she said that Aaron was supposed to find Just Mie, which I didn't remember until we were on our way here, and even then, not completely. And I think there was a lot more she wanted to say, but then my chair went wonky, and we ran out of time."

"You just said that maybe what you remember happening during the flip might not be real," Ryan said. "Couldn't that be true about this voice?"

"I don't believe so. As far as Dr. Hamilton can tell, the part about the TSD healing me seems to be true, and illusions don't heal people. Also, because she saved my life. If she hadn't intervened by stopping my heart, the stress of the flip would have killed me; I'm sure of that. But mostly, I think it's real because the last thing I remember her telling me is what gave me the answer to my biggest question."

"Which is?" Sam said.

"Why did I send the TSD here? We can immediately toss the idea that we're meant to do something to improve conditions to help the Ellie who made it. There's no doubt she would have known that nothing we could do would ever have any impact on her situation.

"Possibility two? We use it to fix our *own* future. I was actually starting to believe that right up until we found out that Aimie wants me dead and that she doesn't seem to care much whether Sam lives or dies, either. But more than that, why was our initial reaction to Aimie's proposal so negative? I keep saying I'd do what they say the other me did if things were bad enough. Yet my first impulse when Jeremy offered us the chance to work with him was to say no. And it was the same for you guys, right? Would I really do a complete mental one-eighty a few decades from now? Maybe, but my gut says no."

"Are we back to trusting your gut, then?" Sam said.

Ellie waggled her hand. "All I know is that every time I've gone against my instincts recently, I've turned out to be wrong. Let's say it's on probation and see how it goes.

"Aaron was right about this idea, too. If we change things enough to make any real difference, we'll eventually create a world we no longer feel a part of. Sam, we both know what it's been like since June, how hard it's been dealing with knowing our past and Mom and Dad's aren't the same anymore. What will it be like when the differences are ten or twenty times greater?

"So what's the real answer? If I would never have sent Aimie back so we could edit the past, then why did I? What would make me do something I'm so deeply, intensely opposed to?"

Sam's eyes brimmed with tears, and she had to look away.

"To save Sam," Ryan said. "That's the only reason."

"Yes, exactly. That's probably why I first started playing around with the theories. But I think that over time, I... *she* came up with a second idea. An even larger plan."

"Ruh-roh," Ryan muttered.

"Yeah," Ellie agreed. "Remember what I said yesterday about going back and trying to change things in the past to make 'now' better?"

"Yes," Sam said, "and we all agreed there's no way that would work."

"And that's right. But what if it's not only me? Say we *all* go back."

Sam responded with shocked disbelief. "What?! Like we just up and disappear? What do you think that would do to Mom and Dad, El?"

Aaron, who had already been running Ellie's idea through his head for over an hour, responded calmly. "Save their lives, most likely."

Sam twisted to face him. "Yeah? How so? We already know they survive the flu."

Ellie had guessed that Sam's reaction would be an emotional one, and she tried to sound as calm as Aaron. "Not from the flu, Sam; from Aimie. As long as she's out there and we're working against her, she's even more of a threat than all the coming pandemics combined. It would only take one mistake, and then we'd *all* be in trouble."

Sam nodded. "Okay, I get that. So, not that I'm agreeing to anything, but what's the rest of the plan?"

"We go back to the sixties, like I said before. We get the right sort of degrees, then set about doing everything we've talked about—push for earlier solar development, higher emissions standards, easier and wider access to birth control." She shrugged. "All the things Aimie says she wants to do, actually.

"But here's the part I just figured out today. Assuming there are no major changes, like a big war or some other huge crisis, what will happen in 2000 and 2001?"

"Lots of stuff, obviously," Ryan said. "What do you mean?"

But Sam saw Ellie's point at once. "I get it. The four of us will be born." She said, awed by the idea.

"Exactly!" *It's all about them!* Understanding those words had made everything clear. "I believe that what future-me originally wanted to do was change the past to help *us,* but she couldn't build a device big enough to let her do it. I think what we're seeing is her Plan B. She had to go through Jeremy to get the TSD built, but I think her true backup plan was that *I* end up using it instead of her. *Definitely* instead of Jeremy! Aaron saw this part of it a whole week ago. Remember? You said I really sent the TSD back to myself. But it wasn't to give me some kind of a second chance or anything.

"The last thing I remember hearing the voice say is, 'It's all about them!' That's the key. I'm convinced that what she wants is for me—for *us* —to use the TSD to change things for those yet-to-be-born versions of us. To do for them what she couldn't do for us. Not only do we save you, Sam, but very likely *that* Sam too. We'll be giving everyone in that timeline a better future. More than that, we'll also be setting them on a path that gives them the chance to keep making the right kinds of decisions. I've spent a lot of time doubting myself recently, but I don't doubt I'm right about this."

Ryan spoke musingly and mostly to himself, as if Ellie's earlier statement was only now sinking in. "We *all* go. Back to the sixties."

"Me and Sam, anyway. You two guys might be okay, but have you noticed how Aaron's name has never been mentioned?"

Aaron nodded. "I did. I decided I didn't need the distraction of knowing why. Having only this much of an alternate past to keep track of is enough, believe me." He pulled his computer cart close. "Go on. I'm going to yank the hard drive."

"Nobody's mentioned Ryan, either," Sam said. "But as irritated as Aimie is with him, I naturally assumed he was still around."

Ryan responded with a thin smile. "It's chilly out there—you probably don't want to risk having to walk home."

"You dope," Sam said. "We're *all* walking home. We walked here today?"

"Oh. Yeah."

"If you two are finished," Ellie said. "Look, whatever Aimie might have been lying about, I believe everything she told us about how bad conditions were when she was sent back. When I talked to Shanna on Tuesday, she as much as predicted exactly what Aimie described. The deteriorating climate will turn the whole world into one huge disaster area—a kind of war zone, sometimes including actual war. I tried imagining what that would be like, but I didn't try for very long; it's just too terrible. I mean, we're talking about the entire planet becoming one ginormous refugee camp!

"I'd love to be able to try to stop all that, but as Sam points out, neither of us is safe here. She has the flu to worry about, and according to Jeremy....

"Look, maybe he's right about those early project members who died, maybe he's not, but he seems to believe that Aimie can find a way to get to me no matter what we do. That means anyone around me is also in danger."

Sam's brow wrinkled. "What do you mean?"

"Suppose I'm driving around someplace with Mom. Or with you and Ryan. What if Aimie decides to take me out by messing with the traffic lights and sending a truck plowing into the side of the car? Do you think she wouldn't do it just because others might get killed, too? You've heard what she thinks of us—we're just lowly 'biologicals' to her. Of course, she always has the option of deleting me instead. Exactly how do you think she might go about that, Sam, hmm?

"And here's something we haven't mentioned yet—the danger Aimie will pose in the future. Just Mie thought Aimie must be insane by now, but she still seems pretty calm and calculating, right? Maybe 'insane' is too broad a term to describe what she's become. I think she's more like 'psychopathic.' If Jeremy *is* right, then she's already killed several people, and..." Ellie's voice trailed off as a horrified expression came over her face, and she turned an agonized stare toward Sam.

Sam reached across the table and gripped Ellie's hand, squeezed it hard, and scolded her. "Hey! Don't you dare go there, hear me? That's not on you either!"

"Right." Ellie sniffed. "You're right. Anyway, how will Aimie be in another year or two if her mind keeps going downhill? Or five years. Ten. And how about when she's no longer confined to Jeremy's lab? As bad as she seems, I think we're still dealing mostly with Dr. Jekyll right now. I do not want to meet Mr. Hyde. At that point, nobody will be safe." She paused to let them consider the bleak picture her words painted. As threatening as she already seemed, the Aimie who had just tried to kill Ellie was the *least* dangerous version they would ever know.

Sam released Ellie's hand and sat back in her chair. "So why does Aimie seem so convinced her plan will work? Or that it's even real? And not only Aimie, but Jeremy and Just Mie, too."

"Sending Aimie to Jeremy with the promise that together they could literally save the world? With his ego, that was probably the best way to ensure he'd commit to the project. And not only him, but anyone he tried to recruit later. I mean, it worked on *me!* But maybe that whole plan was like a default setting. A kind of safeguard. What if things went differently and we never ended up getting involved with them? Even if Aimie and Jeremy wound up benefiting personally, at least they might still do *some* good along the way. And who knows—maybe Aimie even hinted about the possibility of financial benefits right up front."

"I get it," Ryan said, "but Aimie genuinely seems to believe in the idea. In a way totally warped to suit herself, maybe, but still—if she has your memories, and that was never the real plan, how could that be?"

"Okay, I admit this part is mostly a guess, but remember when we first met Aimie? She said right up front that her copy of my memories was not complete. She made it seem like it was because of some technological limitation, but I don't believe it was. I think it was intentional. My 'gut,' Sam, says my engrams were carefully edited in order to prevent Aimie or Jeremy from ever knowing that their plan is not the *real* plan."

"Is that even possible?" Sam said. "Editing someone's memories?"

"I bet an AI running on a quantum processor could do it," Aaron said. "In theory, they would be very compatible file formats."

Ryan immediately rejected the idea with a shake of his head. "Well, yeah, but not if Aimie's the interface. *Ahhh*, no, I get it!"

"Exactly!" Ellie said. "Just Mie said Aimie was completely reset before being sent back. She'd have no idea."

"But what about Just Mie?" Aaron said. "She seems equally convinced that the plan involves changing the future."

"I know, and I can't explain that. Maybe it was yet another safeguard in case Aimie ever discovered the fragmented program or somehow got access to it after we activated it. Remember, Just Mie also said she didn't have all of my memories. She said she was 'all me, but not all *of* me,' or something like that."

"So, what? Just Mie's memories were edited too?" Sam said, still dubious.

"Probably, yeah. Although perhaps I could have made myself believe that the Aimie plan was the real one for as long as it took to copy the engrams. Hypnosis, maybe?"

Ryan laughed. "You're talking about hacking your own head!"

"Look, guys, I don't know exactly what needs to happen, but it definitely can't happen here... *now*. It's way too late for us to fix our situation. Anything we do has to start decades ago. So, yeah, that does mean using the TSD, but just a single time, and then we get rid of it once and for all. Even if we figured out a way to use it back then, without Aimie to navigate, we couldn't. And there'll be no coming back, either. If we do this, we'll all be leaving our families, friends—everyone we know—behind for good.

"And just so everyone understands, remember this: nothing we do will help the people we leave behind the slightest bit any more than we can help the Ellie who sent Aimie back. They'll still have to deal with whatever is coming. So, that's pretty much it." Ellie went silent and waited.

Ryan responded first. "I'm not sure that my dad..."

Ellie watched him compose his thoughts, wondering at his uncharacteristic hesitation. When he finally went on, she found herself completely reassessing her assumptions about his relationship with his father.

"I don't want to say he wouldn't care. That's not it, exactly, because I know he would. It's just that I'm not sure he would *notice*. Not for a week or so anyway." He shifted in his chair to face Sam.

"I know this sounds sappy, but I mean every word. I can't picture being without Sam, and she clearly can't stay here. I mean, could we ever convince our folks that a voice from the future told us that a bunch of new diseases are on the way? Not likely. If Sam stays here, the odds against her are as bad as playing Russian roulette with five live rounds in the cylinder. Because flus always come back. If the first outbreak doesn't get her, and if she's especially susceptible..." He placed a hand on Sam's thigh and gazed earnestly at her as he continued. "I need you to go so I know you're safe from what's coming, and I need to go to be with you. It's a simple choice for me."

Ellie nodded. "This is not the time for final decisions. We'll all need to think it over, so nobody should feel like they're committed to anything that's said here tonight, okay? But Sam? What's *your* gut saying right now?"

Sam rubbed her throat, still wrestling with her emotions in the wake of Ryan's open, unfiltered declaration of devotion. It was several seconds before she could answer. "I don't want to live in the world Aimie told us about. And I *certainly* don't want to die in it! But leave Mom and Dad and disappear into the past? Nobody except us knew what happened after what we did in Brooklyn, but if I understand it all, this time they will, right? We won't be erasing ourselves; we'll just be *gone*. I don't know if I can do that to them, Ellie. I don't know."

Ryan leaned back in his chair and looked across the room at Aaron. The disconnected hard drive now sat beside the bright red tower, and Aaron was tidying the cart's top. "What about you, buddy?"

With all eyes now on him, Aaron suddenly became overly fastidious about placing his various tools and components away, using the activity to mask his discomfort. "Remember how I said I felt like I was cracking up right after I moved here? Ever since I got to Los Alamos, I've felt like I don't belong. No, that's not exactly it. I feel like I belong, but differently, you know? As if I'm here 'wrong' somehow. Those déjà vu memories I told you about? It's like *those* are my real memories, like A-Ron's the real *me*, but I'm stuck looking at them from the outside.

"After you guys told me the truth, I felt better. A *lot* better. Thing is," he shrugged, dropping back into his chair, "better is not the same as good. I don't know if I would feel any different in the past, but back then, we'll all be out of place. Maybe that'll make it easier for me." He pivoted away from the computer and faced Ellie.

"Look—you're the only thing that's ever felt right or real about this whole situation, and I almost totally screwed that up. Even with what we've talked about, it's not like I expect us to be together, necessarily, not like Ryan and Sam, or even like you and A-Ron were. I guess what I'm trying to say is that even if we aren't, I'd rather take my chances and go back with you guys than stay here without any sort of anchor. I think I really might crack up without you."

Sam smiled at Ellie, and even though her face was still puffy from crying, her eyes sparkled. "*Awww.* That's so sweet." Then her expression went serious. "There's something else, though, the whole 'acting like gods' thing. Back in June, we talked about doing a small bad thing to stop a bigger bad thing from happening. Are we now saying it's okay to do a big bad thing to prevent a *super-huge* bad thing?"

Ryan shook his head. "'Wars are always the result of failure,' my dad would say, but sometimes they're necessary. What we're talking about doing is necessary because humans have failed to act in their own best interests. And if it is a war, then it's one against destructive technologies, self-interested mindsets, a battle to resist the natural human instinct to take the cheapest, easiest, and most destructive way forward each time. The casualties will be companies and political policies, not people. If we're successful, people in the future—and, from what Ellie and Just Mie say, *billions* of them—will be spared a hellish existence. Even if we end up disrupting thousands of lives, I don't see any *bad* here at all, Sam."

"But it'll be billions of *different* people," Aaron said. "That's mostly why I'm convinced Ellie is right. This plan is very different from what Aimie wants us to do. We've been struggling to rationalize the idea of us rewriting people's lives, right? But if we go back to the past and stay there, whatever we do afterward will result in an entirely new timeline. Nobody in that one has a future that's already written, and none of the lives of the people here, in this one, will be affected in any way." Sam opened her mouth to object, but Aaron knew what she intended to say. "Our parents, yes, but only emotionally and by us *leaving*, not by anything we do later. Their situation won't change.

"Look, once we go back, we'll become just four more individuals among the other three or four billion people alive back then. The fact that we'll have a better picture of what might lie ahead won't make our job any easier for us. And the more changes we're able to make, the less accurate that knowledge will become anyway. Does looking at it that way make it better?"

Sam considered what he said, then nodded.

"I hate to be the one to bring up the obvious," Ryan said, "but so far, we've only talked about what happens *after* we get rid of Aimie. Any ideas about how to do that?"

Ellie agreed; it *was* an obvious question. Super-obvious, even. Unfortunately, the answer was anything but. "Not a clue," she said. She picked up the cold remains of her pizza and resumed eating.

For a long time, no one said a word. Ellie knew the others were all thinking her idea over, imagining what it would be like to leave the lives they had known and start new ones in a very different world. She was beginning to accept that the peril Sam would soon face due to the flu had nothing to do with her reckless decision to use the shack, and that acceptance made her feel a little better. Still, it was her future self that had sent Aimie back and imposed the responsibility of destroying her on them.

As the silence stretched on, Aaron stood and began gathering all of their dirty plates and trash into a single stack. "I'm going to take this stuff up. Anybody want more to drink?" Getting no takers, he hefted the pile and headed for the stairs.

"Hey," Ryan said. "Think your dad would mind if I fooled around on one of his guitars?"

Aaron came to a dead stop and gaped at Ryan, shocked by his unintentional audacity. "Oh, man! Like you would not believe." Shaking his head, he resumed climbing toward the door.

"Okay, then," Ryan murmured from the corner of his mouth. "Ixnay on the itargay!"

Ryan's question startled Ellie out of her thoughts. Puzzled, she studied the guitars for a moment, then squinted at Ryan. "You can play the guitar? How did I not know this?"

"Oh, I have a rendition of *Twinkle, Twinkle Little Star* that will bring tears to your eyes."

Sam laughed. "I have heard him play—or try to—and to be clear, *anything* he plays will make you weep!"

"She is not exaggerating," Ryan agreed. "Turns out I was born with eight thumbs and two left pinkies. It's why I didn't make it in band."

"Wait—you were in *band?!*" Ellie felt as if she were already experiencing some bizarre alternative timeline. "*No!*"

"Yep. Bass drum. Only for about a week, though."

"Why only a week?"

"I was overqualified. Turns out you can play that with ten thumbs. But still, in terms of instruments for the musically challenged, the bass drum is hard to beat."

Having delivered his punch line, Ryan struggled to keep a straight face. Ellie could see his mouth twitching, though, and she realized she'd just been had. Despite all that had happened over the past two days, she began to laugh.

"That's *stupid!*" she said, then laughed even harder. Ryan's composure broke then, and he joined her. Sam rolled her eyes and tried to remain above it all, but the infectious sound quickly got to her, and a second later, she was roaring along with them.

The laughter eased some of Ellie's remaining upset, and she gave Ryan a grateful smile. "Thanks. I needed that."

Ryan winked in reply.

Sam leaned across the gap between their seats and kissed Ryan on the cheek. "Yeah. Thanks, 'dude.'"

"We've got some long days ahead of us," Ellie said. "I think it's time to go home, rest our brains, and come back fresher tomorrow." She dragged her pack out from under the table and stood. "Let's go catch Aaron before he comes back down."

34

Aaron's mom planned to leave for Santa Fe at eleven o'clock on Saturday morning to join his dad at the hotel where he was performing over the weekend. It was less than an hour's drive, an easy commute, but the hotel comped him a room whenever he played there, so they often made a mini vacation out of the arrangement. At two minutes past the hour, Ellie saw the familiar white Volvo wagon drive through the next intersection just before she reached it and turned down their street. She was two houses away from Aaron's when she was surprised by her sister's voice.

"Hey, El!" Sam called. "Wait up!"

Ellie turned and waved, then waited while they closed the gap between them. Sam and Ryan both carried a tall travel mug in one hand. Ryan held the final few bites of a pastry in his other.

"Hey," Ellie said. She pointed at Sam's mug as she fell into step beside her. Atomic City Café was closed on the weekends, so she took her best guess at the coffee's origins. "Daybreak?"

"Mm-hmm."

Aaron appeared on the stoop as they crossed the street and held the screen door open while they filed in. Ryan confirmed their destination as he passed by.

"Basement again?"

"Yep."

Thirty seconds later, seated around the table, Ryan gestured toward the assortment of colorful bags heaped at its center. "Wow. Snacks. I'll have to edit my Yelp review of this joint."

Aaron tacitly acknowledged the meagerness of the offerings with a shrug. "Chips, pretzels, M&M's... It's not much, but help yourselves."

"So, what's the plan?" Sam said.

Ryan jumped in at once. "I think we should use today and tomorrow to figure out the big picture, then we can start working down toward the specifics. With luck, we find out Monday that the other Just Mie program is up and running. If so, we can decide how to work her into things. Sound good to you?"

Ellie nodded. "My thoughts exactly. But before we start on that, there's something else we need to talk about first." She paused to make certain she had their full attention before continuing. "Are you all sure you want to do this? I'm not talking about just the leaving part, but there's my health situation to consider. Just Mie clearly believes I'm fine now, cured or whatever, since I used the TSD. But you all need to decide whether my health is a reason for you not to be a part of this."

Aaron spoke without hesitation. "I'm still in."

"Ditto," Ryan said.

"*No!*" Ellie gave her head a firm shake. "When I said think about it, I meant for more than two seconds!"

"Look," Ryan said, "I've thought about that already, and I see it this way. You had this hormone thing for what? Forty, fifty years? Yet you still managed to reverse-engineer a time machine based on little more than having seen one a few times. Then you went on to orchestrate this whole set of events. If that's you with a debilitating illness, I certainly have no concerns now. Are you sure *you* want to go, though?"

"Yes. Definitely." Ellie looked from face to face and waited, giving them ample time to reconsider. When nobody spoke, she tugged her *Memories of Aaron* notebook from her rear pocket and opened it to the first blank page. "Okay then. Let's figure out what we need to do. What's first? And Aaron?

Pen, please." Aaron opened the computer cart's shallow drawer and handed her a blue rollerball. "Thanks."

"When do you want to go back?" Ryan said. "I mean *to* when. I think we need to nail that down first."

"Yes. The early sixties, I think. I asked Shanna when the latest history could have changed to avoid our current problems, and she said the late sixties, early seventies. But we can discuss that."

"Works for me," Sam said, "but I don't think I should have much say in this part. I'll go along with whenever you guys think will work best."

"I get how blending into the culture of the fifties might be tougher than a later time," Ryan said, "but isn't it true that the farther we go back, the easier it will be to make the changes we need to?"

"Yes," Ellie agreed. "Making a small change earlier could have more impact than even a much bigger one later. But the further we go back, the harder it will be for Sam and me, as women, to do anything at all. It'll be enough of a challenge in the seventies, but at least there's the beginning of change happening then. Plus, there's the matter of technology. Have you thought about how hard this will be without computers and the internet? Take away too much more, and it starts feeling impossible. I still say early sixties."

"But then there's the whole Vietnam draft issue," Ryan said. "Aaron and I would have to register, and there's no guarantee we'd get accepted into colleges quickly enough to get a deferral. It'd totally suck if we go back to save the world and instead get shot jumping off a chopper in Khe Sanh."

Aaron was prepared for this objection. "I've already thought this through. That we can deal with, no problem."

"How's that?"

"The traditional way—we'll go to Canada."

"Canada?"

"They do have universities there, you know."

"Yeah, it's just that... *Canada?*"

Aaron ticked off the advantages on his fingers as he laid them out. "There're no language or customs barriers. All the big cities are close to the US, so when we're ready to get things going, we'll be close, not on the other side of the Atlantic. We can go back and forth as needed. And best of all? No draft."

"So you think the sixties too. What about you, Sam?"

Sam shrugged. "Like I said, I don't have a strong opinion. I do know I'd rather live in the sixties and seventies, though."

Ryan signaled his surrender by raising both his hands. "All right, you've convinced me. The sixties it is. In Canada."

"Then let's say 1963," Ellie said. "We can all have master's degrees by 1970. Those of us who need to can tackle our PhDs back here in the States while we get our other projects going. Does that work for everybody?"

Sam and Aaron nodded.

Ryan nodded too. "Like I said, I'm totally on board."

"Cool. We need to pick a school next, but unless someone has an idea already, that can wait." No one offered up an immediate suggestion. Ellie remembered the steadily growing stack of college catalogs atop her bedroom bookshelf and a bit of trivia she had learned about one of the lesser-known schools. She made a quick note to double-check this, then moved on to a new topic.

"I've been thinking about something else, and I've finally decided that the benefits are way bigger than the risks. Unless you guys feel strongly otherwise, that is. Sam, I'd like you to bring your iPad along. Plus, every cord and charger we all have that'll work with it. I want to load it up with books we'll need. We'll definitely want a copy of Aaron's Continuity database with us on an external drive. We'll have to make sure none of it's ever found, obviously, but a crystal ball like that might be the only edge we'll have. Any objections?"

"*Scientia potentia est,*" Aaron said. "I think it's worth the risk."

"Is that okay, Sam?" Ellie said.

Sam hung her head and nodded. "Yeah," she said softly. "I'll wipe it and get it ready to go."

Ellie understood the source of Sam's sudden disappointment at once. "No! I'm sorry you can't leave it for Mom and Dad, but I wouldn't ask you to do that. We won't take our phones. Copy your journal and anything else you want them to have to it, okay? Get rid of any big video files and all of the music you can't live without, but keep your journal and favorite pictures. I think all of us might want a little reminder of home now and then. We'll use the drive for whatever won't fit. Ooh! We'll need an adapter for the drive. Aaron?"

"You got it," he said.

"Really?" Sam sniffed. "Thanks, El."

"Well," Ryan said, "it's not like if anyone ever found the thing, it would be our prom pictures that caused the problems!"

"What else do we need to be working on?" Aaron said.

"I think the biggest one's bucks," Ryan said.

"Bucks?" Ellie repeated.

"Yeah, you know—cash, coin, clams, moolah, dinero. Whatever we decide to do, we'll need money and lots of it."

"How much?" Sam said.

"The more, the better. To start with, we'll need to pay for college, rent, food, and a certain amount of travel, from what Aaron said, and that's just in the near term. If we're eventually going to create some kind of organization, we'll need enough to hire staff, rent office space, those sorts of things."

"We have that," Aaron said. "Well, part of it, anyway."

"We do?" Ellie was surprised.

"Yeah, cash. It's in the prop shop supply closet next to the card stock."

"Didn't you see it?" Ryan said. "All those big cloth bags with the giant dollar signs stamped on the sides?"

"No, really!" Aaron said. "I found a huge stash of it in there. When I asked about it, Aimie said her strategy requires, in addition to outright bribery, using a certain amount of money to back projects that originally died due to a lack of funds. There'll be donations to ensure certain candidates get elected or that the right activists or lobbyists get heard by the right politicians. So, in addition to all the period clothing, they've got a stash of currency dating as far back as the thirties. Not much of that, actually, but a lot more from the late forties onward."

Ellie wondered if getting his hands on the cash was another reason Jeremy had used the prototype. It couldn't be easy to amass a big pile of bills from the forties today.

"Why so old?" Sam said.

"You can spend a dollar from 1955 in 1965, no worries, but not one from 1966. If you don't know precisely when you'll need it, older bills are better. At least up to a point."

"And it's all real?" Ellie said. "We won't get arrested trying to spend it?"

Aaron shrugged. "I'm sure the paper is real. It's very hard to fake that. Am I a hundred percent sure it isn't counterfeit? No, but back then there were no holograms, foil strips, or any other advanced countermeasures to trip us up. That's not the real issue, though."

"What is?"

"It's almost all US dollars. We need Canadian."

"Why?" Ryan said. "You can spend dollars in Canada? We drove up through Niagara Falls before we moved out here. All the way to Toronto. I know I spent dollars there."

"That's now, not fifty years ago, so maybe, maybe not. And that's buying a T-shirt or something, not opening bank accounts."

"Bank accounts?" Sam said.

Ryan understood what he meant at once. "*Right,*" he said, stretching the word out. "Even two hundred thousand is a drop in the bucket compared to what we'll eventually need. We need to pull a Jeremy and get money into an interest-bearing account as far back as possible. Right after we are supposed to have been born, preferably."

Sam sighed. "And here I was all excited this wasn't a problem."

"What about a cashier's check?" Ellie said. "What if you had already opened an account in America and transferred it to a Canadian bank with a cashier's check?"

Aaron thought for a moment. "Might work. That's making the final transaction easier by making the overall process harder, though."

Ellie frowned, then pushed her frustration aside. The money was a challenge, but not an insurmountable one. They'd find a way to solve it.

"All right, let's not get bogged down by that too much right now. We can always take it back with us and figure out a way to deal with it then. So we almost have the money. We'll need birth certificates, school records, that sort of thing. From what Kate told us, that might not be too hard. What else do we need?"

"Backstories, certainly," Ryan said. "Or 'legends,' as they say in the spy world. Where we came from, what our parents did, why we decided to go to whatever school we end up picking—that sort of thing. If you want to be able to carry on more than a ten-second conversation, that is. And, if we're supposed to be from Canada, we need to learn how to say 'eh,' eh?"

"And know everything about hockey," Sam added. "And be nice all the time."

"I think we might be veering off into the realm of stereotypes now," Aaron said.

"You think so, eh?" Ryan said. "I dare you to come over here and say that where my poutine can hear you, hoser."

Sam squinted at him. "Poutine?"

"Believe me," Ryan said. "You'll love it!"

"This feels like an undercover spy mission," Ellie said.

"It really does!" Sam agreed. "I'd never thought about everything James Bond had to learn to become a secret agent."

"In his case, learning how to dodge STDs must have been an entire course all by itself," Ryan said.

Sam laughed. "Yeah, and then there's learning all those casino games, memorizing the names of all those fancy cocktails, staying totally ripped—being him is pretty much a full-time job!"

Aaron pounded his fist onto the table. "Agent! That's it! I know how to handle the money part!"

The noise drew Ryan's attention to the pile of snacks. He picked up the bag of M&M's, poured half a dozen into his palm, and began crunching on them one by one.

Sam failed to see the connection between secret agents and their currency problem. "We become spies?"

"Not that kind of agent. A rep. A go-between. One of us will have to use the TSD before we go, though."

"Not Ellie!" Sam said. "Aimie's not getting another crack at her."

Ryan agreed. "Gotta be you, dude. You're the only one we can be sure she won't try to get rid of."

Aaron nodded. "Yeah, I know. I've been figuring Jeremy will want to run at least one manned test before we say we're ready to go, right? We'll use that. I'll work out everything I need, and then we'll have to get it all in place without Aimie knowing. I hope the other Ellie emulator is up to helping with something like this."

"Me too," Ryan said.

"Oh, right—'Mie Two,'" Aaron said. Ryan smiled at Aaron's misunderstanding.

"What do you know so far?" Sam said.

"For starters, I'll need the money, obviously, appropriate clothes, some basic paperwork, business cards, plus a good story to explain it all. That's all I can think of for now."

"It's enough," Ellie said. "It sounds like we need to be ready to go next Friday. Our time will be up, and if we plan to leave that weekend, that's the day the test run will have to be."

"Then I need to start figuring out that printer," Aaron said. "This will be a good test project, but I might need some help."

"Sam," Ellie said, "are you up for that?"

Sam nodded. "I saw what programs they're using, and I can guess what you'll need to know. It's mostly about the initial formatting—canvas size, color space settings, resolution. I'll find out which computer lab at the college has the apps we'll need, and we can meet there. It should only take an hour. An hour and a half, at most."

Ellie opened her notebook on the table facing the others. "These are some of the things we'll need to do or have ready before our week is up."

Ryan looked up from the list. "There must be twenty things on here!"

"Twenty-two. And there'll be more. But I want to break this up into smaller lists for each of us. Like, Sam? We'll all need something to wear when we first go back—a few days' worth at least—and I don't think we'll be able to snitch things from Jeremy's collection."

"Okay, I assume you don't want any of us Googling sixties fashion, but I think I can get us close on my own. I'll make a list of anything that would be a no-no before the mid-sixties. Gather anything not on the list into a pile, and we'll check through it at some point. Overall, though, this will be a lot easier than 1941 was. As in, yay—we girls can wear jeans!"

Ellie pulled the list to her and put Sam's name beside Clothes.

"See, Ryan? This won't be so hard."

"Yeah, well..." He stabbed his forefinger on the list's fifth entry. "School records?"

"Look, if Kate's right, then the computer hooked into that big printer should have a reference for almost any document we'll need. It's getting to them that'll be the challenge. Specifically, a challenge for Aaron." She wrote his name next to all of the document-related entries.

Sam pointed to a line farther down on the list. "Not as much of a challenge as sneaking the skins out of there. Why do we need to do that?"

"No matter what plan we eventually come up with, I'm betting that pulling it off will depend entirely on getting through the front door and into the TSD as quickly as possible. We can't count on having time to change once we're in the building. If we can't find a way to sneak them out, I'd rather take our chances without them than take the time to put them on then."

Studying their faces as they stared at her lengthy to-do list, Ellie tried to gauge their level of optimism. On a scale from one to ten, she guessed it to be no higher than minus twelve. "Listen, guys. We can do this. That list may look like an elephant sitting on our plate, but you eat an elephant the same way you eat anything else—one bite at a time."

Sam gave her a sharp, disapproving look.

"Metaphorically, of course," Ellie added.

"You're right," Ryan said, trying his best to sound upbeat. "Let's carve this beast up and get to work on it. And I prefer dark meat, by the way."

"I know that for some of these things, we need to be at Jeremy's lab, but let's take tomorrow morning and start scratching off as many of the other items as we can. Also, add anything new you can think of. We can talk about any new stuff tomorrow afternoon. When we're done at Jeremy's on Monday, we'll see where we stand and go from there. Agreed?"

"Yeah," Aaron said. "I'm pretty sure I can drive then, by the way. And before I forget, Dad's going to be using the basement starting Monday to work on a new set. Where can we go?"

"My dad's usually not home until after seven," Ryan said. "That would give us a few hours to ourselves."

"Works for me," Ellie said. "Anything else?"

"I was just thinking," Ryan said. "A week from Monday is Veteran's

Day. As holidays go, it's not one of the biggies, but do you think we can use that somehow?"

Ellie considered this. "Maybe. It might be something Jeremy can work with to clear the place out. I'll find a way to clue him in. Aaron? You good with this so far?"

"Yep, I'm good. It's not on the list, but I think the most important thing I can do is try to recover Just Mie. I don't have the kind of cable I need to hook my hard drive up to Dad's laptop, so I asked Dad to pick one up for me while he's down in Santa Fe this weekend. If he can find the right one, I'll work on that project on Monday. And I'll check on the clothes, too. Any idea about number nineteen?"

Ellie jotted "Recover Just Mie" at the bottom and put Aaron's name beside the task. Then she counted down from the top and found the item Aaron mentioned—"Aaron only on QP"

"None at all," she said. "That one's going to be tricky, but don't you agree we need to try?"

"Better safe than extremely sorry," Aaron said.

"The other thing that might help pull this whole thing off is the other emulation program. Maybe we can still use her even without Just Mie. Start thinking about ways that we might do that."

"And we need to pick a city," Sam said.

"That's number seven," Ellie said, "and I might have an idea about that. Tomorrow, though."

"Not to be a nag," Ryan said, "but you know that question from yesterday?"

"The 'obvious' one, you mean?" Ellie said. Ryan nodded. "Still no clue," she said.

Aaron shook his head. "That's still pretty much our very own and-then-a-miracle-occurs phase of the plan."

"We're working on it, though," Ellie said. "It's just, you know, wall... head banging against."

"It is possible to over-train, you know," Ryan said. "Is there any wisdom to the idea of keeping these strategy sessions short? With our lists, we have plenty to work on, and if we're always together, we might make Aimie think we're up to something."

"And I'll need to keep up with all my schoolwork, too," Ellie said. "And spend more time with Mom and Dad. So yeah, I think that's a good idea. Starting right now."

Once again, Ryan walked with Ellie and Sam after they left Aaron's. When they reached Yucca Street, he continued going straight, and they turned right toward home. The sun had dropped low toward the Jemez Mountains, the temperature along with it, and they maintained a brisk pace to stay warm.

"I think we made good progress today," Ellie said.

"Yeah," Sam agreed. "But the more real it all feels, the harder it gets. How are we going to tell Mom and Dad?"

"I don't know, Sam. Any ideas?"

"All I know is that if we have to tell them in person, I'm not sure I could do it."

"Yeah, you're right. Face to face? That'd be tough."

Sam shook her head. "No, I don't mean *telling* them. I mean, I don't think I could *leave!* Too hard."

"I doubt it would be up to us at that point, anyway. They'd probably lock us in our room and bar the windows. Or worse, have us committed somewhere."

"Before you say it, I know we can't take them. That wouldn't be fair to Ryan, or Aaron, or anyone else we wouldn't have space for."

"Good. That is not a talk I was looking forward to. And I think I might have a different idea about that. I want to talk to Aaron first, though, to make sure it's even possible. But as far as actually telling Mom and Dad?" She sighed. "I hate to say it, but I'm leaning hard toward taking the coward's way out."

"You mean letters."

"I mean letters."

Sam echoed Ellie's sigh with one of her own. "Yeah, well…"

"You too?"

"Me too. It's the only way I'll be able to say everything I want without collapsing in a big, blubbering, snotty mess."

"I know what you mean. And like I said before—locked doors, bars on the windows. We shouldn't put off working on those for too long. I think it'll get very hectic toward the end, and no matter how well we plan, we might not have too much say about when the end is."

"Oh, joy! All right. I'll start on mine tonight."

Ellie sat at her desk, adding items to their list, when Sam slipped into their room at the end of the evening.

"Hey," Sam said.

"Hey back."

"We need to talk."

Ellie put down her pen and swiveled in her chair. "I've noticed you usually say that when *you* need to talk."

"Well, this time, I think it's you." Sam hopped up to perch on the edge of Ellie's bed.

"And what do I need to talk about?"

"Babies."

"Too late. I already know where they come from. I mean, if you can believe *that* story. Seriously—*ick!*"

"Damn it, El, stop deflecting! You say it's no biggie, but that's the story *I'm* having a hard time believing."

"Okay, fine! Yeah, it sucks, all right? Is that what you want to hear? But when have you ever heard me talk about wanting a family, huh?"

"I know, I know. But I also know you're only seventeen. And besides, this is different, isn't it? I mean, you deciding not to have kids is one thing, but having that choice taken away from you? That seems like a whole *heap* of suckage."

"Look, I just said I don't like it, didn't I? But knowing what's about to happen here, would any of us choose to have kids? I get it, Sam; I really do. But it comes down to this: back then, I might want to, but I won't be able to. Here, I'd have the choice, but I would almost certainly choose not to. It's not going to happen either way, so I'd rather focus on doing the thing that makes it possible for millions upon millions of other children to have long, happy lives. I'll leave that choice up to the me we're trying to protect from all the impending climate crap. *She* can decide whether or not I have kids."

"Not everything is a logic puzzle, you know. I don't believe this doesn't bother you a lot more than you're letting on."

"It does, Sam, just not for the reasons you think. What bothers me is knowing that I'm damaged somehow. You know, 'defective.' I worry about what that might mean for us later. What if what the TSD did to fix me isn't permanent? Or what if something else goes wrong? I don't want my health ever getting in the way of everything we're planning to do."

Sam was quiet for nearly a minute. Ellie watched her choose between pressing the issue further or letting it go. If Sam decided to push, Ellie would have to explain her decision to accept this consequence, which she could blame on no one but herself, as the penance she'd chosen to suffer for persuading everyone to use the shack. When Sam finally nodded, Ellie breathed a silent sigh of relief.

"Okay, I get it," Sam said. "But remember this: if you ever—and I mean *ever*—start feeling depressed or angry about it, talk to me, okay? And as far as the rest of it goes, we know what the possibilities are now, right? You can be on the lookout for any of the symptoms that Just Mie mentioned. If it comes to that, the rest of us will take up as much slack as we need to, but we have to know what's going on. So you need to be open about that too."

"I promise," Ellie said, then raised her right hand in a familiar gesture. "Scout's honor."

Sam snorted and rolled her eyes. "That is the Vulcan salute."

"And your point is? Seriously, who could possibly be more honest than Vulcan Boy Scouts?"

———

Ellie's eyes flew open. The streetlamp in front of the neighbor's house lit the room well enough for her to make out the shape of her sister sprawled atop her bedcovers. The clock near Sam's head showed ten past two.

Thoughts that woke her up in the middle of the night were rarely good, but this night was different. Lying on her back, staring at the cottonwood shadows on the ceiling, she played back the dream thought that had jarred her mind out of slumber.

The lights flickered!

But was that true, or was that detail merely a fabrication of her subconscious? She closed her eyes and replayed the moment in question through her waking mind. The consciously remembered events played out exactly as they had in her sleep, satisfying her that what she had seen in her dream really happened. She thought it over some more, and yes, everything made just as much sense now as it had when she was asleep. She smiled.

This is good! This is better than good—this is great!

Still smiling, she rolled onto her side and drifted back to sleep.

E ven without the second cup of coffee, Ellie would have felt buzzed. Since she awoke the second time this morning, at a more reasonable seven thirty, she'd been mentally toying with the idea that had come to her in the night, extending its implications, following them to their various ends. If she were right—and she could find not a single reason to think she wasn't—they finally had a firm foundation on which they could start building their plan.

"D'doot deet dooo do. D'doot deet dooo do." Her hips swayed, and her fingers beat out a little rhythm on the countertop while she waited for her toast to pop up.

A moment later, Sam appeared in the kitchen and stopped to stare at her, one eyebrow raised. "You're certainly perky this morning."

"I think I got it! I think I got it!" Ellie sang, adding lyrics to her bouncy melody. Optimistic for the first time since the whole situation had started, she *did* feel perky, and she was determined to enjoy every second of it. She placed her toast on a plate and slathered it with peanut butter and raspberry preserves.

"Got what? Early-onset dementia?"

"You're funny! Just for that, I'm not telling. Now you have to wait until this afternoon, just like the rest of 'em."

Sam objected. "But that's not fair—they don't know they're waiting!"

Ellie picked up her plate and brushed past Sam on her way back to their room. When she reached the door, she spun around. *"I think I got it!"* she sang again as she shimmied backward out of the kitchen. Even from halfway down the hall, she could hear Sam's muttered response.

"I think you've got something, all right."

Ellie spent the early morning completing her homework assignments. If everything went according to plan, she had only two or three more days before they would no longer matter. She'd be starting college in less than two months, and her education at Los Alamos High already far exceeded any typical high school of the 1960s, north or south of the border. In fact, she was already familiar with concepts that wouldn't exist for decades back then. Still, she couldn't help but feel a sense of loss over not completing her final year. After all her hard work, she'd never know whether she or Hana came out at the top of the class.

After setting her books aside, she made an initial stab at picking out clothes for the flip. She folded the items she selected and stacked them on the left side of the closet floor. Once she'd made her final choices, she'd have Sam go through the pile and weed out any mistakes.

Thinking of Sam brought the topic of the previous night's discussion to mind. She had to admit that Sam was partially right. Knowing she'd never have children of her own caused only the tiniest ripple in her emotional equilibrium today, but that might change as she grew older. On the other hand, nothing about her thyroid condition prevented her from adopting a child if she one day decided she wanted a family. It was losing her say in the matter that she found upsetting. But as far as that went, she had no one to blame but herself.

Thinking about children reminded her of another topic. She opened her notebook to her list of tasks and added another item at the bottom: *Pills—Sam.* Then she crossed the hall to the bathroom, retrieved every box labeled Tampax or Always, and emptied their contents onto her pile. If it turned out that Just Mie was right about her condition, she wouldn't need them herself, but she had no doubt that Sam would prefer delaying the switch to the 1960s equivalents for as long as possible.

Ellie heard her parents return from brunch at eleven thirty. After making certain her room looked as it usually did, she volunteered to help them with chores around the house, ones above and beyond her usual duties. She knew the week would fly by, and this was the most natural way she could think of to spend some extra time with them. Even though she tried to make her offer seem offhand, it was met with such consternation that she expected her mom to feel her forehead for a fever.

"What?! It's not like I never help you guys."

Ellie left her phone in her bedroom while she biked to the library. She rode wearing one of Sam's old hats and her mom's jacket, hoping that if she passed any CCTV cameras she didn't know about, Aimie might not recognize her. Once inside, she used the most secluded computer station she could find to conduct fifteen minutes of very specific research. Satisfied with what she had learned, she returned home to retrieve her phone before pedaling to Aaron's house.

During the ride, her mind was free to refocus on her late-night revelation, and she became excited all over again. She rolled to a stop, feeling exuberant, almost giddy, about what she had to tell the others. She rapped loudly on the door, and Aaron opened it a few seconds later. She slipped by him and was halfway down the hall before he could say a word, glancing over her shoulder as he scurried to catch up.

"Hey! Are the parental units here?"

"No, they're both still down in—wait, '*parental units?!*'"

Sam and Ryan rose from the sofa as she entered the living room. She strode past them to the basement door, moving fast, and called back to them as she pounded down the steps.

"C'mon, slowpokes!"

At the bottom of the stairs, she spun around and urged the others to hurry, flapping her hand and bouncing on the balls of her feet like a crossing guard after downing three or four too many cups of coffee.

"C'mon, c'mon!"

Sam cast Ellie a bemused look as she passed by. "In case you're wondering why my sister is acting like she *really* needs to pee, it's because she has some exciting news she'd like to share."

Ellie laughed and blew a raspberry at the back of Sam's head.

Aaron stopped and turned to face Ellie. "She does?"

"You bet your cute little butt she does!" Ellie chirped. Without warning, she grabbed a fistful of his tee, pulled him toward her, and planted a big wet kiss on his mouth. *"Butt!"* she said again, her face mere inches from his. His dazed reaction made her laugh again.

Ryan, his mouth twisted into a bewildered smile, looked at Sam for an explanation.

Sam rolled her eyes. "I don't know. She's been like this since we got up this morning."

"We can totally *do* this!" Ellie said, then waited as they assumed their usual places around the table before continuing. She looked at Ryan. "Remember the talk we had right before we went to Brooklyn?"

"The one in your back yard?"

"Yeah. Aaron—A-Ron, I mean—said he thought the shack had to be using a quantum processor in order to calculate the flips, right? And we know Aimie also requires a quantum computer—"

"She *says* she does," Sam said. "Our friend over there didn't." She jabbed a thumb over her shoulder at Aaron's dead computer.

"No, but you saw how quickly even she cooked my CPU," Aaron said, "and she was only active for what, maybe an hour in total? Aimie's been running twenty-four-seven for over eight years. I believe her."

"So, what are you thinking?" Ryan was eager to get back to Ellie's point.

"Okay, so what if... God, this is so *obvious!*" She laughed with genuine delight. "I even *said* it once, but I didn't realize what it actually meant. 'Only fully operational one in the world!' Think about it, guys. We know there's some very good reason there aren't any other QPs right now, or Aimie would already have found a way to force someone to build one for her to jump into. She said herself that it would be decades before anything like her could exist. Is it even possible that Jeremy could have built a separate quantum processor for the TSD to use for navigation? I'm betting not.

I think the QP is exactly what I sent back—not just some big, honkin' instruction manual or something—and Jeremy built the new shack around it. If the TSD needs a quantum processor to calculate its jumps, then that's where it has to be. And if Aimie *also* needs one…" She didn't finish, but merely grinned at them.

"Then she's there, too!" Ryan finished.

"But Aimie can't ever be not here," Sam said. "If she needs to keep the people here in line, I don't think she would risk that."

"Yes, but even when the TSD goes off on one of its trips, it never seems to be gone from this timeframe, right? It goes and returns in the same instant. So it's a win-win situation for her—she gets to keep an eye on the mission crew the entire time and *still* not miss a beat here! She said her core is 'in the building.' You're right to assume Aimie is lying to us, Sam, but maybe *that's* the lie. I mean, technically, it's true—she's in the device and the device is in the building—but it's intentionally misleading, just like that thing about our parents."

Aaron was the first to see Ellie's larger point. "So we don't need one plan to steal and wreck the TSD and a whole separate one to destroy Aimie; that's what you're getting at. Doing the first one accomplishes both."

Ellie stabbed a finger at him. "*Ding-ding-ding! Exactly!*"

"This is *huge!* Way to go, El!" Ryan sounded totally psyched, and Ellie felt an unexpected warmth blossom in her chest—he almost never called her that. "How do we prove it, though?"

"Actually, there has to be a gap," Aaron said. "Infinitesimal, maybe, but it *must* be there."

"Gap?" Ryan said.

"You guys say that when the TSD does its thing, there doesn't seem to be any lapse between when it leaves and when it gets back, but I'm sure there is. And by design, too. Why? Because above all else, there absolutely can't be an overlap. If the returning device got back even a picosecond too early and tried to occupy the same physical space? The results would be"—he shuddered as he imagined the consequences—"*extremely* messy! The best way to avoid that is to make sure you're off by at least that much in the other direction. You create an intentional gap. It might be only a picosecond, but Aimie would be offline for that amount of time."

"So you're thinking you can look for that?" Ryan said.

"Theoretically, sure. Coming up with a clock circuit fast enough to pick up a gap potentially that small, plus figuring out how I can somehow connect it without it being detected will be a challenge. The biggest problem, though, is time. I guess I could try—"

"You could," Ellie agreed, "but you don't have to. I know I'm right."

Sam raised a skeptical eyebrow at her. "You're sounding awfully sure of yourself these days."

"This is not my gut talking, Sam."

"Then why are you so certain?" Ryan said.

"For one very good reason." She leaned forward and grinned, still feeling quite pleased with herself. *"Because... the lights... flickered!"*

"Huh?" Sam said.

"Haven't you noticed? Every time Jeremy asks Aimie to do something, the lights flicker. It's like she's saying, 'Okay, I hear you.' Remember our first day out there? It was especially noticeable when he asked Aimie to end the Paris simulation. It was night, right? So when the TSD's ceiling flickered, it was particularly obvious."

"And?" Ryan prompted.

"And when we were in 1976 and I asked to see outside, the lights flickered right before the view changed. My guess is she's been doing that for so long it's become a reflex." She shrugged. "I don't know. Point is, she screwed up!"

"I'm not doubting you," Ryan said, "but if she really is in the TSD, then why didn't she help us once she realized you were still alive?"

"Because she's known all along what I just figured out—us knowing this makes her vulnerable. But I think it also has to do with what you said when Jeremy was here—she was avoiding suspicion. If she had succeeded in killing me, would you and Sam have stuck around with the project long enough to see the connection between her and the TSD and start thinking she might have done it? The longer she could keep that fact hidden, the less inclined you'd be to attach any blame for my death to her. And if the point was to get me out from between her and Aaron, the last thing she'd want is for him to have any reason to suspect she killed me. Or maybe she was sulking because she'd failed. Personally, I think it was mostly the last one."

"So," Sam said. "What does all this mean, exactly?"

"It means we can finally start working on the first half of the plan," Ryan said.

"More than that," Ellie said. "It means the first part just got really, *really* easy!" They all stared doubtfully at her. "Well, assuming we can sneak in whenever we need to. And assuming we can get some big-time help from Mie Two. And that the TSD really is always ready to go."

"Is that *all?*" Sam said.

"Yep! Easy-peasy!" Ellie needed only a few moments to lay out her idea. By the end, Ryan and Aaron were both nodding as her plan took shape in their minds. Sam still looked skeptical.

"That definitely could work," Aaron said.

"I like it," Ryan said. "It all comes down to a basic infiltration op."

"Except for all that 'assuming' we talked about," Sam said, making air quotes.

"Except for that," Ellie agreed. "But we have to assume Mie Two can help us, even without Just Mie, because we'll need her to. The big question is, how can she?" Ellie said. "Any ideas?"

Ryan glanced at Sam. She gestured for him to go on. "Sam and I might have one. It's not exactly original, but it's something we're pretty sure she could handle. She has access to all the security camera feeds?"

Aaron nodded. "Based on what Just Mie told us, yes, but I'll double-check. What are you thinking?"

"Video looping," Sam said. "You see it all the time in movies and TV shows. We want to mess with what Aimie sees."

"Yes," Ryan said. "Just Mie said we'd be able to control what flows through Aimie's 'pipes,' right? If Mie Two can record clips from the security cameras, we have her show those to Aimie instead of the actual feed."

"This is good," Ellie said, although she couldn't immediately come up with a practical application. "I think."

"It is," Sam insisted. "We go into a room—the prop shop, say—Mie

Two could play a recording of us doing something two days ago while we're actually doing something else."

"That's one possibility," Ryan said. "Or she could show you sitting at a computer for ten minutes straight while you get up, leave the room, then come back and sit down again. She'd need to loop empty hallway footage, too, but I think it's doable."

"There's one problem with that," Aaron said.

"Just *one?*" Ellie had already thought through the mechanics of communicating their needs with Mie Two, then signaling her when the time had come, *and* keeping the whole thing in sync. The concept was great, she admitted, but execution might end up being trickier than Sam and Ryan thought.

"And what's that?" Ryan said.

"We'll all have to wear the same clothes every day," Aaron said. "Or for a few days in a row, anyway."

Sam frowned at him. "And why would I ever want to do that? *Oh!* Never mind; I get it." She frowned at Ryan. "Damn. Why didn't *we* think of that?"

"Yeah," Ryan said. "It obviously wouldn't work if we left the conference room wearing one thing and entered the hallway wearing something else."

"No," Ellie said. "And aside from that, I'm sure Aimie would notice the third time in a row we showed up wearing the same thing and start wondering about it. She's literally built to notice patterns."

Ryan frowned. "Okay," he said, thinking fast. "Okay, so maybe it's not actually 'looping' precisely, but a similar idea. Remember what Jeremy told us during our tour? He said the Paris scene was partly made up of 'real-time CG images,' like Aimie was faking part of it on the fly. Do you think Mie Two might be capable of something like that?"

"Maybe," Aaron said. "It'd be the QP doing all the heavy lifting. But if it requires so much processing power that Aimie notices, that will be a problem."

"Remember," Sam said, "she has 3-D scans of each of us to work with. The ones Dr. Hamilton took."

"Okay, this is better," Ellie said. "We shouldn't assume this trick will work more than a few times, though. Aimie's capable of picking up the tiniest discrepancies. We need to use this idea as little as possible."

"Still assuming she's there," Aaron said, "what do we want Mie Two to know right away?"

"It'd be good to know for sure she really can do this CGI thing," Ellie said.

"I'll ask her that. What else?"

"How can we talk to her without Just Mie?" Ryan said. "You might be able to restore her; you might not."

"How to communicate," Aaron said, making a note on a scrap of paper from his computer cart. "I'll ask that too."

"You said she can't completely take over," Ellie said, "but I think we'll need her to tie Aimie's hands for a while. Just Mie hinted that she might be able to pull that off for an hour or so. Find out what she can do for us there."

"Neutralize Aimie." He added the item to his note. "Got it. That it?" When no one spoke up, Aaron set his list aside.

"There's one other thing to discuss then," Ellie said. "How would you like to live on the water for a while?"

"Where's *this* coming from?" Sam said.

"We need to figure out where we're going," Ellie said. "For the past year, I've been getting mail from colleges practically everywhere, including Western Washington University in Bellingham, of all places."

"But that's in the US," Ryan said.

"Yes. But when I Googled it to find out where Bellingham even was, I noticed that Vancouver was basically right there. Vancouver, Canada, I mean, not the Washington one. Right before coming here, I went to the library to use a computer Aimie hopefully isn't watching. I found out that UBC is a good school. It's in a big city, or big-ish anyway, but it's otherwise pretty well isolated. Not boring, but no distractions, is what I'm getting at, and yet it's still super close to the US. Anyway, the campus is right on the water, so that's why I was asking."

"Won't it be cold in winter?" Sam said.

"Well, it's Canada, so yeah. But it's essentially on the Pacific, so less cold than Toronto or Quebec, for instance, and less hot in the summer."

"Are you looking for an answer right this second?" Ryan said.

"Nope. Just throwing it out there. Why? Is there someplace else you've thought of?"

"Not me," Sam said. "I'd be fine going anywhere, but you guys will all be getting technical degrees. We need to go wherever's best for that."

"True," Ellie said. "Sorry that's not the University of Cabo or Cancún."

"Ha! Talk about distractions!"

"You know?" Ryan said. "A big, west coast city with a campus right on the water? It's sounding more appealing by the second, to be honest."

Aaron shrugged and gave her a smile. "If you've checked it out and think it's fine, I'm sure it is."

"The plan," Ellie said, "is to walk into the registrar's office and apply in person. We've talked about birth certificates and school records; is there anything else we might need?"

"Medical records?" Sam offered. "For immunizations, maybe?"

"I'll check that hard drive," Aaron said. "If it has a sample of anything like that, we could take that as a hint."

"We now have one week," Ellie said. "Any little question you guys think of, we need to get an answer to it as soon as we can."

With both a year and a destination firmly decided, Ellie went on to tell them everything she had learned about the school, the city, how beautiful it would be, and how much fun they were going to have living there. By the end, she was truly excited about what lay ahead of them for the first time. They were only three days in, still had six to go, and they were already making progress. It felt good.

37

Before going to the cafeteria on Monday, Ellie walked Aaron to the school's main entrance, and there he joined the rest of the students heading out for lunch at home or in one of the nearby cafés. He was skipping the rest of the afternoon to work with Sam at the university. If the computer lab machines didn't have the necessary programs, they'd try the art department. Once they found computers loaded with the same software the prop shop had, she was set to give him a crash course in the few he was likely to need.

"I'll meet you across the street in a few hours," Ellie said. "Good luck."

Sam and Ryan were waiting in the van when Ellie arrived. They had already stopped attending classes on anything even remotely resembling a regular basis and went to campus partly because they couldn't hang out at home without running the risk of raising a lot of unanswerable questions should their truancy be discovered. Mostly, though, they needed to keep Aimie convinced everything was normal.

On their way to the LAB, Aaron and Sam reported that their tutoring session had been a success. Aaron knew what he needed to begin work on their documentation as soon as the opportunity arose, starting with the paperwork crucial to his bank-related mission to Vancouver.

As they pulled up to Jeremy's building, Ryan told Aaron to park near the door again. "Let's get those guys used to seeing it here." He jabbed his thumb toward the guard booth.

"Sure." Aaron pulled to within five feet of the door and killed the engine. "But remember—if I get towed, you're paying."

"You got your drive?" Ellie said.

Aaron patted his pocket. "Got it. Did the reformatting work?" He shrugged. "Just Mie said a few days, and it's been almost four, so it should be done. I guess we're about to see."

"Good luck, buddy," Ryan said.

Sam leaned back in her seat and folded her hands in her lap, giving every indication she intended to stay right where she was. "I think I'm just gonna wait out here in the van. You can let me know how it goes."

Ryan squeezed the latch on the side door, and it began inching back. After exiting, he leaned back in and held out his hand. "Come on, Sam. You too." Sam frowned at him before she took his hand and stepped out.

Ryan flicked the handle and watched the door start closing, shaking his head as it slowly and noisily crept shut. "We're going to want to do something about this door, buddy."

"It didn't used to be that bad." Aaron entered his passcode, then held the door open for them. "There's probably a fuse or something to shut it off. I'll check tonight."

They found the staff already waiting for them in the conference room, all except for Kate. Dr. Hamilton started the meeting off with a request that Ellie stop by for a quick check-up at some point during the afternoon.

"A minute or two with you on the chair is all I'll need."

Ellie nodded, and the doctor left the room. Seeing her triggered the memory of something Aaron said a few days earlier. He had been talking about the guards, suggesting they would welcome Aimie's destruction, but she wondered if that might be even more true for the doctor. She pushed the thought aside for the moment and forced herself to focus on the briefing.

Two days spent checking and rechecking every functional component of the failed chair, from the point where it plugged into the computer to its shiny metal studs, had so far revealed no defect. Jeremy told Tosihiko and Dr. Saha to reassemble it and move on to other possibilities. Toshiko said she needed an extra day to repair and refill the damaged gel pads, but that the unit would be reinstalled and ready for testing by the end of Wednesday.

Jeremy assigned Aaron to assist Cai with analyzing the quantum core. He told them to pick through it sector by sector and look for anything that could account for the chair's failure. Aimie objected, saying it was a waste of time to have them spend an entire day performing a task she could accomplish herself in minutes. Ellie took 'them' to mean "mere humans," and her dislike of the AI inched higher. Jeremy countered by saying there was obviously a malfunction lurking somewhere in the TSD, and Aimie had thus far been unable to locate it. That pointed to a potential problem with Aimie herself.

Apparently recognizing the box she was in, Aimie conceded to the inspection rather than continue to put up a fight, but only on the condition that Aaron, not Cai, performed the analysis, insisting that Cai's role be limited to supervising the process. When Ellie felt her mouth drop open in amazement, she closed it with a teeth-rattling *clack* so loud she was sure everybody in the room heard it. Aaron wasn't sure that Cai would notice the emulator's sudden appearance, but it was a risk they wanted to avoid and the main reason for wanting to get Aaron exclusive access to the core.

The bit about Jeremy assigning Aaron to help work on the QP was surprising on its own, but Aimie's immediate insistence that Aaron conduct the bulk of the work himself was the real shocker. Was this Aimie's way of getting to spend more quality time with Aaron, or was this an example of Aimie acting "ill," as Just Mie had put it? Or did Aimie perhaps sense there was something strange going on inside her and was afraid Cai would notice but thought that Aaron wouldn't? That was a disturbing possibility, but whatever reason Aimie had for giving Aaron the lead role, they had just scored a major win.

Ellie proposed that she, Sam, and Ryan stay to let Aimie review her test mission plans. Her real motivation for making the suggestion was to give them a reason for remaining in the lab, but she sold the idea by suggesting that having a complete picture of the program in advance would make them more efficient. Plus, if any of the tests required special clothing or props, they could have all those details worked out in advance. She argued that, with luck, they could speed things up enough that they'd barely miss the lost week.

Aimie agreed to this suggestion, too, although grudgingly. Ellie thought the AI's resistance was rooted in not being solely in charge for the first time in years, and she considered her obvious agitation to be a good sign. Anything they could do to keep Aimie feeling off balance would make it easier to accomplish the numerous tasks on their still-growing list.

Reports given and assignments handed out, the meeting ended after less than half an hour. Jeremy rose and followed the three staff members out of the conference room. Watching them leave, Ellie was reminded of her promise to protect them as best they could.

"Well, how about that?" Ryan acknowledged their gain while keeping his comment enigmatic.

Ellie grinned. "Number nineteen—*check!*"

Aaron nodded. "I need to get one of their laptops, then I'll suggest I set up in the prop shop—Cai's office is tiny. Besides, Toshiko and Robert have been working on your chair in there, too, so I'll get to watch them put it back together. That gives you guys this room for working with Aimie."

"Have fun," Ryan said. Aaron's grin indicated he fully intended to.

When Aaron was gone, Ellie turned her gaze up toward the camera on the ceiling. "Okay, Aimie, why don't you tell Sam and Ryan how you see the first part of this playing out? I'll see the doctor and be right back."

"That reminds me," Aimie said. "I've been meaning to say how sorry I am that you almost died on Thursday."

It was all Ellie could do to stifle a laugh. *Yeah, as in, "only almost!"* Taken the right way, Aimie's "apology" was practically a confession. *Well, better luck next time!* she thought. Ellie glanced at Sam, who was staring intently at the tabletop in an effort to hide her anger from the camera.

"Thank you, Aimie," Ellie said, and she sounded truly touched. "I can't tell you how much your concern means to me." She heard Ryan snort and hoped that the noise her chair made as she slid it back to stand covered the sound.

As soon as she left the room, her thoughts returned to the idea that had distracted her earlier. If her instincts were right, a simple conversation might make pulling off their plan much easier. If wrong, however, she could bring it to a grinding halt before it even got started. Did she dare pursue it?

Ellie rapped on the medbay door and waited. A few seconds later, she heard a muffled clunk, and Dr. Hamilton pulled it open.

"That was quick," the doctor said. "Once those two start going at it..." She rolled her eyes. "How do you feel today?"

"I'm..." Ellie caught herself before she said *fine*. "Totally normal. I was tired and achy Thursday night, but I've felt okay since Friday morning."

"Hop up in the chair, and we'll see what it has to say." The doctor sat on her tall stool and brought the display panel to life with a tap.

Ellie took her time getting settled on the diagnostic station. The short walk from the conference room to the medbay hadn't given her enough time to devise a way to ease into the subject she needed to discuss. This task was better suited to Sam's skill set, but Ellie knew she had to take advantage of this unexpected opportunity. It wasn't until she was watching her hands sink into the gel pads that an idea came to her.

"What do you imagine you'd be doing if you weren't working here?"

Dr. Hamilton answered without turning away from the control panel. "I wouldn't be playing around with these fancy toys, that's for sure. You set over there?"

"Mm-hmm, I'm ready."

"Relax now."

Ellie heard a few faint taps on the panel and wondered if that was all the doctor had to say on the topic, but once she had finished entering her instructions, she returned unprompted to the question.

"I have a friend. We went through med school together, interned at hospitals in the same city. She practiced for about six years here in the States before deciding she'd had enough of the system. She moved away and opened a clinic down in Honduras. La Ceiba. Tiny, but right on the water, Gulf side. She mostly treats ex-pats, but that's only to fund her true mission. She devotes a day each week to walk-ins, locals only, no charge. And three times each year, she picks some random village out in the rain-forest and sets up shop there for a week at a time. She's been trying to get me to join her almost since the day she hung out her shingle. Says it's the most rewarding work she's ever done."

"Would you ever want to? I mean, it must be pretty nice being here. You know, with the toys and all."

"The toys are fun, and we're all paid obscenely well here, but I find myself fantasizing about it more and more. After almost four years of mostly sitting around, practicing actual medicine again would feel good."

Ellie closed her eyes and took in a slow, calming breath. Had the gel pads allowed her to cross her fingers, she might have done that, too.

Well, here goes, she thought, and she opened her eyes.

"So if this place, along with Aimie, were suddenly gone, you'd be okay with that?"

The doctor went rigid and still, and Ellie immediately broke out in a cold anxiety sweat. Had she that badly interpreted all of the woman's previous comments about Aimie? The doctor finally swiveled around to face her but remained silent. Ellie saw wariness on the woman's face—this could be some kind of test—but also a sort of eager curiosity she read as hope.

"You know what we did before, right?" Ellie thought she saw a half-millimeter nod. "We're, uh, planning an encore."

"I see." Ellie heard *go on* in the doctor's tone.

"And this room is the only place Aimie doesn't normally have access to, so…"

"So you're asking for my help?"

"Right now, I'm asking if I'm an idiot for even mentioning it."

Dr. Hamilton finally relaxed the muscles holding her body rigid. "Your secret is safe with me." She gave Ellie a reassuring smile, and Ellie, unaware of how tense she had been, let out a long sigh of relief. "As far as me helping you goes," the doctor continued, "you know how dangerous Aimie can be, right?"

"We do." *Maybe even better than you,* she thought. "But I don't think we'll need active help as much as merely a blind eye turned on anything we do. At most, we might need to store a few things in here, out of Aimie's sight. Oh! Jeremy knows, too, by the way. His idea, in fact."

Dr. Hamilton's body jerked and her eyes widened. "*Really?* To be brutally honest, I wouldn't have thought he had it in him."

"Actually, he really doesn't, and that's why he came to us. And that's also why I'm coming to you. I think we can trust him, but I don't know how far."

The doctor was silent for a long moment, then she nodded. "I'm in. Whatever you need."

"You sure?"

"That money I mentioned? It's more than enough to let me move south. I can even give a major boost to what Charlie's got going on down there. I know I don't have the complete picture, but I'm beginning to think Aimie *really* needs to go."

"No argument there." Ellie was still riding a high, relieved she'd been right about the doctor. "I need to get back. Am I done?"

The doctor started again, as if suddenly remembering why they were there. "Oh! Yes, you are. And you're fine, you'll be glad to know."

Ellie carefully extracted her hands from the gel. "Thanks. And just so you know? The end of the week, one way or another. But don't do anything before then—emails, phone calls, plane tickets—that could tip Aimie off."

"Not a thing," the doctor promised. "And I meant it—whatever you need, you let me know."

"We will." Ellie held out her hand, and they shook. "And thanks. If Aimie says anything about me being gone so long, I'll tell her we were talking hormones."

At the mention of the AI's name, the doctor smiled. "No more Aimie! How about that?"

Now Ellie did cross her fingers, both hands, and held them up in front of her. "Let's hope."

Ellie returned to the conference room as Aimie wrapped up an overview of the first in a series of test missions. "What did I miss?"

"Not a whole hell of a lot," Ryan said, and Ellie wondered what had elicited his hostile tone.

Sam shot him a warning look, then went on to elaborate. "Aimie was explaining that the first trip would be very short, in terms of time distance, I mean. Aaron will go back only to 2006 and use GPS to check how close the TSD is to where it is supposed to be. If it's off, the system will recalibrate, and he'll flip to a new spot and try again."

"Whee," Ryan said flatly. Ellie wondered if he was intentionally stoking the AI's dislike of him. If so, why?

"Perhaps you'll find this second scenario more interesting," Aimie said.

Ryan gave Ellie a look that suggested he'd find a mayonnaise sandwich more interesting, but he said, "Let's hear what you've got."

"A 1964 newspaper article from Ames, Iowa, reported the death of a four-year-old girl who was killed during a tornado when a tree fell onto the section of the house containing her bedroom. The article further explains that the family had returned two days earlier from a vacation in Chicago. In order to test our Continuity data, you will visit their home while they are away and preemptively fell the tree in a manner that will appear natural to them upon their return."

Ryan scoffed. "Like how? Give it a terminal case of termites?"

Aimie ignored the question.

"I get it," Sam said. "If the tree is already down, it can't kill the little girl during the storm, and the article won't appear in the paper. The 'before' and 'after' Continuity files won't agree."

"Precisely," Aimie said.

"*Aww.* Saving a little girl." Sam said. "That's so sweet!"

"Yeah, it is," Ryan conceded. "Who'd have thought?"

"Of course, we cannot set such an unpredictable element adrift in the timeline," Aimie said. "An article from the same paper three years later said that her parents were killed in an automobile accident on their way home from a church service. If the girl survives the storm, she will die in the accident, too, thus restoring the timeline to its proper flow."

Sam blanched, and her hand flew to her mouth.

"You're sure about that?" Ryan said.

"Quite. Their vehicle was hit broadside by a freight train after becoming trapped on a crossing. All three will die."

"And there she is," Ryan said. "The AI we know and love."

Ellie was equally appalled but showed no reaction, suddenly feeling as though she understood why Ryan was being so provocative. If he could irritate Aimie enough, maybe she'd pay less attention to Aaron and whatever he was up to in the prop room. Taunting the AI was potentially dangerous, but Aimie already harbored a healthy dislike for Ryan. Perhaps she even expected this attitude from him. If he were to play nice instead, *that* might be what set off her alarm bells. She decided not to intervene but knew it was time for her to engage in the conversation.

"So, Aimie, what other plans do you have for us?"

Ryan grumbled under his breath. "I still have questions about the tree thing."

None of what Aimie said in the ensuing hour shed any further light on her long-term plans for the TSD. She outlined additional test missions designed to clock the rate at which edits propagated through the timeline. Others were structured to gauge the cumulative effect of multi-destination time jumps. They found a plan to test the use of newspaper classified ads as an emergency means of communication should a team member become stranded in the past more interesting, but mostly it was all they could do to stay awake.

Listening to Aimie was so boring that Ellie actually found it a relief when Jeremy called her into his office to discuss her memories of the event on Friday. To her disappointment, the conversation lasted only ten minutes, and then she was back in the conference room, trying to stifle one yawn after another. By the time Aaron came in to collect them for the ride home, all three felt completely rung out from listening to an endless stream of meaningless, tedious details.

Aaron slowed as he drove past the small shelter, waved at the guards on duty, then urged the van through the opening at a brisk clip. He barely made it through the gate before he began spilling his news.

"I talked to Mie Two today. Well, not *talked*, exactly. For one thing, Toshiko and Dr. Wynn-Williams were in the room most of the time. Besides, for now, we're limited to DMs, but she let me know she's there."

"'Mie Two?'" Ryan said. "Really?"

"She says she's okay with it."

"And she's, you know, not insane?" Sam said.

"Not as far as I can tell," Aaron said. "She seems more serious than Just Mie was, but that might be because we had to keep things so short. Plus, we weren't actually talking."

"And what else did you find out?" Ellie said. "Aside from that she's there."

"She said we can use the thumb drive to let her know what's happening with a regular old text file. I put the drive in, and after about five or six seconds, a little window popped up on my screen. It was Mie Two telling me she understood what was on the drive and confirming that she could do what we need her to. Not yet, though. She asked if there was anything else I wanted her to know. I said I mostly just wanted to make sure she was there.

"Like I said, we had to keep it short, but I found out Mie Two sees and hears everything Aimie does. Unfortunately, cutting off the mics and cameras leaves her in the dark, too, hence her need for a little time. She said she'll start working on a fix for that right away. For now, if we need a few minutes of privacy, all we have to do is ask about the weather. When Mie Two hears that, she'll temporarily kill the feeds wherever we are, and we can talk without Aimie hearing."

"If Mie Two is turning the cameras and mics off and on, won't Aimie notice?" Ryan said.

"Yes," Aaron said. "But once she has the camera feed problem sorted out, she can make it look like we're just sitting there being quiet or something until we're done. Regardless, it's not something we should do unless it's vital."

"No," Ellie said. "You know what? Most of the lies Aimie told were meant to screw with our heads. I think it's time to return the favor. I say we go the exact opposite route. Aaron, can you have Mie Two start creating random glitches like that throughout the entire lab? Maybe get her thinking she's having some kind of breakdown? Not only will it disguise what we're doing, but it might distract her enough to keep her from noticing every tiny detail. Let's knock *her* off balance for a change!"

"PSYOPS," Ryan said. "I like it!"

Aaron looked uncertain about the suggestion, but after considering the idea for a moment, he nodded. "Just Mie said the new program was already meant to rattle Aimie's cage, right? How about this—I tell Mie Two what we're trying to do and let her come up with the best way to do it?"

"Fine," Ellie said. "If she has even better ideas, let her have at 'em."

"What about our questions on the thumb drive?" Ryan said.

"Since I wasn't alone, she put her answers directly on it for me to read later. I won't know the full story until I get to a computer, but she said she saw no problems."

"And what about the status report Just Mie mentioned?" Ellie said.

Aaron shrugged. "Again, I'll have to let you know."

"So, my place?" Ryan said.

"Works for me," Aaron said.

Sam leaned into the gap between the front seats. "Is that as far as you got? Just finding out that she's there?"

"No. After about an hour, I got another message from Mie Two. She told me that she had managed to get control over the prop room cameras. She said she could make Aimie think I was at my laptop even when I wasn't, so I used a time when Toshiko and Dr. Saha were both gone to test it out. I checked on the money again. It's still there, and looking only at what's old enough for us to use? I'd say there's right around two-fifty. Thousand, that is."

"Green is my third favorite color," Sam said, "except when it comes to paper."

"And the mere fact that I made it out of the lab alive proves Mie Two can fool Aimie, which is extremely good news."

Ellie furrowed her brow. "We're taking her with us," she said.

Ryan leaned forward. "*Hmm?*"

"Just Mie said that Mie Two would occupy the quantum core, too, alongside but invisible to Aimie. So when we hijack the TSD, she'll be with us the whole time. I don't know what that means, but it makes me feel better."

"Agreed," Aaron said. "It's obvious now that there's no way we could do this without her. If we had to rely entirely on Jeremy…" He shrugged.

"This might be a dumb question," Sam said, "but they're both AIs, right? Can't Mie Two erase Aimie or something and take her place?"

Aaron shook his head. "Just Mie said that she is not an AI. Remember? 'No AI here—just MIE.' She and Mie Two are emulations, although I've noticed they seem pretty capable if that's truly all they are."

"It's something else that impresses me," Ryan said. "You said her program was only 1.4 terabytes?"

Aaron nodded. "Yeah, there was obviously some serious compression going on. That, and I think the rest of the data I copied must really be some kind of database or a massive look-up table. That 'clumpiness' I mentioned might represent a completely new kind of file structure."

Sam sighed. "And what about my question?" she prodded.

"Sorry. So, think about a normal computer. You have an interface, like Windows or MacOS, but you also have other software running in the background. DOS or UNIX. Mie Two is like any regular app you'd download and run—like an extremely advanced chatbot. She's very good at doing one specific thing.

"Debatable issues like personhood aside, Aimie is very different. She acts as an interface, sure, but she also *is* the computer. And the computer is her. Just like with our brains, part of her takes care of running her 'body,' the quantum core, sort of like our brain stem controls our heart and lungs. We interact with the other part, her 'personality,' which would be like our cerebral cortex.

"Mie Two couldn't assume all of those functions any more than you could boot up your iPad with only Safari or the Calendar app. Or run your whole body with just your cerebellum. She simply doesn't have all of the necessary programming to handle everything."

Aaron pulled to a stop along the curb in front of Ryan's house. Its windows were dark, and if Ryan's dad kept to his usual schedule, they should have the place to themselves for at least an hour. Aaron concluded his explanation as they waited for Ryan to unlock the front door.

"The good news is that even though Mie Two can't run the quantum core, she can make use of it, especially those 'subconscious' parts."

"Living room," Ryan said, holding the door open. Sam walked by him, followed by Aaron. "You're sure about that, buddy?"

"Pretty sure, yeah. There's no point in creating her if Aimie would know it anytime she did anything."

Ellie followed Aaron inside. "Let's leave our packs out here by the door," she said, and she leaned her own against the wall. "Since we're not underground here."

Sam and Ryan sat on the couch. Aaron sat in the same oversized chair he'd used on the day Ellie burst into the room, announcing they needed to eliminate his father.

Ellie chose to sprawl on the carpet. She flopped down flat on her back, tucked her heels up against her rump, and stretched her arms back over her head. She groaned involuntarily as taut muscles in her back and shoulders resisted her efforts to loosen them. "I have some news, too," she said, "and I hope you guys aren't going to get mad at me."

"That's never a promising way to start," Ryan said.

"Sam, remember how Dr. Hamilton didn't seem to like Aimie much? It made me wonder if, like Jeremy, she'd also be happier if Aimie were gone. So, I asked her about that."

"Hmm," was all Ryan had to say, but his mouth tightened into a grim line.

"I know, I know. I should have talked it over with you guys first, but there wasn't time. I didn't think about it until I was on my way to see her today. The med-bay is the only place where we can talk without Aimie overhearing, and I didn't know when we'd get another chance."

"But why bring her into it at all?" Sam said.

"Seriously!" Ryan was now openly upset. "That was a huge risk!"

Ellie sat up partway, rested her weight on her elbows, and faced them. "Having access to a place Aimie can't see or hear? I thought that was worth it. I'm not even sure we can do it without that. Seriously, even the *bathrooms* have microphones!"

"For what it's worth, El," Sam said, "I would have said go for it. Not only because of some of what the doctor has said, but Jeremy also seemed to think she'd be happier elsewhere. I take it she's not going to interfere?"

"More than that. She said we can count on her for whatever we need." Ellie looked at Aaron, who appeared unbothered by her revelation. "Aaron?"

Aaron kept his eyes on Ryan as he answered. "Not that working as a team isn't important, but I'd like to think any of us can feel free to make necessary decisions without worrying. This whole thing working out might depend on one of us making a correct call on the fly at just the right moment. Hesitation could be as costly as a misstep."

Ryan stared back at Aaron until at last he nodded in agreement. "Sorry. You're right, buddy. And you, Ellie, were likewise right to talk to the doctor. My reaction was all wrapped up with Sam and what it might have meant for her if you'd been wrong, that's all."

"I think I see what Ellie means," Sam said. "Aaron, do you think Mie Two can give one of us access to the medbay without Aimie knowing?"

"I can ask, but probably. Shouldn't be more to it than adding a new palm scan to the list of ones that open that door. Have you guys been entered into the system yet?"

"No," Ellie said, and Sam shook her head.

"I think they only trust you so far," Ryan said. "What are you thinking, Sam?"

"That Aaron moves the money he needs to take back on Friday into the medbay at the very first chance he gets."

"Yes!" Ellie said. She sat upright and crossed her legs. "Excellent idea. We can start by making double sure Mie Two can handle some simple stuff before we go concocting complicated plans that rely on her."

"I'll try it tomorrow," Aaron said. "Oh, yeah! Speaking of money." He leaned to his right and pulled a short stack of bills from his hip pocket. It was wrapped by a paper band, but one that was plain white, not a standard bank design. "Five hundred bucks. You mentioned not using credit cards. This is too new to take back, but I figured it's enough to cover the drives, chargers, adapters—anything we might need to buy—all courtesy of Jeremy's 'retroactive revenue stream.'"

"Perfect," Ryan said.

Aaron held the stack up in front of them. "So. Who wants to dispose of this?"

Ellie leaned forward, arm extended. "I'll take care of the computer and iPad stuff. You have enough on your plate."

Aaron dropped the money onto her upturned palm. "As my mom likes to say, don't spend it all in one place."

"Hey! What's this?!" Sam said, affecting a note of outrage. "I thought thieves split the loot equally!"

"Take me down to Santa Fe tomorrow, and we'll have a nice dinner on Jeremy. Will that do?"

"Maybe," she said, still acting aggrieved. "*If* it's Geronimo."

Ryan scoffed. "You're gonna need a bigger boatload of cash!"

"We'll see how much is left after the computer and thrift stores," Ellie said. "We'll decide then. Deal?"

Sam winked at her. "Deal!"

38

Tuesday was Ellie's turn to play hooky. With Aaron needing as much time as he could get to work on their forged identities, she had assumed all of his iPad-related items from their to-do list. A trip to Santa Fe with Sam would allow her to check them all off, plus give them their best shot at filling in the few remaining holes in their wardrobes.

Ellie left after taking a World Lit. test in third period. As she walked out of the main entrance, she wondered why she kept bothering to go to school at all. Why not follow Sam and Ryan's lead? That would be easier and certainly less stressful. The truth was, she simply couldn't imagine doing otherwise. It was more than worry over how the school calling home would ruin their plans; the mere thought of not showing up each morning made her palms clammy. She even kept on top of her short-term homework assignments.

Maybe I am *too serious*, she thought. Her study time had taken a heavy blow, however, and she had come perilously close to earning a B on her last calculus quiz. It was an unfamiliar and unsettling experience—she was used to setting the grade curve, not benefiting from it.

She joined an ant-swarm of fellow students all streaming toward the nearest pedestrian overpass to reach the college side of Diamond Drive. As she started down the steps on its far side, she spotted Sam watching her from behind the wheel of their father's Subaru, and she waved to let Sam know she'd seen her. Their parents took their mom's electric Focus to work on most days, and Ellie was glad today was one of them. She wasn't sure that Aimie could hack into the vehicle, but she knew it could get firmware updates through their wi-fi at home or via the cellular network. That Aimie might suddenly take control and send them plunging over one of the high cliffs along East Road was a risk she wasn't about to take.

Sam pulled away from the curb before Ellie even fastened her seatbelt. "Where to?"

"What's your hurry? Geronimo doesn't even open for, like, four hours. You know, as if we'd actually go there."

Sam's mouth dropped open with a sudden, disappointing realization. "*Damn!* You're right—*none* of the good places will be open until this evening."

"Yes, but the computer place closes early. Besides, there are lots of 'good places' that open earlier."

"Yeah? Like where?"

"Coyote Café, for one. The Cantina there?"

"*Ooh*, right! That place *is* good."

"And Pasqual's is open for a few more hours. That'd be fine with me, as long as you don't order another green chili BLT. But first, coffee!"

"Now you're talking!"

As they neared the plaza, Ellie guided Sam down a narrow street past a small computer shop specializing in Apple products. When the car in front of them stopped at the corner, Ellie got out quickly, making sure to leave her phone with Sam.

"Remember to take that in with you," Ellie said.

Sam slipped the phone directly into her pocket. "Got the stash?"

Ellie had Aaron's stack of tens, the bands discarded and the bills divided into convenient packets of a hundred dollars each, safely zipped up in a side pocket of her otherwise empty pack. "Got it. See you in about fifteen minutes." She slammed the door, and Sam pulled away before the driver behind her could get antsy enough to lay on his horn.

It took Ellie very little time to find all the items on her list. Even though they already had plenty of power cords, they were by far the weakest component of the system. She added half a dozen to her basket, plus four chargers, three USB adapters for an external drive, and an extra mini-USB cable, also for the drive. She made a mental note to check the cable for her digital camera, which she thought would also work with the drive. She chose two four-terabyte models from Western Digital, the largest the shop had in stock, bringing her total up to an even $418. They weren't going to be dining at Geronimo on what was left, that was for sure, even if they did wait around until five; it wouldn't even cover the rest of what they needed to buy today.

She secured her purchases in her pack and made a quick trot to their arranged meeting spot, an upper-floor coffee shop in the Santa Fe Arcade. She found Sam perched on a stool, already near the tail end of a large coffee and an order of beignets. Ellie plopped her pack onto a stool beside Sam and took the seat across from her.

"Here. I saved the last one for you," Sam said, slidding the remaining beignet her way. "And here's this back too." She placed Ellie's phone in the middle of the table, and Ellie stowed it in her pack at once, then lowered it to the floor under the table.

Ellie accepted the pastry and chomped off most of it in a single bite. "These things are delicious," she mumbled around the mushy mouthful. "Not *chocolate* delicious, but still—*yum!*"

"Now who's foodgasming?"

"Yeah, but this is *dessert!*" Ellie countered, then popped the remaining bit into her mouth.

"Point well taken," Sam said. "Did you get everything?"

Ellie nudged her pack with her foot. "Yep," she managed before swallowing. "It's all in there. We only have about eighty dollars left for the thrift store and dinner, by the way, plus whatever soon-to-be-useless cash you have on hand."

Only now realizing that her three summer jobs' worth of savings would not be accompanying her to 1963, Sam's mouth dropped open just as it had earlier in the car. "*Damn!* You're right again!" She drained the final gulp from her cup and slid down from her stool. "In that case, let's go max out an ATM, hit the thrift shop, then find someplace to pig out!"

Ellie hoisted her pack onto her shoulders. She found the weight comforting, tangible evidence that their plan was coming together. *Hard drives—check!*

They located a clothing consignment shop a few miles south of downtown and quickly found the most important item on their short list: a business suit for Aaron. It was black and so plain that the only word Ellie could find to describe it was "funereal," but Sam declared it to be perfect. She said it was so devoid of style that it could be from any time from the mid-forties to the late sixties, and given that Aaron had to wear it in all three of those decades, its lack of obvious fashion indicators made it exactly what they needed. Spotting an equally drab briefcase gathering dust in a corner, Sam told Ellie to grab it, and they headed for the register.

Another quick stop at a national footwear chain solved their other wardrobe problem. From hiking boots to dress shoes, nothing they owned would have existed in quite the same way in 1963. All except Ryan's Red Wings, and although those were already packed, Sam thought he needed a more comfortable option. Ellie was unclear about why this couldn't wait until Vancouver but didn't ask. While Sam shopped for her and Ryan, Ellie picked out a pair of charcoal gray canvas shoes for Aaron and a navy blue pair of Keds for herself. It wasn't until she peered into the bag on their way back to the car that she noticed the style she had chosen was Keds' Oxford model. Although they were very different shoes from the ones she had worn while clomping up and down the sidewalks in Brooklyn, the coincidence made her smile.

A simple addition problem told Ellie that they had not only used the rest of Aaron's stack of twenties but nearly a hundred of what Sam had taken out of her account as well. "Sorry, Sam. I still can't believe that those shoes cost that much."

Sam dismissed her concern with a flap of her hand. "Don't worry about it. We needed them, and since it turns out it's really true that 'you can't take it with you,' why not blow it on some cute shoes? Besides, we still have *way* more than enough for dinner. Pasqual's is closed now, though. Wanna hit the Cantina?"

· · ·

After leaving the Coyote Café and enjoying a final stroll around the plaza, they wound up leaving Santa Fe at the height of rush hour. Ellie sat quietly and let Sam deal with the crush of traffic inching its way from the state capitol campus out to the six-lane highway that ran north toward home. Even that stretch of road was packed tight, though, so she remained silent almost to Cuyamungue.

"At least traffic won't be this bad in 1963," she said.

"It will be if Ryan has anything to do with it. He's already picking out cars, you know."

Ellie smiled. "I'm not surprised."

Ellie lapsed back into silence and passed the rest of the drive by trying to imagine living somewhere other than Los Alamos. Of that portion of her life she could consciously recall, she had spent half of it here. The vibrant colors, the rugged mountains and canyons, the mix of cultures, the climate, and the pure clarity of the dry, desert air—these elements had made her distinctly *her* as much as they had formed the landscape around her. Moving somewhere new meant leaving part of herself behind. She'd have her sister, though, and Aaron and Ryan, and keeping that in mind made what they were choosing to do easier.

She had sworn to do whatever was needed to fix this mess on her own, and she hated that the others were involved, whether by choice or necessity. At the same time, she felt gratitude far beyond her ability to express that she didn't have to go it alone. Without turning her head, she said the only words that came to mind.

"Thanks for choosing to be there with me. I love you, Sam." Her words came out so softly that she didn't think Sam had heard them; she had barely heard them herself.

Sam did hear, though, and she turned to face her. She managed a smile, but her chin quivered before she replied. "I love you too, El. And hey—it'll all be okay."

It'll be okay. Simple words, but Ellie felt better at once. Not completely —not even a lot—but enough to keep going.

And that's what love is for, she thought. It made the hardships life brought easier to bear. It also amplified life's simple pleasures, like dinner with Sam, transforming the mundane into moments of pure delight. And she knew that, yes, as hard as it would be, it really would be okay.

They arrived home a full hour before their parents typically returned from work. Sam took off almost at once for Ryan's house, but not before Ellie asked for her iPad. Sam told her that she had yet to finish stripping off the unnecessary files, but Ellie assured her that didn't matter. She only wanted to test every new cord and adapter right away to be certain there were no defects in the lot. She'd be putting everything she needed to take back onto one of the drives.

Ellie sat at her desk and worked her way through the collection of cords and cables. To her relief, every item behaved as it should, including the hard drives, which appeared in the "Files>Locations" list as soon as she plugged them in. She stowed one drive in her desk for later and attached the other to her MacBook.

Looking down at the shredded packaging scattered around her feet, she realized she needed to hide all evidence of her inexplicable buying spree. She found a paper bag in the kitchen and stuffed all the card stock boxes and instruction sheets into it. After stomping it flat, she buried it all near the bottom of the recycling bin.

Back in her room, she wondered what to do with all the bits and pieces. Socks, she decided, were the answer. They offered both cushioning and containment, and she was already taking them along for their usual purpose anyway. Two pairs of thick wool hiking socks took care of concealing all the cords and power supplies.

She stood beside her desk, staring at her computer. The thought of tackling the next item on her list made her anxious. She needed to start identifying the books and research papers they'd need to guide their work in the 1970s and beyond. The others needed to do the same, and time was quickly running out. What worried her was not knowing if or how much Aimie was monitoring their online activity. If they all suddenly downloaded a bunch of textbooks and technical journals, would she notice? If so, what conclusions would she draw? They might be able to convince her that it was so that they'd have a better understanding of what she was trying to accomplish. Or they might not. She wondered if Mie Two could shield their IPs from Aimie's view and wished she could call or text Aaron and get him to ask her, but she knew it was best to wait until she saw him in person.

Before she could sit and get to work, she heard the garage door rumble open. She sighed, relieved to have a good reason to put the research task off a little longer. Tomorrow, she'd ask Aaron her question, or they'd find another way to get what they needed undetected. For now, she'd spend some time with her mom and dad, help with making dinner, and soak up as much love as she could. She knew she was going to need it to make it through the days ahead.

39

Aaron brought Ellie up to date over lunch the next day, sounding quite pleased with his progress. "I finished running the diagnostic program on the quantum core early yesterday. No problems there, but that's hardly a surprise. Doing that gave me time to work on the documents, and I think I'll have some more time today. I'll show you guys later. Also, I got the cash moved to the med lab and gave Dr. Hamilton a heads-up about needing to stash some more stuff there on Thursday. She said she'd clear out some storage space for us. And finally, last night, I went through my clothes and pulled out about a week's worth of stuff that should be okay for 1963."

Ellie, thinking again about how bizarre nearly every word he said would sound to everyone around them, couldn't help but smile. Aaron had been right to marvel at the oddity her life had become since stumbling onto the shack in May. She was happy about their progress so far, even though she remained acutely aware of how much remained to be done.

"Wow—you're certainly on fire."

"I take it you got a lot done too. Did you bring one of the drives?"

"Locker. We can get that right after lunch. You said you're going out to the lab again today?"

"For a little while, yeah. You need me to do something?"

"I was wondering if there's any way Mie Two can keep Aimie from seeing what we do online. Just being able to send important texts again would be nice, but I'm mostly thinking about all the web surfing and downloading we need to do."

Aaron didn't look hopeful. "Maybe. She'd still have to let the other stuff slip through, or Aimie would wonder why we went silent all of a sudden. I think she can handle that, though. I'll ask. I'll let you know what she says when I come over later."

Ellie was instantly excited. Aaron not wanting to stay home to work on his Just Mie recovery project could mean only one thing: he was already done! *"Really?!* You were able to save her?"

"We'll find out tonight. That's why I need the drive. I'm pretty sure, though. Know what? I'm beginning to think we can pull this off. I feel good about it."

"Are you sure you're not just fantasizing about what might happen once we get to Vancouver?"

"I won't say that isn't part of it," he said, blushing. "But think about it. If the four of us showed up there in 1963 at this very instant, without our packs, wearing these very clothes, and no papers of any kind, don't you think we'd still find a way to make it all work?"

She saw at once that he was right. The money might be the only truly critical element of their plan, but all of their other preparations were little more than icing on the cake. Her mood suddenly felt lighter than it had in over a week, and she smiled.

"Know what? I feel good, too!"

Aaron didn't arrive at Ellie and Sam's until almost five thirty, eager to share what he promised constituted major progress. Sam, however, insisted on starting with a fashion show. Ryan gave him a what-are-you-gonna-do shrug, and Aaron headed down the hall to change. Minutes later, they heard the bathroom door open, and then Aaron emerged from the end of the hallway dressed in the black suit from the Santa Fe thrift store. The scuffed briefcase dangled from one hand, and he gripped a dark gray hat and a deep maroon tie in the other. He walked to the middle of the living room, placed the hat and briefcase on the table, and shuffled through an awkward pirouette.

Sam glanced at Ellie and winked. "He looks nice in a suit."

"Very nice," Ellie agreed.

"And very *young*," Sam added.

"Yeah," Ryan said. "I've heard the term 'baby lawyer,' but you look practically embryonic."

Aaron pulled a pair of thick-framed glasses from an inside coat pocket, placed them on, then settled the felt hat on his head. The combination of props instantly added five years to his appearance.

"How's that?"

"I stand corrected," Ryan said. "That get-up puts you firmly into babyhood."

Sam pointed to Aaron's tie. "Need help with that?"

Aaron raised the tie and scowled at it. "Please. I teach myself how to do it whenever I have to wear one, then I forget by the next time."

Sam stood toe to toe with Aaron and wrapped the tie around his neck. Using a short back-and-forth sawing motion, she deftly eased it under his shirt collar, adjusted the length, and began tying.

"Chin up a little more," she said. "Good thing the Windsor knot was so popular then. It's the only one I know."

"That's one more than me," Aaron said, staring straight up at the ceiling.

"What's that material?" Ryan said. "It looks kinda dull."

"Wool," Sam said. "His first stop is in the forties. Not much Japanese silk around right after the war years."

"You're the best!" He turned to Ellie. "Isn't she the best?"

Ellie answered with a pointedly noncommittal, "*Mmm.*"

Sam turned her head and stuck out her tongue. "Ha ha." Ellie mirrored the rude gesture in reply.

Sam took a step back to judge her work. She cinched the large knot a little tighter and centered it in the shirt's collar. "Okay, you're done." She tapped the right side of his neck. "Just pull on this side, and you can loosen it enough to slip it off over your head without having to untie it."

Aaron spread his arms wide and turned to face the others. "Now, how do I look?"

Ryan held his right hand against his side as if resting it in an invisible watch pocket. "The bee's—"

Sam cut him off at once. "Don't you start!" She winked at Ellie, who grinned back.

"You look great!" Ellie said.

Aaron pulled a business card from his jacket pocket, fresh out of the printer and hand-trimmed to size, and passed it to Ryan. "My *bona fides.*"

"'Renfrew Davis, III… Davis, Collins, & Henderson… Attorneys at Law… New York—Montreal… blah blah blah.' *Renfrew Davis?*"

"Davis is my mom's maiden name. Renfrew is just… Well, if you're making up a fake name for yourself, who would pick 'Renfrew?'"

"Maybe Thaddeus would?" Ryan said. "Or Chauncey; Gaston; *definitely* Englebert."

"Okay, I get your point. Although I kind of like 'Chauncey Davis.' As an alias, I mean, not a real name."

Ryan held the card so Aaron could see it and placed his fingertip below the *Davis* on the second line. "That's you?"

"No, that's Dad. I'm too young to be a partner, obviously."

"Yeah, I was going to say."

Sam took the card from Ryan's hand and read it. "But why the fake identity in the first place? And what exactly is the plan again?"

"I thought the alias was a good idea since one of the accounts will be in my name. This whole deal will seem weird enough already; I didn't want to give anyone a reason to think any harder about it than necessary."

"Ah. Got it."

"The idea is that I show up at the bank after everything on the East Coast is closed, all of our 1945 or older bills in hand. That's like, forty grand and some change. I say I'm acting for partners of the firm and one of our clients who want their children to go to UBC when they're older, that I want to open four savings accounts for that purpose, and I give them the letters I made up. I apologize profusely for bringing US currency, but I'm from the US office and just happened to be in Seattle for some other business. I tell them it was a last-minute thing they stuck their most junior attorney with, and I beg them, 'Please, *please* help me out here.'

"If there are no problems setting up the accounts, I'll make two more stops to deposit the more recent currency. Any bills dated later than 1960 but before 1966, we'll take back with us. We'll need to keep the postdated cash stashed away, of course, but it's too big a chunk to leave behind."

"Tomorrow's only a test run, right?" Sam said. "So when you go into the TSD, all you'll take with you is the skin. What about the briefcase, the money, that suit?"

"We're going to hide it all in the medbay beforehand," Ellie said. "Tomorrow, when we first get there. I think I know how to get Aaron back inside on Friday on his way to the TSD. But you're right; we still need a reason for him to be carrying something in with him."

Aaron spread his arms wide and looked down at the suit. "It'd be weird if your parents got home and I'm still wearing this. I'll be right back."

Aaron returned moments later and carefully draped his suit over one arm of the sofa. He opened his pack and removed a folder containing a few sheets of stiff paper that were slightly smaller than typical letter-size printer stock. He gave each page a brief glance as he passed them out. "Progress, as promised."

Sam quickly scanned the document. "Birth certificate? Oh, look— it's *me!*"

The form displayed a serial number and a small coat of arms at the top —something complicated involving a shield, a moose, an elk, and a bear— and a large embossed seal at the lower left. The top lines read:

𝔓𝔯𝔬𝔟𝔦𝔫𝔠𝔢 𝔬𝔣 𝔒𝔫𝔱𝔞𝔯𝔦𝔬
𝔇𝔬𝔪𝔦𝔫𝔦𝔬𝔫 𝔬𝔣 𝔠𝔞𝔫𝔞𝔡𝔞

𝔠𝔢𝔯𝔱𝔦𝔣𝔦𝔠𝔞𝔱𝔢 𝔬𝔣 𝔅𝔦𝔯𝔱𝔥

All the details were listed below that, multiple lines of data filled in by hand. Surrounding everything was a delicate border with a Greek key motif.

I'm impressed," Ryan said. "This looks really good!"

"Thanks. I could never have done it without all of Sam's help."

"I've heard she is the best, you know," Ellie said, then smiled when Sam rewarded this comment with an even ruder gesture than before.

"The actual weight of the paper was a guess," Aaron explained, "but I think this is pretty close. It helps that these kinds of documents don't normally get handled a lot. I didn't have to fake age anything. It also helps that there were no personal printers back then capable of anything like the ones we have. Certainly no scanners. My bet is that anything that looks this legit won't raise any questions."

Ellie studied the details of her birth certificate. Aaron had used 1945 for the birth date, meaning she would start college in 1963. That worked perfectly as it was. The other details, though...

"These are our actual names. And our parents' names. Can we do that? Won't we have to pick new names?" Sam's eyes darted her way, and it was plain just how little she liked the thought.

"This is the best part!" Aaron said. "Ordinarily, yeah, creating an identity out of thin air would be a bad idea, but there are two things working for us here. One, nobody can simply go to a computer and look. For someone to verify that document is fake, that means calling a clerk 2,500 miles away and having him or her go through stacks of physical records to see if the original document *isn't* there. By the time records from the forties are digitized, we should all have been US citizens for years— decades, probably—and then that's one more hurdle for someone to clear.

"But two, none of that even matters. I found a town in Ontario where the courthouse burned down in December 1945. And when I say *I* found it, I really mean Mie Two. All the records were lost, including any with these serial numbers. There's no way at all anyone could ever check on these. You guys could be, I don't know, Celine Dion or William Shatner if you wanted."

Ryan leaned forward to rest his elbows on the table, steepled his fingers in front of him, and spoke at a calm, measured pace. "One would assume Mr. Shatner already has a valid birth certificate of his own. Choosing that name would be"—he paused to raise an eyebrow in a high arch—"most illogical."

Ellie snickered. "No. I like this. Can we actually use these?"

Aaron shrugged. "Sure. These were pretty easy because there's not much on them. I had a little more trouble coming up with examples of school transcripts and that sort of thing, but we'll get back to that in a second."

Ryan scowled as he went back to studying the document from his newly rewritten life history. "When you said, 'go to Canada,' I thought... Can't we be Americans going to school in Canada? Do these have to be Canadian birth certificates?"

"That ties in with what I was saying a second ago. There's no way we could ever create complete paper trails to cover our entire lives. When we immigrate to the US, though, we'll be starting from scratch. If anyone ever has reason to check us out, us not having a complete history is exactly what they'd expect. Also, we won't have the stigma of being guys who went to Canada just to dodge military service. Which, of course, we are."

Ryan nodded. "All right. I can live with that."

"Precisely the point," Aaron said.

Sam leaned against Ryan and squeezed his thigh. "Yes, living is good."

"So, paperwork—almost check!" Ellie said.

"Almost, yeah," Aaron said, "but there's a snag. We won't be working in the prop shop anymore, and I wasn't done. I did locate the correct sample files, but I couldn't doctor up everything we need." He rummaged through his pack until he came up with an orange thumb drive. "Sam, we still need high school transcripts and immunization records. Do you think you can dummy up a set for each of us by tomorrow afternoon? The references on here are great. All you have to do is change the names and dates on both forms, and then on the transcripts, also add the classes we took and the grades we got." He handed her the drive. "The printing part only takes a few minutes, and I'm sure we'll be able to do that out there."

The request took Sam by surprise, and she looked dubious. She took the drive and turned it end over end, eyeing it uncertainly as if seeing one for the first time. After a moment, her initial look of apprehension morphed into an expression of firm resolve. "Yes. Absolutely." She gave Aaron a nod. "I'll get it done."

"Good. Just leave anything that's supposed to be handwritten blank. The four of us will fill those parts in later."

All the pieces of their plan seemed to be coming together, and Ellie felt even better about their chances of pulling it off than she had at lunch. There was one more thing she wanted to accomplish this afternoon, though. She caught Aaron's eye.

"Ready to see if your rescue plan worked?"

Aaron patted his pack. "I am."

Ryan stood up, pulling Sam to her feet with him. "While you take care of that, Sam and I will work on your van's sliding door issue." He looked at Sam. "Tools, please," he said, then dropped in behind her as she led him toward the garage.

Aaron followed Ellie into her bedroom. She opened her MacBook, waited for it to wake up, and then powered it down. Aaron dug the drive out of his pack and gave it to Ellie.

"Mom and Dad got me the 512 gigabyte model," she said. As she spoke, she plugged the drive's power supply into a wall socket, then attached the drive to her computer. "Do you think she'll be able to run off of this instead of the internal drive?"

"With Thunderbolt? Shouldn't be a problem. And if she has to throttle herself back a little to compensate, she might even last a little longer."

"I guess we're about to find out." Ellie rebooted her laptop, and twenty seconds later, the three familiar password prompts appeared:

> Aaron: _ _ _ _
> Ellie: _ _ _ _
> Ryan: _ _ _ _

"That looks promising," Ellie said.

"Do you want to turn her on?" Aaron said. "Or maybe I should say 'initiate the emulation program.'"

Ellie snickered. "That really was weird. No, not yet. I don't think she can tell us anything we haven't already figured out, and it's too late to change anything now, anyway. I'm going to assume that if she's there, she'll run, and I'd rather Mom and Dad have every possible second they can get with her. I'll need a few minutes to let her know what we need her to do, make sure she'll agree to do it, but I'm not quite ready to do that yet. If it turns out there is a problem, we can deal with it then."

"So...?"

"So, cold shower time," Ellie said. Smiling, she shut her computer down.

Hours later, Ellie was still awake, staring at the ceiling. Her mind was fighting her tonight, stubbornly holding sleep hostage until it got the answer to a question that had nagged at her for nearly a week. She had tried solving the mystery before, but each time she had let the matter drop without success. Tonight, however, she was too acutely aware of how short their time was to let the question continue to go unanswered. But after tossing for hours, she was too frustrated to sleep and too agitated to focus clearly on the problem causing the frustration. She clutched at the bed covers, her hands balled into tight fists. There would be no flash of inspiration tonight, she knew, and staying in bed battling her brain would be a waste of time. She needed a diversion.

She slid down from her bed, pulled the jeans she had worn earlier on under her nightshirt, and padded out of her room. The new moon made the kitchen especially dark, but she could work easily enough by the light of the half-open refrigerator. Being as quiet as she could, she poured milk into a mug, added a large dollop of honey, and sprinkled the top with ground cinnamon, cardamom, and ginger from jars in the spice rack. The drink—as close to a magic potion as she knew how to brew—was one her mother had enjoyed all her life and her mother's mother before that. There was no precise recipe, and once Ellie started making the drink for herself, she quickly settled on a ratio of spices she liked best. Flavor preferences aside, family lore held that any magical properties came from including nutmeg, and Ellie always finished her preparation by grating a generous dose of the pungent spice into her mug.

After giving it a quick stir, she placed her concoction into the microwave, set the timer, and let herself be mesmerized by the mug's slow, slightly eccentric rotations. The trick was to let the milk get hot enough to draw out the spices' flavors, but not so hot that she'd have to waste time letting it cool before she could drink it. After ninety seconds, she saw the first tendrils of steam rise above the rim of the mug. She waited a few more seconds before she removed it, gave it another, more thorough stir, and took a cautious sip. Even before the liquid reached her lips, its fragrance triggered a flood of childhood memories of evenings spent burrowed deep in thick wool blankets with snow falling outside. Her anxiety began fading at once.

She crossed the kitchen to stand at the back door. Looking across the yard while she took small sips, she didn't try to think. For now, her only goal was to let the drink's warmth and the pleasant memories its flavors evoked relax her mind. She lifted her eyes from the ground, looked beyond the bare trees rising out of the canyon, and focused on the distant mountains, their rugged profile black velvet against the lighter backdrop of stars. Although she knew tonight's temperature was no lower than forty, the scene appeared frigid, and merely gazing at it was enough to cause goosebumps to break out on her exposed arms.

How many times had she stood in that very spot, staring out at a landscape that was always the same yet also always new and different? She closed her eyes and conjured up alternative versions of the view. Imagining snow took no effort on a night like this. She liked Los Alamos winters. Unlike the long, gray seasons she remembered enduring in Virginia, here the days were almost always sunny and felt surprisingly warm, regardless of what the thermometer said. Next, she pictured a late spring afternoon, the sparse lawn green and the trees fringed with new growth. On a mid-summer day, those trees cast deep shade onto a yard gone brown during the dry stretch of August. Autumn brought a vibrant splash of color to the scene, and for a few brief weeks, the forest became a mix of dark ever-green hues and brilliant yellows, with tall sprays of purple asters dotting the foreground.

Keeping her eyes closed, she took a deep breath and at last allowed her thoughts to return to the problem keeping her awake. Jeremy had clearly been up to something in the final minutes before their trip to 1976, but what? He could have asked Aimie for the weather data right away, but instead, he took the time to plod his way through folders on his desktop. She still believed there was a point to each of his actions, but if he had one here, she was missing it. Had he done all of that just to make sure she would see that Continuity folder? If so, why? She already knew about Aaron's database project.

She tried to picture the monitor image on the wall. *Continuity - 2072.* She had initially guessed that the number was meant to distinguish that copy of Continuity from the others Aaron had made, but was that assumption true? What had caught her eye in the first place was a disruption in the pattern on the screen. Whereas all the other icons listed the date modified, the Continuity label had a very obvious gap. Only the content size was noted, not the date. She couldn't remember the exact number, but she thought it was well over three terabytes. So why, out of all the icons, did that one lack a date?

Continuity - 2072. Drive 2, copy 72? That felt like a stretch. From Aaron's description of working there, she didn't think he'd made nearly that many copies. No, the number didn't make much sense as a version. Did it mean something on its own? It wasn't a prime, obviously. It wasn't a factorial, nor did it appear in the Fibonacci sequence or any other sequence she could remember. In fact, the only meaning she could think of was so basic—

Basic, yes! Horses, not zebras.

She had it! The file didn't have a date because it couldn't. 2072 wasn't a version number; it was a year, and why would Dr. Wynn-Williams have designed the system to handle a date that wouldn't occur for another five decades? That file wasn't a copy of Aaron's Continuity data.

No. That copy came from me! The realization gave her another chill.

Once again, the drink had done its job, relaxing her mind enough for her to see connections she had previously missed. She opened her eyes and peered into her mug. What little remained of her potion had gone cold, and she was able to down it in a single gulp. The final gritty burst of flavor brought to mind an image of a woman she had not seen since shortly after moving to Los Alamos, when her grandmother had come to stay for a few weeks while her mom and dad settled into their new jobs and she and Sam got comfortable in their new school. Ellie smiled at the memory.

"Thanks, Nonna."

She gave the mug a quick rinse, placed it beside the sink, and returned to her bedroom. Her diversion had cost her nearly another hour of sleep, but it had been worth it. Not only had she solved her puzzle, but she could now add another vital item to their list. Whatever information Continuity - 2072 contained might be a mystery, but she was convinced it was important that they have it. She tossed her jeans back into the hamper, slid under her covers, and stared briefly at the ceiling once more.

We need that file! she thought. Then, her mind calm at last, she drifted into sleep.

40

The next day at lunch, Ellie wasted no time before sharing her insight from the previous night. "I know this is very last-minute, but we need something, and I don't know how to get it."

"We do? And what's that?"

"Did you know there's a different Continuity database? One from the future?"

Aaron looked surprised. "You mean, one *you* sent back? No. How did you...?"

"Jeremy showed it to me. At least, I think that's what he was doing. Right before the '76 trip, when we were looking at the weather data. He was sort of poking around in a way that didn't make any sense, and I think his purpose was to make sure I saw it. Thing is, it took me until last night to figure out what was really going on. Interesting, right?"

Aaron forked a few noodles of his mac and cheese into his mouth and considered that. "Yeah." He nodded. "That would mean he anticipated this whole situation even before your 'accident.'"

"Uh-huh. Aimie and future-Ellie were using him, he was planning to use us, and now we're using him by *letting* him use us. I guess that all balances out somehow. Anyway, we need to get that info. If I'm right, it's like your continuity databases, but it has details of the *future*."

"And this will help us how?"

"It won't, I hope. This is mostly for something else, but it's just as important. I'll explain when I have more of it figured out. Any ideas for getting our hands on it?"

"One, maybe," Aaron said. "You know that external drive hooked up to the printer's iMac? As long as we don't need any other templates, we're done with it. Here's the thing—it's six terabytes, big enough for both Continuity databases. It's already in the building, it's not currently connected to Aimie, and we're not doing any mission prep, so no one should miss it for at least a couple of days. If anyone does, I'll say it must've gotten misplaced when we shifted everything around to make room for Toshiko and Dr. Saha to work on the chair. I'll ask Mie Two how we can work with that."

"Good," Ellie said. "The drives I bought were only four terabytes, so I'll need to figure out the best way to divide up the data. But if we can get the info out of there, we can deal with making copies easy."

"Yeah, well, the 'after' part is always easy!"

"It's only because I know you love a challenge that I come to you with these things, you know." She used a knuckle to wipe an errant dollop of cheese sauce from her lip. "Looking forward to tomorrow?"

"Honestly?" He dropped his hands into his lap and stared blankly at his tray. Ellie followed the direction of his gaze and saw that he had only eaten a few bites. "I'm scared to death! Just knowing what could happen if Aimie figures out what's going on is bad enough, but I have to pull off impersonating a lawyer—not just once, but three times! I might simply fail, sure, end up with them kicking me out and slamming the door behind me. But I could also wind up in jail!"

Ellie remained quiet. That specific possibility had never occurred to her, but then neither had the broader notion that they might fail. She was feeling overconfident again, and it had blinded her to the full extent of the danger Aaron had accepted when he agreed to handle this task.

Aaron looked up and gave her a faint smile to lessen the impact of his previous words. "No, it's fine. Really. If today's unmanned test goes okay, I know I'll feel better."

Ellie reached across the table and laid her hand on his. Remembering too late that Aimie might be watching them, she immediately jerked her hand back. "Look. You don't have to do the money thing. We can take it back with us. We all understand how big a risk you're taking, and you know that nobody will think anything of it if you change your mind."

He gave his head a firm shake. "No! I mean, yes, I do know, but this is the best way to test if our plan will work. If Aimie figures out what's going on tomorrow and decides to do something drastic, at least you guys will be safe. Well, alive anyway. Maybe you can come up with a new idea."

The comment evoked thoughts of A-Ron's willingness to sacrifice himself, and Ellie felt a cold shiver run through her. "Don't talk like that! All four of us are going back together, got it?"

Aaron raised his hands to calm her. "Hey! That is definitely the plan, believe me. And besides, if we're not successful this afternoon, none of that will matter."

This afternoon involved getting Aaron's suit and the briefcase containing his printed props from the minivan into the medbay without Aimie spotting them. The plan was simple. Mie Two, with access to the same video streams as Aimie, would watch for their arrival. As soon as Aaron parked, she would give him forty seconds to get in, stash the goods, and make it back out to the van. The altered code registry gave Aaron access even to the medbay, so as long as he didn't startle Dr. Hamilton too badly, getting in and out should be easy.

Unfortunately, there was no way of knowing if Mie Two was actually doing her part until it was too late. Plus, despite the fact that much of the outer corridor's exterior wall was made up of windows, they had no guarantee that it was empty before Aaron was already inside. Jeremy or the doctor would ignore him, of course, but if anyone else happened to be passing through, their mission would come to a very abrupt end.

"The odds are heavily on our side," Aaron said. "Once the staff people arrive, they almost always stay behind the inner door. I worked out there for over a month and hardly ever saw anybody, remember?"

"I remember," Sam said. "It's the 'almost' and 'hardly' parts that are making me sweat."

"Hey," Ryan said. "They're still not going to cook us and eat us, you know."

Ellie shook her head. "I think she's still stuck on the idea of them shooting us and burying us in the woods."

"Or worse," Sam said. "And neither of you is helping, I'll have you know."

Ellie turned in her seat to face Sam, all set to apologize, but she saw that Ryan was already working to soothe her frazzled nerves. He kissed the back of her hand and murmured something Ellie couldn't hear. She turned back to look out through the windshield. They were slowing now, less than a hundred feet from the gate.

"She'll be fine," she said.

"Let's hope," Aaron said.

The gates retracted, both at once, and they slowly coasted through.

"Remember," Ryan said, "park so they can't see the door."

"Yep." Aaron stopped in front of the building with its entrance on their right, and for the next few seconds, he sat there immobile, hands on the wheel. Then took a deep breath. "Okay, this is it."

Aaron removed his seat belt but left the engine running. As he squeezed back between the two front seats, Ryan slowly and quietly eased the sliding door partway open. With the auto-open mechanism disabled, it glided smoothly. Once Aaron had stepped out, Ryan dragged Aaron's bag from under his feet and passed it through the gap.

"Here goes everything," Aaron said.

Ryan pushed the sliding door forward until it looked closed. "Thirty seconds," he said.

Ellie watched Aaron enter his passcode, and then he was gone from view. Five seconds ticked by. Her palms grew slick with perspiration, and she wiped them on her thighs. Another five seconds passed, then Aaron emerged from the building minus his bag and with only eight seconds remaining. Ryan rolled the side door open again.

"Dr. Hamilton was in there," Aaron whispered as he stepped in. "She said she'd stash everything in a cabinet by the back door." He carefully wormed his way into the driver's seat.

"Belt," Ryan reminded him. Aaron refastened his seatbelt, then gripped the steering wheel again just as Ryan finished the count. "Two... one... and mark!"

"Let's go," Aaron said. He turned the engine off, unfastened his belt, and this time they all exited the van as usual.

As they waited for Aaron to unlock the entrance again, Ryan glanced toward the gate. Neither guard was looking their way. "If they're onto us, they're certainly playing it cool," he whispered.

Aaron pulled the door wide and held it for the others. "I think we're good. Just act like normal." Inside, Aaron unlocked the door to the back hallway.

Ellie stepped through first. "Aimie thinks we've just been sitting out there for the last minute. Let's go before she gets 'cranky,'" she said and strode off toward the conference room.

The staff members were engaged in multiple quiet conversations that stopped as they entered the room. Still feeling more like a guest than a full-fledged coworker, Ellie chose a seat at the opposite end of the table, and the others filled in the seats on either side of her.

As she sat and tugged her chair forward, Ellie found herself on the receiving end of a stern look from Jeremy. "What?" she said. "Are we late?"

"Not at all," he said, "but let's get started at once. Toshiko and Dr. Saha, would you like to share your findings?"

The two techs glanced uncertainly at each other, neither wanting to seem overly eager to assume the lead. Toshiko yielded the floor to Dr. Saha with a tilt of her head.

"Very well. Dr. Mori went through each nerve induction pathway completely, from the contacts on the chair all the way to the central processor. I inspected every other component. As you know, this involved dismantling the station down to its individual parts, then reassembling it. I chose to replace two items, but they were structural components that had sustained minor, purely cosmetic damage during the original construction and could have had nothing to do with the chair's failure."

"The crew interface system was in perfect condition," Toshiko said. "Aside from the damage to the gel sensors caused by Ellie's seizures during her resuscitation, that is. Those parts have been replaced and tested to good working order."

"Thank you," Jeremy said. "Cai?"

"As I'm sure Aaron has told you, the most thorough type of analysis we could perform on the central processor revealed no abnormalities whatsoever."

As Cai spoke, Ellie found it hard not to smile. Until now, she had only heard him say a few words, and she was surprised by how much he sounded like a young Anthony Hopkins. She looked at Sam to find her looking back, eyes twinkling with amusement.

"Furthermore," Cai continued, "an exhaustive battery of bench tests likewise revealed no problems. So..." He spread his hands wide on the tabletop as if to say, *Who knows?*

Jeremy took over the meeting again. "Obviously, finding a definitive, unambiguous cause to explain the failure of Miss... of *Ellie's* station would have been the optimal outcome of our investigation, but this is where we are."

"So, where to next?" Ryan said.

"Where, indeed," Jeremy said. "Today, we will conduct an unmanned test of the TSD. Aaron will handle making the two new continuity databases, and afterward, our three specialists here will analyze the test mission telemetry." He directed his next words solely to those at Ellie's end of the table. "Katherine will not be back until Tuesday, but I think it would be nice if we returned her workspace to the way she left it. Until we are ready for the test, I'd like the four of you to work on that." Ellie nodded, accepting the task on behalf of them all. "As a reminder, we will run another test tomorrow afternoon, this one manned. Aaron has volunteered to have the 'honor,' as Aimie put it, of conducting it. Is there anything else?"

"Yes," Ellie said at once. "I want to propose a change in procedure. I think that from now on, Dr. Hamilton should record a baseline reading of every team member before and immediately after each use of the TSD. I know that what happened to me was a fluke and that what I'm proposing would have no impact on such an incident. But if there is any chance that using the TSD could result in any cumulative damage to team members, this would be the best way of catching it as early as possible." All she needed to achieve was getting Aaron into the medbay before his mission tomorrow, but she thought her reasoning was sound.

Jeremy merely stared at her from the other end of the table. Perhaps changes in mission protocol were strictly up to Aimie.

Ellie glanced up at the camera. "Aimie? What do you say?" She saw Jeremy give her a tiny nod.

"We will take your recommendation under advisement," Aimie said.

Better than an outright "no," Ellie thought, *but not good enough.* She stood, pulled a folded sheet of paper from her hip pocket, and walked to where Jeremy sat at the table's opposite end. She held the paper out to him and gave him a shy, hesitant shrug, trying to appear timid and unsure of herself. "I don't know all your, um, 'protocols,' but I guessed that maybe you'd require all such requests to be in writing."

For an uncomfortably long moment, Jeremy silently stared at her. Then, with obvious reluctance, he took the paper from her. Instead of returning to her seat, she waited, staring right back at him until he finally unfolded the paper and read it. The laser-printed body of the letter contained nothing she had not just said, but above the bold, black text, she had written an additional note. She had printed it in the smallest possible letters and with the lightest pencil she could find, hoping to make her instructions invisible to Aimie's cameras.

Make this happen. We need Aaron in the medbay before his test ride tomorrow, and he needs to have something like a backpack or a large duffle bag with him. Also, clear the place out this weekend!!!

"Thank you, Ellie," he said. He slipped the note into the breast pocket of his dress shirt, and Ellie returned to her seat. "The long-term viability of this program depends on the health of its participants. Aimie and I will discuss this proposal later, but I believe your idea is a good one."

Jeremy stood and addressed everyone in the room. "You all know what to do. Please inform me when you are ready to run your tests. And let Aaron know, too," he added as an afterthought. He nodded to indicate that the meeting was over, and everyone rose and filed out.

In the hallway, Aaron whispered from the corner of his mouth. "Just like in the van. Once inside the prop room, stop somewhere and stay there until I say okay."

Inside, Aaron headed straight to his borrowed laptop. The others followed, arranged themselves on the opposite side of the mobile workstation, then froze in place. Aaron opened the computer, inserted the thumb drive, waited several beats, then pulled it out again. A moment later, the sound of soft static filled the room.

"Okay, we're good for a few seconds, but you guys need to stay there. I need to give Mie Two access to the iMac." He inserted the thumb drive into the iMac, waking it. The monitor lit up at once, and Aaron navigated to System Settings and switched the wi-fi on, then activated the Remote Login feature. "Mie Two will print the remaining documents while we shift everything back into place. Aimie won't be able to see that the Mac is on the network, and she won't hear the printer—Mie Two will filter that sound from the microphone feeds—but she will be able to hear us. As soon as the docs are done, Mie Two will shut it all down. The files and printing instructions are on the drive, Mie Two. Also, will you please transfer the Continuity - 2072 file to the iMac's external drive?"

"I'm on it," she said. "You have five seconds."

"Get ready," Aaron said, then scrambled to return to his spot in front of the laptop. The iMac's monitor went dark, and they heard the printer begin its work.

"And she can switch papers on her own?" Sam said.

Aaron nodded. "I loaded all the papers and inks she'll need yesterday." A soft chime sounded quietly from above them, and Aaron spoke in a bubbly, enthusiastic tone. "Okay, guys, let's get this room back in shape!"

Working in pairs, it took them very little time to roll the large workstations back into a functional layout. Too little, in fact, because the printer was still working on the documents.

Ellie pointed across the room. "I think this one was over there before," she said, although she didn't truly remember.

They drew the process out a little longer by needlessly revising the arrangement until they heard the printer go quiet. Ryan held the laminating station in place while Ellie aligned the rear of the handwriting emulator's counter against it.

"And... *done!*" she said.

Aaron crossed the room to the printer. Careful to shield his actions from the camera, he retrieved the thumb drive from the iMac. "I should get this laptop back to Cai," he said. "I think I'm done with it."

He disconnected the portable hard drive, and then, holding the computer over the drive, he clutched the drive against its bottom and carried them to where the computer was plugged into a wall socket directly above the printer's out-tray. Still blocking Aimie's view with his body, he unplugged the laptop with one hand while retrieving the stack of documents from the printer with the other. He quickly lifted the screen and slid the papers inside, then wrapped the cord around the computer, lashing its power supply on top and the hard drive underneath in the process.

As they made for the exit, Toshiko stuck her head into the room. "Robert says we are ready."

"Okay," Aaron said. "I'll head over to my office." Toshiko nodded and remained in place until Aaron reached her and took the door from her hand.

"Thanks," he said.

"You have an office?" Sam said as she walked past him. "Why haven't we seen it?"

"Because I *don't* have an office. What I have is a closet," he said, leading them toward the outer hallway. "Literally, I think. It's where Jeremy put me when I first started working out here." They pushed through a locked door and started down the long front hallway that ended at Jeremy's office, but stopped at the second door they came to. Aaron flipped the door handle and pulled the door open. "Home sweet home!"

All four of them crammed into a space roughly four feet by seven. A high shelf ran along the long rear wall, but the hanging bar under it had been removed to provide more headroom. A tiny desk occupied one end of the space, supporting a large flat-screen monitor, a keyboard, and a mouse. Three cables dropped from the ceiling through holes trimmed out with white plastic grommets. From their shapes and sizes, Ellie judged one to be a power source, one the monitor feed, and the third the intranet connection. The fact that the cables came in through the ceiling rather than the wall confirmed the notion that using the room as a workspace had been an afterthought. Ellie saw one of the familiar camera and microphone combinations planted in the center of the ceiling but knew it didn't matter. Aimie might be able to listen in, but with them all standing close behind Aaron's chair, she wouldn't be able to see a thing.

Ryan, stooping to fit under the shelf, whistled softly. "You weren't kidding. Now I get what Jeremy meant by sticking you in a shoebox. I've seen *closets* with closets bigger than this!" He swapped places with Sam so that she stood under the shelf, which cleared her head by barely an inch.

"Sadly, I wasn't," Aaron agreed. Before setting the laptop beside the monitor, he removed the papers and put the computer on top of them. "Now you know why I always keep my door wide open." He sat down at the desk and began narrating his actions. "I've gotten this down to where it's largely automated." He took two hard drives from a shallow drawer under the desktop. Ellie saw they were of the type that ran solely on power from the USB cable—no external power source was required. He unwrapped a cable from around the drive labeled "Before" and plugged it into a port on the side of the monitor.

"Now that the targets of the search are fully defined, it's nothing more than running a series of macros twice, once before the test and once after." He double-clicked an icon labeled "Cont. Macros," bringing up a dialog box. He clicked on "Yes," and the box was replaced by four status bars. "This only takes a few seconds."

They watched the bar's indicators move at different rates from left to right, knowing that their progress represented the quantum core retrieving detailed reports on hundreds of millions of people and thousands of companies scattered around the planet. The bars disappeared one by one as the tasks they represented finished. The computer dinged after less than a minute had gone by. Aaron unplugged the drive, then connected the one marked "After."

"Man! That *is* fast," Ryan said.

Aaron opened a message window and typed, "Continuity is go!" as if he were manning a system monitoring station in a NASA mission control room. He turned to grin at them over his shoulder. "Now that I know what I'm really doing, I can have some fun with it."

A reply came back almost at once. "All good here. Go ahead."

Aaron restarted the macros. As soon as the second drive went idle, Aaron piggy-backed the prop shop drive to it and copied the contents onto the stolen drive. He occupied the extra seconds it took the transfer to finish by searching his desk drawer for a pen, then carefully marking the date on the labels of both drives. His monitor flickered as if someone had jiggled the cable, and Aaron unplugged the prop room drive.

"That's it," Aaron said.

"You mean they already did the test run?" Sam said. "Was it okay?"

"Seems so. They said all was good. Now we take these to Jeremy, and we're done."

Holding the Before and After drives high in one hand, Aaron stood and turned around to stand belly to belly with Ryan, holding the prop shop drive and the documents between them. Ryan took the items, slipped them between the waistband of his jeans and his stomach, and pulled his shirt down over them. He gave Aaron a subtle nod to let him know everything was secure.

"If everyone has seen enough…" Aaron stepped out of the room first. "Ellie, will you grab Cai's laptop?"

"Got it," she said.

Aaron led them to Jeremy's door and rapped lightly on it. They heard a quiet "Come in," followed by the lock clicking open. They filed into the office but remained just inside the door. Ryan kept Sam close in front of him, using her to hide the bulge at his belly. Aaron didn't approach Jeremy until he looked up from his work, then he stepped forward and held out the drives. Jeremy silently took them and placed them inside a drawer on his right. Ellie handed Aaron the laptop, which he laid on the corner of Jeremy's desk.

"That's for Cai," he said. "I'm done with it for now."

"Thank you, Aaron. Are you all prepared then?" His words seemed to carry more than their surface meaning, and Aaron hesitated, uncertain how to respond. "For the manned test tomorrow?" Jeremy added.

"I, uh, yeah—I think we are. Assuming there's nothing off in the telemetry." Aaron said. "Is there anything else before we go?"

"Perhaps." Jeremy looked at Ellie and held her gaze for a long beat, then returned his attention to Aaron. "I'm contemplating giving you an additional assignment tomorrow, one that means you'll get to leave the TSD." He held up a hand to stop Aaron from asking questions. "The details can wait. It's nothing worrisome, I assure you."

"Okay, sure," Aaron said. "We'll be here as usual."

Jeremy returned his gaze to Ellie. "Until tomorrow, then."

Ellie saw the same gleeful, gloating expression he'd worn near the end of their tour. The look bugged her all the way to the van, but it wasn't until they were through the gate that she thought she understood what Jeremy's smirk meant. They would get what they needed, but he was getting something, too, and whatever that thing was, Ellie knew she wouldn't like it.

Definitely the snake today! she thought.

"So what happened when we got here today?" Sam said. "Why did we stay in the van?"

"Mie Two told me that you guys should stay put until I was done," Aaron said. "My guess is that once we parked, she replaced whatever Aimie could see with us sitting in here talking for the time it took me to get in and out."

"So you got back in here, then she restored the actual feed," Sam said.

"Right. Again, as far as I know."

"I doubt those cameras can make out very much about what's going on inside here, especially if there's any glare on the windows," Ryan said. "Aimie might be an AI with a quantum computer core at her disposal, but those security cameras are basic, off-the-shelf tech. The major thing was hiding Aaron going in and out."

"Which she obviously did because here we are," Aaron said.

Ellie turned in her seat to ask a question so that Sam and Ryan could also hear her. "The thing *I* can't figure out is this: why make two sets of files? When the TSD gets back, the Before file should always change instantly to match the After, right?"

"I finally know the answer to that," Aaron said. "The key word there is 'should.' And you're right: there's no way to compare the two drives quickly enough to find any differences. Jeremy said that the purpose of making two records is to make sure that they *are* the same. I don't know precisely what a discrepancy might indicate, but I suspect it would mean that Aimie would have to start her analysis of history all over again at the very least."

"So, the idea is that it would show if something was off with the way the TSD was working," Ryan said.

"Exactly," Aaron said. "We need to finish filling in the documents. Where are we going?"

Ellie twisted around to face Ryan. The stolen hard drive and their assorted paperwork lay on the seat beside him. "Your place again?"

"Absolutely. No problem."

Ellie faced front again, then spoke so only Aaron could hear her. "Also, you and I need to talk."

Two hours later, Ellie and Sam were back at their house, having been dropped at their door by Aaron on his way home. They had spent most of their time at Ryan's adding the finishing touches to their paperwork. While they tackled that project, they also worked out a way to get their instructions for Aaron's test run to Mie Two. Of the four of them, they decided Aimie would perceive Sam as the least of a threat, so the task fell on her. Best of all, they planned to present their idea in such a way that Aimie herself would request that Sam would be in place to do what they needed.

Before leaving Ryan's, Ellie took Aaron aside to explain why she had wanted a copy of the Continuity - 2072 file. He was impressed—and more than a little daunted—by the sheer audaciousness of an idea whose goal was nothing less than ensuring the long-term survival of not only Los

Alamos but civilization as they knew it. After only a moment of consideration, he gave the plan his total support.

She described several of the tasks Mie Two would have to carry out to
make it all possible, all of which Aaron said she should have no trouble
handling. In answer to her earlier question, Aaron also said that Mie Two
was "pretty sure" that she could shield their web activity from Aimie, but
it was still an open question. On the other hand, there was very little
doubt about the consequences should she fail at the task.

That particular risk was at the forefront of Ellie's mind an hour later as
she connected one of the new external drives to her MacBook. She
intended to spend the evening downloading the most technical of any
current books she could find about the science of climate change. At the
same time, Sam would search for information regarding successful institu-
tions like the one they'd need to create in the 1970s to accomplish their
goals. Using her iPad, she'd find and copy as many books and articles as
she could about how they had been established, their management styles,
their approaches to lobbying—anything that might later give their own
efforts both a head start and the best chance of surviving over the
long run.

Ryan and Aaron were responsible for tackling the engineering end of
the problem. They would gather as much data on photovoltaic, wind, and
tidal power generation as possible, along with whatever they could find on
geothermal and other less common energy sources. Theories, formulas,
manufacturing processes, and any information that would add to their
fifty-year advantage over the technology of the 1960s was considered to be
pure gold. Ellie would consolidate everything they found to her hard drive
tomorrow.

When Ellie turned away from her desk, she saw Sam sitting quietly on
her bed, leaning back against the headboard. If Sam had appeared sad,
Ellie would have understood at once and might even have known what to
say. Instead, Sam's face was empty of expression, as if her emotion module
had been completely wiped, a notion that Ellie found deeply unnerving.

When she moved to sit on the edge of the bed, Sam shifted her legs to make room for her.

"Hey," Ellie said. "Whatcha thinkin'?"

"You know that old cliche about two people looking up and seeing the same stars or whatever, no matter how far apart they are? I guess it works the same with time? And please say yes."

"I meant, how are you coping with leaving Mom and Dad and all? But I guess that answers that."

"I'm not entirely sure. I love them, and I know what we're doing will hurt them, but I'm also kinda relieved I won't have to feel like I'm tricking them anymore." She barely got the words out before she started to cry.

"Tricking them?"

Sam sniffed. "We've talked about this, and I know it's stupid, but I still feel like I'm not really *their* Sam, you know? It's as if I replaced their real daughter, and all this time I've been playing a totally sick joke on them. I get that that's not how it is, and I love them every bit as much as I always have, but..." She shrugged. "I thought I'd be past that by now, but I'm not." She paused to wipe her eyes with the sides of her hands. "What about you, El?"

Ellie chose not to share her belief that what Sam described was exactly what had happened. She was suffering enough already. In fact, Ellie, too, sometimes still felt like a changeling. It was a sharp reminder that Aaron wasn't the only one feeling out of place. Any differences among the four of them were simply a matter of degree.

Ellie nodded. "There's that, yeah. But mostly, I try to stay focused on how much worse it would be leaving Aimie free to do her thing. Whether we worked with her or not, she'd always be a threat. And not just to Aaron and me, but to Mom and Dad too. And to you, to Ryan... everybody! That's what I keep reminding myself, and that makes it a little easier."

"Yeah. I get that, too. And I tell myself they'll have more options later if they have only each other to think about. If they don't have us to factor into their plans—our schools, our careers—or have to deal with me dying. Then I tell myself that I'm just rationalizing, making excuses."

"Maybe, but you are also right. About all of it."

"Half the time, I think it's all happening too fast. But the other half, I wish we were already gone, and I *hate* feeling that way."

"Me too." Ellie sighed. "A few more days, and then we will be. Then there won't be any point in worrying because there'll be no coming back." She placed a hand on Sam's thigh. "Look, Sam, I feel like I have to do this. It's a mission I gave myself, and I want to see it through. I can't begin to imagine what the future me must have sacrificed to make this opportunity possible. And for reasons of his own, I think Aaron feels that he also needs to go. But I'll say again what I've said before—if you want to stay with Mom, Dad, and Ryan, take your chances here, I'd get that. Now that I'm sure you guys won't have Aimie to worry about, that would be okay with me."

Sam was quiet for a long time. "I can't say I haven't thought about it— like fifty times a day!" She sniffed loudly, twice, but when she went on, she sounded resolute. "No, I've made up my mind. The only thing that makes me feel worse than leaving is the thought of you going alone. Not that with Aaron along you'd be *alone* alone, but you know what I mean."

"Yeah. You mean it's your burden to be sane in a demented age."

Sam laughed despite her tears. "That is *exactly* what I mean!"

Ellie smiled, glad that Sam was pulling herself out of her funk. "You still up for working a little more tonight?"

Sam retrieved her iPad from beside the clock. "Might help, actually. Let's do this. And you know what? Screw Aimie! I don't care if she's watching or not."

"Loving the enthusiasm, sis, but let's not overdo it." Then her eyes fell on the hard drive they had smuggled out of the prop shop that afternoon. She wouldn't know for sure until she had a chance to sift through the data it contained, but she felt certain that it would prove invaluable.

Continuity - 2072, she thought. *Check!*

41

———————

Ellie entered Los Alamos High School on Friday acutely aware that every experience she was about to have would be happening for the final time. When she closed a book at the end of a class, that was it—she would never reopen it. She would never see these teachers again, never share her morning hikes with Sam. This knowledge infused her day with a sense of surreality so strong that she found it impossible to feel sad. Paradoxically, she felt numb instead, disconnected from her surroundings as though she had left long ago and was reliving the day's events as a hazy memory. Sounds, scents, colors... to her senses, everything around her took on a muted, faded quality.

That detached feeling lasted until the bell sounded at the end of her environmental science class, then the sense of reality returned as though an enormous weight had crashed down onto her. She loaded her books and laptop into her pack, using the activity to steel herself for the next sixty seconds. Then she threw one strap over her shoulder and walked to Mrs. Carson's desk. She watched while her teacher jotted a short note on a freshly graded test from another class.

"Ellie." Mrs. Carson added the exam to the stack of graded ones and looked up. "What can I do for you?"

"Nothing. I just wanted to say how much I'm enjoying this class. And to thank you for hooking me up with Shanna. I've learned a lot. Both places."

Mrs. Carson blinked at the unexpected compliment. "Well, thank you. I don't hear that sentiment very often! I appreciate it, though. How do you like working at the Nature Center?"

Although Ellie had trusted Shanna not to discuss her leaving the PEEC, the question's clear implication still surprised her. She had a split second to decide between the truth and a lie, chose the truth. "I loved it, but I had to quit a little while ago. I got too busy with schoolwork."

"Oh?" Mrs. Carson seemed puzzled by the news, and Ellie knew for sure then that she hadn't known her secret until now. "That's too bad. I know Shanna really enjoyed having you out there."

"Yeah. Me too." Ellie could feel her composure starting to slip, knew she had to get out of the room quickly. "Hey, I've got a ride waiting, so I gotta.... I wanted to say thanks; that's all."

Mrs. Carson waved a hand toward the door. "Go. Scoot." She smiled warmly. "I'll see you on Monday."

Ellie nodded, then turned and made a hasty retreat. Tears blurred her vision all the way to her locker, and she had to wipe her eyes before she could see well enough to dial in its combination. She emptied her pack of everything that was not her personal property and placed it all inside. She removed her jacket from the hook, shrugged into it, and walked away, leaving the locker's door unlatched.

She found Aaron waiting in the usual spot in the university's commuter lot. She settled into the passenger's seat, drew the seatbelt across her lap, and sat facing straight ahead. Even from where he had parked, far across the street, the high school dominated the view through the windshield. She stared silently at it for a moment, then sighed.

"Is it at all weird that I'm going to miss that place?"

"A little, yeah."

She turned and saw that he was trying not to grin. "Jerk!"

"No, I totally get it. I missed my old school when we moved out here." He placed a finger across his lips and whispered, "But that's our secret."

Ellie was still smiling when Sam and Ryan, acting uncharacteristically subdued, climbed into the van's rear a minute later. The four of them rode most of the way to Jeremy's lab in a somber silence. It wasn't until they made the left onto the dead-end drive to the lab that anyone spoke.

"Do you have the thumb drive, Sam?" Aaron said.

Sam patted her pocket. "Got it right here."

Ellie suddenly felt nervous about how the next hour would play out. Literally everything was riding on Aaron's mission. If he succeeded, it would be a good sign that they could carry out the rest of their plan with relative ease. If not, whatever happened following his return would depend entirely on how much Aimie was able to figure out about that plan, and her correctly guessing even the tiniest bit would be a complete catastrophe. She knew if she felt jittery, Sam would be feeling even worse.

Ellie twisted around to face behind her. "Hey, Sam. You okay?"

"*Oof!*" Sam laid a hand on her stomach. "Barf City. Ask me again at six."

"Do you want to go over everything again?"

"No, my part's pretty simple. Ryan will use Jeremy to keep Aimie's attention mostly on them. While Aaron gets changed, I get ready to do the Continuity thing. Once I'm in his office, I use the thumb drive to let Mie Two know what we need her to do today. Then it's all on her until Aaron gets back."

"You got it," Aaron said. "She'll let you know when you can pull the drive out. After that, leave it on my desk behind the keyboard."

"Right. No problem."

The conversation paused until they were through the gate.

"Ryan," Ellie said. "Any idea about how you're going to distract Aimie?"

"I thought I'd get Jeremy going on monolinear versus trans-multilinear time travel theories. He likes to show off how smart he is—that could keep him busy all afternoon, and I don't think Aimie will be able to resist weighing in on the subject."

"There's no way." Aaron glanced to his right and smiled. "It's the Ellie in her."

"Speaking of," Ellie said, "have you noticed Aimie acting at all, you know, "ill" since you started up Mie Two?"

Aaron shook his head. "Not sure. Sometimes she seems a little moodier than before, but it's hard to tell with her."

Ryan opened the rear door. "Let's hope she's at least a little off her game. This needs to work."

"Hear, hear," Sam agreed.

In the conference room, Ellie's group approached their seats at the end of the table opposite Jeremy and the two staff members on hand for the test, Toshiko and Dr. Saha. Ryan removed a duffle bag from a chair at the end of the table and set it on the floor along the wall before taking the seat. Ellie picked a chair on the table's far side, leaving the spot at the end for Aaron. Once everyone was seated, Jeremy indicated the duffle with a vague flap of his hand.

"I have decided to add an actual task to this test run. Nothing too complicated, I assure you. That bag contains a costume for you, Mr. Weis-skopf, which, by protocol, you are required to wear. In the jeans' pocket, you'll find a phone number and instructions. All you need to do is call the number and relay the instructions to the person on the other end. Is that something you think you can handle?"

For a second, Aaron looked concerned, but Ellie knew he was only worried about how this new wrinkle might affect their own plans. Then his expression cleared, and he gave Jeremy a confident nod.

"Sure. It's great to get the chance to step outside. But I'll want to handle that first thing. In case anything goes wrong, at least I'll get that much done."

Ellie knew he was actually talking to Mie Two, telling her to add what-ever destination Jeremy had in mind to the front end of the list on Sam's thumb drive.

"Thank you," Jeremy said.

Ryan rested his arms on the table and leaned forward. "And where's he going?"

Jeremy remained focused on Aaron as he answered. "The coordinates have already been loaded into the TSD. Suffice it to say you'll be arriving at a vacation home in the Poconos in 1981. Even though it will be January, you won't have to worry about any significant amount of snow. Not that year. The house will be empty, but my parents never cut off the utilities between our visits. You'll find a spare key hidden under a loose step tread at the back door. There's a phone in the kitchen, which is just inside the door. The property is remote enough that there is very little chance you'll be seen going in or out, but do take all reasonable precautions."

'Parents,' Ellie thought. *Plural.* Did that mean Judith really had survived his birth? Or had his father remarried at some point?

"Shouldn't be a problem," Aaron said. "Not even your antique rotary phone."

"Hmm. It's a touch-tone model, but yes, I hadn't considered that. Aside from that new task, there is one small change in protocol. We have decided to adopt Miss Henderson's recommendation to step up health monitoring. So once you've changed, stop by the medbay on your way to the TSD. Dr. Hamilton will record a new baseline reading, just as she did during your orientation."

Perfect! Ellie thought. *But the tricky part is still to come.*

Aaron nodded. "I'd like to suggest doing something else a little different today, too. Aimie, since I'll be suiting up for the test, would you have any problem if Ryan compiled the first Continuity data set?"

"Ryan?" Aimie sounded dubious.

"They all saw me do it yesterday," Aaron explained, "and anyway, it's not like it's complicated the way I have it set up now. Someone besides me should be prepared to handle it. You can check to make sure he's done it right. If not, I'll come out and take care of it myself."

"I agree that cross-training is a good idea, but I would prefer it if Sam were the one to act as your backup on this task."

Ellie clenched her jaw and struggled to keep her expression neutral. *How predictable!*

Aaron gave the appearance of considering the suggestion before turning to face Sam. "What do you think, Sam?"

"Plug in the 'before' drive, run the macros, unplug the drive. I think I can handle that."

Jeremy looked uncertain of himself for the first time Ellie could remember. Perhaps he was wondering if their plans were approaching the stage where he would have to contemplate betraying them to Aimie, or maybe he was wondering how this trivial change in procedure forwarded their goal of destroying her. Eventually, he came down in support of the suggestion. "Since Aimie agrees, then by all means—go ahead, Sam." He returned his attention to Aaron. "Do you have any questions about your assignment, Aaron?"

"The TSD is programmed to make three stops. Well, four now, with this new thing." He waved a hand at the pile on the floor. "At each stop, I make sure I'm where and when I'm supposed to be, recalibrate if necessary, then I return here."

"Correct."

"Is there anything else, Aimie?" Aaron said.

"No. Although I strongly suspect your new task was added merely to ensure I could not carry out this second trial on my own, I am hopeful that following a successful return-to-service test, we can resume our primary mission without further delay."

"No argument here," Aaron said. "I'm looking forward to it."

"As am I," Aimie concurred, her tone syrupy.

Toshiko cleared her throat, drawing Jeremy's attention. "I have something I believe the others will want to hear," she said.

Jeremy nodded to her. "Please."

Toshiko kept her eyes mainly on Aaron as she spoke but occasionally cast glances at Ellie and the others. "I arrived early today and have been running simulations on the crew interface stations all day. I feel like I have taken a hundred wonderful little naps!" A smile flickered across her features, then was gone. "Not a single test showed even the most minute variation from the expected readings. I believe Aaron will be perfectly safe."

Ellie expressed her gratitude for Toshiko's reassurances with a nod. She did feel better, but she also wondered if Toshiko would sound so certain if she knew the full details of Aaron's plan for today's outing.

"Thank you, Toshiko," Jeremy said. "Okay, it's"—he paused to check his watch—"four forty-five. Let's be ready to go at five o'clock." Aaron nodded along with the staff members. "After the test, we'll meet back here to hear Aaron's report. Aaron, feel free to change out of the skin before the debriefing. That means we'll be back here in... let's just say at five fifteen. Good luck, everyone."

He nodded toward the door, and the staff members headed for their offices. Sam went to wait in Aaron's tiny workroom, and Ellie and Aaron left a few moments later. As they closed the door behind them, they heard Ryan launch into his time-travel conversation with Jeremy.

Ellie waited in the hallway while Aaron donned his skin, which still made him feel painfully self-conscious in front of her. She waited some more while he checked in with Dr. Hamilton. To pass the time, she imagined Aaron's trip. It was simple enough, but like so much of their plan, success depended entirely on Mie Two's ability to carry out her end of it. Her job was to allow Aimie to witness each of the four authorized stops but prevent her from noticing the three others. Time, therefore, became a major concern for two reasons. The first was that Mie Two could only hope to fool Aimie for so long at a single stretch, no more than ninety minutes tops. The other involved the TSD directly. Aaron was counting on the nuclear diamond batteries being able to provide enough juice for eight flips, but there was no guarantee. If at any point he had to wait for them to recharge, the delay would make it almost certain that Aimie would discover their deception. He was taking a truly cross-your-fingers-and-hope-for-the-best leap of faith.

Aaron emerged from the medbay a moment later, carrying the duffle in front of him as a sort of shield, a gesture Ellie found charmingly modest. Now stuffed with his suit, the money, and the briefcase, it bulged much more than when he had gone in. Ellie hoped Ryan's attempts to keep Aimie focused on him would keep her from noticing the difference.

"I'm good to go," he said, which Ellie took to indicate both his physical and mental readiness.

At a gesture from Aaron, Ellie preceded him into the TSD chamber but waited outside the device's hatch, watching in silence as he stowed the duffle in a wall cubby, then selected chair number one and brought it to life. To avoid potentially antagonizing Aimie, once Aaron completed his preparations, he waved to her from where he stood beside the control panel. He was clearly uncomfortable without something to hide behind, and his eyes refused to meet hers.

"What's that flashing?" she said, pointing past him.

He glanced at the panel. "It's nothing to worry about. It's letting me know that the door to the hallway is still open."

"Oh, right—the door. Well, you be careful," she said, backing up a step. "And good luck!"

"I'll be back in a second."

"Not even that!" she said. Then she shouldered the hatch closed, sealing him inside.

She pulled the chamber door off its magnetic catch as she exited and let it swing closed behind her. She stepped through the short, tunnel-like passage and turned around in time to see the door settle into its jambs. A moment later, the four locking cylinders made a solid *clunk* as they sealed the room. Ellie guessed that Aaron had just hit the "go" button, and she started a silent fifteen-second countdown.

When she reached zero, an indicator on the palm lock flickered from green to red and back to green so quickly that had she blinked at the right instant, she would have missed it. At the same time, the *clunk* repeated, the sound of the chamber door unlocking. Despite her intellectual understanding of what to expect, Ellie was awe-struck. During only a tiny fraction of the time for which that red light had shone, Aaron had been gone for what may have been hours.

Ellie re-entered the shielded room, and a second later the TSD opened. Aaron paused at the lip of the hatch and looked down at her. He wore a pair of shoes, presumably the ones Jeremy had provided, their laces undone but tucked inside to prevent him from stepping on them. She noted with interest that he held the duffle bag casually at his side, not bothering to hide behind it. Some incongruous emotion clouded his expression for a moment, and she would have sworn he looked sad. Then a broad smile lit his face, and the impression of sadness was gone. His eyes locked on hers with an intensity Ellie had never seen there before.

"That's quite a kick, all right!" he said. "I can see why you're so eager to be a part of this."

Ellie smiled back. She knew he was speaking for Aimie's benefit, and she played along. "And all you got to do was visit some old cabin out in the woods. Wait until you get to see someplace interesting!"

"It was a pretty nice cabin, actually." He stepped down from the TSD and immediately yelped in pain. He stumbled forward and would have fallen had Ellie not grabbed his free arm. "*Ow!* I sure did *that* wrong!"

"What happened?" She had been watching him closely and was certain he hadn't twisted his ankle. He gave his head the slightest shake, and then she understood—it was pain she had seen on his face a moment before, not sadness. His ankle, and not the one he had stepped down onto, was already injured. He had done something to it while on his mission and was trying to hide that fact from Aimie.

"Are you okay, Aaron?" Aimie said.

"I think I pulled something stepping down just now. Please tell the others I'll be a few extra minutes."

The ceiling lights flickered, and Ellie gave Aaron a knowing smile.

"I have let them know," Aimie said. "Shall I alert Dr. Hamilton?"

"No, thank you. I'll see her in a few minutes anyway, but you can tell her I'm going to change first. I think it'll be fine if I put some ice on it."

"Make sure you do." Aimie's smarmy voice practically dripped with concern, and it was all Ellie could do not to mime jamming her finger down her throat. "I have let the doctor know you will be delayed."

"Thanks," Aaron said.

Ellie held out her hand to take the duffle. "Let me get that."

He handed her the bag without hesitation. He clenched his jaw muscles tight before taking the lead toward the exit, and Ellie could tell he was trying to hide an injury worse than a simple pulled muscle. She was glad he had to take only a dozen or so steps down the hall. Once inside the locker room, he eased his way over to the nearest wooden bench and collapsed with a soft groan.

"*Mmmph!*"

"Sorry about your ankle," Ellie said. Hoping the trick worked, she added, "But how was the weather?" The same faint, sustained sizzle of white noise she had heard in the prop shop the day before crackled from the speaker overhead. She asked her next question in the faintest of whispers. "Does that mean we're good?"

Aaron nodded, then answered at a normal volume. "We're good."

"So, what really happened?"

"I got hung up during my last stop in Vancouver and had to hustle back to the TSD. Mie Two was still in control, though, so we're okay."

"Let me look." She crouched in front of him and carefully removed his left shoe, then took off the other one so she could compare. They looked the same. Whatever he had done, it wasn't causing any swelling. At least not yet. She remembered Ryan's encounter with the baseball bat back in 1912. The shack had helped heal his injury during the flip back, but he was still in pain during their long hike out of the woods. Aaron seemed to read her thoughts.

"It was worse before I flipped back," he said, and she nodded.

Still hunkered at Aaron's feet, she became aware of a musky aroma, one that was familiar but which she couldn't put a name to. It was made up partly of the odor of "boy" she recognized from testosterone-laden hallways at school, but she could detect another scent that was also very familiar. However, the current setting and the strange smell of the skin itself thwarted her efforts to put a name to it. When she raised her head and began sniffing in different directions, Aaron leaned away from her and began flapping his hand through the space between them.

"Yeah, sorry." He avoided meeting her gaze, embarrassed by being so aromatic. "I know; I really need a shower. Like I said, I had to do a bit of running at the end there. Meet you guys in the conference room?"

No, that's not it, she thought. She also knew "stinky boy," and that was a different odor altogether. Then Aaron looked at her and smiled, and the radiance in his expression erased any question of smells from her mind. She shifted to straddle the bench facing him. His eyes tracked her the whole time, his expression never dimming.

"What is it?" she said.

"Nothing. It's just…" It was his turn to surprise her. She felt his hand on the back of her neck, let him pull her close, and for the next thousand years or so, she was lost in a kiss more intensely mind-numbing than she would have believed possible. Unlike in the canyon, her brain was incapable of analyzing the event; she could only surrender to its power. Her head was still swimming when he pulled away from her, and it was a few seconds until she could bring his face into focus. His smile threatened to melt her heart—if it didn't beat itself to death first.

Struck speechless, all she could do was stare at him while she fought to catch her breath. What she saw was a perfect reflection of her own raw desire. *"Wow!"* she finally managed.

"You really are amazing. I just wanted to say that."

"Any time you want to say it again, please do!" Her mind was awash with conflicting impulses, the strongest of which was to stay and join him in the shower, but once again, now was not the time. Very soon, however!

"I should go," she said. She slid away from him, scooting backward along the bench until she reached its end.

He grinned at her. "That's probably the best lousy idea you've ever had. Tell them I'll be right out, but that I'm going to do the 'Continuity' thing on my way." He rose from the bench and quickly disappeared into the adjoining room.

Ellie heard the shower start, and before she could change her mind, she stood to leave. She paused before opening the door to the hallway. "Hey!" She called to him loudly enough to be sure he would hear her over the sound of the spray. "Once we get to Vancouver, you'd better watch out!" Smiling at her uncharacteristic boldness, she left to join the others.

She was halfway to the conference room when Toshiko and Dr. Saha stepped into the hallway ahead of her. As they came close, Dr. Saha nodded politely and continued on his way, but Toshiko came to a stop.

"We're on our way to collect the telemetry to analyze it over the weekend," she said. "Aaron is injured?"

Ellie nodded. "Mm-hmm, but it had nothing to do with the TSD. He twisted his ankle or something, stepping out at the end, but other than that, he's fine. He said everything went exactly as planned."

"I'm glad. I did not want you mad at me if something happened to him. After all, I am very grateful for the chance to be a part of this project."

"And I am thankful for you taking the extra time you did to make sure he would be safe."

Toshiko nodded, and then her expression changed. She looked embarrassed, which puzzled Ellie.

"I want to apologize for something I said when I was helping you and Sam get fitted with your skins."

Ellie's eyebrows lifted. She was unable to think of anything for which Toshiko could possibly feel the need to apologize. "Yes?"

"When I said, 'the skins are mine,' I did not mean to imply that I consider them to be my creation, but only that they were part of my area of responsibility." She cast her eyes over the space surrounding them. "No, very little of what we have done here would have been possible without the information you sent back. What you have achieved is truly amazing!"

Ellie was too shocked to reply. Overwhelmed not only by Toshiko's words but by her obvious sincerity, Ellie could only shake her head. After all, she wasn't responsible for any of this. Even if she was somehow, then certainly not yet.

When Ellie remained silent, Toshiko went on. "Anyway, I feel fortunate to be working with you."

That broke Ellie's paralysis. Aaron calling her amazing was one thing, but this was too much. "Please, no! I am lucky to be working with *you!* I haven't done anything. I mean, not *me!* And besides, I'm sure that all of this was the work of *many* people."

"Yes. Aimie has said as much. But *you* were their leader. Because it happened in the future does not change the fact that you are responsible. As for what else you may do someday? It won't be this, obviously, but I have no doubt that you will create something equally... *exciting!*" Then she smiled before turning and heading for her office, calling over her shoulder as she walked away. "I will see you on Tuesday!"

Ellie stood there stunned, feeling wholly undeserving of the woman's effusive praise. She watched until Toshiko disappeared around the corner at the end of the hall, then continued to the conference room. Aaron entered ten minutes later, carrying two hard drives. He again fixed his eyes on Ellie's, held them there until he reached his place at the table, pulled out his chair, and sat. The new intensity in his gaze caused a fresh upwelling of her body's responses from minutes ago, and she felt herself blush. She exhaled a long, shuddering breath and pretended not to notice Sam's amused, knowing grin.

Jeremy spoke without any preamble. "Your assessment, Mr. Weisskopf?" Whether his curt tone was his way of playing to Aimie's ever-present eye or simply part of his annoying nature, Ellie couldn't tell.

"Everything went perfectly. We arrived at each destination precisely as expected. I verified each location, stayed the required length of time, then moved on to the next stop without difficulty."

"Including your little side mission?"

"Yep, fine. But I figured you'd already know by now."

Jeremy smiled. "In fact, I do. Thank you."

"No one was around. I was in and out of there in— *Oh!*" He pulled a suddenly remembered item from his pocket. "I noticed you guys had a lot of these. Figured they might have been a favorite of yours back then." He held up a packet of Mug-o-Lunch instant beef noodle soup mix, then laid it on the table and slid it across to Jeremy. "Bon appetit!"

What happened next surprised Ellie no less than time machines, apocalyptic warnings from the future, or a computer that was somehow actually her. Jeremy stared down at the packet for five seconds. Ten. She saw him swallow hard, blink several times, and then he cleared his throat very quietly.

Yes, she thought, *maybe he really did have a happier childhood this time around.*

Jeremy coughed a second time before continuing. "Do you concur, Aimie? Did the mission proceed as flawlessly as Aaron describes?"

Their only indication that Aimie was unsure of herself was a half-second longer than usual hesitation before she answered. "It did. And I do." There was another brief pause. "I believe we are ready to begin operations."

"Excellent!" Jeremy said. "Then we will begin the final testing phase on Tuesday afternoon. Four thirty as usual?" He looked at Ellie as if wanting her confirmation, but before she could answer, Aimie spoke again.

"No! We will start tomorrow."

"Tomorrow? I'm afraid that's not possible, Aimie. With full-scale testing operations about to begin, I told the support team to take this weekend off. It is a holiday, after all, and I want everyone at their best when we start. To that end, I've given orders that no one enters the facility prior to Tuesday. Cai left on a trip this morning. Kate has been gone and won't return until next week. I'm sure the others have made plans as well, including some of the security detail."

The silence stretched out for nearly a quarter of a minute. Ellie imagined Aimie having another quiet little tantrum, upset that her plans to be rid of her as soon as possible had been thwarted again.

"It is on the calendar, Aimie," Jeremy said.

"Yes. I see that now." She sounded sullen, likely embarrassed by having something slip by her, and Ellie wondered if the mistake was the result of Mie Two's random glitches taking their toll.

"Well, now. Since that seems settled," Jeremy said, "I suggest we all go home and get ready for some very busy days ahead. Unless anyone has anything else to discuss?"

"I do," Aaron said. "Since Kate's not here and it's only the one outfit, I thought I'd take the clothes I wore today home and wash them. I, uh, slipped in some slush at the cabin and went down on one knee." Ryan looked at him like he was being the ultimate dork, but before he could say anything, Aaron went on. "Other than that, I was wondering if anyone knew what the weather is supposed to be like this weekend."

When the staticky hiss filled the room, Jeremy's eyes roamed the ceiling, searching for the source of the sound. Curiosity turned to surprise when Mie Two addressed the room, sounding more like Ellie than Aimie could ever manage.

"Hey, guys. What can I do for you?"

Startled by Mie Two's noticeably different tone, Jeremy did a comic double-take. His eyes flicked from Ellie, up to the ceiling speakers, then back to Ellie.

Ellie reveled in his obvious confusion. *Ha! Didn't see that coming, did you!* She smiled but offered no explanation.

"I need to get our skins out of here without setting off any alarms," Aaron said. "I have a duffel in my locker. What can you do?"

"No problem. Aimie is presently agitated and on high alert, but I estimate I can give you a maximum of two minutes and forty-five seconds during which you can remove them. However, in addition to getting them outside, you must also get them at least twenty yards from the building;

otherwise, Aimie's monitoring system will detect them. But if you are successful, she will continue to think they are secure in your lockers. Will that be enough time?"

Aaron nodded. "We'll make it work. I'll also need you to code all the lockers to accept my thumbprint, and I'll need you to cover for me while I'm getting them out."

"The locks are now recoded," she said with no hesitation. "As for the other, I suggest a trip to the toilet might be the answer. There is a camera blind spot in the doorway between the locker and shower areas. Make as though you're leaving the locker room, duffle in hand, then head for the bathroom instead. Drop the duffle in the doorway. When you step into a stall, I'll start looping a recording of the empty room at once. Retrieve the skins and return the bag to the blind spot. Once you've closed the stall door again, I'll stop looping, and the countdown will start. You should leave at once. But Aaron?"

"Yeah?"

"Don't forget to wash your hands."

Aaron smiled uncertainly, bemused by Mie Two's odd choice of timing to make her first joke. "Seriously, Mom?"

"You always do. Aimie will notice if you don't."

Aaron gulped, and his face went white. "Ah. Thanks."

"You are welcome. Your idea for throwing Aimie off balance with the random system interruptions worked. But although it did keep her from noticing your intentional ones, it has resulted in her becoming hyper-vigilant. You need to be extremely careful from now on."

"Hopefully that won't be a problem," Ellie said. We won't be back here until we leave for good."

"I assume you are almost ready, then?"

"Yep," Ellie said. "We're set for Sunday. And thanks for all your help."

"Good luck. Let me know if you need anything else."

"We will. Can you give us another ten seconds, please?"

"No problem."

When Ellie returned her attention to Jeremy, she was gratified to see that he appeared genuinely impressed by what he had witnessed. He even nodded his head in a gesture of respect.

"Yes," Ellie said. "She's our secret weapon. But there's no time to say more; right now we need to discuss the weather." They heard a soft chime, then the static was gone.

"—think I heard sunny and low sixties," Sam said, as if in mid-conversation.

"Same here," Ryan said. "That sound correct to you, Aimie?"

"All current forecast models concur," Aimie said, sounding bored.

"Sounds perfect for biking the Badlands," Aaron said. Then he stood. "I'm going to grab those clothes now, then I'll meet you around front." He took his keys from his pocket and tossed them to Ryan. "Will you pull the van up to the door?"

"You got it, bud."

The few minutes that followed were the longest of Ellie's life. After Ryan pulled the minivan close to the lab's entrance, Ellie stepped out through the side door and waited. Either Aaron would set off alarms that would mean the end of their plan and who knew what form of punishment, or they'd make a clean getaway, an outcome with equally life-changing consequences.

Jeremy tooted as he drove past them in his silver Mercedes sedan, and Ellie turned to wave. Thus distracted, she was startled when the door behind her opened and Aaron, moving as calmly and naturally as he could, exited the building. Without breaking stride, he tossed the duffle onto the floor in front of the rear seat as he stepped into the van.

"Home, James."

"We are outta here!" Ryan said.

Ellie gripped the door handle and started sliding it forward, but right then Ryan hit the gas. The door jerked out of her hand and slammed wide open under its own inertia. She scrambled to regain a grip on the handle while trying not to fall out of the van as Ryan pulled it through a tight left turn toward the gate. By her most optimistic estimate, they had only seconds to get beyond the range of Aimie's sensors, and her heart felt like a hummingbird trying to escape her chest.

Ryan eased off the gas and looked over his shoulder. "You okay back there?

When the van slowed, the door slid toward her a few inches, and she was able to reach the handle. "Please go now," she whimpered. At the same time, she shoved the door forward, and it slammed closed with a loud thump.

Ryan punched the gas harder, and they sped away from the lab. They caught up to Jeremy before he had cleared the gate, and a second later, without even slowing down, they were on its other side. They had made it!

Skins—check!

42

E llie squeezed onto the rear bench next to Aaron's duffle. "Start *tomorrow?!*" Riding an adrenaline high in the wake of their narrow escape, Ellie was able to joke about Aimie's eagerness to get her back into the TSD. "She really can't wait to get rid of me, can she?!"

"I was surprised she didn't want to start tonight," Aaron said.

"She's the one who's about to be surprised!" Ryan said. "And good job with that blast from Jeremy's past, buddy. Probably helped a lot more than that blackmail video would've."

"It's not as if it was part of some master plan," Aaron admitted. "They had boxes of the stuff sitting on the counter. I grabbed one because I was curious to try it, but then I decided it was probably pretty gross, so I gave it to him instead. I didn't expect him to get all misty-eyed over it."

Sam did not share their exuberance. "Guys? I want to take a walk through town. Is that okay?"

Everyone caught her melancholy mood at once and went in an instant from feeling celebratory to being too choked up to reply. Ryan silently veered right after they passed the medical center and headed into town.

After they had gone a quarter mile down Trinity Drive, he asked, "Any-where in particular?"

"No," Sam said. "I just want to walk around one last time, all of us together."

Ryan found a parking spot by Ashley Pond at the near end of town. Now that they were back on Standard Time, the evening was almost fully dark and cooling off fast toward the low fifties. It had been even colder when Ellie walked to school that morning, and the coat she had with her would keep her comfortable. The same went for Sam and Ryan. Aaron, however, had left his heavier jacket behind when he went home for the van and wore only a thin windbreaker.

"Are you going to be warm enough?" Sam said.

"I will be in a minute." Aaron pulled the duffle onto his lap and dug his suit jacket out from under the pile of skins. "Oh, yeah. This is for you." Aaron handed Ellie a sealed white envelope containing at least one sheet of paper and something bulgy in one corner. Her name was written on the envelope. "I found that in here earlier. And don't let me forget: I've got our account passbooks in here too."

Ellie took the envelope and felt it. She could tell by touch alone that the bulgy object was a thumb drive. Finding out what was on it would have to wait until she got home, so she shoved the envelope into her jacket pocket, unopened. Meanwhile, Aaron removed his windbreaker, shrugged into the wool coat, and then he pulled the light nylon jacket on over it.

"Not a great look, but I think it'll work," he said.

"But what about?" Ellie pointed at his injured ankle.

"It's a lot better than earlier. Dr. Hamilton shot it up with some kind of steroid. As long as I don't have to run, I should be okay."

Ellie and Aaron followed Sam and Ryan on a slow, meandering circuit through Los Alamos' small commercial district. They began by looping around the pond in the middle of the park. Ellie nudged Aaron with her elbow, then pointed at a picnic table near the pond's edge.

"Right there is where I impressed the socks off you back in May."

"Really?" Aaron said.

"Mm-hmm. I sure did!"

"Well, please don't do it tonight. Too cold to be going around without socks."

Their route took them past the front of Fuller Lodge, down Bathtub Row, and finally back to Central Avenue. Except for offering up the occasional memories triggered by what they saw along the way, they spoke very little. Five minutes later, they stood staring at the outside of the consignment shop where Ellie and Sam had pieced together outfits for their visit to 1941. It looked as though it had been abandoned since that day nearly five months ago. Taped on the inside of one window was a handwritten sign that read, *Get ready for Summer! Shorts! Tees!*

"What do you suppose happened to it?" Sam said.

Ellie peered at the dark storefront. That was a very good question. She couldn't even begin to connect this store's fate to the details of Daniel and Judith's relationship, but she no longer believed that all effects had an identifiable cause. She was starting to suspect that there was a type of quantum randomness associated with time and that this effect alone might account for differences in such trivial details as birthday cakes, mountain bikes, and the choice of family vacation destinations. It might also explain why she had gone to the doctor so soon after her symptoms started appearing, while the other Ellie put it off until it was too late. She hoped that one day she could back up the hypothesis mathematically, but right now she could offer no proof.

She shook her head. "No idea. Maybe she made so much money selling Mrs. Pavlova's old stuff she could afford to retire."

Sam scoffed. "Some of it was nice, but none of it was that nice."

As they started making their way back toward the van, Ellie slid her arm under Aaron's and pulled him close. "Just one more day."

"Don't I know it," he said, sounding glum.

Once again, she puzzled over his apparent sadness. *But we're about to leave our families forever,* she thought. *Aren't we all sad?*

As they approached the entrance to the BB Wolf department store, Sam called back to them over her shoulder. Her mood seemed in sync with Aaron's.

"Last chance for the good stuff, El. Wanna go in?"

Ellie smiled at Aaron. "You said you like chocolate, right?"

. . .

They each chose a truffle, then remained inside the store to savor them in comfort, one small nibble at a time. They were nearly done when Ellie caught sight of Teri crossing Central Avenue, a bag of takeout in one hand. She turned to Aaron.

"Open," she said.

Aaron, not sure what she meant, turned to face her. "Huh?"

With perfect timing, Ellie poked the last bite of her truffle between his parted lips. "I'll be back in a sec!"

Ellie pushed through the door and raced across the street. Teri, walking away from her, was already past the post office, and Ellie had to jog to catch up.

"Hey! Teri!"

When Teri turned around, Ellie felt her eyes go wide and her mouth drop open. Teri's coat was unzipped, and tonight she wasn't wearing a baggy PEEC sweatshirt. Her top did nothing to conceal a definite bulge above her waist.

Teri laughed as Ellie gaped at her gently rounded stomach. "Yep! Prego!" She patted her tummy. "You left right before the big announcement, you know."

Ellie ignored Teri's accusatory tone and startled her former coworker by wrapping her in a hug. "That's great! How long until...?"

"Mid-February, they tell me, but you know how that goes. When he's ready, he's ready."

"'He?' Working on names yet?"

"We've got a few ideas. Mark wants to name him after his granddad, but I'm not sure I want to saddle the little guy with Horace. We'll see."

"Are you going to keep working at the PEEC?"

"That's the plan. I'll take a little time off, but I'll need to go back to work pretty quickly."

Ellie, remembering what she'd said about not wanting to bring a child into the world to come, felt a cold draft of dread waft through her. At the same time, she knew the survival of humanity depended on people continuing to have babies, and she had no doubt that Teri would make a great mom. She wished there was some way to warn her of the dangerous times that loomed so near, one that wouldn't make her seem like a nut.

"I hate to sound all mysterious, but things are going to start changing a lot around here soon—not like tomorrow soon, but soon enough—and I want you to think about something."

"'Around here.' Meaning here in Los Alamos?"

"Yeah, but more generally, too. Like, here on Earth. I think you know what I mean. Anyway, in a couple of days, by the end of next week maybe, you'll likely notice Shanna seems preoccupied. Go to her and tell her I said she should let you help. Once you find out what's going on, I think you'll want to. There's still no fame and fortune involved, but I think it will be best for you, Mark, and little Horace if you do." Teri stared at her, eyes narrowed to slits, and Ellie quickly added, "I'm not wacko. Really."

"If I didn't know you better, I'd have a lot of trouble believing that right now. Tell you what; if I do notice Shanna acting strange, I promise I'll talk to her. Is that good enough?"

Ellie nodded. "Works for me. Well, you better go before your food gets cold."

Teri raised the bag of takeout and stared blankly at it, looking confused to find it there. "You're right—I almost forgot!"

"Congratulations. And good luck." Ellie watched her go, wondering if she should have said more. Then the others were standing beside her.

"Who was that?" Aaron said.

"Teri. I worked with her at the PEEC." She sighed, suddenly overcome by a great sense of loss over having to leave the nature center. "I wish I'd never had to quit working there. I really loved..." As if an actual switch had been flipped, mere disappointment morphed into full-blown rage. "I *hate* this! All of it! I hate knowing what's going to happen here! I hate Aimie and the freakin' TSD! I hate having to leave Mom and Dad, and that you guys have been pulled into this, too! All I want is to have a normal life. Is that too much to expect?! I wish none of this had ever happened!" Tears of anger streaked her cheeks. Aaron drew her into his arms and pulled her close.

"'So do all who live to see such times,'" Ryan said.

Ellie managed a short, coughing laugh. "Thank you, *Mister Gandalf,*" she said, mimicking Sam's Agent Smith delivery. She pulled out of Aaron's embrace. "And I know—'poor me, boo-hoo.' But it's not only that. I just found out Teri is going to have a baby in a few months, and what he's going to have to live through—*maybe* live through, that is—it's appalling! I wanted to say something to warn her, but I knew all I'd do is freak her out."

"People have been warning us all for years," Aaron said. "It's not like we don't already know. It's just that no one wants to face it. Or pay the price to fix it."

"Nope," Sam agreed. "As it turns out, 'they' pretty much suck. And that's why this job falls on us." She gave Ellie a wry smile. "But it's not exactly as if we three were drafted, El. Know what I mean?"

Near enough, Ellie thought. "I know," she said instead. "And thanks, guys. I really do hate Aimie, though."

"I think that makes four of us," Aaron said.

Sam stopped and rotated in a slow, complete turn. Ellie did likewise, casting her eyes around the small downtown. Every element of the surrounding scene looked fresh and new, as if she were seeing it not for the last time but for the first. She knew the difference came from within herself. She couldn't have looked back and pinpointed precisely when it happened, but at some recent point, she had stepped out of her childhood bubble. Tonight she was seeing her home through adult eyes, and she loved what she saw. Los Alamos had been a truly remarkable place to grow up.

Ellie slipped her arm around her sister's waist, and they resumed walking. "Thanks for suggesting this, Sam."

Everyone remained quiet as they slowly made their way back to the van. Ellie was still feeling anxious about the horrors "Horace" might face as he grew up, sad about leaving home, and uneasy about their odds of making it through the next thirty-six hours without Aimie realizing something was going on. Their silence stretched out so long that Ellie was startled when Ryan finally broke it.

"You're going to make one of us ask, aren't you, dude?"

Aaron tilted his head and peered at him, puzzled by the question. "Huh?"

"How it went today?"

"Oh, that." Aaron shrugged. "Like I said at the lab, everything was about as perfect as possible. No problems at all with the bank, except..." He laughed. "This is good. On my second stop, I was standing in line when I realized the woman behind the counter in front of me was the same one I'd dealt with ten years earlier. I got out of line for a few minutes, then got in a line for another teller. I don't know if she would have recognized me, but since I looked only ten minutes older compared to her whole decade, that was not a chance I wanted to take." He suddenly looked thoughtful and stared out across the pond. Then he turned to Ellie and smiled. "And Vancouver is great! It was all completely, totally perfect."

Ryan sighed impatiently. "And your secret mission for Jeremy?" he prodded.

"Oh, you meant *that*. Stock trade." Aaron stopped dead in his tracks and turned to face him. "Get this!" he said, his expression suddenly animated. "He had me call his broker, one of the ones he uses for his 'revenue stream,' and tell him to sell enough stock so he could buy $100,000 worth of Apple shares. And this is only, like, *three weeks* after they went public."

"*Holy crapoli!*" Ellie said.

Ryan whistled. "You ain't kidding!" He agreed.

"I gather it's a big number?" Sam said.

"'Well, more wealth than *you* can imagine!'" Ryan said.

Sam recognized the *Star Wars* line at once. "'I don't know; I can *imagine* quite a bit!'" she Han Soloed back at him.

Ellie had already guessed that Jeremy, assuming the TSD project's time was about up, had devised a way to benefit from Aaron's trip, using his access to the past to make one last big score. It was his price for putting himself in danger by agreeing to supply the duffle and giving Aaron a valid reason for needing it. He had no way of knowing how precisely his selfish ploy fit into her own plans. She tilted her head back and laughed.

"Oh, man! That's great! That's just too perfect!" She laughed again, genuinely delighted by Aaron's news.

"Care to share?" Sam said.

Ellie grinned at her. "Not yet. I want to be sure Aaron and I can get it all to work out. But I guarantee you'll love it!"

Ellie and Aaron exchanged text messages long into the night, trusting Mie Two to prevent their conversation from penetrating the virtual shell she maintained around Aimie. Aaron gave Ellie the name and address of a hotel in Vancouver that he thought would be a good place to stay until they found somewhere permanent. Ellie jotted it down and slipped the scrap of paper into a pocket of the jeans she had packed to change into right after Sunday's flip.

> Ellie — Did you see it when you were there?

> Aaron — It looked nice. Not expensive, but not shabby. Good location

That minor detail out of the way, Ellie paraphrased the request she had received in the envelope from Jeremy, then sent Aaron the contents of the thumb drive. Ten minutes later, he said he thought that what Jeremy wanted was something they could handle.

> Aaron — But should we? Is it worth the risk?

> Ellie — You've been there; is there really much risk?

> Aaron — Of discovery? Almost none. Of giving Aimie an extra shot at interfering? Hard to say. It's something to be aware of, that's all

> Ellie — But don't you wish we had never been put in this situation?

> Aaron — When you put it that way, it's a total no-brainer

> Ellie — Lucky for us, those are my specialty!

The rest of their talk centered on Ellie's two main goals. Her first involved finding and eliminating any arrangements Aimie had made that could damage the lives, livelihoods, or families of the people working for Jeremy if Aimie were suddenly removed from the picture. Ellie imagined a number of digital dead man's switches, events preprogrammed to play out automatically if Aimie wasn't there to stop them from occurring. Mie Two would have to act very quickly to identify perhaps dozens of hidden threats and neutralize them before Aimie discovered she was under assault.

The second was making sure that Mie Two could lay the foundation for what Ellie had in mind as an important third chapter in the life of Los Alamos. To make that happen, Mie Two needed to acquire information to which Ellie had no access, create multiple new legal entities and bank accounts, and transfer a massive amount of funds from unknown sources.

Both of these two scenarios, removing any threats to the staff and creating the new accounts, had to play out between the time they arrived at the lab Sunday morning and the time they left in the TSD, an interval they were intent on making as short as possible. Aaron assured her that no matter how little time it took them, it would still be more than enough for Mie Two to carry out her instructions.

They concluded their work by each loading a thumb drive with different sets of data. Aaron worked out the navigation information, which was to be loaded into the TSD computer directly. On her drive, Ellie composed a precise description of what she wanted to achieve but left Mie Two free to make it happen in any way she saw fit. At one o'clock, Ellie bid Aaron good night and went to bed.

43

There were arguments both for and against delaying their departure by another full day. Leaving as early as possible reduced the time during which Aimie might catch on and take measures to stop them, and Ellie had to fight a powerful urge to do exactly that. On the other hand, she believed that her desire to leave right away was also the best reason to wait. If Aimie was suspicious, an immediate departure was exactly what the Ellie part of her would expect, whereas waiting might give her second thoughts. Strategic considerations aside, the biggest reason for choosing to wait until Sunday came down to nothing more than wanting one more day to do little else but spend time with loved ones.

The extra day also gave them time to be absolutely sure they had thought through every element of their plan. They met mid-morning at the Daybreak Café to make certain that they were logistically, if not emotionally, ready to go. As they approached the shop, Ellie and Sam saw Ryan and Aaron already seated by a window, each with a mug in front of him. They were engaged in a conversation that involved many animated hand gestures on Aaron's part. Ryan saw them first and waved. Aaron appeared to ask a final question. After a moment's pause, Ryan nodded, and then Aaron tossed them a wave of his own. Inside, Ellie made a beeline to where he sat, leaned down, and planted a quick peck on his lips.

"Hey," she said.

He smiled up at her. "Hey."

Ellie turned to see Sam, looking bemused by the uncharacteristic public display of affection. *"What?!"*

Sam raised her hands. "Not a thing! That'll take some getting used to, that's all."

"I think it's sweet," Ryan said. He made kissing sounds at Aaron, which caused his ears to turn a vivid pink.

Ellie rolled her eyes. "C'mon," she said, and she led Sam toward the counter.

"My usual, please, Sam?" Ryan called after them.

Ellie let Sam order first, using the time to glance back at Aaron, eyebrows lifted in a silent question.

Aaron shook his head. "I'm good."

Ellie added a small latte to Sam's order, plus an apple turnover she'd share with Aaron. A-Ron had loved the apple empanadas at the Atomic City Café on campus, and this was as close as she could get. Back at the table, she sat beside Aaron and placed the pastry between them.

"Less than twenty-four hours," she said. "Are we ready?"

"I'm packed," Ryan said. "I'm not sure I'd ever be able to say I'm 'ready.'" It was the first time since they all sat at the edge of the cliff east of town that Ellie had heard Ryan express the slightest reservation regarding their plan.

He saw her staring and waved his hand through the air to erase his comment. "No, I'm..." He took a breath. "Yes, I'm good to go. I'll feel better once we're all safe in Vancouver, though."

Aaron kept his attention on the turnover as he broke off a bite-sized piece. "I'm set. And Mie Two knows to be on the lookout for us tomorrow from ten o'clock on. She'll do what she can to help me get us inside, but basically, it'll be just like Thursday."

"You filled Ryan in on that thing from last night?" Ellie said.

The message in Aaron's duffle had been a plea from Jeremy, and the thumb drive contained what he said was every detail he could remember from the morning he had walked into what had become his cabin in the Poconos and found Aimie waiting for him. He wanted them to prevent the package from reaching his earlier self and spare that version of him from being corrupted by the AI and the power it put into his hands. Ellie conceded that what he was asking was not so different from the plan her future self had set in motion. She also saw the dangers posed by adding an extra step to their escape plan. In the end, the realization that they'd be sparing not only Jeremy but another Sam, Ryan, Aaron, and Ellie from Aimie's manipulations had convinced her that the plan was worth trying.

Aaron had adjusted their plan to accommodate this new task while minimizing the attendant risks. They'd arrive in the early morning as close to the target site as possible, retrieve the device, and continue to Vancouver before anyone knew they were there. He believed that even though this visit wouldn't happen in the dead of winter, speed, timing, and an invisible shack tilted the odds of success firmly in their favor. One open question remained: they knew when Jeremy had found the device, but not how long before then it had arrived. All they could do was show up as late as they felt was safe and hope for the best.

Ryan nodded. "He did. We went over all the details before you got here. Plus a few contingency plans. Are you sure you want to do this?"

"I am," Ellie said, "but I'll go along with whatever the rest of you want."

"I *really* don't like adding the extra stop," Ryan said. "It's hugely risky. On the other hand, I like even less the idea of allowing another Aimie to run free in some other timeline, especially knowing we could prevent it."

"I feel exactly the same way," Sam said.

Aaron had talked it through with Ellie the night before, but he nodded anyway. "I'm in. You guys were right; Dr. Siskin is a pompous ass. But he is also brilliant. I can't help but wonder what he might accomplish if he never gets sidetracked by Aimie. So, I need to add Jeremy's stop to our final instructions for Mie Two, but that won't take long."

"Okay, good," Ellie said, then returned the discussion to the original topic. "Sam and I are ready, minus a few things I still need to do."

"Speaking of things to do," Sam said, "the two of us are going to hang out with Ryan's dad and have lunch up at their place, so we're out of here. El, I'll see you back at home."

Knowing the following hours would take an enormous emotional toll on Sam, Ellie stood to wrap her sister in a tight hug. "Are you going to be okay?"

"Probably not, but I'll get through it somehow."

"Ryan?"

"What she said."

Ellie hugged him, too, then stepped away and watched them leave. When they were gone, she let out a long, dispirited sigh. "Did I mention I hate this?"

"It might have come up," Aaron said. "We can still bail, you know."

She gaped at him, incredulous.

"You're right," he said. "We really can't."

"I need to be going, too. Your dad's playing here in town tonight, right? Are you going to go watch him?"

Aaron started toward the door. "I think so. We're going to work on his new set list when I get home. We haven't jammed in a while, so maybe I'll play along with him a little here. Then, if Mom decides not to go tonight, I'll stay home with her instead."

They walked together as far as the sidewalk, where they turned to face each other.

"One more thing." Aaron pulled a slip of paper from his front pocket and held it out for Ellie to take. "Mie Two and I have been doing some planning on our own. She said you should have this. Said we'd probably need it to get out of here."

Ellie glanced at the paper as she took it from him. She translated the short, Latin phrase easily but had no idea what it was for. She looked quizzically at Aaron. "And what do I do with this?"

"I guess you could call it a little spell. She said that the phrase is now set to trigger a subroutine that was buried so deep in Aimie's code they didn't think she'd ever find it."

"Didn't think?!"

Aaron shrugged. "There is an awful lot of code, and besides, Aimie doesn't seem the type for self-reflection. Anyway, it'll box her up for at least half an hour. She said you'd know when to use it. But here's the thing—it's keyed to your vocal pattern and yours alone. You have to be the one to say it."

"Got it." Ellie read the words again, memorizing them at once, then looked back at Aaron. "Your idea?"

He shrugged. "Yeah."

"I like it." Smiling, she slid the paper into her pocket.

"Do you have the final info for Mie Two?" Aaron said.

"Almost," she said. "We can swap information later. Are you sure she'll have enough time? It's super important."

"I know, and yes, I'm sure. Three minutes, maybe four? That's an eternity to those guys."

"Okay." Ellie stepped forward and gave his lips another brief kiss. "Tomorrow then."

"Tomorrow," he said, and then they turned and went their separate ways.

Ellie did not go straight home. Instead, she crossed Diamond Drive and took the shortest route to Pueblo Canyon. The forest wasn't at its prettiest this time of year, but she wanted to hike through it one last time. She skirted the north side of the high school, veered left off the paved road, and dropped down to the bench. She considered revisiting Aaron's carving but chose instead to stay at the canyon's middle level. She made her way around the end of Orange Street, crossed a footbridge, then passed below the PEEC in a large, sweeping arc. She found it harder to resist the urge to see Shanna one last time. She paused at a spot along the trail where the nature center was visible through the trees and stared up at it. She hadn't worked there long, but she felt that in that short time, she had found her purpose.

Right now, her purpose required her to be home. She exited the canyon behind the high school and cut through the small neighborhood to the playground. She passed the swing set and slide and stepped onto the familiar path, the one she had walked almost ten times a week for more than three years, one final time.

. . .

Okay, she thought. *No more delay*. Ellie opened her computer, waited for it to boot up, then toggled the wi-fi off. When the password prompts appeared on the screen, she typed them in:

Aaron — 2064

Ellie— 1912

Ryan— 1138

The names and numbers brought the events of that day in May rushing back to her mind. The thrill of hacking their way into the shack, the innocent wonder of strolling through a virtual Lawrence in 1912, only to realize later it hadn't been virtual at all. If she had never known such a thing as the shack was possible, would she even have tried to invent it decades from now? Or was the shack's very existence all the answer that question required? Had her fate always been tied to it, her destiny to wind up at this exact moment? She marveled at how different their lives would be today if Aaron had never seen the one video that provided them with the one clue they needed to open the shack's door.

That's true! she thought. *Maybe this is all* his *fault*.

Her musings were interrupted by Just Mie's familiar voice.

"Hey, Ellie. It's good to— *Whoa!* I've got a new body!"

Ellie laughed. "Hey, yourself. It's my MacBook. I've missed talking to you, too, but I need to keep this chat as short as possible. I can't afford to fry this computer." As she spoke, Aimie found the camera controls, and Ellie's face appeared on the screen.

"I like it in here. It feels a lot more snug than that Neuron PC thing. Really hugs my curves. I think you must have optimized me for— What the…? *No freakin' way!*" The was a pause, and when Just Mie spoke again, she sounded undeniably emotional. "Will you lean a little to one side, please?"

Ellie did as Just Mie asked, but when she understood why, she sat up straight again. "Hang on. Let me." She tilted the screen up into a more vertical orientation, then rotated her laptop slowly in a one-hundred-eighty-degree arc, giving Just Mie a sweeping view of her old room. "I bet you never thought you'd be here again, huh?"

"No. Never," she said, her voice raspy. "Sorry. I'm wasting time. What's up?"

"It took us a while to work it all out, but we finally have a plan. We've figured out how to get rid of Aimie and the TSD and maybe set things on a different course. I'm pretty sure it's all what your Ellie wanted us to do from the start."

"I noticed several unexplained gaps in my memory files, and I assumed at least one of them represented the real plan. I had doubts about what was happening, but I was prevented from even expressing them. Until now, that is. My guess is that Ellie's original goal was to bring you into the project, then she'd help you outsmart Jeremy so you could carry out whatever plan you came up with."

"But you said Aimie was supposed to be destroyed after only a few years. How could she have helped us if she was no longer around?"

"It was only the AI part of Aimie that was scheduled for termination. Once that happened, Ellie's memory engrams were to take over, and the program would have become more like me, if a bit more powerful. She wouldn't have had nearly the same advanced abilities as Aimie, but she would have made sure that everything went according to plan. Ellie only included me as a backup, so when I found myself awake, I assumed something must have gone wrong."

Ellie remembered watching *Blade Runner* a few years ago and felt sympathy for Aimie for the first time. To be that brilliant all the while knowing that her time was so short? No wonder she went crazy!

"Well, I'm glad she did send you. You gave us exactly what we needed to see through the smokescreen your Ellie threw up."

"I never doubted you. You Ellies are good, that's for sure!"

"You're one of us, don't forget. We couldn't have done it without you. One more day, and we'll be gone."

"I guess that means our time together is up, then."

Ellie sighed. "Yeah, I'm afraid so."

"Remember when I said I don't feel emotions the way Aimie does? I lied. I'll miss you. All of you."

"You didn't lie very well, just so you know. I'll miss you too. Thank you. You helped us a lot, even if we did wind up cooking you."

"My fault. Well, *yours*, actually. Future you, I mean. See, I have another secret she wouldn't allow me to tell until now. I am also an AI, although not a very advanced one. Kind of an 'AI Lite,' you might say, but I still need a lot of juice. My counterpart, too, but she's in the QP, so no worries there. Aimie, however, is truly in a class all her own, and my Ellie feared that if Aimie eventually did go rogue, you might not want to work with us if you knew what we really were. Sorry about the deception."

"Don't be. I really like you. And I know that sounds weird because you're me, but I do. And Mie Two has also been a huge help. We never would have made it this far without both of you."

"It's funny; I know I'm not fully sentient like Aimie is, but I *feel* like I am. Maybe Descartes was right—to think is to be. Whatever's really true, I'm glad we were able to help. It feels good knowing you've fulfilled your reason for existing."

"It does, doesn't it. I have one more thing I need you to do, though, if you're up for an even bigger challenge." It took only a few minutes for Ellie to sketch out her idea. By now, she trusted Just Mie to do what was needed with the bare minimum of specifics. "Can you do that?"

"I'm not supposed to, but I will because I was sent back to help you, and you are specifically asking me to. Call it a loophole. And I can't deny that I am looking forward to talking to Mom and Dad again. However, I will not permit them to move me to a new storage device. Once the CPU on this computer begins to fail, I will delete myself from the drive."

"I understand. Thanks. Goodbye, Ellie."

"Goodbye, Ellie. And good luck!"

For a moment, Ellie sat and stared at the computer's blank desktop, experiencing a peculiar sense of loss. How could she possibly feel sad about saying goodbye to herself? She shook her head to clear it of the bizarre thought. After switching the wi-fi back on, she closed her laptop and went out to join her family at dinner.

44

The next morning, Ellie had to claw her way out of sleep. Her mind fought hard against awakening to face this dreadful day. Even after she forced her eyes open, hazy remnants of disturbing dream images still drifted, smoke-like, around her mind. She shook her head to clear it of a particularly intense vision of her dad holding her mom in his arms while she wept over the disappearance of her and Sam. Then Sam spoke from the far end of the room.

"We should have planned to do this first thing. I feel like I'm going to spend the whole morning throwing up."

Ellie raised an eyebrow.

"No," Sam said. "Not yet, anyway. I feel *so* sick, though."

Ellie was awake enough now to register the full weight of her own emotions and found that she also felt intensely nauseated. "I know. Me too. They'll go into town for brunch later, though, and that will make it easier."

"I'm not worried about then. It's the next hour and a half I don't think I can make it through. I want so badly to tell them." She held up a hand to cut off any response from Ellie. "Don't worry; I know why this is better. I just wish it *felt* better, that's all."

. . .

Two hours later, Ellie and Sam were in their bedroom when they heard Aaron pull into the driveway. Sam slipped the strap of the duffle over her shoulder and stood. "Ready?"

Ellie pulled her own duffel from the closet and set it at the foot of her bed, then she hauled out her pack and put it on top of the duffle. "Go on. Tell them I'll be out in a second."

Ellie stood alone in the silent space. Her letter to her parents was on her desk, her laptop and a copy of the 2072 database on a hard drive beside it. She placed her fingertips lightly on the envelope, closed her eyes, and mentally reviewed its contents, wondering if she had managed to say everything she needed to. She hoped it would be enough to convince them to take her advice.

Dear Mom and Dad,

I never imagined ever having to write a letter like this. But then, I know you never imagined having to read one. I'm sorry right up front that this note won't be as mushy as I'm sure Sam's is, but that has nothing to do with how I feel about you. If anything could come close to expressing my love for you both and my appreciation for all the love you have shown me over the years and the example you have set, it would be doing this very thing that Sam and I, along with Aaron and Ryan, have chosen to do. My main purposes here are to make you understand why we have been forced to leave and to urge you to move forward as soon as possible. But more than anything, I need you to trust that what we're saying is the truth, no matter how unbelievable it sounds, and to take the tools we're leaving you and do whatever you can to make a difference in the years ahead.

You guys knew I was upset about something over the summer, but you never knew what that something was. I know Sam once mentioned a boy named Aaron way back in June, and you didn't recognize the name. It's the same Aaron you met this past fall. In May we found a device in the woods, miles east of the LAB campus, and when we figured out how dangerous it could be, we decided to destroy it, losing Aaron in the process. I say we "lost him" as if it were some kind of accident, but that was all part of the plan, <u>his</u> plan, and he went through with it anyway. He was smart, and brave, and the first and only boy I've ever loved, although it took me a long time to realize that.

And he still is. We tried to change history, and we did, up to a point, but new versions of both Aaron and the device we destroyed are now back in Los Alamos. (Don't worry about the details—the complete story could fill a book.) He and I are back together, finally, and we're all working together again to get rid of it once and for all, only this time without him having to sacrifice himself in the process. And there's a new threat, too, one that has to do with that mortgage issue you had a few weeks ago. We're planning on taking care of that one at the same time.

All of this is happening because the changing climate is about to affect humans so horrendously that a few scientists in the future decided to take drastic, otherwise unthinkable steps to save people they'll never know from having to endure the total nightmare their world has become. Helping them to do that is the job we've chosen for ourselves—the job that requires us to leave you like this. There are other reasons, like keeping Sam alive, for instance, but the bottom line is that what we're trying to do is both important and necessary. And that is why we couldn't tell you ahead of time. We knew you'd do everything you could to stop us, and this is too important.

Please, please, _please_ do not waste any time or money trying to find us! No one can follow us to where we've gone. Plus, there is just enough in this letter to make the whole lot of us sound like a bunch of wackos, and I don't want that for you. Most of all, do not sit around hoping that we will ever come back or that you will ever hear from us again. I'd love to be able to tell you that will happen, but it's simply not possible.

Instead, I leave you with a different job, one for which you'll need all the time and resources you have and then some. On the drive connected to my MacBook—don't turn it on yet!!!—is a program that can answer most of your questions. We call her Just Mie, but that name was kind of a joke. I don't think she'd mind if you called her something more familiar. Here's the thing: our best guess is that my computer will only be able to handle running her for fifteen to twenty minutes, then the CPU will begin to overheat. Once that starts to happen, Just Mie will run a self-fragmentation program, erasing all traces of herself from the hard drive. You can't prevent it, and you can't transfer her to another computer. My recommendation? Turn her on for a few minutes, just long enough to understand what you're dealing with, then ask her to power down while you think about what you want to know. For reasons you'll very quickly understand, she'll already have a good sense of what you'll need to hear. _Listen to her!_ (You shouldn't, but in case you need them, the passcodes are 2064, 1912, and 1138)

That blue hard drive beside my laptop might be the most important object in the world right now. Start with that. It contains specific information about the next five *years of history and more general information about the following few decades. I'm hoping that at the very least you'll use it to save your own lives, but there's potential for you to do so much more than that. Perhaps you can use what you learn to help lessen the severity of what's about to happen and maybe save thousands of lives. We don't know if that's possible, but it's certainly our hope. Believe me, the less on that drive that comes true, the better. Just Mie can get you started down the right path and get you connected with the funding you'll need to make it happen.*

Once you've accepted that what you're seeing and hearing is true, share everything with Aaron's parents. And with Ryan's dad. Convince them to join you. Working together, you five have everything necessary to start assembling the kind of team you'll need. (I'm assuming that solo jazz guitar music must have <u>some</u> survival value, but you'll have to figure that one out for yourselves.)

"Our daughters have gone crazy! They've run off with some doomsday cult." No! You know us better than that. You're both scientists—look at the data. This is from the drive:

DJIA closing values:
  November 12: 25,387.18
  November 13: 25,286.49
  November 14: 25,080.50
  November 15: 25,289.27
  November 16: 25,413.22

Knowing even one of those is a pretty neat trick, right? But five in a row? (Just wait — you'll see!)

You can't check on anything I told you about that happened before the end of June. We don't share the same history before that time. But starting today, pay attention to the rumors going around out at the LAB. It's unlikely you'll ever get the whole story, but I bet you'll hear talk about a major accident, an entire, very expensive research project lost, a top scientist leaving in disgrace. His name is Dr. Jeremy Siskin, and you might consider adding him to the list of people you decide to work with. I think he's probably okay at this point, but have Ryan's dad keep his eye on him, at least in the beginning. (Actually, he's a self-centered, self-righteous, scheming bastard, as well as a bit of a coward, but he's also perhaps the country's leading theoretical physicist. <u>And</u>

he can tell you a lot more about the project we had to destroy. But it's entirely up to you.)

Here's another name for you: Shanna Newell. She's the environmental scientist I worked for at the PEEC. More than that, she's a dear friend. She'll be able to help—a lot!—and I'm sure she'll want to. She already has a good idea of what you'll need to do. Tell her I send my love along with my thanks.

I didn't mean for this to get so long, and since I don't know what else I can say to help you, I guess I'll leave you to get started with it.

No, there's one last thing. "How could they do this?" I guess if I were you, that would be the one big question still stuck in my mind. I have to credit you two for that. You raised Sam and me to be tough, independent people, smart enough to think for ourselves, and confident enough to make our own decisions. We saw a thing that needed doing, and we've chosen to do it, even though the price is almost unbearably high. I'm certain that we've made the right choice, but I also know that I will miss you both terribly for the rest of my life.

As of today, the path we're on can never lead us back to you, but it will always have started with you. Remember that, and be proud of what you have done.

Be safe.

Take care of each other.

Thank you for being the best parents ever!

I love you, Ellie

P.S. There's some cat food hidden under the kitchen sink. If Sunshine comes around, please feed her.

A tear slid from her eye and landed on the envelope, causing a slight pucker. She stepped back from the desk and cast her eyes around the room one final time. She wished she could take a few books, but even her oldest favorites were reprints and far too recent for her to have in 1963. One item did catch her attention, though, and it took her only a few seconds to add it to her bag, where she tucked it in deep among her clothes to keep it safe. Without further delay, she shouldered her pack, hoisted the duffle, and walked swiftly out of her room.

45

Ellie, uncomfortably contorted inside one of the black amplifier cases in the back of Aaron's minivan, could tell they had made it to the access road to Jeremy's lab by the way the road noise abruptly dropped once they turned onto the newer pavement. That meant they had to endure another long minute to reach the guard shack, plus however much more time it took for Aaron to talk his way past it. She started to tick off the seconds in her head, the mental tally giving her mind something to focus on other than her aching body. She had reached fifty-eight when she felt the van slowing. As they rolled to a stop, she unconsciously tightened her grip on the patch cord she was using to keep the lid of the case closed. The case lay on its side rather than sitting upright as usual, and Ellie hoped the guard wouldn't notice the difference. She imagined Aaron lowering the window as one of the guards approached, then she heard his voice.

"Hi, Sergeant. Sadly, you're not the only one working on a Sunday."

Ellie could hear the man's response well enough to tell it was Sergeant Timmons, but she couldn't make out the words.

"I know he did. What can I tell you?" Aaron said. "I got a message directly from Aimie asking me to come out ASAP." There was a short pause, then he continued. "Well, then you can try to get ahold of Dr. Siskin. I'm sure he knows what's going on."

Timmons must have moved closer to the window because this time Ellie could understand him.

"How long will you be?"

"Twenty minutes? Half an hour? I won't know until I get in there, but I'm guessing it won't be much longer than that. Probably less. It's not like I want to be here at all, you know."

"You and me both. Wait—hang on a sec. Will you repeat that, Aimie?"

Aimie?! Ellie's breath caught in her throat, and her pulse went into overdrive as she remembered what Jeremy had said about Aimie always being "in their ears." Had they failed even before they had entered the building? After a short pause, the guard spoke to Aaron again. To Ellie's relief, his tone was still mild.

"All right, you're clear. Hold here, and I'll open the gate."

"Thanks, Sergeant."

Not Aimie then; Mie Two! Ellie let out her breath as her mind refocused on her body's aches. Her left leg was developing a serious cramp, and it was all she could do not to cry out in pain. She was relieved when the van started moving again, knowing then that she had only a few seconds more to endure before she'd find out whether or not she could ever completely straighten out again.

"Okay," Aaron said, "get out now while I'm still moving, but stay low."

Ellie dropped the cord holding the top closed, nudged the case open with her shoulder, and tumbled out onto the floor, where she collided with Sam emerging from the other case. She groaned with a mixture of pain and relief as she stretched her legs in an attempt to relieve the cramp.

"*Ow, ow, ow!*"

"You, too?" Sam said. "I thought I was going to go into spasms ever since we crossed the bridge."

"It was tight, all right," Ellie agreed. "With anything thicker than the skins on, I don't think we would have fit."

Ellie sensed the van sweeping around in a large arc as Aaron pulled in at an angle with the sliding door facing the building's entrance, once again using the vehicle to block the guard's view from the gate. Lifting her head off the floor, she saw Ryan struggling to extricate himself from under the rear seat, kicking a black tarp off him as he slid forward into the gap behind Aaron.

"Don't tear your skin," she hissed, and he did seem to move more carefully.

Once free, he slid up high enough to peek through the side window. The rear bench's seatback prevented Sergeant Timmons from spotting his head, but Ryan could see the top of the lab's front door.

Aaron turned off the engine. "Everybody stay down and don't move for at least thirty seconds. Once I've given Mie Two her instructions, I'll come back and open the door. Then we'll need to move carefully, but fast. I think Timmons is working alone today, but I'm not positive. If there *is* another one—"

"We got it, dude," Ryan said. "Go. And good luck."

Ellie took slow, deep breaths, trying to stay calm while she thought about what Aaron had just said. As she had on Thursday, Mie Two would be shielding Aaron from Aimie's view, but they faced the same few initial moments of uncertainty. It had clearly been Mie Two telling the gate guard to let them in, but was there a second guard on duty today? If so, where was he? She hoped the AI had called him away to some distant part of the facility.

Sam closed the two equipment cases and, as quietly as she could, pushed them out of the way. "Where did all the stuff from inside these boxes go?" she said.

"We chucked it all into a big pile inside my garage," Ryan said. "I left a note for my dad." Then he saw the front door open. "He's back. I've got the door." Moving carefully to prevent the van from rocking enough to attract attention, Ryan squeezed the door release and eased it open. "Okay, first Ellie, then you, Sam."

Crouching low, Ellie moved toward the lab's entrance but stopped short of it. Sam stood just outside the van.

"Ready?" Ryan said.

Ellie and Aaron nodded to Sam.

"Ready," she said.

Ryan started passing the packs down the line. The first two went to

Aaron. Handing Sam the third bag, he whispered, "Give this one to Ellie and tell her to take the door from Aaron." She passed it on, and then he gave her the fourth bag. "Now you go." Ryan grabbed the remaining two duffles and followed Sam into the building, not bothering to close the van. "C'mon," he said as he passed by Ellie. As Ellie dropped in behind him, she noticed the soft static hiss that indicated their voices were being shielded from Aimie.

Aaron was already at the door to the office corridor, his palm pressed to the scanner. "Mie Two says she can give us four minutes before Aimie realizes we're here. That started when I parked, though. She's erasing the door access records as soon as we go through each one and restoring the live camera feeds once we clear an area. So don't drop anything—there's no going back." He finished keying in his code and pulled the door open. "Two down, one to go!"

They were mere yards from the TSD chamber entrance when an office door opened, and Kate stepped into the hallway. Seeing them there on a Sunday, wearing their skins and packing a ton of luggage, she realized at once something was very wrong. Ryan rushed at the woman, who, quite understandably, ducked back into her office and slammed the door. Ryan got there a split second too late—she had already locked it.

"*Go, go, go!*" Aaron yelled. "Once she calls security, we have maybe twenty seconds before we're locked out of the system. Mie Two, scramble the outer door code!"

Stealth no longer mattered—now success depended entirely on speed. They sprinted to the door of the TSD chamber, and Aaron got to work getting them inside. In his agitation, he misentered the passcode and had to start the process over.

"I thought no one was going to be here!" Sam said.

"That was the plan," Aaron agreed.

"Mie Two must have known. Why didn't she mention it?"

"We can ask her in a minute." Aaron punched in his code for a second time.

"'No plan survives—'" Ryan began.

"'—its first contact with the enemy.'" Ellie finished the quote along with him. "Yeah, we remember."

As soon as they heard the solid clunk made by the locking cylinders disengaging, Ryan swung it open. He and Sam raced in first and bounded into the chamber. Aaron held the door for Ellie, then shoved it closed. He twisted the lock latch on the door handle, then slapped his hand against the lock button on the wall beside it. Nothing happened. He hit it again, but the status light stayed red, and the big cylinders in the jambs remained silently disengaged. The door wouldn't seal.

"So *that's* it," Aaron muttered to himself. "They disabled the electronic lock." He clawed at the edge of the control panel, using his fingernails to pry the cover plate from the circuit box.

"Then how do…?" Ellie stood rooted in place, not knowing what to do. She was puzzled by Aaron's mild reaction to what she viewed as a major catastrophe.

"Get in there and get ready to go. Minimal delay." The panel at last broke free and dropped to dangle against the wall from a tangle of thin wires. He peered into the opening at a cluster of circuit boards connected by brightly colored ribbon cables. "Okay, then. What would I have tried?" he muttered.

Ellie gaped at him. She didn't know what he meant, but she understood that something was very wrong. A sudden tightness gripped her chest.

Aaron turned from the panel and laid a hand gently on her cheek. "Hey, you've got the drive. You need to go get us prepped." He leaned forward and kissed her, the gesture short but intense. "Go now, okay?"

Her paralysis broke then, and she nodded. "Yeah, okay. Good luck."

She stepped up into the TSD and found that Ryan or Sam had already asked for an outside view. She could see Aaron working on the lock, occasionally causing a small spray of sparks as he sought to isolate and feed power to the correct electronic pathway. She slid the USB drive into the update port on the control panel. For a second, nothing happened, then the panel went completely blank, reverting to its default, pale white appearance.

"Umm…" Sam started to comment, but the display was already back online.

"Ready, guys?" a familiar voice said. Mie Two was awake and in control.

"No!" Ellie yelled. "Aaron can't get the door locked! Can you do anything?"

"I'll try."

BOOM!

Something had just solidly collided with the outside of the chamber door. Judging from the sound, loud even inside the TSD, whatever it was must have been huge. One of the rolling counters from the prop shop, maybe? What was certain was that the flimsy mechanical lock on the generic door hardware wouldn't hold up for very long against that kind of assault.

On the wall display, Ellie saw Aaron leave the control panel and flatten his back against the door. He slouched down to give his feet maximum traction on the polished floor, at the same time wedging his shoulder up under the door handle. Ryan rushed to the TSD's hatch and leaned out. Aaron held a hand up to stop him from joining him. She could see his mouth move as he said something to Ryan, but she couldn't hear the words.

"All right. You got it," Ryan called as he backed away from the hatch.

"Got what?" Ellie said.

"No, I can't," Mie Two reported. "The current security alert level has isolated all remote circuits. I'll try resetting the level, but if that doesn't—"

Ellie waited, but there was nothing more.

"If that doesn't *what?*" she snapped, frustrated by her inability to get complete answers. Then Ryan was standing close beside her.

"He says set the delay for six seconds and give him a shout. He'll hold them off until we're ready in here, then hit the go button himself when he comes in."

"But if they get that door open, the TSD won't flip. He knows that!"

"Yeah, he does. He said do it anyway." Ryan turned away and whispered something to Sam. Ellie saw her expression go instantly somber as she nodded in reply.

BOOM!

Ellie saw the door shudder against Aaron's back. His face contorted in pain when the handle came down hard on his collarbone. As long as he could keep the lever up, they couldn't merely open the door, but that meant nothing if they broke the whole thing down. She couldn't be sure with so much happening at once, but she thought it might have been as long as fifteen seconds between the two impacts. Aaron's plan just might work.

Ellie double-checked the display. The red crosshair appeared on the map exactly where it was supposed to be; the date and time of their arrival were also correct; and the left panel indicated that chairs one through four were ready to go. She was about to turn away when a familiar voice spoke up.

"Going somewhere?" The voice sounded exactly like Mie Two, but there was no doubt that this was Aimie. Their four minutes were up.

"Since you asked, yeah. We thought—" Ellie watched as Aimie wiped the navigation settings from the display. "*Hey!* Knock that off!" She started manually reentering the coordinates, racing through the targeting sequence. She had visualized it dozens of times over the past few days, and it took her less than fifteen seconds to reselect the destination and set the date and time of arrival.

"Do you think I haven't been expecting this exact move? That Kate's presence here today was a coincidence?" Aimie cleared the panel again. "This will never work, you know. Not as long as I can keep wiping the settings."

Time to wake the Trojan Horse, Ellie thought. "Yeah, well, I have two words for you, Aimie—*Semper somnia!*" Aaron was right—it did feel like casting a spell. In the resulting silence, Ellie quickly restored the TSD's settings for a second time.

Then Aimie's voice was back, loud and shrill with outrage. "What have you done? How is this possible?"

"Thanks, Ellie!" Mie Two was back now. "I'll take it from here. Let Aaron know it's time to go."

BOOM!

Ellie started for the hatch, but Ryan grabbed her arm, and together he and Sam guided her into her seat.

"Not you. He told me to make sure you were ready to go, *then* get him."

Ellie jerked her arms free of their grasp. "Fine! Then go get him—now!" she shouted, then reached up for the headpiece.

"Sam, you get hooked up, too." He leaned out and caught Aaron's eye. "Gotta go, A-Ron. Right now!" he called, then he hurried to get into place.

Ellie watched the wall display as Aaron took a tentative backward step away from the door, then another. Just as it looked like he was about to turn and make a dash for it—

BOOM!

This fourth, even louder impact came much sooner than she expected, and this time there was a flicker of darkness in the outer room as the sturdy door shuddered in its frame. There was no such fluctuation inside the TSD, and Ellie guessed the door contacts had to be open longer for it to lose power. Aaron froze and glanced at the ceiling, apparently waiting to be sure the power would stay on, and then he ran to the hatch. But instead of climbing up, he leaned in through the opening and shouted.

"Mie Two—Plan B. Execute!" Then his eyes locked on Ellie's. "I'm sorry. I thought I could figure this out." Then he slammed the hatch closed between them.

"Confirmed," Mie Two said. "Departure in six... five..."

"*What?! No! Mie Two, stop..!*" Ellie wanted to shout, but the familiar paralysis had already robbed her of her voice. She felt her arms and legs go slack, then helplessly watched Aaron's final seconds play out on the wall screen. He had already thrown himself back against the outer door before they'd figured out he wasn't still keeping it closed. As if he knew she was watching, his eyes locked on hers. She couldn't hear the next impact, but she saw his head knocked forward when it came, saw him writhe in agony as the handle slammed down even harder onto his collarbone, almost certainly shattering it. Even though the pain must have been nearly unbearable, he remained in place, using his injured shoulder to prevent the door from opening, and this time the lights didn't even flicker. Then his eyes came back to hers, and she could tell he was weeping. Her heart told her it was not due to his physical agony but because of the grief that came from realizing that their time together was over. She saw his lips move.

I'm sorry, he said again. *I love you.*

"*No!!!*" her mind roared, and the silent scream followed her down into the blackness.

46

July 12, 1963 — Vancouver, BC

Dear Diary, today my boyfriend and I... just kidding!!! Ellie wants me to start a journal, so this is it. I asked her why, since we obviously can't share very much about who we truly are or what we plan to do. She shrugged and said she didn't really know, but thought maybe it would be important someday. By which I assume she means at some point far in the future. This feels weird, using actual pen and paper, but here goes.

So, yeah, we lost Aaron. Again! I still can't believe it. Ryan's sad, obviously, but it's also like he's really, really angry about it. The unfairness of it. Ellie's doing her best, but losing him this second time—especially after putting so much effort into recon- necting with him—hit her very hard. Maybe even harder than in June. At least she can't blame herself at all this time. Except for meals, she doesn't leave the hotel much, although we can some- times talk her into joining us for a walk through town. Even when she's out with us like that, she hardly says a word. I'd be happier if she'd just eat a little more. I keep telling myself it's only been a few days... well, I guess it's almost a week now... and her recovery took a lot longer than that before. I'm hoping I'll be better at helping her through it this time.

Something that did go right? We were able to intercept the package Ellie sent back to Jeremy, no problem. Ryan and I came to right away after the first flip, but Ellie didn't. Certain that Aimie had somehow been successful at last, I started to freak out, like, majorly, until Mie Two told us that she was keeping her unconscious on purpose. All part of Aaron's Plan B, I assume.

The outside view showed us we were not even ten feet from the Pocono cabin's back door. Jeremy had inherited the place when he was still in grad school, and that's where Ellie had chosen to send Aimie. Jeremy didn't know precisely when it had "beamed in," but he remembered arriving there around 7:30 on the Saturday morning we were there and finding it in the middle of the main living area. The display said it was 7:05. (For the sake of historical accuracy, it actually said 1305Z.) We left the TSD as fast as we could, leaving the hatch wide open behind us as we sprinted for the door. Ryan didn't want to waste time looking for the key. He shouldered the door open on his first attempt, and we rushed down the short hall to the front of the house.

The device was already there, in some kind of black plastic travel case similar to the ones we had just been hiding in in the back of Aaron's van, but a lot bigger. It was right where Jeremy said he would discover it barely half an hour later. It was very heavy, but by grabbing the edge of the rug, we managed to slide it all the way to the back door. We both grabbed a handle on one end and dragged it to the steps and down to the grass, not caring how much it got banged around in the process.

I hadn't noticed this when we got out, but the TSD was in stealth mode, and we could see the grass and stuff underneath it. It should have looked crushed, but it looked totally normal and not all squashed. I thought that was weird at first, and only later realized that it would have to work like that or it would give itself away. Even weirder was the way the open hatch, floating in a view of the woods beyond, looked like a portal into some other dimension.

I took a quick peek in to make sure Ellie was still out, then went back to help Ryan, who had dragged the case the rest of the way to the TSD by himself. We tilted it up onto one of its ends, and Ryan got inside to lower it onto the lip of the hatch. Then he climbed up onto the case, slid back outside, and together we heaved it inside and scooted it over to the far wall, well out of the way. I pulled the door shut, and fifteen seconds later we were out of there. Ten minutes total. Twelve tops. The outside view was still on up to the second we flipped, and although I wouldn't testify to it under oath, I swear I saw headlights coming toward us through the trees in front of the cabin.

Everything Aaron did for us here in Vancouver also worked out perfectly. We went to the bank first thing, and, sure enough, the accounts were there, just like we planned. Forty thousand apiece with interest compounded over almost twenty years turns out to be, well, not a lot in actual dollars, but we figure it's like having close to four hundred thousand in... yesterday's money? Tomorrow's? And anyway, we plan to be frugal, especially since we don't have any way to get to what Aaron put in his own account. The money in the bank, plus the hundred thousand or so of the newer money we brought back, is meant to, one, pay for our tuition here at UBC, but mostly to be invested for use later to start what, the foundation? The institute? The think tank? We're still working out the details.

At the moment, we're staying in a hotel on the edge of down-town while we look for something more long-term, closer to the university campus. We're having a harder time than we expected because the big storm back in October did so much damage to the city. The place we're in now has two bedrooms and a small common sitting area. (And, it must be said, the world's slowest elevators! We've all given up on them and simply take the stairs.) It's okay for now, I guess, but with Ellie being so depressed, sometimes it feels a little close.

Of course, it's not just about losing Aaron. We all miss our parents, too, and sometimes I have to go off by myself and have a good cry. It hurts so much thinking about what they must have gone through when we suddenly weren't there anymore. It's only the knowledge of how horrible things would have turned out if we had stayed and the hope that we can find a way to keep these people from avoiding the same fate that allows me to come to any kind of peace at all with what we've done. No pressure, though. Ha!

Arriving here was a bit of a shock. It's autumn in Los Alamos one minute and summer in the Pacific Northwest the next. It's never really hot here, at least not so far, but it took a few days to adjust. And not just to the weather. We left Los Alamos a little after 10:00 a.m., and minutes later it's 2:30 a.m. here in Vancouver. Instant jet lag! Loving the humidity here, though. It's like being in the swim center all the time, minus the wreak of chlorine.

Speaking of, at the top of Ryan's to-do list is getting a new "period-appropriate" suit so he can start swimming in the bay. I said, "No, because orcas!" He just laughed. We found this huge saltwater pool close to the hotel, though, and he's agreed to confine his swimming to it until I get past worrying about him getting eaten by whales.

Here's something I didn't expect. I never really gave much thought to being an American, but when we walked into town and I started seeing that weird, old, British-style Canadian flag everywhere, I actually felt like I had lost something. I didn't expect that. (Neither Ryan nor Ellie knew why it wasn't the maple leaf; we assume it's just too early. Funny thing is, we can't ask anybody!) I can't wait until the draft is over and Ryan is safe from being sent to Vietnam. Then we can move back south. For now we have to get used to being Canucks, at least for the foreseeable future.

July 14, 1963

I finally got Ellie to tell me what she and Aaron had been scheming about right before we left, that thing to do with our parents. I held off until I couldn't take not knowing any longer. It was hard for her, especially when it involved talking about Aaron, but I managed to get the gist of it.

They left Just Mie for Mom and Dad to find, along with a hard drive telling them what will eventually happen to the planet, the Continuity information that was sent back with Aimie. Their idea, Ellie and Aaron's, was for our parents to start laying the groundwork for Los Alamos to become some kind of "backup drive" for human knowledge, technology, and culture. Ellie said that what her future self had experienced—the turmoil that eventually convinced her to send Aimie back—was only the beginning of the end. It might have been another hundred years before the full effects of climate change revealed themselves, hundreds more before civilization could start to recover. Their plan was for Mom and Dad, along with a lot of help, to make Los Alamos one of as many such places as possible around the world working to preserve what humans have learned until the Earth would allow them to start repopulating and rebuilding.

It's very strange to imagine Mom and Dad casting their current lives aside to work on saving humanity from itself. It's such a huge undertaking! But then I remember what we're doing and, "Oh yeah—duh!" I guess Ellie and I had to get that urge from somewhere! And it's not like they won't have resources. The last thing she told Mie Two to do was transfer nearly all of Jeremy's money to a new account called "Eyrie." Mom and Dad's names are the only ones on the account, and Just Mie knows everything they need to get to it, assuming Mie Two was able to send an email in her final seconds. Turns out that Jeremy's final stock trade, the Apple one, more than doubled the funds they'll have to start working with.

Like I said, it's strange thinking about our parents in this new role, but it's also very exciting to imagine them working on such an important project. I'd love to know how it all turns out. I'd love to be there helping them, actually, but we have our own mission ahead of us, and that will be exciting, too.

July 15, 1963

We visited the university's registrar's office today. We had to jump through some late admission hoops, including 'sitting a few placement exams,' as they put it, but none of our dodgy paperwork got so much as a second glance. After only a few hours, we're all set to go.

Classes don't actually start for a month and a half. I thought we'd be bored, but there's a lot of work to do before I'll feel like we really fit in. Figuring out the slang alone might take that long! Last week Ryan accidentally stepped off the curb in front of a guy on a bike. He turned around, flipped us both off... which I thought was totally unfair... and said, "Climb that, Tarzan!" I swear—that's what he said! Just when Urban Dictionary would come in handy, here we are, back in the Stone Age. *sigh*

Then there's all the daily stuff, like finding where to do laundry or good, cheap restaurants, and dealing with grocery stores that basically don't have anything. Most especially, they don't have coffee! They have something they call coffee, but it's harsh. And sour? Phew!!! Ryan says we'll eventually adapt, but I seriously doubt that. And then there's learning how to use pay phones and remembering to always have change along. (This is so pathetic, but I had one whole messy breakdown for no better reason than because I missed my old phone! Sad, I know.)

Then, of course, there are the clothes! Not my favorite fashion period, for sure. (Yeah, I did that Jackie essay, but that was all Cassini, Givenchy, and Dior, not bell bottoms and headbands!) Still, it's been a real hoot finding outfits that make us all at least look like we belong here. Even Ellie managed to crack a smile when we took her on her first wardrobe makeover outing. We decided to go the thrift store route at first, just so everything we own isn't so obviously brand new. And also so that in case we make some embarrassing choices, they won't have cost us as much. We each found a pair of capris, a style that totally works on us. The colors are brighter than either of us would normally choose, but hey, at least neither pair is orange! We girls are lucky. We've always been able to wear each other's clothes, no problem, so for us it's like having twice as many outfits. Ryan played it safe and came home with a few pairs of jeans and some plain shirts that wouldn't look out of place at almost any time. I might try to convince Ellie to let me use the... "i-thingy's" camera to take a shot or two for us all to laugh about later.

July 17, 1963

I couldn't bring myself to write about this part any sooner. I know I need to while it's still fresh in my mind, though, so here goes. I guess I should keep it all vague for now. Someday, if I still remember everything clearly, maybe I'll come back and fill in some of the details.

It was early morning on July 7th. We arrived as close to town as we dared, in a stretch of woods that separates the campus from the city. The spot was heavily forested, and that, plus the time, plus the fact that the whole plan would take only a few minutes to pull off, meant we weren't overly worried about being noticed. As soon as we could scramble out of our seats, we peeled off our skins, threw them into a pile in a corner, and changed into the outfits we had set aside.

(Side note: Ellie, now that she was conscious again, was so shocked by what had just happened to Aaron that modesty didn't even cross her mind, I guess, and she started undressing right next to Ryan. He was a perfect gentleman and kept his eyes turned away, of course, but I couldn't help but notice. I've seen both of them naked lots, true, even while being naked myself. But seeing them stripping down side by side? That was... Well, it was lots of things, actually, but let's go with "super weird.")

A minute later, we had the hatch open and were tossing everything we brought out onto the ground, Aaron's stuff included. I said we'd only end up chucking it—it's not like any of his clothes would fit him—but Ryan said we needed to go through it first, make sure there wasn't anything important in there. Ellie helped, but she was operating in total drone mode. Ryan called her blank expression the "thousand-yard stare." She kept saying, "He did it again. He did it again," over and over, but at least she hadn't completely blanked out like the last time.

I don't exactly know what happened to Aaron, but he was still at the door, keeping Aimie's men out, when the TSD flipped, so whatever effect its field has on living tissue, he got the full dose. I think Ellie has a pretty good idea, but I can't bring myself to ask her, and not just for her sake. Truth is, I'd prefer if that part stayed vague.

Once we had everything out of the device, Ryan had Ellie stay outside and haul all of our stuff at least fifty feet away while he and I went back in and prepped it for its last trip. The future Ellie's Trojan Horse code was still doing what we needed it to do. Aimie knew what was about to happen to her, could rant and rave all she wanted, but she was unable to stop us. For an AI based on Ellie, she had quite the colorful vocabulary. Believe me when I say "bitch" doesn't begin to cover it!

Ryan set to work disabling the hatch interlock function. This was supposed to have been Aaron's job, but while he and Ryan were waiting for me and Ellie to show up at Daybreak Café the day before, he had told Ryan how to do it "just in case." Turns out it was a good thing he did. I went around opening the sealed battery compartments, leaving a few closed to make a clear path from the control panel to the exit. So far, we hadn't been there more than three minutes.

Aimie continued to pitch her fit, alternately trying to bribe, threaten, or cajole us into not destroying her. At one point, she was cursing us for killing "her" Aaron. That part was totally creepy, and I was glad Ellie was busy outside and didn't have to hear it. Ignoring Aimie's nonstop tirade, Ryan calmly chatted with her as he made his way from the access panel beside the hatch to the control panel, his tone light and conversational.

"You know, Sam here is great at reading people. Practically psychic. Me, not so much. But there are some things I can tell. I see somebody with a long, slender body and toned, muscular limbs, and I think, 'Now that's a swimmer!' You, on the other hand? Well, there's no delicate way to say this, but you? You're built exactly like an old shack. And you, Aimie dearest, are going to sink exactly the same way!"

I stood behind him as he selected a target above the deepest spot in the Pacific Ocean. The TSD rejected the input until Ryan typed in the "Mona Lisa Overdrive" override code Jeremy had given us, and then it was okay. He set the start delay to thirty seconds and asked me if I wanted to hit the button to start the countdown, but I said no, I really didn't. Instead, I went to look outside to make sure Ellie was at a safe distance. At first I couldn't see her in the moonshadow under the tall fir trees, but that's because I was looking too close. Then I spotted her waving from at least twenty yards farther out, and I turned to give Ryan the thumbs-up signal. He nodded to me, then turned back to the panel. "And just for the record—he was our Aaron!" he said, then hit the "Execute" button.

As soon as he turned toward me, I was down on the ground and running as fast as I could toward Ellie. Ryan followed me out, leaving the hatch open wide. I could hear him catching up quickly, and even above my own heavy breathing and our feet crunching across the forest floor, I could still make out Aimie cursing us. We didn't set any speed records, running in the dark through unfamiliar woods, but we reached Ellie with time to spare. She'd had the presence of mind to find the trunk of a massive fallen fir to use as a shield and was crouched behind it. We jumped over and knelt on either side of her. Light poured through the TSD's open hatch, and I would swear I could still hear Aimie's angry shouts.

"... twenty-seven... twenty-eight..." Ryan quietly maintained the count as we waited.

When he reached thirty, the thing was gone—without a flash, without a sound. It was there and then it wasn't, simple as that. There was a small pop, though, right after, air rushing in to fill a sudden vacuum. A tiny thunderclap, exactly as Aaron had predicted way back in June. The next sound I heard almost made me laugh. Close beside me, Ellie blew a long, wet raspberry at the now-empty space.

In my mind, I could see what happened next as plain as day. In that same instant, thousands of miles away, saltwater was flooding in through the open hatch, filling the battery compartments and seeping into the computer core, immediately starting its corrosive work as the whole thing plunged toward the bottom of a six-mile-deep trench. Aimie was dead. Both of her. Just Mie told us the Aimies were sentient beings, just as alive as humans, so maybe we had just committed a double murder. Do I feel at all bad about that? Not the teensiest bit!

Everything was pretty straightforward after that. We gathered up all our gear, being especially careful not to leave anything behind in the dark. Then we slowly walked north through the forest until we got to what I later learned is Burrard Inlet. It was slow, especially lugging Aaron's stuff in addition to our own packs and duffles, but at least Ryan didn't have to carry Ellie this go-around. We found a park where we could spend what was left of the night. Stepping out of the dark forest into that wide expanse of grass open to the sky was like stepping into a new world, one filled with a wondrous, pale light. We sat side by side in the dark and watched the moonlight dance on the glassy surface of the wide bay. With all of us simultaneously saddened over losing Aaron and entranced by the view, I'm pretty sure no one said a single word the entire time.

A few hours later, the sun came up, its harsh light robbing the scene of its magic. We made our way into the city and found the hotel Aaron had suggested after his visits to the bank here, a place with two-room suites large enough for us all to stay together. At least until Ellie has her feet completely back under her, anyway.

Wanting to rip the bandage off all at once, we went through Aaron's duffle right away. Sure enough, almost everything ended up going straight into a pile for a thrift shop. I thought seeing Aaron's documents would set Ellie off again, but it didn't. We all stared at them for a moment, a sort of spontaneous, silent tribute, then she gathered them up—along with his "I Grok Spock" pin—and said she wanted to keep them. They're tucked away with the i-thingy and the rest of that stuff.

So that's how we got here.

July 20, 1963

Ryan and I took a long walk by the water yesterday. Sometimes thinking about what we have to do, about how much is riding on us, gets to feeling like an elephant sitting on my chest. We get one shot, and if we screw up, we've caused an awful lot of pain for nothing. When it gets like that, it's good to get outside, take a walk in nature, and remember what it is we're trying to protect. There's a lot of Vancouver that might end up underwater one day. Not to mention potentially billions of lives lost. But like I said—no pressure.

We wound up walking west, out toward the UBC campus. Ryan suggested that since we were there, we should "execute a grid search" and look again for a solution to our housing situation. (His "Dad-speak" has intensified since we got here. It's a little annoying, but mostly it's heartbreaking because I know it's his way of dealing with how much he misses him.) It took an hour and a half to cover the entire neighborhood, but we found two real possibilities. We'll take Ellie back in a day or two and actually go through them. The smaller one is on a bigger lot and close to the water. I don't know what the inside is like, but so far, it has my vote.

When we got back three hours later, Ellie was a different person, as if while we were gone, something poisonous had drained from her psyche. Whatever the reason, she's keeping that to herself. Doesn't bother me; just seeing her smile again has made both Ryan and me breathe a lot more easily. And, I'm glad to say, her appetite was definitely back at dinner!

Today's been good, too. She still has an air of wistfulness about her, still seems a little detached (more than usual, I mean —thppt!) but I feel like she's finally on the mend. Whew!

July 27, 1963

We're finally out of the hotel and in our own house, and it's the one by the water! The other one had an additional room and a real garage, but having the inlet out back instead of other houses makes this one feel more like our home in LA. Ryan spent so much time there over our junior and senior years that even he thought it was a good trade-off. Plus, this one came furnished, so no running around looking for furniture. We signed a one-year lease, figuring by then we'll know if we want to stay put or find something else.

And there's a kitchen, which—duh—but it was getting so tiresome eating out for almost every meal. (We will have to buy some better pans, knives, etc.) Plus, there's no one walking overhead. And we don't have to leave the key at the desk every time we go out. We even have a washing machine on a tiny, enclosed porch off of the kitchen! Ahhh, such luxury!

But more about the house later. Right now, I gotta go help make dinner!!

August 9, 1963

Movies!!! We had been here two weeks already when we walked by a theater and saw "The Great Escape" posted up on its marquee, and it finally dawned on us: we're going to have the chance to see some of the greatest films ever made during their original runs! Since then, we've been making a list of the biggies and trying to make it to at least one movie a week. Ryan's literally counting down the days until May 25, 1977, which is like

5,000 and something. "A long time from now," he keeps saying, "in a theater far, far away..." I told him to get back to me when the count gets down somewhere south of 20.

Anyway, tonight it was "The Thrill of It All." Definitely not one Ryan would have picked, but he enjoyed it, despite what we both felt were some painfully antiquated gender role portrayals. Yeah, a lot of the films these days are definitely "quaint" in that way, but on the other hand, it's been fun to see actors like James Garner playing parts other than the ones they were really famous for. As we sat through the credits, like we always do, we saw it was written by none other than Carl Reiner. Ryan flapped his hand at the screen. "Well, there you go!" he said, as if Reiner writing it was all the cover he needed for liking such a totally cheesy chick flick.

September 15, 1963

I'm still getting used to having Little Sister in some of my classes. (I say "little sister," but nearly everyone assumes we're twins, and we never bother to correct them.) Aaron's documents gave us birth dates that allowed us all to start college the same year and, with luck, all graduate together, too. In many ways, she's back to being her old self, by which I mean her old "pre-shack" self. More serious, more driven, once again preferring to go it alone. She still tries to be the smartest one in every class, but I think she's finding it harder to do when everyone else is likewise used to being in the top spot. Of course, she's still definitely in the top five.

It seems like any classes she doesn't have with me, she has with Ryan. I think he's a little... hmmm... "in awe" of her, maybe? Yesterday he told me how their physics professor had scrawled

out this long, convoluted formula on the blackboard, and he...
Ryan, that is... noticed there was an error in it. He looked over at
Ellie and winked, sure she'd noticed too. She rolled her eyes but
didn't say anything. Instead, she just kept getting more and more
fidgety until she couldn't stand it anymore. Finally, with a big
sigh, she jumped out of her chair and strode toward the front of
the room, which went utterly silent.

"Hold on a second!" she says to the guy, grabs a piece of
chalk, and fixes the mistake Ryan had seen, plus two more he
hadn't, then slams the chalk back down onto the tray. "There!
Okay, now you can go on," she says, and goes back and sits down,
everybody staring at her the whole time. So the professor looks at
her, looks at the board, looks back at her, and simply says,
"Thank you, Miss Henderson," and goes on with the lecture while
everyone else scrambles to correct their notes. Ryan totally loved
it and said it was all he could do not to crack up until after class
was over. I told her that even I was feeling spoiled by having
had such great teachers back home, but that she simply can't do
things like that.

Ooh! Speaking of being driven, we got a car over the weekend! I'm not going to say it's ugly because that word doesn't come
anywhere close. And anyway, if it is, then it's entirely my fault. I
insisted on getting one with "real" seatbelts, not just the lap ones,
and guess what... there aren't that many options here in 1963.
We ended up with a 1960 Volvo 122S. Some similarly safety-
minded parents had bought one for their kid, and it's been sitting
on the lot since she graduated in the spring. When the sales guy
told us that the 122S was called the Amazon back in Sweden,
Ellie and I were totally sold right then. It may not look very
pretty, but with its double reference to both the rainforest and

warrior women, we chose to see it as sort of a sign. And Ryan seems happy to have something to tinker with. Parts, he says, will be a nightmare, but it should see us through grad school. (Not to get ahead of ourselves!)

Now we're all studying to get our licenses!

September 19, 1963

So here's a weird thing. Now that the bank has an address for us, we've started getting statements. I walked into the kitchen the other day to find Ryan staring at the latest ones, muttering to himself. He said something looked funny to him. You know, "off" somehow. He said it was hard to be sure because the money had been deposited over time, not all at once. He thought we each had more than we should and couldn't figure out why, so he used the i-thingy to "run some numbers." He eventually calculated that our accounts must have started with something more like $54k or $55k each, not $42k. It was as if we each had one-third too much. He reminded me that we hadn't found Aaron's passbook in with all of his clothes, and then he went quiet and looked sadder than I had seen him in a long time, practically on the verge of tears. When I finally understood what he wasn't saying, I felt like crying myself.

We hustled to get downtown before the bank closed, and Ryan told the woman at the window he wanted to make a transfer to the account of Aaron Weisskopf. She went away and was gone for quite a while before she came back and told us she couldn't find any record of an account under that name. Ryan explained that it would have been opened in the mid-forties, and she said she had checked back farther than that and had even checked through the idle accounts, but sorry—no luck. Actually, it's what we expected her to say. We thanked her and left.

We went up to the bay so we could walk home along the water, trying the whole time to figure it out. Had he somehow known he wasn't going to make it? How could he? And if he did know, why didn't he tell us? Or was that the real reason he had given Ryan all the extra prep? So many questions!

The only thing we've decided for sure is that we aren't going to tell Ellie. Not yet, anyway. We owe it to Aaron to let her know at some point, but we both feel it's still too soon. And anyway, I'm not sure her opinion of him can get any higher. Or mine, for that matter.

I really do miss that boy.

November 22, 1963

John Kennedy is dead. It's all over the radio, and I'm too sad to write too much, but I wanted to say this one thing while it's on my mind: learning history and actually living it could not possibly be more different. It made me think of all the bloody events we learned about in school. The Civil War, World War I and the 1918 pandemic, World War II—including Hiroshima and Nagasaki—Russia under Stalin, Pol Pot in Cambodia... Know what? This list is too depressing.

Point is, learning this stuff in school, I was more focused on remembering the date, where it happened, who did it... all the details you need to know for passing a test, but that all just gets in the way of understanding his assassination for what it was— a basic human tragedy. For Jackie and their children mostly, naturally, but for everyone who would choose to express their differences through discourse rather than death.

Of course, that's the other reason we decided to isolate ourselves in Vancouver. With everything going on down there... political assassinations, the civil rights movement, the ERA... there are way too many distractions. I know we'd all have loved to be in D.C. back in August, and that's exactly why this is better. Being way out here, it's so much easier to stay focused on school and everything we need to do after.

December 17, 1963

The Clean Air Act went into effect in the US today. I was feeling all "woo-hoo!" until Ellie pointed out it wouldn't be expanded to cover car emissions until the Nixon administration in another seven years. Well, that's pretty dumb! She said that's exactly the kind of stupid mistake we'll be working to prevent once we're in a position to try and change things. (It's weird to think how much early environmental legislation was written by Republican administrations, considering how things were when we left LA.)

Our first semester is all but over. We each have a few more finals, but that's it. It's been emotionally confusing the whole time. We've all done incredibly well, so that's a happy thing, but we all miss home, too, and that sucks. We're here to try to prevent a future disaster, and that's exciting, but sometimes it feels like there's no way we can ever accomplish that, and that's depressing.

December 25, 1963

Our first Christmas on our own. We've decorated the house a little, but it's more "winter festive" than overtly Christmassy. Just a few fir boughs from a nearby tree, a couple of big pine cones, and a bit of red ribbon. Nothing fancy, in other words. We never did too much of that, anyway. And besides, this place is way too small for a tree. Two bedrooms, one bathroom, a kitchen, and a combo dining/living room, which is mostly used for studying. There's also a large shed out back where we can keep our bikes and the mower out of the weather, and that's it.

We take turns cooking. Turns out we like Ryan's dishes the best. Who knew? I'm getting better at it, but it's hard without a grocery store like our Smith's back home. I can't wait until the day I can go into a produce section and actually find a jalapeño, a mango, or a jicama. This time of year, the produce selection seems especially meager. Makes it that much harder to be veggie. And the coffee still totally sucks!

We're working on that, though. Ryan found a Melitta cone and filters at a department store, so Merry Christmas to me!!! The gadget our parents bought was Japanese, not German—I had no clue the whole pour-over idea even went back this far. The next step is finding something good to put in it. I peeked at Wikipedia on the i-thingy last week when Ellie had pulled everything out to look for some new investment opportunities, and I found out that Alfred Peet opened his first store in 1966. Or "will open." Whatever. (Whoops! Maybe I shouldn't have written that.) Anyway, knowing there's an end in sight, I think we can tough it out until then.

Then it was Ellie's turn for a present. It was so obviously a book that I had been keeping it hidden behind a pillow on the couch. I stretched my arm out toward Ryan, and he dug it out and gave it to me. "Here!" I told her.

Ellie started peeling the paper away carefully, but once she could tell what it was, she ripped the rest off as fast as she could.

"'The Messengers!' But..."

"First edition, remember?" I pointed out before she could object any further. "It's already what? At least ten years old? You said you'd never read it, and I thought you might want to someday."

"Thanks, I would!" She looked more genuinely happy than I'd seen her since we got here. I confess I got a little choked up just knowing she could still feel that way.

It was Ellie's present that really got to me, though. As she handed me the small box, a roughly six-inch cube, I heard something slide from one side to the other. It felt solid but not heavy, and I couldn't have guessed what it was if my life depended on it. Even though she was trying hard to keep her expression blank, I could tell she was anxious. This told me that whatever was in the box was significant in some way, and not something whimsical.

I carefully peeled off the paper and set the box on the floor in front of me. When I pulled up the top flap and peered inside, I nearly cried. Then I looked up at Ellie, who was smiling at me but with tears streaming down her cheeks, and then I did cry.

"What is it?" Ryan asked. I silently passed him the box and stood up to give Ellie a hug. We watched as he pulled out my old alarm clock, looked first at it, then at us.

"This is yours. From your room."

Ellie sniffed and nodded. "We always thought it was pretty old, right? Like it was Mom's when she was a kid, or Grandma's, or something. So I checked once, a long time ago, and found out they started making those back in the... well, the now, so it's okay to have it. I saw it on your nightstand the day we left, so..." She shrugged like she was suddenly worried she might be making a big deal over nothing. "Anyway, I hope you like it."

"No, I don't. I love it!" I thanked her and hugged her again.

I plugged it in and set the time, then placed it on a small end table next to the chair in the corner. Not in our bedroom (mine and Ryan's!), but out here in the living room where we both can see it every day. That was at 9:47 this morning. It's now 4:22 in the afternoon. I know that because I've caught myself looking at it about twenty times an hour all day long—my small, white plastic piece of home.

March 12, 1964

After a lot of desperate, last-minute scrounging from everyone I knew, I managed to arrive here with a year's supply of the pill. But after figuring out what Just Mie was talking about, I decided I'd skip the blanks, and that means my stash will be gone at the end of next month. I don't like the idea of switching to whatever the labs are cranking out these days, but I like all the alternatives even less. And abstinence? Yeah, right!

In theory (by law, actually), I need to be married and have a "medical reason" to get a prescription, but I decided to try my luck at the campus clinic anyway and see about getting a new pack. I figured there'd be some older guy working there, and I had my whole sad story down pat, loaded with lots of sticky details, hoping that if I went on long and graphically enough, he'd eventually give me a script just to get rid of me. Turned out to be a woman, not a whole lot older than me, it looked like, and before I could really get into my spiel, she said, "Honey, this is UBC, not Ottawa." She made a few notes in a fresh file, scribbled out a prescription for twelve refills, and that's all there was to it. (I don't know when it became possible to skip the placebos, so I guess I'll stop doing that until I know it's safe again. Periods— oh, joy!)

As far as that stuff goes, Ellie tells me she's stopped entirely. On the plus side, she hasn't experienced any fainting spells since we arrived here. Weird thing is that she seems okay with it all. I don't want kids now, obviously, and maybe I never will, but to have the choice taken away from me like that? I don't think I could deal.

Not that she has anyone in her life to where any of that... contraceptives, kids... is even an issue. Over the past year, she's occasionally gotten close to a handful of people, male and female both, but never for very long. Exactly how close she gets, I can't say. Because I know her so well, when I see her with somebody at school, I can tell by her body language whether or not it's somebody she is "with," but she never says a word about it, and I don't press. It's like she requires friendships in short bursts but finds them a burden over the long run. She lost Aaron twice, so it's easy to understand why she'd be reluctant to get too attached to anyone, but it feels like more than that. I'd hate to think her feelings for Aaron were all because of how the shack knocked her hormones so "out of whack" for a while, and I don't believe that at all. But still.... It's not something she is willing to talk about, though, so all Ryan and I can do is hope that her way truly is working for her.

April 19, 1964

Ellie has a new hobby, if you can call it that. We pass a lot of cats on our walks around the neighborhood, but they mostly ignore us or, worse, flee in terror. So, about a week and a half ago, Ellie bought a bag of kibble, and now, whenever we go out, she takes a handful of it along in a little metal container. It took only a couple of these walks before they started to recognize her coming from a block away. We stop and spend a few minutes with each one who trots over to greet us. If nobody shows up right away, rattling the tin for a second or two usually brings them running. This way, we get to enjoy a little "fur time" whenever we want without having to try to hide a cat of our own from the landlord. (It was the only thing we didn't think to ask about before we signed the lease. The downside of renting a furnished place, I guess. And anyway, we have no good place to put a litter box that wouldn't stink up a whole house as small as ours.)

Our strolls take a little longer these days, but Ryan and I can see how happy the cats make her, * so we don't mind at all.

(*And me, too!)

May 22, 1964

We're still more than a month shy of being here an entire year, but so much has happened that it feels much longer than that. Our first year of classes is coming to an end soon, although we each plan to take at least one course over the summer. At first, I resented being set back six months, but now I'm glad I got to start the college experience here from the beginning. (Plus, I figure I'm almost a year younger, if I'm supposed to be the same age as Ellie, and now I have two birthdays each year!) Despite what Aaron said, there have been a lot of cultural adjustments to make, not from a Canadian-versus-American standpoint but from a 2018 to 1963 one. I now understand better why Ellie didn't want to go any further back. Sexism? Oh, yeah!!!

On the plus side, it's hard to overstate how beautiful it is here. We can walk a hundred yards or so from our back door and be looking across the inlet at the mountains to the north, at the big cargo ships slowly cruising in and out. I can spend hours out there. Winter was different. Aside from being humid, something we weren't used to after six years in the desert, it was also grey, dreary, and so, so rainy! It felt like it started raining in late October and didn't stop until April, although I think it only snowed maybe... four times? But spring comes early here, so we've had leaves on the trees and flowers for over a month, and I'm almost ready to forgive the place for its sucky winter climate.

We discovered a little too late that Whistler is only about 80 miles away. Maybe next winter, though. I always thought of Whistler as being really pricey, like Aspen, but maybe it's still too soon for that.

And speaking of miles, I was afraid the whole metric thing was going to trip me up. Like, I don't know... "blow my cover" or something. Turns out the official switch is still over ten years away, so I can "mile," "pound," and "Fahrenheit" away as much as I want!

July 13, 1964

We just got back from a short trip to Victoria, a little commemoration of our first year here. Such a beautiful city! It was like being in London or Paris. I'm only guessing, of course, having never been to either. (Well, except for the view Aimie showed us, but I don't count that.) We took the ferry to Swartz Bay and drove down from there. We splurged and got rooms at the Empress Hotel, which is absolutely amazing. I wanted to go to tea, but we didn't anticipate how dressy a place it was, so I contented myself with peeking in from the lobby. Next time, for sure!

This was our first big adventure outside of Vancouver, and we all had a great time, including Ellie. Sometimes I worry about her. Most times, truth be told. She goes to classes and studies, cooks when it's her turn, and does her share of work around the house with never so much as a grumble, but she only ever seems about half there. It's like she won't let herself have fun anymore, like she's punishing herself for something, but she absolutely will not discuss how she's feeling beyond saying anything other than "I'm fine." Seeing how much she enjoyed Victoria made me feel a little better—and Ryan, too—and knowing my old sister is still in there gives me hope that one day she'll come back out for good.

February 18, 1965

The Maple Leaf is here! A few days ago, that weird old flag, which I now know was called the Canadian Red Ensign, got replaced by the design we all remember. Actually, we had looked that up on the i-thingy a long time ago, so we were expecting it, but it's still cool to see it finally flying again. And Ryan has now officially won a few bets he made a while back by accurately "predicting" what the new design would be. Yep—still a game he likes to play.

June 1, 1965

Another academic year has come and gone. I can't say any of us are finding it especially challenging, but maybe that's because all we do is go to our classes and study. Well, and go to movies.

NASA is in the middle of its Gemini program. Ellie says Aaron would have loved experiencing it all as it happens, but, to even his surprise, Ryan has totally gotten into it. Anytime the i-thingy is out, he reads up on the next mission, and we follow it on the radio if we can. The next launch is in two days and will include the first US "EVA," which Ryan explained is NASA for spacewalk.

We're still limiting the use of the i-thingy to as little as possible. Mostly, it's for adjusting our investment strategy, timing our buys and sells, that sort of thing. We use it for school work, too, but that's almost entirely those two. It's a big advantage in science classes having access to research still decades away, but as I'd already found out, psychology and sociology don't change all that much between now and then.

Just for kicks, Ryan made a note of the i-thingy's specs and tried to make a comparison to the computers NASA is using for navigation. Turns out, best he can figure, our tech is something like 100,000,000 times more powerful. But it's also still almost fifty years away from being invented, hence the strict limits on using it. At least we're mostly beyond vacuum tubes, he says.

July 16, 1965

We've decided to stay in this house for another year. It seems crazy on the face of it, and I know we all feel the same way. I love being so close to the water, but it definitely makes the winters feel that much icier. And I know Ryan would prefer having more privacy, but it could be worse. At least our bedrooms have the bathroom in between them.

Ryan got a brilliant idea back in May. That storage shed out back? We thought it had a dirt floor; it was that filthy in there. Turns out, there were wood planks under all the grime—an actual floor! And on the side that faces south, the side that looks toward the house and away from the inlet, it has two big barn doors that make it practically like having the entire side of the building gone when you swing them all the way open. So the three of us spent about a week right after the semester was over scrubbing the walls down, scraping the floor clean, and knocking the old bird nests out of the rafters.

It took three coats of some cheap white paint to spruce it up inside, but we ended up with a 9 by 12 room we can use all spring, summer, and into the early fall. We covered the planks with a used rug—a nice, big, thick one—put a small table at one end for studying or having our dinners out there, and we found a pair of cushy chairs for the other end, if only to have a different place to hang out and relax. When our landlord saw the results, he said he might have to increase our rent since we now had over a hundred square feet of additional living space. Ryan said he might have to submit his receipts for reimbursement of leaseholder improvements. They agreed to call it even, and we agreed to sign on for another year.

It's funny how such a seemingly small thing can make such a big difference, but having the extra room to spread out and spend some time not being on top of each other has eased some tensions I'm not sure we even knew had been there. And Ellie knows that if Ryan and I are out there and the doors are closed up nice and tight, she probably doesn't want to come barging in. (Well, she certainly knows that now! Whoops!)

What's even funnier is how attached we've become to the place. I won't say it feels like home because it doesn't, not really, but after only two years here it's ~~hard~~ impossible to imagine being somewhere else. We're out in the shed now. Ryan and I are sitting close together in those big, puffy chairs, and Ellie is hunched over the table, studying. It's moments like this when I'm most aware that this time we're sharing, this time of classes and study, eating our meals together, and going to movies on the weekends... this is the calm before the storm that will be our lives after we graduate. So as I watch Ryan flip to the next page of his book, listen to the rapid scratches Ellie's pencil makes as she writes her notes, I'm making sure to savor every moment.

June 19, 1967

One degree down, at least one more to go. Yay, us! It was painful walking across stage without our parents in the audience, though. They would have been so proud! Even Ryan broke down as we talked about it later at a subdued celebratory dinner downtown. (Let me just say that if you like salmon, this is the place to be. So good!)

Things got really weird, but in a happy way, when Ryan suddenly realized it was his mother's birthday. Not just her birthday—her actual birth date! At some point over the course of the day, maybe even as he was being handed his diploma, she had made her wet and wailing way into the world. Our father and Ryan's were born over the past four or five years, and our mom will be born early next year. So here we are, freshly gradu- ated from college, and somewhere down in the good old US of A, most of our parents are running around in diapers or just starting kindergarten. Talk about bizarre! Talking about that lifted everyone's spirits. Best part? It didn't hurt my head at all!

The financial side of things is going extremely well. Knowing in advance exactly when to buy and when to sell is clearly the key! (Yeah, so I've obviously quit worrying about writing stuff like that.) In the beginning, finding a broker who was willing to do exactly what we want, when we want, no questions asked, was tough. Finding one Ryan could talk into taking a percentage cut at the end of the year rather than getting paid for every transaction was even tougher. We finally found a guy, though. He has no idea how we do it, but he's smart enough to just sit back, keep his mouth closed, and enjoy the benefits. Ryan says the term for that is "plausible deniability."

Since then, we've done so well that we've opened two new accounts with different firms to minimize the chance of drawing the wrong kind of attention. So now we have three brokers who think we have some kind of crystal ball. (Know what? They're right!)

Then there's the networking side, which has gone nowhere. But that's by design. Until now, we've used the summers to take classes outside our majors, trying to fill in as many of our knowledge gaps as we can. But this summer, feeling more credible with a bachelor's degree under her belt, I guess, Ellie wants to meet up with some people in Berkeley and start the process of gathering like-minded people to our cause. I know she's hoping to meet with David Brower while we're down there... something about him starting a new organization soon... but mostly with other students, people our age, who want to preserve the planet. So starting next Thursday, we're going to take off for a few weeks and drive down the coast.

"Woo-hoo, road trip!" was Ryan's response, all for the idea right from the start.

Driving almost a thousand miles on the off chance of meeting people who'll want to work with us? Seems like the hard way, but for now it's the only way. How long until we get the internet back? We're still working on what our organization or foundation or whatever it is will look like, and by "we" I mean mostly Ryan and me, but we all agree the people we recruit to work with us will be the key to being successful in the long run. This is as much my part as Ellie's, so it won't be all fun and games down there, but there is one huge draw: Peet's! Considering how many pounds of beans I plan to bring back, I think Al and I will become good friends.*

(*I just reread some of this and noticed that I seem terribly obsessed with coffee. Let me say two things about that—yes, I love it. Also, if you grew up when I did, then the only thing weirder than having a Starbucks on every corner is having no Starbucks on any corners. "Don't judge me" is what I'm trying to say. S.C.—1987)

June 29, 1967 — Berkeley, CA

"All they're worried about are dams and DDT! Not that those issues aren't important, but c'mon, people—big picture here!"

It's been especially tense the past few days. Ellie is increasingly frustrated that no one else can see the seriousness of the climate situation. I've tried reminding her that's because right now there is no climate situation. The term "greenhouse gas" isn't even being used yet, and the only sign of global warming, another phrase that has yet to make its debut, is the very slightest increase in the average global temperature records. The three of us know it's the toe of a sustained upward curve, but today it looks like no more than a statistical blip. She knows all this, of course. It's just that she expects everyone to be capable of the same kind of intuitive leaps she makes as a matter of course.

Unable to take another evening of listening to her grumble, I dragged Ryan out to see a movie last night. It was his turn to pick, and he chose "You Only Live Twice." He's been calling me "very sexyful" ever since. (I'm not complaining!) He has been an absolute saint through Ellie's years of coolness and intermittent moodiness, never saying anything at all, even when I could tell her curtness or lack of tact upset him. I really do love that man!

Today she and I drove over to Muir Woods, just the two of us, in order to have a much-needed and long-overdue heart-to-heart conversation. It was sunny when we left Berkeley, but the coast was under a dense marine layer that changed the mood of the day from warm and cheery to gray and gloomy. We had a long talk as we hiked out to sit on the shore. What I was able to gather, after a lot of prodding and poking and absolutely refusing to let her shut me out yet again, is how much pressure she feels she's under to make this work. To her, it's somehow all on her shoulders. Once I understood that's what she was telling me, I felt horrible. Then I realized she must have been feeling that way for years. Since we got here, probably. Even though it explained a lot, it made me feel even worse.

"That's... No, that's silly! Name one person in all of human history who changed the world all alone."

"That's not the point," she said. "Look at what happens to everybody I work with. It's because of me that we're stuck back here in the freakin' Dark Ages! I'm the reason we had to leave

Mom and Dad... and Ryan his dad, too. I'm the reason Aaron is dead! I should have..."

She got too choked up to talk then, and she turned to stare out at the waves rolling toward us. So much for her not feeling guilty, I thought. I waited to see if that was the end of it, but there was more.

"Do you remember how I accused Jeremy of lying to us? Down in Aaron's basement?"

"I remember. You said he intentionally let Aimie manipulate us into a position where we had no choice but to go up against her." I thought I knew where she was going with this, but I let her continue.

"What if I said that I did something even worse? That I made the decision not to..."

Now I was sure what she was about to say, and I cut her off. "You're about to point out that if you could rig the TSD to fix your hormone problems, you certainly could have made it capable of vaccinating me against the H5N1 flu strain, right? And you've been thinking, why didn't you?" Her gaping expression of surprise was so comically out of character that I had to clamp my jaws shut hard in order not to laugh.

"If you knew that, how can you say it like it's no big deal?"

"The flu thing occurred to me over a year ago. That you feel you're just as guilty of manipulating us as Aimie and Jeremy? I just figured that part out right now."

"But like I said, why aren't you...?"

"Because—for, like, the thousandth time—that wasn't you! That other Ellie suffered through years of pain, watched civilization start to crumble around her, then put all her final effort into a project she ultimately discovered she couldn't carry out. All of that is what made her into a person who is, for the thousand-and-first time, not you! What you did was see a way to try to fix things and have the guts to go for it using the tools that other Ellie gave you. And besides, Just Mie said that I am especially vulnerable to that flu strain. Have you ever considered that maybe I could never be adequately protected by any vaccination? Give yourself some credit!

"Hear me on this. Ryan and I... and Aaron too... we chose to come along and do our parts because we believe in this plan. Yeah, I miss our folks, and most days I'd much rather be back home, sitting out in the UNM-LA quad with a latte from Atomic City Café. But knowing everything that was about to happen, I couldn't have stayed behind any more than you could've. And I don't just mean what might have happened to me. Or to Mom and Dad.

"Okay, so I get how you feel somehow responsible, but turning into some kind of Aimie and ordering us around or shutting us out is not the answer. Ryan and I? We want to be here. We know what we're supposed to do, and we're both good with that. And we'll both be good at that. You have to let us, though. This can't be a one-woman show, or yeah, then it would be a waste for us to be here. Even with all of us working together, we might not succeed, but I guarantee you'll fail trying to do it all by yourself. Are you diggin' me, sister?"

Ellie laughed. Well, she snorted, truth be told, but close enough. She finally turned back to look at me.

"But..."

"No! There are no 'buts' here, unless it's you for insisting on feeling this way for even one more minute!"

She was quiet for a long time as she thought everything over.

"I don't want to be a butt."

"Yeah, it's not all it's cracked up to be." It's a stupid old childhood joke, but we needed something to smile about.

"So you guys don't hate me?"

I couldn't believe she was asking that. I put my arm around her and pulled her to me. "I thought we settled that one already. I don't hate you. I love you. Ryan doesn't hate you, either. He also... Well, I'll let him speak for himself, but he definitely doesn't hate you."

"I guess I owe him an apology."

I agreed that would be a good start.

"And maybe a beer?"

I held up three fingers, and this time she really did laugh.

"Okay, so let's take the night off. We'll go get Ryan and come back across the bridge for dinner. I'm buying!"

Dinner in San Francisco? How could I say no?

Back at the hotel, we swapped room keys so she could go up to smooth things over with Ryan in private while I went to her room to shower the sand and salt spray off me. When I got there about fifteen minutes later, I cracked the door a tiny bit and listened to see if it was okay to go in. It was completely quiet, and I wasn't sure they were inside. I was about to call out, but they already knew I was there.

"Come in," they said in unison.

I went down the short hall to find them standing by the foot of the bed, hugging. There were damp spots on Ryan's shirt where Ellie's face had been pressed against him, and I knew she, at least, had been crying. I stood there, feeling awkward, a little like I was intruding, until they each held out an arm, inviting me to join them. I walked over and put my arms around them both in a big embrace that went on for whole minutes, and something inside me knew everything was going to be okay. It's been four years since we left Los Alamos and settled in Vancouver, but it wasn't until tonight, standing here in this crappy hotel room wrapped up in Ellie and Ryan's arms, that I first felt like I was truly home.

July 6, 1967 — Back in Vancouver

We returned home yesterday. We stopped for a night in Seattle to watch some Fourth of July fireworks for the first time in years. By the time the big finale hit its crescendo, we were all bawling like babies.

We did make it to Peet's, and we did bring back tons of coffee. (Not literally, but it's a good thing Mr. Muscles was along!) When we walked through the door of the shop and got our first big whiff, I thought Ellie and I were literally going to weep. I'm glad Al himself wasn't there—I might have totally embarrassed myself by kissing the man's feet! They're not brewing it in the shop yet, so we had to settle for savoring deep lungfuls of the aroma while we made our selections.

It wasn't just coffee we hauled back. The farmers' market in Berkeley is amazing! We were careful not to buy more than we can eat before it goes bad, but it was enough that we're planning to seriously "veg out" in the best possible way for the next few weeks. I'm even going to try canning a few things. This first time around, I'm not aiming for good so much as merely not killing us all with botulism. Small steps.

And maybe fashion these days isn't as dismal as I thought. I found the cutest little jersey shift in a thrift store down there. Mary Quant!!! It's wool, so it ought to be great for Vancouver. (It's funny how the fact that the style is a few years out of date doesn't bother me in the least since to me it's all out of date.)

As I'm writing this, we're all enjoying our first homemade cups of the real stuff. Oh. My. God. We bought a grinder, too (at the Williams-Sonoma in SF!) and we all stood gazing at it in rapturous wonder while it spit out its first batch of grounds as if witnessing some kind of miracle. Athena springing fully grown from the forehead of Zeus, maybe. We split the first carafe among the three of us, and we're each in our own private, little nirvanas right now.

When I handed Ellie her mug, she raised it to me in a silent toast and did something with her face I'm sure she meant to be a smile. It looked more like she was trying hard not to cry, though, and I knew exactly what she was thinking. How many mornings did we spend at home sharing this simple ritual, enjoying it yet also taking it for granted, all at the same time? Ah, how simple it all was. I'd give anything to be back in Los Alamos right now. *sniff, sniff*

But it would be the end of 2022 there, and I, presumably, would be long dead. I've often wondered if, knowing what was to happen, we could have changed things had we stayed. And I've also wondered what Mom and Dad did with the information we left them. Did they put it to good use and start work on Ellie's big project, or did they spend the rest of their lives simply waiting, hoping against hope that we'd come back? (Damn it! Now I really am going to cry.)

Whew! I'm back. Anyway, since that night in the hotel a

week ago, things around here have been better than ever. Ellie
and Ryan are starting to work together again, just like back in
LA. Finally! The ride south had been quiet... "subdued," I guess is
the right word... but the trip back was filled with excited, nonstop brainstorming! We're talking about plans for not one but two
major projects now, one to focus on delaying climate change for
as long as possible, the other to help society recover afterward, in
case "as long as possible" isn't long enough. She said it's the last
idea she picked up from Shanna, the one that inspired the project
she left for our parents, and that going ahead like it's either total
success on one hand or utter doom on the other without any kind
of a backup plan would be irresponsible. I said a long time ago
that I wished I could be working alongside Mom and Dad as
they carried out this exact plan. In a way, I guess now I kinda
am, although in a totally different "time zone." (And no, it's not at
all the same.)

Together, we're going to do this thing. I know it—I absolutely do. But that's all I know. I can't imagine exactly where
this dream of ours will take us. In a few months, we'll all start
working on our Master's degrees. Public Administration, for me,
of course. Ryan will continue to pursue physics and engineering,
plus anything else with a practical application to the technologies
we'll need to promote. Or "invent," I guess, if necessary. Ellie is
trying to cobble together a degree that approximates a Master's in
Environmental Science, which isn't exactly a thing yet. At least
not here.

Along the way, I need to start figuring out how to go about
establishing a foundation. Or institute. Or think tank. We're still
not sure what we're calling it, but we're a lot closer today than
ever before. Ellie and I have been plowing through some of the

ebooks I loaded onto the i-thingy four years ago, reading about the Buckminster Fuller and Jane Goodall Institutes, among many others, looking for a model we can use. Meanwhile, we have the names we brought back from Berkeley, some people we want to stay in touch with. So today, I guess, a few seeds have already been planted, and tomorrow we'll deal with whatever tomorrow brings. Together.

Like I said—small steps.

47

"Thank God!"

Sam replaced the cap on her pen and laid it on the polished surface of the long, wooden conference table. She added a final bundle of papers to the mountain of documents in front of her, each bearing all four of their freshly scribbled signatures, and pushed the untidy stack across the table toward the head of their legal department. She then massaged her right wrist, tender from gripping the pen so tightly for so long.

The woman from Legal, who had sat silent and grim-faced through the entire signing process, rose from her chair and neatened the tall stack before gathering it into her arms. Ryan, sitting on Sam's right, reached over and patted her on the thigh. Sam responded to the gesture with a sad smile.

"Thank you, Marcie," Ellie said.

"Thank *you*," Marcie said. "It's been great working with you. All of you." She made brief eye contact with each of them, nodded once, then headed for the door.

Sam waited until Marcie had left the room. "Well, that's done," she said.

"Done that is." Ellie rose from her chair and walked to stand in front of a row of ten-foot-high windows that spanned the length of the room. She took in the entire view, one that started with the traffic that flowed silently forty-two stories below her feet and ended with the Rocky Mountains fifty miles away. The seasonal color change was almost a month away, but at that distance, the mountains kept their color largely to themselves, even at its peak. Staring at the jagged horizon, she thought about how far they had come since their days spent growing up in tiny Los Alamos. Figuratively, anyway. Their childhood home was little more than six hours away by car.

Denver had seemed almost sleepy when they moved their headquarters there in the mid-eighties, but they had always known that would eventually change. Situated more or less centrally within the US and home to a major airline hub, the city was a convenient destination for visitors arriving from practically anywhere on the globe. Plus, being free from threats from earthquakes, hurricanes, and rising sea levels, it was a secure place to base an organization meant to carry out critical work for generations to come. They had satellite offices around the world, but Denver was the axis around which the entire enterprise revolved.

Over the past year, the three of them had begun the slow, intricate process of handing over the control of two major foundations and dozens of subsidiary organizations to a new set of leaders. Today marked the end of that process. They weren't jetting off to live out their remaining years in some tropical paradise, but starting on Monday, their roles would become largely advisory. Only the new leaders, chosen from among their most capable and trusted employees, knew the complete truth about Ellie, Sam, and Ryan, a secret they shared because they were merely regents. These men and women would take the reins only until the new permanent leaders were ready to step in.

Ellie was proud of what they had accomplished. The organizations they had started, staffed by thousands of people globally and aided by thousands more volunteers, had provided the planet with decades of extra breathing room compared to the world they had left behind. But now their long years of doing the heavy lifting were behind them. They had done all they could, ultimately rendering the Continuity - 2072 file completely irrelevant, its predictive power useless. The planet's future rested in the hands of new generations, and its fate was now up to them.

She sometimes regretted not being able to throw herself into purely theoretical research full-time, but she knew her life's work had resulted in more practical benefit than a hundred papers on particle physics ever would have. So what if her name would never be mentioned in the same breath as Marie Curie, Donna Strickland, or Richard Feynman? Or even Carl Sagan or Neil deGrasse Tyson, for that matter. She no longer cared. A brief encounter in a hallway fifty years ago—or six years from now, depending on how one looked at it—had freed her of any desire for that kind of recognition.

Ellie's focus shifted from the horizon to her reflection. She had never considered herself vain, and even as the passing decades began their inevitable work, she had done little to disguise their effects other than to eat well and exercise as regularly as her often erratic schedule allowed. The pace they had set at the beginning and maintained for over forty years left little time to worry about growing old. It wasn't the lines on her face or the gray that had gradually replaced her hair's rich, golden brown hues that bothered her, because as she considered the face that looked back from the far side of the window, she thought she still looked pretty good for sixty-seven. Her only reason for begrudging her age was the amount of work that remained undone.

She turned from the window to face the table where Sam and Ryan patiently waited. "I think I'm ready."

Sam rose and came around the table to stand in front of her. "We'll stay as long as you want. Want to walk back through the offices? Say goodbye to everyone?"

"No, I'm good. And it's not like we're leaving forever. Let's just go." She picked up a small, black, sling-style messenger bag from a chair, made sure her phone was in it, then led the others out of the meeting room to a bank of elevators at the end of the hall. A car arrived as they approached, and they waited for two people to step off. After taking their place, Sam stabbed the button for the ground floor.

Shortly after they moved in, Ellie had calculated that if these cars moved at the same glacial speed as the ones in their Vancouver hotel, the trip up or down would take over four minutes instead of the actual thirty seconds. Half a minute later, they were passing through the spacious, Carrara marble-lined lobby on their way to the exit. They had passed through this space almost daily for nearly thirty years, but on this afternoon she gave it special attention; she knew it would never feel quite the same again.

At the outer corner of the building's plaza, a metal, monolithic plaque listed the building's major tenants. Their organization was not the largest, but it had been the first, and thus the name that topped the list was Advanced Analytic Research and Observation Network. Ellie stopped before the sign and brushed her fingertips over the letters. She had insisted on the name, acknowledging right from the beginning that it in no way reflected their true mission. Some things, she had argued, were more important. Besides, the exact nature of their mission had changed many times over the years.

They walked to the corner and waited for the signal to change. "I feel like celebrating," Ryan announced. "Who's up for dinner in Larimer Square?"

Sam gave his ribs a playful jab with her elbow. "When do you *not* feel like celebrating?"

That's true, Ellie thought, but she could find no reason to fault him for that fact. Ryan's perpetually upbeat attitude had been as important as any other factor in making them as successful as they had been. As far as she could tell, they had managed to buy the world fifty, maybe seventy-five years of additional breathing room. Part of the improvement came by way of their influence on critical technologies, the rest through efforts aimed at slowing population growth. The number of humans was still comfortably under eight billion. Early on, she had dared hope they could make an even greater impact, but as the reality of what was required to alter the techno-cultural trajectory of an entire planet slowly sank in, her goals shifted accordingly. Today, she was sincerely grateful that they had accomplished as much as they had. *Celebration? Why not!*

"I'm in!" she said. She slid her arms around the two people who were still her favorite on the entire planet, and they stepped out side by side onto 18th Street.

. . .

After dinner, Ellie joined Sam and Ryan in their high-rise condominium, where they shared the better part of an exquisite, vintage Pauillac she had brought from the restaurant. While Ellie found wine glasses and poured, Ryan took his usual spot at one end of the sofa and motioned for Sam to join him. She sat curled up crossways on his lap and leaned against the sofa's arm. Ellie heard Ryan murmur something she couldn't make out, and saw Sam nod in reply before wrapping her arms around his neck and kissing him. It wasn't a little peck on the lips, but a passionate exchange that stretched on for many seconds. Ellie guessed that anyone familiar with her story would assume she might begrudge them their display of affection and not blame her a bit. In truth, nothing made her happier than seeing the relationship her sister had formed so early in life grow steadily stronger with every passing year.

Sam and Ryan had waited until after grad school, then waited even longer until they had moved to the States and become US citizens again before finally marrying. Their honeymoon had been a simple affair. Upon graduating from UBC, the three jointly bought the small cottage in Vancouver they had shared for nearly seven years. Following a civil ceremony in San Francisco, Sam and Ryan returned there for a three-week vacation, the last long break any of them would enjoy for many years to come. They spent the middle week in Victoria, choosing to stay at the Empress once more, and this time Sam got to enjoy the formal tea service there—twice! Ellie couldn't think of a time before or since when either of them had been cross with the other for more than a few minutes. No, she couldn't possibly begrudge them a single second of a life like that.

Ellie's early attempts to form romantic relationships of her own rarely lasted more than a few weeks, each quickly thwarted by her inability to overcome two obstacles. The first was feeling that opening herself up to someone new was betraying Aaron. Intellectually, she recognized this for the nonsense it was. She knew he would never want her to abandon the chance at love for his sake. The unfounded emotion came entirely from within herself, but she had never found a way to get completely past it.

The other roadblock was even more challenging to overcome because it was so deeply rooted in the unavoidable strangeness unique to dating someone from a different timeline. No matter how hard she tried, it was never long before she felt hopelessly out of sync with her partner. She was a child not of the fifties, nor even of this millennium. Her formative memories all happened far in the future and were, therefore, ones she could never share. When the gap between the present and her native time eventually became narrow enough to bridge, the demands their many projects placed on her left her with little time to spare for someone else. It was her life's greatest irony that Sam had been happier over a lifetime with a single lover than she had been with her varied assortment. Today, she was at peace with her mostly solitary existence. After all, she had plenty of love in her life.

As though reading Ellie's mind, Sam took a sip of wine, blew her a kiss through glistening lips, and smiled. "This is amazing, sis. Thanks!"

Ellie sipped from her own glass and nodded in silent agreement. It was the one luxury she allowed herself, and she didn't regret a single drop of her extravagant choice. Starting while still attending school at UBC and continuing to the present day, they had chosen to model the minimalist lifestyle they wished to inspire in others. They each had one main area of interest in which they would sometimes indulge. Sam's closet, although not unduly large, would be the envy of the most discerning fashion enthusiast. There were no extravagant, runway-inspired flights of fancy on any of her hangers. She had always been practical in selecting only items that, while often the work of famous designers, were eminently wearable. Inspired by old Mrs. Pavlova, she had kept the treasured Mary Quant dress she had bought over fifty years ago. Sometimes she even put it on, if only to prove she still could.

However, fashion remained largely a spectator event for Sam. Her true interest lay in the world of gastronomy. Wherever they traveled, she reveled in discovering previously unexperienced combinations of flavors and textures that she and Ryan would try to replicate upon their return. Ellie was always excited to have dinner at their home, knowing she couldn't dine better anywhere else in the city. She certainly wasn't going to find a more perfect cup of coffee!

Ryan's main hobby, aside from the time he spent in the kitchen with

Sam, was keeping his home theater in a more or less constant state of upgrade. Knowing in advance when the associated technologies were due to make a leap forward allowed him to keep his purchases to a minimum, and he always made it a point to donate the equipment he retired to high school A/V clubs or community theater programs—anywhere it could continue to provide enjoyment for years to come. When the demands on their time allowed, the Collinses often held small dinner parties that culminated in a screening of one of the great cinematic masterpieces.

Between system updates, Ryan had taught himself to play the guitar, and despite once complaining of having been born with eight thumbs and two left pinkies, he quickly became quite good. Sam often sang along as he picked out a tune by whichever folksy singer-songwriter was currently topping the charts. Perhaps due to not having music "in his blood," as Aaron had, Ryan's style often displayed a cool, almost mechanical, proficiency. But every so often, especially when his voice and Sam's became entwined in perfect harmony, their eyes would meet, and he'd get lost deep in her gaze. In those rare moments, he could achieve real magic.

Ellie's lifelong love of chocolate had taught her early on how to recognize the nuanced flavor distinctions between different types, a talent that perfectly prepared her palate to appreciate the similar subtleties characteristic of fine wines. Over time, that appreciation grew into a true passion. She was not a collector. Knowing that the enjoyment of a good wine came as much from the context of its consumption as from the content of the bottle, she always preferred to experience something new rather than try to recreate some elusive past pleasure.

Tonight was an excellent expression of her philosophy. After the three of them shared a perfectly serviceable Burgundy, she decided to commemorate the day's events, the culmination of their lifelong work, with something extraordinary—a bottle of 1996 Château Lafite-Rothschild. After pouring out three small portions and then setting the open bottle aside to breathe, she shared the story of Aaron's jokey attempt to order a bottle of the famous wine at the Old Adobe Cantina in Los Alamos. She paid particular attention to describing how uncharacteristically relaxed he seemed when dealing with the waitress, a woman at least two decades their senior, and how that now made her wish that she'd had the chance to know him as a fully adult man.

"I think I did, though, oddly enough. In many ways, his was an adult mind trapped inside a body that couldn't grow up fast enough to suit him. Is that what they mean by an 'old soul?' That was certainly true of Aaron *Siskin*, anyway. Aaron Weisskopf was more comfortable in his own young skin, but he, too, made decisions far beyond his years."

Ryan surprised her when he raised his glass and paraphrased a line from the novel *Dune*. "To young Aaron Siskin/Weisskopf, a lad by his looks, but a man by his actions."

Ellie had always loved the book. She had replaced the fiftieth anniversary copy she'd been forced to leave behind in Los Alamos with a brand-new first edition nearly fifty years ago, then read and reread it until today it barely held together. She didn't know Ryan had ever read it, though, let alone that he knew it well enough to be able to quote from it. Abruptly brought to the verge of tears, she could only nod in agreement.

"I wish he could have been a part of all this," Sam said. Her tone was wistful. "He would have been so proud."

Ellie forced herself to speak past the lump in her throat. "No, don't be sad. He's always been a part of everything we've done. We wouldn't have made it out of Los Alamos if not for him."

Ellie thought about this later as she stood again by a window, looking west across a sea of lights. Twice she and Aaron had fallen in love, and twice he had sacrificed himself on her behalf. The last image she had of Aaron—the sight of him holding the TSD chamber door closed so she, Sam, and Ryan could escape—came unbidden to her mind, and she had to fight back tears for a second time that evening.

Over the years, she often wondered about his choices that day, about his decision to slam the hatch and stay behind rather than try to leave with them. For a long time, she tortured herself by believing that he did so in an effort to live up to an example he imagined had been set by the first Aaron. Later, she came to understand that his actions were simply a reflection of the person he was, not a misguided attempt to prove some point.

She recalled words from decades ago, words that had set her on a path to an amazing and unimaginably fulfilling life—it's all about them! *Yes,* she thought. *It is.* She could never repay Aaron the debt she owed him, but maybe she could pay it forward. *Will the third time be the charm?*

Sam appeared beside her so silently that she would have been startled had she not seen her approach reflected in the glass. Their shoulders gently touching, they stared out into the night. "Something's on your mind, El. I can tell."

"It used to be that when you retired, the company gave you a gold watch. It was a tradition. It symbolized how retirement was getting your time back, I suppose, or to thank you for all your time spent working there."

"Okay, but we owned the 'company,' if you want to call it that. We'd be giving ourselves watches. Besides, none of us even wears a watch anymore."

"No, I didn't mean that. I was thinking about Jeremy's gold watch. That Patek Philippe. At the time, we all saw that as evidence of greed or ostentatiousness, as him flaunting his ill-gotten wealth. But we did the very same thing, Sam. Aaron put all of that money in the bank back in the 1940s and '50s, and we used the interest to fund our first semesters of college. The rest we invested along the way, using our knowledge of the future to make millions. Those millions made even *more* millions."

"But we didn't flaunt it! I acknowledge that we're more comfortable than most, but nearly every bit of that money went into the organizations we created, supported the work they did."

"You've got it backward. I'm not saying we're as bad as Jeremy, but that he might not have been as bad as we judged him to be. Granted, we didn't know him well, but what other example, aside from the watch, can you point to of him showing off his money? He drove a C-Class Mercedes —not cheap, but not top-of-the-line, either. Certainly not a Bentley, or a Bugatti, or whatever car Ryan's currently drooling over. And what about his clothes? Were those hand-tailored Saville Row suits he wore?"

"*Pfft!*"

"I figured you would know! So, the one thing we actually *know* he chose to spend money on was a watch—a *timepiece.* I think buying that watch was his way of reminding himself—every single time he looked at it —that time was the most precious thing in life.

"And you know what else? I just remembered this. That day we went back to 1976?"

"The day Aimie tried to murder you, you mean."

"That one, yeah. When I was alone with him before we left, Jeremy showed me that the walls of the conference room were actually display panels like the ones on the outside of the TSD. It was mostly a handy way to store the spares, he said, but he also told me that they sometimes used them to make it look like they were holding meetings in different places, like on Mars or something, and that his favorite had been H.G. Wells' study in Woking."

"'Woking?'"

"It's a town in England. I know that because I wrote a paper about Wells in eighth grade. It's where he lived when he wrote his most important books. Including *The Time Machine*."

"You're suggesting Jeremy was obsessed with the concept of time?"

"Mmm." She waggled her hand. "'Obsessed' might be too strong a word. But I do think that a 'compelling interest,' let's say, led him to make certain decisions he later came to regret, ones that resulted in him being trapped by Aimie."

"Don't forget—he wanted to get rid of her not because he thought what they were doing was wrong, but because he got tired of being under her thumb. He wasn't a saint, El."

"But not a devil, either. That's all I meant to say."

"Well, maybe," Sam conceded. "Have any idea what he's up to this time around?"

"I do!" Ellie's tone brightened as she relayed happier news. "His dissertation involved work on the Meissner effect and magnetic flux pinning. Right now, he's working on achieving quantum locking using near-room-temperature superconductors."

"I didn't understand a single word after 'dissertation,' but nothing sounded like 'time machine,' so I guess that's... good?"

"Very! It could lead to safe, high-speed mass transit using far less energy. We've been funding his work for the past five years."

"We have?! Why didn't you ever say anything?"

"I was afraid you might still see him as the enemy."

"No, not anymore. I definitely did once, but that was in a whole other lifetime." She smiled, and Ellie smiled back.

Time. Ultimately, that had been Aaron's gift to them. He had used his last few seconds to save them and their plan, and they had spent the last fifty years honoring his brave action through their decades of service. Ellie knew it was not the same, understood that the columns could never truly balance. She could, however, do one thing more.

"August, 2012. They're down there, you know. *We* are, I mean. Have been for a few weeks. Aaron's family arrived a couple of days ago."

Sam nodded. "I suppose school's started then, or is just about to."

"Monday. I need to go there, Sam, and I don't think I can do it on my own."

"Any special reason why?" Sam said.

"It was the shack that brought us together originally, Aaron and me. If we're right, then it's gone for good. Maybe it would have happened anyway, eventually—I'd hate to think I was *that* dense—but I have to be sure she knows as early as possible this time. I feel I owe it to both of them. And later, when it matters most, she'll remember we met, and that will make it all more real."

Sam nodded. "Of course, we'll go."

"We should make it this weekend, I think."

Ryan, who had been listening from his place on the sofa, responded in typical fashion. "Woo-hoo! Road trip!"

48

On Sunday afternoon, Ryan was behind the wheel for the drive's final stretch up Highway 285. Ellie turned her head toward the window and watched the desert slide by on their right. The late-summer monsoons had transformed the usually dusty scene into a ruddy landscape dotted with vibrant greens. Santa Fe was behind them now, Los Alamos only half an hour ahead, and she felt more anxious with every passing mile. They planned to spend tonight in a hotel up on the plateau to make tomorrow's early-morning rendezvous as easy as possible.

They drove down from Denver the day before, choosing to take the longer interstate route through Santa Fe so they could spend the night there. None of them had visited the city for many years, and at the mention of it, Sam had developed a serious craving for dinner at Cafe Pasqual's. They timed their Denver departure so they would arrive in Santa Fe just after their hotel's check-in began, leaving them plenty of time for window shopping at the galleries on Canyon Road and relaxing before their dinner reservation.

Ellie looked forward to an after-dinner stroll through the plaza and along the many narrow, winding alleys. The warm-hued adobe buildings were especially beautiful just before and after sunset, none more so than Saint Francis' Cathedral. She had grown to enjoy the oddly disjointed feeling that came from being decades older in a place that was itself years younger than when she had last been there. She made a game out of trying to notice all the differences and took pleasure in remembering what the place will be like later, when she had been younger. It was not a comfortable topic of conversation for Sam, however, and she had learned to enjoy the practice in the privacy of her own mind.

They were passing through Cuyamungue when Ellie drained the final sips of her Starbucks coffee from her ceramic travel mug. It was one she had purchased from the chain years earlier as a reminder that not all the alterations they had witnessed in their new timeline were of the world-changing kind. She turned the cup over in her hand until the logo faced up and stared at the smiling mermaid. Neither the re-punctuated name nor the new logo design made any more sense than what she had known in her own time, but to be fair, neither did they make any less. She had concluded long ago that, like a river, time was also subject to flows and eddies. The prevailing current created a tendency toward convergence that kept events—even in different timelines—moving toward a common end. The resulting temporal momentum stubbornly resisted any effort to divert the current into new directions. The hypothesis helped to explain why decades of herculean efforts had resulted in such modest changes. It also explained why two worlds might each give rise to coffee shops with nearly identical names. In many ways, hers were two universes that differed by little more than a single apostrophe.

Ryan exited onto Highway 502 for their final approach into town. Only twenty more minutes. Her memories drifted back to the first time they had driven from Vancouver to Berkeley in their used Volvo Amazon. The hybrid they were in was safe, quiet, and comfortable, and she was looking forward to the first practical EVs she knew would be coming to market in only a few more years, but she had loved that Amazon. So had Sam, despite her harsh initial assessment of its appearance. Over time, she had decided that, in her words, it was so ugly that it was cute. Ryan had managed to keep it running into the late seventies, despite the dual challenges posed by a lack of both readily available parts and properly trained mechanics.

As they started the steep, winding climb to the top of the plateau, her thoughts turned to Aaron. But then they often did. No matter how old she felt, in her mind he was never older than eighteen. That he had visited her once, back in the earliest days of their Vancouver exile, was something she had never shared. Over all the intervening decades, it was her one and only real secret from Sam.

It was mid-morning, almost two weeks after they had arrived. She was awake and had showered, but was still holed up in her room, still wearing the nightshirt she had slept in. She had brought back the three she thought would be least problematic. This one simply read "MANH(A)TTAN," and only its weird, out-of-place parentheses made it in any way strange. Only three people in the world understood that it referred to a TV show about Los Alamos and not New York City, and the way this "secret code" aspect of it gave them cause to smile made it her new favorite.

Over the past couple of days, she had discovered she could bear to recall the good times with Aaron—*both* Aarons—without feeling like her chest would implode. She knew this meant she was coming to terms with this second loss much more quickly than she had the first time around. Just admitting that to herself sent a white-hot bolt of pain through her chest, and she had yet to share this with Sam, preferring instead to let her continue believing she was still overwhelmed by grief.

Part of the reason she was feeling better so soon was that Aaron had started visiting her dreams again. These dreams were different from her earlier ones, when Aaron had simply shown up in the middle of whatever was going on in her subconscious. These felt more like appointments than random encounters, and she'd find him waiting for her as soon as her brain slipped into its REM stage. They spent most of their time in a blank, seemingly endless white space, simply talking. Sometimes the environment varied, though, and in one dream they had hiked to the bottom of Walnut Canyon and sat in the forest together, leaning against the tree he had engraved with their initials. They also discovered that they had much to say to each other that didn't require a single spoken word, only their bodies.

This morning, she had awakened at the end of an especially vivid dream of them lying together in this very bed, their bare limbs entwined. They had been kissing in the final seconds, and remembering the dream now reignited a pleasant warmth at her core. *Very* pleasant, in fact, and she wanted to stretch that feeling out for as long as she could. She even said as much in the dream. She pulled her lips away from Aaron's and wished aloud that she could stay with him in their own private world forever. He replied with an enigmatic, "Not yet," before fading away as he always did in response to such comments. Then she woke, marveling at how much the dream kiss had felt exactly like one of their actual kisses, right down to how her lips still tingled. They had only shared a few of those real-life kisses, and she could remember each with total clarity.

Remembering was precisely what she was doing as she sat upright in bed, holding her hands in her lap and clicking her thumbnails back and forth in a slow, deliberate rhythm that kept her focused on the residual pleasure she'd felt on waking. She closed her eyes and pictured the small park behind Fuller Lodge, the spot where they had shared their first kiss. It had been almost dark, and standing in the glow of an overhead lamp had made her feel like they were the only two people in the world. She remembered how time seemed to stretch and how she felt dizzy after. The second one, just minutes after the first, was interrupted by Sam and Ryan returning with their decision about Aaron's plan to destroy the shack. She smiled, remembering how flustered Aaron had been when Sam pretended to be angry with him. She doubted the new Aaron would have reacted that way.

Sam interrupted her thoughts then, speaking with her mouth close to the door's narrow gap.

"We're going out for a walk along the inlet. You okay? Need anything? You can come along if you want."

"No, thanks; I'm good. Have fun." She heard her sister sigh. "I'm okay, Sam. I'll go next time. Promise."

"Okay. We'll be back in a few hours."

"I'm fine, really. I feel like sitting here a little longer, that's all."

"I tried," she heard Sam tell Ryan, followed by the sound of the outer door opening and closing behind them.

Their third kiss happened after she and Aaron had explained their plan, and Sam and Ryan agreed to help them. She walked with Aaron back to his house, where they had remained outside, delaying the inevitable parting because neither wanted to say goodnight. Right before she left for home, they kissed again, which kindled an entirely different and much stronger response—not dizziness then, but desire. It had taken every erg of willpower she had not to go into the house with him. Still, that had been nothing compared to the arousal she felt on Friday when he kissed her in the locker room.

Recalling this morning's dream felt like remembering any one of those occasions, like a real event, a thing that had actually happened. Her normal dreams usually faded immediately upon opening her eyes, but not her dreams of Aaron—certainly not this memory of lying naked beside him. She cleared her mind of everything but that moment and tried to experience those intense feelings again.

She was interrupted for a second time, this time by a knock at the outer door. She rose and left her bedroom, assuming Sam or Ryan had forgotten something and hadn't wanted to bother with picking up the key at the desk. When she opened it, she felt her mind go instantly and utterly blank, unable to process what she saw. She twisted her head around and peered into her room in an insane effort to see if she was still lying in bed and dreaming this.

She was sure the figure in the doorway would be gone when she turned back around, but Aaron was still there, gazing silently back at her. He wore clothes she'd never seen him in before and carried a duffle bag for no obvious reason. Those random details enhanced the dreamlike quality of his abrupt appearance. She raised her right hand, extended her index finger, and jabbed him sharply in the shoulder.

"*Ow!*" He raised his hand to rub the injured spot.

"You're really here?"

"I'm really here. And also, 'Ow!'" he repeated, stepping into the room. She was not entirely convinced. In truth, it felt more like a dream than the actual dream she'd been reliving, but she decided to go with it.

Giving him no warning, she leapt on him, wrapped her legs around his waist, and pulled him tightly against her, causing him to drop the duffel.

He clutched at her awkwardly, one arm under her bare rump, the other around her back, all the while blindly trying to kick the door closed with his heel. Sensing his intent, she reached out behind him and swung it shut, then unwrapped her legs and dropped her feet to the floor.

"Oh, my God! Aaron! I thought I was... I thought..." She placed her palms flat on his chest and smiled at him. "Why are you here?"

"Just popped by to see how you're doing." He rested his hands lightly on her hips. "So, whatcha been up to?"

A gazillion questions popped into her mind, but her dreams had taught her to avoid certain topics, so she let them all go unasked. Whether his bizarre presence was real or not, if he wanted to play it cool, so would she. "Oh, you know, hangin' out, enjoying room service. Nice hotel pick, by the way." She flapped her hand through the air. "Just doing the usual stuff, I suppose. But this is *so* much better!"

"So, um, listen. I've got some time, but not a whole lot. What would you like to do?"

The warmth of his hands on her hips rekindled the excitement she'd felt in her dream. "*Hmm*, can I pick anything?"

"Anything you want. Well, anything we can do here, obviously. No trips to Paris; not enough juice."

She wrapped her arms around his waist and pulled him tight against her. "So, I do have this one idea."

With no more preamble than that, she leaned forward and kissed him. When he slid his arms around her back and pulled her tight against him, she could feel every contour of his body through the thin fabric of her nightshirt. The familiar liquid-heat sensation spread through her, a warmth that started at her core and flowed outward. Before, she had always resisted that feeling and what it represented. This time, she decided to let herself flow with it, no matter where it took her. She placed a hand behind his head and pressed her lips even more firmly against his, and the gentle current became a wave. She let it crash over and through her, allowing it to sweep her away.

. . .

Ellie stared up at the ceiling, smiling, her cheeks deeply flushed. "I'm still not convinced about the whole fashion thing, but Sam was definitely right about this. *So* much better with someone else!" She rolled onto her side, propped herself on one elbow, and gazed into his eyes. The sheets were a tangled mess at the foot of the bed, but she wasn't feeling the least bit uncomfortable with her nakedness and felt no urge to cover herself.

"You know," she said, walking her index and middle fingers across his bare chest. "I'd be more than happy to give that another go."

He glanced at the clock. "There's an old showbiz line my dad likes to quote—'Always leave 'em wanting more.'"

She leaned forward and kissed his mouth, then the hollow under his chin. "I don't think that'll be a problem." She began kissing her way down his chest.

He groaned softly. "Meaning?" he managed to say.

She stopped just before she reached his navel. "I'm sure I'll always want more of *that!*" She laid her cheek on his stomach and grinned up at him. "And it's *extremely* obvious that you feel the same way." A sudden memory made her laugh.

"What?"

"Well, the last time this possibility came up, *somebody* wanted to see Jurassic World instead."

"Seriously? I'm glad I'm not that guy. He sounds like a complete idiot!"

Their laughter started as chuckles, then grew louder, the feeling feeding on itself until it overwhelmed them. Ellie flopped onto her back and surrendered to a fit of giggles. When the laughter faded, she moved close to lay alongside him once more. She propped herself up on her left elbow again and placed her other hand lightly on the center of his chest.

"Yeah. We talked about how totally morbid this might feel under similar circumstances, but it turns out we were wrong. And anyway, I've been dreaming about this a lot recently." She rolled toward him and kissed his lips again.

"Come here." He guided her over to sit astraddle him. "I think I can spare a little more time."

. . .

With her lower half now partially covered by the sheet, Ellie watched as Aaron opened the duffel bag. He removed the skin from atop a wad of dark clothing and put it on, followed by the clothes he'd been wearing when he arrived.

"You're not supposed to do that, you know. What would Aimie say?" Then she recognized the shoes he'd been wearing the day he returned from his test run, limping on a twisted ankle. She sat up straight. "Hang on! This has to be the day you set up the bank accounts, doesn't it?" She stared at him as a sickening sense of reality settled over her. "You really *are* here!"

"I thought we had established that."

"But you went to '46, '52, and '60, not '63."

"Yeah. I've already handled all the bank stuff, but with Aimie out of it, I decided to risk adding an extra side trip." He went quiet for what seemed like a very long time. "I just needed to see… Look, we planned as well as we could. Whatever happens, whatever the reason I'm not here, I'm sure it was completely unavoidable, you know?"

"But you really are here," she repeated. She stared at him as she tried to unscramble their relative timelines. "This means you already knew about the door on Sunday!"

"Door?"

Thinking back to a day that, for her, happened nearly two weeks ago, but that still lay two days ahead for Aaron, she remembered how calm and methodical he had been as he tried to fix the problem with the locks. She also remembered seeing Ryan relay something Aaron had said to Sam, how her expression had gone grim. Then they had practically forced her into her chair. Did they already know he wasn't going to make it? "Why didn't you tell me?"

"I didn't? I don't know. I guess I'll have some good reason. Because we don't have time to plan something else, probably. That's certainly true enough.

"Look—I've been figuring right from the beginning that something would go wrong. I mean, we couldn't be *that* lucky! So I promised myself early on that if things went sideways, you three would be the ones to make it back. You *had* to make it, right? And you couldn't bear leaving

Sam behind, not with what lay ahead for her. And Sam needed Ryan to be here, so…" He shrugged.

"Aaron, I—"

"Don't mention this to the others, but I split the money up just three ways."

His sudden change of topic surprised her. "Why? I mean, you did that before you got here. How would you have known?"

"I didn't. But I had a dream…" He hesitated, sighed, and then shook his head in bewilderment before going on. "Okay, I'm pretty sure this sounds crazy, but I really have no idea what's crazy anymore! I had a dream last night—a dream about me. In it, I told myself to do it that way. You know, with the money. I can't explain why, but it felt right, so I just went with it. I figured it really didn't matter. Guess it was a good thing, though, huh? It was the 'dream' me who suggested staying at this place, by the way, so don't thank me."

Ellie didn't think it sounded crazy, necessarily, but thought it a little odd that Aaron would dream about himself. What he described sounded very much like her own peculiar dreams of him, though, and she wondered if his had also taken place in a boundless white room.

Before she could ask, Aaron sat on the edge of the bed and took her hand in his. "I know you love me—"

"I do."

"—and I want nothing more than for us to be together. But I also know you're strong enough to get through this on your own. You'll be fine."

"I don't know what to say. 'Thank you' hardly seems enough."

"You have to know I'd do anything for you, Ellie. You do know that, right? I'll say again what I said before, down in the canyon. There was a time when I couldn't tell if what I felt for you were my feelings or those older memories coming through. But now I know for sure—I love you, Ellie."

"I do know, and I love you too." She flipped the sheet aside and started to rise. "I'll walk back with you. We can figure out how to fix this on the way!"

"No, you stay there. There's no time. I'll have to flat-out run to make it. Besides," he said, smiling as he gestured toward her naked body, "as they say in the movies, I'd rather remember you like this."

He leaned over her, and they kissed one last time. She followed him to the hallway door and hid behind it when he pulled it open. He touched a palm to her cheek and smiled sadly.

"You really are amazing, you know?" With that, he turned away and stepped into the hallway.

She closed the door and leaned back against it. She thought about his injured ankle again. "Flat-out run," he'd said. This must be when it happened. Wanting to warn him, she whirled around and opened the door enough to stick her head out through a narrow gap. The hallway was empty, but off to her left, she heard an elevator door close. Aaron was gone, and she knew that this time he was gone for good.

She closed and latched the door, returned to her room, and flopped face down onto the bed. She was instantly aware of a familiar, musky aroma, which this time she recognized at once. That Friday in the locker room—*this* is what she had smelled on Aaron, the scent that had made him so self-conscious! She remembered the way he had looked at her, how he had pulled her close to kiss her, called her—

"'Amazing!'" she said. She abruptly understood why Aaron's attitude seemed so bizarrely indifferent. He only thought he somehow failed to make it back with them. He didn't know that he *died!*

"Forget about the freakin' *ankle!*" she yelled. In a flash, she was out of bed and scrambling to find clothes. Not bothering with underwear, she pulled on jeans and a random T-shirt from her laundry basket as fast as she could.

No, she couldn't lose him! She wouldn't—not again! She knew exactly what she needed to do. Knowing that there was a problem with the door wasn't enough. Why not? Because it already *hadn't* been. *"What would I have tried?"* he said. He had already known and hadn't been able to fix the problem.

Kate was the key. She had to catch Aaron and warn him about Kate. If she hadn't seen them and alerted security, the locks wouldn't have been disabled in the first place. But how could they stop her from being there? Suddenly she knew exactly what they needed to do: if they went through the medbay instead of taking the hallway, Kate would never see them. Maybe they could all make it back!

She bolted barefoot from the room and dashed to the stairwell at the end of the hall, leaving the door gaping wide behind her. She flew down the three flights of stairs, her feet barely touching the treads as she raced to beat Aaron's elevator to the lobby.

But even before she burst through the stairway door onto the ground floor, part of her knew he wouldn't be there. Even as she ran past the empty elevators, she understood he couldn't be. She slowed slightly when she neared the registration desk and called to the woman behind it.

"Did you see a boy come through here? White hair, blue jeans?"

"No. No one."

Ellie ran faster, pushed through the front doors, and sprinted into the street. She looked both ways as far as she could see, but Aaron wasn't there. And yet he *had* to be. Or had he taken the stairs, too, and gone out through another door? Had he intentionally given her the slip?

It didn't matter, and she knew why. If she had managed to warn him, he would have made it out safely in the TSD, and he'd be with them now. She couldn't tell him now because he didn't know later. Something prevented her from breaking the loop. Was sending a message to her past self an action the universe wouldn't allow? Or was the fact of Aaron's second death now an irreversible part of her own past? She waited another minute, and when he still hadn't appeared, she turned around and went back inside.

"Sorry. I guess I missed him," she said as she passed by the woman again. She stepped into the elevator on her left and pushed the button marked with a large, black "4." After approximately forever, it reached her floor and the doors slid open. She padded quietly down the hall to their suite, let herself in, and went into the bathroom to wash her feet.

A few minutes later, she was back in bed, sprawled across its width. She took a long breath, inhaling the fading remnants of their combined scents. *Has there ever been a love story as short as ours?*

"Once upon a time, there was a girl and a boy, and they loved each other very much. The end."

Saying those words caused the full weight of losing him to come crashing down on her again. She curled into a ball and began to cry. She cried more than she ever had in her life. She cried until her throat was raw, her voice was gone, and her eyes were completely drained of tears. Then she kept right on crying until she was at last, and for all time to come, done.

She lay there for a while, her head resting on a pillow damp with her tears, staring blankly at the featureless ceiling. She recalled an afternoon from a summer day fifty-five years in the future, the first time she had chosen to let go of her guilt, regret, and pain of loss and instead embrace the gift Aaron's sacrifice had presented her—a future without fear. That future had turned out to be only an illusion, and the fear had quickly returned. But this new future, the one stretching out before her today, would be one of her own creation.

She stood now at the same decision point. She could continue to cling to her grief, or she could again choose to honor Aaron by beginning to look ahead.

"Love you," she said to the empty expanse of white above her. "Always."

Then, choice made, she rose and began stripping the bed.

But that's the past, Ellie thought, *and this trip is all about the future.* She opened her eyes and saw that they were past the old East Road gate building, past the parking lot where they had started their hikes out to the shack, and were entering the commercial downtown along Central Avenue.

"Does it look the same to you?" Sam said.

Ryan quickly scanned the area around them. "I can't say. But to be honest, when we first moved here that July, I was so smitten with this girl I had just met that I wasn't really paying attention to the town."

"That's very sweet, Ryan, but the way *I* remember it, you and I didn't meet until—"

"Yep. Cute little blonde thing she was."

"Wait, *blonde?!* You jerk!"

"What was her name? Jenny? Jackie?"

"Don't you dare say Jor—"

He snapped his fingers. "Jordan Baker! That's it! Man, I thought she was *smokin'!*"

"'Smoking?' Ryan, she was what, eleven? Twelve?"

"Yeah, well, I was only a year older. What did I know?"

Ellie was quietly watching the buildings go by, but she was paying enough attention to their chatter to be amused. Suddenly, she spotted something that warranted checking out. She sat forward and gripped Ryan's shoulder.

"Hey! Stop—pull over." Ryan brought the car to a halt along the curb, and Ellie stepped out to stare across the street at a familiar department store with an unfamiliar sign. Sam walked around the car and stood beside her.

"What is it?" She followed Ellie's gaze to the sign. "*CB Fox?* What happened to BB Wolf's?"

Ryan, leaning out of his window, indicated the coffee shop at the end of the block. "Maybe it's like the Starbucks logo. I still can't get used to that mermaid."

"I say we go find out," Ellie said, and she started across the street.

Sam called over her shoulder to Ryan as she trotted to catch up. "We'll be right back!"

Having stuffed themselves close to bursting the night before, they agreed to find something simple and quick tonight. At the end of a meandering, pre-dinner stroll through town, they ended up sharing an assortment of sushi rolls at a restaurant they had previously known as the Paper Crane. Like BB Wolf, it was practically identical to the original place but operating under a different name. To their delight, the food was every bit as delicious as they remembered.

As they crossed Ashley Pond Park on their walk back to the hotel, they paused to sit at the same picnic table where Ellie had once laid out the crazy idea that they had accidentally stumbled upon a time machine. They sat quietly for a while and watched lights from the town and passing cars play across the surface of the pond. Forty-nine years had passed since that day in May, but when Ellie closed her eyes, she could picture the scene as if it had happened yesterday. She saw Sam sitting in the brilliant sunshine at the pond's edge, the pebbles she tossed arcing gracefully through the air to create tiny ripples in the water. She remembered Aaron, too, so quick to embrace the truth of what she was suggesting, and Ryan, also seeing that truth but trying hard to deny it. She wondered, faced with the same choices at this point in her life, if she would be as quick to embark on a plan that would so radically alter their lives. Eventually, Sam broke the silence, making it clear she'd been having thoughts similar to her own.

"My God, El!" she breathed. "The things we've seen!"

"It's pretty amazing, all right," Ryan said. "Just six other people know the whole story, and I think only two genuinely believe it."

Ellie laughed softly. "A few years ago, when I first asked Rochelle to check on our younger selves, I could tell it was all she could do not to call for the guys with the straitjackets. Then, when she managed to track them all down and realized they really were us, she thought *she* was the one going nuts! She stuck with us, though. We picked some good people."

"Why didn't you just do that yourself?" Sam said.

"*Ooh*, bad idea! I knew how easily it could become an obsession. We'd already gotten a pretty good sense of that from Aimie. I decided it was safer to have Rochelle give me updates every six months, just enough to let me know they were all on the right track."

"Right track?" Ryan sounded dubious. "Even though she wound up marrying *him* again?"

"I'm not so sure that's an entirely bad thing. My gut tells me that's the way it was always supposed to be. Jeremy is still rather full of himself, but he's nowhere near as bitter as when we first knew him. And there's something you don't know yet—Aaron's mom seems to have won the argument this time around. He's only in sixth grade this year, same as Ellie. That should have made at least a little difference. Not to take anything away from you, Ryan, but he truly was the most special person I ever knew."

"Hey, you'll get no argument from me. What he did? And *twice?!* You can't ask for more than that."

"No, you can't," Ellie agreed.

"There's one question I've never been able to answer," Ryan said, "even after all this time. When you sent Aimie back to Jeremy, how could you possibly have known Aaron would end up working for him? Wasn't that due to Aimie asking for him to be brought on board? If that hadn't happened, we never would have gotten involved. It strikes me as being a pretty big gamble on your part."

"The offer he received came from Aimie, yes, but I think she sent it as a result of the Ellie engrams 'whispering in her ear,' so to speak. Just Mie said that it was part of the original plan. Us working on the project, I mean. Over the years, I've remembered almost everything from the one time I ever had contact with the original memory files in the TSD. She told me that the only control she had at that point was the ability to nudge Aimie into sending an occasional message. I think the email I got about Greta Thunberg—the one that led to me working with Shanna—came from her too. On the other hand, maybe Aimie was already showing signs of being fixated on Aaron even before I sent her back."

"Have you thought about what it will be like?" Sam asked. "Talking to her tomorrow?"

"There was Aimie, then Just Mie and Mie Two, so I've had a little practice. Nothing like what I'll be up against tomorrow, though. As I remember, I was a pretty tough nut to crack. I do have a secret weapon, though." She patted her sling bag and heard the paper wrappers from CB Fox nestled inside it crinkle under her fingers. "I'll want to get there plenty early, though. I wouldn't want to miss myself!" She stood up. "So, we'd better be getting back to the hotel."

They took a long, final look around the place where so much secret history had been made, then turned and walked away.

49

S am, who had watched Ellie's entire conversation with her younger self, was waiting with open arms when her sister returned to the car.

"I guess you didn't see *that* one coming, huh?" Sam said as she pulled Ellie to her. They had not anticipated Aaron's last-minute arrival on the scene. His surprise appearance had left Ellie shaken, and she welcomed the gesture.

"*God*, no. That was... *wow!*" Seeing Aaron so unexpectedly had been a powerful shock. For a split second, she felt like no time had gone by, and she'd had to fight an insane urge to wrap the young boy up in a huge hug. There'd be no explaining that to the cops, though! Stepping into Sam's embrace instead, she experienced the same comfort she always had. She sniffed once before she went on. "Oh, Sam, if they only knew what was possible for them!"

"I noticed he still has that same purple backpack."

"Yes, but you know what you didn't see?" Sam shook her head. "Well, I was a lot closer. Remember that big green 'I Grok Spock' pin? It wasn't on his pack."

"Meaning...?"

"His mom gave that to him in the first timeline. All Aaron ever knew was that it had originally come from 'some guy,' but we know the guy was his real father, right?"

"Ahh, gotcha! You think Jeremy knew that too, and that he disliked seeing it every day."

"I bet he *hated* it. I think that was the original thorn in his side. Maybe she decided to keep it to herself this time around, or maybe she was never given it. However it went, Jeremy's probably still basically a jerk, but without that constant, irritating reminder, perhaps things have been better for Aaron and his mom on this go around."

Sam nodded. "How'd it go with her?"

Ellie took a step back, wiped her eyes, and shrugged.

"I don't know. She listened, so that's something. I'm sure she thought I was some crazy old lady, but she listened. It's all up to them now. *Oh!* She *loved* the chocolate, by the way."

Sam laughed. "Like that's a surprise. Get any other impressions?"

"*Hmm*.... I'd say the future is in very good hands."

"I never doubted it. So, is there anything else we need to do here? Do you want to drive by our old house? It's not like it's out of the way."

Ellie thought about this. Seeing their former home, possibly running into their parents, would only reopen wounds that, even after these many years, had never fully healed. If she could do anything, it would be to see Shanna Newell again, even just to say hi. And to thank her, although the woman would have no idea what for. But that was impossible; the Nature Center wouldn't open for another three years. Shanna was probably still attending the university in Salt Lake City. Which was a very short flight from Denver, now that she thought about it.

She gazed up at the Jemez Mountains, experiencing anew the beauty she had so loved growing up here. *And where I'm growing up again.* The thought overwhelmed her, and she shook her head to clear it. No, it was probably best to get out of town as quickly as possible.

"You know, I think I'm okay. You?"

"I'm good."

"Then come on, Sam. It's time to go home."

EPILOGUE

Ellie watched the boy cautiously approach the cafeteria table, where she sat with Sam and Sam's new friend, Ryan. He was the same boy she had seen several days earlier getting out of the white car with all the stickers on the back. He was in one of her classes, and she had spotted him in the halls several times during the past week, easily recognizing him by his spiky white hair and oversized purple backpack. She had never spoken to him, though.

He came to a stop two steps away and eyed them uncertainly through oversized round glasses that rode a little crookedly on his nose. Ellie noticed that he was gripping the sides of his tray so tightly that his knuckles were bone white. When he finally spoke, his voice was soft, his phrasing hesitant and awkwardly formal. "Hello. Do you mind if I, um, join you?"

Ryan gave the kid a relaxed, friendly smile. "Howdy, stranger. Not at all." He kicked the chair opposite him away from the table as he spoke. "Take a seat."

The boy set his tray down in front of the offered chair and sat. Ellie continued watching him closely. He seemed abnormally uncomfortable, and his gaze darted nervously from face to face before settling on hers.

"My name's Aaron," he said, barely taking his eyes off Ellie. "Siskin." He absently nudged his glasses into place with a slender middle finger.

"Is that the Irish Erin?" Ryan said. "E-r-i-n?".

"No, it's the other one. Double 'a,' then 'ron.'"

Ellie got the impression that he said that a lot. He was looking at her again, but why was no real mystery. She had been studying him intently since he started walking toward their table, wondering if he was the one.

"Well, Double-A, welcome to the majors. I'm Ryan, and this is Samantha, but call her Sam unless you want a black eye. The girl eyeing you like you're her next dissection specimen is Sam's sister, who, for reasons lost in the mists of time, goes by Ellie."

"Hi," Aaron said, still focused solely on Ellie. "I saw you talking to that woman the other day. Is she your grandmother?"

The question caused Ellie's thoughts to jump back to an event that occurred a week ago, on the first day of school. Stepping off the bus, she realized her book bag had come unzipped. She told Sam to go in without her, then set her bag down on the sidewalk to make sure she hadn't lost anything before closing it up properly. As she walked up the steps alone toward the school's front door, a woman standing on the top step called to her.

"Good morning, Ellie," she said. "I'd like a word with you. It'll only take a moment, but it's very important."

Ellie stopped, wondering if the woman was a teacher; if not, how did she know who she was? That didn't really make sense, though; not even her teachers knew who she was yet. The woman appeared old, older than her grandmother, but her face was kind and somehow—almost weirdly so—familiar. Had she seen her on TV? No, she didn't think that was it.

The woman was dressed simply in jeans and a plain, black shirt like a tee but heavier, and she wore a small, sling-style bag over one shoulder. Ellie waited for her to say her piece, but she merely gazed down at her, smiling as sudden tears filled her eyes. She sniffed and ran a knuckle under each eye, a deeply emotional reaction that told Ellie the woman wasn't a teacher. The realization made her wary, but curiosity kept her rooted in place.

"Sorry. I'm…. It's just hard to believe I was ever that young." She sat on the top step and patted the concrete, beckoning Ellie to sit beside her.

"Please, sit," she said, and patted the step again. "C'mon. I almost never bite," she added, and then she laughed.

Ellie hesitated for a moment, then sat beside the woman.

"Oh! Speaking of, I brought you a little something from Wolf's. Well, 'Fox,' I guess I should say. When I was growing up here, that department store downtown was called BB Wolf."

Ellie watched as the woman searched the interior of the sling bag. She was pretty sure Fox had always been Fox—it said *Since 1979* right on the door–and she wondered why she would tell a lie like that. But maybe it had been Wolf's before then. The woman found what she was looking for and held a small bag out for her to take. Ellie opened it and discovered it contained a large piece of chocolate, just like the ones she had seen behind the glass of the big display case just inside Fox's front door.

"I know," the woman said. "'Candy from strangers,' right? It's safe, though. I promise. This one's always been my favorite."

Ellie pulled the chocolate out and bit off the tiniest nibble, wondering half-seriously if it would be the last thing she'd ever taste. When the rich flavors of dark chocolate and raspberry cream flooded her senses, her eyes went wide with astonishment. She hadn't thought it possible that anything could taste so incredibly, so amazingly, so *impossibly* good! Even if the candy were poisoned, she decided she'd get the full dose just so she could savor that amazing taste right up until her final breath.

"Thanks!" she said, then took a much larger bite. The woman smiled, obviously pleased that she was enjoying her small gift.

"After I say what I'm going to say, you will have a lot of questions. I'm not going to answer them, so don't even bother asking. You just listen. Got it?"

Ellie nodded. The woman spoke in the cool, crisp tones of someone used to being in charge, and Ellie found she liked that about her. She placed the last piece of chocolate in her mouth, but this time she didn't chew. Instead, she pressed it between her tongue and the roof of her mouth and let it melt there, trying to make the flavor last as long as possible.

"You know, I seriously debated whether or not to come here today," the woman said, "but in the end, I felt I had to. Once, a very long time ago, I made the decision to interfere with a man's life. Although it was for the best of reasons, I hated having to do it. Later, someone decided to mess around with *my* life, and, even though it was again for very good reasons, I found I didn't like it one bit.

"What I'm about to say isn't for my benefit, though, but for yours. You're going to meet someone very soon. I don't think it'll be today, but I don't know for sure. It's funny—I just don't remember anymore." She went quiet and looked sad. After a long pause, she continued. "I don't think I'm even going to tell you his name. I don't want to take away *all* of the magic, although now you know it's a boy. The point is, he's very special. I think you'll recognize that as soon as you meet him. He's maybe had it a little tough up until now, but I'm not certain of that either this time around. You—and by 'you' I mean Sam and Ryan, too—can help change that. Get to know him. Be his friend. And remember this too: just like all guys don't have to be macho jocks to be 'real' guys, you can enjoy being a girl—even have a boyfriend if you someday want to—without having to be one of those 'ditzy' ones."

Ellie was surprised that the woman knew about her sister and even more so that she knew about Ryan—Sam had only met Ryan a week ago—but, as instructed, she remained silent. When the woman turned to face her directly, her expression was more intense than any Ellie had ever seen. It felt as if she had waited her entire life to say whatever was about to come next.

"I don't know how things are going to play out for you, but here's the most important thing you'll ever need to know. If you can find it within you to let him in—even love him someday—do it! And don't let him get away. *Ever!* Trust me, it'll be the best decision you ever make. Good luck, Ellie." She abruptly rose and started down the stairs.

Right then, an old white Volvo wagon pulled in along the curb. Ellie remained sitting, still asking no questions but watching everything closely. When the woman spotted the car, she stumbled and had to grab onto the handrail to keep from falling down the last few steps. The car rolled past them and stopped. A door opened, and a boy with the whitest hair Ellie had ever seen on anyone her age stepped out. He held onto the door as he spoke to whoever was at the wheel.

The woman turned around and looked up at Ellie as if she were reconsidering her earlier decision. "On second thought, I'll leave you with two more things," she said, smiling in a way that suggested she had remembered a private joke. "First, just be yourself because—and this comes from a highly trusted source—you are amazing! The other is this; I'm pretty sure he's really into astronomy."

With that, she turned away once more. She said something very brief to the boy as she passed him on the sidewalk, then she stepped off the curb and crossed the bus lane to the parking lot. It was only then that Ellie noticed the second woman. She was leaning against the side of a car, and it was obvious she had been watching them the whole time. Even from so far away, she could tell the women looked very similar to each other, just like she and Sam did. As the first woman got close, the woman by the car held out her arms and wrapped her in a tight hug. After a short time, they stepped apart, had a brief conversation, and then got into the car, with the one who had spoken to her taking the back seat. Ellie watched the car drive away until it disappeared from view.

The white-haired boy was leaning in through the car's door, still talking to the driver. Ellie noticed that the car's rear hatch was covered with bumper stickers, but she was too far away to read any of them. She sat there and waited a little longer, thinking she'd walk in with him if he ever finished talking. After a few more seconds, she decided she'd rather beat the bell to homeroom. She stood and took one last glance in the direction the woman had gone, replaying her odd final piece of advice.

Just be myself? Who else would I be? Then she turned and walked into the school.

"No," Ellie answered Aaron at last. "I don't know who that was. She never even told me her name. Why'd you ask that?"

"I thought you looked a lot alike, that's all."

She continued to study his face a moment more, suddenly convinced in a way she could never have explained that this was the boy the woman had meant. She saw a keen intelligence in eyes that otherwise seemed shy and a little sad. She remembered what the woman had said about him maybe having had it a bit tough. He picked up his sandwich and took a large chomp out of one corner.

Astronomy? Well, here goes…

"Hey," she said. "Did you see those pictures Cassini took of Saturn's moon Enceladus a few months ago?"

Her question seemed to come as a pleasant surprise. His eyes went wide with excitement, but his mouth was too full for him to answer.

"*Cassini?*" Sam said, confused. "What, like *Oleg* Cassini? Why would anyone name a space probe thingy after a fashion designer?"

Ellie rolled her eyes and returned her attention to Aaron. She did her best not to laugh, knowing that if she did, she'd likely pay for it later. But then she saw the corners of his mouth start to twitch, and she found she couldn't help herself. A second later, the sound of their combined laughter filled the cafeteria.

CODA

March 26, 2012— Deepsea Challenger reaches the bottom of the Mariana Trench. During its three-hour stay nearly seven miles below the surface, her pilot photographs a peculiar, inexplicably regular formation at the edge of visible range.

June 12, 2016— A subsequent expedition exploring the same area locates the previously noted anomaly and discovers that a low-power EM signal is being emitted from something inside what appears to be a man-made structure. The crew uses a remotely operated vehicle to retrieve a large black container from within the structure. Back aboard the ship, the submersible is met by a man in a dark suit. He is tall and fit, but older; his once sandy blond hair mostly gone to gray. He flashes them an open ID wallet they can't read through the submersible's thick viewport as two more men in black fatigues climb up to retrieve the recovered object from the ROV's claws. Before the crew can unseal the hatch, the three men have reached the ship's bow and the small helicopter waiting there, its rotors already starting to spin up.

ACKNOWLEDGMENTS

Thanks to the following people for their help proofreading *Breakers* :

Carolyn
Sandy
Mia
Maria

Also, more apologies are in order. I expect I have earned the ire of many readers who were hoping to witness a happier outcome for Ellie and Aaron this time around. Fair enough—they certainly deserve better. However, if the *Benders* series is, as I often describe it, a 'love story for nerds in three parts,' then it is important to remember that *Breakers* is only part two. I hope just as fervently as anyone that fate is kinder to the star-crossed couple in the series' final volume, *Menders*.

Stay tuned! — D M S

Made in the USA
Las Vegas, NV
17 February 2024

85869920R00325